THE
Sentimental
JOURNEY
ROMANCE COLLECTION

9 Love Stories from the Memorable 1940s

THE
Sentimental
JOURNEY
ROMANCE COLLECTION

Cathy Marie Hake, Kim Vogel Sawyer,
Dianna Crawford, Joan Croston,
Kelly Eileen Hake,
Sally Laity, DiAnn Mills,
Janelle B. Schneider, Lynette Sowell

BARBOUR BOOKS
An Imprint of Barbour Publishing, Inc.

Print ISBN 978-1-63409-471-9

eBook Editions:
Adobe Digital Edition (.epub) 978-1-63409-398-9
Kindle and MobiPocket Edition (.prc) 978-1-63409-399-6

Published by Barbour Publishing, Inc., P.O. Box 719, Uhrichsville, OH 44683, www.barbourbooks.com

Our mission is to publish and distribute inspirational products offering exceptional value and biblical encouragement to the masses.

Member of the
Evangelical Christian
Publishers Association

Printed in Canada.

Contents

Of Immeasurable Worth

by Joan Croston

Chapter 1

London, 1940

A gust of wind scattered twigs along the sidewalk, then swirled around the ladder as Ann Heydon stepped on the first rung and inched her way toward the top. "I don't like heights," she muttered as her stomach churned, "but Grandpa can't climb up here to do this." She grasped the ladder with her left hand and stretched as far as she could to wipe dirt from the sign on her grandfather's shop. Her weight shifted, and the ladder began to tilt. "Oh, no!" she cried out as she and the ladder headed for the sidewalk.

"Taking flying lessons?" Below, hands steadied the ladder and helped her to the ground.

She looked up into the face of Peter Austin and felt the dreaded blush creep over her. "Oh no, sir. The shop sign was dirty so I climbed up to clean it, but the ladder slipped, and I. . ." She stopped in embarrassment as he chuckled at her rambling.

"After you've risked life and limb up there, the least I can do is check the results." He stepped back to inspect her work. "You did a great job!" The sign again clearly identified her grandfather's establishment:

WORTHINGTON'S BOOKSHOP
BOOK REPAIRS AND RARE EDITIONS
NIGEL WORTHINGTON, PROPRIETOR

"That's a relief! I never want to climb up there again!" Ann collected her cleaning supplies and smiled. "You haven't been by the shop for a while, Mr. Austin. You must keep busy with that book you're writing, or is it those literature classes you teach at the university?"

"A bit of both, I'm afraid." He shook his finger at her, a teasing glint in his eyes. "But how many times do I have to remind you? My name's Peter. After all, we're fellow Americans here in jolly old London. 'Mr. Austin' makes me feel too old." He wagged his eyebrows at her. "Unless you're trying to tell me something. . . ."

She fought to keep the red from her face. "No, of course I'm not. You're not old, but I'm used to calling teachers by their more formal names. I know you're not my teacher, but you do teach at the university and—"

"Hold it!" He burst out laughing. "Don't be so serious. It's 1940. The world's not that formal anymore. It may be falling apart around us, but that's even more reason to enjoy it while we can." He picked up the ladder. "I'm here to see your grandfather about a book. I'll take this in for you."

Ann let out her breath and collapsed against the shop as a woman stepped out of her gift shop next door and bustled over.

"Are you all right, dearie?" Mrs. Chumley stopped in front of her and peered over her glasses.

Ann brushed off her cardigan sweater. "I'm fine—at least physically. I'm not so sure about the rest of me."

Her neighbor planted her hands on her ample hips. "I saw that handsome young man rescue you. It was so romantic!"

Ann sighed. "I know I'm a dunce when it comes to men, Mrs. Chumley, but why does that man always leave me in a dither? I'm foolish to think he could be interested in a plain Jane like me. After all, he's tall, dark, and handsome, a writer, and a professor, but. . ." She twirled the empty bucket in her hands.

Mrs. Chumley folded her plump arms across her chest. "And who says you're a plain Jane?"

"I have mirrors, Mrs. Chumley. I don't look like the girls who make themselves up the way movie stars do. No pompadour. No long red nails. Mousy-colored hair. I'm just a plain Jane who's more at home with books than people."

Mrs. Chumley shook her head until her bright red curls bobbed on their dark roots. "So you think you need to look like a movie star to get a good man. I don't look like none of them, but my Albert says I'm classy." She gave her hair a pat. "And I do have a sense of style, if I may say so myself."

Ann looked at her neighbor's orange dress and bright red hair and stifled a chuckle. "But you—"

"Let me finish, dearie. Those women may look all fancy, but they're probably pretty stuck on themselves, if you ask me. Maybe your young man has better taste, like my Albert. Think about it." A woman approached her store, and she hurried away.

As Ann turned, Peter stepped out of her grandfather's shop, waved, and walked briskly toward the bus stop. With a sigh, she entered the store, her heart thumping. There were no customers, so she was startled when suddenly a raucous voice screamed and ranted from the workroom at the back of the building. When it paused, a crowd roared, "*Sieg heil! Sieg heil! Sieg heil!*" She knew her grandfather was glued to his radio, and she gave a shudder as the harangue continued. She didn't understand German, but from the sound of Hitler's voice, she knew he wasn't saying anything good. As she picked up a feather duster, the voice disappeared and her grandfather approached the counter, bristling with anger.

"There's no hope of a peace treaty?" she ventured.

He spread his hands on the counter and stood silently a moment. "No, my dear, Hitler is a liar who thinks he can grab whatever he wants." He gave a snort. "He talks about peace; then in the past two years, he's taken the Rhineland, Austria, Czechoslovakia, and Poland. In April he invaded Norway and Denmark, and now a month later he's taken Belgium, Holland, and Luxembourg with that Blitzkrieg of his." He shook his white head slowly and pounded his fist on the counter. "And mark my word. By the end of June, he'll have France. How long 'til we're not safe here in London?"

Ann watched the pain in her grandfather's face as he recited the litany of Hitler's conquests. She braced herself for what she knew was coming next.

"We've talked about this before, Ann. You must go back to America. It's not safe here." His voice was firm. "You have to leave while you can still get out."

Ann moved the feather duster back and forth over the counter. "I won't leave you over here alone, Grandpa, and that's final. Besides, why should I run away? You've always assured me God's with us."

He sighed and rubbed his hands together slowly. "And that He is, my dear, but He also gave us brains and expects us to use them. We're not to act foolishly and wait for Him to bail us out." He picked a book off the counter and returned it to a shelf.

"England's my home country, Ann. Those years I spent in America as a young man were wonderful, but it wasn't home." His face took on a nostalgic look. "That's where I met your grandmother. She returned home with me, and we lived here all those years. But when our daughter grew up, she wanted to see America, so across the ocean she went. When she met your father there, she decided to stay, and you were born American. So, we each have our homeland." He looked at her with a sad smile.

"But, Grandpa, there's tradition. I have to find the love of my life in another country as you and Mom did. Don't send me away now. Please. Wait to see what happens. Maybe this war will be over soon. Hitler can't take over the whole world!"

He shook his head. "You understand so little of what's going on. We'll talk about this again. I have a book to repair; I'll be in the workroom."

Ann leaned on the counter and stared out the window. "I won't leave Grandpa," she muttered, "and I can't lose my chance to have the great adventure of my life and find the man of my dreams. After all, I'm twenty-five years old already. Nothing will make me give up and go home!"

Chapter 2

Peter Austin leaned back in the chair and rubbed his neck, enjoying the warmth of the sun's rays streaming through the windows of his flat. He sighed and tapped his pencil on the manuscript before him. He needed to do more research for his book on England in the Middle Ages, but with the country at war, it was no longer a matter of *if* he went home but *when*.

He twirled the pencil between his fingers. At the rate students were leaving school to help the war effort, he wouldn't have enough people in his classes to keep teaching here much longer. He should collect the information for his book and do the writing back home in America.

He walked to the window and stared out at the city he'd come to love. He could feel its history and tradition all around him. If he left now, how many valuable books and documents would be sacrificed to finance the Nazi cause or be destroyed when war came to London? He couldn't desert his colleagues and the efforts they were making to preserve things that couldn't be replaced.

Another image, this one soft and sweet, floated through his mind. He loved the way Ann's face turned pink at the least little thing, and he chuckled at her tendency to ramble when she was flustered, but once they began discussing books, she was relaxed and fun. Then he'd turn around and she'd start acting so...well, so strange—almost as if she really didn't like him. If he went home, he'd never know why she kept popping into his mind.

He walked back to the desk and stared at the manuscript. He was stuck without the material Nigel had ordered for him. If he stopped by the bookstore, it might be in—and maybe he'd have a chance to talk to Ann. He grabbed his tweed jacket and headed for the bus stop.

◆　◆　◆

Customers were in and out of the bookstore all morning, and it was midafternoon before Ann climbed the steps to the upstairs apartment she shared with her grandfather to make a list of groceries she hoped to buy. Planning meals had become a challenge with so many items either rationed or in short supply. She put the list in her purse and hurried down the stairs, poking her head into the workroom. "I'm going shopping, Grandpa. I'll stop by the bakery to see if Mrs. Wilson saved you any sweets."

He nodded and turned back to his work.

She stepped outside and slowed her pace, taking a deep breath and enjoying the warble of birds and fragrance of late spring blossoms that brought a touch of home to a country girl in the big city. She glanced up to check a street sign only to find it gone. Signposts and street names had been taken down to confuse German forces should they invade the country, more evidence that life wasn't normal these days.

She turned the corner and faced the inevitable line. With shortages, lines grew long as people waited in hopes of purchasing the items they needed. Somehow the wait seemed more tolerable when she thought of them as queues. She smiled to herself at the English expression.

Back on the sidewalk with her purchases, her ration books tucked in her purse, the air took on a sudden chill as she stared at sandbags piled high to form a protective wall in front of the post office and the bank. The city was changing from a place of adventure to one of uncertainty. She gave a shudder.

She needed a few moments to refresh her spirits, so she headed for an area of the park across the street adjacent to St. Andrew's churchyard. The park seemed eerily quiet now. No children played and shouted. A year ago, most of them had been sent to homes in northern England, where they would be safer should the Germans attack. Women were working up to sixty hours a week in the war industry.

Ann entered a sheltered corner near the churchyard, set her packages down, and plopped on a bench that offered a view of green grass and flowers. The rest of the park was marred by trenches dug to serve as quick shelters if German planes attacked, but in this corner, irises bloomed in shades of purple and lavender, and dandelions brought bits of sunshine to the lawn. At least here in her sanctuary the world seemed the same.

"Is this seat taken?"

"Oh!" Startled, Ann looked up to see Peter smiling at her. She shook her head and tried not to blush as he settled down on the bench beside her.

"I often stop here on my way to the bookshop. I'm pleased we have the same tastes." He paused and sniffed the air. "Hmm, speaking of tastes, either I smell something tasty, or you have very unusual perfume. You've been searching out some sweets, I believe." He leaned over and sniffed the bag she had set beside her.

"No, it's my new perfume," she teased as she put her hand on the bag. "I'd never tell you if I had goodies in there. I've seen how you and Grandpa devour a tin of biscuits!" She moved the bag to the other side of her.

"Oh, ho, trying to sound English, are we? That smells like my favorite cookies to me!" He tried to reach around her for the sack. "I'll take a look to be sure. Scarce as sweets are these days, I may have to walk you home to protect them."

"Oh, no, you don't!" Ann grinned and slapped at his hand. "Mrs. Wilson has a soft spot for Grandpa and saves him treats whenever she can. If I let you see them, there won't be anything left!" She put her hand on the bag.

Peter hung his head and gave a dejected sigh, then winked at her. "It's good to see you relax and have a little fun."

The smile quickly left her face. "There's something wrong with *me*? How can you be so cheery when the world's falling apart, *Mr.* Austin? When I came over here, I didn't expect this." She looked down at her hands. "I know that sounds self-ish when countries are being overrun by the Nazis, but I loved it here so much the way things were."

Peter leaned back and crossed his legs. He looked over at her and spoke quietly. "I do understand, Ann. Don't forget; I've come to love England, too. I'm not through with my research, so I try to hang on a little longer. I love my work, and I like the friends I've made here, especially two in a little bookshop I frequent." He patted her hand and gave her a lopsided grin.

Ann could feel the color rise in her face and took a deep breath. "Seriously, Peter, do you think Germany will attack London?"

He reached down to pick a blade of grass and twisted it between his fingers. "The signs are all around, Ann, and they're not hopeful. We're under a blackout every night. Street signs are gone. Think how long it's been since you've heard a church bell. Headlights have to be covered so no light shows at night." He looked over at her. "I don't want to frighten you, but you need to be aware of what's going on."

Ann nodded without looking at him. Her fingers played with the top of the bag.

"You do know what's happening at Dunkirk, don't you?" His tone was somber.

"Some. I guess I try to ignore as much as I can. As if that will make it go away, I suppose." She shrugged.

He paused a moment. "Ann, the Germans are taking France. They've pushed the French and English forces to the coastal areas around Dunkirk, right across the English Channel from us. The troops are trying to defend themselves, but they won't last. There's a big operation underway to evacuate them. Fishermen in their boats and men in every kind of vessel that will float are risking their lives to bring these men home."

"But the channel separates us from the continent. Hasn't that always been a good protection?"

Peter slapped his hand against his forehead. "You do wear blinders! Today's wars aren't like those of years ago, Ann. You read a lot. You should know that. Planes can fly over the English Channel in twenty minutes, and guns fire long distances today. France thought its Maginot Line of defense fortifications would protect them from the Nazis, but those concrete bunkers and the wooded hill country of the Ardennes were nothing to Germany's planes and tanks. By the end of June, France will no longer be free, and that's only a few weeks away. Then we'll be looking right across that channel at German troops and planes."

"If you're trying to make me feel selfish and ignorant, it's working. I know wishing won't make things the way I want—"

Suddenly the piercing wail of an air-raid siren drowned out her words. Peter grabbed her hand as she reached to pick up the groceries. "Leave everything," he shouted above the noise. "We need to get in the church!" They ran to the small old building and pulled the door open. The interior was dim and cool, but as their eyes adjusted, they could see people sitting here and there in the pews with their heads bowed.

A side door opened, and the vicar hurried into the sanctuary. "Follow me to the basement," he called out. "You'll be safer down there." He held the door while people rushed past him. Ann and Peter were halfway down the aisle when the all-clear signal sounded. A sigh of relief passed through the church as people came back into the sanctuary and stopped to gather items they had left in the pews.

Peter followed Ann from the church, still holding her hand as she tried to stop trembling. "Are you all right?" He looked at her with concern. "It was probably just a drill."

She nodded, enjoying the security in Peter's hand covering hers.

"After we pick up your groceries, I'll walk you back to the shop." He led her to the bench where they had left her packages. He was loading his arms when she reached over to grab the bag with her grandfather's sweets. "Hey, don't you trust me?" He looked at her, crestfallen.

Ann shook her head. "Not on your life. That would be like asking the fox to give the chicken a lift home. I'm carrying these, *Mr.* Austin!"

Peter chuckled. "I guess I'll have to consider your company my sweet treat for the day then." He shifted the bags of groceries and grinned at her, and she felt her cheeks flush.

The breeze was soft as they walked along the sidewalk. Lofty chestnut trees arched over the walk, leaving it dappled with sunshine. Ann looked up at the sturdy branches. "Just think of the stories they could tell."

Peter's eyes followed her gaze. "They've survived for many years. That's a hopeful sign."

Ann watched the changing patterns of the shadows on the sidewalk. "When I sat in the park, everything was so peaceful and beautiful that I had one of my *now* moments—like I was completely in the present and it would never change. It was so real." She smiled sheepishly. "That probably sounds stupid."

Peter stopped at the curb and glanced down the street before starting across. He smiled at her. "Not at all. I've always thought you had poetry in your soul."

Ann stepped onto the sidewalk and looked up at the sky. "It doesn't happen often, but sometimes the moment seems to spread and connect with other times in my life when I've had that same feeling. Then they run together, and it becomes so real the rest of the world fades and becomes unreal. I'd like to stay in that moment forever." She laughed softly. "Grandpa would say it's a little taste of heaven." Embarrassed at revealing so much of herself, she concentrated on the displays in the shop windows with their diminishing supplies of watches and clocks, fabrics and clothes.

Suddenly Peter grabbed her elbow and pointed to a notice. "Look—a poetry reading! Would you like to go? I said you have poetry in your soul, so how can you refuse?" He grinned at her.

She hesitated, wondering if he was teasing or really asking for a date. "I, uh, well, I—"

"You don't have to go, but I thought we'd both enjoy it. If it's no good, we can take a walk or do something else." Peter looked at her, uncertainty on his face.

She took a deep breath and smiled. "I'd like that."

"Good. We'll call it a date then." He gave her a smile, and her heart raced.

As they approached the shop, a short, middle-aged man stood on the sidewalk staring at the building. "Are you looking for something?" she asked when they walked up to him.

He gave them a quick glance. "I see this is the shop of Mr. Worthington. He's known far and wide for the rare and valuable books he's able to procure for his customers. No one else has his connections." He spoke briskly with the touch of an accent she couldn't place.

Ann felt uncomfortable, but knowing she needed to be polite to a potential customer, she took a deep breath. "Is there something I can help you with, sir? I work at the shop; Mr. Worthington's my grandfather."

The man continued to inspect the building. "I'm told Mr. Worthington's ancestry goes back to persons of position in Germany. Rare books must run in the family." One side of his mouth turned up in more of a smirk than a smile.

Peter shifted the packages. "Come inside, sir. We'll get Mr. Worthington for you."

"Another day, I think." The man glanced at his watch. "I just wanted to know where to come when it's time." He tipped his hat and hurried away.

"An odd man," Ann remarked as she opened the shop door. After a trying afternoon, the comforting smell of old books wrapped around her, giving her a sense of warmth and security. She motioned toward the counter. "Leave the groceries there. I'll put them away."

Footsteps approached from the back of the shop, and her grandfather hurried into the room. "My good friend, I was hoping you'd come by. I've gotten in some books you'll want to see."

Peter placed the packages on the counter and smiled at Ann. "I enjoyed our afternoon. Don't forget our date."

Ann returned the smile and turned to pick up the groceries, hoping he couldn't hear her heart pounding. She couldn't believe it! Peter hadn't made fun of her when she shared her special feelings, and he'd even asked her for a date!

Chapter 3

Peter followed his friend to the workroom, where Nigel handed him a book. "It's perfect," Peter said as he sat down and leafed through the volume. "As always, you've come to my rescue."

Nigel sat at his cluttered worktable, books stacked all around him in various stages of repair and an open Bible in front of him. He rested his elbows on the table and brought his fingers together, tapping them lightly, then resting them under his chin. "I want to thank you for walking Ann home today. I was afraid for her when the sirens sounded." He shook his head. "I've tried to convince her to return to America, but she's stubborn." He winked at Peter. "She gets that from her grandmother."

Peter laughed and ran his hand over the book. "I refuse to touch that one, sir. But I do understand your concerns; I have the same ones. To stay or not to stay; that's the question. I have research to finish, and I don't want to desert our project."

Nigel nodded. "Your help has been invaluable. With the Nazis stealing art treasures to finance their war effort, it's important we get valuable books and materials to places of safekeeping. And if bombs should fall, I shudder to think of the treasures we'd lose."

"I'm honored to serve as a link with our colleagues at the university who are working to preserve materials from either disaster," Peter replied. "I hope my coming here for research material has kept me above suspicion."

Nigel sighed and moved a stack of books to the side. "And if you leave, I'll not only lose your help, I'll lose a good friend."

Peter rested the book in his lap and glanced around the room. Books were everywhere. "It's easy to see you consider books your friends as well as your treasures. Did I ever tell you about the collection of Bibles my grandmother left me? Some go back several generations."

Nigel studied him for a moment. "That Bible collection. You've read the books as well?"

Peter felt a stab of guilt. "I can't say I've read them as much as I should have. They've been more a treasure to preserve than something to read. Not that I don't believe them," he added quickly, "but I've been so busy with other things I . . ." He felt as if Nigel were looking into his soul and finding it wanting.

Nigel leaned forward. "Since rationing and shortages, the value of food has become more apparent. Would you stock your cupboards and leave the food on the shelves only to look at?"

Peter felt Nigel watching his response and shifted in his chair. "You're talking about food for the soul. You sound like my grandmother. She said the body couldn't be nourished by cream puffs, nor would the soul be nourished by the fluff we try to feed it."

Nigel nodded. "A wise woman." He rubbed his hands together. "Peter, you have that collection because men risked their lives to translate and preserve God's Word many years ago. They didn't sacrifice themselves so the Bible could be collected. They wanted people to read it and store it in their hearts, not their bookcases." He peered over his glasses.

Peter raised his hands. "I admit I have no excuse. The world is too much with us, as they say, and too often it takes times like the present to try men's souls and make them think of things spiritual."

"Every generation is the custodian of God's Word, Peter, and must see that His truths are learned and passed on. When that doesn't happen, we have the violence that's in our world today." Nigel paused as if making a decision before closing the workroom door. He walked to a bookcase and rolled it aside. Behind it, he pushed on a part of the wall, and a narrow door popped open to reveal a tall safe.

Peter stared at him and had opened his mouth to speak when Nigel continued.

"I keep the most valuable books in here. Some are priceless, but there are people willing to pay any amount for what they want. I protect them here until they go to their new owners. And some of these are my own family treasures." He took out a bundle secured with a cord.

Peter watched as Nigel placed it on his worktable and removed the paper. Inside lay a large, worn book with a brown leather cover. Nigel carefully opened it at random. Peter stared, and words caught in his throat. "That's. . .it's. . . it couldn't be what I think it is." He blinked and looked up to see Nigel smiling gently. "It is, isn't it? It's a Gutenberg Bible!" He let out his breath and stared at it in awe.

"Yes, Peter, it's one of the first books produced by a printing press, somewhere around 1455. It's been in my family for many generations. I'm its guardian in this time. Ann will have to protect it after me, in these times perhaps a dangerous task."

"May I?" Peter looked at his friend.

Nigel nodded, and Peter reached out to touch the book, feeling overwhelmed as he leafed through it. Two columns of Latin ran down each page. Some of the pages were plain. On others, curling vines decorated the sides along with colorful birds and flowers, or vines curled down the center between the columns. The letters at the beginning of each book were elaborate designs done in shades of green, blue, and red. Peter stared at the book, mesmerized.

"This is volume two," Nigel explained. "Somewhere along the line the first volume was lost. The Gutenberg Bible was so large, it was usually bound in two volumes—sometimes three. Mine includes Proverbs through the rest of the Old

Testament and the entire New Testament." Nigel rewrapped the book and put it in the safe, and Peter moved the bookcase to its place in front of the panel Nigel had opened. Neither spoke as they worked.

Peter let out his breath and picked up his book. "I feel as if I've been on holy ground."

Nigel smiled. "You have been but not because of the Gutenberg Bible, old and rare as it is. With any Bible, you're on holy ground. This is God's Word to us, written so we can know Him. Through it, He reveals His love, comes into our hearts to redeem us, and then shows us how to live. Just knowing that should bring a sense of awe."

Nigel studied him a moment. "Your Bible collection. I think you take it for granted. Have you ever thought about the men who preserved God's Word for you? What they sacrificed? Men like William Tyndale, one of the first to translate most of the Bible into English in 1526? He dedicated his life to the task but had to flee England for his safety, was finally betrayed in Antwerp, strangled, and burned at the stake—just for putting the Word into our language. And yet all many people do with Bibles is collect them."

Peter felt his face take on a sheepish look.

"I'm not chastising you, my friend, but there are forces today trying to destroy this Word or, in the case of my treasure, use it to finance their evil purposes. The Bible I have would bring a lot of money. And so I have to ask, 'Who is willing to defend God's Word in our time?' When you go home, Peter, spend some time in your Bible."

Peter nodded and extended his hand. "I will, sir. Thank you for sharing this with me. I feel very honored."

Nigel placed his other hand over Peter's. "I didn't do it for that reason, my friend, though I knew what the book would mean to you. Someone needs to know about my Bible besides Ann. I won't always be here, and with the country at war, I want someone trustworthy to help her with it if need be." He walked with Peter to the workroom door. "I shudder to think what would happen if the Nazis knew of that book."

At the words, Peter felt a chill. "Is the book in danger? Are you?"

Nigel shook his head. "I pray not. My name is English, and the family lost its connection with Germany many years ago, but we must always take precautions."

They walked into the shop, where Ann was handing a customer his purchase. Peter put his hand on Nigel's shoulder. "Thank you again, my friend. You've shared with me an experience I'll always cherish. And I will go home to spend some time in my own Bible." He gave Ann a warm smile and followed the customer out the door.

Ann glanced quickly at her grandfather. "What experience? What's this about his Bible?"

He turned toward her. "I showed him our Bible, Ann. Someone besides you needs to know. We live in dangerous times."

"You trust him that much?" Ann was astounded.

He nodded. "My friend at the university trusts him completely, and he's been a loyal friend to me. He knows the value of the book, and I think he went home to ponder the value of its contents as well."

◆　　◆　　◆

Peter walked toward the bus stop, thinking about the treasure he'd seen. When he looked up, he saw he had passed his stop and quickly retraced his steps as the bus pulled up and he scrambled on.

He took a seat and stared out the window as thoughts and questions assailed him. Why had this Bible had such an impact on him? He'd touched many old books and had held many Bibles. Nigel had chided him for collecting Bibles but not being fed by their content. His face felt warm as a thought nagged at him. If all Bibles disappeared, would it matter to him? Would it change his life?

The bus pulled up to his stop, and he got off, carrying the bag of books Nigel had sent with him. He entered his flat and absently put the books on the table. Nigel had told him about the man who died for translating the Bible. War was coming to London, and he could die. What had he stood for that would matter?

The troublesome thoughts continued as he sorted through the books and put them away for safekeeping until he could deliver them to his colleagues. He walked over to the bookcase, picked up a Bible his grandmother had given him, and frowned. If the Bible was holy ground, why wasn't he feeling the same awe from this one that he did from the Gutenberg Bible? Was he in awe of the book's age instead of its contents?

He paced the floor and stopped suddenly as a Bible verse he'd learned in Sunday school popped into his mind. "*For where your treasure is, there will your heart be also.*" He swallowed hard as he thought about things that were treasures in his life—even Ann settled comfortably among them—but the list didn't include God's Word.

"I think I understand," he spoke aloud as he stared at the book. "The Gutenberg Bible is a reminder of the value men placed on the Word and what they were willing to give up for it. I could sense their commitment. The man holding this book hasn't made such a commitment. It's not the treasure of his heart; he doesn't even read it."

Peter sat down in the overstuffed chair by the window and opened the book. In his twenty-nine years of life, this would be the first time he had read the Bible as God's Word to him.

Chapter 4

Ann had unlocked the glass case beneath the counter and bent down to run the feather duster along the shelves when the bell over the door jangled. She peered through the glass case as a man entered the shop. Peter! He looked so handsome, her heart beat faster, and she straightened quickly, banging her head on the frame of the case. Taking a deep breath and squeezing back tears, she stood as Peter approached the counter.

"Good afternoon, Miss Heydon. Ready for the poetry reading?" Peter smiled at her and folded his umbrella. "I know I'm early. I need to speak to your grandfather before we leave."

Her heart gave a flip, and she smiled. "I'll get ready and meet you in here." She hurried upstairs to change and run a comb through her hair, taking care to avoid the bump that had formed.

A date with Peter! Her stomach had a strange, nervous feeling, and she hoped she wouldn't babble or, even worse, have nothing to say! She added a fresh coat of pink lipstick and returned to the shop, where Peter was examining the books in the glass case. "I'm ready," she announced. He offered her his arm, and they stepped out of the shop and into the rain.

◆ ◆ ◆

Peter quickly raised his umbrella and pulled Ann close so they could share its protection. The patter of raindrops on the umbrella grew loud as Ann's nearness left him tongue-tied. He looked down at her, and all he could think of was flowers. Her perfume smelled like some kind of spring blossom, and in her pink blouse, she reminded him of the delicate blooms he saw in window boxes near his flat. Her light brown hair and the pink in her cheeks added to the soft look. He swallowed hard as she smiled up at him.

"Watch the puddle!" He pulled her to the side but not before her right foot splashed into the water. "Do you need to change shoes?" he asked apologetically.

Ann shook her head. "I'm fine. I don't want to make us late."

"We'll let it go then—unless you start quacking," he teased as her shoe sloshed with each step.

Ann wrinkled her nose at him and gave him a gentle push toward a puddle.

"Truce!" he declared. "From henceforth I promise to carry you across all puddles."

They approached their destination and saw a notice taped on the door. "Poetry reading canceled," Peter read. "So much for that. And it's not a good day for a walk, so how about a cup of coffee? There's a shop right around the corner."

"I'd like that." Ann smiled at him.

Inside, they sat down at a table and soon held cups of steaming coffee. Peter took a careful sip and watched as Ann wrapped her hands around the cup. Her blue eyes sparkled and seemed to hint at something deeper within, something he longed to know better. He cleared his throat. "So tell me. Why did you come to England to work in a bookshop?"

Ann carefully twirled the cup. "I'd always wanted an adventure. When Grandma died, I talked my parents into letting me come over to stay with Grandpa. It's been the most wonderful time of my life. I love books, and I'd like to learn all I can about Grandpa's business so I could take over the shop someday." Her face grew red, and she looked down at her cup. "That's one reason going back to America upsets me so much."

Peter reached out and squeezed her hand. "Believe me, I understand. I don't want to leave, either. I know it doesn't feel like much consolation, but at least we have a safe country to return to."

Ann nodded. "I know all that. And I know God will watch out for Grandpa better than I can, but leaving him and the shop would be so hard. I keep hoping a miracle will change the direction the world's headed." She looked up at him and smiled. "Pray and think positive, you know."

"A miracle's certainly what we need." Peter swallowed the last of his coffee and picked up the umbrella. "Ready to brave the elements?"

They stepped out into the rain and hurried along the wet sidewalk. At the shop door, Peter suddenly dropped the umbrella and scooped her up in his arms, making an exaggerated step across a small puddle. "I keep my promises!" he said with a chuckle.

Ann laughed as he set her down, bowed gallantly, and opened the door as the bell jangled. "Would you like to go out again sometime?" He raised his eyebrows, and she nodded. "I'll try to find something interesting and let you know."

Footsteps could be heard coming from the backroom as Peter bent to give her a quick kiss before her grandfather appeared. "I had a great time," he said softly. "Watch those puddles!" He touched the tip of her nose gently and stepped outside.

A warm sense of Ann's presence stayed with him as he walked along the sidewalk, trying to figure out why she fascinated him so. She was a surprising mix of spunk and softness, and they had a mutual love of books, but there was something more, something about the way she captured special moments and stored them inside to enjoy on bleaker days. He ambled along, oblivious to the raindrops until they trickled down his collar. The umbrella! He quickly retraced his steps and paused at the shop window, hoping for a glimpse of Ann, but the room was empty. He picked up the umbrella. *What's that woman doing to my mind? Or is it my heart?*

◆ ◆ ◆

The next morning, Ann's grandfather was rearranging a shelf of books when she came downstairs after completing her morning chores. He looked up and smiled. "I'm pleased you had a good time with Peter yesterday. He's a fine young man."

Ann felt her face grow hot. "I. . ." She paused as the bell jangled and a man entered the store. From his clothing and stocky build, he looked like someone who spent much of his time outdoors.

"What can I do for you?" her grandfather inquired as he stepped down from a stool.

The man walked up to the counter and looked around. "I'm interested in old Bibles. Ones like that Gutenberg Bible. You don't have one of them I could look at, do you?" He looked her grandfather in the eye without smiling.

Ann could feel her heart beat faster and watched her grandfather take a quick breath. "There aren't many of those left, sir, and most are in museums," he answered truthfully, watching the man's face.

"I heard there are still some around. They were made in Germany. Too bad they're scattered around the world instead of staying in their own land." He ran his hand over the counter, his mouth smiling slightly, but his eyes remaining cold.

"I'm sorry I can't help you. Would you like to order some information on the subject?" her grandfather offered.

"No, just asking." The man turned and left the shop.

Ann let out her breath. "Grandpa, you don't think. . ."

He shook his head. "Just a coincidence, I'm sure." He climbed back on the stool and searched through the books on the top shelf.

Ann stepped to the window and looked out to see the man a short distance down the sidewalk in a conversation with. . .Peter Austin? Her heart gave a flip. Peter would be here in a few minutes! She busied herself at a bookshelf as minutes ticked by, but Peter didn't appear. Finally she walked to the window and looked out. The sidewalk was empty. Why had he been out there if he didn't come in the shop?

She was jolted back to reality as her grandfather called out, "Ann, unload the box of books that arrived yesterday and stack them on the counter. I need to take a look at them." He climbed down from the stool and stepped out the shop door.

Ann returned to her work, but her mind was on Peter's soft hazel eyes instead of the books she took from the box. Sharing her thoughts with him had seemed so natural, even her dreams and her feelings deep down inside. And when he picked her up to step across the puddle, it felt so right to be in his arms. She jumped as the shop door slammed.

"I knew it would happen!" Her grandfather entered the room, staring at the day's newspaper. "France has fallen! They signed the surrender yesterday. Now England stands alone between Hitler and the free world!"

Ann stared at him in disbelief.

"I've been trying to get you a ticket home, Ann, but we've waited too long.

Everything's booked. It won't be long before German submarines make it unsafe for ships to cross the Atlantic." He slapped the paper against his leg.

"It's June twenty-third, and nothing's happened here in London, Grandpa. Maybe Hitler will stop with France."

"If wishes were horses, beggars would ride," he snorted. He picked up a small package and handed it to her along with some money. "Take this to the post office for me, please. It needs to go out right away." He rubbed his forehead and sighed.

Ann stopped to pat him tenderly on the shoulder. "We'll be all right, Grandpa." She opened the door and stepped out onto the sidewalk.

"Yoo-hoo, Ann," Mrs. Chumley called out. "How's the romance coming along?" She wore a bright purple dress, and her red curls bobbed as she swept the sidewalk in front of her shop.

Ann stopped to tell her about the date. "And he wants to take me out again!"

"What did I tell you? You come talk to me if you need advice on romance," she said smugly. "That's what my Albert always says."

Ann chuckled. "I'll remember that." She glanced at her watch. "I have to get this package to the post office. Talk to you later, Mrs. Chumley."

◆　◆　◆

A frown creased Peter's brow as he hurried along the sidewalk and entered the bookstore. "We need to talk," he said to Nigel abruptly and looked around. "Is Ann here?"

Nigel shook his head. "She went to the post office. Come, have a seat by my desk."

Peter joined him and took off his hat. "Things have been happening that make me uneasy. Did Ann tell you about the man we talked to on the sidewalk a while back?"

Nigel put down his pencil. "She told me."

"A few days ago, a man stopped me in front of your shop and asked if I worked here. I told him I'm doing research for a book, and you help me find material. Then he asked if I had heard of a Baron Ravenhurst or the Earl of Pembroke. I had no idea what he was talking about and told him so."

Nigel paled as Peter completed his story. "What did he look like?"

"Stocky, sportsman type. I was afraid he suspected I help move valuable materials to safekeeping. I didn't want to jeopardize our work, so I went on home."

Nigel got up and paced, a deep frown on his face. He let out a sigh. "Peter, those men he named were my ancestors. It's through their line I received the Gutenberg Bible." He pounded his fist into the palm of his hand.

"You think someone suspects you have the Bible?" Peter watched his friend carefully.

"I'm concerned, Peter, but I won't let anyone use the Bible to finance an evil cause. It must stay with the family." He continued to pace. "I've been praying for a way. . ."

"Sit down, my friend. Let's talk about this."

Nigel joined him and put his head in his hands. "I'm not worried for myself, Peter, but I don't want either the Bible or my granddaughter hurt. Why didn't I get her a ticket and make her go back to America with the Bible?" His voice was filled with anguish.

Peter thought a moment. "Maybe there's a way. I also came to tell you I sail for America in September. My colleague got me the ticket and is sending boxes of material with me for safekeeping. I'd be honored to take your Gutenberg Bible along—if you'd trust me with it."

Nigel took off his glasses and rubbed his eyes. "I trust you completely, Peter, but that would solve only half my problem. How do I get Ann to leave? There won't be more chances soon."

"I could give her my ticket," Peter began.

Nigel shook his head. "No, you need to go home. And even if I had a ticket, how would I get her to leave?"

"Convince her she has to take the Bible to America to keep it out of Nazi hands?"

Nigel looked doubtful. "But would she leave me to save the Bible? And if she knows you're leaving, she'll tell me to send it with you. I need to get both of them to America."

Peter stood. "My colleague got my ticket. Maybe he can come up with one more to save the Bible. I won't reveal the item we're talking about, but if I hint at its importance, maybe he'll do something."

Nigel grasped his hand. "I'd be so grateful, Peter. The Bible and my granddaughter are of immeasurable worth to me. It will be hard to part with them, but my heart will be at peace knowing both my treasures are safe. Let's keep this from Ann for now."

Peter nodded. "I'll talk to my colleague this afternoon and let you know if I find out anything." He walked to the door, then turned. "Oh, I haven't had a chance to tell you, but I've been reading my grandmother's Bible. It's become more than something I collect. The road ahead may be rough, but the Word is a light for my path in this very dark world. Thanks, my friend."

Nigel looked pleased. "Let God's Word keep you focused on the One who holds the world in His hands. And indeed the days ahead will get rough. The Germans have taken the Channel Islands, and they're bombing airfields and industrial plants in the south of England. I'll be praying He puts a ticket into your hands soon."

Chapter 5

The last customer had left the shop, and Ann was collecting the day's receipts when the aroma of fresh bread filled the room. Mrs. Wilson stepped through the doorway, carrying two large loaves, and smiled at Ann's grandfather. "I brought your favorite bread," she said. "We didn't have sugar to make anything sweet today."

He got up and walked to the counter. "Thank you. We'll enjoy it as a special treat." He took the bread and smiled at the dainty, white-haired woman.

Pink appeared on Mrs. Wilson's cheeks. "If I can find enough meat to buy, I wondered if you and Ann would share a pot of stew with me. Maybe after church one Sunday?" Her hands clutched her purse tightly as if for support.

He glanced over at Ann, and she nodded. "We'd be delighted. And we'll bring some tea for the occasion."

Mrs. Wilson walked to the door. "So many things are scarce these days. I'll let you know when I'm able to buy the meat." She gave a small wave and stepped outside.

Ann watched her grandfather return to his work with a quiet smile on his face. She'd been hoping he would find someone with whom to share his life, and, as a widow, Mrs. Wilson would be perfect. She got up to lock the shop door, hoping meat wouldn't be so scarce it would take all year before they got together!

◆　◆　◆

Midsummer arrived. To Ann, the shop had become stuffy, and she fanned herself with a book from the shelf she was rearranging. As she worked, her mind drifted to the afternoon they had spent with Mrs. Wilson. Peter had been invited to join them, and after the delicious stew, the four went for a stroll. She and Peter had found a grassy spot in the park, where they talked while her grandfather strolled along the paths with Mrs. Wilson holding his arm. The day had been so fresh and peaceful, one she'd always cherish.

She stepped down from the stool and looked through a pile of books. The constant blare from her grandfather's radio frayed her nerves as unearthly screams from Germany's Stuka dive bombers shrieked from the backroom. As he worked, her grandfather was listening to BBC reports of the German Luftwaffe sinking British merchant ships in the English Channel and attacking navy bases and airfields in the south of England.

And where was Peter? He hadn't been by the shop lately. Suddenly she felt suffocated and hurried to the workroom. "I need some air, Grandpa. I'm going for a walk."

His face reflected concern. "Be careful, my dear, and be ready to take cover at a moment's notice."

Ann nodded and hurried out the door. She walked along block after block, looking in store windows at the meager selection of goods now available and remembering the days when window-shopping was a pleasant pastime. Around her, the English went about their daily routines and searched the stores for the rapidly diminishing items they needed. She sighed and turned toward the bakery for a chat with Mrs. Wilson, who had become a dear friend.

◆　◆　◆

Peter entered the bookshop as Nigel was turning off the radio. "Hello, my friend." He smiled and looked around for Ann.

Nigel walked to the counter and placed his hands on it. "She went out for some air. The shop felt stuffy, and the radio broadcasts were too much for her."

A look of disappointment crossed Peter's face.

Nigel's forehead creased in an anxious expression. "Do you bring me good news, my friend?"

Peter shook his head. "People know time is running out, and everyone wants a ticket to go home. I'm sorry."

Nigel slapped his hands on the counter. "Please keep trying, Peter. There must be some way."

Peter paused a moment. "I'd like your permission to try one last thing. I haven't told my colleague about the Bible, just that Ann has something of value to take to America. He says everyone else does, too." Peter stopped and looked at Nigel. "If I could tell him about the Bible, he might be willing to pull some strings to get her a ticket. I can't think of anything else."

Nigel paced, praying softly, then stopped and faced Peter. "I don't see we have a choice, but reveal as little as possible." He gave a deep sigh.

"These people know how to keep quiet," Peter reassured him. "I'll be here for another month, and I'll keep working on it. Now, I have to run. I'm trying to do as much as I can in the time I have left." He paused. "Tell Ann I haven't forgotten her."

When Peter left the shop, he hurried toward the bench in the park to spend some time in his quiet place. He had just sat down and bowed his head when a sound on the sidewalk caused him to look up. Ann stood there, looking uncertain.

"I don't mean to intrude," she began.

He smiled at her and patted the bench. "I'm always glad to see you."

Ann sat down, and he reached for her hand. Pink appeared in her cheeks as she looked up at him. "It's coming, isn't it? The attack on London, I mean. Even I can't pretend any longer."

Peter nodded.

"Grandpa tried to make me leave, but I refused to look at reality."

"Are you sorry you stayed?" Peter raised his eyebrows.

"I'm glad to be here for Grandpa; he'll never leave. I have to admit I'm afraid, though." She looked up into the leaves above them. "Sometimes I can't take any more of the news about the war, and I come here. This place has become my sanctuary." She looked over at him. "Are you sorry you didn't make arrangements to leave when you could?"

Peter paused, remembering Nigel's request that he not tell Ann about his ticket. "I'm not sorry to spend more time with someone who's become very special to me," he answered evasively. "And you have become very important to me, you know. When I pray, I ask that I not lose the opportunity to know you better and find out what happens from here. War is not the easiest time to develop a relationship!"

Ann's face filled with color as he squeezed her hand. "I've. . .we've missed seeing you at the shop lately." She looked at him with questions in her eyes.

Peter picked a leaf and smoothed its surface. "I've had to take on more responsibilities at the university." He stood and pulled her to her feet, gently putting his arms around her and resting his chin on the top of her head. As she nestled against his chest, the world faded away, leaving nothing but the two of them in their sanctuary.

He sighed when she pulled away and spoke. "I'd better go. I've been gone so long, Grandpa will be worried." They looked at each other silently, the uncertainty of the times hanging between them.

"I'll walk you back." Peter reached down and picked a daisy to tuck in her hair. "A beautiful flower for a lovely lady. I've been praying I'll have the opportunity to give you many more." He lifted her chin and gave her a soft kiss, then took her arm and walked her to the shop.

Chapter 6

As the weeks of summer passed, Ann tried to avoid the incessant radio broadcasts. Her grandfather listened to them religiously, so she no longer minded the hours she spent waiting in long lines for the food they needed. German air attacks had now reached the outer suburbs of London. As she walked through the city, she couldn't ignore the sandbags piled high in front of most stores.

Again it seemed so long since she'd seen Peter. She sighed as she remembered the walks they'd taken, sharing their thoughts and dreams as they ambled along, and the day they took a picnic lunch to the park to enjoy their favorite poetry. Why did he disappear for periods of time?

The August day felt warm as she hurried home with her few purchases. She entered the shop, relieved to be met by quiet as her grandfather sat with his Bible open. "I bought what I could," she told him. "We won't starve, but meals may be strange."

He nodded. "And Mrs. Wilson brought some bread. We should invite her to share a meal with us; she's been very kind." He gave a soft smile.

"I agree." Ann hesitated a moment. "Has Peter been here lately? I've been standing in line so much, I thought perhaps I'd missed him." She shifted the packages with exaggerated concentration.

Her grandfather looked up at her, his eyes tender. "You don't need to pretend, my dear. I can see how much you care for him, and I certainly approve. He's a young man I'd be honored to have in the family. And yes, he has come by while you've been running errands." He rummaged through the desk. "He left something for you. I forgot all about it."

Ann took the package he handed her and hurried to the door to their living quarters. "I'll take these upstairs and see what I can fix for dinner." She ran up the steps and pulled out a small book, *Poems for the Heart*. She opened it to see a note in Peter's handwriting. "We missed the poetry reading, so I hope you'll enjoy reading some poetry on your own. When I read this one, I thought of you. Peter."

She quickly looked at the pages where Peter had placed the paper. On the left she saw one of her favorite poems by William Wordsworth. Peter had remembered! She skimmed to enjoy the lines she loved:

29

I wandered lonely as a cloud

. . . .

When all at once I saw a crowd,
A host of golden daffodils;

She ran her finger down the page to the last verse:

For oft, when on my couch I lie
In vacant or in pensive mood,
They flash upon the inward eye
Which is the bliss of solitude;
And then my heart with pleasure fills,
And dances with the daffodils.

She caught her breath. Peter understood! He knew she spent time in quiet places like her sanctuary near St. Andrew's, reflecting on memories to refresh her mind and spirit! She ran her hand over the page. Peter hadn't laughed at her when she'd shared her deepest feelings. Instead he said she had poetry in her soul. Peter was the man she'd longed for all her life. Did she dare hope he'd be more than her friend?

She shifted her glance to the page on the right and stared. *"How do I love thee? Let me count the ways. . . ."*

A shiver ran through her as the words of Elizabeth Barrett Browning leaped from the page. *He couldn't mean this one, could he?* She tried to catch her breath as her grandfather's footsteps sounded on the stairs. She quickly took the book to her room and started on the evening meal. Which poem did Peter mean?

◆　◆　◆

On the morning of August 24, Ann opened the blackout curtains and stared at a wall of white: Fog had spread across London. She had straightened the shop and was getting ready for the day's business when the bell on the door jangled and a man stepped into the room. "Peter! What are you doing here so early?" She smiled and put down the keys to the cabinet as her heart beat faster.

"I didn't know I was on a schedule." He raised an eyebrow and grinned. "After struggling to get here in this pea soup, that's all the welcome I get?"

"No, you don't need a schedule. You're welcome anytime. This is a business. It's just that we weren't expecting you. Grandpa's in the back." Ann stopped as Peter chuckled at her rambling. *Which poem did he mean?*

"I thought we could—" Peter stopped suddenly as the air-raid sirens began to wail.

"Follow me!" her grandfather called out as he hurried into the room. "We need to take cover, just in case!" He led them to the storeroom in the basement, where he closed the door and turned on a light. "We'll be as safe in here as anywhere." He reached for their hands and asked God's protection as the piercing sounds continued above. Then he took a Bible from a shelf and opened it.

Ann and Peter sat down on a small sofa. He put his arm around her and drew her close so her head rested on his shoulder. She could feel his heart beating rapidly and hoped it was because of her nearness as well as the sirens.

Time dragged while the wailing continued. Suddenly there was a loud silence. Her grandfather listened a moment before he opened the door. "Stay here. I'm going up to see what's happened."

Ann stood quickly. "We're not letting you go up there by yourself!" They followed him up the stairs.

Her grandfather opened the shop door, and they stepped out, relieved to find their street unchanged. The fog had thinned, and they anxiously scanned the skyline through a wispy veil. In the distance, smoke billowed above the treetops, and a church spire pointed toward the sky in the midst of boiling black clouds.

"The city was hit," her grandfather said softly. "People over there need our prayers."

As they stared in disbelief, Mrs. Chumley stomped out of her shop and scanned the skies. In spite of the disaster, Ann chuckled at their neighbor. Her red hair stuck out in all directions, and she had two different kinds of shoes on her feet. Her bright green summer dress was buttoned with one side hanging lower than the other. As she searched the skyline, her red curls bobbed and her glasses moved up and down on her nose. "If those Germans think they're going to march in here and find us quaking in fear, they don't know the English!" she declared, then looked around and gave a huff. "Well, what are you standing here for? This is a business day. Let's get to it!" She turned and marched into her shop.

Peter stared after her and shook his head. "I'd better get back to the university to see if all's well. We'll plan to do something another day when things are quieter, Ann. I'll try to come by soon." He touched her cheek gently and hurried down the walk.

◆　◆　◆

On Monday morning, Ann finished the breakfast dishes and came downstairs to find her grandfather hunched over the newspaper. "The situation is about to get worse, mark my word. British planes made a raid on a Berlin suburb last night in retaliation for what the Germans did here. Hitler won't let this pass. He'll be back!"

Ann shuddered at the danger that lay ahead for the city and people she loved.

Tense days followed. To Ann, they crept by as she waited impatiently for Peter to appear. She was sweeping the stockroom when the bell jangled and a customer entered. As she had so often lately, she paused to listen for that familiar voice.

"Peter!" she heard her grandfather exclaim. "Ann and I were beginning to worry about you."

She dropped the broom and hurried into the shop. "Where have you been?" she blurted out. "I was afraid you'd gone back home and hadn't had time to tell us." She stared at him as her heart thudded and the warmth came into her face.

"I've been busy at the university. I'm sorry I worried you." Peter quickly glanced at her grandfather.

"Why don't you fix some tea, Ann? We've been saving it to enjoy at a time like this." Her grandfather smiled at her.

Ann nodded and hurried from the room.

Peter sat down and put his hat on the desk. "I told our friend about the Bible, Nigel, and he met with those higher up in our work. They were astounded at what you have and very concerned for its safety. It took time, but they were able to pull strings and book passage for Ann on the same ship I'm leaving on." He reached in his pocket and took out an envelope. "Keep this ticket safe. I couldn't get either of us passage until the middle of September, but things seem to have calmed down for a while anyway."

Nigel reached out to grasp Peter's hand firmly. "The Lord's been good to us, and you have my deep gratitude, my friend, but let's not tell Ann about this yet. The less she knows, the better. I'll tell her at the last minute, and it's essential she not discover you're on board until she gets there." They could hear the rattle of teacups and Ann's footsteps on the stairs. "Come by late Wednesday morning," Nigel said. "I'll see that Ann's out on an errand, and we'll plan the details."

Peter nodded as Ann came into the room carrying a tray. He hurried to take it from her and smiled into her eyes. The room was quiet as she poured the hot but weak tea and handed Peter a cup.

Nigel cleared his throat. "I have a book I need to work on. I'll leave you two to solve the world's problems." He took his cup of tea and left the room.

"I'm sorry I worried you." Peter set his cup on the desk, reached over, and took her hand. "There's much going on at the university that takes my time. With the war moving closer, we need to ensure records and important items will be safe."

Ann drew a deep breath. "I was afraid you'd left for America." As she looked at him, tears filled her eyes.

"You can't get rid of me that easily!" He smiled and handed her a small bag. "Here. Sweets for someone sweet."

Ann sniffed. "Cookies! Where did you get them?" She peered into the sack. "One for each of us!"

"My friend at the university gave them to me. I wanted to share them with the most special people in my life." He put his hand on the sack and winked. "One's for your grandfather, don't forget."

She handed him a cookie, and they ate slowly, savoring each bite. "When I was little, I'd raid the cookie jar and eat until my stomach hurt." She sighed.

Peter chuckled. "And I remember one time my grandma taught me a lesson. I'd been eating cookies she'd baked for her ladies' group, so she put extra salt in the next batch. Was that awful! I was a more cautious cookie thief after that!" He smiled at the memory and wiped the crumbs from his hand. "Ann, I—"

The bell jangled as a customer walked in, and Peter stood. "Your help is needed. I'll come by as soon as I can." He smiled at her and headed for the door.

Ann's heart dropped as she watched Peter leave. Something felt different, but she couldn't put her finger on it. She sighed and turned to help the customer.

Chapter 7

On Wednesday morning, Peter arrived at the shop to find Ann out running errands as Nigel had promised. He took a seat beside the desk. "So, how do we get Ann to the ship without arousing suspicion?"

Nigel sat back in his chair. "I've thought of nothing else, Peter. I've decided to tell her about the ticket right away. The ship leaves in a few weeks, and we need her possessions taken from here a bit at a time in case the shop's being watched. We'll want her to slip away from here at night. I'm hoping you can arrange all that."

Peter nodded. "I'll work on it with our friends. They've reserved a very small but private room for her aboard ship. Now we have to decide how to protect the Bible. Ann will be transporting it, but we don't want to put her in jeopardy. We can always keep it in the ship's safe, if we can trust those with access to it, but these days there are too many people who will do anything for money."

Nigel got up and paced to the counter, rubbing his chin. "She'll have her suitcases with her. We can ship some books on her ticket, but we want the Bible to remain in her possession." He paused. "Maybe I can disguise it so it looks like some ordinary book that wouldn't arouse suspicion."

"How about Shakespeare?" Peter suggested.

Nigel tapped his fingers together. "An excellent idea!"

Peter paused. "But the Gutenberg Bible's twelve by seventeen inches and thick. That's too large for her to carry as casual reading."

Nigel was silent a moment. "Mrs. Wilson keeps her knitting in a large cloth bag. Maybe she has an extra one that would hold the Bible."

"And we could fill it with knitting supplies so the book wouldn't show," Peter added. "Mrs. Wilson could teach her to knit—"

"Perfect!" Nigel's eyes gleamed. "I'll talk to Mrs. Wilson and start on the false cover right away."

"Passengers will be carrying all their possessions on this trip, so a bag that's a bit heavy won't be out of place," Peter commented.

Nigel placed his hand on Peter's shoulder. "I want you to know how much I appreciate this, and if I may speak out of turn, you and Ann have my blessing. . . ." He paused and looked at Peter.

Peter smiled broadly. "I was hoping to hear those words before we left. But how I wish you were going with us. Ann will be very sad to leave you, and I'll miss a dear friend."

"We'll be together again one day, Peter. If it's not until heaven, take good care of Ann for me."

"You know I will." He looked at Nigel solemnly and stood to warmly clasp his friend's shoulder.

"If you have time, Peter, stop by late this afternoon. I should have the information you ordered, and maybe I can talk Ann into fixing us something to eat," Nigel suggested. "We need to enjoy an evening together while we can."

Peter's face lit up. "A real dinner? Tell her I'll be there!" He was smiling in anticipation as he hurried out the door.

◆　◆　◆

Ann finished the errands and returned to find her grandfather again listening to his radio, a Bible in his lap. He looked up as she walked in. "The fighting's fierce and the bombing heavy in the south of the country," he reported. "And with the Germans bombing areas around London, be sure the basement is well stocked with food and water." He paused to listen again before he said, "Oh, and Peter will be by later to look at some materials. I invited him to join us for dinner. I didn't think you'd mind. Mrs. Wilson will be here, too."

Peter was coming! Ann hurried upstairs to plan the menu, hoping she had enough food on hand to make a decent meal. The afternoon passed quickly, and soon she heard her grandfather leading Peter and Mrs. Wilson up the stairs. The table was set, and she was dishing up the food as they walked in. Her grandfather seated Mrs. Wilson, and Peter joined them at the table, smiling at Ann warmly.

"This isn't fancy, but at least there was plenty of fish available when I shopped this morning," she explained as she set the platter on the table, then added bowls of potatoes and green beans and the plate of bread Mrs. Wilson had brought. "I wish we had butter, but we've used our ration coupons. We'll have fresh fruit for dessert; I didn't have sugar to make anything."

"No need to apologize." Peter chuckled. "You wouldn't want to know what I usually eat for dinner!" He bowed his head for the prayer her grandfather offered. The conversation was light as they enjoyed the meal, and Ann felt her spirits lift as thoughts of war faded.

When they finished, her grandfather ushered Peter and Mrs. Wilson into the sitting room, where they discussed England in more peaceful times. As Ann was bringing a pot of the tea they had saved for special occasions, she paused and looked at the three people so dear to her. Maybe someday she and Peter could invite her grandfather and Mrs. Wilson to dinner at their apartment. Suddenly her face grew warm. Where had that idea come from?

She served the tea as Peter told stories about his family in America, and Mrs. Wilson and her grandfather shared tales of their childhood days in nineteenth-century England. Mrs. Wilson worked on her knitting and offered to teach Ann how to make an afghan. "I volunteer to be your first victim, er, recipient," Peter teased. He chuckled as she flicked a piece of yarn at him.

Finally her grandfather left to walk Mrs. Wilson home, and Peter stood. "I have to catch the bus. Will you see me out?" At the shop door, he turned to her. "The dinner was delicious, Ann. Imagine, a poet who can cook! I'm impressed!"

She smiled. "Thank you for the compliment, but I only read poetry."

"I wish we had time to share our special poem, but this will have to do." He bent to give her a long, warm kiss and smiled into her eyes. "I'll see you soon."

Ann closed the door behind him and tried to catch her breath. *Which poem did he mean?*

Upstairs, she cleaned the kitchen, then headed for her room to get ready for bed. She paused at the book of poetry and turned to the pages where Peter had placed the note. What was he trying to tell her? She fell asleep, her dreams filled with images of a bookshop and a cozy home with Peter.

Suddenly, she sat straight up as the air-raid siren wailed, a feeling of terror racing through her at the deafening sound of antiaircraft guns and exploding bombs. "Let's get to the basement!" her grandfather called out over the noise. He reached for her hand, and they hurried downstairs, where he closed the door carefully and turned on a small light.

Explosions sounded in the distance, and Ann felt the terror build in the pit of her stomach. Even down here, she could hear the planes overhead, some droning and some like a swarm of bees buzzing in terrible anger.

She sat on the edge of the sofa and clasped her hands tightly to keep them from trembling as she prayed for their safety. Trying to escape the sounds, she closed her eyes to picture Peter's teasing smile and his hazel eyes that seemed to say he understood her deepest thoughts. Her heart ached for the security of his presence.

Her grandfather got out a kerosene lamp. "We'll need this if the power goes out." He sat next to her on the sofa and put his arm around her. Ann laid her head on his shoulder and closed her eyes as he stroked her hair gently. After reading the Twenty-third Psalm and praying, they listened to the terrifying sounds until both fell asleep.

Suddenly Ann awoke. Silence! The light was still on, and she could see the room was unchanged. She touched her grandfather's shoulder, and he sat up quickly, looking around in confusion for a moment before hurrying to the door. All was quiet above. He motioned to her, and they ascended the stairs to find the first floor unscathed. Ann breathed a sigh of relief.

"But others somewhere will not be so fortunate this morning," he remarked as he unlocked the door. "We need to check on Mrs. Wilson today."

In the early morning light, they could see thick, dark clouds of smoke billowing above the trees. Their neighbors' homes, however, appeared undamaged. They were staring at the scene when Mrs. Chumley tromped out of her shop, dressed in her nightclothes. Her red hair stuck out from under a green hat with a feathered plume, and she wore work boots on her feet. She shook her fist at the sky and tromped back inside.

Ann chuckled. "Leave it to Mrs. Chumley to bring us a smile at a time like this!"

"Let's thank the Lord for His protection and pray He extends it to others in the days ahead," her grandfather said as he stepped back inside. "Then you work in the shop this morning, Ann. With the attacks increasing, I have things to do in the workroom."

Throughout the day, Ann looked up quickly whenever the shop bell jangled, but Peter didn't appear. When she expressed her fears, her grandfather reminded her Peter had said he'd be very busy for a while, but she knew she wouldn't have peace until he walked through their shop door unscathed.

With night raids occurring on a regular basis, her grandfather set up cots in the basement, where they would sleep until the bombing raids ceased. She spent the afternoon moving their bedding down from upstairs and seeing there was a supply of food and water.

After their dinner of scrambled eggs and toast, her grandfather stood. "Leave the dishes for now, Ann. We need to talk." He walked to their sitting room and sat in his overstuffed chair. When Ann was seated, he stared at his hands for a moment, then looked up at her. "It's about our Gutenberg Bible." He ran his hand over the arm of the chair slowly. "We can't let it be destroyed by the bombs, and we can't let it fall into the hands of evil men."

Ann watched him carefully. The conversation seemed to be very difficult for him.

He looked at her and took a breath. "I think some men know I have it, and now in the confusion of the bombing, I'm afraid someone will try to steal it. We can't let that happen."

Ann caught her breath.

Quietly, he continued. "The book has to be taken to America. I can't do it. If someone is watching the shop and I leave, they'll know I have the Bible with me, and it would be in jeopardy. I don't like putting you in danger, my Ann, but it's also your possession. You have to be the one to save it." He reached in his pocket and took out an envelope. "I was finally able to obtain a ticket to America. You need to take our Bible to safety."

Ann stared at him. "You expect me to leave you here alone? I've told you before I will not do that, Grandpa! Can't you ship it?"

He shook his head. "Boxes can be searched. It needs to travel with someone who will have it in her possession and look out for it." He stood. "I have a plan. Come downstairs with me."

Protesting, Ann followed him to the workroom, where he opened the safe and took out a book. She stared at a worn copy of *The Works of William Shakespeare* and frowned. "I don't understand."

He smiled. "I'm pleased to see you're confused. I put a false cover on the Bible."

"It doesn't look like the Gutenberg Bible at all." She touched the metal latches he had added at the opening to secure the closure.

He breathed deeply. "I hope others will think so, too." He returned the book to the safe and handed her a large cloth bag. "You'll carry the Bible in this, and we'll add balls of yarn to conceal the book. When you're aboard ship, you'll need to work on the afghan whenever people are around so they'll believe this really is your knitting bag."

All Ann could do was stare.

He rubbed his chin. "Now, we need to have your possessions taken from here a bit at a time so nothing will look suspicious. Your ship sails in two weeks, so we need to get started."

She tried to speak but couldn't seem to get any words out.

He looked at her, waiting. "Don't be afraid, my Ann. I'll be praying for you. And don't worry about leaving me here. You couldn't protect me from the bombs anyway. Only God can do that. The truth is, I'll be safer when the Bible's on its way to America."

Ann took a deep breath and swallowed hard. "I didn't realize you'd be in danger if I refused." She nodded. "I'll go. I love you too much to see you hurt, Grandpa, and I couldn't live with myself if I helped the Nazi cause." Her heart felt like a leaded weight. She blinked back tears as she patted his shoulder and forced a mischievous wink. "Besides, Mrs. Wilson will be more than happy to see you're well fed." She noticed a spot of pink appear in his cheeks.

He turned quickly. "Good. Then it's settled. Now we need to pack your things." He headed to the basement. "I'll get your trunk and suitcases."

Chapter 8

Peter sat at his desk, reviewing the plans. Arrangements had been made for the removal of Ann's possessions, and she would be spirited away at night for the journey to the ocean liner. He felt guilty knowing he could make the trip in the safety of daylight while Ann would be at risk from night raids and vehicles with covered headlights.

He ran his hand over his forehead and walked to the window. In the far distance lay areas of the city that had been bombed, and he remembered the day he had walked through the streets to view the damage. Walls jutted into the sky, and the ruins resembled archaeological sites with remnants left here and there. Smoke rose from smoldering fires. People picked through the rubble for any belongings that survived, and some were staying in the remains of their houses without windows or walls.

"Hitler's wrong if he thinks he can crush the English spirit," he said aloud. "He'll only make them fight harder. They're carrying on with remarkable courage." He turned to finish packing before he made one last trip to the bookshop to say good-bye to Nigel and review the plans.

When he entered the store, Ann looked up quickly, a big smile spreading over her face. "Peter! It's so good to see you! Where have you been?" She hurried over to greet him. "Grandpa, Peter's here!"

"I'll stay away more often if this is the welcome I get!" He smiled at her and took her hand. She looked so trusting and happy to see him, he hated to think what lay ahead.

Nigel hurried into the shop. "Peter, my friend, come, see what I've found for you." Peter smiled at her and followed him into the workroom, where Nigel handed him some papers. They reviewed the plans, prayed together, and said their good-byes.

As they returned to the shop, Peter turned to Nigel. "Now, may I borrow your granddaughter?"

He nodded. "Keep her safe."

"We can go to our special spot for a bit of peace and quiet." Peter paused with his hand on the doorknob.

Ann gave him a shaky smile. "I'd like that."

◆ ◆ ◆

They were quiet as they walked to the park. Ann's heart ached, knowing she might never see Peter again. They entered their secluded spot and sat on the bench. The place that had been such a solace now seemed strange and different, she thought as she stared at the late-summer flowers, not trusting herself to speak. The wind rustled the leaves above them and moved through the trees with a mournful sigh. To Ann, it was the sound of her heart being broadcast for all to hear.

Peter picked up a wilted daisy and straightened the petals. "I'll be praying for you, Ann. Your grandfather told me about your plans to go home." He leaned forward with his elbows on his knees. "I wish. . . ." He paused and looked up at the trees and sky. "Maybe when this is over, we'll be back here someday."

Ann couldn't hold back the tears. She pulled a handkerchief from her pocket and mopped at her eyes. "It will be so hard to leave. I'll worry about you and Grandpa and the city, but this is something I have to do. Others have sacrificed things they cared about. Now it's my turn, and I have to give up all this for something I believe is right. I just didn't expect it to be so hard." She wiped her eyes again.

Peter reached over and took her hand. "Courage is doing the right thing even when it breaks your heart. Think how sad it would be if you could leave everything without caring." He pulled her into his arms and stroked her hair gently. His chin rested on her head, and her tears made wet splotches on his shirt.

Ann sat up and wiped her nose. "Please take care of Grandpa for me, Peter. I know Mrs. Wilson will see that he has food. They care about each other so he'll have someone after I'm gone, but promise me you'll come by often and see that he's safe. You've been a dear friend to him; I'll never forget that."

Peter stared at her, then looked down. "I'll, uh, I'll get there as often. . .as I can. I'm sure Mrs. Wilson will do a better job than I could, though." He stood quickly and pulled her to her feet. "Now, you need to stop worrying and enjoy the rest of your time here. I miss that smile of yours." He lifted her chin. "We'll see each other again, I promise. You can't get rid of me that easily."

Ann couldn't stop the tears that streamed down her face. Peter took her in his arms and kissed the top of her head. "Okay, kiddo, time to get you back to the shop before we have a flood here. I didn't bring a boat!" He grinned at her, and she managed a wet smile. He bent to give her a tender kiss, then took her arm and walked her home.

When Peter left her at the shop, Ann went to the window to watch him walk away. Instead he approached a tall man she'd seen out there before. Why would Peter be talking to him? By the time Peter had finished the conversation, curiosity had replaced her tears.

◆ ◆ ◆

The following days passed quickly, and most of Ann's possessions had been sent ahead. As she made a last tour of the neighborhood and talked to people she had grown fond of, she chuckled to herself. Mrs. Chumley felt something was up and decided Ann was eloping with Peter. "You can't fool me," she insisted. "I know romance when I see it!" She thrust an object at Ann. "From Albert and me." Ann stared at the framed picture of King George VI. "Deserves a place of honor in every proper home," her neighbor declared proudly.

Ann took a deep breath. "I can't take it now. Please keep it for me." She tried to make her smile sincere.

"Sure thing, dearie." Mrs. Chumley gave a wink. "A person don't need much on a trip like that. It'll be here when you get back."

Bombing raids had continued every night starting at dusk, so Ann was thankful their area of town remained unscathed. She glanced at the clock—one hour left. Now she had to face the good-bye she dreaded, and she hurried into the workroom, where her grandfather was repairing a book. Keeping busy was his way of handling the pain of her leaving, she realized.

"Grandpa, please stay safe and let Mrs. Wilson see that you're properly fed. She cares for you very much, and I have a feeling it's mutual. You have my blessing." They spent the hour reminiscing, and her grandfather reviewed important points for the safety of both her and the Bible.

Ann clasped and unclasped her hands. "I thought Peter would come by one last time. Tell him—" Suddenly, there was a soft tap on the back door, and she jumped.

Her grandfather stood. "Ann, your ride is here." He put his arms around her, and she hugged his neck, fighting back tears. "Grandpa, I can't leave you here. Come with me. Please."

He patted her hair gently. "God will watch over me—and I'm sure Mrs. Wilson will, too. I'll be praying for your safety, as you will mine. God will keep us safe." He reached out to wipe a tear from her cheek. "Now you must go. And do what these people tell you; I'm trusting them completely with my two greatest treasures."

Her grandfather turned and opened the door to admit a man who reached for Ann's suitcases. "We need to leave right away, miss." Ann nodded and hugged her grandfather one last time before following the man out the door and into the night, carrying the knitting bag into which was tucked a well-worn copy of Shakespeare.

Chapter 9

Ann stepped into the ocean liner's tourist-class entrance and stared at the chaos around her. Everyone in London seemed to be boarding the ship. How would she ever find her cabin in this confusion? She spotted a ship steward and quickly asked directions.

"Follow me, miss." Looking relieved to get away from the clamor, the steward took her suitcases and led her down the grand staircase to her corridor, finally stopping at her cabin door. "As you can see, this won't be a normal passage. We're carrying as many refugees as we can hold, so you'll find cots set up in the ballroom, lounges, and everywhere we can put them. People want to get to America while they can." He unlocked the door and set her suitcases inside.

Ann took a deep breath and asked the question that had been plaguing her. "Will the ship be in much danger from German submarines?"

He paused at the door. "We'll be escorted by a convoy of navy ships until we're several hundred miles from the English coast," he explained briskly. "Then we'll be on our own until we approach North America and pick up another convoy. The United States is still neutral in this war, so the Germans haven't been targeting her passenger liners. Once we're on our own, we'll do everything we can to make it clear we're hauling civilians and not military personnel."

Ann let out her breath. "So, there's no danger?"

"We can't guarantee that." He gave a frown. "There have been maverick attacks against neutral ships, but the captain will do all he can to make this a safe trip." He took some papers from a folder. "We're carrying so many extra passengers, meals will be served in shifts. We ask that you come to the tourist-class dining room promptly at your assigned hour." He handed her a schedule and a list of wartime regulations and hurried down the hall.

Ann put the bag on the bed and looked around the small cabin. It was compact with a single bed, dressing table, a tiny closet, and bathroom. How did her grandfather get her a cabin of her own, especially one this nice? She had come over third class. She glanced at the beautiful wood finish of the furnishings and paneled walls.

The ship rocked gently. This didn't seem real. One day she was in London, and now she was on a ship sailing for America in the middle of a war. The old worry nagged at her as she thought of leaving her grandfather and Peter to the mercy of the bombing raids.

After hanging her clothes in the closet, she set her suitcase on the dressing table and put her smaller travel bag on the floor of the closet. Now what? Her grandfather had said to keep the Bible with her at all times. There was no place she'd be more comfortable than in the ship's library, and she had time to locate it before dinner. She checked a map of the ship she had found on the dresser and picked up the knitting bag.

After carefully locking the cabin door, she hurried down the corridor and up the grand staircase. To the left, she could see the main lounge filled with row after row of mattresses and cots. People sat against the walls with their possessions and children around them. Ann swallowed hard and turned in the opposite direction to the library.

Inside, she walked around the small room, checking the titles before sitting down and taking out the afghan she had started with Mrs. Wilson's help. As she struggled to remember the instructions, the door opened and a distinguished-looking gentleman entered. He nodded to her and picked up a magazine.

She fumbled with the knitting and was relieved when she glanced at her watch and saw it was almost time for her dinner hour. She put the afghan in the bag and hurried down the staircase. Suddenly her heart gave a lurch, and she gasped as she saw the back of a man's head standing out above the crowd. Her eyes had to be playing tricks on her! The man looked like Peter! He quickly turned a corner, and she lost sight of him. Suddenly she felt very alone.

When she finally arrived at the spacious dining room, she found long rows of tables had been set up to accommodate the increased number of passengers. She took a seat and was inspecting the lovely room when a voice spoke at her left. "Is this seat taken?" Looking up, she saw it was the gentleman from the library and shook her head. With his white hair and blue eyes, he reminded her of her grandfather. Somehow she didn't feel as alone when someone seemed familiar.

"You're the lady from the library," he said as he sat down. "When I travel, I spend most of my time in the ship's library, too, though not to knit." He smiled. "I'm Winston Humbolt, and you're. . . ?"

"Ann Heydon," she replied. "I notice you don't have an accent; you're American?"

"Yes, I'm returning from a business trip. I'm an importer."

As she unfolded her napkin, a woman took the empty seat across from them. Her hair was smartly coifed, and her face carefully made up. She smiled across at Mr. Humbolt and gushed, "I'm so glad to find an empty seat at your table. I can see you're a person of quality." She sniffed. "I can't believe I'm stuck with these. . . these. . ." She waved her hand toward the other passengers as her perfume engulfed the table. "Who did they think they were, denying me first class!" Voices around them grew still. The woman reached out her hand as large gems sparkled on her fingers. "I'm Mrs. Van Peldt. My late husband was Herbert Van Peldt, the shipping magnate. I'm sure you've heard of him."

Mr. Humbolt took her hand and introduced himself, and the woman chattered on about her social status. The food was soon served, and conversations again buzzed around them. "An adequate meal but not up to their usual," he commented. "And I don't enjoy having my meals rushed."

"I do agree," Mrs. Van Peldt replied. "We have so much in common."

Ann finished her dinner, picked up the knitting bag, and stood, almost colliding with another diner as she stared at a man leaving the room. He could be Peter's twin! She hurried to the corridor, but the man was nowhere in sight. With a sigh, she headed for the staircase, her feeling of loneliness deepening as she entered her dark cabin and switched on the light. All windows on board were tightly covered to help the ship proceed undetected for this part of the voyage.

Her nerves felt frazzled, so she decided to stay in her cabin. Maybe Peter wouldn't feel as far away if she read the book of poems he'd given her. As she opened her suitcase to pick out clothes more comfortable for lounging, she gasped. Someone had searched through her suitcase and left everything in a mess! A jolt of fear ran through her.

Her hands shook as she carefully checked each item; nothing seemed to be missing. What was happening to her? She had imagined she saw Peter on the ship and now this! Were worry about the war and the responsibility for the Bible weighing heavier than she thought?

She sat on the bed and tried to read, but her thoughts drifted from the mess in her suitcase to her grandfather and Peter. The ship's motion was comforting, and her eyes grew heavy. At least she felt rocked instead of seasick! Her mind drifted back to the days she and Peter had spent in their special place in the park. The memories brought a warm feeling, but too quickly the worry intruded. Was Peter safe, and was their part of town still undamaged? Finally she fell asleep, longing for the security she had found in Peter's arms.

◆ ◆ ◆

That was close! Peter closed the door to his cabin and threw the key on the bed. He never dreamed he'd be assigned to the same meal schedule as Ann. He had promised Nigel he wouldn't let her know he was on the ship until they were a day out at sea. He'd have to be more careful.

He paced the room, trying to quell another worry nagging him. Ann was going to feel he'd deceived her when she learned he was on board. He couldn't let that destroy their relationship.

Pacing wasn't going to help, he realized. He got out his grandmother's Bible and turned to the Psalms to calm his spirit, something he'd never have done a few months ago. Now with so many things he couldn't handle on his own, it had become a comforting habit.

Chapter 10

The next morning, Ann woke late and rushed into the dining room. Looking around for an empty seat, she ran into the back of a steward carrying a loaded tray. "Oh, no!" The contents began to slip, and she gasped as a man's hands grabbed the tray to steady it.

When the steward bent to set it on the table, Ann looked into Peter's face. "Peter! It *is* you! What are you doing here?" All she could do was stare. He had known she was leaving. If he had gotten a last-minute ticket, why hadn't he told her? Something was very strange.

"Ann." Peter finally spoke up. "I, uh, you. . .you'll have to be seated, or you'll miss breakfast. The next group will be here in a few minutes." He thrust his hands into his pockets and jingled some coins.

Ann's stomach knotted, and she shook her head. "I'm not hungry anymore, Peter, but I do want to know what's going on. The last I knew, you were in London. How did you get here, and why didn't you tell me?"

People around them were staring as Peter took her arm and led her from the room. "There's a small lounge down this hall. We can talk there."

Neither spoke as Ann followed him down the corridor. Suspicious scenes flitted through her mind. Peter talking to the men who seemed to be watching the shop. Peter avoiding the shop for so long. Peter being the only one on board who knew she was taking the Bible to America. *Who is Peter Austin?*

When they were seated in the lounge, Ann couldn't hold her thoughts in any longer. "Something strange is going on, Peter, and I want an explanation. Does Grandpa know you're here? You knew which ship I was sailing on; why didn't you contact me?" She frowned at him and held the bag tightly.

Peter took a deep breath. "I was able to get a ticket, and I planned to find you, but there are a lot of people on this ship. The staff is overworked, so I thought I'd wait until things settled down."

Ann continued to frown at him. "Not good enough, Peter. I thought. . ." She paused. Even under these circumstances, she could feel the red start to cover her face, and her eyes filled with tears, so she quickly looked down.

Peter reached out to cover her hand, but she pulled it away. He let out his breath. "We're far enough out at sea that I guess I can tell you. I promised your grandfather I wouldn't say anything until we were well underway."

Ann's head jerked up. "Promised Grandpa? What's he got to do with this?"

Peter sat back and rubbed the arm of the chair slowly. "I've had my ticket for a long time, Ann. Your grandfather wanted you to go home, and the Bible needed to be taken to safety, but you wouldn't leave. He was afraid if you knew I had a ticket, you'd have me take the Bible. He wanted both his treasures safe, so he had to send the Bible to America with you. And I had to promise I wouldn't let you know until we were far enough out that you couldn't change your mind."

"And what did you think I was going to do? Swim back?" Ann spat out. She grabbed the knitting bag and hurried from the room as tears ran down her cheeks.

She stumbled along the corridor, her mind full of disturbing questions. Was Peter ever who she thought he was? Who were those men he talked to outside the shop? A chilling thought ran through her mind. Peter was the only one on board who knew she had the Bible. Did he go through her luggage last night? Was he connected with those men hoping to steal it?

Her heart felt torn as she opened her cabin door. She couldn't let the Bible fall into the wrong hands. Whom could she trust? *Lord, please show me what to do!* She stared at the knitting bag. Her grandfather always said the Bible wouldn't do her any good if she didn't read it. She washed the tears from her face, then took her own copy out of the suitcase and opened it to the Twenty-third Psalm. It brought a sad comfort as she remembered the night her grandfather had read it aloud while the bombs fell on London.

◆　◆　◆

"I really blew that!" Peter muttered as he walked back to his room. "And I must admit the situation looks pretty suspicious." He nodded at a distinguished, white-haired gentleman who turned toward Ann's corridor. He could show Nigel's letter to Ann and clear up the misunderstanding, but he needed to know if she really trusted him. He stopped and turned around. He couldn't take a chance on losing her. They had to talk this out, and he had an idea where he'd find her.

◆　◆　◆

Ann checked her suitcases again, memorizing the position of the contents. If anyone went through her possessions, she'd know for sure. She locked the suitcase, picked up the knitting bag, and headed for the library. When she entered the room, Mr. Humbolt was reading a newspaper. "So, we meet again, my dear. Are you enjoying the voyage?"

Ann started to reply, when suddenly the door opened and Peter stepped into the room. She stiffened and quickly looked down. As he took a seat beside her, she could feel Mr. Humbolt watching them before he got up and left the room.

"Ann, please listen. I'm telling you the truth. Your grandfather is doing what he thinks is best for you. He loves you so much and so do I. . . ." He stopped as if shocked at his own words.

He loves me! The puzzling scenes and Peter's words jumbled together in Ann's mind—the suspicions on one hand and their precious moments together on the other. Of all the times to hear the words she'd been hoping for!

Peter grabbed her hand and wouldn't let go. "Ann, this is a dangerous trip. The convoy has left us, and the ship's on its own. They're turning all the lights on, windows are being uncovered, and spotlights will be turned on the ship's name and the American flag so the Germans will know this is a passenger ship, but it's still dangerous. I don't want to be fighting with you under these circumstances."

Ann looked down at their hands and spoke in a whisper. "Peter, you're the only one who knows what I'm carrying. If you didn't go through my suitcase, who did?" She looked up and stared at him.

Peter's mouth dropped open. "Someone went through your suitcase? When?"

"Yesterday when I came back from dinner, I opened it and found everything in a jumble."

"Ann, if I wanted to take the Bible, I'd know where to look. I wouldn't have to rummage through your suitcase. Apparently someone suspects you have it, and that puts you in jeopardy."

Ann longed to believe his words. "But I saw you talk to those men watching the shop. Who were they?"

Peter let out his breath. "Your grandfather and I were part of a group working to keep valuable materials both from the Nazis and from being destroyed by bombs. When we realized someone might be watching the shop, we arranged for a man from our side to keep an eye on things. That was the tall, thin man. We assume the others were looking for treasures to steal, either to sell to the Nazis or because they were Nazis."

"Oh." Ann swallowed hard, suddenly feeling foolish as she remembered her grandfather had told Peter about their plans for keeping the Bible safe. "What should I do now?"

"Check your suitcases when you get back to your room and let me know what you find. I'll keep running into you. People can think I'm the ship's Romeo chasing after a beautiful girl. And the last part's true." He smiled and winked.

Ann felt herself blush. "I'll check my luggage and then come back to the library. I feel more comfortable here." Peter nodded and she left the room.

Back in her cabin, she went straight to her suitcase and opened it to find the contents as she had left them. Quickly, she pulled her travel bag out of the closet and placed it on the bed. As she opened it, she gasped. Someone had rummaged through it and left everything in a jumble! Her hands were shaking as she picked up the knitting bag and hurried to the library.

No one was in the room. She had taken out the afghan when the door opened, and Mr. Humbolt walked in. "Ah, so we meet again." He smiled at her. "And how is the afghan coming?"

Ann greeted him, and as she shifted in the chair, her foot caught the knitting bag. It plopped on its side with a *thud*, and balls of yarn rolled across the floor. "Oh, no!" She quickly grabbed as many as she could and turned to stuff them in the bag but instead stared in horror when she saw the copy of Shakespeare lying exposed.

She felt Mr. Humbolt stop beside her with the yarn he'd collected and looked up to see him staring at the book. "I see you enjoy Shakespeare." He motioned toward the book. "It must be very special to carry it with your knitting."

Prickles ran down Ann's spine. "It was a gift from my grandfather."

Mr. Humbolt bent over. "I collect old books. This one's very unusual. May I—"

As he reached out to pick it up, the door burst open and a wave of heavy perfume filled the air. "There you are, Winston!" Mrs. Van Peldt stalked into the room. "I saw you turn down this corridor." She gave a haughty smile and put her arm through his. "Let's leave the tourist class to itself." She patted his arm with a hand covered in sparkling rings.

Ann smiled weakly as she watched Mr. Humbolt's face turn a dark red and a frown cover his brow. The woman pulled on his arm and led him to the door. Ann sighed in relief. In the Bible God had used some unusual characters to accomplish His purposes; it looked like He still did!

When the door opened a moment later, Ann quickly reached for the knitting bag, then let out her breath as Peter stepped into the room. "I saw the gentleman leave and hoped you'd be alone." He took a seat and peered at her. "You look pale. Was something wrong with your suitcases?" As Ann related what she had found in her cabin, Peter gave a deep sigh. "Someone knows there isn't much time left to steal the Bible. Fortunately, no one realizes what you carry in that knitting bag."

"Oh, but now someone does!" She told him about spilling the contents of the bag and Mr. Humbolt's attempt to examine the book.

Peter was quiet a moment. "Ann, do you trust me? You know how much I care about you, but are you really convinced I'm who I say I am?"

The question caught Ann by surprise, and her suspicions and feelings struggled with each other. She knew she loved him, but did she believe him and trust him? It was true; he could have stolen the Bible a long time ago, and he'd been nothing but a help to her grandfather and her. She said a prayer for guidance, then nodded. "I trust you, Peter. What do you want me to do?"

"Let me take the book. If you don't have it, you won't be in danger." He watched her face carefully.

Ann couldn't breathe for a moment. *Lord, this is Your Word. Don't let anything happen to it!* She hesitated, then handed him the knitting bag.

Peter looked relieved and took an envelope from his pocket. "Your grandfather asked me to give you this when we met on the ship."

Ann blinked in surprise as she opened it and read the brief message. Relief washed over her, and she looked up at Peter. "Grandpa confirmed what you told me. I'm so sorry I suspected you." She flashed him a mischievous smile and motioned toward the bag. "Ready for some knitting lessons?"

"Knitting lessons, no, but I am counting on lots of hugs and kisses to even the score!" Grinning, Peter pulled her to her feet for a tender embrace. "You won't have to worry about the Bible now, so let's pretend this is a pleasure cruise and enjoy the rest of the trip. Those Germans are supposed to think this is a normal voyage. Let's show 'em!"

She felt her heart racing. "That sounds wonderful!"

"I need to take care of the Bible. You get ready, and I'll meet you by the main lounge in an hour." He lifted her chin and smiled into her eyes.

Chapter 11

For the rest of the voyage, Ann and Peter tried to forget the war as they swam in the pool and lounged on deck chairs. They strolled the enclosed promenade hand-in-hand, admiring the ocean view outside the sliding-glass windows. As they turned at the class barrier isolating the tourist-class promenade from that of first class, Ann chuckled. "Any minute I expect to see Mrs. Van Peldt leaping the class barrier so she can be on the first-class side."

Peter stopped at the windows, and they watched the ocean moving in rhythmic waves before he spoke. "Ann, when we dock, I don't intend to have you disappear from my life. I want some promises made between us." He glanced over at her. "Your grandfather said he'd welcome me into the family—if you so desire."

Ann's heart was pounding, and she could feel the red start to cover her face.

Peter held her close, then glanced at his watch and sighed. "I'll walk you to your cabin. We dock this afternoon, so we both need to pack. Then we'll continue this conversation and thank the Lord for a safe journey both for us and the treasure we carry."

"And let's ask Him to keep Grandpa and Mrs. Wilson safe," she added as they headed for her corridor. "I pray constantly their area of town has remained undamaged."

Back in her cabin, Ann rechecked the room, then closed her suitcases. She was putting the keys to her luggage in her purse when a knock sounded at the door. She opened it to find Mr. Humbolt standing there. "What are you doing here?" she asked as he entered and shut the door.

"Since we're about to disembark, I didn't want to miss my chance to inspect your unusual book," he said with a smirk. "I've never seen one like it. It's odd how you always kept it with your knitting but never read it. So, how about a look for a fellow book lover?"

Ann stood speechless. "But I don't have it anymore. I gave it to someone who wanted a book for the voyage."

"And who might that be? Mr. Peter Austin? Is he keeping it safe for you? My, my, you are clever, my dear. But he'll find he has a choice to make—you or the book. Which do you think he'll choose?" Mr. Humbolt looked at her with cold eyes.

Ann couldn't catch her breath. *Lord, please help me!* She jumped at a sudden knock on the door.

"Stay where you are. I'll answer it." He jerked the door open and stared.

"So this is where I find you!" Mrs. Van Peldt stalked into the room, bristling with anger. She glared at Ann, then turned her ire on Winston. "All that sweet talk, and here you are chasing some young floozy. I've seen you come here before. Don't think you can take me for a fool!" She jabbed him in the chest with her long red nails.

Despite the serious situation, Ann chuckled to herself.

"It will take more than an apology before I forgive you, Winston." She pulled him toward the door. "We need to talk before the ship docks."

As she opened the door, Peter stepped inside, followed by a ship's officer, who quickly grasped Mr. Humbolt's arms. "You're not going anywhere, Humbolt. We checked you out and found you're nothing but a thief who preys on people aboard ship." Winston Humbolt struggled, but the officer kept a firm hold. "After a tip from Mr. Austin, we followed you here."

Mrs. Van Peldt gasped. "Winston, a thief? He can't be! I. . .uh. . .we. . .well, I never! That's what I get for lowering myself to traveling tourist class!" She thrust her chin in the air and stalked out of the room as the officer led Mr. Humbolt away.

Shaking, Ann sank against the wall. "How did he know I had the Bible?"

Peter shuddered as he let out his breath. "It's worth a lot of money, and word gets around. I'm sure those men outside your grandfather's shop weren't working alone. Someone must have had access to the passenger lists."

"The Bible! Peter, where is it?" Ann straightened quickly and stared at him in alarm.

"In a box with a note on it," he said with a smug grin.

Ann frowned. "I don't understand."

Peter picked up her suitcases and headed to his cabin. "I put it in a box I got at the ship's gift shop." He opened the door and pointed to a box sitting on his suitcase. His coat was carelessly thrown on the pile. "I disguised it as a gift to someone special."

He picked up the box and turned it so she could read the label: *Kramer's Nativity Scenes—authentic reproductions of original works; 15"x20" set includes ceramic figurines, manger, and stable.* He placed the box in the knitting bag, then repacked the yarn around it. "I took out the heavy figurines and laid the Bible on the bottom, then put the stable walls on top and ended with straw and the small figures." He chuckled. "It's true; the box does contain nativity scenes!" He handed her the cloth bag, then led them back to the promenade, where they set their possessions on a bench.

Ann frowned. "But the box looked as if it had never been opened."

"Ah, another of my hidden talents, my dear." He winked and reached in the bag to retrieve a paper that lay on top of the box. "I said this was a gift for someone special. Read the note I left on it. It's addressed to you."

Ann took the paper. *"To the one who makes my life complete. Will you enjoy this nativity scene with me every Christmas for the rest of our lives? I love you with all my heart. Peter.*"

Ann couldn't speak as she blinked back tears. Peter raised an eyebrow, and she nodded her answer.

He took her in his arms. "There are two treasures in my life that are of immeasurable worth—God's Word and you. I don't intend to live without either again."

Ann nestled against his chest. "Peter, haven't you guessed why I blush whenever I'm around you? I've loved for you for a long time, but I knew I was a plain Jane while you're handsome, a writer, and a prof—"

"Hmm, keep talking!" He wagged his eyebrows at her. "Seriously, my love, you're anything but plain. And your sweet blush is what attracted me in the first place. Never change it."

She looked up at him and took a deep breath. "That note you left in the poetry book. Which poem made you think of me?"

His lips curved into a teasing grin. "Which do you want it to be?"

She felt her face grow warm as she answered softly, "I'd like to hear you count the ways you love me."

He smiled into her eyes. "My dear, I promise to spend the rest of my life telling you all the ways I love you, but for now I'll let Elizabeth Browning say it for me: 'I love thee with the breath, smiles, tears, of all my life! . . .'" He lifted her chin. "The only thing I can add is a kiss for punctuation!"

JOAN CROSTON
Joan and her husband, Lee, live on Route 66 in the beautiful Missouri Ozarks. They have two married daughters and six grandchildren whose ages range from 4 to 14 so life can become delightfully hectic at times. After spending over half her life on the West Coast, Joan loves being a Midwest transplant where she enjoys gardens and country living. Bible study and writing are at the top of her love-to-do list along with reading anything anytime anywhere but especially when curled up by a crackling fire on a snowy winter day. Her love of history has led her to compile her families' histories, one of her lines going back to 1482 in Norway and her husband's to an ancestor who was with George Washington's troops at Valley Forge. She's currently recording her own family's story and loves seeing how God has been at work blessing their lives.

A Flower Amidst the Ashes

by DiAnn Mills

Dedication

To Margaret Harry, who served England
as a member of the Women's Auxiliary Air Force
during World War II. May God bless.

"He giveth power to the faint;
and to them that have no might He increaseth strength.
Even the youths shall faint and be weary,
and the young men shall utterly fall.
But they that wait upon the Lord shall renew their strength;
they shall mount up with wings as eagles; they shall run,
and not be weary; and they shall walk, and not faint."
Isaiah 40: 29-31

Chapter 1

*"I would say to the House, as I said to those
who have joined this government: 'I have nothing
to offer but blood, toil, tears, and sweat.'"*
WINSTON CHURCHILL

November 1940

In the twilight between sleep and consciousness, Corporal Margaret Walker of Britain's Women's Auxiliary Air Force suddenly woke to the familiar call of air-raid sirens alerting London to another round of German bombings.

"Oh, no." She moaned and covered her head with the pillow. *I'm not moving. I'm not going anywhere. I'm staying right here in this bed. I spent the entire day transporting pilots back and forth from the barracks to the hangars, and I'm exhausted.*

Margaret closed her eyes as her body relaxed, despite the death-screech echoing around her. The day had been too long. . .too exhausting. . .with too many Royal Air Force pilots not returning from their combat missions. She didn't want to consider the ongoing nightmare since September seventh, when German bomber and fighter planes first razed London. In August the enemy hadn't been successful in forcing the island to surrender when they bombed the navy and later the coastal factories involved in airplane assembly. Now, the Luftwaffe attempted to level the capital, hailing the city with bombs and leaving destruction in its wake. Although Britons young and old, men and women, had prepared for the ordeal, no one really anticipated the decimation of property and the loss of lives in their city. At least she hadn't.

Someone shook her. "Margaret, are you awake? Come on, we have to hurry."

She recognized the voice and lifted the pillow from her head. "I'm not going, Beryl. I'm tired and I want to sleep."

Her friend continued to shake her. "If you don't get up, I'm going after the lieutenant. She'll get you moving."

Margaret threw back the thin coverlet and scurried to her feet. "All right. I'm up and going. Be glad I hadn't run the bath before the sirens."

Beryl laughed. "You'd have worn your blanket, I'm afraid."

Margaret smiled in spite of her interrupted sleep. How long had it been since she enjoyed a long, leisurely bath instead of the brisk showers housed beyond their quarters? She adjusted her trousers and quickly buttoned the shirt of her blue-gray work uniform. Her desire to sleep quickly fled in light of the servitude she owed her beloved England. To ignore the warning sirens would be folly, and meant she'd do her country no good dead. Without another word, they raced with the other WAAFs from their barracks to their designated shelter.

Pulling back the tarp to the entrance, Margaret ushered the way for Beryl. Downward they trod to the damp, dimly lit underground shelter protecting them from bombs. They found an empty spot near the back on one of the long benches and waited.

"I thought you had night duty," Beryl said. "I was surprised to see you on your cot."

"No, that's tomorrow night," Margaret said, closing her eyes for a minute's respite. "Perhaps the Germans will cease their bombing, and all will be quiet. The last time I drove an ambulance during an air raid, the cries of the injured kept me awake for nights."

"When will it end?" Beryl whispered. "My Patrick risked his life every time he flew against the Germans until the day they shot him down." She took a deep breath. "My heart longs for him and my dear boy, Christopher."

Margaret knew how Beryl grieved her husband's death and how she missed her young son tucked away safely in an Irish country home. "God will protect Christopher and save England from invasion. We must have faith and trust that not one Nazi will set foot on British soil."

"Faith is all I have left." Beryl released a faint sob. "One day I'm going to ask for a long pass, and then I'll go see my precious son. Holding him will help ease the pain. Oh, he looks like his father, you know."

Margaret smiled in the darkness and gently took Beryl's hand. Her friend held a secret, one of bittersweet memories. New life nestled within Beryl's womb, but Margaret had promised not to disclose the information until Beryl could talk to their lieutenant. "We knew this war would be difficult, and we'd have to make sacrifices, but it's so hard to keep our minds centered on our duties when we hurt."

"I need your strength." Beryl patted the hand over hers. "I thought others would be killed, nameless faces who might never touch my life. I never thought the war would affect me or take my beloved Patrick, just like you never thought your brother would be shot down."

Margaret swallowed her own pain. She welcomed the darkness to hide the tears coursing down her cheeks. Sometimes she believed her heart held visible scars of the war's carnage. How did one live without the reassurance of God's provision?

The low timbre of men's voices captured Margaret's attention. Why did men sit among them in a women's shelter? Straining her ears to listen and not concentrate on the roaring challenger above them, she heard a distinctly male laugh.

"Ladies, there's only two of us and even though none of you are our mums or sisters, have mercy on these two poor pilots," a man said, his voice laden with merriment.

She heard the women giggle, and for a moment she welcomed the man's humor in the dismal place, but the question still plagued her as to why they were there at all.

Irritated, Margaret shook her head. The men had obviously strayed beyond their own barracks and were caught by the sirens. She glanced about in the darkness and didn't see the profile of her lieutenant. In fact, she could barely make out Beryl beside her.

"What rank are you men?" Margaret said.

"I'm Lieutenant Stuart, and my companion is Corporal Harris of the Royal Air Force," came a different, quieter voice. "We're in the area on business."

I dare say you had RAF business among the women's barracks. "I see," Margaret said. Gentlemen officers among the women's quarters infuriated her.

"And your rank?" the lieutenant said.

"Corporal Margaret Walker."

"Kindly forgive us, Corporal, for invading this shelter. We had no choice."

At least the lieutenant possessed the courtesy to address her properly.

She said nothing in response. Tomorrow she'd investigate the matter, but right now she wanted the all-clear signal before sleep overcame her.

For the next thirty minutes, Margaret leaned her head back against the cold, moist wall and dozed until the familiar wail broke the air.

"Moaning Minnie is telling us it's over for the moment," Beryl said. "I wonder how bad the damage."

Margaret shrugged. A lot of wounded meant she'd be robbed of sleep to drive an ambulance. She'd been caught out in the open in enough air raids during work hours to appreciate the shelter's safety. In those times when she had to remain aboveground, her work went on: dodging bombs and tending to the needs of the injured. Immediately she regretted her selfish thoughts. The wounded always took precedence, as it should.

Margaret longed for sleep and a reprieve from her responsibilities. Rarely did she feel melancholy, but rather she took it upon herself to boost the morale of the other women. Light-heartedness gained her respect among the WAAFs along with a keen sense of love and commitment to the women in her barracks. Her current mood must be caused by exhaustion and by thinking about poor Beryl's sad circumstances.

At least I have no one to worry about. How distressing to be among the parents who had to send their children away from the cities.

Numbly, Margaret stood in line to leave the shelter. Tomorrow she'd feel better. Tomorrow she'd find her wit and humor.

"Excuse me, Corporal," a male voice said once they stepped aboveground. She recognized the voice of the reserved Lieutenant Stuart.

Margaret stiffened and turned in the darkness to face the officer. "Yes sir." His face was silhouetted in front of her, but she could make out nothing more.

"In defense of Corporal Harris and myself, we were here in search of a couple of our pilots who may have been wandering among the women's barracks."

"I appreciate your clarification," she saidd. "In all due respect, sir, I hope you understand how suspicious your presence sounded."

"Yes, I do, but it's the truth."

She knew he didn't have to clarify his motives since he held the higher rank, and the fact he offered an explanation impressed her. "Thank you, sir. If I observe anything out of protocol, I'll notify you."

"Thank you for your cooperation and dedication to those in your charge. Have a good night, Corporal."

Margaret saluted and stepped beyond the shelter without taking a look back. She trudged back to the barracks with Beryl, too tired to speak. The acid smell of destruction alerted her to fires in the distance. She heard the cries of ambulances rushing to the aid of victims and felt the flow of adrenaline through her veins. In a strange way, she wished they did need her to drive. At least then she'd feel like she'd accomplished something instead of only bemoaning her lack of sleep. This was reality: another war-torn night on the edges of London.

◆ ◆ ◆

Two weeks passed, each day the same as before. Margaret pursued her optimism, encouraging those around her and always finding victory in the bleakest of defeats. She took pride in her job, operating whatever vehicle the Royal Air Force needed. Sometimes her assignment led her to drive pilots in tarp-covered lorries to the hangars, move the injured to hospitals, pick up mail, deliver food and medical supplies, or simply chauffeur an officer to his or her destination. After all, she had trained for six weeks to learn how to drive, and it didn't matter what manner of vehicle.

On a mid-November afternoon, Lieutenant Elizabeth Fitzgerald issued Margaret an order. "I need for you to transport two pilots from the hangars to an officers' meeting immediately. I've been told you'll need petrol before you leave."

Margaret grasped the keys to the government vehicle and saluted the lieutenant. She'd taken pilots earlier that morning and wondered why these two fliers returned alone. After missions, the men normally tarried at the hangars until radar determined hostile airplanes en route over the English Channel. Praise God for this system of warning, for it hastened bombers and fighters to the skies.

Her stomach curdled. Surely nothing had happened to the other men. Generally, downed pilots parachuted into the water, where sea vessels rescued them.

Another possibility occurred to Margaret. The two officers could have taken pictures over enemy territory and now needed to report their findings. For certain, though, it had nothing to do with her duties.

Winding the officers' car through the outskirts of London could have been a rough assignment if Margaret had not known the way. Road signs had been removed in the event invaders prowled over their land. Let the enemy stumble about. Britons valued vigilance.

The government had initiated various protective measures for its people. The air-raid alerts and underground shelters saved many lives. Blackout shields covered the headlights of what few vehicles were permitted to roam the streets. Lampposts were painted white so drivers could find their way during the night. All children ages fifteen and under had been removed from the larger cities to safety in the country. Rationing and training the citizens of England to protect their lives and property became an integral part of life. This and so much more kept the enemy at bay.

Women did more than their share by filling men's jobs. They delivered the mail, trained for the home guard, joined a branch of the military, and worked in factories. Everyone had a job. Everyone had a purpose.

At the hangars, Margaret parked the car where two pilots stood talking with the mechanics. She rounded the front of the lorry and saluted two RAF officers, one a lieutenant and the other a corporal. Perhaps their rank supported special treatment or an undisclosed mission. She opened the passenger side of the back-seat for them.

"To the colonel's office," the lieutenant said, his voice oddly familiar.

"Yes sir." Her mind spun as she searched her memory for the officer's identity, but nothing came to mind.

As soon as Margaret started the engine, the corporal began to talk endlessly about nothing important. She recognized his voice as one of the two officers in the air-raid shelter. Glancing in the rearview mirror, she instantly met the most incredible brown eyes she'd ever seen. They belonged to the quiet lieutenant. He smiled at her, a shy smile, almost innocent looking.

A moment later, she swerved to keep from hitting a huge rut in the road, but the maneuver proved too late. She tore her gaze away from the mirror while warmth rose from her neck to her cheeks. Had she gone daft? Embarrassment continued to flow through her veins, and she wondered how she could avoid facing the lieutenant, but she must. Once they did reach their barracks, she must open his door and salute him. What fun he must be making of her.

Stiffening, Margaret vowed to regain her composure and will away the redness she knew colored her cheeks. She tightened her fingers around the steering wheel and focused her attention on the road ahead, but her mind could not shut out the endless chatter of the corporal. He could hold his own in a host of women.

Once they reached the officers' area, Margaret summoned the strength to complete her assignment. After all, she was a WAAF and certainly above petty nonsense about a man's eyes. Yet she had driven poorly by hitting the hole in the road.

Lieutenant Stuart waited beside the car, while Corporal Harris, the more muscular of the two, exited. "Go on ahead. I'll be there in a moment," he said.

She watched the chatty corporal walk toward the colonel's office, all the while expecting a reprimand for her driving.

"Corporal Walker?"

"Yes sir." She lifted her chin.

He smiled, the half grin she'd seen before, the kind that could easily melt a woman's heart. But not hers. "What time do you get off duty today?"

"Seventeen hundred hours, sir."

"Would you consider a stroll?"

Her pulse quickened. "Well. . .have I violated a procedure? I mean, I apologize for not minding the bumpy road."

His pleasant demeanor remained intact. "No, ma'am, I'm not concerned with your driving expertise. I'd simply like your company."

Her emotions bounced between relief and caution, and she wavered. This could be official RAF business. "Yes sir. I mean, that would be fine with me."

He touched the brim of his cap, where a tousle of sandy-colored hair slipped onto his forehead. "Thank you. I'll be at your barracks around eighteen hundred?"

"Do you know which one, sir?"

A hint of amusement glistened in his eyes, and she felt her color mount. "Yes, Corporal, I do."

The rest of the day sped by, and in those moments of idleness Margaret questioned the lieutenant's motives. If this had nothing to do with the defense of Britain, then he must be interested in her as a woman, and she had no intention of becoming involved with any man until the British won the war.

Visions of the young pilots who never returned flashed across her mind. Her brother's demise had caused her to avoid all men. Shaking her head in denial of the pain, her thoughts turned to Beryl and how she mourned the death of her husband. With four-year-old Christopher and another babe yet to be born, Beryl's future looked frightening, even without considering the events of the war.

Margaret had only one love—the Lord—and when the fighting ceased He'd be the one to initiate any kind of a relationship between her and a man.

Promptly at seventeen hundred hours, Margaret raced to the showers, hoping a quick spray of water would soothe her rattled nerves. Moments later, she slipped into clean work trousers and shirt. She huffed. If Lieutenant Stuart had stated the purpose of their time together—professional or personal—she would have known whether to wear her dress uniform.

Beryl met her back at the barracks. "Where are you going?"

Margaret fluffed at her hair, then held up a mirror to make sure the curls fell just so on her shoulders. She noticed a thickening around Beryl's middle but refused to mention it. "Business, I think," she said, avoiding her friend's scrutiny.

"You don't know?"

Dare she tell Beryl what occurred this morning? "I'm supposed to meet Lieutenant Stuart at eighteen hundred."

Beryl touched her finger to her lips. She reminded Margaret of a mere girl with her oval face encircled in blond curls. "The name is familiar. Female or male?"

"Male," Margaret whispered, glancing about to make sure no one listened.

"Weren't you briefed on your assignment?" Beryl's forehead crinkled.

"Not exactly." Margaret slipped the mirror back into her personal belongings. "Oh, Beryl, you remember him. The night in the shelter when those two pilots joined us?"

"Which one—the chatty or reserved one?"

"The reserved lieutenant."

Beryl smiled and nodded. "Is this something special?"

Margaret felt the color rise in her cheeks. "I have no idea. He invited me for a stroll, but I don't know why."

Her friend giggled and positioned her hands on her hips. "I say he's a man who has taken a fancy to a lovely young woman, and you're fancying him as well, or you wouldn't be so flushed."

"Nonsense. I'm sure this is RAF related."

"Your lip is quivering."

Margaret cringed. "Is it? Oh, dear, what am I to do?"

A woman's voice from the door of the barracks diverted Margaret's attention. "Corporal Walker, there's a Lieutenant Stuart waiting outside for you."

Chapter 2

"It is to wage war, by sea, land, and air,
with all our might and with all the strength that God can give us;
to wage war against a monstrous tyranny, never surpassed in the dark,
lamentable catalogue of human crime.
That is our policy. You ask, what is our aim?
I can answer in one word: It is victory, victory at all costs,
victory in spite of all terror, victory, however long
and hard the road may be; for without victory, there is no survival."
WINSTON CHURCHILL

Lieutenant Andrew Stuart toyed with the crease of his cap. He flecked imaginary dust from his albatross insignia and shifted from one foot to the other. What had gotten into him to invite the lady for a stroll? He didn't have time for such nonsense when he had a job to do. Hadn't he and the other men been warned by a superior about allowing women to interfere with duty? He'd been better off to spend his time in a dart tournament. The war effort was the utmost priority. Victory outweighed every selfish desire.

Unfortunately, once he'd met Corporal Margaret Walker in the shelter, she'd haunted him until he found out all he could about her. Only curious, mind you. He couldn't see her face in the blackness of night, but something about her intrigued him.

This morning he saw the sun's rays pick up reddish highlights in her thick, rich brown hair. Those tresses were the kind a man could weave through his fingers. When she spoke, a sparkle lit up her arresting eyes and drew him even closer. In the past, he held little regard for men who lost themselves in a woman's beauty, and now he threatened to do the same.

All he ever hoped to find in these dark days was friendship. He wanted a woman friend to talk to when the day ended, when he wanted to put behind him the peril of his beloved country and the terror raging over Europe.

What he'd learned about Margaret also saddened him. She'd lost a brother in '39. Her brother had flown a Wellington on a mission to destroy a German naval ship and met up with the Messerschmitt 109 bombers. Andrew's source said he doubted if any pilot could convince the lovely Corporal Margaret Walker to do anything other than transport fliers back and forth to the hangars, much less befriend a chap. Couldn't blame the lady for her apprehension. Britons were noted for their sense of humor and hopefulness in the midst of bleak times, but that attitude didn't stop the pain of losing someone they loved.

Although his chums refused to believe it, Margaret had agreed to accompany him on a stroll, and no matter the outcome he planned to enjoy the company of a beautiful woman.

No sooner had his thoughts scattered about in his head, than the subject of his musings appeared in the doorway. She looked a bit flustered with her reddened cheeks and crinkled brow, reminding him of earlier when he caught her observing him through the rearview mirror. To his amusement, she hit a rather large bump in the road. The force jolted him up off the seat. She'd been embarrassed, but he'd found it delightful.

"Good evening, Lieutenant," she greeted, smoothing her trousers.

He grinned like an awkward schoolboy. "Hello, and my name's Andrew." He noted his sweaty palms gripping the crease of his cap. How many missions had he flown with less turmoil waging his insides? "You look lovely."

"Thank you, and I'm Margaret."

She returned a measure of congeniality, while he battled his increasing nervousness. He hooked his arm, and she linked hers into his. Margaret's touch unnerved him, leaving him stumbling for words. They walked for several minutes while he searched for something clever to say—he so wanted a topic aside from the war.

"I'm not good at conversation," he finally said.

"Unlike your friend, Corporal Harris?"

"Perhaps I should have taken a few notes the night we invaded the women's shelter."

Margaret appeared amused. "Quite the talker, isn't he? Does he ever run out of subjects?"

"Only the queen has more subjects than James Harris. I once saw him make friends with a lamppost. He's a fine chap, though, an excellent fighter pilot."

"Ah, so you're the witty one," she said.

For the first time, he relaxed slightly. "Not exactly. More like the quiet one. I prefer watching and listening."

"I prefer quiet," she said.

He felt his heart do an upward climb, level off, spin, and soar even higher.

"Why don't you tell me about yourself, Lieutenant?"

He'd rather be outnumbered by Nazi aircraft ten-to-one than talk about himself, but he didn't have a choice. "I attended Cambridge before the war and plan to finish there when it's over. My family lives outside of Northamptonshire, and I fly Spitfires for the RAF." He managed to say it all in one breath.

She laughed. He liked the sound of it, light and cheery as if inviting him to join along.

"Andrew, must I ask more questions to find out about you? What did you study at Cambridge?"

His heart hammered louder than gunfire riddling his Spitfire. "Philosophy. I almost have my master's."

"Then what?"

"Oh, I imagine myself as a professor someday, once I receive my doctorate."

Andrew felt decidedly uncomfortable. Blood rushed through his veins and heated him despite the chilly temperatures of the November day.

"Splendid." Her eyes seemed to dance. "And do you have brothers and sisters?"

"Ah, yes I do. Three older brothers and two younger sisters." His voice faltered.

Margaret tilted her head. "I see I've touched on something sad. I'm sorry."

Andrew thought he masked his sorrow. "I'm the one who must apologize. It's my sister. She died in childbirth about five months ago. Hard on my family, you know. Luckily they live in the country and the babe is with them, while his father commands an army post."

"I'm so sorry. Times are hard for England. Everywhere you look is some type of devastation, but we have to go on."

She offered kind words and no false expectations. He liked that.

"Are you Christian?" Margaret said.

Startled, he nodded. "My faith is what helps me climb into my cockpit. Either in this life or the next, God will give England peace, but until then I will fight for those things He declares important. I firmly believe He will see the free world reign over the atrocities of the Germans."

"I do as well. God guards the way of those who fight for His principles, and He will not allow this to continue forever." She stopped and turned to him. "I lost a brother to the cause. It grieves me, but like your sister, he is in a better place."

Andrew stared into the young woman's face, realizing her empathy was sincere and not a mixing of words to gain his attention. "Thank you, Margaret." He didn't know what else to say, especially when he'd already spoken more than usual.

They walked a bit farther in silence, and he felt his spirit strangely exhilarated with her arm coupled in his. He grappled for another topic and forged on. "Enough nonsense about me, tell me about yourself."

"Oh, I'm a country girl, Andrew, and I long to one day return. Strange as it sounds, I'd never been in a large city until joining the WAAF. Before then I had plans to become a teacher, and I'll finish my degree once the war is over."

She didn't dwell on herself, either. "Whereabouts?" he said.

"Northwest of Manchester." She sighed as if remembering another place in time. "A beautiful piece of land: tranquil, lush green, and full of unusual gardens. It's my own promised land."

"How commendable to know what you want. I've met people who strive to merely end the war and don't know what they will do afterward. We need dreams of a future to keep us alive." He hesitated, a bit self-conscious for speaking his mind and mentioning the war. "Do you have a large family?"

"Just my parents now. We're all doing what we can. My mum took in six children without consulting my father. When he found out, he added two more."

Andrew allowed his laughter to roll about them. "I neglected to mention my family is housing several children as well. How are your parents faring with the additions to their home?"

"Quite well. They both insist having little ones about keeps them young."

He took a gander about them and realized they'd walked farther than he anticipated. Evening shadows danced about, and with the promise of night also came the reality of bombing.

"We should make our way back before the Germans bestow us with their gifts," he said.

"Yes, I suppose you're right." She glanced upward.

For a moment he permitted himself to think she didn't want the evening to end any more than he. They stopped at a crossroad. One building stood, while another lay in shambles beside it. The philosophical side of him compared the sight to all affected by the war. He knew where he stood. He'd stepped across the line separating the weak from the strong, the resolute from the defeated. God held his destiny in the palm of His hands as well as all Britons who'd willingly give their lives.

"What are you thinking?" Margaret said. "Or is it none of my concern? You look hundreds of miles away."

"Simply thinking about the war—a topic I vowed not to discuss this evening." They slowly walked back toward the barracks.

She nodded. "I understand, but it's quite all right, you know. It consumes us but will not overtake us."

"Good show, fair lady. I admire your spunk, but I'd rather speak of dearer things." He stared into her flawless face. "Thank you for agreeing to meet me."

"You're welcome, Andrew. I've enjoyed our time together." She glanced at the sky with its pressing shadows. He saw a frown, and they increased their pace. "Now tell me about your boyhood. What was your most favorite thing to do?"

They chatted all the way back, and much too soon they stood in front of the round-roofed wooden building she referred to as home.

"Sometimes I think I'd like to plant flowers around these barracks," she said. "My friends think the idea foolish."

He attempted to envision a spot of color around the drab quarters. "What kind would you plant?"

For a moment, she closed her eyes, and he marveled at the serene smile gracing her face. "Oh, roses. I can only imagine how lovely they'd look, and their sweet fragrance would make the days brighter."

Andrew remembered a matter of importance. He shuddered at his actions in complete disregard for his careful upbringing. "Margaret, I never asked. You missed the evening meal, didn't you?"

"Yes, but it's perfectly fine. Did you not eat as well?"

He refused to confess his thoughts had been on her and not his stomach. "I'm sorry. So much for my being a gentleman."

She laughed. "If I'd been hungry, I'd have stated so."

A strange silence enveloped them, and she slipped her hand from the crook of his arm. "I best be going inside."

"Of course. Thank you again for joining me. I had a grand time."

"You're a fine man, Lieutenant Stuart." Her eyes fairly glistened.

"May. . .may we do this another time? I'd like to see you again."

Margaret took a deep breath and hesitated. She appeared to carefully form her words. "I don't think so, Andrew. It wouldn't be a good idea."

With her decision made, she hurried inside the barracks, leaving a whipping blast of chilling air behind her.

◆　◆　◆

Margaret braced herself and slowly made her way down the narrow row of iron cots to hers. She smiled at the women who greeted her, hearing them but not truly seeing them. Some would want to talk. They always did. She had the gift of listening to their problems and offering prayer and encouragement. Beryl said Margaret reminded her of a mother hen with her chicks—always drawing them close and fussing over each one.

Tonight, Margaret's heart felt heavy. She'd find it hard to cover her burden and take care of these precious ladies. The truth lay before her plain and simple. She couldn't see Andrew again, in fact not ever. He reminded her too much of the dreams she'd put aside until after the war. Someday she wanted to build her life around a man like Andrew, have his children, and grow old with him according to the plan God designed for a man and a woman. But not until the free world won the war. Worrying over a man flying missions against the enemy didn't fall into her plans.

Andrew held the same ideals as Ross, her sweet brother, and she didn't dare let her heart feel such intense grief over a man again. Some scars bled easier than others, and caring for men who knew the probability of their destiny made them easier to love—if not for the man, for the integrity of their values. All she needed to do was consider Beryl: a widow with one small child and expecting another.

Every time Margaret transported a lorry full of pilots to the hangars, she couldn't help but count them and calculate how many would not return. That's why she declined invitations to dances, the theater, and social events sponsored by the churches and the air force. No relationships for her, not even friendships. She couldn't involve herself casually and learn later they'd been shot down.

"Margaret, you look a fright," Beryl said. She rose from her cot and tossed aside a newspaper. "What happened?" A fierce look passed over Beryl's round face, and she whispered, "Did the lieutenant have dishonorable intentions?"

Margaret pretended to smooth her blanket. "Oh, no. He acted quite the gentleman."

"What happened?"

"I liked him."

Tears pooled her friend's eyes. "Then why are you so sad?"

Margaret eased down onto her cot, unable to gaze into her friend's eyes. "Because I don't dare see him after tonight. It makes losing him harder to bear. Oh, Beryl, I know we only had a brief walk together, but he's a good man, a Christian who puts others before himself."

"Maybe God means for you to know a man like him—like a gift from heaven." She sat beside Margaret and lightly squeezed her shoulders. "For all the hardships and sorrow, I don't ever regret loving my Patrick." She muffled a sob. "And now I'll have two wonderful pieces of him to cherish forever."

Margaret choked back her own emotion. Sweet Beryl, she always saw past the storm to the rainbow. "I don't think I can be like you. Right now the only thing consuming me is my desire for victory, but if I can avoid some of the costs I must."

Much later, long after the sirens ceased and the other women lay sleeping, Margaret lay on her bed and sorted through her turbulent thoughts. A reserved lieutenant occupied her mind—those incredible brown eyes and a sprinkling of tan-colored freckles. Finally Margaret turned to the only solace she knew, that of prayer.

Oh, God, I believe I acted rightfully in refusing to see Andrew again, but now I wonder if I'm being selfish. I can't get involved. Please don't ask me to give my heart to a man and then have him killed in this horrid war. I'm so frightened with all that goes on around me. Leave me in my shell, God. It's safer here.

The following day, Margaret transported several pilots to the hangars. She understood they were to be briefed on a special mission, and her orders were to wait until a commanding officer dismissed her. After awhile, she grew bored and exited the lorry to stretch her legs. Keeping her distance from the mechanics, she studied the planes waiting for takeoff: Spitfires with narrow noses and straight lines, known for their speed in fighting, and Hurricanes, the workhorse fighters. All stood ready, fueled up, and armed for their mission.

How many young pilots would come back? She wanted to believe the RAF could crush the Luftwaffe, but from her point of view, Britain's success looked bleak. Hitler's military had cast terror into the hearts of all of Europe. She'd never whisper a hint of her fears to anyone. Yet sometimes she wondered if the newspapers stretched the truth about the British successes. Not that she'd ever doubt Churchill—"Winny" some called him. He kept up their morale with his hopeful speeches and spurred them on to continue one more day. Even so, the year 1940 had been a rough year for the men and women who fought for Britain.

She offered a prayer for the pilots' safety and turned back to her lorry. Climbing onto the seat, she saw a piece of paper. Curious, Margaret picked it up and found a sketch of a rose, perfect in petal and formation. At the bottom, a note had been carefully penned.

For Margaret:
Never has a rose in England looked so fair. I wish I could have given you a real, brilliant red beauty, but none could compare to you—a royal flower amidst the ashes of London.
Lieutenant Andrew Stuart

Chapter 3

*"Centuries ago words were written to be a call
and a spur to the faithful servants of Truth and Justice:
'Arm yourselves, and be ye men of valour,
and be in readiness for the conflict;
for it is better for us to perish in battle than
to look upon the outrage of our nation and our altar.
As the Will of God is in Heaven, even so let it be.' "*
WINSTON CHURCHILL

Andrew didn't know why he'd sketched the rose and left such a ridiculous note for Margaret in the lorry, but he had. He didn't want to consider what she might think of him after he'd followed his foolish impulse. Hadn't he resigned himself to steering away from relationships until after the war? Of course, his action could merely be his pride reacting to her refusal to see him again. Or could this be something else? He recalled her clear eyes, sparkling with laughter, and the honesty in her voice.

Margaret, have you already pushed me from your thoughts?

Andrew realized he'd lost his common sense. After spending less than an hour and a half with the lady, he thought she might be the one God intended for him. What happened to his plans for friendship, a chum to share idle hours?

Lord, help me with this. Am I reaching out to Margaret instead of clinging to You? I'm wondering if I should be bothering You at all with my turmoil.

Andrew pushed aside the burdensome thoughts of the lovely Corporal Walker and considered his flight pattern for the day. He pulled his jacket around him in the frosty morning air and watched the ground crew load ammunition into the fighter's wing guns. This had to be done with expertise or the guns could fail during battle. Glancing about, he felt intense pride in being a part of the RAF. The foresight in camouflaging fighters and bombers from German planes was one of the reasons why the RAF still ruled the skies over England. Other European countries who had fallen in a matter of days had lined their aircraft along the runways. Those planes had been perfect targets for airborne Germans.

Climbing into the cockpit of his Spitfire, Andrew pulled the hatch closed. The frigid air chilled him to the bone. Last winter while he flew for France, the weather had grown so cold he thought he'd never be warm again. He didn't look forward to another season like it.

With a heavy sigh, he glanced upward. The sky tinged a bit cloudy, but it did not hold the black, curling smoke of combat. Too many times he'd heard the burst of gunfire finding their mark in aircraft and heard the screams of falling planes. A smart man wouldn't want to take on these assignments, but he had neither the intelligence nor the will to be anything but bold and stubbornly courageous. He followed orders and his gut instincts, praying all the while for God to lead him in the right direction.

Some hailed Britain's pilots as heroes, but he laughed at those titles. The RAF did what it deemed necessary because it had no choice. In his estimation, the real heroes were the mechanics who bore the brunt of German fire to repair and patch the bullet-riddled planes. He certainly didn't want their job.

◆ ◆ ◆

Margaret pondered Andrew's rose and poetic words for three days before summoning the courage to approach him about it. She'd written a proper note thanking him, but it seemed too proper and impersonal in light of his tender gift. She placed the picture under her pillow and studied it in her spare moments, putting his written words to memory and tracing the flower with her finger as though watching him draw it.

Through Beryl, who packed parachutes at the hangars, she learned Andrew's schedule. One evening she lingered outside the men's dining hall in hopes he sat inside. She'd planned a brief encounter, one to express her appreciation and not in any way commit her to seeing him again. But in the confines of her heart, another flower budded in a garden of secret dreams.

Margaret stood several feet back from the entrance of the dining hall, not wanting to attract attention from the other men. The pilots filed out, some laughing, some talking. The unmistakable lively voice of Corporal Harris swelled above the others and caught her attention. Beside him stood Andrew. Even the talkative corporal said nothing as Andrew sauntered toward her.

"Good evening," she managed through a ragged breath. She swept her tongue across dry lips and braved forward. "I wondered..." She studied her shoes to avoid the stares of the other men until they passed by. Glancing up into his face, she offered a faint smile. "I wondered if you would have a moment to speak with me."

"I do." Andrew jammed his hands into his trouser pockets. "We could take a walk."

"An excellent idea." A nip of icy air caught her hair and whipped it back from her face. She'd taken great pains to arrange it, but for naught.

"Winter is wanting to overtake us," he said.

"I agree." She wrapped her arms around herself, more from the undeniable emotions Andrew's presence gave her than the cold.

He pointed to an area shielded by buildings. "We can venture in that direction. It'll block the wind."

"Yes, thank you." Suddenly her carefully formulated speech escaped her.

"You wanted to talk to me?" Andrew said.

She nodded. "The rose and your note were beautiful, and I wanted to tell you so in person."

"I got your post thanking me."

"But it didn't express my gratitude suitably. I was deeply touched."

He shrugged. "I'm pleased."

Silence overtook them, and she searched her mind for one of the million things she wished she could discuss with him.

"Have you eaten?" he said.

She shook her head. "I didn't have much of an appetite."

"In better days, I'd have offered to take you to a fine restaurant."

"In better days, I'd have accepted."

He laughed then sobered. "Is that the problem, Margaret? Are you living in memories of pre-war England instead of reality, or do you truly not enjoy my company?"

His question stopped her colder than the November temperatures. "I did enjoy our walk and your company. I'm not certain I can explain my reluctance to see you . . . It's rather personal. . . Certain things need to be kept private, even sacred during war times."

"Some things are always sacred in God's eyes, no matter what is going on around us."

"Even if the time is not right?" Why did she feel like crying? Betrayed by her own fragile feelings, Margaret could not bring herself to look into his face.

"God's timing is always perfect."

She glanced at the building behind them, stone and hard. Sometimes she wondered if her heart had become the same. "Andrew," she began softly. "Do you know what happens when you plant flowers in the wrong season?"

He nodded sadly.

"They die for lack of nurturing," she finished.

"But not if they are sheltered within a greenhouse. The flowers still flourish, because the gardener tends to them."

"Do you believe this gardener decides which flowers will grow?" she whispered.

"No. I believe the flowers choose to live or die according to the riches of the gardener's care."

Margaret forced herself to look at him. "I'm afraid, Andrew." No longer could she conceal her tears.

He brushed away the wetness on her cheek. "I, as well. Remember, we Brits are known for not turning our backs on adversity and being prepared for hard times. Can't we begin as friends, Margaret, for isn't that how it should be?"

"All right," she said. "I can be your friend."

◆　◆　◆

As the weeks poured into December, Andrew found every spare minute to spend with Margaret. He longed for her laughter and wit. She made him laugh with a single phrase, and she appeared to enjoy his company. At least she no longer refused to see him.

"Good news," Corporal James Harris announced one evening. "I see a new band will be entertaining the troops next week. Oh, it will be a jolly good time, don't you think?"

Andrew's mind raced. Margaret loved music. Perhaps she'd want to attend the event with him. "Are you sure about the band?"

"Quite," James said, his mirth ringing through the roof of the barracks. He patted Andrew on the back. "Old boy, I see the light of love in your eyes. Have you fallen for the pretty corporal already?"

Andrew furrowed his brow. "It's only been four weeks, much too soon to be proper."

"Whoever said love had to follow socially acceptable timetables?"

"She's a friend, and that's all for the time being," Andrew said more gruffly than he intended. "We're a country at war."

"No need to get upset about it," James said, "just making conversation."

Immediately Andrew regretted his rash words. "I'm sorry, old chap. Margaret is special, and I don't want to make light of her."

"Of course. All of us are a bit ill tempered these days. So would you like for me to get more information about the band? It's better than most of those they've had in the past."

"I surely would, and I'll ask Margaret about it as well."

James turned to go, but Andrew stopped him.

"Thanks for being understanding. With our missions increasing into Germany, my mind is torn between the war and Margaret."

"God is with us." James looked as stalwart as Andrew had ever seen him. "With all my talking and joking, I have faith we will prevail, and I believe God wants us to enjoy the friendships of those who bring us joy."

"Well said, James." Andrew took a deep breath and reached for his fur-lined jacket. "How about a cup of tea and a game of Ping-Pong? I'm in the mood to beat you."

"If you do, it will be a first in a long time."

Andrew knew James's observations about Margaret were true. He had fallen hard for her, something he hadn't planned to do. The logical side of him said his feelings escalated because of the loneliness and uncertainty of his job, but his heart told him otherwise. Every minute he spent with her seemed more splendid than the last. He appreciated what he saw and how she related to other women.

Andrew's thoughts returned to the day before, when he and Margaret had returned from a lively game of darts at the Naffi. Beryl, Margaret's dear friend, met them along the way. Andrew hadn't thought Beryl looked ill, but obviously Margaret did.

"Are you all right?" Margaret had said to the woman.

"Oh, I'm very well, just out for a stroll," Beryl said hastily, her gaze darting about.

"You need your rest." Margaret's face tilted and concern edged her words. "Don't overdo yourself."

"I won't," Beryl said with a smile. "A bit of fresh air will do me good." She glanced at Andrew. "It's good to see you, Andrew. Are you keeping Margaret out of mischief?"

He grinned. "I certainly try. You should have joined us. Corporal Harris asked about you, wanted to know if we all could do something together."

Beryl braced herself against the wind. "I think not, but kindly thank him for the invitation." Turning her attention to Margaret, she added, "I'll be going now. Cheerio."

Andrew watched her plod toward the dining hall. "Is her health not good?" Andrew said once Beryl disappeared. "I mean, she looks fit, and her cheeks are rosy."

"She's as well as can be expected," Margaret said. "Beryl hasn't been a widow long, and often his absence grieves her. Plus she has a young son living with family in Ireland. I'm afraid she doesn't take good care of herself, and with the winter. . ." Her voice trailed off.

"Don't neglect her," Andrew said. "I know I take up a lot of your time, but friends are important. Should I apologize for suggesting she keep company with James?"

"No, that's not necessary. I've told her what honorable men you are. She knows you mean the best." Margaret smiled appreciatively, while her gaze swept back to Beryl.

He saw a tear trickle from Margaret's eye, and once more he felt convinced of her tender heart. "Is there something else troubling you?"

Instantly her violet pools flashed into his. Did he see panic?

"Nothing I can tell you," she said. "I need to go inside where it's warm."

Andrew started to hurry after her but stopped. He understood Margaret enough to realize when she needed to work through things on her own. He wished she'd confide in him instead of running, but maybe he was the problem.

Chapter 4

"We shall fight on the beaches,
we shall fight on the landing grounds,
we shall fight in the fields and in the streets,
we shall fight in the hills; we shall never surrender."
Winston Churchill

A few days later, Margaret waited for Beryl to return from the nurse's station. Her friend had reached her sixth month and couldn't hide the rounding stomach any longer. Besides needing medical attention, Beryl needed to take care of her position with the WAAF and obtain a proper discharge.

A few days earlier, when Andrew stated Beryl looked fit and noted the color in her cheeks, Margaret feared he suspected the pregnancy. She'd heard the other women talking among themselves and whispering their suspicions. They felt sorry for Beryl—a new widow with two children to raise alone, but she needed to declare her condition.

One of the women approached Margaret. Jenny had lived in the slums of East London before the war. A smile played on her lips, and she carried a piece of paper.

"How can I help you, Jenny?" Margaret motioned for the tall redhead to sit beside her. "You look more radiant than usual."

"My children are so happy." She sighed. "They tell me they love the country and want me to join them." She handled Margaret the letter. "Read for yourself."

Margaret took the note but sensed Jenny needed to voice more of her feelings.

"I know I'm lucky to know where they are and even hear from them, but my heart aches for 'em. My dear boy says he ain't never took so many baths, and he's gotten bigger since eatin' regular. My thirteen-year-old daughter says she can milk a cow and make good stew." Jenny clasped her hands together. "I couldn't offer them none of those things before, and look what they have now."

"Then it's God's provision." Margaret patted Jenny's hand. "He's taking care of them like we ask in our prayers. Isn't our God wonderful?"

Jenny nodded and a tear slipped from her eye. "Up until this very minute I doubted if a God really existed, but I see a miracle in my children. Matthew wants to always live in the country—doesn't want our tiny flat anymore." She toyed with a button on her shirt. "Of course the rats plagued us, and most likely it's blown to bits."

Jenny's story drew the attention of several others. The letter proved to be a blessing not only for Jenny but also for many women who pondered over the plight of their children.

Margaret pulled a handkerchief from her trouser pocket and wiped Jenny's cheeks. "See, the Germans did you a favor, and they didn't have the sense to know it. Got your children out of a bad situation and into a home where they're well-taken care of."

Suddenly one of the women began to laugh, and soon the others joined.

"I hadn't thought of the Germans doing any of us a favor," a thin young woman said. "When we chase them off once and for all, I'll get me a new house, and it won't have a thatch roof either to catch every fire spark."

"Me and my husband will have us a fine butcher shop again," another woman added, "without a bomb in the middle of it."

Soon they all were laughing and joking about their misfortunes. That's what Margaret liked the best about being British—strength and humor.

Beryl wiggled her way through the crowd to her cot. She wore a smile, but Margaret doubted if it held much substance.

"I have an announcement to make," Beryl said, waving her hands to quiet the others. She nodded at Margaret. "As much as I love all of you, I will be departing from your delightful company."

"Where ya going?" Jenny said.

"To Patrick's family in Ireland. . .to be with my dear boy, Christopher, and. . . to give birth to another babe." She lifted her chin, while silence echoed around the barracks. "Would someone say something, please?"

A moment later, a dozen arms wrapped around Beryl, and the hum of well-wishers sounded livelier than a beehive.

"When are you leaving?" Margaret said, feeling immense relief for her friend but realizing how much she'd miss her.

"Shortly, I believe. Lieutenant Fitzgerald is making the arrangements." Beryl embraced Margaret and hugged her tightly. "Thank you for supporting me these months since Patrick died. I couldn't have made it without your God-given friendship and all of the wonderful ladies here."

Margaret responded with a nod. Later they could talk in private. Right then, emotion blocked her every thought.

"What will you name the babe?" Jenny said.

Beryl smiled genuinely. "Patrick Winston if it's a boy, and Elizabeth Clementine if it's a girl."

"Ah," Jenny said. "For our Mr. Churchill and his wife."

"Bravo," the cheers rose. "To God and England."

"And His blessing on our families where'er they may be," Jenny added.

The conversation continued with names of children and mothers' fond memories of peaceful days. Without warning, the sirens sounded.

"Soon you'll be free of this," Margaret whispered to Beryl as they raced to the shelter.

"But a piece of my heart will always be here with you, my friends," Beryl said as they hurried to go, "and all of the RAF. Here is where Patrick and I found purpose to the lives God gave us."

♦ ♦ ♦

Andrew watched Margaret and Beryl hug each other one last time before Beryl departed. A train would take her northwest to Liverpool, where she would cross the Irish Sea to Dublin. Now he understood Margaret's concern for her friend and the reason she protected Beryl.

"So you'll be home for Christmas?" Andrew said heartily. "I envy you with family and all."

Beryl laughed. "It seems like a fantasy come true." She clasped Andrew's hand. "Oh, I don't mean to sound selfish or shirk my responsibilities."

"Not at all," Andrew said, peering into her eyes. "You have the responsibility to take care of another loyal subject. Motherhood is the finest profession I know."

Beryl tilted her head. "You are so kind, Andrew. I wish you the best, and take good care of Margaret for me."

"I will, be certain of that." Andrew winked at Margaret.

The conductor called for all to board, and Beryl glanced longingly at the train.

"Wait up," a voice shouted.

The three turned to see James racing toward them. He closely resembled a rugby player hurrying for the ball. "I wanted to see Beryl off," he said between frosty breaths. He turned to her and removed his cap. "Hope you don't mind."

"Not at all. I'm humbled you took the time in this bitter weather." She drew her coat around her bulging stomach.

The train whistle sounded.

He glanced up with a smile. "Godspeed, Beryl. I wondered if I might write you."

She nibbled at her lip and glanced down at her suitcase setting beside her. "I'd like to hear from you, Corporal Harris."

"Call me James," he said above the roar of the train.

She nodded and made her way up the steps. Turning, she waved. "Merry Christmas to you. I'll be praying for you and England."

Margaret stared after the train until it disappeared. No tears, only a trembling smile. *How wonderful for Beryl. May God bless her with a healthy baby and a good life.*

"Are you all right?" Andrew said.

"Very well," she whispered. "Things will be fine for her. I'm sure of it."

He wrapped his arm around her waist and longed to take her into his arms and kiss her soundly, but he hadn't ventured past friendship yet. Christmas Eve he planned to tell her of his growing feelings, and he prayed she felt the same.

♦ ♦ ♦

The winter seemed to be colder than usual, or perhaps the bleakness of the war held its own bitter temperatures. In London, a few fragile restaurants still stood and served four-course dinners—if one could pay for them—and the theater still drew the attention of the elite. Although dust from the bombings fell on the stage, the "show must go on" philosophy kept the actors and actresses returning for repeated performances. English and Americans alike entertained the troops, often using the bomb shelters as a hotel.

"Wish I could find a small gift for Andrew," Margaret said wistfully to Jenny. The two had just finished breakfast and were walking back to the barracks.

"I understand," the tall woman said. "With the cost of everything in London so dear and everything rationed, what can you do?"

Margaret contemplated the matter once more. She'd always sent much of her money home to Mum and Dad, and she couldn't justify not continuing to do so. "He says our Christmas will be celebrating the Lord's birthday and a carol-sing, but I wish for a token of our friendship."

"Friendship, aye?" Jenny said with a soft laugh.

"Of course. We're good chums." Margaret knew she inched closer and closer to something more with Andrew, but she found it difficult to admit the truth to herself, much less confide in Jenny. At times Margaret's growing attraction angered her as if her heart had a will of its own. Other times she allowed the sweet bliss of love to envelop her like a garden of fragrant roses. She tried not to think about the many missions Andrew flew—only to be grateful when he safely returned.

Jenny leaned closer and whispered, "I know where you can get a chocolate bar."

Margaret nodded. "Perfect."

Unfortunately, on Christmas Eve, Margaret received orders to drive high-ranking officers to a special meeting and remain near the lorry until they finished. After she transported them to their destination, the air raid sounded as usual. She took shelter, then resumed her position and waited for the officers to finish. In the wee hours of Christmas morning, she returned to her barracks.

Christmas Day, Andrew flew an unscheduled flight. Margaret had learned he and James often flew these types of missions to take critical pictures for future bombings.

On the afternoon of December twenty-sixth, Margaret and Andrew were finally able to grasp a few moments alone to wish each other merry Christmas.

"I have something for you," she said, pulling the rare sweet treat from her trouser pocket.

His smile warmed her like the fireplace at her mum and dad's home. "Hmm. I'll make sure James doesn't know I have chocolate. Thank you so much, and I have a gift for you. I hope you'll be pleased."

She held her breath, unable to image what Andrew could have gotten for her.

He carefully reached inside his jacket and produced a sheet of paper. She knew he had sketched something special, and judging by the rose he left in her lorry, she knew it would be magnificent.

The moment Margaret saw the drawing, she gasped. She touched her fingers to her lips to keep from crying aloud. There before her, a quaint, moss-covered cottage stood surrounded by a garden of roses. Some climbed the stone walls trailing up onto the roof, while smaller bushes and other flowers dotted the earth's floor. A winding rose vine arched the doorway, spreading blossoms over the entrance. In the middle of a pebble-laden path sat a young woman dressed in the manner of an eighteenth-century maiden. She inhaled the sweet fragrance of a rose and possessed a face identical to Margaret's.

"If I had my colored pencils, I'd have given her dark brown hair and violet eyes," he said. "I hope you're not disappointed."

"Oh, Andrew. This is the most extraordinary gift anyone has ever given me. Thank you ever so." She stared into his eyes and saw her own reflection and something else—the warm glow of love. The sensation both frightened and pleased her at the same time.

"Margaret," he said, "may I kiss you?"

She'd thought about his kiss—more than she cared to admit—but with this bridge between friendship and a relationship came a commitment. Could she brave forward?

"It's a step beyond. . .well, where we are now," she whispered, more for her own understanding than his.

"Yes, it is. I'm ready, but are you?"

She nodded and lifted her face. "I think so."

He wove his fingers through her hair and drew her close to him. His lips touched hers, gentle at first then deepening with his embrace. Trembling, she responded, desiring to hold back her own delicate emotions and yet losing the battle. With one hand firmly gripping the sketch, she wrapped the other arm around his neck and leaned into the curve of his body. She knew she'd given him her heart—no matter that the time seemed too soon and uncertainty lay around them. She could love him and he'd never know.

The kiss ended, and when they parted, Margaret traced her finger along his jawline and lightly touched his lips. He gently caressed her fingers and kissed them lightly.

"Merry Christmas," he whispered, still holding her fingers.

She glowed from the inside out. "Thank you for making my holiday perfect."

"My pleasure, but the thanks go to you. You're all I need, all put together quite nicely in one lovely package."

Margaret could not reply. She wanted to say the thoughts wafting across her mind, but until Andrew made his declaration, she'd not have to respond. Truth be known, any feelings of love were best unsaid until after the war.

On Sunday, December twenty-ninth, Margaret was assigned to night duty delivering much-needed medical supplies. The Germans' nightly bombing had continued to shake London, leaving their city collapsing in rubble and the injured storming the hospitals.

Britons refused to give in to the siege against their capital and plodded on, unwilling to accept defeat as an option. The air-raid shelters were full at night, while the cleanup and search for victims persisted by day. Some of those seeking shelter sank into wells of depression, while others spent their time singing songs and rallying England. The shared danger seemed to make them more sociable, or perhaps they learned to value those things money could not purchase.

Shortly after the medical supplies were loaded, the sirens sounded, and heavy air strikes began, stronger than she could remember in months. Instead of seeking shelter, she watched the bombs illuminate the night sky as if a demon had lit a giant torch. The incessant attack left her feeling empty and fearful. One prayer after another flowed from her heart.

As soon as the all-clear siren sounded, Margaret climbed into her lorry and drove toward the hospital, all the while wondering about the horrendous devastation. This had to be the worst barrage since the Battle of Britain began in late August.

Fires raged in the distance. Their flames leapt into the blackness like giant tongues hungry for more. The attack appeared to concentrate its efforts on central London. Soon afterward, she learned that in Westminster and the City regions, fires spread out of control and destroyed docks, factories, and offices.

Dear Lord, when will it all end? We can't take much more of this. I pray for those whose livelihood has been destroyed, for those who have lost loved ones this night, and for Britain to survive.

Chapter 5

*"Let us therefore brace ourselves to our duties,
and so bear ourselves that, if the British Empire
and its Commonwealth last for a thousand years,
men will still say, 'This was their finest hour.' "*
WINSTON CHURCHILL

High winds carried sparks from rooftops to melting stained-glass windows, but Saint Paul's Cathedral towered erect as though the hand of God halted the bombs destroying everything around it. For Margaret, the magnificent church symbolized Britain's ability to withstand Germany's assault.

She leaned her head on Andrew's shoulder. Twelve hours ago, she'd watched in horror the sight of London plummeting into ruins thirty miles away. Yet, today, Home Guardsman and firefighters worked diligently to extinguish the blazes and pull victims from the wreckage. The casualty count had been much lower than anticipated, since the areas hardest hit were commercial. In truth, it looked like the Germans had caught the British off guard by focusing their bombs on the heart of Britain's financial security district. News reports claimed it was the greatest fire in recorded history.

Beautiful old buildings—the pride of many Britons—had vanished beneath smoldering ashes. History in the making had destroyed the relics of the past.

"The Thames nearly ran dry," Andrew said. "Hitler chose to do his work during low tide. Can't put out such an inferno without water."

"What will Churchill say now?" Margaret said, grasping his hand in the bitter cold.

His lips pressed firmly together. "I have no idea, but we are still here."

She fought the rage inside her over the violation of her homeland. "I shall not give up," she said. "Not as long as I can breathe."

He smiled and brushed a kiss in her hair. "We all feel the same. The more Hitler bombs, the more we rally onward."

"Do you suppose the United States will join the war now?" she said, believing the Americans' entry would give Britain the edge to stop Germany.

"We already have many of their fine pilots joining our ranks." He sighed. "They're good chaps to volunteer and help us. Perhaps Churchill can convince them."

"I've heard speculation about Germany's plans," she ventured.

"I have as well. I believe Hitler would not stop at merely controlling Europe. He has even set his sights on the States."

Margaret felt a deeper cold seize her. "And would not Japan attack them on their west coast?"

"Who knows? We will not let it come to that."

Neither whispered a word for several moments.

"You and I are like England," Andrew finally said.

Puzzled, she merely stared up into his face.

"We can withstand any adversity. Nothing can separate us. We'll make it through this war and live to tell about it."

She smiled sadly, not wanting to consider the fact that every time he flew, the odds increased of his not returning.

He began to hum "There'll Always Be an England," a popular wartime tune. Together they softly sang the chorus.

There'll always be an England,
And England shall be free
If England means as much to you
As England means to me.

◆　◆　◆

The winter persisted with work and missions halting when the pilots were hampered by ice and snow. Germany eased the intense bombing that had occurred during late August through the end of 1940. It appeared the island had passed the test for control of England.

Spring arrived, and Andrew wanted to take Margaret to the country. He felt they would gain new hope in the midst of fresh air and the landscape unscathed by bombs.

"I'd like to take a few days to go see my mum and dad," he announced one March morning. "I'm sure I could help with the extra children, and I want to see my nephew before he's walking."

"Splendid idea," Margaret said. "You need a break."

"Would you care to join me?" he said, all the while praying she'd agree. "My mum has plenty of room, even with the children."

"Are you sure? I mean, it sounds wonderful."

"Positively." Oh, how he treasured the joy of the woman beside him. "The garden will be blooming in spring color, and there's a special spot I'd like to show you."

Because Andrew and Margaret had not taken any passes for several months, their arrangements were quickly made. The end of March, he escorted her to London, where they boarded a train to Northamptonshire. From there they'd take bicycles to Andrew's family estate.

The moment London lay behind them, he felt his spirits lift, much like in his schooldays when he traveled home for a holiday. So many things he needed to tell his parents. With no end of the war in sight, they should hear of his love and respect for them. Andrew also wanted them to meet Margaret. He knew they would love her as much as he did.

Andrew hadn't revealed his true feelings for Margaret. He prayerfully waited for the right moment. In the confines of his heart, he feared she might not share the same love. Whenever he spoke of the future, she veered from the subject and irritation took over her demeanor. He knew her commitment to the war and her apprehension about his dangerous position, but her eyes betrayed her. He'd seen the love, and he'd guessed her feelings.

In Northamptonshire, they purchased bread and cheese for a picnic and secured bicycles for the remaining distance to the Stuart Estate. He was anxious and excited, wanting to leave the dark months of war behind and enjoy three days of peace. Glancing at Margaret pedaling beside him, her hair flying free, he saw the weary lines vanish from her face and her cheeks grow rosy in the chilly air. They sang songs and teased the other over forgotten words to the tunes, and laughter rang from the budding trees. He stole a kiss, which nearly wrecked them both.

Once they walked their bicycles so they could hear the birds, although he believed the lilt of her laughter far sweeter than any sound of nature. The light-heartedness reminded him of a proper courtship, the way it should be.

"Up ahead is home." Andrew pointed to a huge manor rising in a clearing behind ancient stone walls.

"Oh, Andrew, it's beautiful. I had no idea it would be so grand." She stopped her bicycle to view the rugged estate.

"I want to show it all to you." He shielded his eyes from the sun. "Have I gone daft, or do I hear children?"

She lifted her chin and turned in the direction of the merry sound. "I hear them. How many are your parents keeping?"

"A dozen, I believe, in addition to my nephew."

Over the ridge, an army of small children filed in a haphazard line. They clung to shirttails and hems of dresses while marching like miniature soldiers. Their little voices echoed like fairy-tale magic.

"Oh, Andrew. It's been so long since I've seen or heard little ones. I want to hug them all." She peered at the group hiking down a grassy knoll. "I believe there's closer to fourteen than twelve."

"My word," Andrew breathed. "There's my dad and Mr. Hardy, the gardener."

Abandoning his bicycle, Andrew called out to a white-haired gentleman taking up the rear of the procession. "Father!" Andrew waved and raced toward them. He didn't care if he looked like a child himself, for at that moment the war lay far behind.

◆　◆　◆

Margaret studied each child seated around the long wooden table. She recalled Jenny commenting about her son's letter—how he loved the country and never wanted to leave. She envied Jenny's children and the precious hope of Britain's future.

Mr. and Mrs. Stuart had trained the children well, especially since most of them had come from poverty-stricken areas. Andrew's mother had told her in private the sad condition of some of them: lice infested, dirty, underfed, and without manners. Even with the rationing, Mr. and Mrs. Stuart had provided for them all. Their bright eyes held the glow of promise.

"I simply mother them and enjoy every minute of it," Andrew's mother had said, her ample cheeks swelling with pride.

Andrew looked more vibrant than Margaret had ever seen him. He laughed more, and she appreciated the gentle way he dealt with the children. She felt at peace with herself in a way she couldn't remember since before the war, maybe not even then.

"Would you like a bit more stew?" Mrs. Stuart said, interrupting Margaret's contemplations. The older woman brushed back sandy-colored hair, the same shade as Andrew's.

"No, thank you, ma'am. I'm simply admiring all of these precious children."

"Oh, they can be a handful," Mr. Stuart said, lifting his knife to emphasize his words. His voice rose above the cherub voices. "Not so loud, children. Our guests will think we're not proper." He feigned a stern look at the brood, in particular one little girl who had not ceased laughing.

A boy about eight years old asked if there would be sweets tonight.

"Possibly," Mrs. Stuart said with a smile. "When everyone has eaten their stew, I might find a treat. In fact, I believe Mrs. Hardy made gooseberry tarts today sweetened with honey."

The children cheered, and those who had not finished their stew and bread hastened to clean their bowls.

After dinner Margaret helped Mrs. Stuart and some of the older children wash and dry the dishes. Once the wet towels were draped over the sink, the older woman announced bath night.

"How do you manage to bathe them all?" Margaret mentally calculated how long the task would take.

"Mr. Stuart and I split them up—girls and boys. Then he heats one tub and I the other. It doesn't really amount to a long time, and the older children help the younger ones undress and dress."

Andrew marched into the kitchen carrying his nephew on his shoulder. "Tonight it will go twice as fast, for we intend to help. Right, Margaret?"

She grinned and laughed at another toddler tugging on his trouser leg. What a lovely day. A part of her wanted it to go on forever—or maybe she wanted to live in this make-believe world with Andrew forever. Margaret forced her feelings for him from her mind. The memory of her brother's death and Beryl's circumstances still shadowed her heart. Perhaps when Germany ceased to plague the world, they could talk of a life together.

The following morning, after breakfast had been eaten and the kitchen scrubbed spotless, Margaret and Andrew offered to entertain the children until lunch. Normally his parents and Mr. Hardy took over those duties while Mrs. Hardy busied herself in preparing the day's food.

"We will go exploring," Andrew announced to the children. "Who knows what we might find?"

The children's voices mounted as each tried to tell Uncle Andrew their most prized find. A short while later they proceeded in single file across the hillsides, grasping shirt and dress tails, just as Margaret and Andrew had observed the previous day.

"Why is it you have the little girls after you?" Margaret called to Andrew while they hiked along a brook's edge.

"I have no idea, but the boys appear to like you best," he said and lifted a wee girl to his shoulders.

"True. I must be prettier," she said, feeling the sweet weight of two little boys pulling on her arms.

He swung a grin over his shoulder, mesmerizing her with his tender glance. "This afternoon I'd like to show you the garden. Perhaps just after tea?"

"Wonderful." She visualized a lovely array of spring color. Everything about Stuart Manor filled her senses with beauty and delight.

Andrew and Margaret enjoyed tea in delicate demitasse cups, poured from a family heirloom pitcher and served on a silver tray. They added a precious lump of sugar and ate cucumber sandwiches and biscuits. She tucked away every memory to open like a treasured book when the days ahead sought to overwhelm her.

◆　◆　◆

"Close your eyes and let me lead you," Andrew coaxed, once they'd left the manor. "I want this to be a surprise."

"I might peek," she said with a giggle.

"Ah, fair lady, then must I blindfold you?"

"Probably so."

He reached into his pocket and produced a clean, white handkerchief. She nodded approval before obediently turning for him to secure it over her eyes.

Andrew couldn't resist and lightly kissed her neck. He detected a shiver. "Cold, are you?" he said.

"Not exactly." A smile played on her lips. "How far are we going?"

"Miles, my lady. Just hold tightly to my hand."

On they walked, beyond the back of the manor and dark yew hedges to a place where dreams were made. He drank in the earthy smells and watched the light splay through the tree limbs. Never had he truly appreciated the garden's beauty and Mr. Hardy's labor until today.

"Here we are," he said, stopping several feet in front of a winding brook beside a small, stone cottage. Andrew removed the handkerchief from Margaret's eyes, watching every movement on her face.

She held her breath and tears fell from her eyes. "It's my picture, my Christmas picture." She studied each delicate spring flower, fern, and grass. She stepped across a rock path to the bubbling brook, then bent to examine a patch of daffodils and red tulips. As though in her own world, she noted each blooming array of primrose, crocus, and white narcissus. A light laugh sprang from her lips as she gingerly scooped up a cherry blossom petal that had fallen among the grasses.

As if a symphony played in the background of rustling water, Margaret slowly stood and approached the cottage.

"The roses." She closed her eyes. "I can only imagine all this paradise when they're in full bloom."

Andrew's heart raced at the sight of his beloved Margaret posed at the threshold of the small structure.

"In summer the scent of the roses mixed with honeysuckle will take your breath away," he said, choosing to join her.

She touched the moss-covered wall. "And the beauty of them, just as in my picture."

"Nearly as lovely as you."

She blushed, and her gaze followed a vine trailing up the side to the roof. "Thank you," she said, so quietly that her voice blended with the gentle sounds of nature. "This is a sacred place. Surely Eden could not have been more colorful and alive." She whirled to face him. "Oh, Andrew, God is here. I can feel Him."

"That's why I've chosen this place to tell you how I feel." His heart pounded and his mouth felt dry, but he dare not lose courage now. Lifting her chin with his finger, he gazed into those beloved pools, more radiant than the blossoms from spring and summer combined. "I love you, Margaret. I want us always to be together. Marry me and let me take care of you."

Her face paled, and she stepped back. "Marry you. . .while the war rages around us?" Her gaze darted like a trapped animal.

Andrew's heart plummeted. "This war will not last forever."

She shook her head. "I can't. I can't possibly marry you. What if I lose you like my brother? Or how Beryl lost Patrick? Forgive me, Andrew, but what you ask is impossible. Perhaps after the war. . ." Her voice trailed off, and in its wake her sobs broke the spell of the garden.

Brushing past him, Margaret rushed toward the house beyond him and the call of the garden.

Chapter 6

"This is a war of the Unknown Warriors;
but let all strive without failing in faith or in duty."
WINSTON CHURCHILL

Margaret raced from the garden toward the Stuart manor, her tears falling uncontrollably. She needed to leave this place and get back to London where she belonged. There in the real world, she had duties and responsibilities that mattered. Andrew had tricked her into coming to Northamptonshire. He knew she'd never agree to marriage while on base. By taking her to the country, he'd played on her sentiments. How selfish of him to ask her to wed when pilots faced death every moment they were in the air. Andrew had taken her affections for him and used them to his advantage.

"Margaret!"

She hurried faster.

"Margaret!"

Anger laced every syllable.

Before she could consider a reply, he grabbed her arm and forced her to face him.

"You're a coward?" Blood pumped its power through his face and neck. "Life doesn't give any guarantees, Corporal Walker. What will your excuse be after the war? I might get sick? I might get hit by a trolley? I might choke on a poached egg? England's weather doesn't suit you?"

"You have no right to talk to me that way." She shook loose his hold and took a step back. Their fury split the picturesque countryside. What happened to her quiet lieutenant? "You don't understand."

He raked his fingers through his hair and expelled a heavy sigh that seemed to come from the soles of his feet. "Oh, I understand perfectly. Do you think you have the market on heartache? Look at the thousands of children living without their parents. Think of the parents who have no idea of their children's living conditions. What about Beryl and Patrick? Do you think they stopped loving because Hitler decided to wage war?"

"Leave me alone," she said through her tears.

"First tell me you don't love me." He intensified his demand with a piercing stare.

"You don't deserve an answer. You brought me here under false pretenses, thinking the country and its garden would twist my mind and heart into seeing things your way."

"Since when is the love God gives a man and a woman something to be reckoned with like a formidable enemy?"

She balled her fists, more angry than she could remember. "He instructs us to be discerning," she spurted through a ragged breath.

Andrew lifted his chin. "It is you who cannot perceive what is clearly before you. How sad. You cannot make a commitment, and you're using anything you can clutch as an excuse." He paused, then stiffened. "Tell me you want me out of your life." His voice softened. "Tell me now, and I won't ever bother you again. I give you my word."

A lump settled in her throat. Her lips quivered and she swallowed hard. She turned and raced back toward the house.

"Go ahead, run," he called after her. "I won't come after you. You've made your choice."

◆　◆　◆

Sunday morning, Andrew rode the train back to London alone. Margaret had gathered up her things on Saturday afternoon and left the house before he'd walked off his anger and talked to God.

He'd been prepared to apologize for losing his temper, and when he found out she'd left his parents' home, he wanted to go after her. But he held on to his pride. He recognized it, and still he could not humble himself to make amends with her. She'd tested him once too often. Margaret would have to come to him.

As he buried himself in the RAF—flying at a moment's notice and often several times during the day or night—Andrew attempted to cast aside his love for her. He avoided the places they'd ventured together, believing he could tuck her memory into a remote corner of his heart. A few times she'd driven the lorry transporting the pilots to the hangars, but he refused to look her way.

Bitterness erupted when he least expected it like a land mine, damaging his relationships with other flyers. He apologized and the others said they understood, but it didn't stop the guilt.

A month later, Andrew settled his plane into formation with other Spitfires above the waters of the English Channel. Radar had indicated German fighters en route to Britain's shores, and the fighters churned their engines to meet them. The RAF planes flew twenty thousand feet above the clouds, making them invisible until the right moment to swoop down behind the unsuspecting German Messerschmitts.

Andrew waited until he knew the enemy swarmed beneath them before ordering the fighters to separate, turn, and dive for the attack. Sadly outnumbered, the RAF utilized their offensive position to fire the enemy from the skies.

The surprise attack left black swirls of smoke and the decimated end of many German planes. Andrew saw two of his friends' planes burst into flames, but one pilot parachuted out. The other man now rested in God's hands.

Angry at the loss of his friend's life, Andrew flew down through the middle of six German fighters and pumped bullets from every angle. He knew he took too many chances lately, and although he'd earned the title of a relentless fighter, he understood his daring came from his wounded heart.

One enemy aircraft met his demise and two others took on heavy damage. He quickly lifted his plane above the clouds to strike again.

Within seconds, he detected three enemy fighters rapidly moving in from his rear.

"You think you have me?" he shouted. "We'll see who wins this round."

The hair on his neck bristled when a fighter zoomed in faster than Andrew anticipated. He pulled his Spitfire up, narrowly missing an onslaught of bullets. Beads of sweat trickled down the side of his face despite the winter temperatures.

"Lord, I need Your help," he said.

Through the white veil concealing him, Andrew spotted a Messerschmitt looming behind. Andrew lifted the plane higher and quickly swung to the right. He aimed his wing guns, fired, and watched the enemy aircraft disappear in an explosion. Another fighter appeared just ahead. Andrew ascended on the plane and sent it spiraling downward.

He no sooner recovered than the third German fighter trailed after him. Andrew used the same maneuver, except this time he swung to the left. The enemy stayed on him as though sensing Andrew's moves. Again he lifted his Spitfire and repeated a wide turn to the left.

The Messerschmitt followed, now within firing range. Enemy bullets ripped into Andrew's fighter.

Lord, this German is smarter than I am. I need You to direct me.

Following his instincts, Andrew sank below the Messerschmitt and prayed for guidance. He glanced at the amount of fuel remaining and assessed the damage done to his plane. He wondered if the right wing guns would work at all. Taking a deep breath, he moved from under the enemy and twisted to the right, but not before taking a bad hit to the side.

Pressing on, he finally secured a rear position and pumped all he had into the German fighter. The aircraft exploded, but the Spitfire would never make it back to base.

Thank You, Lord. Please be with the other pilots as well.

Andrew parachuted out and saw his landing would be on English soil and not the water. He breathed a prayer of thanks, for he had no inclination to drop into the icy waters of the Channel or set up a rescue boat as a target for airborne Germans. He cringed when his fighter plane crashed into the coastal terrain long before his feet found safety. He rather fancied that little fighter, but like Margaret, all had been lost.

◆　◆　◆

On May tenth, Andrew picked up his Bible and read through Isaiah forty. He had long ago put the verses of twenty-nine through thirty-one to memory and often prayed through them in flight. This morning the Scripture held a different meaning. He closed his eyes and allowed the words to flow through his body and soul.

"He giveth power to the faint; and to them that have no might He increaseth strength. Even the youths shall faint and be weary, and the young men shall utterly fall. But they that wait upon the Lord shall renew their strength; they shall mount up with wings as eagles; they shall run, and not be weary; and they shall walk, and not faint."

Andrew felt as though a knife had thrust through his heart and twisted. *"...the young men shall utterly fall."* His pride was destroying him. For weeks he'd been depleted of strength, not the strength required to fly his Spitfire but his ability to hold on to the Lord. His broken heart had stopped him from forgiving Margaret and apologizing for losing his temper. The time had come to stop asking God why she'd refused him and accept he might never know until he saw God face-to-face. For now, God had allowed this upheaval in his life, and He did know best.

Forgive me, Father, for my hard heart. I will find Margaret today and apologize. Thank You for caring enough to point out my sin and for providing a way for me to seek forgiveness. You know my love for her, and now I see my love must be unconditional, like Yours.

Andrew closed his Bible. He did not have to fly until tonight. He'd make amends with Margaret and not go another day with the shame tormenting his soul.

"I'm praying for you, chum," James said from his cot. Their friendship had grown to the point where oft times neither had to speak a word to sense the other's mood and thoughts.

"Thanks, James. I've been a fool not to patch up things. At least Margaret and I could be friends. At times I can't help but wonder if I'd gone after her that afternoon things might have ended differently."

"No word from her at all?"

"Nothing, but I haven't tried to contact her either." Andrew shrugged. "I misjudged her feelings and then judged her myself." He glanced up. "I've had a nasty disposition lately, but I promise things will be different."

"We all know it's been rough."

"No excuse for taking out my wounded pride on you and the other chaps. I'll make sure I talk to them today."

After apologizing to the other pilots and assuring them that God had dealt with his bad temperament, Andrew scoured the camp for Margaret but couldn't find her. He asked some of the women at her barracks, but none knew where she could be found. He prayed he'd have an opportunity to speak with her before heading to the hangars.

As the day drew to a close, he prepared himself for flight. Although his heart felt the burden of not righting things with Margaret, he sensed a peace. Laughter came naturally, and optimism for the future returned.

When the call came to board the lorry, he filed out with the other pilots. If only Margaret drove, but he couldn't see the driver's seat from the vehicle's angle.

"Did you see the driver?" he said to James once they were en route.

"'Tis Margaret," James said. "I spoke to her, and she acknowledged me. She looks as unhappy as you."

Andrew felt a spark of hope. "I'm going to do my best to have a word with her once we get to the hangars."

"Jolly good idea."

Once they reached the aircrafts, one of the pilots cornered Andrew about a downed plane from the preceding day in which a pilot lost his life. "Sir, about yesterday, the pilot confided in me about a concern he had with his fighter."

Andrew lifted a brow. "Did he discuss it with a mechanic?"

"Not to my knowledge."

"Let's talk inside and see if we can pinpoint the problem."

As they stepped into the wooden building, the lorry drove away. Regret washed over him, but safety for his pilots came first.

Shortly before darkness wrapped its blanket over England, the fighter pilots were summoned to the skies. Andrew raced to his plane and pulled the canopy over his head. He felt the familiar adrenaline pump through his veins as he waved to James beside him and mouthed "tally-ho." Taking his position on the runway, Andrew breathed a prayer before lifting his Spitfire into the air.

◆　◆　◆

Margaret's misery increased every time she thought of Andrew. She missed him terribly and despised their harsh words. So many times she wanted to go to him and apologize, but in doing so she feared he would press her about marriage. Couldn't they love each other until the war no longer existed, then discuss a future?

Today she'd transported him to the hangars. It took all of her control to avoid him. She wanted to ask how he fared and seek the warmth in his deep brown eyes. A part of her realized his feelings for her had vanished. She'd ruined it in Northamptonshire—the day in the beautiful garden when he proposed. Admittedly, Margaret didn't know what she wanted, nor did she know what God intended for them. All she knew was the ache in her heart for Andrew. Perhaps her misery stemmed from the fact she refused to seek God's will. Her heavenly Father might ask more of her than she could give.

She'd told her friends in the barracks not to breathe a word of her whereabouts if Andrew came looking. He'd done so today, and now the pain ravaged her heart.

Early evening, Margaret delivered a document to one of Churchill's advisers in London. Within minutes, she climbed into the lorry to head back to base. Evening had drifted into night, and along with the darkness came the sirens alerting London of imminent German bombing.

They never give up.

She glanced up at the skies as the warnings assaulted her ears. Sometimes she simply didn't care when it sounded. Other times she prayed for those who would be affected. Praise God Britain had the early detection radar, for without it they'd have fallen months ago.

Margaret picked her way along the road, avoiding deep crevices and rubble resulting from previous bombings. In the war-torn city, she felt uneasy, trapped by the probability of falling bombs and collapsing buildings. She'd feel much better once safely away on base.

She heard the roar of enemy planes above her and the zoom of their engines cutting through the darkness to drop their destruction. To Margaret, there appeared to be more than usual, reminding her of December twenty-ninth's raid. Bombs fell like a shower of hail, igniting fires that burst into yellow-orange flames. They raised their fiery fingers to the sky as though paying homage to the German bombers.

An apartment building exploded in front of her, sending shattered glass through its walls directly into her path. A man, obviously wounded, emerged from the fiery mass and stumbled in her direction. Pulling the lorry to a halt, she rushed to his side.

"I'll get you to a hospital," she said above the deafening roar. As the fire lit up his face, she saw blood stream down his forehead and cheek.

He leaned heavily on her until she fell. Together they struggled to their feet and inched their way to the lorry.

"My wife's inside," he said, attempting to gain his breath.

She helped him onto the seat and patted his shoulder. "I'll look for your missus."

He uttered a feeble thanks as she shut the door.

Margaret scanned the burning area but saw no one. The heat nearly took her breath away. Why hadn't the couple gone to a shelter? Another bomb crashed on the same building, eliminating any chances of the woman's survival. Margaret needed to get the injured man to the hospital and away from the fire. Even the street was laden with fire.

She rushed to the driver's side and in one fluid motion slammed the door and stuck the key into the ignition. "I'm sorry, sir, but I don't see your wife, and I can't get inside the building to find her." No need to tell him it had been destroyed. She hoped her words sounded compassionate, but in truth fright tore through her senses.

With trembling hands, Margaret jerked the lorry into gear. She backed up, all the while taking in the devastation. The man slumped against the passenger's door and moaned before whispering something inaudible. She wished she could have helped his wife, but only God could deliver the woman now. Terror gripped Margaret as she steered away from the site.

The burning mass disguised the normal landmarks, and she wondered what street to take to the hospital. An explosion in front of them caused her to slam on the brakes. She screamed as a mighty force pulled her from the vehicle and threw her into the inferno.

Chapter 7

*"Never in the field of human conflict was so much
owed by so many to so few."*
WINSTON CHURCHILL

M argaret opened her eyes. Fires blazed, while the deafening sounds of falling bombs echoed around her. From where she'd been thrown, she could
see her lorry in flames. She called out for the injured man inside, knowing
full well the futility of her cries. A moment later she prayed he'd been tossed from it
as well.

Her mind dulled to everything around her except her tormented body. She felt
as though every bone had been broken, but a fierce determination to survive compelled her to move. Every muscle and nerve screamed out in protest, and blood
trickled into her eyes. Fighting the pounding in her head, Margaret tried to lift her
right arm to find the source of the blood, but excruciating pain hindered any
movement. Her head dropped back onto a rock.

I have to see the rest of my body. Oh, dear Lord, I'm scared.

She tried to suck in air, but the smoke caused her to choke and sputter. After
several long minutes, she slowly raised her head and studied her body sprawled out
on a mass of rubble. The lights from the fires showed what she suspected. Her left
leg curled in an awkward position away from her torso. She had to lie there until
one of the fires tasted her body and devoured her.

Listening to the crackling and crashing going on around her, Margaret prayed
for strength to endure whatever happened. Although she tried to stay alert, she
drifted in and out of consciousness. Sometime during the night, she awoke and her
thoughts turned to Andrew.

Dear, sweet Andrew, who only wanted a chance to love her. She'd been so cruel
to make light of his feelings.

*I can't ever tell him how sorry I am for that afternoon in the country. Never tell him
how I wanted to spend the rest of my life with him and be the mother of his children.
He'll never know how much I truly love him.*

Her past harsh words spilled across her mind like ink blots. In the recesses of
her heart, she knew he'd been right. She was a coward—afraid of getting hurt and
being left alone. She was paralyzed by the memories of her brother, Beryl loosing
Patrick, and the countless faces of pilots who never returned. Other women in her
barracks grieved the family members who gave their lives in the war effort.
Margaret didn't want to think about being in the same situation. She didn't have
the courage to love a man no matter how hopeless the future.

But with God all things were possible.

She well knew this Scripture. Why hadn't she remembered it before? Guilt for her inability to be bold and courageous assailed her heart and mind.

Precious Lord, forgive me for not seeking Your will about Andrew. I know I'm going to die, and all of this time my fears were for him. The irony of death, Lord. I've been such a fool.

A wave of blackness drew her back into its web.

Later she woke again to the sound of German bombers still releasing their fury on London. Opening her eyes, she strained to see a hint of daylight, but a thick film coated her eyes. With the searing pain invading her body, she prayed for death's release.

◆ ◆ ◆

Andrew wearily opened his eyes. Throughout the previous night he'd flown repeated missions until at last the Germans ceased their attack that morning. Glancing at the clock, he noted six hours had gone by, and he felt like sleeping another six.

"I see you're awake," James said from his cot.

"Trying to be," Andrew said. "How long have you been up?"

"About an hour."

Andrew swallowed hard. "So what's the word?"

"Gloomy, at best."

He stared at his friend. "How bad?"

"I heard nearly seven hundred acres of London burned." James stared at the ceiling. "This is the first time I've really felt low about the war—asked myself why go on."

"I've felt the same way from time to time, more so when a chap parachuted beside me and still didn't make it." Andrew hesitated. "Tell me more about the bombings."

James expelled a heavy breath. "A number of places were hit: Scotland Yard, Westminister Abbey, most of the City, and all the bridges across the Thames. None of the telephones are working, and I'm sure there's more, but I heard enough to know the Germans must have dropped every bomb they had on us."

"What about casualties?"

James's gaze appeared to bore through Andrew. "I'd hate to speculate. Fires raged for miles."

Andrew prayed for all those innocent people and for England. "We only lost one fighter plane and shot down fourteen of theirs. At least that was the count this morning."

James nodded. "Our radar has helped tremendously, and I know we did well last night, but the devastation is horrible."

"Are you praying?" Andrew said.

His friend gave him a faint smile. "I have to. Without God, we are nothing."

Their conversation ceased when a pilot stood before their cots.

"Lieutenant, a woman is waiting outside to speak to you."

Andrew reluctantly rose to his feet. Suddenly the possibility of Margaret seeking him out brought a new surge of energy.

Outside his door, he recognized Jenny, one of Margaret's friends. Although disappointed, he would not reveal it.

"You wanted to speak with me?" he said. He saw the tension in her face, and it alarmed him.

"Yes, sir." Jenny glanced nervously about and back to Andrew. "Margaret has been seriously injured. She was caught in the bombing last night."

Andrew felt the color drain from his face. "Is she here at the hospital?"

"Yes, sir. I'm on my way now. I thought you might. . .well, might want to join me."

"Not my Margaret," he said, his stomach threatening to retch.

He rushed back inside for his jacket and to ask James to pray. A moment later, Andrew and Jenny rushed to the hospital. If only he knew the extent of Margaret's injuries. The thought of losing her had a strangling hold around his neck. He hadn't been able to apologize, and now she lay injured in the hospital. His pride, his stubborn, foolish pride.

Dear Lord, hold her in the palm of Your hand. Heal her body.

Inside the busy hospital, Andrew located a nurse and asked for assistance in finding Margaret. She directed him to a women's ward at the far end of the building. Another nurse met him outside the room.

"I'm Lieutenant Stuart. We're looking for Corporal Margaret Walker," he said. "I understand she's in this ward."

The nurse nodded. She wiped a loose strand of hair from her face with her arm. Blood had splattered her apron. "She drifts in and out, Lieutenant. You can visit, but she needs her rest."

"Thank you. We won't stay long," he said, peering anxiously into the room.

The nurse hurried down the hall, then spun around. "Lieutenant, is your first name Andrew?"

Startled, he stared at her a moment before replying. "Yes, it is."

"Good." She smiled. "Corporal Walker has repeated your name several times."

Tears welled in his eyes, and he hastily blinked them back. "I've got to see her." He stepped aside for Jenny to enter, although it took all of his might to uphold his proper upbringing.

Margaret's bed sat midway down the ward in a room filled with injured women. His pace couldn't get him to her side fast enough. At the sight of her, Andrew again swallowed his emotion. In his worst expectations, he didn't think she would look so battered. A bandage wrapped around her head, and her swollen face revealed a mass of bruises, making her barely recognizable. A cast encased her right arm and another wrapped around her left leg. He prayed there were no internal injuries. She appeared to sleep, but Andrew wondered if she lay unconscious.

"Margaret," he whispered. When she didn't respond, he spoke her name again.

"Do you think she hears us?" Jenny said, reaching out to stroke Margaret's arm. Instantly she drew back her hand. "Poor lamb. I'm afraid I'll hurt her."

"If she's asleep, then she's not in pain," he said. Andrew could only stare into Margaret's face. "Jenny, do you know any of the details of what happened?"

"Not much more than what I already told you. She had to deliver something into London and got caught in the bombing. Lieutenant, I'm not surprised Margaret called out your name."

He raised a brow.

"She's been miserable since you two stopped seeing each other." Jenny sighed. "Oh, yes. I don't know why you two decided to go your separate ways. . . Guess it's none of my business."

Andrew chose not to reply. So many things needed to be said to Margaret, and even then he wouldn't want to discuss their relationship, or rather the lack of it, with anyone else.

"Andrew," Margaret uttered though her eyes were still closed. "Is it really you?"

He bent to her face. "Yes, it is." He wanted to hold her, kiss away the bruises and cuts. "Don't try to talk, just rest."

"I'm so sorry," she said, her voice barely above a whisper.

He held his finger a hair span above her bruised lips. "Hush. You just concentrate on getting better. I'll visit you tomorrow and every day until you're well. Jenny's with me. She needs to say a word with you."

He stepped back for the woman. "Hello, love. Please do what Andrew says and listen to the doctor. All of us will be praying for you."

Margaret wet her lips and her face relaxed.

For the next three days, he visited Margaret at every opportunity. On occasion Jenny and a few of the other women from the barracks accompanied him, and sometimes he went alone. The doctors kept Margaret sedated, and he knew she rarely comprehended his presence. While he sat and waited by her bedside, he watched her lovely face and longed for the day when she would be well. He couldn't help but allow his thoughts to drift toward dreams of Margaret by his side forever.

◆　◆　◆

Margaret stirred. Had she been in another world, or had Andrew actually been there? She glanced about and realized she lay in a hospital. With her uninjured hand, she felt the bandage on her head and noted the casts on her arm and leg. Instantly her mind reverted to the night of the bombing: the wounded man, the fires, and the explosion throwing her from the lorry.

Thank You, Lord, for sparing my life. I pray the injured man fared as well.

Glancing about her, she saw the crowded beds and the women occupying them. Margaret could only imagine the stories they had to tell—tales of tragedy and heroism. When she felt better, she'd talk to those patients and make sure they had a relationship with Jesus.

Something drew her attention to the door. She must be hallucinating, for she believed Andrew stood there, looking more handsome than she could ever remember. As he approached her bed, tears sprang to her eyes.

"Andrew, for a moment I thought I might be dreaming." She reached out her left hand, and he took it firmly into his.

"How are you feeling today?" he said in the same quiet tone she remembered. And those incredible brown eyes were only a few feet from her.

"Much better, I think. I know where I am and the pain has subsided."

"Good, then my prayers are answered."

"Thank you for coming to see me."

He smiled. "I've been here every day since the accident."

"You have? I had no idea." She took a deep breath. "Andrew, I'm sorry for the things I said to you in the country. You were right. I'm a coward, and I did make excuses to not commit myself."

He shook his head. "I'm the one who needs to apologize. I lost my temper and demanded things you weren't ready to give."

She allowed her stinging eyes to close for a moment and asked the Father for the courage she desperately needed. Forcing them open, she continued. "I love you, Andrew. I don't want to ever lose you again—I mean, if you'll still have me. It took the accident and believing I was going to die in my foolishness to make me realize how much I love you."

He bent over her, his arms on each side of the bed. "Oh, my sweet Margaret, I never stopped loving you. My pride got in the way."

Gazing up into his beloved face, she wept.

"Don't cry, darling. We'll work this out. The war can't last forever," Andrew said, brushing away a tear with his finger.

"It's not the war," she said. "I'm happy, Andrew. When I get these casts off, would you? I mean, if you still want to. Would you marry me?"

◆　◆　◆

In August of 1941, beside a moss-covered, stone cottage outside the city of Northamptonshire, Lieutenant Andrew Stuart and Corporal Margaret Walker held hands on a pebble-laden path lined with white lilies and pink phlox. In the midst of vibrant pink and red roses, the flowers' sweet scent mingling with the fragrant honeysuckle, Andrew lifted her hand to his lips. Margaret smiled and blinked back a joyous tear that threatened to glisten her cheek. She dared not gaze anywhere but into the eyes of her Andrew for fear this wedding blessed by heaven might disappear.

They both wore their blue-gray dress uniforms, and she carried a bouquet of the garden's pink and red roses. Never had she known such happiness.

The moment came when the minister raised his hand and pronounced them man and wife. She realized they were so much more than a wedded couple— foremost children of God, loyal subjects of England, and fighting members of the Royal Air Force dedicated to preserving the freedom of their country.

Epilogue

Andrew shifted the bouquet of vibrant red roses and hurried down the long corridor of the London hospital. He slid between an empty bed and a metal cart of medicines without slowing his pace. A nurse called for him to slow down, but he ignored her.

Finally he stood outside Margaret's door. Taking in a deep breath, he steadied his exhilaration and stepped into the room. Not since the day he and Margaret were married had he felt such pride and thankfulness to his Father God.

Margaret glanced up and met his gaze. A smile graced her lips and held him spellbound.

"Come see your daughter," she whispered. "Have you decided on a name?"

He nodded and laid the flowers on her nightstand. Kissing first Margaret and then his tiny infant daughter, he pulled a chair closer to the bed.

"Thank you for the flowers, sweetheart. They're lovely," she said, her face as radiant as the day they wed in the garden.

"You and our daughter are no match for them," Andrew said, gently brushing his finger over the baby's hand. "I'm one lucky man."

"And the name?" Margaret said. "Oh, Andrew, I can't wait any longer to hear what you've chosen."

He grinned and straightened his shoulders. "I want to call her Audra Rose. Audra means noble strength, and I want our daughter to never forget the strength and courage God gave us to save our England."

DIANN MILLS

DiAnn Mills is a bestselling author who believes her readers should expect an adventure. She combines unforgettable characters with unpredictable plots to create action-packed, suspense-filled novels.

Her titles have appeared on the CBA and ECPA bestseller lists; won two Christy Awards; and been finalists for the RITA, Daphne Du Maurier, Inspirational Readers' Choice, and Carol award contests. Library Journal presented her with a Best Books 2014: Genre Fiction award in the Christian Fiction category for Firewall.

DiAnn is a founding board member of the American Christian Fiction Writers; the 2015 president of the Romance Writers of America's Faith, Hope, & Love chapter; a member of Advanced Writers and Speakers Association, and International Thriller Writers. She speaks to various groups and teaches writing workshops around the country. She and her husband live in sunny Houston, Texas.

DiAnn is very active online and would love to connect with readers on any of the social media platforms listed at www.diannmills.com.

To Sing Another Day

by Kim Vogel Sawyer

Dedication

For Mom,
whose faith could move mountains

*[Charity] beareth all things, believeth all things,
hopeth all things, endureth all things.
Charity never faileth.*
1 CORINTHIANS 13:7–8

Chapter 1

Henry, are you upset with me?" Helen Wolfe held her breath as she waited for her brother's answer. Henry's pose—elbows on knees, head slung low—indicated sadness. Henry was a good boy, helpful beyond his years, but at fifteen his moods were often mercurial. Although in the past she'd reprimanded him for moodiness, she wouldn't blame him if he spouted angrily at her now.

Slowly Henry lifted his head and met Helen's gaze. "I don't like it. Wish it didn't have to be. But. . ." He released a deep sigh. "I understand."

Helen's breath whooshed out in an expulsion of mingled relief and regret. She leaned forward from her perch on the red velvet sofa. Reaching across the expanse of faded cabbage rose carpet, she grasped Henry's hand. They both squeezed hard—a silent communication that spoke more eloquently than words. Tears stung Helen's eyes. Henry'd already lost so much. This wasn't fair, but what else could they do?

"I'll get it back for you somehow." She stated the promise with more confidence than she felt.

Henry nodded then pushed to his feet, releasing Helen's hand. "I'll fetch it." He scuffed from the parlor, his heels dragging over the scarred pine floorboards that led to the bungalow's bedrooms.

Helen covered her face with her hands, fighting tears. She wouldn't cry. She wouldn't! Would tears bring back Mom and Dad? Of course not. Would tears make Richard change his mind and marry her? No. Tears fixed nothing. They served no purpose except to frighten her younger brothers and sister. She drew in fortifying breaths, and when Henry emerged from the hallway, she was sitting upright, her chin high and her eyes dry, although her insides still quaked.

Henry pressed the twenty-dollar gold piece into her palm. The engraving glared up at her, accusing her with its message: "Love never fails." She certainly felt like a failure, taking Henry's inheritance—his only belonging of value—from him.

Closing her fingers over the coin, she rose and wrapped one arm around Henry in a fierce hug. Then she stepped back and assumed a brisk tone to conceal her inner heartache. "Check on Lois if I'm not back in an hour, and give her another dose of tonic." The medicine stifled the child's cough enough to allow her to rest, and rest was important the doctor had said.

"I will. Don't worry."

"I'll put supper on the table when I return, so tell Carl to stay out of the icebox." Their twelve-year-old brother would devour the entire baked chicken in one sitting if Helen let him.

"I'll tie it shut if I have to."

Helen headed for the pegs beside the front door, where her knitted cap and scarf hung next to Mom's old wool coat. Outside the oval window, rain fell in a drizzly curtain. Helen grimaced. The heavy coat would do little more than absorb the moisture, but she had no other covering, so she tugged the plaid wool with its round wooden buttons over her simple cotton dress and covered her curly hair with the bold red cap. Her hand on the doorknob, she sent Henry one more sorrowful look.

Henry waved at her, scowling. "Just go already." Then his lips quirked into a grin. "Hope you get a lot for it." His bravado pierced Helen more deeply than pouting or fury would have.

The coin in her pocket, she set out into the dreary late afternoon.

◆　◆　◆

Bernie O'Day swished the feather duster over the shelves climbing the wall behind the tall wooden counter of his family's pawnshop. His pop had dusted twice a day—once before opening and again before closing—and Bernie followed the familiar routine partly out of habit, partly because it felt right to do what Pop had done.

He whistled as he worked, the tune for "There Is Power in the Blood" warbling from his pursed lips. Pop's whistling had been clear and sweet, where Bernie's sometimes hit a sour note or rasped into breathy blasts, but there wasn't anyone in the shop to complain, so he continued onward to the chorus. With each shrill hoot for "power," he gave the stiff feathers a sharp flick. By the time he finished, the rows of the little ceramic figurines and gold-plated statues stood completely devoid of so much as a speck of dust.

Satisfied, Bernie wheezed out the final note and plunked the duster under the counter. He glanced at the pendulum clock tick-tocking on the wall. Three more minutes till closing. His stomach rumbled in readiness. But even though he hadn't seen a customer all afternoon, he wouldn't put out the CLOSED sign one minute early. Pop had instilled a solid work ethic in Bernie—*Always stand true to your word, son, and you'll never have reason to hang your head in shame.* The painted sign above the plate-glass window of the O'Day Pawn Shop stated HOURS: 9:00 AM TO 6:00 PM MONDAY THROUGH SATURDAY, and he'd honor the hours, just as Pop always had.

At one minute till six, Bernie removed his bleached apron and hung it neatly on a hook on the back wall. Then, sliding his hand over his short-cropped hair to smooth the strands into place, he headed for the door to lock up. Just as he turned the cardboard placard hanging on a string inside the door to CLOSED, a young woman in a rain-soaked plaid coat and bedraggled knit cap trotted to the opposite side of the glass door.

Her gaze fell on the sign, and her blue eyes widened into an expression of panic. Then her shoulders wilted, and she turned away, shoving her hands deep into the pockets of the threadbare coat. Her dejected pose stung Bernie's heart.

Without a second thought, he gave the brass lock a twist and flung the door wide, causing the little bell above the door to clang raucously. The girl spun around, her rosy lips forming an O of surprise. Brown curls framed her cheeks, which were pink from the cool breeze.

Bernie smiled. "Did'ja need something?" He suspected she could use a new coat. He had several from which to choose, and he'd make her a good deal.

She pointed to the little sign. "Aren't you closed?"

"Haven't locked up yet. C'mon in."

Uncertainty marred her brow. She hunched into her soggy coat and nibbled her lower lip.

Bernie held the door wider. "At least get out of the drizzle for a minute or two. You look chilled all the way through."

A shiver shook her frame, and it seemed to spur her to action. She darted forward, scooting past him into the store. Bernie let the door close then turned to face her. She stood rooted between aisles, dripping, her hands clasped in front of her. "I'm sorry to be so late," she said, her voice very prim although it quavered slightly. "It took longer to walk than I thought it would."

Bernie offered a smile, hoping to put her at ease. "No need to apologize." From the looks of her, she'd covered a fair distance in the rain. He wondered why she hadn't taken a trolley. Quicker—and drier—than walking. Her drooping curls and waterlogged coat gave her a sad, waiflike appearance that stirred his sympathy. He gestured to the stove in the far corner of the room, where a few coals still glowed in the round belly. "Why don'tcha move closer over there—warm up a little. Then you can tell me what you're shoppin' for. I got pretty much anything a person needs." Pop had prided himself on their wide array of merchandise. Bernie felt certain whatever the girl needed he'd have it.

She hung her head, toying with one limp curl. "Actually, I'm not here to make a purchase. I. . .I'd hoped. . ." Her voice trailed away, and she stared off to the side.

Since she still hadn't moved toward the stove, Bernie headed in that direction. To his relief, she scuffed along behind him and released a little sigh when she reached the warmth radiating from the black iron. She stood stiffly beside the potbellied stove, her arms folded over her ribs. He waited, but she didn't speak.

Leaning his elbow on the counter, Bernie assumed a casual air he hoped might put her at ease. She seemed as skittish as a newborn colt. "What is it you're needing today, miss?"

She jerked as if roused from a sound sleep. Her hand slipped into her pocket, and she withdrew a round gold coin. "I need to sell this."

Bernie pinched the coin between his thumb and finger and held it to the bare bulb hanging overhead. The Liberty twenty-dollar piece had been rubbed nearly smooth on the front side, and someone had carefully engraved the words "Love never fails" in an arch on the upper part of the coin. Below, "W.W." and "Central Park" filled the bottom half. Bernie rubbed his thumb over the engraving, his brow puckered.

"William Wolfe was my grandfather," the girl said. She bobbed her chin toward the coin, her eyes shining. "He gave this coin to my grandmother as a token of his affection after fighting in the Civil War. It's been in our family for almost a hundred years."

Bernie wondered why she would part with it when the coin clearly meant a great deal to her. He turned it over to examine the back side. The tips of the eagle's wings were marred by some sort of grayish blobs. Bernie angled the coin toward the girl. "What happened here?"

"My father soldered a pin back onto it so my mother could wear it as jewelry, but the fixture fell off. Does...does that diminish its value?"

Bernie hated to tell her a defaced coin held little monetary value even without the lumps of solder on its back. He rubbed the coin between his thumb and finger, trying to decide what to say. Then, without conscious thought, he blurted, "Why are you selling it?"

The girl ducked her head, her cheeks flooding with color. "To be honest, Mr. O'Day, I'm sorely in need of the funds. My sister has been ill for over a month. I had to quit my job to take care of her, and the doctor bills have eaten up what little reserve I had in my bank account."

He wondered why she was caring for her sister. Where were her parents? But he decided not to be nosy. He'd already made her uncomfortable with his blunt question. He stepped behind the counter and pulled out his cash box and pad of tickets. "I tell you what. . . Since this is a twenty-dollar piece, I can give you a straight trade—twenty dollars for the coin. Does that sound reasonable?"

The stricken look on her face gave the answer. Bernie bit on the inside of his cheek, his business side warring with his sympathetic side. He'd never recover even twenty dollars for the coin. Who would want it besides the Wolfe family? But the girl clearly needed money. A Bible verse flitted through the fringes of his mind: "Inasmuch as ye have done it unto one of the least of these. . ."

Bernie pulled three ten-dollar bills and two fives from the cash drawer then slammed the lid closed before he could change his mind. He picked up a pencil and quickly scrawled the amount—$40—on the ticket and added a description, reading it aloud as he wrote. "One twenty-dollar gold piece, inscribed with 'Love never fails. W.W. Central Park.'" He looked at the girl, who hovered next to the stove, her fingers woven together. "Your name?"

"H–Helen Wolfe." She skittered forward, her gaze on the short pile of bills. "You're buying it?"

Bernie shot her a quick grin. "Isn't that what you wanted?"

She nodded, her drying curls bouncing around her cheeks. "Yes. Yes, that's what I wanted." Yet sadness lingered in her blue eyes. "Th–thank you very much, Mr. O'Day."

"Bernie," he said. At her puzzled look, he added, "My pop's Mr. O'Day. I'm just Bernie."

A soft laugh trickled from her lips. An enchanting, lighthearted sound that broadened Bernie's grin. It pleased him more than he could understand that he'd brought that laugh out of her.

"Thank you, Bernie."

He liked the way his name sounded in her musical voice. "You're welcome. Now. . ." He turned the ticket pad to face her. "This is how things work. I put the coin away for thirty days, and anytime during those thirty days you can come in and reclaim it with this ticket and the same amount of money I gave you. After thirty days, I put the coin out as merchandise with a price on it, and if you want it back, you'll have to pay the full price. Does that make sense to you?" The only way he'd break even on this deal was if she returned. Bernie didn't hold out much hope of that happening, and it saddened him. But not for himself.

Her blue eyes dimmed, but she nodded. "Yes, that makes sense."

"All right then. Sign here." He pointed to a line at the bottom of the ticket and watched as she picked up the pencil and wrote her name in neat, slanting script. He tore the ticket from the book and handed it to her. "Don't lose that now."

She folded the yellow sheet and slipped it into her pocket. "I won't." Her gaze seemed to caress the coin, which lay on the counter. "I truly hope to reclaim it. It. . .it means a great deal to my brother since my father left it to him."

Bernie wished he could coax another smile from her lips. He dipped down slightly, catching her eye. "I'll say a prayer that it finds its way back to you. God has a way of workin' things out even when we don't think it's possible."

She didn't smile, and when she spoke, her words chilled him with their finality. "I thank you for the prayer, Bernie, but it's been a good long while since I felt as though I could trust God to answer my prayers." Snatching up the bills, she wadded them in her fist and darted for the door. The bell clanged wildly when she departed, hurting Bernie's ears nearly as much as her pained statement had hurt his heart.

Bernie lifted the coin and tipped it this way and that, watching the play of light on the carved surface. His gaze drifted to the doorway, where Helen Wolfe had disappeared. He didn't know what hardships she'd encountered, but he did know God could bring healing. And he sensed the coin could play a role in her receiving that healing.

Crossing to his rolltop desk—the desk where Pop had sat to do paperwork, pay bills, and study his old leather-bound Bible—he pulled a silver key from his pocket and unlocked a tiny drawer. He placed the coin in the drawer and locked it again. Then, his hand on the drawer's handle, he closed his eyes and offered a solemn prayer. "Lord, I'm trusting You to find a way for Helen to reclaim this coin. Bring it back to her, and when she holds it again, let it serve as a reminder of Your perfect presence in her life."

Peace chased away the feelings of melancholy his brief encounter with Helen Wolfe had brought. With a smile on his heart, Bernie hurriedly closed the shop and headed up the back stairs for his supper, satisfied the Lord would work, as He always did.

Chapter 2

Helen waited until Carl had mopped up the shiny patches of grease from his plate with the last slice of bread before instructing him to get started on his homework.

The boy scowled and slumped in his chair. "But tomorrow's Saturday! Got the whole weekend to do it. Why do I gotta do it now?"

Helen missed her parents the most in these moments when she was forced to be the disciplinarian. "Because that's always been the rule, Carl. Homework before play." She softened her tone. "Besides, if you get it tucked out of the way, you can enjoy your weekend without the task hanging over your head. Wouldn't that be better?"

Carl grumbled under his breath, but he pushed away from the table and clomped to his bedroom. A door slamming let her know he wasn't pleased.

Helen sighed and reached to begin clearing the table. Lois, her pale cheeks and thin hands giving evidence of her lengthy bout with pneumonia, picked up her bowl and spoon and started to rise. She wobbled. Helen rushed to her sister's aid. "Here, honey, let me do that. You go stretch out on the sofa with a book and rest."

Lois sighed and scuffed her way to the parlor, where she flopped onto the sofa, the too-short hem of her nightgown exposing her skinny ankles. Helen's heart caught. Lois had lost so much weight over the past month. Somehow she'd have to encourage the child to eat more than broth and crackers now that her fever was finally gone, hopefully for good. With the money she'd received for the coin, she'd buy some of Lois's favorite foods. Perhaps that would entice her to eat.

Pushing aside her worry for Lois, she carried the stack of dishes to the kitchen and placed them in the sink. As she reached for the tarnished brass spigot, Henry moved in front of her. "I'll wash," he said.

Helen shot her brother a startled look. Henry hated housework. She had to battle with him to pick up his dirty socks. She teasingly pressed the back of her hand to his forehead. "Are you sick?"

He offered a sheepish grin. "Need to talk to you. Figure this's as good a place as any." He angled a quick look over his shoulder toward the parlor, where Lois now snoozed on the sofa with a book open, upside down, across her knees. "Didn't want to talk at supper and upset the youngsters."

Helen's chest ached. At fifteen, Henry was a youngster, too, but he was being

106

forced to grow up too quickly. She put her hand on his shoulder, all teasing forgotten. "What is it, Henry?"

Henry snapped off the water and shifted to look at her. His face—still boyish despite the hints of impending manhood—turned serious. "I think I need to look for a job."

Helen's hand fell away, and she shook her head wildly. "No, Henry! You know how important school was to Mom and Dad. They'd roll over in their graves if—"

"But that money you got for the coin won't last forever. Some groceries and a load of coal—that's all it'll cover." Henry spoke in a fervent whisper, his brow pinched tight. "You've used up the money Dad saved for you to go to the Conservatory. And your job cleaning at the hotel. . .it doesn't give us any extra. How're you gonna go to the Conservatory now?"

Henry's words stabbed as fiercely as a knife. Her dream, and her parents' dream for her, had been to complete the music courses at the Music Conservatory and become part of an opera company. But Mom and Dad's death two years ago had stolen Helen's opportunity. She'd allowed the dream to fizzle and die, too. With her brother's mention of the Conservatory, the dream tried to rekindle itself from the ashes in her heart, but she couldn't allow so much as a flicker to rise. Only a selfish person would continue chasing a dream when she had three younger siblings dependent upon her.

"You know I've given up on the Conservatory." Helen angled her way in front of Henry and began slipping dishes into the sink before the water turned tepid. She scrubbed, the activity a means of dispelling the longing that filled her as she considered singing on a stage.

"But you shouldn't give it up." Henry lifted a coarse towel and dried the plate she handed him. "Even Richard said—"

Helen dropped the plate and dishrag and whirled to face Henry. "Do not speak his name again."

Henry gawked at her, mouth open.

She drew in a breath, gentling her tone. "Richard Mason has no bearing on anything anymore, Henry. He's gone. Talking about him is too. . .painful."

Henry gulped and placed the dry plate on the shelf. "I just know he really wanted you to become a singer—the same way he's doing." Henry flicked a glance at her. "So you don't think if you go to the Conservatory, he'll change his mind and marry you after all?"

Helen frowned. "Is that why you want me to finish the music course? So Richard will marry me?"

Henry shrugged, his head low. "Thought that's what you wanted. To travel together. Sing together, as husband and wife."

At one time, it was what she'd wanted. How many nights had she lain awake considering her future with Richard? But Henry didn't know Richard hadn't broken their engagement because she had no money for the Conservatory. And she'd never tell Henry—or Carl or Lois—the truth. Why burden them?

She sighed. "Sometimes things just don't work out." A man who could callously demand that she place her beloved brothers and sister in an orphanage had no place in her life. "Besides that, singing on an opera stage is a rather childish desire." Her voice caught. Childish or not, letting go of the long-held plan had proved much harder than letting go of Richard. "I'm twenty-one now. It's time for me to let go of youthful daydreams. But as for you—" She sent him a stern look. "You are going to finish school. And that's that!"

Henry drew back his shoulders. His jaw jutted stubbornly. "Helen, you might be the oldest, but I'm the oldest male in our family. That makes me the man. And I've made up my mind. We need more money coming in, so I'm going to find a job." His eyes squinted as he glared at her. "And you can't stop me."

◆　◆　◆

Wednesday afternoon, while Bernie assisted a customer in perusing his selection of gemstone rings, the little bell above the pawnshop door jangled. Bernie glanced past Mrs. Horton's flowery, kettle-shaped hat to smile at a young man who hovered in the doorway, allowing in a rush of cool, damp air. Winter seemed to be sneaking up on them early this year.

"I'll be with you in a minute," Bernie called, gesturing. "Step on over by the stove, if you like, and warm your hands."

The boy, gloveless, blew into his cupped palms for a moment before inching his way toward the potbellied stove. "Thanks, mister."

Bernie nodded then turned his attention back to Mrs. Horton. The older woman already wore a ring on every finger, yet she searched the flat display case for another gem to add to her collection. Bernie appreciated Mrs. Horton's business, but sometimes he wondered if she sought happiness in places that would never satisfy.

While Mrs. Horton fingered each ring by turn, Bernie flicked a surreptitious glance at the youth who hunkered beside the stove. Brown curly hair stuck out from beneath the brim of his newsboy-style cap. A tan jacket with patched elbows looked to be at least one size too small for the boy's lanky frame. Despite the boy's somewhat ragged appearance, his face and hands were clean, his clothes neatly patched. Bernie'd had trouble in the past with teenage boys pilfering stock, but he suspected he could trust this one. He turned his full focus to Mrs. Horton.

"All right, Bernie, I believe I'll take this opal ring." Mrs. Horton's wrinkled face bloomed into a bright smile. "I counted eighteen stones in all, perfectly matched! How much is this one?"

"Thirty-seven fifty."

The woman didn't even flinch. She opened her pocketbook and withdrew crisp bills. Bernie noted the youth watching, his eyes wide. The boy almost seemed to salivate.

"There you are," Mrs. Horton said. "And if you receive earrings that might coordinate with the ring, you send me a message, will you? I prefer drop earrings, with a back that screws into place rather than simply clamps." She slipped the ring onto her right pointer finger, above a sapphire and diamond ring, and held her hand straight out. The opals shimmered with color in the light. "This ring will be lovely with my blue dress."

Bernie gave Mrs. Horton her change and then walked her to the door. When he turned from closing the door behind the woman, he discovered the youth next to the counter, very near the cash box, which Bernie had left on top of the wooden surface. But even though his eyes were on the box, his hands were deep in his pockets, as if controlling an urge to snatch the box and run. Bernie hustled to the counter and put the box underneath before temptation overcame the boy.

"Now then." Bernie brushed his palms together and fixed his attention on the young man. "What can I do for you?"

The boy whipped off his cap, revealing thick, tousled hair in need of a cut. He glanced around. "You run this place on your own?"

Bernie frowned, unease wriggling through his middle. Had he misjudged this boy's intentions? He hoped the kid wasn't scoping out his shop. Bernie chose to answer with a question of his own. "Why do you want to know?"

The boy raised his chin and met Bernie's gaze squarely. "I was hoping maybe you could use some help. I need a job."

Bernie looked the boy up and down. Tall, slender, with an open face holding a hint of defiance. Or desperation. Bernie couldn't be sure. He examined the boy's face more closely. No whiskers dotted the youth's smooth cheeks. He frowned. "Aren't you a little young to be job-seeking?"

His jaw jutted a little farther. "I'm old enough."

"How old?"

For a moment, the boy pursed his lips, his eyes flicking around as if afraid to look directly at Bernie. If the kid lied, Bernie would boot him out in an instant. He couldn't trust a liar.

The boy drew in a breath that straightened his shoulders. "I turned fifteen in August." He rushed on. "But I'm strong for my age, and I'm a fast learner. I'm willing to do anything you need—cleaning, deliveries, anything you say. And I can start tomorrow if you'd like."

Bernie rested his elbow on the counter edge. Pride nearly pulsed from the boy. Although he'd encountered many young men seeking employment and had turned down every one of them—he just didn't need the extra hands in his small shop— there was something about this boy that tugged at him. He chose his words carefully. "Seems to me a fifteen-year-old ought to be spending his days in school instead of at a job."

The boy hung his head. "I'll finish my schooling. . .someday. But right now. . ." He raised his face, and the desperation Bernie thought he'd glimpsed earlier returned. "My family needs the money I can make." He blew out a frustrated breath. "I've been walking the streets since last Saturday, and nobody'll give me a chance. If you say no, too, I don't know what I'll do."

Bernie ambled from behind the counter and curled his arm across the boy's shoulders. He drew him to the pair of rocking chairs that had sat in the corner for as long as Bernie could remember. He and Pop had sat there on evenings, sometimes talking, sometimes not, but always at ease with each other. Even though Pop was gone now, Bernie still viewed the rockers as a place of comfort. He gave the boy a gentle push toward one, and he sank into the other.

Holding his hand out in invitation, he said, "Why don'tcha tell me why your family needs money so badly. Might be there's a solution that wouldn't involve you dropping out of school."

The boy sat erect in the chair, his feet planted wide. "My folks died a couple years back, and my sister's been taking care of my little brother and sister and me ever since. She has a job, but it doesn't pay as much as the one she had to give up when my little sister came down with bad pneumonia. She was supposed to go to the Conservatory—become a singer—but she had to use her Conservatory money to pay our bills while my little sister was so sick. Now we've got hospital and medicine bills and not enough money to cover it all."

Bernie's scalp tingled. This story sounded familiar.

"Winter's coming on, and the doc says if we don't want Lois to get sick again, we gotta keep the house warm. Takes a heap of coal to keep the furnace going, and I don't see how we'll be able to do it on my sister's measly salary. So. . ." The boy gulped. "I need a job."

Bernie looked into the youth's earnest face, the blue eyes glowing with determination. Suddenly another face flashed in Bernie's mind's eye. He sat upright. "Your sister—is her name Helen?"

The boy's jaw dropped. "How'd you know that?"

Bernie set the rocker into motion, trying to combat his churning emotions. The sympathy that had compelled him to overpay Helen Wolfe now spilled over on her brother. Even so, a hint of suspicion tickled the corners of his mind. "Did she send you here to ask for a job?"

"No, sir." The boy shook his head, making the brown curls—so like his sister's—bounce on his forehead. "She's plumb irate with me for even hunting for work. Wants me in school. We've argued about it every day, but we need the money, so. . ."

Bernie pinched his chin, thinking. The boy's sister was wise to want the youth to finish his schooling. In these changing times, an education was becoming more and more important. But clearly the family needed help, and for reasons Bernie couldn't begin to comprehend, he wanted to help them. "What's your name?"

"Henry, sir. Henry William Wolfe."

"Well, Henry William Wolfe, I could use someone around here to organize the stockroom, keep the sidewalk outside cleared of leaves and snow, and do some general cleaning."

The boy's face lit. "Oh?"

"But I don't need somebody full-time."

The elation died. "Oh."

"And I happen to agree with your sister that you should be in school."

Henry crunched his lips in a tight line.

Bernie stifled a chortle. "But if you're willing to work after school and all day on Saturdays, I'm thinking maybe we can find a compromise that'll help your family and also satisfy your sister. What do you think?"

Henry bounded to his feet. He stuck out his hand. "I think we got a deal!"

Chapter 3

Although Bernie had hired Henry out of sympathy, thinking he was doing the boy a favor, it took less than a week for him to change his attitude. Henry became an unexpected blessing, providing not only assistance but a level of companionship Bernie hadn't even realized he needed. After working side by side with Pop from the time he was knee-high, he'd missed his father's presence in the shop. Busyness had held the loneliness at bay, but now that Henry came in every day, Bernie discovered the pleasure of having someone around to talk to, laugh with, and teach the trade.

As Henry'd said, he was a quick learner, and by the end of the boy's third week in the shop, Bernie felt secure enough to leave Henry in charge for brief periods of time so he could go next door and sip a cup of coffee or fetch a newspaper from the stand on the corner. He enjoyed the new sense of freedom having an employee offered, and he wondered how he'd managed so long on his own.

Bernie started out giving Henry a fifty-cent piece at the end of each school day and two silver dollars at closing on Saturday. As a boy, he'd always liked the larger coins, and he figured Henry would, too. So it surprised him when he held out the round half-dollar the third Friday of October and Henry sheepishly asked to receive his pay in dimes and nickels.

Bernie coughed a laugh, dropping the coin back into his cash box and fishing out four slim dimes and two nickels. "You wantin' some rattlin'-around money in your pocket?"

Henry shrugged into his jacket. "No, sir. I don't carry it long—just hand it over to Helen. But my little brother, Carl, has been doing my chores since I'm here in the afternoons. I figured it might be nice to give him a little something now and then—a dime or nickel—so he could go see a picture show or buy a candy bar as a treat."

Carl nodded in approval. "That's a right good idea." He tipped his head, giving the boy a serious look. "It'll also make it easier to tithe." Henry had indicated he and his brother and sisters attended Faith Chapel each Sunday. "You're givin' a portion of your earnings to the Lord, aren't you?"

Henry hung his head. "To be honest, Mr. O'Day, I haven't been. I know Dad tithed. Saw him drop money in the offering plate after every payday. But since he and Mom died…" He scratched his head, making his newly cropped hair stand on end. Those curls, even short, were untamable. "Just never seems as though there's enough to give to the church."

"You know, Henry, it's always been my experience that when we give God a portion of what He's given us, He makes the rest stretch to meet our needs. Not that we give to get, understand—we give because we love Him and want to honor Him. But I think you'd find a real blessing in giving God a portion of your earnings."

Henry examined Bernie's face, his brow puckered thoughtfully. "I'll do some considering on that, Mr. O'Day. And talk to Helen about it, too."

The mention of Helen sent Bernie's pulse racing. Although he hadn't seen her since that day over six weeks ago when she came in to sell her grandfather's gold coin, she'd often crept through his thoughts. Having Henry in the store each day talking about his sister contributed to Bernie's fascination with the young woman. He'd had no more than a few minutes of time with her, yet he felt as though he knew her from Henry's description of her hardworking attitude, her willingness to care for her siblings, and her desire to keep the family together. He found he admired this woman, whose sweet face and beguiling curls haunted his dreams.

"You do that," Bernie said, "and tell her if she has questions about tithing to come see me. I'd be glad to share some scripture with her."

Henry plopped on his hat and turned toward the door. "I'll tell her, but don't count on her asking. Ever since our folks died and Richard ran off, she hasn't been too interested in talking about God. I think she believes God let her down, and even though she takes us to church 'cause Mom and Dad went, she doesn't really want anything to do with Him anymore." The boy waved on his way out the door, unaware that he'd just thrown icy water over Bernie's heart. "See you tomorrow, Mr. O'Day."

◆　◆　◆

Helen awakened early on Saturday, teased from sleep by a recurring dream that pricked her conscience—a dream in which Bernie O'Day, attired in fine clothing including a top hat that glistened as if covered in sequins, offered her his elbow and invited her to attend the opera with him. Why couldn't she set that dream aside?

Bernie had been exceedingly kind to her family. Besides purchasing the coin, his putting Henry to work after school and paying him a fair wage had eased their financial burdens significantly. Henry's pay covered their weekly groceries, allowing her to put extra toward the hospital bill that had seemed insurmountable after Mom and Dad's accident followed by Lois's lengthy illness. In another few months, the bill would be paid in full, and then she'd be able to put money into the bank to save up for—

No! She needed to stop thinking about the Conservatory. That time was past. She had to focus on the children—getting them raised, putting them through school, seeing to their needs. Lois was only nine. Helen would be far too old for the Conservatory by the time Lois grew up enough to be on her own. Helen resolutely pushed aside the sting of regret. The children were more important than some silly aspiration about singing on a stage.

So why did she continually dream about being taken to the opera by Bernie O'Day?

She sat up, careful not to bounce the bed and awaken Lois, who slept on the other half. On tiptoe, she crept out of the room and down the hallway, past the room Henry and Carl shared, and on to the closed doorway behind which Mom and Dad's bedroom remained undisturbed. She rarely entered their room because it brought back too many painful memories, but on this morning she discovered a need to visit it. To visit them and the days before they'd left her.

Almost feeling like a burglar, she creaked the doorknob and stepped into the room. A musty odor tickled her nose. Sheets covered the bed and bureau, protecting the furniture, but she stirred dust with her feet as she crossed the wood floor to the bed and sat on the edge of the mattress. She closed her eyes, allowing memories to surface. The first one to rise from the dark corners of her mind was a Sunday-morning memory—Mom and Dad in their church clothes, Bibles held in the crooks of their arms, leading her and the children down a sunshine-splashed sidewalk toward the chapel.

Helen tried to push the memory aside to focus on something else, but it persisted. The memory collided with her dream, and Henry's comments at supper last night rang through her mind: *"Mr. O'Day says God can make what's left over meet all our needs when we bless Him with our tithe."* And she finally understood why the dream and memory were so closely intertwined. They both pertained to God.

Longing filled Helen's breast—a longing to return to the carefree days when she truly believed God cared about her, heard her prayers, and met her needs. Mom and Dad had believed it, and they'd taught her to believe it. But first Mom and Dad died from injuries in the awful trolley accident, and Richard said he didn't want to be responsible for three snot-nosed kids and deserted her when she needed him most, and then Lois fell ill and came so close to slipping away. And somehow in the midst of all that heartache, Helen had lost her belief in a caring God.

But Bernie O'Day believed in Him and now encouraged Henry to believe. Would Henry one day suffer the same deep disappointment that plagued Helen by placing his trust in a God who kept His distance? She couldn't allow that to happen. As much as they needed the money Henry made at the O'Day Pawn Shop, she'd have to tell Henry to stay away from there if Bernie was going to fill his head with unrealistic notions.

A scuffling sound in the hallway intruded on her thoughts, and moments later Henry poked his head in the room. He scowled across the shadows at Helen. "What're you doin' in here?" He stayed in the hallway, not even the loose toes of his socks crossing the threshold.

"Thinking." Helen pushed off from the bed, the creak of the springs discordant in the quiet morning hour. She stepped into the hallway, pulling the door shut behind her and sealing away her parents' room the way she wanted to seal away the troubling thoughts that plagued her. "Henry, when you go to work today, I want you to turn in your notice."

Henry gawked at her. "What? But why?"

"We're caught up on bills now." Her conscience pricked. They weren't caught up, but the more time Henry spent with Bernie O'Day, the greater the chances for his heart to be broken. "We don't need the money."

"Oh yes, we do." Henry folded his arms over his chest. He'd grown so tall in the past year—he now peered down his nose at his older sister. "And I'm not quitting."

"Henry. . ."

"No, Helen. It's a good job, and I can still go to school, just like you wanted." Henry inched backward toward his bedroom. "Both of us working is better than only one of us, and I'm going to do my part to take care of the family. I'm keeping my job." He stepped into the bedroom and clicked the door closed behind him.

Helen stared at the closed door, her heart pounding. Should she go after him, insist on him quitting? Dad wouldn't have allowed Henry's backtalk, but she wasn't Dad, and she had no real authority over Henry even if she was responsible for him. She buried her face in her hands, the longing rising to have someone else to help her with her brothers and sister. Someone on whom she could depend. She wished she could still rely on God.

Lifting her face, she pressed her fists to her hips and scowled at the ceiling. She had no help anymore—not from her parents, from Richard, or from God—and she'd manage. If Henry wouldn't quit that job, then she'd just have to make sure his boss understood what he could and couldn't say to Henry. On her way home from work today, she'd stop by the O'Day Pawn Shop and have a firm talk with Bernie O'Day.

Chapter 4

Tired, footsore, and frustrated by her nearly empty pockets, Helen trudged down the street toward the O'Day Pawn Shop. Cleaning hotel rooms wasn't beneath her—it was honest work, and she was grateful to have been hired—but her dependence on guests leaving a few coins behind as a thank-you for her service worried her. She never knew from week to week what she might be bringing home to pay bills. Even on a good week, the money barely stretched to cover their needs. And now Henry, thanks to Bernie O'Day's prompting, wanted her to give some of her precious earnings to the church? The man obviously didn't understand how much she needed the money she made!

We also need the money Henry makes. The thought had plagued her all day as she planned exactly what she would say to Bernie O'Day. She wished so much she could say, "Henry doesn't need a job, so please release him from your employment immediately." But wishing didn't change the facts. They did need Henry's money. All of Henry's money. So Mr. Bernie O'Day would simply have to understand he was Henry's boss, not his preacher or father or even his friend. No more advice-giving.

As she approached the shop, she saw the door open and Henry step out. He paused to wave at Bernie, a smile on his face, then he trotted down the street in the opposite direction, heading home. Helen slowed her footsteps to allow Henry to get well ahead of her. When he turned the corner at the end of the block, she hurried to the door, which now sported a CLOSED sign, and rapped on the glass.

Moments later, Bernie O'Day appeared on the other side. A smile broke across his face when he spotted Helen, and he opened the door quickly. "Miss Wolfe! How good to see you. Please come in."

His cheerful greeting stung, considering the purpose of her visit. How she hated to see his bright smile fade. Just as she'd noted from her dreams, Bernie was a handsome man, with neatly combed sandy-colored hair and thick-lashed hazel eyes. If circumstances were different, she'd be drawn to him. But her intention was to push him away. Away from Henry, and consequently away from herself. She swallowed a lump of regret and forced herself to meet his friendly gaze.

"Mr. O'Day, I must talk to you."

His smile faltered, but then he released a light chuckle. "From the sound of your voice, I'd say it's serious. Should we have a seat?" He indicated a pair of cozy-looking rocking chairs nestled in the far corner of the store.

Although her sore feet and tired body yearned for the comfort of one of those chairs, Helen shook her head. This wasn't a social call, and she must remain brisk and impersonal. "I'll only be here a short while. Mr. O'Day—"

"Bernie, remember?"

She pursed her lips. Would he stop being so kind? This task was growing more difficult with each second that ticked by. She cleared her throat. "Bernie, I've come to request that you do not speak about God with Henry. He holds a great deal of respect for you, and he likes you as well. Everything you say, he takes to heart. If you continue to speak of God, Henry could very well begin to accept your words as truth. And I know all too well that God is not the loving Father my parents believed Him to be."

Sadness clouded Bernie's hazel eyes, bringing a rush of sorrow through Helen's frame. He slipped his hands into his trouser pockets and set his head at a thoughtful angle. "Exactly how'd you come to the conclusion that God isn't a loving Father?"

Helen nearly snorted. "A loving father gives good gifts. He doesn't bestow hardship and trials on his children."

"He doesn't?"

Bernie's genuine surprise took Helen by surprise. She blinked at him. "Well, of course he doesn't!"

Setting his feet widespread, hands still tucked in pockets, Bernie gazed at Helen with twinkling eyes and chuckled. A low-in-his-throat chuckle like distant thunder that sent a tremor of pleasure down Helen's spine. "Miss Wolfe, when you were growin' up, did your father ever find it necessary to bestow a little pain on your. . .er, sittin'-down place?"

Heat flooded Helen's cheeks. She looked sharply away. "I suspect most fathers inflict the occasional rod of discipline. Mine was no exception."

The chuckle rumbled again. "And did that make you think he didn't love you?"

She jerked her face around to meet his grin. "Of course not! If he didn't love me, he'd let me grow up without any sense of right and wrong."

Bernie nodded. "That's exactly right. Your father—being the loving man he was—guided you with painful lessons every now and then, knowing there'd be a good result." He shrugged slowly, his eyes never leaving her face. "So why is it so hard to believe God wouldn't do the same? Use painful lessons for a good result?"

Helen couldn't think of an answer. Which irritated her. She glared at Bernie.

For long seconds they stood in silence, staring into each other's eyes. Finally Bernie sighed. "I don't wanna overstep any boundaries, Miss Wolfe. I like Henry. He's a good boy, and I'd like to keep him employed here. But I can't promise not to talk about God. You see, God and me. . .we're pretty close. I can't shut Him in a drawer and pretend He doesn't exist when Henry's around. So I'll probably keep talking about Him." He shrugged again. "I just can't help myself, Miss Wolfe."

Helen suddenly realized she'd think less of him if he agreed to change. The thought confused her. Her tongue refused to form a retort.

Then Bernie confounded her even more. "Miss Wolfe, do you and your brothers and sister enjoy picnics in Central Park?"

Immediately, memories swept through Helen's mind of the many summer picnics she'd shared with her parents and siblings when she was a girl. She gulped. "Y–yes. Yes, we do."

"Would you care to join me for a picnic after church tomorrow? My treat. Nothin' fancy—just sandwiches and fruit. Maybe a jug of sweet tea. But I'd like to get to know you and Carl and Lois after hearing Henry talk about you all so much."

Helen shook her head. "Tomorrow? But. . .it's late October. Not summertime."

He used his chuckle again to disarm her. "There some rule says you can only have picnics in the summertime? I happen to think October's a fine time for a picnic. No leaves to hide the blue sky from view. Nice crisp breeze drifting from the lake. And no flies."

Helen's lips twitched, fighting a giggle.

"We can spread a blanket on the bridge at the pond and toss bread scraps to the ducks. What do you say?"

Deep regret pierced Helen. She lowered her head so he wouldn't see the desire to join him glimmering in her eyes. "I'm afraid it's out of the question. My sister, Lois, is still recovering from a very serious illness. She shouldn't breathe in the cool air." She flicked a gaze upward and caught a disappointed frown on his face. "I appreciate the invitation, though." She did appreciate it. No wonder Henry liked his boss so much. Bernie O'Day was a very kind man.

Flustered, Helen turned toward the door. "I need to get home. My brothers and sister expect me."

He reached past her and opened the door. "Thanks for stopping by, Miss Wolfe, and thanks for letting Henry work for me. He's a fine boy, and you should be proud of him."

Helen scurried out the door without answering. Not until she was halfway to her bungalow did she realize she'd completely failed in what she'd set out to do. And to her chagrin, she discovered it really didn't matter.

◆　◆　◆

Sunday morning Lois pushed her barely touched bowl of oatmeal toward Helen and wrinkled her freckled nose. "This doesn't taste right."

The milk had started to turn. Helen had hoped, mixed into the oatmeal with a tiny dash of cinnamon for flavoring, no one would notice. But the way Henry and Carl stirred their oatmeal rather than eating it, Helen knew she hadn't managed to mask the slightly spoiled taste. Even so, they couldn't waste food, so she assumed a brisk tone. "You're probably just hungry for something else, so your taste buds are feeling fussy." She sent a nod around the table. "It's all we're having for breakfast, so eat up or you'll be awfully hungry by lunchtime." She scooped a bite and resolutely swallowed, ignoring the little tang on the back of her tongue.

With sighs, her brothers and sister followed her example. Within minutes, the bowls were empty. Helen gathered the spoons and bowls. "Go dress in your Sunday clothes now. And bundle yourselves well. The wind howled all night, so it's likely to be chilly this morning."

"Wonder if it rained, too." Carl screeched his chair from the table and bounded toward the door. He swung it wide and stuck his head out, looking left and right. "Nope. It's not wet, but—hey!"

Helen's hands stilled in their task at her brother's excited exclamation. "What is it?"

Carl darted onto the porch, letting the screen door slam behind him. Moments later, he clomped back inside with a large basket in his arms. "Look what I found on the porch!"

Lois and Henry bustled forward to meet him, and Helen followed, curiosity filling her. She reached past Lois to lift the checked cloth covering several lumps within the basket. When she revealed the contents, she gasped.

"Lookit all this!" Carl's face glowed with wonder. "Sliced ham, deviled eggs, sweet and dill pickles. . ."

Lois reached into the basket and withdrew a fat jar. She squealed. "Spiced peaches! My favorite!" She hugged the jar to her skinny chest, beaming.

Henry pushed items around, continuing the recitation. "A whole loaf of bread, white cheese, two packets of cookies—looks like Snickerdoodles and oatmeal raisin. Mmm."

Helen's heart began to pound. Spiced peaches for Lois, Snickerdoodles for Carl, deviled eggs for Henry, and oatmeal raisin cookies for her. All of their favorites were nestled in the basket, wrapped in wax paper and cushioned with checked napkins. Only one person besides Mom and Dad could have put this basket together with each of their favorite items. The person who'd often joined her family for summer picnics in years past. Richard. . .

Dashing past her clustered siblings, who continued to gaze into the basket and ooh and aah in delight, she clattered onto the porch and searched the street. Her heart thudded almost painfully against her ribs. When she'd broken off their engagement, Richard had vowed to make her change her mind. An entire year had slipped by without any contact from him, and she'd given up hope of reconciliation. But now, this basket of treats both she and the children loved ignited a flame of emotion that couldn't be quelled.

She hugged herself, seeking any sign of Richard, both hopeful and apprehensive. Was he back? And more importantly, did she want him back?

Chapter 5

Bernie could hardly wait for Henry to arrive after school on Monday. It had taken some doing to gather the food items he recalled Henry mentioning as family favorites, but putting that basket together had brought more pleasure than anything he could remember in quite a while. After Helen had left his shop, he'd prayed for a way to show God's caring to her. Feeding her physical body seemed a good place to start. Would she recognize the gesture as evidence of God wanting to meet her needs?

Henry sent the bell above the door clanging at 3:45 p.m., prompt as always, and darted directly for an apron and the broom. "Lots of leaves out front. I'll get to sweeping, and when that's all done, I'll—"

"Hold up." Bernie caught Henry's jacket sleeve. In the past weeks, Henry'd grown even taller, and at least three inches of his arms stuck out from the bottom of the sleeves. His current jacket wouldn't last him through the winter. Bernie led Henry behind the counter then held up a brown corduroy jacket with a sturdy zipper and pockets that buttoned shut. "Can you make use of this?"

Henry took the jacket and held it up in front of him.

Bernie said, "It isn't new. It's a trade-in, but it looks to be your size. If it fits, you can have it."

Henry removed his old jacket and slipped on the brown one. He wriggled his shoulders, as if testing the fit, then stuck his arms out. The cuffs reached halfway to his knobby knuckles. Bernie nodded in satisfaction. Plenty of growing room remained, which was good since a boy of Henry's age would probably keep adding to his height for a while yet. The heavy corduroy with its wool lining should keep Henry warm.

"So what do you think? You like it?" Bernie examined Henry's face, seeking signs of approval.

Henry sighed, rubbing his hands up and down the chest of the jacket. "I like it plenty, Mr. O'Day, but I can't keep it." He removed it and offered it to Bernie.

Bernie didn't take it. "Why not?"

"Helen'd have a fit." Henry laid the jacket on the counter and stood gazing at it, longing on his face. "She's got a lot of pride. Wants to take care of us herself. She'd feel like she'd failed if I brought this jacket home."

"Helen won't let you accept a gift?" Bernie wondered what she'd done with that

120

basket of food. He sure hoped she hadn't tossed it out!

"Well. . ." Henry scratched his head. "Don't really know what she'd think if I called it a gift." He looked at Bernie, his brow puckered. "Are you giving it to me outright, or am I earning it? 'Cause if I did something extra for you—something beyond what I usually do around here—then I could say I earned it."

"And then Helen would let you keep it?"

Henry nodded.

Bernie's thoughts bounced around erratically. He'd wanted the jacket to be a gift—a sign of God meeting her family's needs. But he didn't want to insult Helen. That would distance her even more. Distancing her was the last thing he hoped to do. But only to draw her to God, of course. He nearly laughed. He wasn't fooling himself any more than he could fool God. Sure, he wanted to draw Helen back to God, but he wanted to draw her to himself, too.

But getting her focused on God was most important. Therefore, he couldn't ask anything in return for that coat or it would destroy the message that God cared enough to meet her needs.

Bernie put his hand on Henry's shoulder. "Henry, this coat is a gift, pure and simple. God laid it on my heart that you needed a new coat, and this coat—a coat just the right size for a boy like you—showed up in my shop. It would be wrong of me to take payment for it, because it really came from God, not me. Does that make sense?"

Henry crunched his face into a scowl of indecision. "It kind of makes sense to me, but I don't know how I'm gonna explain it to Helen."

Bernie scooped up the coat and pressed it into Henry's arms. "You just tell Helen your loving heavenly Father wanted you to be warm this winter and leave it at that."

Henry pushed his arms into the sleeves and closed the zipper all the way to his throat. He smoothed his hands over the sleeves, noting how they reached beyond his wrists. He sighed. "Thanks, Mr. O'Day."

"Don't thank me," Bernie said. "Thank God."

Henry gave a solemn nod.

◆　◆　◆

Over the next weeks, as Thanksgiving approached, Bernie spent a significant amount of his prayer time lifting up Helen Wolfe and her siblings. He'd learned from Henry that their parents died in the horrific trolley accident that claimed more than a dozen lives two years ago. It gave him a start to realize he and Pop had prayed together for the accident victims' families, unknowingly praying for the Wolfe siblings even before he met them. It connected him more firmly to Helen, Henry, Carl, and Lois, and made him all the more determined to reawaken the faith their parents had lived.

Henry seemed to enjoy talking to Bernie, and Bernie filed away everything the boy said about his sisters and brother. He learned Helen loved to sing but now rarely lifted her voice in song, too busy working and caring for a household. He learned Carl was a good baseball player, and that Lois hoped to learn to play piano someday. He also discovered Henry had a head for business and possessed a number sense that exceeded Bernie's. Henry could add in his head faster than most people did on paper. A boy like that should think about college, and Bernie began praying for a way to make sure Henry had the chance to further his education after he graduated twelfth grade.

Learning bits and pieces of the Wolfe siblings' lives offered lots of ways for Bernie to reach out to the family. He began a practice of leaving packages on the porch of the Wolfe home. Never anything elaborate, fearful Helen would reject items of great monetary value, but little things he knew they needed or that would bring one of the family members some pleasure. Baseball cards for Carl, new gloves for Lois, paper tablets for Henry. And song sheets for Helen—vocal arrangements for a mezzo soprano. According to Henry, she had a rare gift, and her parents had encouraged her to use it. Apparently, her song died when she buried her parents. Bernie hoped holding those song sheets would entice her to sing once again. And he prayed raising her voice in song—using her God-given talent—would help her open her heart to God again.

The Wednesday before Thanksgiving, Henry arrived early since school let out at noon. As soon as he donned his apron, he offered an apology. "I hope it's all right, but I can't stay clear till closing today. Helen asked me to stop by the grocer and get everything we'd need for our Thanksgiving dinner." He flapped a sheet of paper, covered on one side with neat lines of script. "She's been saving up so we could have a good dinner. If I wait too late to choose our sweet potatoes and roasting hen, all the good ones'll be picked over."

Bernie smiled. "That's fine, Henry. In fact, I rarely get much business the day before Thanksgiving—people are too busy cooking. So why don't you just take today off? Tomorrow I'm closed, too, so that'll give you a nice break."

"Are you sure?" Henry fiddled with his apron ties. "I don't wanna shirk my duties."

Bernie clapped the boy on the shoulder. "Henry, if there's one thing I would never suspect you of doing, it would be shirking your duties." He pointed to the hooks. "Hang up that apron and scoot on out of here. Pick your sister the biggest, freshest sweet potatoes you can find. But. . ." He stepped around the corner and grabbed the crate he'd put together that morning. "You won't need to spend money on a roasting hen. There's a fine turkey in here—enough to feed your family and then some." Bernie had also packed in bags of flour and sugar, a dozen eggs, and two loaves of bread—one for slicing and eating, the other to chop into pieces for stuffing. The Wolfe siblings would have a veritable feast.

Henry stared at the crate. "A–are you sure?"

"Yep." Bernie thumped the crate on the counter. He rested his elbow on the corner of the crate, peering at Henry over the slatted side. "Y'know, it's not uncommon for employers to give their workers something at holidays. Your sister won't fuss about this, will she?" Bernie hadn't asked about Helen's reaction to the gifts he'd been leaving. Partly because he feared Henry would say she resented them, and partly because he wanted to remain anonymous.

Henry shrugged, zipping up his brown jacket. "I think she'll appreciate it. Getting harder and harder to satisfy Carl's appetite. He eats more than the rest of us put together."

Bernie snorted out a laugh.

Henry balanced the crate against his belly. "I'll let her know it's from you, though, so she doesn't think Richard gave it to us."

Richard. . . That name had come up before, and every time he heard it, Bernie prickled. He didn't want to feel jealous of the man who'd once asked for Helen's hand in marriage, but despite his best efforts, the emotion welled. His voice tight, Bernie said, "Why would she think it's from Richard?"

Henry waddled toward the door. "He's been leavin' stuff on the porch for us. Helen's sure it's him, 'cause he leaves things somebody who'd have to know us pretty good would leave."

Bernie's mouth went dry. Helen credited Richard for the gifts? But that meant she wasn't seeing them as God-blessings. "She—she's certain it's Richard?"

Henry shot Bernie a puzzled look. "Who else could it be?"

Bernie clamped his mouth shut so he wouldn't blurt out the truth. He swallowed. "Is she. . .happy. . .that Richard's leaving her presents?"

For a long moment, Henry stood silently, rubbing his lips together. Then he shrugged. "I dunno about happy, necessarily. It hurt her pretty bad when he broke off their engagement. But I know she's lonely. I know she'd like to have somebody to help her out with the youngsters. So maybe she's happy Richard's back. I haven't really asked."

Bernie shuffled past Henry and opened the door for him. "Well, I better not keep you. You've got some shopping to do." He shifted out of the way so Henry could push through. It made a tight fit with the bulky crate in his arms. Once the boy was on the sidewalk, he said, "Have a good Thanksgiving, Henry." He heard his sad undertone and forced his lips into a smile. No sense in worrying the boy.

Henry angled his head to peer over his shoulder at Bernie. "Thanks. You, too." He took one step then cried, "Oh!" Henry whirled around, nearly tipping the crate. "Mr. O'Day, what're you doing for Thanksgiving?"

Slowly, Bernie lifted his shoulders in a shrug. He had no plans. He'd just be here at the shop, probably going through unmarked inventory in the backroom. Things tended to stack up back there. "Not much. Why?"

Henry's cheeks streaked with red. "Helen told me to ask you if you'd like to eat Thanksgiving dinner with us. A thank-you, she said, for giving me this job."

All of Bernie's sadness washed away in one swoop. A smile broke across his face. "I'd like that, Henry. I'd like that a lot."

"Good." Henry flashed a quick grin. "See you tomorrow then, around six. Can't eat earlier than that 'cause Helen has to work."

"Six o'clock." Bernie touched his forehead in a mock salute. "I'll be there." He closed the door and danced a quick jig, excitement stirring in his middle. Helen had invited him to dinner! As a thank-you. But not for the gifts he'd sent. She didn't know they'd come from him. Bernie's feet paused midstep. The joyful feeling faded and a lump of consternation settled in his stomach.

Had Helen invited Richard, too? And if she had, how would he be able to sit at the same table with the man who'd so wronged this woman who'd sneaked her way into the center of his heart?

Chapter 6

S tanding on the porch of the Wolfe family's bungalow, Bernie adjusted his bow tie one last time. Nervousness, excitement, and apprehension created a flutter in his belly. He hadn't been to a real family Thanksgiving since he was a boy, when his grandparents were still alive and the aunts, uncles, and cousins all gathered together. With Grandmother's death, the family get-togethers ceased, and not until he'd received the invitation from Henry had he realized how much he missed being part of a family gathering.

But today, thanks to the Wolfes' kindness, he'd once again have the chance to sit at a noisy table. But exactly how noisy, he couldn't help but wonder. Would Helen have invited the man named Richard as a thank-you, too? A thank-you he didn't deserve?

Pressing one palm to the buttons of his best blue suit coat, he raised his other hand and gave the doorjamb several brisk knocks. Within seconds the door creaked open, and a young girl with a thin, pale face and a tumble of shoulder-length sausage curls gazed up at him. Thick black lashes swept up and down with each blink of her bold blue eyes.

Bernie found himself immediately smitten. "Hello there. You must be Lois." He stuck out his hand. "I'm Bernie O'Day."

The child hunched her skinny shoulders and took his hand in a quick, embarrassed shake. "Hello, Mr. O'Day. Will you come in, please?"

Wonderful aromas greeted Bernie's nose as he stepped over the threshold. His stomach turned, but this time from eagerness rather than apprehension.

Lois closed the door behind Bernie then fixed him with a serious look. "May I take your hat?"

Her impeccable manners and formal speech belied her tender years. Bernie swallowed a grin and mimicked her courtly attitude. "Why, of course, miss. And thank you."

A tiny giggle found its way from the little girl's throat. She placed his hat on a chair in the corner then gestured toward a wide doorway at the far side of the simple parlor. "This way, please." She led him through the doorway to a dining room where a long table covered in a crisp white cloth, flowered china plates, and gleaming silverware sat ready for Thanksgiving dinner. Bernie gawked in amazement. Helen had gone all-out to make this dinner a festive affair. He quickly counted the chairs—six in all, but the one at the foot of the table had no place setting. Apparently he was the only guest. He nearly collapsed in relief.

Lois gestured toward a chair on the left-hand side of the table. "Helen, Henry, and Carl are dishing up the food right now. We'll be eating in a few minutes. You can sit down, an' we'll be out in a little bit." She dashed through a doorway in the corner of the dining room, her voice trailing after her. "He's here, Helen! We can eat now!"

Bernie stood behind the chair, unwilling to sit until his hostess had taken her seat. Clanks, scuffles, and mumbled voices carried from beyond the doorway, painting a picture of busyness. He wished he could go in and offer his help, but he didn't want to intrude. So he stood, gaze aimed at the doorway, alternately smoothing his hair into place with his palm and checking the buttons on his jacket while he counted down the seconds.

In less than two minutes, his patience was rewarded by a small parade led by Lois, who carried a basket of sliced bread and a round dish of creamy butter. Henry came next, his hands filled with bowls of steaming mashed sweet potatoes and buttery green beans. A shorter version of Henry—Carl, no doubt—clomped behind Henry with some sort of green wobbly tower balanced on a plate. And finally Helen emerged, holding a platter containing a beautifully browned turkey and a mound of moist stuffing. Bernie barely noticed the bird, however; he couldn't take his eyes off the woman.

She'd done something different with her hair—pulled it up so it formed a smooth sweep from her slender neck to the crown of her head. Soft curls spilled toward her forehead. Her cheeks sported soft pink, and the color also graced her full lips. The deep blue of her two-piece, well-fitted suit brought out the bright blue of her eyes. She was beautiful. Breathtakingly beautiful.

The three younger Wolfe siblings placed their offerings on the table and settled into chairs with a noisy scraping of legs against the wood floor. Lois took the chair next to Bernie, and Henry and Carl sat side by side across the table, leaving the seat at the head for Helen. She wiped the back of her hand daintily across her perspiration-dotted brow and sent Bernie, who stood stupidly behind his chair staring at her, a shy smile. "Welcome to our home, Bernie. Won't you be seated?"

Bernie darted to her chair and pulled it out. "Ladies first."

Henry coughed into his hand, and Carl smirked. Bernie chose to ignore the boys and kept his focus on Helen. Her cheeks deepened—a natural blush much more appealing than the powder she wore—and she slipped into the chair, her head low.

"Thank you, Bernie."

"You're welcome."

She smoothed her skirt over her knees and lifted her face slightly. "You already met Lois, and of course you know Henry. Please meet our other brother, Carl."

The freckle-faced boy grinned at Bernie. "Hi, Mr. O'Day. Nice to meet'cha."

Bernie stifled a chuckle at the boy's lack of formality. He gave a quick nod in reply then returned to his chair, feeling clumsy compared to Helen's swanlike motions. As soon as he sat, Carl reached for the nearest bowl—green beans—and started to serve himself.

Automatically, Bernie cleared his throat. "Would you like me to say grace?"

Carl's hands froze on the serving spoon.

Bernie wished he could kick himself. He was a guest—he had no business inflicting his belief system on this family. But how could they sit down to such a fine feast and not offer thanks? He flicked a glance at Helen. She wasn't smiling, but neither was she frowning. Her sweet face wore a pensive expression Bernie wished he could translate.

After a few tense seconds of silence, Helen folded her hands. "Please do so."

Everyone folded their hands and bowed their heads, and Bernie delivered a short prayer of gratitude for the food and the hands that had prepared it. He finished, "Thank You, our Father, for Your bountiful blessings. May we be ever mindful of Your presence in our lives. Amen."

◆　◆　◆

Helen swallowed the lump that filled her throat at the sweetness in Bernie's tone as he talked to the God he called Father. Dad had spoken to God with the same ease and familiarity, and as a child she'd experienced such security while listening to her father pray. Bernie's prayer sent a spiral of warmth around her, as comforting as a cozy quilt on a winter day, but at the same time a chill whisked through her heart. The emptiness that had plagued her since her parents' deaths and Richard's departure returned, coupled with an aching realization: The emptiness was due to more than burying her parents and her dreams of a future with Richard; it was due to her decision to refuse God any part of her life.

Her hands shook as she carved the turkey and placed succulent slices on each plate. But no one seemed to notice her turmoil. Her brothers and sister passed the bowls and dove into the hearty meal. While they ate, they chatted with each other. And with Bernie. Carl and Lois seemed as at ease with this newcomer as if he'd visited a dozen times. Bernie, too, appeared completely comfortable after his initial shyness. He teased Lois, talked to Henry like a peer, and drilled Carl on baseball facts. Helen found she needed to contribute nothing to the conversation, which suited her—she couldn't think of a thing to say—yet also left her feeling left out. Her topsy-turvy emotions confused her, and the food that she had so anticipated lost its appeal.

When they'd nearly emptied the bowls and consumed a good quarter of the turkey, the boys clamored for pie. Helen brought out the sweet potato and pecan pie made from Mom's recipe and cut it into six equal portions. Conversation ceased while they ate dessert. Helen wasn't sure if they'd all run out of words or if they were just too full to speak, but in the silence that fell—only the clink of forks on plates and satisfied sighs creating a soft backdrop—she grew more and more unsettled. If only she could make sense of her tumbling emotions!

As soon as the boys were finished eating, they staggered to their bedroom to change out of their church clothes, which Helen had insisted they wear for the dinner. Lois yawned widely and asked to be excused. Looking into the child's dark-rimmed eyes, Helen decided not to insist Lois help with cleanup. Lois scuffed around the corner, and Helen and Bernie were left alone at a messy table with chairs all askew.

Bernie sat back and patted his stomach. "That was delicious, Miss Wolfe. Thank you so much for including me."

"You're very welcome." Helen's voice sounded unnaturally high. She cleared her throat and tried again. "After your kindness toward Henry, it's the least we could do." She hadn't intended to intimate she'd invited him out of obligation, but she realized her statement could offer that meaning. She scrambled for a way of rephrasing, but before she could think of anything, Bernie spoke.

"Henry gives as much as he gets. He's proved himself invaluable."

Relieved that he hadn't seemed to take offense, Helen rose and began stacking dirty plates. "He loves his job, and—truthfully—his income is very helpful."

Bernie gathered silverware, filling both fists with forks, spoons, and knives. "I'd like to keep him on until he's finished with school. But after that. . ."

Helen gestured for Bernie to put the silverware into the empty green bean bowl. When he'd released the handfuls of clattering silverware, she put the bowl on top of the plates and lifted the stack. "After that. . .what?"

Bernie sent her a serious look. "I'd like to see him quit working for me and go on to college. He's a bright boy. He oughta aim higher than being the helper in a pawnshop."

Although he'd paid her brother a compliment, his words stung. Mom and Dad had wanted college for Henry. But how would she provide it? Forcing a laugh to hide the hurt his comment had inflicted, Helen turned toward the kitchen. "Well, if Henry's to attend college, my gift elf will need to leave more than school supplies and woolen socks on the porch. We'll need a bag of gold."

Bernie scurried after her. "Your gift elf?" Humor and interest tinged his tone.

Helen placed the dirty dishes on the counter then faced her guest. "Have you ever heard the story about the elves and the shoemaker?"

Bernie nodded.

"Apparently we have our own version. Someone. . ." It had to be Richard, trying to butter her up. Helen's stomach churned. ". . .has left items on our porch once or twice a week for the past couple of months. It reminds me of the little elves seeing to the needs of the shoemaker when he isn't looking."

A smile twitched on Bernie's clean-shaven cheeks. He smelled of bay rum, too. He must've cleaned up and shaved right before coming over to look so fresh. Helen hurried to the dining room before the temptation to run her fingers along his smooth cheek overcame her.

He followed. "That story always reminded me of a Bible story—the one about a pitcher of oil that never ran dry. God made sure the widow and her son's needs were met."

Helen paused in gathering the dessert plates. She shifted slowly to look at Bernie. His open, honest gaze met hers. "Do you really believe God meets our needs?"

Without so much as a moment's hesitation, Bernie nodded emphatically. "I believe that with all my heart. He might not meet them the way we think He ought to do it, but He gives us exactly what we need."

The past months of worry, frustration, and heartache rose up in one mighty tidal wave of emotion and spilled from Helen's mouth before she could stop it. "What I need most is a helpmate, and if God puts him on my front porch, maybe I'll finally believe He really does care about me."

Bernie stared at her, openmouthed and red-faced. Embarrassed, Helen spun away from him. She reached for the last dessert plate, but as her fingers closed around it, a loud knocking sounded on the front door. "Excuse me," she muttered and bustled through the parlor.

The knocking came again—harsh and impatient. Helen called, "I'm coming!" She threw open the door then stumbled backward in shock.

Richard Mason swept his hat from his head and gave a dapper bow. "Happy Thanksgiving, Helen!" His gaze roved from her head to her toes and up again. A knowing grin climbed his cheek. "You're just as pretty as you always were." He held out his arms. "How about a hug, honey?"

Chapter 7

ernie strode around the corner from the dining room in time to see a well-dressed young man with a dark mustache step into the house and wrap his arms around Helen. Helen stood within the circle of his embrace with her arms dangling, as if she'd suddenly turned into a giant rag doll. The clatter of footsteps intruded as Henry, Carl, and Lois thundered into the room. The man released Helen and turned his broad grin on the children.

"Well, lookit here, if it ain't the whole gang! How you doin', Hank? Looks like you've grown a foot since I saw you last." He punched Henry's shoulder then whirled on the younger two. "Carl! Little Lois!" He rubbed his hand over Carl's head, further tousling the boy's unruly hair, then swooped Lois in the air. The moment he released her, she scooted behind Henry. The three stared at the man, unsmiling. But his wide smile never dimmed. "Good to see you all." Finally his gaze found Bernie, and a scowl quickly marred his brow. He pointed. "Who's that?"

Henry answered. "My boss, Bernie O'Day. We invited him for Thanksgiving dinner."

The man's lips formed a smile, but his eyes remained narrowed slits of distrust. "That so? Well, nice to meet you, Mr. O'Day. I'm Richard Mason, Helen's fiancé."

Helen delicately cleared her throat. "My former fiancé." She folded her arms across her chest. "Children, would you please finish clearing the table for me?" She raised her brows at the trio, and they trooped past Bernie. Still holding her arms in the defensive position, Helen faced Richard Mason. "Richard, I wondered when you'd finally show your face."

From her tone, Bernie couldn't determine whether she was pleased, apprehensive, or controlling herself for his sake. He knew he should leave—he had no place here—but his feet seemed mired in concrete.

Richard tossed his hat onto the sofa and leaned his shoulder on the doorjamb, his easy smile pinned directly on Helen's face. "Aw, you know how busy stage life can be, doll. Hardly a minute to spare. But I couldn't let the holiday go by without at least popping in and saying hello."

Helen inched backward, her fingers holding tight to her elbows. "Well, I suppose I should thank you for the gifts you left on the porch."

Mason smoothed his finger over his mustache. "Gifts?"

Helen's curls bounced with her nod. "I know they're from you. Who else could have known that spiced peaches are Lois's favorite, or that Carl loves baseball cards?"

Bernie nearly bit through the end of his tongue, trying to hold back the truth. Helen needed to hear it from Mason rather than him. He waited for Mason to admit he had no idea about the gifts.

Mason cleared his throat, his head ducked low as if modesty held him captive. "Yes, well, spiced peaches are a delightful treat. And of course what boy doesn't like baseball cards, hmm?"

Bernie found the ability to move. He stormed forward, his elbow brushing against Mason's sleeve as he went. "Thanks again for the invitation to dinner, Miss Wolfe. I enjoyed my time with your family." Aware of Mason's steely glare on him, he paused long enough to give Helen a soft smile. "You and the children enjoy the rest of the holiday. I'm sure we'll talk again soon." Without waiting for a response, he charged out of the house and down the street, his strides wide and arms pumping.

He was halfway home before his chilly ears reminded him he'd left his hat behind. With a disgruntled huff, he slowed his pace. Should he go back and get it? Part of him itched to turn around. To check on Helen and make sure that weasel Mason—because he was certain the man was a weasel—was behaving himself. But in the end he let out a sigh of resignation. His breath formed a cloud of condensation in the evening dusk then dissipated. Watching the puff disappear, Bernie wished he could make his feelings for Miss Helen Wolfe float away so easily. It hurt more than he cared to admit to think of her taking up with Richard Mason again. Especially if what Henry said was true and the man callously tossed her aside when she gave up her dream of singing in lieu of caring for her siblings. A woman who acted so unselfishly deserved a man who would cherish her.

Lord, what's Your will for Helen. . .and me? The prayer whispered from his heart. *I want to show her Your love in action, but would it be all right if I let her see my love in action, too? Can I be the helpmeet she's seeking?*

Bernie didn't receive an answer, but he felt better having asked the question. In time, God would answer. He trusted his Father to lead him when the time was right. He set his feet in motion again, determined to leave Helen and her needs in God's hands, where they belonged.

◆　◆　◆

Sunday morning as Helen dressed for church, her thoughts drifted back to Thanksgiving Day. Bernie's prayer and the emotions it had stirred contrasted with the surprise of the visit from Richard. He'd stayed well past bedtime and had apologized repeatedly for his hasty exit from her life. She still wasn't completely sure she wanted him back—not in the way he wanted to be back—but she couldn't honestly say she was ready to permanently sever her ties with him. They'd known each other since they were youngsters, and they shared a common goal of singing on the stage. Surely they'd be able to build a life together if only she could learn to trust him not to abandon her again.

Carl's and Henry's voices drifted to her ears—fighting over first turn for the washroom. She should go break up the argument before it turned into fisticuffs, but she stood behind Lois at the mirror and shaped her sister's naturally curly hair into fat rolls instead. While brushing, she idly asked, "Lois, would you like it if Richard moved in here with us and became part of our family?"

"Richard?" Lois wrinkled her nose at her reflection. "He's a dandy."

Helen snorted out a laugh. "Where did you learn a word like that?"

"From Henry. He called Richard a dandy, and I think Henry's right. Richard smiles funny—like he doesn't really mean it—and he's afraid to get his hands dirty. He wouldn't even help you with the dishes the other night. He laughs too loud, and sometimes he laughs when you don't mean to be funny, which I think is mean."

Helen supposed she should scold Lois for speaking ill of Richard. But she couldn't make herself condemn her sister for her honesty. The things Lois mentioned were things that bothered Helen, too, yet Richard also had good qualities. He was very talented and already had a good-paying job with the opera company as their lead singer. He'd claimed he could easily get her hired into the troupe, as well, allowing her to live out her long-held dreams. When she'd asked about the children, he'd said, somewhat disparagingly, "Well, this isn't a traveling troupe, doll." She took his comment to infer she'd be available to them.

Lois stepped away from the hairbrush and sucked in a big breath. "None of us are very fond of Richard, Helen. He's hardly the cat's meow."

Helen clapped her hand over her mouth to keep from laughing out loud.

Her hand on her hip, Lois tossed her hair. "But if you like him, then. . ." She flounced out of the room in a perfect Mae West imitation.

Helen sank onto the edge of the bed, shaking her head. She'd have to forbid Carl from taking Lois to the picture show if her sister was going to pick up such habits. But she had to admit, Lois's antics were amusing. And her depiction of Richard far too accurate. Helen sighed. She wished her parents were there to advise her concerning making a commitment to Richard. Without warning, her mother's voice echoed through her memory: *You should pray before making any decision, Helen, and ask for God's guidance.*

Helen whispered, "But I don't pray anymore." She waited, her head tipped, expectant and hopeful. But her mother's voice didn't return. With another sigh, she pushed off from the bed and retrieved her black pumps from the closet. She'd be late getting the children to church if she didn't hurry.

As she buttered slices of toast for a simple breakfast, another thought crossed her mind, carried with the remembrance of Bernie's easy prayer at their Thanksgiving table. Helen no longer prayed, but Bernie did. And Bernie obviously cared about Henry's future, which meant he'd want the best for her brother. If she asked Bernie to seek God's guidance about allowing Richard back into their lives, she had no doubt he'd do it.

Helen desperately needed answers. She could send a message with Henry tomorrow to give to Bernie, and he'd probably send a reply on Tuesday. But she really wanted him to begin praying now. She needed financial help now. She needed an emotional helpmate in her life now. She didn't want to prolong seeking an answer.

Setting aside the butter knife, she dashed to the hallway and called, "Henry?"

Her brother poked his head out of the washroom. "What?"

"Which church does Mr. O'Day attend?"

"The big brick one on the corner of Fourth and Applewood."

Helen nearly groaned. The church was huge! How would they locate Bernie in that massive sanctuary? She tapped her chin, thinking. If they sat in the back, they could scoot out the doors quickly at the end and watch every parishioner leaving. If they were lucky, they'd spot Bernie in the crowd.

"Everyone, hurry now," she ordered, clapping her hands to emphasize her words. "We're going to Mr. O'Day's church this morning, and it's quite a walk." The distance to his church was much greater than to their own little chapel, so she'd need to bundle Lois well and make sure she kept her scarf over her nose and mouth.

For a moment she hesitated, uncertainty holding her captive. Was she doing the right thing, taking her siblings to meet Bernie O'Day and placing such an important issue in his hands? And why did she trust him with her dilemma? She hadn't a clue. She only knew, for the first time in a long time, she believed she'd found someone who wouldn't let her down.

"Please let my trust in this man not be misguided," she mumbled as she hurried back to the kitchen to pour juice. But she told herself the plea wasn't a prayer.

Chapter 8

Bernie rose after the closing benediction and turned toward the aisle. His heart felt burdened by the minister's impassioned plea for the parishioners to pray for the people in Europe caught up in war. Here in his cocoon of security, Bernie admitted to giving little thought to the horror raging overseas. While he moved toward the double doors leading to the street, a man brushed against him, nearly knocking his Bible from his grip.

"Sorry about that," the man said.

Bernie grinned. "No problem." He slipped the Bible into his jacket pocket and glanced around. "Crowded today—hard to walk without bumpin' each other."

The man nodded. "Holiday Sundays always bring in a lot of visitors."

Bernie agreed. He wished those who flooded the pews at Thanksgiving, Christmas, and Easter would make church attendance an every-Sunday event. He couldn't imagine getting through the week without the nourishment his soul received each Lord's Day. As he stepped from the warmth of the sanctuary into a blustery Sunday noon, his gaze roved across the small groups of people chatting together. Although he glimpsed many cheerful faces, he also noted somber ones. He passed between groups, overhearing snatches of conversation, and realized many of the sober expressions accompanied comments about the war. Bernie blew out a little breath of relief. Apparently he wouldn't be the only one praying for peace in Europe.

He stepped from the crowds and turned his feet toward home, but then a female voice—a familiar female voice—called his name and stopped him in his tracks. He whirled around to see Helen, with the younger Wolfe siblings on her heels, scurrying toward him. She wore the same blue suit she'd worn on Thanksgiving Day, but a cream-colored hat with blue feathers and red beads sat at a jaunty angle over her curls. Bernie gulped. Had any woman ever been as appealing as Helen Wolfe?

She reached his side, and the fervency in her blue eyes nearly stilled his heart. "Oh Bernie, thank goodness we caught you."

Bernie whisked a glance over each of their faces. Rosy cheeks and bright red noses let him know they'd waited in the cold for quite a while. "Is something wrong?"

"I needed to speak with you." She curled her hand through his elbow and turned to her brothers and sister. "Wait right here. I'll be back in a minute." Then she guided Bernie a few feet away to the curb, where she released his arm and clasped her gloved hands in front of her. "Bernie, you're a praying man, and I need to ask you a favor."

Bernie's heart swelled. She'd just paid him the biggest compliment ever. Whatever favor she needed, he was ready.

"Remember Richard Mason? He came over Thanksgiving evening as you were leaving."

Bernie stifled a growl. He gave a brusque nod.

"Well. . ." Suddenly Helen turned shy, angling her gaze away from him. "He's asked to begin seeing me again—courting me. But I'm very confused about whether or not to allow it. You see, he. . .he. . ." She didn't directly meet his gaze, but her eyes fluttered in his direction. "He broke off our engagement when I refused to send Henry, Carl, and Lois to an orphans' home. He didn't want the responsibility of seeing to their needs."

"Is that so?" Bernie tried to rein in his contempt for a man who'd ask Helen to cast aside her siblings, but when she blanched he knew he'd failed.

"But he must have changed his mind," she hurried on, once again looking off to the side, "because he's back, and he's been very kind to the children. So I was wondering if, maybe. . ." Very slowly she turned her face to look fully into his eyes. "Would you please pray for me to know what to do? I desperately need someone to help me support the family. If I were to marry Richard, our financial problems would be solved. He's well established with the opera company, and he says if we're married, he'll secure a spot for me, too. The salary would far exceed what I make now as a hotel maid." Her words tumbled out faster and faster, her breath forming little clouds of condensation that drifted beneath Bernie's chin. "The children deserve security, Bernie, but I want to make the right decision. Will you pray for me?"

Bernie lifted his hands to cup her shoulders. Her tight muscles beneath the fabric of the blue suit spoke of her inner turmoil. How he wished to draw her into his embrace, to offer her comfort. But she'd only asked for prayer. A lump formed in his throat, and he swallowed before speaking. "I already pray for you, Helen. Every day I pray for you, and for Henry, Carl, and Lois."

She blinked up at him, her pink-painted lips slightly open. "Y–you do?" Tears flooded her eyes, deepening the blue irises.

"God put you on my heart, and I've been praying for Him to give you peace and strength."

One tear broke free of its perch on her thick lashes and rolled down her cheek. Gratitude glowed from her eyes.

"So now I'll pray for God to make clear to you what you're to do. But, Helen?" He paused, uncertainty making his pulse pound. "Be careful. Don't be looking for a man to meet your needs. Men'll let you down. They can't help it—they're human, and they fail. But God? He can't forsake you. It's not in His nature. So lean on Him before anything or anyone else. Trust Him to meet your needs. Will you do that?"

She swished away her tears with her fingertips. Her chin trembled. "I–I'll try."

He knew what effort it took for her to make the concession. He squeezed her shoulders and then let his hands fall away. "It's cold out here, and you need to get the youngsters on home. You ridin' the trolley?"

"We never ride the trolley."

Bernie understood. He reached into his pocket and withdrew two quarters. "Then take this—get a taxicab."

She stared at the coins. "Oh, but. . ."

He grasped her wrist and pressed the coins into her palm. "For me, Helen, so I don't hafta worry about Lois catching a cold. Please?"

With a deep sigh, she closed her fingers over the silver disks. "Thank you, Bernie. You're a very kind man." She gestured to the children, and they dashed to her side. Curling her arm around Lois's shoulders, she offered Bernie a quavering smile. "Thank you for your prayers, Bernie. I promise, I'll be listening for God's voice."

◆ ◆ ◆

Over the next week, Helen honored her promise to Bernie. As she cleaned hotel rooms, she kept her heart tuned to guidance concerning continuing the job or taking up singing in the opera company with Richard. While she saw to the children's needs, she searched her mind's eye for images of someone stepping in beside her to help her parent her siblings. When she lay in bed at night, she petitioned God to give her the peace and strength Bernie had mentioned. And, although her circumstances didn't change, she discovered she slept more soundly and felt less burdened than she had before. Could that mean God was answering her prayers? Her heart fluttered with hope that maybe, just maybe, God was near.

Richard began the habit of visiting each evening. He always brought gifts— frivolous items like lace handkerchiefs for Lois or chocolate bars for the boys. Helen tried to be grateful, but she wondered why he'd ceased leaving items they could really use, the way he'd done before. With each visit, she tried to envision him as a permanent fixture in their lives. He was willing to accept her and the children—he'd said so—but somehow she couldn't get comfortable with the idea. So although he pressured her continually to set a wedding date—"*And make it soon, darling,*" he'd whispered into her ear—she hesitated. Only when she knew for certain Richard was the helpmate God wanted for her would she give her answer.

Sunday morning, December seventh, bloomed like many other December days. Cold, crisp, with snowflakes dancing on a stout breeze. Helen held a steaming mug of coffee between her palms and looked out at the gray morning. Both Carl and Lois had the sniffles, so although she hated to skip church services, she chose to let them sleep. Henry was dressing, however, unwilling to miss attending church. He'd stated firmly he could go on his own.

Her heart swelled, thinking of the fine young man her brother was becoming— responsible, caring, mature beyond his years. And much of the change she'd seen in the past months was the result of Bernie O'Day's influence. Henry quoted Bernie, emulated Bernie, and respected him as a mentor. Henry didn't have a father anymore, but he had Bernie, and Bernie filled the hole their father's passing had left in Henry's boyish heart. *What a kind, good man is Bernie O'Day.* A flutter in her chest accompanied the thought.

"Sis?" Henry bustled into the room, interrupting Helen's musing. "Want me to stop at that hamburger stand and pick up some burgers for our dinner? They'll be yesterday's leftovers, so only a nickel apiece."

Both Lois and Carl loved the greasy sandwiches with ground beef and grilled onions. They might be enticed to eat if offered such a treat. Although Helen had little money to spare, she retrieved her purse and gave Henry two dimes to purchase burgers. Then, as if something—or Someone—encouraged her fingers, she plucked out one more dime and dropped it into Henry's waiting palm. "Put that in the offering plate."

Henry beamed in approval. He dashed out the door, his knitted cap tugged low over his ears.

The house quiet, Helen curled on the sofa with her coffee and her Bible. If she couldn't attend service, she could at least read from God's Word. She flipped pages, scanning passages, and finally settled on one of the letters to the Corinthian churches. Nestled in the corner of the sofa, she read, content. When she reached the thirteenth chapter of First Corinthians, her reading slowed, her finger underlining the words describing God's idea for love.

Without conscious thought, she began to read aloud. "Charity suffereth long, and is kind; charity envieth not; charity vaunteth not itself, is not puffed up, doth not behave itself unseemly, seeketh not her own, is not easily provoked, thinketh no evil; rejoiceth not in iniquity, but rejoiceth in the truth; beareth all things, believeth all things, hopeth all things, endureth all things. Charity never faileth. . . .'" She closed the Bible, the final line replaying in her thoughts. Charity—love—never fails.

An image of the engraved coin she'd sold to Bernie O'Day flashed before her mind's eye. Slipping to her knees, she clasped her hands and offered a heartfelt prayer: "God, Bernie told me Your love never fails or forsakes. I want so much to believe You'll always be there and You'll meet the needs of my brothers, sister, and me. Bernie is praying for my strength to find You. I'm seeking You. Will You please make Yourself known to me? Make Yourself known to me in a way I cannot misunderstand, because I need You, God. I need You. . . ." Her last sentence choked out on a sob.

She pushed to her feet just as the front door burst open and Henry charged into the room. He dropped a grease-stained brown paper bag as he raced to her and took her hands in his icy grasp. "Helen! The burger man said there's a rumor that Japan attacked the United States!"

Chapter 9

In all of his twenty-eight years, Bernie had never kept a radio going day and night, but the events of December 7th, 1941, changed that. For the next three days he hovered near the Philco, determined to stay abreast of the latest developments concerning the United States' involvement in the war that, up till now, had seemed distant.

When Henry arrived after school, he, too, drifted to the radio frequently, and more than once Bernie overheard the boy mutter, "Soon as I'm old enough, I'm puttin' on a uniform and going to battle. Won't let nobody attack my country and get away with it!" Bernie admired Henry's determination, but at the same time, his heart quaked. He prayed the war would be over long before Henry reached his eighteenth birthday. At the same time, a desire to do as Henry stated—don a uniform and march in defense of America—continually played at the fringes of his mind.

Posters of Uncle Sam with his finger extended and the words *I Want You!* appeared in windows all over town. Banners claiming the army's need for fighters hung from lampposts. Everywhere Bernie went, the tug followed him, and by mid-December, he'd made a decision: After Christmas he'd close the shop, visit the Army Recruitment Office, and sign up to defend his country.

He had only one concern. What would Helen do without the income Henry earned? He added another prayer to his list of daily petitions. *Lord, help me find a way to ascertain the Wolfe family won't go hungry. Even if I'm not here, meet their needs, my Father.*

◆ ◆ ◆

"What are you saying, Richard?" Helen stared at the man, disbelief raising her voice several decibels.

"It isn't difficult to understand," Richard retorted, his eyebrows fixed in a supercilious angle. "With the U.S. focus on that European skirmish, people will lose their interest in attending operatic performances. We have no choice but to move the opera company into Canada."

"But. . .but I can't move to Canada!" Helen held her hands outward, indicating the simple yet homey parlor in which they sat together on her parents' sofa. "This is my home."

Richard huffed out a breath, adjusting the lapels of his suit jacket. "Then stay. Honestly, Helen, you can be so stubborn."

Helen reared back, her pulse thudding so hard she felt as though a bass drum beat in her head. A snippet from her reading in First Corinthians whispered through her heart—"Charity. . .seeketh not her own." Richard claimed to love her, yet he was willing to walk away from her to pursue his own interests. Again.

She jolted upright and marched several feet away. Aware of her brothers and sister studying in their bedrooms, she deliberately kept her voice low although every part of her wished to rail at him in righteous indignation. "Richard, why did you bother to come back? You haven't changed. All you really care about is seeing to your own selfish desires."

He glowered at her. "What about you—insisting on holding on to this little house and wasting your life taking care of a bunch of kids that aren't even yours? You aren't concerned about me and what I want or need. We had plans, you and me, and you threw them all away!"

"If you truly loved me, you'd understand how much Henry, Carl, and Lois mean to me. You'd never ask me to discard them."

Richard rose and advanced at her, his lips curled in contempt. "I thought a year of separation would be enough to bring you to your senses—to make you see what a fool you'd been. But apparently I was wrong." He released a derisive snort. "Well, I'm going on to Canada, where I will continue to build my career. And by the time the war ends, my name will be up in lights. But what of you, Helen? What will you have achieved?"

Helen shook her head slowly, silently berating herself. How could she ever have desired this man's presence in her life? He was right when he'd called her a fool, but he'd chosen the wrong reason to accuse her of foolishness. Now that she recognized the truth, she was more certain than ever that she did not want a future with Richard. Not even for the financial security he could provide.

She spoke softly, her voice quavering with conviction. "I love singing—I always have and I always will—but I love my brothers and sister more." Peace swept through her, assuring her she'd made the right choice. "Someday, Richard, God will give me the chance to sing again. But not for myself. When I sing again, it will be for Him."

Another snort blasted from Richard's sneering lips. "That won't bring much fame and fortune, my naive little Helen, but who am I to stand in your way?" He buttoned his jacket and headed for the door.

Helen called after him, "Before you go. . ."

He turned back, his expression impatient.

She drew in a breath, gathering the strength needed to set aside her pride and utter the thank-you so she'd owe him nothing. "I appreciate the boxes of food and the other items you left. They helped us a great deal."

He rolled his eyes. "Helen, I don't have the foggiest notion about any boxes. I didn't leave anything here."

"Y–you didn't?"

"No." He wrenched the doorknob. "Good-bye—this time for good." He stepped out, slamming the door into its frame behind him.

Helen stood in the middle of the room, confusion coiling through her middle. If he hadn't left the boxes, then who had?

"Sis?" Henry's voice sounded from the hallway. Helen turned and spotted her brother half-hidden in shadows. He held the brown corduroy jacket he'd been given. "I've got a loose button on the pocket. Can you fix it?"

Helen stared at the jacket. Comprehension tickled the far corners of her mind. Could it be. . .? Hopefulness tried to rise in her chest, but she refused to allow it free rein. She'd made a grave error in assuming Richard was the mysterious gift-giver. She wouldn't jump to another conclusion. She needed solid proof.

She held out her hands. "Give me the jacket, and I'll stitch that button on securely for you." As Henry placed the warm coat in her hands, she smiled. "Come sit beside me while I stitch. I need to talk with you about something important."

◆　◆　◆

Bernie rose from his knees in prayer. His knees and shoulders ached—he'd remained on the wood-planked floor of his bedroom, hunched over the edge of the bed, for nearly an hour—but he smiled in satisfaction. God had answered his prayers in bigger ways than he could have imagined. The plan was perfect. *If only Helen agrees.* He winged up one more petition for God to move in Helen's heart as effectively as He'd moved in his own so they could be in one accord.

He headed down the darkened stairway to the lower level of the building. He tugged the overhead string dangling from the single light bulb just inside the shop. Light flooded the room. For several minutes Bernie stood in the glow and examined the shop, allowing memories to creep from every corner. He'd lived his entire life in the upstairs of this shop. He'd worked side by side with his father, learning the trade, earning an honest living. He loved this shop—loved serving people. How it had pained him to think of it closing. And now it wouldn't have to.

Thank You, God. Thank You.

Gratitude warming him, he moved to the storeroom and rummaged around for a suitably sized box. He had one more task to complete before marching into war. One final gift for Helen and her siblings. Then he could leave, secure that she—and his shop—would be just fine.

◆　◆　◆

As the calendar inched toward Christmas, Bernie took advantage of every minute to prepare for his time away. In the past, he'd only given Henry cleanup and organization chores. Now he taught the boy every aspect of running the pawnshop. He drilled Henry on the value of items so he could offer a fair exchange without losing money on the transaction. He taught the boy how to keep the meticulous records and to make out tickets as well as how to rotate stock on the shelves so his regular customers wouldn't miss any new arrivals.

Henry soaked up the information, never questioning an instruction. Instead, he listened attentively and applied the lessons, proving his trustworthiness. Yes, Bernie had made the right decision.

During the evening hours, Bernie accumulated items for one last, special delivery to the Wolfe family. Clothing in sizes he hoped were appropriate for Lois, Carl, and Henry. Bolts of fabric so Helen could sew suits and dresses. Canned goods and bags of beans, flour, and sugar. Necessities—those things needed for survival. Satisfied with his choices, he turned his attention to things intended to bring pleasure.

For Henry, he selected a set of *Encyclopedias Britannica*—the 11th edition, published in 1911—but still very serviceable and containing information perfect for a studious young man like Henry. He chuckled as he wrapped a Little Slugger baseball bat, mitt, catcher's mask, and chest gear for Carl. He wished he could be a fly on the wall when Carl spotted the signature in the mitt's pocket—Jumbo Brown, pitcher for the Giants in 1940. A baseball fan like Carl would take excellent care of the mitt—Bernie just knew it.

The biggest gift—too big to wrap—lurked in the corner beneath a moth-eaten white sheet. Bernie'd had to promise the produce stand owner a silver dollar to borrow his horse and cart to deliver the clavichord, but it would be worth it to please Lois. The old clavichord wasn't a piano, but it was pretty with its elaborate paintings of flowers and vines, and it would take up less space in their parlor. He needed to find someone willing to give the little girl lessons, but he had a few more days to work out that detail.

Helen's gift was the smallest. It fit perfectly in a foil-covered box with a hinged lid. And he knew the item nestled in the velvet interior would deliver a message directly from his heart to hers. His fingers trembled as he tied a bright red bow around the box. Only two more days, and he'd make one more trip in the darkness of night to leave gifts on the Wolfe family's porch. Then, on Christmas evening, he'd visit to share his plans. And after that, he'd leave.

Pain stabbed. It would be hard to leave them, but it was the right thing to do. His country needed him. And he was leaving his shop in good hands. God would carry them through. Bernie had no doubt.

Chapter 10

Lois and Carl awakened Helen early Christmas morning, bouncing on the bed and squealing for her to get up now! Although Helen would have considered it a gift to sleep in a bit on her one day off, she stifled a groan, tugged on her robe, and allowed the rowdy pair to drag her to the parlor, where they'd decorated the tree the evening before. Their cries of delight at the sight of the packages she'd tucked beneath the sagging branches of the little tree chased away the vestiges of sleepiness, and she instructed Carl to fetch Henry so they could open their gifts.

Although the presents were simple and mostly practical, the children raved anyway, pleasing Helen. How proud Mom and Dad would be of them—so unspoiled, so unselfish. Despite her misgivings and stumbles, they were growing up just fine. She whisked a prayer heavenward in gratitude to God for working in their hearts, even when she'd wished to refuse His presence.

Henry bestowed Helen with a package marked "To Helen from all of us," and Helen pretended great surprise before removing the ribbon and lifting the lid. Inside she found a neat stack of yellowed music sheets—hymns and ballads and even a couple of haunting spirituals. The desire to burst into song exploded through her chest as she fingered the music. *Someday, God, I know You'll let me use my voice again.* She thanked her siblings enthusiastically, giving each of them a heartfelt hug, and then they trooped to the kitchen for a Christmas breakfast of pancakes with globs of strawberry jam.

When they'd finished, Helen shot an impish grin around the table. "All right, are we ready to deliver our Christmas surprise?"

Carl and Lois cheered, and Henry pushed away from the table. "Let's go!"

"Dress warmly," Helen admonished as the trio raced for their bedrooms. She followed, trying to imagine Bernie O'Day's face when they showed up outside his shop. Over the past two weeks, they'd practiced Christmas carols in three-part harmony, with Henry singing baritone in his newly discovered man's voice, Carl and Lois sharing the alto line, and Helen carrying the melody. Although they had no other gift for Bernie, she was certain he would accept their offering with much appreciation. His kindness knew no bounds.

Carl led the family out the front door, but he came to a stop just over the threshold, causing Lois to slam right into his back. Henry—hunched over Lois's short frame like a gargoyle in his attempt not to run her down—scolded, "What're you doing, Carl?"

"There's stuff out here," Carl bellowed.

Helen peeked past her siblings and gasped. Stuff indeed! Their gift elf—whoever he was—had outdone himself this time. She couldn't believe the bounty! They dragged everything inside and then spent a happy half hour examining it all. Helen watched her siblings with the little box bearing her name on it held between her palms, unopened.

When the clamor died down, Lois pointed at the red-ribboned box and said, "Aren'tcha gonna open yours?"

Curiosity battled with apprehension. The box—the kind of box that held jewelry, specifically a ring—certainly would reveal their unknown benefactor. She knew who she wanted it to be. Her heart nearly twisted in agony, hoping. What would she do if it turned out to be Richard once more trying to manipulate her into bowing to his will?

"Open it, Helen," Carl prompted, and Henry and Lois added their encouragement.

Painstakingly, Helen removed the bright red ribbon and set it aside. Then, holding her breath, she eased back the lid of the box. Gold glinted at her. With a gasp, she snapped the box closed and shoved it in her pocket.

"Helen!" her siblings protested, but she jumped to her feet and urged them up from their spots on the rug. They had a concert to deliver. When it was over, she'd share the box's contents with them. But not until she'd had a chance to look into Bernie O'Day's face and find the truth in his hazel eyes.

◆ ◆ ◆

Bernie sat at his little table tucked beneath the front window and sipped his third cup of hot black coffee. He looked at the clock—10:35 a.m. Only ten minutes had passed since he'd last peeked at the round face. He'd told himself he wouldn't intrude on the Wolfes' Christmas until evening, but the day stretched endlessly before him. How could he while away the hours? Before he settled on a suitable pastime, something reached his ears.

Music. Voices. Sweet voices, the highest line delivered so beautifully gooseflesh broke across his arms. Feeling like the man in Clement Moore's " 'Twas the Night before Christmas," he threw the sash open. Cold air blasted him, but he stuck his head out the window and looked down at the street. His heart galloped happily in his chest—Helen, Henry, Carl, and Lois stood in a half circle on the pavement below, their faces lifted toward him and "Joy to the World" pouring from their throats.

He couldn't stop a joyful laugh from escaping as he peered downward. They finished the carol then launched into "O Little Town of Bethlehem," followed by "Hark! The Herald Angels Sing." By the time they finished with "We Wish You a Merry Christmas," tears stung Bernie's eyes. He'd never received a sweeter present.

When the last note trailed away, he waved his hand and called, "Wait right there!" He nearly skidded down the stairs in his eagerness to get to the door, his slippers treacherous on the slick stair treads, but he made it without mishap and flung the door open, nearly bopping Carl, who stood too close. Laughing, Bernie ushered them inside then stood staring at them with a goofy grin on his face and his hands shoved in the pockets of his sloppiest pants.

"Merry Christmas, Mr. O'Day," Lois chirped, and Carl and Henry echoed the sentiment.

"Merry Christmas," Bernie said, bouncing his smile across each of the younger Wolfe siblings before allowing it to rest on Helen. Her sweet face, bold pink, wore the most tender smile he'd ever seen. Her blue eyes bored into his, shimmering with a myriad of emotions. Looking into her eyes, Bernie found it difficult to draw a breath.

Then, without speaking, she reached into her pocket and withdrew a little foil box. She held it aloft on her mitten-covered palm, giving it a gentle bounce. "All this time, it was you."

Bernie gulped. He didn't know what to say, so he simply nodded, aware of three pairs of eyes looking back and forth between Helen and him in curiosity.

Helen tipped her head, her brown curls brushing the shoulder of her plaid coat. "Why didn't you tell me?"

He shrugged slowly. "Didn't want you to thank me. Wanted you to thank. . ." Would she understand? Would she accept the gifts once she knew?

Understanding bloomed across her face, her rosy cheeks deepening. "I do thank Him." She swallowed, tears winking in her eyes. "Mostly I thank Him for bringing you into our lives."

Bernie forgot all about Henry, Carl, and Lois. He lurched past them, reaching, and moments later he held Helen in his embrace. Cold air scented her hair, and he buried his nose in her curls, savoring the aroma of Christmas. She laughed against his chest, the little box digging into his back where she clung to him. But he didn't mind. Not at all.

"Merry Christmas, Bernie," she whispered, her breath caressing his cheek.

"Merry Christmas," he replied. How he longed to press his lips to hers, but whispers and soft giggles reminded him they had an audience. With reluctance, he released his hold on her and stepped back. "I was going to come see you all this evening, but since you're here, should we go upstairs? There's something I need to tell you."

The four of them preceded Bernie up the stairs to his apartment, Lois and Helen in the lead with Henry and then Carl trailing. Bernie resisted the urge to hurry Carl—the boy's gaze bounced here and there, taking in every detail of the shop. Now that the time had arrived to share his plans, Bernie experienced a sense of urgency. What would he do if Helen said no? He pushed the anxious thought aside. God had planted this idea in his heart, and he'd prayed about it. If it was meant to be, Helen would see the sense and agree. He needed to trust.

They entered the big room that served as sitting room, dining room, and kitchen. Bernie pointed to a long, low settee, and the four of them lined up on the peach-colored cushions. Bernie took his father's overstuffed chair across from the settee and rested his elbows on his knees. For the next several minutes, he spilled his intentions to enlist in the army and his hopes that Henry and Helen would assume management of his pawnshop while he was away. They were silent and attentive as they listened, eyes wide.

Sitting up, Bernie heaved a sigh. "That's about it, I guess. I know I'm asking a lot. Don't know how long I'll be gone—I'm praying the war won't drag on, but I don't reckon any of us can know for sure. But while I'm away, whatever the shop brings in, it'll be yours. I won't have need of anything while I'm off fighting. And—if something should happen and I don't come back—I've already drawn up papers to transfer the shop to Henry." Warmth filled Bernie's chest as he gazed at the serious-faced young man seated so straight between Lois and Carl. "I know I couldn't place it in better hands."

Henry swallowed twice, his Adam's apple bobbing in his skinny neck. "I won't be taking it, Mr. O'Day, 'cause you'll be back. I know you will."

Helen added, "We'll all be praying for your safety every day. You can rest assured of that, Bernie."

Both Carl and Lois nodded, adding their agreement.

Helen still clutched the little box in her hand, and she now placed it on her knee. She opened the lid and withdrew the gold coin she'd brought into his shop only four months ago. Such a short time, but such a changing time. Bernie felt as though his life had turned completely around since the afternoon she'd entered his shop, breathless and needy. She held up the coin, and the gold glinted as brightly as the twin tears shimmering in her eyes.

"Bernie, you've showed me that love—God's love—never fails. You've taught me to trust again, and for that I will be forever grateful."

Thank You, Lord. The words sang from Bernie's heart. His life had changed but so had hers. God had answered his prayers.

◆ ◆ ◆

On January 3rd, 1942, Helen and the children accompanied Bernie to Grand Central Station. Snow dusted their caps and froze their noses, but she was determined to keep a happy face for Bernie's sake. They'd spent part of each day since Christmas together, and in those precious hours she'd grown to love him more than she'd thought possible. It hurt to send him away, yet pride filled her as she thought about him serving his country. Everything about Bernie—his kindness, his strength, his steadfastness, and mostly his love for God—pleased her.

As they walked hand in hand along the boarding ramp with Henry, Carl, and Lois trailing behind them, she inwardly prayed for God's protection over him while they were apart, and she knew he prayed the same thing for her and her siblings. Their hearts were in one accord, just the way God designed them to be.

At the end of the ramp, a cluster of men in matching green blouses and baggy trousers with duffel bags lying in piles around their black boots, waited in a noisy throng. Henry pointed. "Guess they're all goin', too, huh?" A thread of longing colored Henry's tone.

"Guess so," Bernie said. He curled his hand over Henry's shoulder. "But don't be thinking their job is the only important one. Taking care of your family—that's your job, Henry. I'm trusting you to work hard in school and keep the shop running." A lopsided grin climbed Bernie's smooth-shaven cheek. "Gotta have something to come back to, y'know."

"Yes, sir." Henry stood straight, his chin high. "You know I'll see to everything."

"I know you will." Bernie turned from Henry to deliver hugs to Carl and Lois. The pair clung hard, their fingers catching handfuls of his shirt fabric. He held them as long as they wanted while Helen battled tears, waiting her turn.

Finally the two stepped back, rubbing their noses. They shuffled over to Henry, and Bernie reached for Helen. She held on to him as tightly as Carl and Lois had. Maybe more tightly. It didn't seem fair to have to let him go after only just finding him—this man she loved and trusted, with whom she longed to build a lifetime of memories. But she respected his desire to go, and she wouldn't stand in his way.

He cupped her face between his palms and pressed his lips to hers, the kiss sweet and warm and rich with feeling. A whistle blared, and he stepped back. Although his arms hung at his sides, he caressed her with his eyes. "That's my cue," he said, his tone gruff.

She nodded.

Henry darted forward, his hand extended. "Here, Bernie."

Tears distorted Helen's vision when she recognized the object Henry pressed into Bernie's hand.

Henry said, "My grandma held on to this as a promise. Now I want you to hold it as a promise from all of us"—he gestured to Carl, Lois, and Helen by turn—"to you. That we'll be here waiting when you come back."

Helen closed her hand over Bernie's, the coin pressed between their palms. "And on that day, we'll take a picnic to Central Park."

Bernie winked. "What if it's October?"

Helen thought she might cry, but she managed a smile instead. "Is there some rule that says you can't have a picnic in October?"

Bernie laughed—the sound like music. He pocketed the coin and gave a nod. "You got a deal. We'll meet at the bridge."

"And throw bread to the ducks," Helen said. Tears filled her eyes, making his image waver.

The whistle blasted again, and the men at the end of the ramp began boarding. But Bernie didn't move. Then Carl let out a huff. "Mr. O'Day, if you don't leave, you can't come back. So would'ja please hurry up and get goin'?"

Her brother's petulant query was just the splash of humor Helen needed to cast aside her doldrums. Rising up on tiptoe, she planted a kiss on Bernie's cheek and gave him a little push. "Go, Bernie. God be with you."

"And with you." He offered a quick salute, yanked up his bag, and trotted to the train car. Just before stepping inside, he looked back and lifted his hand in a final wave. And then he was gone.

Helen remained with her arms around Carl and Lois's shoulders until the train rolled out of the station with a screech of wheels on iron and mighty huffs of steam. Lois sniffled and Carl stood with folded arms and distended lower lip. Beside them, Henry held his chin high and proud, his fingers on his brow in a salute until the train disappeared from sight. Then he lowered his arm and turned to Helen.

"Well, guess it's time to get busy. Got a shop to run."

Helen nodded.

Henry's eyes twinkled. "We'll be all right, you know."

Again, Helen nodded, a smile growing on her lips without effort. "We will be. God will carry us through."

Together, they turned toward home.

KIM VOGEL SAWYER,

Kim Vogel Sawyer, a Kansas resident, is a wife, mother, grandmother, teacher, writer, speaker, and lover of cats and chocolate. From the time she was a very little girl, she knew she wanted to be a writer, and seeing her words in print is the culmination of a lifelong dream. Kim relishes her time with family and friends, and stays active in her church by teaching adult Sunday school, singing in the choir, and being a "ding-a-ling" (playing in the bell choir). In her spare time, she enjoys drama, quilting, and calligraphy.

A Living Doll

by Cathy Marie Hake

Chapter 1

Virginia—January 1941

P aul Kincaid paused outside the sanctuary as the bells pealed an invitation to worship. "Mrs. Ainsley, you've been busy." He smoothly robbed the old woman of the blue-and-lavender-striped afghan she carried and used his other hand to brace her elbow.

She grinned up at him. "Knittin' for Britain."

"This is nice and warm. Someone will be glad to receive it." He patiently helped her up each of the shallow marble steps. Last night's rain had left them slick, and he didn't want her to take a tumble.

"It breaks my heart," she murmured, "thinking of those poor folks over in England, doing without."

Beneath his fingers, her coat was threadbare. The contrast between her thin, old coat and the thick, soft afghan bothered him. She'd spent money she could ill afford on yarn. "I can't knit, Mrs. Ainsley. What if I donate some yarn?"

"Why, that's a generous idea!"

"I'll need specifics—or better yet, why don't you tell Abel Nannington what you'd like?" Paul opened the church's heavy oak door and helped her across the threshold. "He can deliver it with your groceries this week."

"Yes, yes, we could do that."

Paul escorted her over to the donation box. The women of Gethsemane Chapel had been busy; dozens of multicolored afghans spilled over the brim. *Mrs. Ainsley ought to have the joy of adding hers on top,* Paul thought. He handed the afghan to her, glanced up, and did a double take.

Rosemary Fulton walked by. This time it wasn't her stunning Nordic blond hair or serene smile that captured his attention. The basket on her arm did. In that moment, Paul felt a bolt of sheer relief. *God, is that Your answer to the problem?*

He slid into a pew and tried to still his thoughts and prepare his heart for the message. As the congregation worshiped, the Lord seemed to be speaking directly to him. They sang "A Charge to Keep I Have," and Rosemary Fulton's grown daughter sang the solo "Children of the Heavenly Father."

Pastor Smith took his place at the pulpit. "Today's scripture begins in Exodus two, beginning at verse six. 'And when she had opened it, she saw the child: and, behold, the babe wept. And she had compassion on him, and said, This is one of the Hebrews' children.' "

Carefully, precisely, Paul moved the black silk ribbon marker in his Bible to that page. God's will was clear to him.

◆   ◆   ◆

"Mr. Kincaid. What a surprise." Rosemary wiped her hands on the hem of her apron and wondered why Paul Kincaid had come calling. They'd exchanged social pleasantries at church; stood side by side in the kitchen, serving the church Thanks-giving meal; and occasionally bumped into each other around town, but here he stood on her doorstep, hat in hand as a show of respect. The chilly breeze ruffled his thick, tawny hair. "Please, come in."

"Thank you. I'll only be a minute."

She inched back as he stepped across the threshold. Though her daughter often had friends from the youth department come over, it had been years since a mature man had crossed the threshold. Between Mr. Kincaid's impressive height and the spicy scent of his aftershave, she felt engulfed by his masculinity.

"I came to ask about the dolls you had this morning at church."

"Mom," Valerie called, "the chicken!"

"Oh!" Rosemary cast Mr. Kincaid an apologetic look.

"I didn't mean to impose."

"Forgive me." She waved toward the gleaming brass hooks on the wall as she started toward the kitchen. "Please, take off your coat. You're welcome to stay for supper."

A moment later, she turned the golden brown pieces in the frying pan. *These didn't burn. Thank You, Lord!*

No footsteps sounded, but Mr. Kincaid appeared in the kitchen doorway. His Windsor double-breasted, charcoal wool suit accentuated his height and the width of his shoulders. "Something smells wonderful."

"Mom's chicken. It's the best." Valerie sat at the table, mashing potatoes.

"There's plenty." Rosemary turned down the heat. "You're more than welcome to join us."

"Yeah." Valerie bobbed her head. "Have a seat."

He smiled at Valerie. "I enjoyed your solo this morning—your voice is very expressive."

"Thanks."

As he reached to pull out a chair, Rosemary hastily suggested, "How about if you take the chair next to that one? Valerie's ankle—"

"It's just a sprain. I was clumsy," Valerie confessed wryly as Paul's brows raised at the sight of the ice bag on her ankle.

"I'm sure Mr. Kincaid has had his share of sprains, too." Rosemary stirred the green beans, then set another place at the table. "I hope you don't mind. We prefer to eat in here."

He looked around the kitchen, taking in the cheery yellow gingham curtains and white cabinets. His brow lifted as he spied the white ceramic canisters she'd brought from Denmark when she had come here as a bride.

"Your kitchen's cozy. I like it. Do you really keep barley and oatmeal in those?"

The deep green lettering across the front proclaimed what each piece held. *Mel, Sukker, Kaffe, Te, Salt*—he could have guessed those. The other two should have been a mystery. "You speak Danish?"

"Enough to get by." A whimsical smile made him look years younger. "When I was growing up, our housekeeper kept treats in those two canisters."

Rosemary waved her tongs at the canister with *Havregryn* painted on it. "I do keep oatmeal in there."

He pointed toward *Byg*. "And the barley?"

"Cookies." Valerie laughed. "But you're out of luck. I ate the last one yesterday."

He chuckled. "I've been unforgivably rude to pry. Had they been English, I wouldn't have asked. For a moment, I became a boy again."

"It's understandable." Rosemary turned a chicken wing as the pan sizzled. "I keep only mint tea in the tea canister because the fragrance reminds me of my grandmother's house."

When Valerie awkwardly tried to scrape the side of the bowl, he lifted it away from her. "You're at a distinct disadvantage, trying to do this while seated." He proceeded to continue mashing the potatoes, went to the icebox and added a splash of milk, and whipped them to a satisfying texture.

"You know how to make potatoes?" Valerie's voice held the surprise Rosemary felt.

A grin lit his face. "My first father was Swedish and insisted Mom hire a top-notch cook. By staying in the kitchen, I got treats. While I was there, she put me to work."

Rosemary grimaced. "That's a handsome suit. You don't want to get food on it."

"It wouldn't be the first or last time."

Five minutes later, the meal sat on the table. Rosemary didn't know what to think. Paul Kincaid managed to act as if he were part of the family. It boggled her mind how he stepped in, decided what needed to be done, and set to work. After finishing the mashed potatoes, he'd sliced half a loaf of bread. Rosemary couldn't recall the last time a man had asked the blessing at their table, and she gladly accepted his offer to say grace.

Once they started eating, Paul looked at her intently. "Had I known you could cook this well, I might have come asking for dolls months ago!"

She smiled. "Thank you. So you're looking to buy a doll?"

"I'd like several. I'd also like another slice of bread. I haven't had homemade bread for nine years."

"Nine years!" Valerie hurriedly passed the basket to him.

As he helped himself to a slice, he said, "Widowers don't bother to bake. We buy those convenient, already-sliced loaves and make fools of ourselves over fond memories of cookies."

Rosemary shook her head. "I found your memory charming."

Paul pensively spread butter on the bread. "Your dolls are charming."

Rosemary figured he didn't want to discuss having lost his spouse and the odd ways little things could trigger the memories and make the loss feel new all over again. How often had she felt that same way? She took his cue and asked, "Do you have a preference as to the size or hair coloring?"

He shrugged. "A variety—blond, brunette, black-haired. More dark-haired ones, though. The size you had at church today looked perfect."

"Little girls tend to like dollies that look like them. Do you need plaits or short curls?"

He chewed slowly, appreciatively, then swallowed. "A variety. It'll allow me to be flexible."

"Oh. I just assumed they were for a niece or—"

"Well, I do have two nieces; however, they're close to Valerie's age. I have several business associates, and I thought the dolls would be suitable gifts for their children. I'm willing to pay whatever you feel is fair."

"That's very generous of you." Rosemary dabbed the corner of her mouth with her napkin. "I'm more than happy to make them, but if you're in a hurry, girls seem to love Raggedy Ann dolls."

"No, no. I want these all to be homemade. That personal touch is what makes them special. Each should be unique."

"When would you like them, and how many do you need?"

He turned to Valerie. "Will you help your mom?"

Valerie burst out laughing. "Me? Sew? Oh, I'm sorry, Mr. Kincaid, but I'm hopeless if you put a needle in my hands."

"But you can sing. You can't be good at everything." He turned back to Rosemary. "I don't want to pressure you, but I'd love a bunch of them as soon as is reasonable."

"How about a week and a half? I'll have some done, and when you come get them, if you still want more, you can tell me. I'll need to figure out what the cost is since I just used scraps to make the ones for the church nursery." She picked up the platter and passed it to him. "Help yourself to more chicken."

"Thank you, I will." He accepted the plate and forked a crispy thigh onto his plate. Paul said he traveled extensively, acquiring art for museums and private collectors.

"How do you manage to travel now?" Rosemary couldn't fathom how he got around.

"We're not at war, Mom," Valerie said. "We probably won't be, either. The America First group is strong enough to hold us back."

"Even if we aren't, Roosevelt declared us the 'Arsenal of Democracy.' " Rosemary frowned at Paul. "Hasn't that angered Hitler?"

"America's isolationist stance is crumbling." He grimaced. "Entering Nazi-held countries is forbidden now."

Rosemary and Valerie exchanged a baffled look. "Then how do you manage?"

"Sweden is neutral, and Germany needs its iron, so Swedes are the exception. My legal name is actually Lindhagen. Though my stepfather had me informally assume his last name, my citizenship was never altered."

Valerie tilted her head to the side. "So do I call you Mr. Kincaid or Mr. Lindhagen?"

He smiled. "There's less confusion if I go by Kincaid here in the States."

"How often do you go over there?" Valerie's questions echoed what Rosemary wondered. At times, she'd rued Valerie's curiosity and spunk. Today, those qualities were a blessing.

"Quite frequently now. Many private collectors are discreetly selling off things in neutral countries because the Germans are claiming art as war bounty."

"I read it was bad in France." Rosemary's fingers tightened around her cup.

"Hitler has a special task force called the *Einsatzstab*. They're crating up everything they can get their hands on. The Rothschild family alone lost over five thousand works." He paused. "It saddens me to buy family treasures, but on the other hand, I'd rather allow the owners to receive the money and have the artwork end up in a reputable museum."

He cleared his throat. "My apologies. I didn't intend to spoil a pleasant meal with ugly politics."

"Not at all." Rosemary lifted the bowl of potatoes and passed them his way. "Do you favor any particular style of art?"

He set aside the bowl without taking more. "Though the Oriental art has been well received, I lean more toward the European works. Oils, watercolors, sketches, bronzes, icons—" He held both hands wide. "I like it all. Speaking of art, I noticed the picture in your living room as I came in."

Rosemary smiled. "The one of the little girl?"

He nodded.

"Mom loves that picture. Dad bought it for her when they went to Copenhagen," Valerie said.

Paul's eyes lit up. "So it's an original Aigens?"

"Yes. You're welcome to take a closer look."

He let out a throaty laugh. "Now there's a quandary I don't mind: having to choose between the company of two lovely ladies and a tasty meal, or gazing at a fine piece of art." He winked at Valerie. "I'll stay put. The painting will still be there after lunch."

To Rosemary's delight, Valerie laughed. It was a rare sound these days. Her fiancé had gone to Canada, enlisted, and been killed in action. Grief still held Valerie in its grip, so moments like this when she found happiness were particularly precious.

They spent the remainder of the meal in pleasant conversation, then Paul admired the painting before he left. As Rosemary washed the dishes, Valerie eased back into her chair. "It's not fair."

"What's not fair?" Rosemary looked over her shoulder at her daughter.

"He makes better mashed potatoes than I do."

Rosemary moaned dramatically. "And you used my recipe!"

◆　◆　◆

Paul slipped behind the wheel of his Duesenberg and set his hat on the gray mohair seat next to him. He'd hoped to catch Rosemary Fulton right after church, but by the time he arranged a delivery of things to Mrs. Ainsley with Abel Nannington, Mrs. Fulton was gone. A sense of urgency drove him to the door of her stately old home. He hadn't planned to go inside, but her warm smile and the mouthwatering aroma of fried chicken drew him in.

Now he'd return to get the dolls. Last Sunday, Mrs. Fulton had seen him at church and invited him to come for supper on Friday. He'd promptly agreed.

Mrs. Fulton was a widow, but with her daughter at home, there was nothing shady about a gentleman stopping by. He curled his hands around the steering wheel and started down the street.

Truth of the matter was, he'd been watching Rosemary since June. Her nephew, Axel Christiansen, was one of Paul's contacts in Denmark, and he'd requested the favor of knowing if his aunt and cousin were faring well on their own. Even if Axel hadn't asked, Paul would have paid attention to Rosemary. The first time he met her, attraction sparked.

Most women wore stylish full sleeves and French cuffs, but Rosemary wore a white silk blouse with a lace collar. Rich waves rippled her platinum blond hair, framing Delft blue eyes. He thought she looked like an Old Master's painting come to life. Had he not been slated for a mission, he would have asked her to the church's July Fourth picnic.

Other than being home during the holidays, he'd been gone on "business" more often than not. Courting a woman under those circumstances rated impossible. Nonetheless, he'd jockeyed to be next to her to serve turkey at the church's Thanksgiving dinner. He'd learned right away that she was blessed with the gift of works—Rosemary didn't sing solos or chair committees. She was the woman who cooked meals for the new mothers of the congregation, weeded the church rose garden, and replaced the felt in the bottom of the offering plates when it looked worn. Her quiet grace and servant's heart appealed to him.

Only he'd just stepped onto a tightrope. He wanted to get to know her better—much better—but he couldn't be completely honest with her. At least not yet. He hoped she'd forgive him when the time came for him to tell her the full truth.

Chapter 2

Isn't she a charmer?"

Rosemary smiled as Mr. Kincaid pulled the first doll from the wicker basket. "I'm glad you think so."

His large hand dwarfed the doll, and muslin legs flopped on either side of his wrist. He fingered the looping, dark brown yarn curls and grinned. "Some little girl is going to be lucky to get her."

"I made a dozen." She watched as he fiddled with the ruffled apron and reached for another doll. "I didn't know how many—"

"At least one hundred."

His quick answer had her laughing. "I'm glad you like them, but seriously, Mr. Kincaid—"

"It's Paul, and I am serious."

Rosemary sank onto the brown-and-beige-striped chesterfield and blinked. "You really are sincere, aren't you?"

He pulled a few more dolls from the basket and stuck them on his forearm as if they were riding a toboggan. All of them leaned into his chest, but he added yet another. "I'll break hearts if I don't have enough."

"But one hundred?"

He gave her a patient smile.

"I never thought there were that many art dealers."

"There aren't. It is a small circle, but as such, it's good form for me to know about my associates' families. It would be novel for me to give gifts for their daughters and granddaughters. A doting grandfather, seeing all of his granddaughters playing with the dolls I gave them, is more likely to think of me when a work of art becomes available. Surely you can see it's good business."

"So you've given gifts before?"

"You'd be amazed at some of the things I've given as gifts." He flashed her a smile. "A couple of years ago, I had a collector strike a bargain with me, and the thing that motivated him was the Monopoly game he learned I was giving to my associates."

Laughter bubbled out of her.

"Duncan yo-yos are great, too. They take up very little space in my attaché case."

"You can't mean to carry dolls in your attaché case!"

157

"Why not?" He rubbed his thumb over a mop of yarn hair. "Most will be in a crate, but I'll keep a few with me. No one will think anything of it. Art dealers put a single etching inside a huge container. I've carried containers the size of your wood box that held a carving smaller than my hand. In their own way, your dolls are each a work of art."

"That's quite a compliment."

"An honest one." He studied them. "No two are alike."

"You said you wanted them to be unique. I used four different patterns."

He slid the dolls onto the coffee table and added the last few. Tilting his head to the side, he pursed his lips. "This one—" He lifted the one with inky braids that had been her favorite of the bunch. White eyelet pantalets peeped from beneath a pink-and-white-striped seersucker dress. "Was she hard to make?"

"Actually, she's the easiest pattern of them all. The one in the blue plissé was the hardest."

His mouth twisted wryly. "Plissé?"

"The light blue on your left." Rosemary winced at the memory of having to restitch the seam at the top to catch all of the hair. She'd taken it out three times before it was right. "If you truly want lots of them, that model will slow me down. Of course, I can ask a few women to help me."

"No." His chin came up. "I want them all by you. These are special, and I can give them with the assurance that you'll make each one so she'll hold together. I know they'll be cherished, so they have to be well made."

"I suppose since your contacts are accustomed to quality art, they'll be particular." She looked at the rag babies. "I used everyday fabrics—organdy, gingham, calico. Should I be using silk or rayon?"

"I've never had children, but it seems to me if a doll is dressed in silk, she'll sit on a shelf instead of being played with. The endearing part of your dolls is they are made to be cuddled and dragged around."

"Valerie had one of those." She smoothed her skirt and confessed, "As did I. Mine was dressed just like the one you chose."

"Do you want to keep her for yourself?"

Shaking her head, Rosemary stood up. "I had my fun making her. Let some little girl enjoy her. Pardon me. I need to go check on supper."

He'd come to his feet the moment she rose. Paul's impeccable manners made her feel special.

"I'd like to help. What can I do?"

"Nothing, really. I have a roast in the oven. I'll just make some gravy."

He followed her into the kitchen and grabbed the hot pan holders from her, then opened the oven. "Is your brown gravy as good as that chicken gravy you made the last time I was here?"

"Better," Valerie said as she finished setting the table. "Would you like coffee or tea with your supper, Mr. Kincaid?"

◆   ◆   ◆

As meals went, it was plentiful, but that was all Rosemary remembered about the food. Seven years of widowhood had left her accustomed to living without a man, but she still felt the loss of masculine presence, strength, and support. Paul Kincaid filled her home with all of those qualities, and she couldn't shake the sense of rightness and balance.

He entertained them with tales about some of his travels. Humor and intelligence sparkled in his stories. Just as important, he proved to be an apt listener. Rich, deep laughter rolled out of him when Valerie told them about the crazy customer she'd had at the bank that afternoon.

After taking a final sip of his after-dinner coffee, Paul methodically rolled up his sleeves, baring strong forearms. "I'll wash the dishes."

"Oh, no." Rosemary gasped. "That's not necessary at all. Valerie and I—"

"Valerie needs to rest her ankle. She's been on her feet all day."

"Actually, I was sitting." Valerie propped her elbow on the table and rested her chin in her palm. She looked thoroughly entertained by this turn of events.

"Good. We want her to heal completely, don't we?" Paul started running water in the sink and added Palmolive. As the bubbles started to pile up, he asked, "What time is it?"

Rosemary glanced at the clock. "Just after seven."

"Great. The Tommy Dorsey Orchestra comes on now. How about if Valerie tunes in some music for us?"

Valerie fiddled with the dials on the Zenith console. After a Nature's Remedy ad, strains of Frank Sinatra singing "I'll Never Smile Again" filled the air. Paul scrubbed dishes in time to the music and occasionally whistled a few bars.

Rosemary rinsed and dried the dishes. Each time she stepped from the cupboard back to the sink, confusion crackled through her. Even when her husband was living, he'd not done dishes. The coziness of sharing such a mundane task was unmistakable but wholly innocent. It felt so good to have Paul there—in their kitchen, by her side. He just seemed to fit.

Lord, don't let me make a fool of myself. Occasional company for a business dealing— that's what this is. Help me to guard my heart and tongue.

His soapy hand brushed hers as he plunged the roasting pan into the rinse water. She shivered.

"Chilly?" He swiped the dish towel from her. "Grab a sweater. We're done in here, and we still need to firm up a schedule and costs."

Rosemary didn't argue. She needed a moment to gather her wits.

"I've been thinking," Paul said as they walked into the living room after she donned her sweater. "The doll that was hard to make—forget making more of her. In fact, you can just stick to the one pattern that you said was the easiest if you'd like."

"I can still dress them differently and embroider different expressions on them."

159

"Great." He stood in front of the Aigens painting again. "I've seen several of his paintings. He's particularly good with children's portraits. Do you have any idea who the little girl is?"

"None at all." Rosemary smiled. "There's just something so sweet about the way she's nestled into that window seat, looking at the bluebird."

"It's unusual for him to paint a portrait in profile. It adds to the allure of the piece." He turned around. "What kind of sewing machine do you have?"

The change of topic took Rosemary by surprise. She stammered, "Singer."

"Is it a new electric one, or one of the old treadle ones?"

"I have both."

He nodded. "I couldn't imagine you making so many dolls with an old one. You'd wear yourself out. I'm assuming you've calculated the cost of material. What's a fair price for the dolls?"

She crossed the richly colored Aubusson carpet and opened the drop desk front of the antique oak secretary. Handing him the slip of paper, she said, "I made a list of the yardage and costs. I can get two dolls from a yard of muslin, so that's four cents apiece. It depends on which fabrics you want for the clothing."

"I know what gingham is, but the rest of this. . ." He hitched his shoulder. "Plissé didn't make sense to me, and neither do challis, batiste, or percale." Studying the page, he mused, "It's all in a similar range. A few pennies here or there don't make much difference when you can get this many outfits per yard."

"Gingham is sixteen cents—the other is far less."

"Nine to eleven cents?" He chuckled. "I'm not going to quibble about a penny per doll, Mrs. Fulton. Put together whatever fabrics you think a little girl would like."

She'd carefully put everything on the ledger—the embroidery floss, yarn, thread, and cotton stuffing. It would cost about seven cents per doll.

"You don't have a figure here for your labor." He looked at her expectantly.

"I don't know how to do that." She lifted her hands in a gesture of helplessness. "I enjoy sewing. As a banker, my late husband provided well for us. Valerie and I live quite comfortably."

"How long does it take to make one doll?"

"I'm not sure. I cut them out and sew them like a Ford production line."

His dark eyes glimmered. "The average man earns about two thousand dollars a year. I'll pay you. . .fifty dollars a week."

"Mr. Kincaid! Minimum wage is thirty cents an hour for a man. That's far too much, and I'm not sure I want to be chained to my sewing machine."

"You won't be chained to your sewing machine. I'd want you to feel free to have luncheons with your friends and help out at the church and such. As for pay—you're working as an artisan, so that's worth more."

"I always heard artists were supposed to be starving."

He swept up an armload of her dolls. "But those artists don't know me!"

◆　◆　◆

Paul adjusted the light and carefully wrapped the glittering ruby in a section of a handkerchief he'd torn off. He'd bought a dozen handkerchiefs Thursday at Nannington's with the grand hope of needing to buy many, many more. Nannington had been busy relating how pleased old Mrs. Ainsley had been when she'd found the coat Paul bought for her at the bottom of the basket of yarn, but Paul wouldn't chance buying more handkerchiefs there. No detail was too small to ignore.

Tucking the wrapped gem into the doll's head wasn't all that easy, considering how small he'd made the opening and how wide his fingers were. Still, if he opened the seam any farther, it would mess up her yarn hair and draw attention to the stitching. After poking in a tiny wad of cotton batting over the gem, Paul pinched together the gaping inch and painstakingly sewed it back together.

This was the last one. He'd been up all night finishing the task. Every poke of the needle felt awkward. Perhaps he could have Rosemary show him how to sew . . .maybe if he took a shirt that needed mending, that would provide a good excuse to spend more time with her. He'd been coming up with all sorts of reasons he should drop by. The initial attraction he'd felt for her had grown each time they were together.

"Ouch." Jerking back, he glowered at the drop of blood on his fingertip and knew he needed to concentrate on finishing with this batch without bleeding all over it. As he wiped away the blood, he couldn't take his mind off of Rosemary. She'd worked hard to get the dolls done just in time.

He'd set sail at noon today to obtain an Abildgaard oil for a private gallery. That provided his cover for the trip. Once done with that, as a Swede on business, Paul Lindhagen would slip over to Denmark.

It was there Paul would drop off the dolls.

He'd served in the navy and knew his knots. A figure-eight knot seemed to work well, but the thin thread might still slip through the weave of the fabric, so he repeated another figure eight, then snipped the thread.

He picked her up and examined his handiwork. "Ah, sweetheart, I have big plans for you."

Chapter 3

The voyage to Sweden was uneventful, and the small case of dolls didn't raise any eyebrows. The same customs official examined Paul's belongings on the next trip three weeks later. He opened the much larger crate of dolls and commented, "Someone must have liked your samples last time."

Paul accepted his stamped passport and nodded. "I'd like to see them do well. A widow makes the dolls."

He smiled as he thought of Rosemary. There hadn't been any reason for him to see her other than to pick up the dolls, but he'd been drawn to her serenity and warmth. His working world was full of darkness; Rosemary was a beacon of light. During his time in Virginia, he found himself making excuses to go see her. He'd bought yarn and delivered some to old Mrs. Ainsley and dropped off the rest for Rosemary's rag dolls. Twice, he went over for Sunday supper.

Rosemary couldn't bear to just sit at her table and allow him to fix the second meal. They'd enjoyed puttering around in the kitchen together and took a refreshing walk after cleaning up. They'd spoken about all sorts of things—surviving the loss of a beloved mate, current events, her antics of having learned to drive her husband's old Pierce-Arrow. He took that opening and invited her to drive them both to a small art exhibit that weekend. Their date went smoothly. She happened to mention she hadn't read *Grapes of Wrath*, so he used that as justification to stop by later in the week to lend her his copy.

"Ahh." The customs official drew out the sound and waggled his brow. "So the widow—she is pretty?"

"Beautiful." Paul shoved his papers into a coat pocket. "I'd like to take her a gift. Is there a jeweler you recommend?"

Early the next morning with his Swedish passport that identified him as Herr Lindhagen, Paul boarded a small Swedish vessel bound for Denmark. Danish fishing vessels were out, but the Germans made their presence felt. Paul minded his own business and exchanged a few desultory comments with a *Wehrmacht* officer just before they reached shore. *Lord, thank You for Your mercy and protection. Bless this trip, Father. Let it be successful so we can rescue innocents in Your name.*

Not long thereafter, Paul delivered the crate to Axel, just as he had the first. They stood in the backroom of Christiansen Enterprises in Copenhagen and exchanged all but ten of the dolls for a watercolor and two antique miniatures. Those miniatures would provide Paul's *raison d'être* for being in Holland. The Germans had invaded and were starting to round up Dutch Jews. Greedy Nazi officials looted each country of art. Surely these pieces would allow Paul access to the "right" people.

He already had contacts in Germany, Holland, and France—some because of his previous trips, but others courtesy of his friend "Wild Bill" Donovan. If Bill weren't so incredibly patriotic and bright, he'd be downright unnerving. He'd approved the concept of the dolls, though. In fact, he'd managed to slip Paul several *reichsmarks* and loose gems to put inside them.

A small, highly secret cell of people had formed and resolved to do their utmost to ransom the Jewish children. Paul played a pivotal role. The booming gray market in fine art provided an ideal cover.

If Germans looked at his papers and searched his luggage, they were welcome to confiscate the art pieces he would be dealing. The dolls would hide in plain sight.

Axel boxed his share of the dolls into two smaller crates. "I'll make a receipt for these just as I did the last time. That way, it'll be on a manifest so you can deliver more in person or have them shipped with us. We've already showed the import was established, and I'll be able to point out that with the effort going toward agriculture and munitions, the poor children won't receive toys if my business doesn't import them."

"Good." Paul glanced around and asked softly in Swedish, "How many children do you think your network can smuggle?"

"Several families in our church have already taken in children. Can you bring film?"

"Here." Paul pulled three rolls from his suitcase. He'd brought them with the expectation that they'd be used in forging identity papers. Denmark was starting to form an underground and would require far more than those three rolls as time passed. "Next trip, I'll bring more. Anything else you need?"

"I want my sister to go back to America. She refuses and says her place is here with me and our grandmother. Could you talk sense into both of them? Aunt Rosemary has more than enough room to put them up."

Someone entered the warehouse. Paul hadn't heard any footsteps, but the hairs on the back of his neck prickled. He stuck out his hand. "It's a pleasure, Mr. Christiansen. I'd be happy to see those watercolors."

Axel shook his hand. "It's very exciting news." He turned and gave an excellent imitation of surprise. "Herr Torwald! What can I do for you this fine day?"

The pinch-faced man approached. He lowered his voice, "I saw the American come here. I came to beg a favor."

"I'm afraid you're mistaken," Paul said in flawless Swedish. "But I won't take offense that you mistook me for one of them. I couldn't resist buying a new overcoat the last time I went to New York."

Herr Torwald grabbed the sleeve of Paul's suit. "I have a nephew. He's eight."

"You must be proud." Paul shrugged away and pretended not to understand the request to smuggle the boy out of Denmark. He sensed this was a trap. "But I am confused by your request. I don't paint portraits—I am an art dealer."

"Mr. Lindhagen knows my Aunt Rosemary in America. She told him about the watercolors in my grandmother's home." Axel beamed. "He's going to come examine them."

Paul held up a hand. "Now, don't get too excited, Mr. Christiansen. They might not be anything at all. I wouldn't want you to be disappointed."

"Oh, but they're from the same set." Axel bobbed his head. "Aunt Rosemary has the winter field. My mother had the summer scene, and when she came back, my sister brought it along. Spring and autumn were still on the wall, and Grams hung summer back between them."

"America's National Gallery of Art is due to open in March. It would be quite a feather in my cap to buy—"

"Americans," Herr Torwald spat. "They think they can buy anything. And you Swedes—you're growing fat, living off both sides of this war." He glowered, then slowly shuffled off.

Axel cleared his throat. "My apologies, Herr Lindhagen. Desperation leads people to grasp at straws. Shall we go? You must stay to supper. Grams is a wonderful cook."

"I'd be honored."

They walked out of the warehouse, and Axel locked the doors. "I'm able to offer you a ride. The Germans allow me to keep a vehicle since my business helps provide well for the region." He got into the car and muttered under his breath, "I want my sister out of here. This place is overrun with spies."

"You threw him off with the talk about the pictures. If you have watercolors and paper, I'll do a quick set to back up your story."

Axel cast him a sly smile. "I was telling the truth. You're about to stumble onto a treasure."

Paul shook his head in disbelief and chuckled. He took a deep breath. "Actually, I already found a treasure. I wanted to tell you: I've started courting your aunt and intend to marry her."

◆　◆　◆

"There you are." Rosemary walked into the living room and waved toward the basket. A sense of sadness swamped her. How quickly she'd come to anticipate Paul's visits! His intelligent conversation, witty insights, and warmth lingered after his visits. She didn't want this to be the end of their times together, but nothing was more pathetic than a lonely widow chasing after a man. She pasted on a perky smile. "That's the last of the dolls."

Paul let out a crack of a laugh, but it died quickly. "I hope that was an April Fool's joke."

"You said you wanted one hundred dolls." Slowly sitting by the basket, she lifted one and smoothed its sunny yellow skirt.

"That was just the first order." Paul sat down and gave her a patient look. "Those little rag babies are the rage. If anything, I need more, faster."

"Surely you can't have that many associates!"

"I have a special associate." He leaned forward. "Axel Christiansen."

"Axel!" Rosemary nearly dropped the doll. "You know my nephew?"

"I do." Paul patted the striped cushion of the chesterfield in silent invitation.

Rosemary hastened to his side and pled as she took a seat, "How do you know him? I can't believe this!"

"Since he's in the import-export business, he's been of help to me at times in following proper protocol. I've found him to be well informed about all of the increasingly stringent rules."

"Yes, that sounds like Axel. How is he? Is he well? I haven't seen him in almost five years! Letters—they don't come through well anymore."

"Yes, he's well. I have letters for you from him, from your niece, and one from your mother." He drew an envelope from the inside pocket of his suit coat.

"Oh, Paul! You can't know how much this means to me!"

He slipped the crinkled envelope into her hands. "Please don't wait to read them. Axel told me how he and his sister lived with you."

She bobbed her head and tore the envelope in her haste. "Yes. They're such good children." She let out a nervous laugh. "I guess they're not children anymore. Axel went back to take care of the family business after my papa died. . . ."

Her voice died out as she unfolded the pages and began to read. Tears misted her eyes as she saw her mother's handwriting. Paul slid his arm around her shoulder and drew her into his sheltering strength. His other hand pressed a crisp, white handkerchief into her lap.

Rosemary hungrily read each letter, then reread them. "They sound okay. Are they really safe?" She looked up at Paul.

"Axel looks strong and well fed. He wants more of your dolls to sell."

"I'll make as many as he wants. Can I send letters back with you when you deliver them?"

"Absolutely. Rosemary, even if he didn't want another doll, I'd still like to spend time with you." He tenderly cupped her cheek. "You're becoming very special to me."

Chapter 4

Rosemary looked into Paul's face. "I care for you, too." Here she'd thought this was the last time he would come to her home, and now he wanted to pursue more than a business association—he wanted to pursue *her!* The very thought made her breathless.

The corners of his eyes crinkled. "I'm out of practice with courting. I've been a widower for a long time."

"I've been a widow for almost as long. Even then—" She laughed. "My first courtship was just two visits and several letters. I'm afraid I'm not just out of practice—I never had much to begin with!"

"We'll just do things our way. How does that sound?"

She smiled. "I'd like that."

"Then it's not bad form for me to ask about how you married someone you barely knew? You led me to believe it was a happy marriage."

Rosemary rested her head on his shoulder. "I was a schoolgirl and thought I knew Lief well. Our families did business together, and we seemed well suited. Now that I look back, I can't imagine what I was thinking. After he made two visits and we exchanged letters for nine months, I came to the States and we married. God looks out for fools and children—and in that instance, I think I was both. Yet it was a good marriage."

"I was in my last year of college. I was so poor, all we did was ice-skate or take walks." He chuckled. "It's a marvel Elsie looked at me twice."

"Not at all. Simple pleasures are the best. That time together let her see how smart and fun you are."

"If you keep complimenting me like that," he said, his voice deepening, "I'll be tempted to kiss you."

Rosemary gasped—as much from her reaction as from his comment. She wanted him to kiss her!

"I know," he sighed. "It's far too soon. You'll have to forgive me for forgetting to bring flowers."

"You brought me something much better."

"The letters?"

They crinkled in her hand. "I forgot about them. I was just glad you came home. I worried about your safety while you were gone."

"Mom!"

Rosemary jumped and looked up. Valerie stood in the doorway, eyes wide with shock. At that moment, Rosemary realized just how close she'd managed to cuddle into Paul's side.

"Mom—" Valerie stared at the wet handkerchief. "You've been crying?"

Rosemary let out a watery laugh. "I'm happy, honey."

Valerie crossed the floor and shot a wary look at Paul.

Paul didn't seem bothered in the least. To Rosemary's surprise, he curled his arm a bit more. "Valerie, I'd like to speak with you for a moment, too."

Valerie perched on the edge of the overstuffed armchair. "What is it?"

"Being away made me realize how much I enjoy your mother's company. We're adults and can make our own decisions, and I've prayed about it. I feel the Lord has brought us together, but I'd also like to ask your blessing as we court."

"It's about time." Valerie grinned at them.

Rosemary felt as if a weight had lifted from her shoulders. Even though Valerie was nursing a broken heart, she was generous enough to wish them well. "Thank you, honey."

Paul let out a relieved sigh. "Good."

"So why were you crying?"

"Oh! I forgot!" Rosemary held out the pages. "You'll never guess who Paul knows—Axel! He brought letters!"

"Wow!" Valerie hopped up and grabbed them. She promptly plopped back down sideways in the chair, with her legs dangling over the arm.

Rosemary winced at the sight.

Paul dipped his head and whispered, "Don't. I'm glad she's that comfortable with me around."

A few minutes later, Valerie looked up. "It sounds like they're okay and Annelise is finally over that guy. Thanks for bringing the letters, Mr. Kincaid."

"You're welcome. So now that I'm courting your mom, do you think you could stop calling me Mr. Kincaid like I'm some old grandpa?"

"Just how old are you?"

"Valerie!" Rosemary couldn't believe her daughter's nerve.

Paul chuckled. "I'm forty." He squeezed Rosemary. "It was a reasonable question."

"Since you don't mind questions. . ."

Unsure what her daughter would ask next, Rosemary cringed.

"Yes?" Paul sounded downright blasé.

"What did you do to the mashed potatoes? Mom and I are dying to know."

"It's an old family secret." He pressed a kiss against Rosemary's temple. "Someday, I might have to share it."

◆　◆　◆

Paul shuffled across the linoleum floor along with the beat of "Chattanooga Choo Choo," which played on the Zenith. Washing his hands at Rosemary's kitchen sink, he said, "You're low on oil, and the tires look a bit worn."

Rosemary set down her shears and frowned. "I just bought those tires last year."

"It's not bad at all. They could last awhile yet." He opened the *Byg* canister and helped himself to an oatmeal cookie. That momentary delay allowed him to weigh his words carefully. "I think it would be wise to buy a set now."

"Surely you don't think there'll be a shortage of rubber?" Rosemary picked up her shears again and started cutting more doll parts from the muslin spread across the kitchen table.

"I'd feel better knowing you and Valerie had them in reserve. The rest of the world is suffering from shortages of several things. I don't advocate stockpiling, but since we know you'll need the tires, it's smart to anticipate. I'll pick them up tomorrow."

"If it makes you feel better."

"It does."

"Father McCoughlin was speaking on the radio. He said Roosevelt is wrong and we have no business getting drawn into Europe's war. Even Charles Lindbergh is part of the America First movement. With so many opposed, how do you think America could come to the point of being so involved with what's going on over there that we'd find it difficult to get basic supplies here?"

"With Roosevelt passing the Lend-Lease Act, we're using resources differently, sweetheart. We're bound to see some changes."

"Not like Europe, though. The news said Holland is rationing milk! Can you believe it? Those poor children."

Paul didn't want to tell her it would get much worse. From what he'd seen on his last trip, the Nazi war machine was systematically stripping the countries of their resources. Instead, he reached over and picked up a thin strip of material that ended with a mitt shape. *The arm.* "You're doing something for the children, Rosemary."

"It feels like precious little. Paul, I want to show you something." She left the kitchen and returned with a magazine. "What do you think?"

The words *Jewish Crisis* jumped out at him as he accepted the magazine. The profile of a mother and little boy on the cover made his heart twist.

"It's from 1938." Rosemary's voice shook. "And it talks about the persecution of the Jews in Germany. It says we need to worry that it'll cross the Atlantic."

"I've read similar things. The stories of what's happening over there are true, sweetheart. It's not just Germany. Poland, Bulgaria, France, Holland, Romania—nearly every country the Reich invades develops a policy of mistreating the Jews."

"So it's not just a bunch of lies to try to rope us into the war?"

He said very quietly, "It's the truth."

Tears filled her eyes. She swiped the material into a heap on the table. "What good is this?"

Paul reached across and tilted her face to his. If only he could tell her the truth about how her dolls would save little children—but he couldn't. It wasn't safe. "Sweetheart, children over there don't have toys. Having something to cuddle matters a lot to those little girls."

The door opened, and Valerie swirled in with the spring wind. "I'm back! Mrs. Ainsley said—whoops!" She halted abruptly and shot her mother a guilty look.

Paul regretted only telling a thin slice of the truth, and he was relieved the conversation had been interrupted. He broke contact with Rosemary and folded his arms across his chest. "What did Mrs. Ainsley say?"

Valerie blushed. "It was nothing."

Rosemary laughed. "It's okay, honey." She turned to Paul. "We gave Mrs. Ainsley a kitten to keep her company, so Valerie takes fish to her a couple times a week."

"Fish for Mrs. Ainsley, or fish for the cat?" Paul was sure of the answer, but he wanted Rosemary to know he was on to her.

"You have no room to grin, Paul Kincaid!" Valerie's chin tilted at a challenging level. "Mom and I both know who bought her that nice coat she's been wearing."

Paul pretended not to hear her. "Mrs. Ainsley's not very spry. I don't suppose you'd know who planted all those bulbs that are sprouting in her garden."

Rosemary laughed, and Valerie's cheeks went pinker. She couldn't meet his eyes and suddenly exclaimed, "Oh, I smell something wonderful!"

"Paul's cooking Swedish beef stew." Rosemary played along with the change in subject and wrinkled her nose. "I don't remember the name. It sounded like *Cyclops.*"

Paul chortled. *"Kalops."*

"Whew. I was afraid you were going to feed me eyeball soup." Valerie finessed the radio dial. Bebop filled the air. "Much better."

"Dizzy Gillespie." Paul nodded. "Great jazz player."

"I like Thelonious Monk better." Just then, the music stopped and an update came across the air about the Canadians pulling American planes across the border that had been provided through the Lend-Lease arrangement. Valerie's smile faded. She turned off the radio, then pointed at the magazine on the table. "No matter where I go, I can't get away from that war."

"Honey. . ."

Valerie held up a hand. "Don't tell me you're sorry. I'm tired of everyone giving me sympathy. Words won't bring back Frank. We're all sending Bundles for Britain and acting as if all they're getting from us is soap, medicine, and blankets. The truth is, lots of American boys like Frank are going over there and joining their army, and Britain doesn't even bundle them back to us for a decent burial! All those mothers from America First went and knelt in prayer by the Capitol building. Instead of old women, maybe it should have been girls like me.

Then maybe everyone would see what wars really cost—bridegrooms, young husbands, and babies' fathers!" She ran from the room.

A door slammed shut, but it couldn't completely muffle her sobs. Rosemary buried her face in her hands. "We're only making it worse, you know."

Paul pulled her from her chair and enveloped her in his arms. "You and I understand grief. She's right—no matter where she turns, she's surrounded by reminders. We'll just love her through the sorrow."

Rosemary wound her arms around his waist and rested her cheek on his lapel. "She really does like you."

"Yeah, I'm pretty crazy about her. You. . .well, you, I'm wild about." He threaded his hands through her silky hair. "I never thought I'd fall in love again, but I have. I'll just pray God will bless her as generously as He's blessed me."

Chapter 5

R osemary let out a small, disappointed sigh as she looked in the butcher's case. "Better just make it the roast closest to the back."

Mr. Twisselman bobbed his bald head in understanding as he pulled out a tiny one and thumped it onto his scale. "Two pounds even. If Mr. Kincaid were in town, you would have gotten one twice this size."

Rosemary let out a small laugh. Her courtship had become cause for comment around town. The butcher's observation was right, and she enjoyed the fact that Paul shared supper with her and Valerie more often than not when he was in town. Because she tended to shun the limelight, the attention others cast on her on such occasions left her feeling a bit self-conscious. Having Paul in her life more than made up for such fleeting moments.

Mr. Twisselman's mustache twitched as he wrapped the roast in white, waxed butcher paper. "Mr. Kincaid seems like a nice man. He can pick out a good cut of meat, too. Not often you find a man who can do that."

Understanding that was high praise, Rosemary nodded. "He makes a great stew. The bacon looks nice and lean. I'd like a half pound, please."

"As much Spam as is being sent in Bundles for Britain," he said as he took a handful of rashers and flipped them onto the scale, "you'd think there wouldn't be an ounce of pork left in these United States!"

"I saw those striped quilts Nelly and Wanda made for the bundles. They reminded me of Joseph's coat of many colors." Rosemary watched as he added two more rashers.

My life is like one of those colorful quilts. I thought all I had left were worn scraps, but God brought color and texture back by bringing Paul into my life. There's so much more warmth and purpose.

"Yeah, Bundles for Britain keeps my girls busy," Mr. Twisselman said, oblivious to Rosemary's musings. "Today Wanda's making a baby blanket, though. Marcy Heath had her baby."

"I hadn't heard the news!"

"A boy." He puffed up as if the baby were his own. "Tipped the scale at eight pounds."

"Eight!"

"Yep. Hospital-born, no less!"

"Well then, I won't buy a chicken to roast for them until next Wednesday. The hospital will keep her for a week, you know." She decided she'd go home, gather flowers from her garden, and pay the new mother and baby a visit this afternoon, though. Paul had helped her cultivate the soil for her flower and vegetable gardens. They'd gotten dirty as could be that day. On the days he was so far away, she still found comfort in walking barefoot where he'd worked.

"Anything else today? Ground beef's on sale."

"Oh." She snapped out of that fleeting memory. "What kind of fish do you have?"

"Mrs. Ainsley was just in." He winked. "She bought some snapper for the cat already."

Rosemary sighed. "Then I don't need anything else today."

"Paul Kincaid better get back soon." The butcher wedged himself behind the register. "Seems to me a certain lady gets mighty lonesome when he's gone."

"The cure for loneliness is hard work. This woman needs to occupy herself instead of mooning around. Nothing's more useless than a lady who sits and pines for a man." She glanced out the window, then sighed again. "But I'm antsy. Since Paul left, the Germans sank the *Robin Moore*."

"Roosevelt declared a state of emergency. Ships are being careful, and the navy's on alert. Don't worry. Paul will make it home in one piece."

"That's my prayer," she said softly.

"That's $1.59." Mr. Twisselman accepted her money and grinned. "Absence makes the heart grow fonder, Rosemary. A little pining's not bad."

She nodded and left. Truth be told, she kept her hands busy. . .but Paul kept her heart and mind tied up in knots.

◆　◆　◆

Paul spied the Nazi officer and continued to walk through the door of Christiansen Enterprises. As Paul Lindhagen, he had every reason to come here. Balking at the sight of a German would ruin his cover. Instead, he cleared his throat. "Mr. Christiansen, if this is an inopportune time, I can return."

"No, not at all." Axel motioned urbanely toward the Nazi. "May I introduce Captain von Rundstedt. Captain, this is Herr Lindhagen, an art dealer."

"Herr Lindhagen." The captain nodded his head curtly and studied Paul closely. "What business does an art dealer have with an import-export enterprise?"

Paul made a vague gesture. "You know how it is. Times change. We all adapt as necessary. Of course, the fact that a pretty widow makes dolls I can import is good motive."

"Dolls?"

Axel chuckled. "Yes. I'll have to show them to you. The fact is, the lady in question is my aunt."

"Ahh, I see."

"Speaking of her, your aunt sent you a gift." By openly setting out the bulky package, it made everything look perfectly innocent. Had Paul waffled or tried to hide the package, the officer would have become suspicious.

"A gift? How thoughtful of her." Axel smoothly set the package aside.

"Do not let our presence hold you back." The Nazi motioned toward the bundle. "By all means, open it."

"Thank you." Axel promptly tore through the brown paper. "A camera and film—oh, my!" He shuffled through a half dozen photographs with notable glee. "Pictures of Aunt Rosemary and my cousin Valerie."

"*Sehr schon,*" the captain said.

Axel chuckled. "The gift is very beautiful, or my aunt and cousin?"

"The ladies are both very beautiful. The Aryan ancestry is much evident in the coloring and features. Why do they not live here, with you?"

"Rosemary met her husband in Sweden."

Paul patted himself on the chest. "And if things continue to go well between us, her next husband is Swedish, too."

Axel straightened his shoulders and extended his hand. "Congratulations. Rosemary is a wonderful woman. I approve."

"Thank you." Paul shook Axel's hand.

"So the camera is Swedish, *ja?*" The captain picked up the camera and read the label. "Hessco Model B. The camera is known to me. I personally prefer my Swiss-made Jaeger. It is clever because it can take both glass plates and rolls of film."

Paul nodded. "In my travels, I'll be passing through Switzerland. If you have need of plates or film, I'd be happy to keep an eye out for some."

"So you are a *resourceful* fellow."

Paul shrugged. "It is a small matter. Axel, your aunt expects pictures of you and your family in return. Don't forget. She'll be upset if I go home without them."

"We'll take pictures tomorrow morning. I can just send the film back with you then. You must come to supper and tell Grams the good news. Captain, would you care to join us?"

For a moment, it looked as if the captain planned to agree. Then he shook his head. "I have other obligations."

"Perhaps some other time."

"Yes, another time. Herr Christiansen, Herr Lindhagen. Heil Hitler." He marched toward the office door.

Axel pulled out a ledger book. "Let me find that account here. . . . How many dolls did you bring this time?"

"Fifty. I plan to take a few with me as gifts for my clients, though."

The captain turned around. "I should like to see these dolls."

Chapter 6

P aul pried the lid off the crate as Captain von Rundstedt leafed through the paperwork. The captain set the sheaf of pages off to the side with a decisive shove. "The stamps on the forms are in order."

"Naturally." Paul pulled out several dolls. "Here we are."

The captain pulled two from his arms and tossed them back into the crate. "Dark hair does not appeal to me."

"How many would you like?" Axel's voice took on the schmoozing tone of a businessman.

"One. I have a niece."

Paul didn't so much as blink an eye. The whole rescue operation would be destroyed if this went poorly. He'd planned for such an eventuality, though. A few dolls of each shipment didn't have gold or a gem inside them. He purposefully chose blond, blue-eyed dolls and exchanged their clothing so they wore red, white, and black—the colors of the Third Reich. Those dolls would serve as bribes for any German who got too nosy.

"The flowered dress—it is something a girl would like." The captain started to stuff the bribe doll back into the crate.

"I agree." Paul moved to throw the last two in his arm into the crate as well. "This pale blue—that color doesn't catch the eye, even if her face is sweet. There is something cheerful about this one, though."

Axel chuckled. "She reminds me of Annelise playing Little Red Riding Hood. All she needs is a cape."

"That story is in a book I bought for my niece." The captain took the doll. He nodded decisively. "*Ja*. She is the one."

"Take her as a gift." Axel smiled.

The captain left, and Axel tugged out a few dolls. "How many do you need to take?"

"Make it a half dozen. Give me another red dress. The Red Riding Hood angle was great."

"I have no idea what made me say that."

"God gave you the words. The minute I saw that Nazi, I prayed for protection. How did we do on the first shipment?"

Axel grinned. "The underground distributed all of the dolls. We were able to

174

forge documents for twelve children. Four are with families here in Denmark—ostensibly they are orphans who came to live with distant relatives. The other eight were taken to safety in Sweden. The second shipment: I don't have all of the information yet. So far, I know two dozen children have gone to safety carrying a rag doll from that group."

"God be praised," Paul said softly as he closed the lid on the crate. "May there be hundreds more."

◆　◆　◆

"Turn down the radio, honey." Rosemary dashed for the phone as Bing Crosby crooned "Only Forever." Breathlessly, she said, "Hello?" into the receiver.

"Hi, sweetheart!"

"Paul! Are you home?"

"Yes. I've been trying to call you all afternoon. The line's always busy."

Rosemary sighed. Most of the families on their party line were considerate, but Myrtle Louis seemed to live on the phone. "It's a problem. I'm sorry."

"It's not your fault. I—"

The line clicked, and Paul stopped speaking. "Hello? Paul?"

"I'm still here. I think we have company."

"I need to use the phone." Myrtle's voice radiated with petulance.

"We just got connected." Rosemary tried to squelch her irritation. "I'm sure you heard the call come through—long and two short rings, which is my signal. You couldn't have mistaken it for your single short ring."

"Well, it's only Paul." Myrtle *tsk*ed. "He's at your house all the time anyway."

Paul cleared his throat. "Ma'am, I'm sure Mrs. Fulton's more than considerate of you when you're on the line."

"Well, I never!" Myrtle slammed down her receiver.

"Never?" Paul snorted. "I have a hard time believing she's never on the phone."

Rosemary sang along with Bing Crosby on the radio as her response, "Only Forever."

A deep, rich chortle came over the line. "I must be crazy to travel. The only thing that makes it worthwhile is coming back to you. Go put on a pretty dress. I'm taking you out to supper tonight."

"We can just eat here, Paul. I'm sure you're tired."

"Nope. I'll be there in an hour." He made a smooching sound and hung up.

"I know that smile," Valerie teased. "It's the Paul's-home-and-I'm-thrilled look."

"He's taking us out to supper."

"Not me. You. Mom, it's a date, not a family meeting! Besides, I have plans." She rubbed her hands together. "So what are you wearing?"

"What about my Easter dress?"

Just shy of an hour later, Rosemary heard Paul's Duesenberg come to a halt outside her house. Whistling Jimmy Dorsey's "Green Eyes," Paul came up the walk.

Rosemary hurriedly latched her pearls and patted them in place. She hoped he'd like her dress. Made of pale green silk, it nipped in at her waist and swirled just an inch and a half below her knees. She'd gotten it for Easter, but he'd been away on business that week. This was only the second time she'd worn it.

As he knocked at the door, Rosemary's heart beat twice as fast. She wanted to run down the stairs and fling herself into his arms like a starstruck teenager. *It's his fault. He makes me feel like a young girl again.* As Valerie greeted him, Rosemary dabbed on a little Evening in Paris perfume. The silk of her dress and stockings whispered as she descended the stairs.

Paul waited at the foot of the stairs. Aware their reunion wasn't private, he pulled Rosemary close and brushed a kiss on her cheek. "You look beautiful, sweetheart."

"Thank you." She straightened his tie. "You look very handsome."

"Mom, I'm going to Angela's."

Rosemary frowned at her daughter. "Not until you change, young lady."

"We're not going anywhere, Mom. This isn't the olden days. There's nothing wrong with wearing slacks."

Paul cleared his throat. "I'm not meaning to horn in here, but even if you don't go anywhere, plenty of people might show up."

"Angela wouldn't do that." Valerie shook her head.

"She wouldn't, but her parents might." Paul slipped his arm around Rosemary, and she nestled into his side. "I happened to overhear Mr. Zilde this afternoon. He was grousing about his wife throwing a surprise birthday party for Angela tonight."

"Swell!" She ran up the stairs yelling, "It's a good thing I already bought her that record she wanted!"

Paul's breath stirred Rosemary's hair as he confessed, "I had a bracelet in my car, just in case."

"Did you really?" She smiled up at him.

"Yes, but I'm just as glad. I'd rather give it to Valerie."

His warmth and generosity never ceased to surprise her. She gave him a hug. "I'm sure she'll treasure it."

"Speaking of treasures. . ." He reached over and took a bag from the corner of one of the steps and handed it to her.

Rosemary squeezed the bag. "What is it?"

He started whistling "Green Eyes" again and waggled his brows at the bag.

Laughing, Rosemary opened it and peered inside. "Buttons?"

He reached in and pulled out a fistful. As he let them spill back into the bag, he gloated, "Green eyes. And blue. And brown. I was watching you embroider doll faces the last night I was here. It occurred to me that if you show me how, I could sew on buttons for eyes. Wouldn't that be faster?"

"But these aren't just ordinary buttons." She held one of the bright notions. "These are darling!"

He grinned. "I hoped you'd like 'em. I found them in Switzerland. Look. Black centers, just like a pupil. Black thread won't even show."

"But these are glass. They must've been expensive, Paul."

"You're not fretting over the cost of a bag of buttons, are you?"

Valerie pattered back down the stairs. "Boy, am I glad I read that mix-and-match article in the magazine!"

"You look snazzy," Paul said. "I wish I could match my ties and suits that easily."

"Why should you? Dad couldn't. The pastor doesn't." Valerie gave him a silly smile. "I don't think there's a man alive who isn't color blind."

"Oh, yeah?" He grabbed several of the buttons and jabbed the blunt end of his forefinger at them one at a time. "Look. This one is blue. This one is green. Blue. Brown. Red."

Rosemary and Valerie burst into laughter. He'd purposefully misnamed every last color. "Red?"

"Bloodshot." He flipped it over his shoulder. "Can't use it. Poor kid will think her doll is drunk!"

"Oh, you! Mom, he's impossible!" Valerie opened the door and scampered out. "Good-bye!"

Shutting the door, Rosemary nodded. "What am I to do with you? Each time you come, you bring gifts. You can come to visit with empty hands, Paul. Just having you here fills up my heart."

"Just being with you fills up my heart, too." He tugged her into the living room, grabbed the bag from her hands, and poured the buttons into her lap. "But there's one more gift in here. . . ."

He knelt by her side, pretended to search through the buttons, and muttered to himself, "Where is it?"

She dipped her head closer to his and stirred through the bright buttons that filled her silk skirt. "What?"

"I remember now." He pulled something from a pocket and held it out to her—a ring. It shone as brightly as the love in his eyes. "Rosemary, I love you. I was going to ask you at the restaurant tonight, but I'm acting like a kid who can't wait. Marry me, sweetheart."

"Oh, Paul!" Rosemary looked at him through tear-misted eyes. The man she'd grown to love had taken her by complete surprise. In quiet moments alone, she'd dared to dream their courtship might blossom into marriage, but after years of widowhood, they'd seemed just that—dreams. Only he was here, making her dreams come true. "I'd be honored to become your wife."

Chapter 7

W e'll check with the church calendar," Paul said two days later as his fingers laced with Rosemary's. He'd invited some friends over for a barbecue so he could introduce his future wife to some of his associates. "I'm hoping for August."

"Congratulations." Bill flipped hamburgers on the grill and winked at Rosemary. "As for you, I suppose someone ought to warn you that Paul snores something fierce. Last summer when he left the bedroom window open at night—"

Rosemary gave Paul a questioning look.

"Bill, you're not supposed to lie and scare the bride-to-be." Paul squeezed her hand. "I should have warned you about Bill. He's known for his lousy sense of humor, but he's been a fair friend."

"Yeah, well, you could have introduced me to Rosemary instead of keeping her for yourself."

"Not a chance. She's mine."

Rosemary smiled up at Paul, and he could see love and joy sparkling in her eyes.

Paul released Rosemary's hand and slipped a plate to her. He set two hamburger buns side by side on the plate and motioned Bill to serve up a pair of sizzling patties. "I heard you might be interested in renting my house. Rosemary's place will be better suited to us."

"Why?"

"My place is too small." He cast her a smile.

"You're not going to have kids, are you?" Bill blurted out the question, then cleared his throat. "Sorry. That's none of my business."

The color in Rosemary's cheeks tickled Paul. He shrugged. "No telling what God has in store for the future."

Later, as Rosemary carried the condiments into Paul's house after the last of the guests had left, she asked, "Do you want children, Paul?"

"We have Valerie." He took the mustard from her and stuffed it into the icebox. "It seems like a mighty late start for us, but I'm willing to tackle whatever God sends our way. What do you think?"

"We'd hoped to have other children, but Valerie was our only one. I don't know that I could carry another child." Tears filled her eyes. "I should have said something. I'm sorry. With Valerie this old, it never occurred to me—"

"Shhh." Paul wrapped his arms around her. "If anything, I'd be worried sick about you the whole nine months. Thirty-nine isn't ancient, but I know it's more dangerous for a woman to carry a child at your age."

She snuggled closer.

"How would you feel about adopting? I think it would be a great option."

"Could we?" Her face shone with hope.

"Sweetheart, God's given us an incredible love for one another. If He has little ones out there He wants us to rear, He'll fill our hearts with love for them, too."

"So maybe someday I'll be sewing a doll for our little girl?"

He laughed. "Who are you kidding? You'll have a whole family of dolls for her, and they'll be the best-dressed rag dolls the world ever saw!"

As she laughed, he held her tight. He trusted her implicitly, and Wild Bill had come to the cookout just to check her out. He'd let Paul know that Rosemary had his resounding endorsement. Paul would have married her regardless, but with Bill Donovan's approval, he could occasionally "socialize" and continue to conduct business on the sly.

Rosemary probably would never know that most of his trips carried a clandestine purpose. It was the only way he could protect her—both from danger and worry.

Brakes squealed outside. "Hey, Mom!"

Rosemary wheeled around. "What does Valerie think she's doing, driving like that?"

"Mom!" Valerie sprinted through the wide-open door. "Mrs. Ainsley fell."

◆ ◆ ◆

"Thank you, Valerie," Mrs. Ainsley said. "You're such a good girl."

Rosemary smiled as Valerie carried the breakfast tray out of the downstairs guest bedroom. Thankfully, the old woman hadn't broken any bones, but she'd been badly rattled and bruised by her fall. Rosemary insisted on having her stay with them for a week or so until she recovered.

As Valerie left for work a short while later, she raised her voice and called from the front door, "Mom, don't forget to make those dolls for Paul."

"Dolls?" Mrs. Ainsley perked up.

Rosemary knew Paul didn't want the doll business to be general knowledge. She understood why, too. Many of the folks in the community and especially in their church had been hard-hit by the Great Depression. They'd welcome the opportunity to make dolls and earn money, but Paul's reputation rested on the quality of the dolls. She didn't want to lie, though.

"Paul takes rag dolls to Sweden."

"Well, that makes sense." Mrs. Ainsley fussed with the edge of her sheet. "If they don't have blankets and soap, those little girls over there won't have toys, either. What can I do to help?"

"Would you like to embroider a face or two?"

179

"I'd love to! Back when my girls were little, I always used the scraps from their dresses to make tiny clothes for their dollies. It brings back such fond memories."

That first morning, Mrs. Ainsley sat propped against the walnut headboard in the blue-and-white bedroom and embroidered three faces. She threaded red floss through her needle, then glanced at Rosemary, who was tying tiny bows on the ends of flaxen yarn braids. "You go ahead and cut more. It won't hurt for us to make a couple extra for your nice young man to take on his next trip."

"He is nice, isn't he?" Rosemary smiled.

Mrs. Ainsley let out a cackle and waggled her finger. "I knew it! You didn't argue about him being yours."

"He's asked me to marry him."

"Well, glory! Now, isn't God good to give you love again? I remember when you lost your husband. Now, here you are, alight with that special glow only love gives. And I thought I saw a new ring on your finger."

"God is good." Rosemary handed Mrs. Ainsley a glass of water. "Dr. Harwell wanted you to rest. Why don't you take a nap?"

"Only if you promise to let me do more dolls when I wake up."

Rosemary laughed.

"Oh! And if you give me my crochet hook and some yarn, I can make a few blankets and dresses!"

"You're a prize." She gave the old woman a kiss and left her to take a nap. During the next week, Rosemary sewed in the mornings as Valerie kept Mrs. Ainsley company before going to the bank. She also sewed up a storm in the hours Mrs. Ainsley napped. Even then, it wasn't possible to make as many dolls as usual.

Each evening, Paul would come over and escort Mrs. Ainsley to the table for supper, then to the living room where they'd all chat, listen to the radio, and play Monopoly or Sorry! Valerie sat at the piano and played, or Rosemary would accompany her so Valerie could practice the solo she'd promised to do the next week at church. Amid the chatter, crocheting, and cooking, the new balance of having a man there felt so good, so right. Hearing Paul's deep, resonant voice, watching his gentleness with Mrs. Ainsley, and relishing the warmth and strength in his good-night hugs made Rosemary glad they'd set a date for their wedding.

Friday night, Paul came for supper. His step dragged a bit, and his smile seemed forced when she met him at the door.

"What's wrong?" She brushed the roguish lock of hair back from his forehead.

"I got a telegram. Some art's coming available that a client wants. I need to leave as soon as possible. I've booked passage on a ship that sets sail tomorrow."

"Oh." Disappointment flooded her. "You haven't been home long at all—only nine days."

"I know." He came on into the house. "Good evening, Mrs. Ainsley, Valerie."

"I didn't mean to eavesdrop, but I heard you. I'll be going home in the morning. Perhaps Rosemary can drive you to the port."

"You're welcome to stay here, Mrs. Ainsley." Rosemary turned to him. "But I'd love to drive you."

"How about if I come here and pick you up for lunch? We could spend a few hours together. My ship sets sail at four."

"I'd like that."

◆　　◆　　◆

Paul dialed again and drummed his fingers as he waited for the call to go through. He'd been trying to reach Rosemary all morning. Bad enough he was making another trip this soon, but if he stood her up for lunch, then left—well, he didn't want to think of that.

Lord, please help me get ahold of her.

All morning long, the phone had been busy. He had several uncharitable thoughts about Myrtle what's-her-name being such a phone hog. The one time he got through, the phone rang and rang. Rosemary was probably taking Mrs. Ainsley home.

She's got to be home by now.

The phone rang.

Lord, thank You—now please let her be home.

"Hello?"

"Rosemary! Listen, sweetheart. I've gotten tied up in a meeting and have to go to the museum, then the bank. I'm afraid I'll have to cancel lunch."

"Oh."

"I know. I'm disappointed, too. I wanted to spend more time together before I had to leave."

"I guess I'd better get used to you popping in and out. It's part of your job."

He could hear the sadness in her voice, but Paul admired how she wasn't kicking up a big fuss. Rosemary's serenity was one of her best traits. "There are supposed to be a few big lots for me to cull through. If I find the right pieces, I might be able to satisfy my stateside clients for a while."

"I'll be thinking of you and praying for you. Do you need me to go to your place and pack for you?"

"No. Not at all." He kept his voice level, but alarms inside jangled. He'd left home in a hurry after receiving an emergency call from Bill. If anyone else saw what was on his desk, it wouldn't be a big deal; if Rosemary did, he'd have a huge problem on his hands. "I packed last night. I'm an old hat at it."

"I suppose as often as you travel, you have to be."

He forced a laugh. "Actually, Valerie's probably right. I might not have things matched up."

She laughed, too—a slightly thin sound. "I'd love it if you didn't have to go back for a little while after this trip. I noticed your blue suit's getting a little shiny. When you come home, we'll go to the tailor."

"And you'll help me pick out ties that don't all look the same?"

"I like your ties. You just don't put them with the right suits."

"That's proof that I'm in desperate need of a wife. Want the job?"

"More than anything in the world!"

They clung to the phone and spent every last second of the time his nickel bought. She told him she loved him half a dozen times in as many ways. He assured her of his devotion and love, too. He promised to pray for her, and she committed to praying for him. One last "I love you," and the phone clicked.

The empty sound echoed in his heart and mind. He already missed her.

◆　◆　◆

Rosemary's Pierce-Arrow purred to a stop in Paul's driveway. She couldn't bear to think of him leaving without them saying good-bye. Besides, after he'd left last evening and she'd tucked Mrs. Ainsley into bed, Rosemary and Valerie had stayed up most of the night, making more dolls. They'd worked like crazy and made six more. Added to the ones they hadn't been able to sneak out to his car, that would be twenty-two—maybe not a lot but certainly better than what he'd expected to take.

A whirlwind trip through her garden yielded lettuce and tomatoes for BLTs. She packed a picnic lunch including his favorite oatmeal cookies and tossed the dolls in the car.

Paul would come home to a surprise.

Thrilled, Rosemary slipped out of the car and headed toward the house with the wicker laundry basket full of dolls. No one ever locked the door in this neighborhood. She knew she could slip in, put the dolls in his study, and come back outside to spread the red plaid blanket in a shady spot beneath the tree. It was a perfect day to eat outside, and it was also a wise move. They weren't married, and avoiding temptation and preventing gossip were important for their witness.

The wooden floor echoed with her footsteps, then the Persian rug in his study muffled the sound. He'd mentioned this was where he usually kept the crate of dolls, so it seemed like the natural destination for her now.

She liked his study. Shelves of books lined two walls, and a solid-looking desk commanded the wall by the mullioned window. A large oil painting of Christ kneeling at Gethsemane hung on a wall. When she'd first seen it, she gasped and Paul wrapped his arm around her. "I prize it. It's not by anyone famous, but of all the works I've ever seen, it speaks to me the most. It makes me reflect on the cost of my salvation and the depth of His love."

As soon as she set down the basket of dolls, she'd spend a few moments admiring that painting again. Paul was right—it did make her reflect on God's infinite love. But Rosemary didn't get that far. She stopped cold when she saw what was on the desk.

A needle with a length of tangled thread had been jammed into a sponge—which was odd enough—but alongside it were two of her dolls. The seam along the head had been carefully snipped open.

Chapter 8

The wicker basket made a squeaky creak as Rosemary set it down. Actually, it tumbled to the side and dolls spilled across the floor. She didn't pick them up. She couldn't stop staring at the table. Surely she was mistaken. Maybe a seam had come loose.

No, it couldn't have. I'm careful, so careful. And even if a seam did come loose, it would be on one doll—not two.

She picked up the first doll. A pair of manicure scissors lay on the desk blotter beneath where it had lain.

He did it. He cut her open. Why? What kind of stupid question is that? The answer is obvious. He's smuggling something.

Pain speared her heart.

Smuggling. *But what? Why?* She could barely breathe. *What has he gotten me into as well? I've been making these!* The next thought made her knees go weak. *Lord, help me. Oh, please, God, help me. Valerie has made them, too. And we're sending them to Axel.*

Wildly, she looked around the room. Everything looked so ordinary, so orderly. Tears made her focus waver as she stared at the picture of Christ. Was that just part of Paul's ruse? How deep did his deception run? Had he merely bought a religious painting to use as a prop in his home?

"You never really know a man." Her sister's bitter words echoed through her memory. Elsa was a loving wife, a good housekeeper, a fine mother to Axel and Annelise, yet her husband, Frederick, had abandoned the family and run off with another woman. Years of trust had been shattered in a single night.

Do I really know Paul?

Rosemary carefully set down the doll. The gaping seam taunted her.

He's not the man I thought he was. How could I have let him sweep me off my feet? Is it love or loneliness that made me promise to marry him? How did I ever think I knew him well enough?

As she pivoted, her toe nudged one of the rag dolls on the floor. She stooped and picked them up one at a time. With each doll she placed into the wicker basket, her heart tightened more.

Lord, I thought this was Your will. I thought I was doing something to help all of those poor, frightened children. I thought I was helping my man with his business. It was all so clear, so simple. I've been such a fool! Show me what to do. Help me. . .

Tears slipped down her cheeks as she held the last doll to her aching heart.

◆　◆　◆

Paul glanced down at his watch. If he grabbed his luggage and took the shortcut, he'd still be able to squeeze in almost an hour-long visit at Rosemary's. He refused to leave without seeing her once more. He turned the corner onto his street. Her car was parked at the curb.

The flash of joy dissolved at once. *She's inside. What if she found the dolls?*

Paul parked and immediately headed for his home, for Rosemary. He didn't know what to expect from her. An oppressive silence filled the house. He went from room to room, looking for her. Then he saw the wicker basket full of dolls right by his desk. One of the dolls on his desk had been moved, and the scissors lay in plain view.

She knows.

Everything inside rebelled. What would this revelation cost? Their love, their future? Would she understand? Would she forgive him for keeping such a secret? If she told anyone, lives hung in the balance. He had to find her.

As he stepped into the hallway, Paul felt a draft. The kitchen door was ajar. He walked through it to the backyard and spotted her sitting on a blanket. Rosemary tensed, and he knew she'd heard him, but she didn't look up. Each step he took, he prayed. *Lord, I love her. Make this right. Father, please. . .*

No one in the neighborhood had fences, and Mrs. Sawyer was out at her clothesline, taking down her laundry as J.J.'s kids scrambled in and out of their tree house. They were out of earshot, but he couldn't be sure what Rosemary would do.

Paul disciplined himself to stroll over to her instead of yielding to the temptation to sprint. He halted at the edge of the blanket and cleared his throat. "I planned to whiz over to see you before I left. Why don't we go for a drive?"

She tilted her face up to his. Her red-rimmed eyes made his heart lurch. "Rosemary—"

"I'd like to speak first." She gestured toward the picnic blanket. Anyone who cared to look would see a casual invitation. Paul saw how her hand shook—from fear, or from anger?

He nodded. He owed her the right to speak her mind. "Maybe we ought to go inside."

She arched a brow. "I don't think so. No one will overhear us in your backyard, but anyone who cares to can see an engaged couple having a pleasant meal. You're very good at hiding in plain sight. This is in keeping with your style."

He winced. Her words carried accusation, and rightly so. From the start, he'd discovered Rosemary was an intelligent woman. He needed to find out just how much she suspected or knew, then proceed with damage control—if that was possible. Slowly, he sat opposite her.

She looked directly at him. "You're smuggling." Her words hung between them as she drew in a deep breath. "I saw your desk. You're using the dolls."

When he didn't give any reply, she handed him a sandwich. "Eat that. It'll help keep up pretenses. That's all a part of the game, isn't it?"

The serenity he cherished about her was gone. Rosemary hadn't fled upon seeing the doll's tampered seams. Clearly she planned to give him the opportunity to explain himself. Even now as she asked for information, he would dole out as little as possible. Keeping secrets from her went against his grain. But he didn't have a choice. This underground operation was all that stood between those children and disaster.

"I never meant for you to be hurt."

"I have a lot of questions. I'm upset. I deserve to know what you've involved me in. It's not just me. You've drawn in my daughter and my nephew, too. You came to me asking for dolls for children. What are you really doing?"

"I've left you in the dark on purpose, Rosemary."

"No more. I expect answers."

"I'm not supposed to discuss this. I'm breaking confidentiality to say anything at all." He stared at her, willing her to open her heart and know the truth even though he'd have to limit his words. "The dolls are going to children."

"But what are you doing with the dolls? What are you putting in them, and why?"

He couldn't lie. In fact, he couldn't ask for more dolls if he didn't confess the truth. Most of all, he simply didn't want to conceal things from the woman he loved. "I'm inserting a little bit of gold or a small jewel. They go to a contact who uses that to fund forged documents and bribe or buy children's freedom."

"The Jewish children in Nazi Germany," she deduced softly.

"Yes."

"No one would expect you're carrying out this plot because you have the ability to travel under your Swedish passport and have a legitimate business. Your art purchasing serves as a perfect cover."

He gave no reply. He didn't need to. Sitting there, he could see her mentally shuffling the facts and reasoning out the puzzle.

Her eyes narrowed. "Axel?"

"Rosemary, I need to protect you and others. I can't reveal anything that would endanger any part of the operation. It's why I never said anything in the first place."

"On no account would I ever tell anyone."

He reached over and took her hands in his. "I trust you for that. When we started out, you were a mere acquaintance. I couldn't risk letting you know. Even now, we have to keep this between just the two of us."

"Promise me you won't involve Axel without his full knowledge."

"You needn't fret on that score."

Rosemary shook her head and let out a mirthless laugh. "No, I suppose not. I ought to know better. If anything, my mother or Annelise is just as involved."

He gave no reply.

"How bad is it?"

Paul looked down at their intertwined hands. "Very little is being revealed about the Nazis' actions. Jews' passports are stamped with a *J* now. They can't own businesses or eat at cafés. Torahs are being burned. They're rounding up Jews from several cities in conquered countries and shipping them into the interior of Germany. They've slaughtered all of the men in at least two villages and many women, too."

Rosemary's fingers tightened around his. "Why aren't people doing anything about it?"

"Nazi cruelty is unspeakable, and their capacity for evil is boundless. Jews, gypsies, people who are mentally or physically 'inferior'. . .they're all being mistreated or shipped to unknown destinations."

"Shipped?"

"Rounded up and put in trucks or railroad cars. I'm not talking about a one-time occurrence, though that would be bad enough. Amsterdam, Poland, Romania—every country that's been conquered by the Reich."

He saw the dawning horror in her eyes and hated stripping away the innocence that insulated her from such ugly facts. It sickened him to make her aware of the depths of evil in their world. She'd asked for the truth, and he prayed she was strong enough to handle it. Now that she knew, she also had to understand the risks that came with her knowledge.

"Warfare between the soldiers—I don't like it, but I understand that much. But they show no mercy to civilians?"

"None. Hitler's reign owes as much of its success to fear as it does to power or might. Europeans are frightened. If someone tries to be a good Samaritan and help what the Nazis term an 'undesirable,' they themselves are punished. Some people are trying to hide Jews; most won't."

"If a neighbor tattled. . ." Her voice died out.

He nodded. "Everyone lives in terror. Denmark is doing better than other countries at trying to shield the Jews, but I can't be sure how much longer they'll succeed. Sweden is one of the last safe holds—and that's because the Germans need Sweden's iron to make steel for their war."

"How can you make a difference, Paul?"

"One person can make a difference, and if I had to do it alone, I would. Praise God, there are others. Several people have organized. There's an underground."

"Like the Underground Railroad that helped Southern slaves to freedom?"

The faint twinkle in her eyes that accompanied the question made hope flicker in his heart. "Yes, Rosemary. We're doing our best to spare lives."

The twinkle disappeared, and wariness replaced it. "It's dangerous for you."

He hitched a shoulder. "I can't say there's no danger. I can't live with myself if I do nothing, though. Innocent children deserve mercy and help. I can't close my eyes to the need, Rosemary. As a man, as a Christian—I have to be involved."

"Don't you think I'm willing to—"

"Rosemary." He sighed her name. "It wasn't a matter of whether I thought you'd be willing to take part. Fact of the matter is, I came to see very quickly that you'd jump in with both feet. But I wanted to shield you. The German Bund is exceptionally active in the States. We have no reason to believe they're on to this—it's a tiny operation. On the other hand, we don't want to underestimate their network. I didn't like withholding facts from you, but it was for your safety. The dolls are just a simple cottage industry—nothing more."

"I know that look in your eyes. I'm every bit as stubborn as you are, Paul Kincaid. Everything hinges on appearances. I'm making innocent dolls; you're an art dealer. I can play that game just as well as you can."

He watched her pick up a cup. "We need to end the conversation. I can't reveal any more details. I've already said far too much."

"I'm not a security risk, Paul." She tilted the cup to her lips.

Paul knew the cup to be empty. She was carrying on a charade, and the least he could do was play along. He picked up his sandwich and took a big bite. Something told him the matter wasn't settled yet.

She looked at him over the rim of her cup. "My sister's husband betrayed her trust. He left her for another woman."

"There's no other woman in my life!" He blurted out the words.

Rosemary set down the empty cup and nodded. A small smile tugged at her lips. "If I suspected such a thing, I wouldn't have stayed to talk." He nodded, and she continued. "When I thought about Frederick, I realized it was in his character not to be true to my sister. He always thought of himself first and was never satisfied with life. You are different."

In his line of work, patience was essential. Paul couldn't think of a time when his patience was so hard won.

"The first time I saw you, you handed your hymnal to someone else and sang by memory. Such a little thing, really." She shrugged. "But little things are telling. Like the way you listen respectfully to Valerie and the way you hold Mrs. Ainsley's elbow to help her. When we pray together, I feel in my heart that we are one. I don't doubt that you love me as I love you."

Paul felt part of the burden lift. They'd make it through this.

"Your character is clear to me. I fell in love with a man who has integrity. Old memories shook me for a moment, but I asked God to help me seek the truth. The one thing I don't understand is why you didn't trust me. Love means trusting, Paul."

He looked at her and let out a deep breath. "Love does trust, Rosemary. A man's love for his woman also compels him to protect her. I'd hoped to shield you."

"I understand your motive now."

"I'm glad, sweetheart. I know this cut you deeply, and I can't tell you how sorry I am. Now that you know I'm part of clandestine matters, I admit I kept a huge secret about myself from you." The words stuck in his throat. "It's only honorable for me to give you a chance to end our engagement."

Chapter 9

P aul!" Tears sprang to her eyes. "Is that what you want?"

"*No.*" He shook his head. "I love you more than I can say. I just told you: You can always be certain of that love. The only question is, is your love strong enough to survive the fact that I'll still keep secrets from you? If you still want to be my wife, I'll have to rely on your trust, because I'll never be able to tell you certain things. There will be times you'll get curious. What I want you to know, through it all, is that you can always be sure of my unwavering love for you."

"I love you with all my heart, Paul, and I'm not a young girl. As a woman, I understand that the need for discretion must come ahead of my personal interest. You can't keep from helping others—and that makes me love you all the more. Now that I know what's behind your actions, it's plain that you never hid who you are. You just concealed part of what your compassion compels you to do. I wouldn't ask you to stop, and I'm not about to let go of the man I love. I want to help in every way I can. I'll be the best wife to you that I can, with God's help."

"And I'll be the best husband I can be to you, with His help."

"Then you need to eat and keep up your strength." Finally, she smiled and slipped an oatmeal cookie into his hands, and he knew things were going to work out well. "I have a hunch God's going to keep us busy."

◆　◆　◆

"Yes, yes. Careful, now." Paul directed the purser as Rosemary stood by his side at the dock.

"Wow." She looked at the latest crate. "You managed quite a sizable transaction."

He patted the crate. "It's bound for the National Art Museum. They'll be more than pleased."

She nestled into his side, and he held her close. "I missed you," he growled.

"Not as much as I missed you." She laughed. "Valerie told me she was glad you were coming home. She said she's sick of me moping around without you."

"Moping, eh?" They walked alongside the cart containing his luggage and a few other smaller crates. The ship-to-shore phone allowed him to arrange with the museum to have a truck waiting. "And here I thought you were going to tell me all she wanted was my secret mashed potato recipe."

"You are the only man of my acquaintance who even knows a recipe."

"Keep it that way." He squeezed her tight and dipped his head. "I'm dying for us to get alone so I can kiss you properly."

Rosemary felt her face grow warm. "Me, too."

"Six weeks 'til the wedding. Did you get your gown yet?"

"I'm not sure I need one. I thought maybe my Easter dress. . ."

"Since when did a bride need an excuse to have a new gown?"

"I'd rather use the money for a project."

"Over my dead body. I brought back some Belgian lace."

"Belgian lace!" She blinked at him in amazement. "How?" She smiled and recovered quickly. "How thoughtful of you!"

"Anything for my girl." He saw to the truck being loaded, then took the keys to her car and drove behind the truck to the museum. "I'm sorry we're tied up like this, but some shipments require immediate signatures."

"What did you get?"

"There's a collection of incredible little carved ivory and jade kimono toggles that are called *netsuke*; a small bronze sculpture of a ballerina by Degas; a very Rembrandtesque painting that I suspect might be by Willem Drost; the central portion of a gilded medieval altarpiece; a few etchings; and a handful of other paintings. The Correggio *Madonna and Child* is the *pièce de résistance*."

"Are you serious? Paul, how can people stand to part with such treasures?"

"It's heartbreaking. So many of them are trying to sell, though. They know the Nazis will take anything of interest. Selling is the better of the two choices." He stopped. "The situation is already ugly. I want you to know I'm trying not to cheat anyone. I do my best to pay a fair price."

"That went without saying."

They stopped at an intersection. Paul leaned over and kissed her. "I want to haul you off to the church today."

She laughed. "Valerie would throw a fit, and Mrs. Ainsley would have a conniption."

He didn't laugh at all. "I'm noticing you didn't object."

"Paul, we can't do that." She blushed. "I'm not about to have anyone think I had to hurry up to get married."

The honk of the horn behind them cut short his laughter. "If we don't get going here, the whole town is going to think that's the case!"

He pulled into the back of the museum. "Sweetheart, it's going to take me a couple of hours. I want you to go buy a wedding dress now. Come back to pick me up, and we'll swing by to collect Valerie and go out for a bite to eat."

"I'll stay—" She stopped. "Okay. I'll go. You can unpack and do whatever you have to."

"But get your dress now."

"Why are you so worried about my wedding dress?"

He traced his fingers down her cheek. "You deserve a beautiful dress." He ran his thumb across her lips and added, "I like silk. I want you to wear silk."

"Any particular color?"

"Not especially. But the government is about to put an embargo on silk. I don't want you to get stuck without a choice."

"I'm getting my first choice. I'm getting you."

He groaned. "Are you sure I can't just haul you off to the pastor's house? His wife and a neighbor could be witnesses."

"Go play with your paintings. I have a dress to buy."

◆　◆　◆

Valerie declined the invitation to go to dinner with them. She and "Grandma" Ainsley were "busy." Paul escorted Rosemary out to the car and muttered, "The two of them are thick as thieves."

"I know. I have a funny feeling they're up to something."

"If it were Valerie and her friends, I'd be worried. Mrs. Ainsley's involvement is reassuring."

Rosemary gave him an incredulous look. "Don't be too sure of it. Mrs. Ainsley can be feisty."

"That sweet old woman?"

She leaned close and whispered in his ear, "A spy ought to be more observant. Mrs. Ainsley is wearing nail polish these days."

He hooted. "Well, that makes her a floozie, doesn't it?"

They had a lovely dinner at Giovanni's. Afterward, Paul wanted to take a walk. They meandered through the park, and to his relief, she didn't pump him for any in-depth information about his trip. She asked general questions and didn't pry if his answers were less than direct. He told her how her relatives were doing, but most of all, he spoke of how he had missed her and how he was glad to be back home.

"How long do you get to stay home now?"

"I told them we're getting married. I figured I'd refrain from any more business trips until we come back from our honeymoon. If I do that, I'll need to slip away right after we return."

"I understand why."

He nodded.

"I'm taking you suit shopping tomorrow. Your blue suit is shiny."

"You're sounding wifely already."

"I'm out of practice. It's been almost eight years since I was married."

"I'm not worried in the least. You're the most practical woman I've ever met. Speaking of practicalities, are there any of my furnishings that you want to bring on over?"

She grinned. "Now that you mention it, I love your oak hall tree. Wouldn't it look great by the front door?"

"Yeah, it would."

"My late husband used the small parlor beside the guest room as an office. We cleared everything out years ago. Would you like to bring over your desk, bookshelves, and picture of Christ?"

"That would be great!"

He took off his suit coat and slipped it around her shoulders. "You're getting chilly."

"Silly, isn't it? It's summer!"

"As long as you're not getting sick."

Rosemary turned and gave him a peck on the cheek. "I am sick—lovesick!"

The two of them sauntered all around the park, then drove back to Rosemary's. When they walked up to the house, Valerie pulled open the door. "You've been gone a long time. Mom, I need to tell you something."

"Okay, honey. Paul, would you please excuse me?"

Valerie shot her a wary look. "Could we go upstairs?"

Rosemary followed her daughter up the steps. What would be so urgent that her daughter would drag her away from Paul on their first evening back together? Valerie practically pushed her down the hall and into the master bedroom. Once inside, Rosemary fumbled with the switch.

When the lights went on, she let out a cry.

Chapter 10

S urprise!" Mrs. Ainsley crowed from over in the corner.

"Well, do you like it?" Paul slipped up behind Rosemary and wrapped his arms around her.

"It's—it's gorgeous!" She stared in disbelief at the antique bedroom set.

"I couldn't resist it," he confessed.

Valerie ran her hand across the front of the huge mirror-fronted oak armoire. "Have you ever seen anything so beautiful?"

Rosemary turned and slipped her arms around his waist. "How did you do this?"

"Valerie and Mrs. Ainsley helped. I called, and they agreed to be here to tell the deliverymen where to arrange everything."

"We put the old set in that empty bedroom down the hall," Mrs. Ainsley said. "It's nice and solid, but this—well, this is something else entirely."

"I knew they were up to something!" Rosemary poked Paul in the back. "You knew they were, too, and you didn't let on."

"Some secrets, sweetheart, are well worth keeping."

◆ ◆ ◆

He'd hoped he wouldn't have to go back for a while. Bill had arranged for a courier to take another shipment of dolls. Everything was arranged. Then the phone rang.

"We need to get together for lunch," Bill said.

He never called unless it was imperative. Paul straightened. "When are you free?"

"I just had a cancellation. Why don't we meet in an hour?"

"I'll be there."

◆ ◆ ◆

Just like that, he was gone. He'd only been home four days. Rosemary kept a positive attitude. She understood they'd live by a capricious schedule and he'd dash off on trips without much warning at times. She loved him; it was a concession she'd make. Compared to the dangers and sacrifices others made, it was nothing.

Two days after he'd pressed her to buy her wedding gown, the government announced a silk embargo. Things like that made her aware of the fact that he had his fingers on the pulse of what was happening in the world. With all of those things weighing on his mind, he'd still made sure she'd have a silk gown. That thought made her love him all the more. He understood the little things that made a difference.

She went to pick up the suit they'd ordered. "It'll fit him perfectly. I guarantee it," the tailor promised.

"I hope so. What about the ties?" She'd selected some ties the day they ordered the suit. One, in particular, would look perfect for the wedding. The blue in it matched the wool in the suit exactly, but the pale blue stripe in it was precisely the same shade as the silk gown she'd be wearing.

"You're lucky I set them aside for you. Once they announced the embargo, folks have suddenly snapped up ties. Cost of wool's starting to hike. I've ordered some extra bolts just in case."

Rosemary studied the tailored lines of the suit jacket. "Why don't I go ahead and order another suit for Paul now?"

"I have his measurements on file. It'd be ready in a week."

"Wonderful."

Rosemary went home and sat down at the sewing machine. As it was Saturday, Valerie was home. *The Adventures of Ellery Queen* played on the radio as they worked together.

The bobbin thread ran out. As the radio touted the excellence of Bromo Seltzer, Rosemary suddenly jolted. *Paul knew about the price of wool. He made sure Mrs. Ainsley had a coat. He said he wouldn't quibble about an extra penny or two per yard of fabric for the dolls. . . .*

"Valerie!"

Valerie stopped stuffing a doll and looked up.

"We need to go buy fabric!"

By the time they carried the third load of fabric to the upstairs bedroom that evening, Valerie gave her a disgruntled look. "How many little girls do you think there are in Denmark, anyway?"

Rosemary diverted her by laughing. "I know you hate to sew, but complaining isn't going to make a difference."

"One yard. One stinking little yard of twenty different materials. That's weird enough, but you did that at—I lost count. How many stores did we end up going to?"

"Enough." The empty chest of drawers came in handy. Rosemary quickly tucked yard after yard into the drawers and filled all five. She'd also bought three bolts of muslin.

The clerks at the store all chattered about quilts. Rosemary didn't lie, but she hadn't corrected their assumptions, either. Paul had insisted on buying tires for the car because supplies would be distributed differently. Well, she figured she'd learn from his example. On Monday, she'd go buy wool yarn for doll hair.

Days passed. The closet in the spare room overflowed with dolls. Rosemary tried to tuck the dolls into the closet without her daughter seeing the "finished" product because she'd been leaving the one seam open. Since Valerie hated to sew, it hadn't been too hard to have her concentrate on sewing on button eyes and stuffing the dolls. Once, as they hugged good night, Valerie whispered, "I know something's up."

"We're up. We should have been in bed about thirty minutes ago."

Valerie gave her an indulgent smile. "Pleasant dreams, Mom."

That night, Rosemary's dreams were anything but pleasant.

◆　◆　◆

"Ah, Captain von Rundstedt! I have a special package for you." Paul plowed through the crate and pulled out a small box. "For your niece."

"How very kind of you." The captain gave him a calculating look.

"Actually, I am in your debt. It was your idea."

The captain opened the box. Inside was another doll. This one was flaxen-haired and dressed in a long dress. A small copy of *Sleeping Beauty* accompanied her. "Very clever."

"The cleverness was yours, Captain," Axel said. "It's too difficult to import books right now, so I cannot carry this line, but Herr Lindhagen said he'd be happy to bring in one of each type when he can."

"That box has a red cape for your Red Riding Hood," Paul mentioned casually.

"My niece will be pleased."

"Good."

The captain looked around the warehouse. "I see you are still able to keep a fair business going, Herr Christiansen."

"I've changed some of the items I carry. A good businessman is always flexible. I'm thinking of dealing with a South American firm. They can fruits, vegetables, and jam. It might be a lucrative venture."

"Be sure such shipments do not end up on the black market." The captain stared at him. "I would expect careful bookkeeping. Such things will not be tolerated."

"Naturally." Axel dipped his head in assent. "It occurred to me that certain products such as that might appeal to desirable persons."

"Keep me informed if they become available. Heil Hitler." The captain started to leave.

Paul cleared his throat. "Captain? Just one thing. I was asked by two families in Sweden to see if I might locate their grandchildren. Is there any assistance in such matters?"

"Give me their parents' names. I can have an aide check on it."

"Death notices were received. That is why the grandparents asked my assistance in finding the children. They're from Flensburg."

Rundstedt shook his head. "I cannot help you. It is not in my jurisdiction. It is a lost cause. Tracking orphans in a time of war is impossible."

"A shame, to be sure," Paul murmured.

"Indeed. Heil Hitler."

After the captain left, Axel gave him an incredulous look. "Do I dare ask what that was about?"

"No." Paul slapped Axel on the shoulder and walked off. He couldn't share the details of this mission with anyone. This time, he had nothing more than Paul Lindhagen's passport, an attaché case, and three dolls.

◆　◆　◆

Rosemary closed the door to the magnificent wardrobe, hiding her silk wedding dress from view. She caught her reflection in the mirrored front and forced a smile. She couldn't let Valerie see her concern.

Over the past few months, Valerie had finally begun enjoying life again. She'd gotten through the freshness of grief and was starting to mention Frank every now and then in casual conversation. "I need some of her resilience and spunk," Rosemary whispered to her reflection.

Paul had never been gone this long. It was supposed to be a short trip. He ought to have been back by now. . .only it had been four and a half weeks, and she hadn't heard a word.

The dangers of his profession loomed in her mind. It was just six days before their wedding, but she couldn't be sure he'd be home in time. . .if he came home at all.

She shuddered at that thought.

As the days passed, she prayed for him. She asked the Lord to protect him and to bless the dolls so children would find safety. Her prayers became increasingly urgent.

Mrs. Ainsley came to spend the day. They made applesauce together. As she added cinnamon to the sauce, Rosemary said, "This will give the applesauce a little zing."

"Like Paul Kincaid puts zing in your heart?"

Rosemary laughed. "Yes. He does that."

"Paul is wonderful." Mrs. Ainsley licked applesauce from her finger and gave Rosemary an impish grin. "I want to marry him if you don't."

"He's mine. You're out of luck."

Mrs. Ainsley pretended to huff. "Well then, I'm going to go home." She rose.

"Be sure to take some applesauce." Rosemary tucked a trio of pint-sized jars in a bag.

After Mrs. Ainsley left, Rosemary slumped into a chair and let out a sigh. No matter how busy she stayed, she couldn't distract herself. Worry gnawed at her. *Where's Paul? Is he okay?*

Soon Valerie arrived home from work. "Mom, you need to get out. You can't brood like this."

"Haven't you ever learned Danes are good at brooding?"

"Yuck. I never liked Hamlet. Let's forget about that and go outside." Valerie pulled her into the backyard and chattered as they gardened. The late August sunlight cast a golden glow around them, but Rosemary couldn't shake the feeling that something was terribly wrong. When they finished gardening, Valerie took the basket of vegetables into the house. Rosemary stayed behind. She knelt in the soil and wept as she prayed.

◆　◆　◆

Two of them were out. Safe. Both little boys had the big haunted eyes of children who had seen far too much in their short years. Nonetheless, Paul knew they'd soon be nurtured by their grandparents back in New York. He'd passed them off to a contact who met them at the appointed time. Paul waded back to shore. Squinting at the horizon, he knew he had to hurry to find cover before the next patrol came by.

It was said anything could be bought for a price. Tonight, he almost believed that. The wealthy grandparents of those boys had gladly donated a sizable fortune—one that would fund the escapes of countless more children. The trip had been what Bill termed a "calculated risk." To Paul's way of thinking, the only calculation involved was that any child was priceless.

He rolled down his pant legs, donned his shoes and coat, and struck out walking. In the distance, he spied an overturned fishing dory. It would conceal him well enough. He ducked beneath it just in time. The patrol came and went.

Another several miles on foot, and he reached a thinly wooded area. The body of a man lay twisted in an unnatural position on the ground beside a thicket. A small sound made Paul take a second look. He knelt down and could scarcely believe his eyes. From beneath the undergrowth, a little child stared back at him.

He pulled her free and hastily checked the man's body for some identification. There was none. Young as she was, this little girl had become one of the orphans Captain von Rundstedt said were untraceable. Paul scooped her into his arms, and she clung to him. They'd barely gone ten yards when footsteps and a stream of harsh German orders sounded not far away. Paul shoved the girl between the gnarled roots of a tree and curled around her. *Lord, please make seeing eyes blind tonight.*

Chapter 11

F ive weeks. He'd been gone now far, far too long. Rosemary spent her days gardening and sewing. Friends from church dropped by with offers to help with the wedding. Rosemary pasted on a smile and acted as if Paul's prolonged absence was understandable. But batch after batch of cookies grew stale.

Inside, she was crying to the Lord with every breath. Once already she'd lost a husband. Was God taking Paul from her, too? She couldn't help fearing the worst.

Five days to go until the wedding. Rosemary sat down at the sewing machine and buried her face in her hands.

Lord, You know what's happening. I'm so confused, so scared. Love is such a rare gift. You gave Your Son as a gift of love. He said a man had no greater love than to lay down his life for another. Paul is risking his life. . .but, Father, please don't take him from me. I love him so much. I long to be his wife. You put us together—please don't tear us apart. Bring my beloved back safely to me.

"Rosemary."

She wiped the tears from her face. She wanted Paul so much that she could hear his voice.

"Sweetheart."

She spun around. "Paul!"

He looked thinner and tired, but his eyes sparkled with love for her. In his arms, he held a little dark-haired, doe-eyed girl. "I'm sorry it took me so long to come home to you. I brought you a wedding gift. Her name is Rebekkah."

"And she's a living doll," Rosemary said as she ran to them with her arms open to pull them close to her heart.

◆ ◆ ◆

one month later

"Up, Daddy. More." Rebekkah tapped her own little cheek to show him where he'd missed a spot.

"There can't be more flour on my face. I'm wearing most of it on my shirt!"

"I wearing flowers, too!"

Rosemary burst out laughing. "Yes, honey, your pretty new apron has flowers on it."

"She's smart as a whip." Valerie dried the mixing bowl. "Learning English fast as can be."

"Yes, she is." Rosemary hugged their little daughter and kissed the white fleck on Paul's cheek.

"Hey, stop that before the cookies burn!"

"I can't believe we only filled two cookie sheets." Paul made a face as Valerie pulled the treats out of the oven.

"Neither can I!" Rosemary wiped Rebekkah's hands. "As much cookie dough as you and Bekkah swiped, I didn't think we'd manage even one sheet."

"Be nice, or I won't share my family's secret recipe for mashed potatoes."

"You'll share it." Valerie laughed. "We *are* your family."

Bekkah's dark curls bounced as she nodded.

Rosemary and Paul exchanged a glance. They did that all the time now—carried on conversations with just a look. It never ceased to thrill her how deep their love had grown in such a short time.

"Rebekkah's eager for these cookies," Valerie said. "Look at her—she got the milk."

"That's buttermilk, sweetie." Rosemary knelt down. "We need the other milk."

Bekkah shook her head and handed the bottle to Paul. "Daddy. 'Tatoes."

He chortled. "This little scamp doesn't miss a thing."

"You use buttermilk?" Valerie gaped at him.

"Among other things. We need baking soda, cayenne pepper, white pepper. . ."

"Who would have guessed?" They all sat down at the table after he gathered the ingredients. Paul picked up the masher.

"Wait!" Rebekkah pressed her little hands together. "Pray. Pray first."

"Yes. Bekkah, would you like to say the prayer?"

She nodded and closed her eyes. "Thank You, Jesus. God bless all the boys and girls. Amen."

Rosemary looked across the table at her husband. Love radiated between them as they said in unison, "Amen."

CATHY MARIE HAKE

Cathy Marie is a Southern California native who loves her work as a nurse and Lamaze teacher. She and her husband have a daughter, a son, and two dogs, so life is never dull or quiet. Cathy Marie considers herself a sentimental pack rat, collecting antiques and Hummel figurines. She otherwise keeps busy with reading, writing, and bargain hunting. Cathy Marie's first book was published by **Barbour Publishing** in 2000 and earned her a spot as one of the readers' favorite new authors. Since then, she's written several other novels, novellas, and gift books. You can visit her online at www.CathyMarieHake.com.

Filled with Joy

by Kelly Eileen Hake

Chapter 1

December 1941

R oy Benson stared at the all-too-familiar turquoise wall. Some dingbat had decided the color was soothing, but that person certainly never stayed in traction for a month with nothing else to look at. It felt like living in a package of Black Jack gum, but the antiseptic smell provided a constant reminder that this was a hospital.

Martha, the grandmotherly nurse, bustled in to pick up his lunch tray. "Hello, Mr. Benson. Did you have a good day?"

He grinned. Every day she asked the same question, and his answer always stayed the same. "Yes, Miz Martha."

"Oh, please." Martha shot him a wink. "Ashley told me you've been restless all morning. Looking forward to tomorrow, I suppose?"

"True." Roy leaned forward as she fluffed his pillows. "A cast and crutches mean I can move around again."

"We're happy for you." She picked up the tray, stacked it on top of several others, and headed for the door. "I know you're itching to get out of here."

More than you know. Lying in bed for weeks on end was slowly driving Roy up the wall. He was accustomed to hard work and missed the sense of purpose he found in serving his country. The moment he'd turned eighteen he'd enlisted in the U.S. Navy, just as his father had done twenty-two years before.

His education at a Swiss boarding school stood him in good stead. Since Roy boasted fluency in English, Swiss, German, and French, in addition to having a knack for mathematics, he'd been recruited to serve the naval cryptography division OP-20-G. Now, eight years later, he'd immersed himself in decoding the Japanese naval code JN-25, as Japanese-U.S. relations became increasingly strained.

Entrusted with top-secret documents to deliver to the capitol from Station Hypo in Hawaii, he'd planned to return to duty immediately. Unfortunately, the spoiled son of a senator had climbed behind the wheel of his daddy's Benz as drunk as a skunk and lost control of the vehicle. As he plowed through the street, somehow the youth drove up on the sidewalk and rammed into Roy. After weeks of traction for his broken leg, tomorrow would bring crutches. Crutches meant recovery, and recovery meant getting back to work.

With those comforting thoughts, he reached over and turned on the bed-side radio Martha had brought him. WOR broadcast live, up-to-the-minute commentary on football games every Sunday. This afternoon, the New York Giants played the Brooklyn Dodgers.

"You fellas ready for the game?"

"Yeah!"

Static from the radio mixed with the men's cheers; then the channel tuned in. "Wagner, can you hear it?"

Wagner waved from the far corner of the ward. "Yes, sir."

Roy settled in and got caught up in listening to the play-by-play calls, hearing the crowd roar, and wishing he could be out enjoying the day.

"We interrupt this broadcast to bring you this important bulletin from the United Press." The sudden news bulletin jerked him back to the present. *"FLASH, Washington—the White House announces Japanese attack on Pearl Harbor. Stay tuned to WOR for further developments, which will be broadcast as received."*

Roy's outraged bellow blended with those of his ward mates before a deathly silence fell over the room. *Pearl Harbor. It's not Station Hypo, but it's so close. Is my division okay? If only I wasn't stuck here in this bed. I could have been there helping break the Japanese code. This might not have happened.*

The bulletin repeated. The announcer also gave nonspecific information that the battle still progressed. Roy's hands clenched around the cold metal bed rail. *Lord, why am I in this bed when my country is under attack?*

◆ ◆ ◆

"Ow!"

Valerie Fulton shot a commiserating grin at her stepfather as he set down the needle and popped a poked finger into his mouth. Paul had a difficult time sewing glass buttons onto the much-needed rag dolls—a fact that made her like him even more. She glanced down at her own much-pricked hands and sighed. "You'd think after making so many of these, we'd be pros by now. Whoever said practice makes perfect never took up sewing."

Her comment earned her a smile from Paul and a cheery laugh from her mother.

"Maybe for some of us it's just hopeless," Paul agreed.

"No." Rosemary expertly tied a minuscule knot. "This project is all about hope. Every poked finger is another child rescued."

Paul and Valerie shared a purposeful glance and concentrated on the work at hand with renewed vigor. These weren't just dolls; they were the means through which the Lord looked after His own.

The dolls, and their lifesaving purpose, were what had brought Rosemary and Paul together this past year. Paul had come up with the idea after seeing Rosemary carry a basket of the dolls to the church nursery. At first, they'd simply made the dolls as requested, but eventually, Paul asked for Rosemary's hand in marriage and revealed the true mission of the dolls.

As the Nazis overran Europe, Jews were being chased from their homes or incarcerated. In an effort to help, Valerie and her mother stitched the dolls, and Paul made sure valuables were buried deep in the stuffing. When the dolls arrived in Denmark, the money funded the production of crucial documents. There, Valerie's cousins Axel and Annelise smuggled the dolls with the documents to Jewish refugees. Then the children were funneled to Sweden, where they would be safe from the Nazis.

On his last trip to Europe before the wedding, Paul had brought home a surprise—a Jewish toddler named Rebekkah. They'd adopted her, and she filled their hearts and home with a special joy. Rosemary called the little girl her living doll, and she'd just tucked her in bed.

To Valerie, Rebekkah was the sister she'd always wanted and the opportunity to help raise a child in the Lord's grace. Every time she sewed another doll, she pictured another precious Rebekkah waiting to be saved.

As the days passed and political relations became more tense, the entire operation gained a frightening urgency. American imports to Denmark were already few and far between; the Nazi regime could stop accepting shipments of the dolls at any time. Every doll made was another child saved.

Valerie finished plaiting a doll's red yarn hair and held it up for a brief moment before placing it with several others in a crate by her chair. She threaded her needle with rose-colored floss and grabbed more material to embroider another face.

Moments later, as she pressed her handkerchief to the red stain spreading across her thumb, Valerie saw her mother watching out of the corner of her eye. "Well, practice makes patient, at least!"

After a shared chuckle, Paul became solemn. "Speaking of patient, what would you two say to bringing an injured soldier into our home for the holidays?"

"You know your friends are welcome anytime, Paul, but through New Year's?" At his nod, Valerie's mom asked, "What about the dolls?"

Valerie bit her tongue. This wasn't just her decision to make. She and her mom weren't alone anymore. Paul brought up the topic, but Valerie knew he and her mom would respect her opinion. Through Paul, God had blessed their home with continued harmony, but they were now a trio instead of a duet when decisions needed to be made.

"We'll have to guard our speech more closely, but we can still make the dolls and tell him we're sending them to Denmark to help Valerie's cousins."

"That's true. . .but what if he does happen to find out?" Valerie asked. Some things just weren't worth the risk.

"If it comes to that—and I'm not saying it will—he's a naval officer. I've known his father for over two decades, and whenever I was sent to Switzerland or the outlying area, I stopped by his boarding school to check on him. Right now he's laid up with a broken leg. Some drunken fool got behind the wheel and hit him. He's a bright young man and loyal as they come. We can trust Roy Benson."

Valerie could tell Paul had spoken his piece. She couldn't ask for a better reference. Clearly Mr. Benson must be an exceptional man. As her mother quirked a brow in silent question, Valerie bobbed her head.

"We'll do it." Rosemary patted Paul's arm. "I can't stand to think of anyone being alone in the hospital over Christmas."

"Besides. . ." Valerie grinned. "If all else fails, we can teach him to sew!"

◆　◆　◆

Roy listened to the morning news. The announcer listed ships and carriers that had sunk to the depths of Pearl Harbor since yesterday's sneak attack. No matter what the government revealed, the information missing told Roy far more. The lack of statistics alone hinted at a devastation he could imagine all too vividly. He'd had a one-day stop in Pearl Harbor; he knew full well the size of the contingent there. The United States had moved the bulk of its naval force to Hawaii just last year as a show of power.

Though none would call the attack honorable or courageous, it had been brutally effective. *Still no word on the number of casualties, but that's to be expected.* The American naval fleet had been all but destroyed, and hundreds of families would bear the scars of what President Roosevelt named "the day which shall live on in infamy." These deaths would not be the last—America and Britain had jointly declared war on Japan.

As the news ended, promising listeners frequent bulletins and updates, the station began Benny Goodman's "There'll Be Some Changes Made."

Roy switched down the volume on the radio in disgust. His new cast itched, but not as much as he itched to rip it off and hop on the first plane back to Hawaii. All his antsy movement had caused a big wrinkle to form on his bottom sheet. He didn't want to bother the nurse, so he yanked at the sheet and let out a moan of relief. Bed. He hated it. This was the last day, too. After the cast dried, he'd be able to use crutches. . .and not a minute too soon.

He turned his head as footsteps clicked smartly down the hall. The tall honey blond in the doorway caught his eye immediately. It felt like years since he'd seen a woman wearing something other than a nurse's uniform. A leaf-green wool coat parted as she moved, revealing a beige sweater and brown skirt. The skirt flirted around the top of her calves, drawing his gaze toward trim ankles. She was a sight for sore eyes and well worth notice, but one of the men in the ward let loose a low, appreciative whistle.

"Show some respect," Roy growled and glared at the man before turning his attention back to the vision as she stepped into the room. She waited for an older woman and man to follow her. *Not timid. Bright enough to have backup before she gets in too deep.* She shot a questioning glance at the older man, who nodded in Roy's direction.

The man seemed strangely familiar. . .yes, more gray hairs, but that was definitely. . .

"Paul Kincaid." Roy broke out in a grin at the sight of his father's old friend.

Paul used to bring him letters and news when he dropped by the boarding school.

"Roy." Paul strode over to his bed and clasped his hand in a warm greeting before frowning at the fresh plaster on his leg. "I just learned you were here yesterday, or I'd have dropped by sooner. Just get out of traction?"

"I got casted today."

◆　◆　◆

Valerie followed Paul's lead toward the bed in the far corner, where a young man with an enormous cast sat listening to the radio. She listened quickly to make sure it wasn't a news update and caught the opening strains of Horace Heidt's "I Don't Want to Set the World on Fire."

Too late for that. This will be a world war, and none of us will escape unscathed. She pushed aside memories of Frank and smiled as Paul introduced her to Roy Benson. "This is my new bride, Rosemary, and her daughter, Miss Valerie Fulton."

His intense hazel gaze and full beard gave him an air of mystery, and the disreputably long, light brown lock of hair on his forehead lent a boyish charm that made her heart skip a beat. Despite the cast covering his left leg from foot to thigh, he struck her as a man of action, chafing at enforced inactivity. The smile that lit Roy's face couldn't completely mask his restlessness.

"I'm glad to meet you." Valerie dipped her head in acknowledgment.

"The pleasure's all mine. Paul, you're a lucky man." As the injured soldier gallantly kissed the back of her mother's hand, Valerie couldn't suppress a grin. Anyone who made her mother giggle was all right in her book.

"Would you like a stick of gum?" She fished a package of Black Jack gum from the pocket of her coat and held it out.

"Thanks."

Before she tucked the remainder of the pack into her purse, she noticed that the gum wrapper matched the teal walls almost perfectly.

"That's right." Amusement colored Mr. Benson's voice as he caught her glancing from the gum to the walls. "You'd better not drop that pack."

"I'd never find it, would I?" She chuckled and stashed it in her handbag. When Roy's smile reached his eyes, he seemed younger.

"Well," Paul began, "we didn't just come for a social visit. My new family and I would like to have you stay with us for the holidays. What do you say?"

Chapter 2

M
r. Benson hesitated, looking at their faces with a measured gaze. Valerie gave a slight nod to encourage him. She wasn't sure why, but she wanted him to feel comfortable coming to their home. He seemed so independent, she almost wanted to make sure he knew other people cared. Maybe it was because Paul had mentioned Roy had grown up in boarding schools. The thought of anyone being away from family for so long left her wanting to make up for the loneliness he must have experienced.

"Please say you'll come, Mr. Benson," Rosemary entreated.

He cast one last glance at the turquoise walls and took a deep breath. "I'd be honored."

"Good. We'll come by later this afternoon when your cast is set." Paul rubbed his hands together. "Dr. Reeves already gave his permission, since we promised to make sure you rested up."

Valerie didn't miss Mr. Benson's grimace at that last part. It seemed as though their new houseguest had had enough rest. Well, if he thought their home would be more fast-paced than the hospital, just wait until he spent a week sewing!

◆　◆　◆

Roy rubbed his jaw and appreciated the brisk December breeze on the back of his neck. Paul had stopped at a barbershop on the way home and made sure Roy got a long-overdue haircut and shave. He didn't look like a bum now. What would pretty Miss Fulton think of his transformation?

Expecting wallpaper embellished with florid pink roses and lacy curtains blocking the window, Roy followed Paul through the house to the downstairs guest bedroom. Even if the room looked like a powder puff, it would be a welcome change. A room to himself was a luxury he'd hardly ever known. He'd shared quarters with other boys in boarding school, then during the first years of his service in the navy. Even the hospital ward packed several men along the long walls.

Now he'd have peace and quiet—time to think about what he would do with himself once he got out of this cast. The doctors told him he'd never fully recover. Cold weather would make his leg ache, and he'd always have a slight limp.

I won't be fit for active duty. Other men are marching off to protect their country, and I can't go with them. Ever. The sooner he could get back to breaking the JN-25, the better. *If I can't offer my life, my mind will have to do.*

He maneuvered his crutches through the doorway and surveyed his new home. Decorated in blue and white with sturdy walnut furniture, the room contained nothing that could be called purely feminine—except her.

Valerie Fulton looked up from the small vase of flowers she'd obviously just placed on the bedside table. She offered a welcoming smile and quickly stepped away from the bed.

The faint blush coloring her cheeks made her even lovelier than he recalled from this morning. Honey-colored curls brushed her shoulders, and now he knew her eyes sparkled a deep emerald green.

Paul didn't notice the awkward moment. "That's nice of you, Valerie."

"Thank you," Roy added quickly.

"You're welcome, Mr. Benson." She came closer. "Why, you hardly seem the same person!"

"Is that good or bad?" He liked how easily she met his gaze. She stood at the perfect height. He didn't have to bend his head, and she didn't need to crane her neck to have a conversation.

"I don't think it would matter how you wore your hair, Mr. Benson, though this suits you well. It's more important that you seem so much happier. I suppose you're just glad to be moving around a bit?"

"Exactly." He grinned. Not every woman would have realized the true change—Miss Fulton looked to the core of a man and understood what she saw.

"Well, Mom asked me to tell you both that dinner will be ready in about twenty minutes."

"Something sure smelled good when we walked in. Nothing like good home cooking, eh, Roy?"

I wouldn't know. "I'm looking forward to it." Roy moved back as she moved toward the door.

"Well." Once she reached the hallway, she regained some of the energy he'd seen in her earlier. "We aren't having green gelatin!"

Roy watched as she whisked around the corner and heard her little heels clicking smartly on the kitchen linoleum as she joined her mother. Belatedly realizing he'd gazed after her like a fool, he snapped his attention back to Paul, only to find the older man giving him a knowing look.

"She's single. Not seeing anyone, either."

Roy scrutinized a painting of an old ship. Its sails swelled in the wind, and Roy could practically smell the salt in the air. *I may not be back on a ship for some time, but there are definite advantages to staying here for a while. Still, it does no good to foster expectations.*

"I didn't ask."

"You know that sometimes a man doesn't have to use the words to ask a question like that." Paul cheerfully ignored Roy's casual dismissal. "But she just lost her fiancé a year ago, so be careful."

"What happened?" Roy gave in to his curiosity. No man with a lick of sense would leave a woman like her.

"Frank signed up with the Canadian Air Force and was shot down over Germany. Valerie had a rough time accepting the loss." Paul's expression became serious, and he crossed his arms over his chest. "If you hurt her in any way, you'll answer to me."

"You sound just like we're back in Switzerland when the headmaster told you I'd hidden a puppy in my closet."

"Some things never change."

"And others do." Roy gestured to his cast. "I'm not in any condition to pursue your stepdaughter, so rest easy." *Besides, now that I'm lame, I can't be the brave young soldier she'd want.*

The older man raised his hands in mock surrender. "All right. But you've been warned. Now let's go get some food!"

◆　◆　◆

"This is excellent," Mr. Benson complimented before loading his fork again.

"Thank you, Mr. Benson." Rosemary, ever the gracious hostess, refilled his iced tea.

"I helped!" Valerie smiled at her new sister's pronouncement. Rebekkah clapped her hand to her heart and explained, "I washed the 'tatoes!"

"Well, I'll bet that's why these are the best baked potatoes I've ever had in my life."

His compliment made Rebekkah positively beam. Their houseguest's personable charm and easy good looks made him a welcome addition to the table. Surely Paul appreciated some masculine company in the house as well.

"What's running through that mind of yours, Valerie Jane Fulton?"

"Nothing special, Mom. Why do you ask?"

"Even I know that satisfied little grin," Paul teased. "It means you're up to something."

"Honestly, I was just thinking how glad you must be to have another man around the house. You've been pretty outnumbered for a while." Valerie loved teasing her stepfather because he always played along without taking any offense.

"I manage to hold my own!" he protested.

"Of course you do, sweetheart." Rosemary's reassuring pat drove the point home, and Mr. Benson chuckled.

"I think Miss Fulton's got you there, Paul!"

"Traitor!" Paul shook his head. "I'd expected better from you, Roy. You're no help at all."

"Sorry." Mr. Benson's hazel eyes sparkled for a moment as he reached for the green beans.

That's the first time his smile has reached his eyes, Valerie realized. *I know these are hard times we live in, but if we forget the good, we do a disservice to those fighting to protect it! I want to see that smile more often.*

Her sister's yawn caught her attention and reminded her that the time was getting late for the little tyke. "Come on, Bekkah." Valerie scooted her seat out and lifted the three-year-old to the floor. "Let's go get the Advent calendar."

Rebekkah clasped Valerie's hand and toddled over to the living room, where she carefully picked up the colorful cardboard before scampering back.

"Here, Momma!" She raised on tiptoes to hand it over.

Rosemary scooped Rebekkah in her arms and laid the calendar, with seven little peekaboo doors open, on the table.

"See the pretty angel, Rebekkah? Up here," she said, tapping the corner, "is an eight. That's today."

"Why is it an angel, Momma?" Rebekkah traced the angel's wings.

"Do you remember what we already learned about Mary? This is when an angel came to talk to her husband, Joseph. Let's read what the angel says."

Rebekkah carefully pried open the tiny door, and Valerie read aloud: " 'And she shall bring forth a son, and thou shalt call his name Jesus: for he shall save his people from their sins.' "

"Jesus born on Christmas!"

"That's right, darling."

"Why did the angel come to tell him that, though?"

"Rebekkah, do you remember that Jesus is God's Son?" Rosemary waited until Rebekkah finished bobbing her head. "The angel is telling Joseph that it's all right to be Jesus' father here on earth."

"Oh!" Rebekkah's eyes shone brightly as she crawled down from her mother's lap and tugged on Paul's pant leg. "Like God told you to be my papa."

Valerie blinked back tears as Paul scooped up the little girl and bounced her on his knee. "That's exactly right, sweetie." He smiled tenderly. "I think it's time to get you ready for bed. We'll hear more of the story tomorrow night."

"Yes, Papa." She willingly went into Valerie's arms but stretched out her chubby little arms for a few last hugs and kisses.

"Ni-night, Papa. Ni-night, Momma."

"Good night, sweetie. We'll see you in the morning."

"'Kay." Rebekkah circled her arms around Valerie's neck and leaned her head against her shoulder. Valerie planted a kiss on those soft brown curls and headed upstairs to the nursery, where she helped her little sister change into a warm flannel nightie before leading her to the bathroom.

"Open wide." Valerie squeezed a dab of Ipana toothpaste on a brush and gave it to Rebekkah, guiding her hand to make sure every tooth was brushed.

Tucked snugly in her new "big girl" bed, Rebekkah followed Valerie's lead and recited her bedtime prayer:

> I pray the Lord my soul to keep.
> Guide me safely through the night,
> And wake me with the morning light.
> Amen."

Valerie hummed softly until Rebekkah's eyelashes brushed her cheeks. It was better to stay with her until she fell asleep—it cut back on the nightmares she'd suffered since her arrival.

Lord, You've blessed us so in Rebekkah. Every time I look at her, I see the reason You brought Paul into our lives and how important those dolls really are. If it isn't in Your plan, I may never have a child of my own, but this precious child fills such a void in all our lives. Thank You for letting Paul bring her to us. And while I'm at it, thank You for making my mother so happy with her new husband and second daughter! Amen.

She made her way downstairs and found her mother, Paul, and Mr. Benson drinking coffee in the living room, listening to the evening news on the radio.

◆　◆　◆

The past two weeks had flown by far more quickly than even a single week at the hospital ever had. Tomorrow would be Christmas Eve.

He'd quickly gotten used to the routine around the house. Getting up and shaving took him far longer than it used to, but by the time he made it to the kitchen, Rosemary or Valerie had laid the table with something fresh and delicious.

Valerie would leave for the bank, where she worked hard promoting the new war bonds, and Paul would go to work as well. Between reading the newspapers from front to back and listening to the radio for news about the war, Roy had plenty to map out.

Determined to be back on his feet in the best possible condition, he'd begun taking daily "walks" around the house on his crutches. Unfortunately, the icy winter sidewalks kept him indoors. After lying in a hospital bed for so long, he needed to work up his strength again.

Aside from the freedom of movement—and good cooking—the real bright spots were the people sharing their home with him. Rosemary fussed over him like a fond mother hen while Rebekkah would toddle up to him at various times clutching a children's Bible or her favorite game—Snakes and Ladders.

Paul had shared with him that he and Rosemary had decided to adopt the child but evaded going into any more depth. The little girl brought an innocent joy that lit the whole house, but at nighttime, Roy could hear Rosemary comforting her as unnamed nightmares haunted her sleep. Roy knew vague details of how the Third Reich systematically deprived Jews of their rights and even homes. The fact that they were just teaching little Rebekkah about Jesus made him wonder whether she could be one of those children. Besides, when Rebekkah cried at night, he heard her speak in German, and that bore out his suspicions as to why Paul had brought her here. Still, it wasn't his place to ask. They'd been more than generous and hospitable to him.

The days flew by, but his favorite hours were in the evenings, when Valerie and Paul would come home, bringing stories and smiles to share. After dinner, they'd open another Advent window before Rosemary or Valerie put Rebekkah to bed. Then they'd gather in the living room for coffee and news.

Rosemary and Valerie were forever sewing tiny rag dolls to ship to their family's business in Denmark, where they apparently needed every import they could get. Paul even pitched in, so Roy didn't mind picking up a needle.

After Roy spent a few minutes hemming a minuscule apron, Valerie realized what he was doing. She stared in astonishment before letting loose a muffled squeak. The small sound caught Paul's and Rosemary's attention, and they all watched him for a while before Paul guffawed.

"Well, if that doesn't beat all. Must be all those years looking after your uniforms, eh, Roy?"

"That's right. But I'll never be able to hold my own with Mrs. Kincaid. Some people just have natural talent at stitching."

"I know!" Valerie dabbed another spot of blood with her handkerchief and moaned, "And you're far better at this than I'll *ever* be!"

Chapter 3

I'm home!" Valerie unwound her blue scarf and hung it on the coat tree in the hallway.

"Sissy!" Rebekkah shot down the hall and squealed as Valerie hoisted her high in the air, then snuggled her.

Roy watched the sweet scene for a moment before clearing his throat. "Did you get more cinnamon? We sorely need it."

"Yes." Valerie gifted him with a wide smile.

"Tomorrow's Christmas!" exclaimed Rebekkah.

"Right you are. Come on, let's go help." Valerie cocked her head, including Roy in the invitation.

"Sounds good to me." Roy hobbled along behind them on his crutches as Rebekkah chatted like a magpie.

"Mr. Benson took me out, but I'm not s'posed to talk 'bout it." The child sent him an exaggerated wink.

"Is that right?" Valerie murmured as she slanted Roy a look over her shoulder.

"Maybe." He'd taken Rebekkah for a walk over to Mrs. Ainsley's place and given her a list of things to buy with the money he folded inside the note.

More than happy to oblige, the old lady trundled off immediately. The only hitch in the plan came when he told her he'd included a bit extra for her to use however she'd like.

Mrs. Ainsley had puffed up like a pigeon, using every single bit of her four-foot-eleven height to glare at him with sharp blue eyes.

"Now, Mrs. Ainsley, you've been so good to me that I want to get you something for Christmas, but I've no idea what you'd like. Besides, this is such a big favor you're doing for me that I absolutely insist." With that spur-of-the-moment speech, he'd won her over. He'd just finished stashing the bags she'd brought him when he heard Valerie come in.

"I get the message." Her eyes twinkled up at him. "I won't ask any more questions."

"That'll be the day." Paul strode into the room with Rosemary right behind him.

"Oh, honey, I sure am glad you didn't have to work today!"

Roy couldn't agree more with Rosemary's loving words. Valerie's company made time fly faster than the snow.

"I could use help making gingerbread men for after the service tonight."

In no time at all, everyone became engrossed in the project at hand. Rosemary threw together the ingredients, then handed the batter to Roy to beat into dough. He passed it on to Paul, who rolled it out and waited for Rebekkah to help him press down the cookie cutter, while Valerie laid the little figures on cookie sheets and popped them in and out of the oven.

"I've never baked before." Roy sniffed appreciatively. "But I could grow to like it." He reached out to snag a warm cookie, only to pull up short when Valerie smacked his hand away.

"What?" He tried to look as innocent as possible.

"I saw that, Roy Benson. Seems to me like we don't have as many of these little guys as we should."

The warm fragrance of ginger and cinnamon filled the house as the final batch baked to a perfect golden brown.

"It wasn't me! That would've been only my fourth one." Roy poked one of the cookies. "They have legs, you know."

"Sure. I suppose they just walked off." Valerie plunked more cookies onto the table, where Roy mixed a large batch of frosting.

"If they didn't, I'd look at the other side of the table, if I were you." He pointed at Paul, who gave a noticeable swallow.

"Don't you be pointing at us!" Paul put his arm around Rebekkah's shoulders. "We haven't swiped very many at all, have we, sweetie?"

But Rebekkah, cheeks puffed out like a greedy chipmunk, just kept sticking Red Hots on the tiny dabs of icing to serve as buttons.

After a hearty laugh, they packed up the remaining gingerbread men for the churchgoers. While they finished up, Rosemary laid out dinner in the dining room, since cookies covered every available inch in the kitchen.

After supper, they all piled into the red Pierce-Arrow, Roy taking the front seat since he couldn't bend his left leg, and rode down to Gethsemane Chapel for the Christmas Eve candlelight service.

◆　◆　◆

"Merry Christmas!" Roy hobbled into the kitchen, where Valerie pulled cinnamon rolls out of the oven.

"Merry Christmas." She smiled to see him so full of energy. "Everyone else will be down soon. I expect they're just getting Rebekkah dressed."

"I'll get the coffee started," Roy offered.

"It's already done. But if you could grab some milk from the icebox for Rebekkah, I'd appreciate it."

He'd just put the milk on the table when the rest of the family filed in and took their seats.

"Dear Lord," Paul prayed, "we thank You this fine morning for all You've given us. Today we remember how You forsook Your powers to come as a man and save us. Please bless this food on our table and watch over our boys not at home as they protect this nation. Amen."

After they'd eaten their fill and the dishes were finished, they made a beeline for the living room, where bright packages waited.

Valerie turned on the radio, changing stations until she heard "God Rest Ye Merry, Gentlemen."

She and Paul passed out all the gifts before anyone opened a single package. Rebekkah fidgeted but stayed polite as ever.

In no time at all, wrapping paper and ribbon lay scattered across the floor, and a barrage of "thank yous" echoed.

"The diary is wonderful, Mom. You remembered that my two-year journal would be all filled up come January!" Valerie hugged her mother joyfully.

"You're welcome, honey. I love my little music box." Rosemary lifted the lid, and the spritely tune competed with the radio.

Valerie got up and shut off the radio, instead opening the Victrola to place her brand-new Jimmy Dorsey album on it. "Green Eyes" filled the air as she thanked Roy.

"Every time I hear that song, I think of you—you're the first girl I've ever known with green eyes, Valerie." Roy's thoughtfulness tugged at her heart. He was such a special man—and it went beyond his thick hair and deep gaze. Despite his frustration over his leg, he stayed patient with Rebekkah, kind to her mother, and companionable to Paul.

Although Valerie had never heard him utter a single word of complaint about how much his leg must hurt, every time he heard about the war, the pain in his eyes deepened. The physical discomfort of his broken leg didn't hurt him half as deeply as the reminder that he wasn't out there protecting the country.

Lord, help me, but a part of me is glad his leg will never completely recover. It means he'll be safe from the war. I couldn't bear it if I lost another man I care for to the Nazis.

"And thank you for the Chinese checkers," Roy said as he set the box on the coffee table. "You'll have to give me a chance to try it out this afternoon."

"Gladly. It'll be fun." Valerie looked at the box. "You know, I think we could all play tonight—it says up to six players."

"Count me out." Paul held up two books. "I've got other plans. Thank you both—Roy for *Call It Courage*, and Valerie for *Daniel Boone*. I'm going to enjoy these."

"I'm up to a game." Rosemary pulled on her new fleece gloves and wiggled her fingers. "These are perfect, Roy. Thank you!"

"You can use my special Christmas table." Rebekkah dragged over a tiny chair and whumped her new teddy bear on top of it.

Valerie was glad Rebekkah liked Teddy. She hoped it would help to have another cuddly friend in bed when the nightmares came again.

"I'm gonna draw a picture for Uncle Roy with my crayons." Roy had given

Rebekkah a set of Crayolas, and she busily scribbled on a sheet of scrap paper until it was time for lunch.

◆ ◆ ◆

"When are you going to tell me what's going on?"

At Roy's pointed question, Paul peered over the top of his newspaper. "You already know that Hitler took complete command over the German army and that Churchill arrived in Washington just before Christmas. . . . And as of the New Year, the U.S. and twenty-five other countries have signed a contract of war against the Axis powers and pledged no separate peace—"

"I'm not talking about what I can read in the newspaper or hear from the radio, Paul," Roy said, cutting into the older man's recitation. "Level with me."

"Listen," Paul said as he put aside the newspaper, "the news is about as accurate as we can get. You know that preliminary data is always sketchy. I will tell you that for the first time in our nation's history, we've established a federal office of censorship to filter information concerning the war, but that's more for the protection of our troops' positions than to keep anything from the public. It's not designed to infringe on our rights."

"Interesting, but that's still not what I mean." Roy held up a rag doll. "And you know it."

Paul shrugged. "We already told you—the dolls are sent to Valerie's cousins Axel and Annelise in Denmark, where they are trying to keep an export-import business afloat." He picked up his paper and raised it once more as he added, "They distribute them there. The dolls are quite popular, I hear."

"Don't try to pawn a surface cover story off on me. You should know better."

"What makes you think there's anything else going on?" Paul tried to sound casual, but Roy sensed the purpose behind the question. If he could convince Paul that his suspicions stood on solid ground, he'd be let into the fold.

"First, why can't they just transport the raw supplies and contract the work to be done in Denmark?" Roy led off with an easy question.

"Rosemary and Valerie are happy to help their cousins. This way, they don't have to pay for the dolls to be made," Paul explained. "It's better business."

"That's what I figured at first, but too many things don't add up." Roy dove in. "What about that letter Valerie received yesterday? She started to read it aloud but got slower the farther down she got. After the news that the Nazis were forcing Dutch physicians into serving them, she stopped altogether. What did she leave out?"

"How would I know?" Paul scoffed. "I don't read her mail."

Obviously Paul wasn't going to cave in easily. But the more he denied, the more important the matter truly was, and Roy didn't intend to be left in the dark. He brought out the big guns.

"Don't forget I was practically raised in Europe. Rebekkah is no little Danish girl. Even before I saw Valerie write her name yesterday as winning tic-tac-toe, I had my suspicions. She's Jewish. Those nightmares she has are part of the reason you brought her here. She was in danger." Paul met his gaze steadily and gave a slight nod. Good. He was making headway.

"So what do you think is going on?"

The question was more than a challenge—Paul had thrown down the gauntlet. If Roy's suspicions didn't come close to the truth, this conversation would be over.

Lord, You know how much I want to be a part of defeating the Axis. If this is Your plan for me, let my words be true.

"Rebekkah has one of those dolls. As far as I can figure out, they're used to smuggle something into Denmark—small things." Roy put the pieces together, building his case. "I would've guessed ammunition, but that'd be too heavy. For some reason, you're sending money over to Denmark. More than Valerie's cousins would need for just themselves. And the last time you visited, you brought home a Jewish child. You've worked out some system where you're using the dolls to save Jews from the Nazis."

"Well done, Roy. I'd hoped you would catch on. The navy can be proud of how well we trained you."

"What are the specifics?" Roy carefully kept his voice neutral and waited eagerly.

"We send valuables in the dolls. In Denmark, they take out the jewels or cash or what have you and use it to fund the creation of documents enabling Jews to leave the country. Rebekkah is one of the children who depended on us."

Roy sucked in a deep breath. "Do the women know?"

"Rosemary and Valerie do. Rebekkah doesn't understand it. She just knows that I came for her, and we're her family now."

More questions raced through Roy's mind, but he knew better than to push. "Then why are we sitting here reading the paper?" He stood up.

"You're right." Paul heaved a resigned sigh. "A man's gotta do what a man's gotta do."

"Sir, yes sir." Roy saluted him, then grinned. "I'll go get the needles and thread."

Chapter 4

"Y ou could just give up now," Roy suggested, looking entirely too happy with himself as he lounged in his chair.

I would be annoyed, but his eyes are sparkling again. If it makes him smile to win a game of Chinese checkers, that's a small price to pay. Not that Valerie would let him know, though.

"Never!" she shot back, giving her hair a saucy flip and reaching for the board as Paul walked into the room.

"Losing again, is she?"

"I don't think she'll ever admit that naval officers can't be beat when it comes to strategy."

Roy's comment proved to be the straw that broke the camel's back. Valerie pretended to ponder her next move; then, just when Roy shifted in his seat, signaling his restlessness, she sprung into action, hopping one of her green marbles over the "bridge" he'd just finished making for his own use.

"Nice one, honey." Rosemary walked up beside Paul.

"Well, what do you know? Maybe you're in trouble after all, Roy!" Paul teased, but their smug smiles faded when Valerie hopped her final marble into its slot, beating Roy by at least three moves.

"Well, Roy, I think you've met your match." Rosemary winked at Valerie before leaving the kitchen.

"I certainly have." Valerie's breath caught at the intensity of Roy's gaze. He gathered his pieces and gently placed them in her palm, the marbles still warm from the heat of his hand.

"It's time to go to the store, Val!"

"Coming, Mom!" Valerie held the marbles a moment longer before putting them away and rushing outside.

When they got to town, Rosemary took off the gloves Roy had given her and stepped into Nannington's General Store. "Hello, Abel."

"Good morning, Rosemary. What can I get you today?"

"A bit of everything, Mr. Nannington." Valerie laughed.

"I need a book of three-cent stamps, a loaf of bread, a gallon of milk," Rosemary rattled off, "two yards of green flannel, a dozen eggs, and twenty pounds of sugar—the ten-pound bags, please."

"See?" Valerie quirked an eyebrow at the shopkeeper.

"I reckon your daughter had the right of it, after all." Abel grinned as he rummaged through the shelves, plunking down the requested items. "But I'm fresh out of the ten-pound bags of sugar." He hopped down from his step stool. "Had a run on it since we declared war. People remember how it was with the Great War not so long ago. I have three five-pounders left. I can call you soon as I get more in, if you'd like. You're probably real low after all those cookies you made for the Christmas Eve candlelight service. Those sure were tasty."

"Thank you, Abel." Rosemary took out her wallet. "What does that come to?"

Valerie gasped when she heard the price.

"Sorry, ma'am. Prices have gone up a lot in the past month. Bread and eggs are a full cent more per order, and milk is on the rise, too," Abel explained. "It'll be worse before the war is over."

"I expected that." While Rosemary paid the bill, Valerie grabbed the box of provisions and carried it out to the car.

"I hate to break it to you, honey," Rosemary said, sliding into the driver's seat, "but a time may come when we can't get some of these things at all. War leaves no family untouched."

◆ ◆ ◆

The door creaked open. Roy hurriedly jabbed his needle deep into the doll he was working on and stuffed it behind his back just as Valerie walked into the room.

"What are you doing?" She gave him an odd look as he swung the Duncan yo-yo Rebekkah had given him for Christmas into a perfect cat's cradle.

"Nothing much," he evaded, reaching for the paper. "What were you gals up to?"

"We went to the store. Just finished putting things away." She strolled over and stood behind his chair. "If you're going to read, you'll need more light."

He caught a whiff of violets as she reached over to turn on the lamp. . .and instead snatched the doll he'd been hiding.

"I knew it!" she crowed triumphantly, only to have her grin replaced by a puzzled frown. "Do you really like sewing that much?"

"Not really." He prayed she'd drop it. No such luck as she spoke once more.

"So you figured out most of it, and Paul filled you in on the rest." She tossed the doll onto his lap.

"Yep." He cautiously lowered the paper. He waited for her to say something more, but she just started filling another doll with cotton batting. He put down the paper and resumed work on the one in his lap. They worked in companionable silence until he finally asked, "How'd you know Paul didn't just tell me?"

"This was our only concern about bringing you here. Paul promised he wouldn't tell you unless you figured it out, and his word is his bond. Besides, you're too smart for your own good." Her smile softened the words, making them a compliment. "Oh, and that's what happened with me, too. You have to put the pieces together yourself before anyone will tell you if you've done it right. Discretion is vital."

"Your secret is safe with me," he vowed.

"I know." She met his gaze in earnest, those green eyes giving her words meaning beyond the conversation. "I trust you."

◆　◆　◆

The next evening, as the adults sat in the family room, stitching as rapidly as possible, the news came on the radio.

"As you all know, last Friday saw the creation of the U.S. Joint Chiefs of Staff. This week is shaping up to bear just as many historic occasions. Yesterday, Washington sanctioned the establishment of the National War Labor Board to oversee wartime economy. This sparks fears of rationing, as was the norm in the Great War, so women around the nation are flocking to their neighborhood stores to stock up on essentials such as sugar. . ."

The voice droned on, speculating about probable shortages of various items, until Valerie got up and changed the station.

"We went to the store yesterday, and everything now is just predictions anyway." She fiddled with the dial until cheery strains of bebop filled the room. "That's better."

"He's right, though," Rosemary noted. "Abel Nannington didn't even have twenty pounds of sugar on hand yesterday, and we bought him out." She handed Valerie a doll to fill with stuffing.

"It's all right, Rosemary." Paul worked at untangling his thread for the umpteenth time that evening. "If there'd been anything else important or new, they'd have covered it at the beginning. Every station is on the lookout for updates anyway, so no matter what we listen to, we'll hear whatever special bulletin comes along next."

"No sense rehashing what we already know." Roy set another completed doll in his nearly full box.

◆　◆　◆

The next Sunday, Valerie stood in the choir as they led the congregation of Gethsemane Chapel in worship. The director had worked with the pastor to choose pieces befitting the sermon to come. As they sang the final piece before the pastor took the pulpit, Valerie closed her eyes at the power of the words:

A mighty fortress is our God, a bulwark never failing;
our helper He amid the flood of mortal ills prevailing.
For still our ancient foe doth seek to work us woe;
His craft and power are great. . .

How true and right those words rang as a prayer set to music. Valerie became swept away by the music, and before she knew it, they were in the midst of the third verse:

And though this world, with devils filled, should threaten to undo us,
we will not fear, for God hath willed His truth to triumph through us. . .

Soon the song was over, and the pastor bowed his head in prayer. "Lord, please defend us against the war. Our cause is just. Bless those families pulled apart by it, and let our faith remain strong that Your will may endure. Amen."

The choir filed off the platform and took seats in the front pews. In light of the escalating war, the pastor chose to speak from Psalm 144.

He read the first two verses, speaking of faith and justice, recalling David's words when he faced war. "Blessed be the Lord my strength, which teacheth my hands to war, and my fingers to fight: My goodness, and my fortress; my high tower, and my deliverer; my shield, and he in whom I trust. . . ."

After drawing the parallel between David's situation when he wrote those words and the situation faced by the members of the congregation, the pastor exhorted his parishioners not to curse the consequences of the war but rather to pray to the Lord in thanks for His blessings of strength.

Roy listened intently to the pastor's words, drinking in the promise of strength as America fought in Christ's name to protect the innocents of the world. As the pastor led them in a final prayer, Roy took the time to offer his own request.

Lord, is there no way I can serve You and my country other than through those dolls? Have I truly spent eight years learning all I could to be of use in the navy only to be relegated to sewing during a war engulfing the entire world? Lord, help me understand Your plan—and to accept Your will, whatever it may be. Amen.

As Roy lifted his head after the pastor finished, he saw Valerie standing at the fore of the entire choir. The organist began strains of a familiar hymn before Valerie's clear alto rang throughout the chapel:

'Tis so sweet to trust in Jesus, and to take Him at His word;
just to rest upon His promise, and to know, "Thus saith the Lord."

For the refrain, the entire choir joined her, and the music swelled with life as they praised the Lord and asked for *"grace to trust Him more."*

Roy watched Valerie's eyes close as she sang the words to the second verse, her face lit with joy and hope. Her voice sounded pure and sweet above the others as the entire congregation rose to join her.

Lord, this woman means more to me than I ever would have thought possible, but what do I have to offer her? Help me trust in Your plan, for now more than ever I am nothing without Your grace.

Chapter 5

In the first week of February, Paul took Roy in to get his cast off, but the doctors told him he'd have to use the crutches for another two weeks, minimum, as he began physical therapy.

"Is there any way to speed this up, Doc?" Roy pumped the physician for information.

"You'll recover better if you take it slow. Too much too fast will do you more harm than good." Dr. Harwell fixed him with a penetrating stare. "First we'll work on stretching to get back your range of motion. Only then is it realistic to work on strengthening the muscle. You've been off this leg for over two months already; it isn't possible for you to just resume walking."

"I was afraid of that." Roy looked down at his legs and grimaced to see his left side so thin compared to the right.

"When you regain your muscle, they won't look so disproportionate." The doctor took a moment to jot down several notes on his clipboard before pronouncing, "I'll see you after two weeks of physical therapy. I want to be perfectly clear: You're still confined to crutches. On the bright side, it'll be a lot less unwieldy without that big cast. But no trying to walk on that leg yet. That's an order."

"Yes sir." Roy grudgingly gave his word, seeing the wisdom in the doctor's order. He'd come too far to let a lack of patience land him back in traction.

◆ ◆ ◆

"Quit scowling, Roy." Valerie handed him a hot water bottle, which he gratefully placed on his shinbone. He put every ounce of determination he possessed into his daily exercises and received each measure of it back in stiffness afterward.

"Sorry, Val. I don't mean to be a grouch. I'll make it up to you with a game of Chinese checkers." His offer made her chuckle.

"All right. Who knows? You just might win this time." She opened the cupboard, grabbed the box, and set up the game on the side table next to his recliner. Since elevating the leg helped make him more comfortable, it had become his favorite chair.

"Yeah, yeah. Let's just play." He pretended to grump just a bit more to coax another smile from her beguiling lips.

"Listen." She perched on the chair she'd pulled up and rested a soft hand on his forearm. "In a week or so, Doc Harwell will decree you're ready to begin strength training. You'll be walking in no time."

He placed his hand over hers and gave it a slight squeeze. "Thanks, Valerie. I hope you're right."

"Well, I *know* I'm right." She tossed him a mischievous smile. "Now, let's get this game going."

A short half hour later, Roy beamed over his hard-won victory.

"Hail the conquering her–o," Paul sang as Roy hopped over to the dinner table. "It's about time you won that game."

"Well, I hope you both learned a lesson." Rosemary ladled heaping portions of thick beef stew into bowls and passed them around.

"Oh, they'll think twice before they say anything about how women can't beat navy men when it comes to strategy." Valerie nonchalantly buttered Rebekkah's biscuit.

"True," Roy admitted. "I should've remembered that you work in a bank, so you're good with numbers and logic." He raised his iced tea. "To a worthy opponent."

"I'll drink to that." They all raised their glasses, then made a special to-do about clinking cups with Rebekkah, who giggled and sloshed her juice down the front of her dress.

Dinner remained a merry affair, and before she knew it, Valerie sat next to Roy in the living room again, listening to the evening news on the radio.

"Top news tonight, February 9. We'd like to remind everyone to set their clocks back an hour as daylight saving war time goes into effect. Although we'll all lose an hour's sleep tonight, we'll gain extra daylight every day. The increased productivity is expected to be a valuable contribution to the home-front war effort. When you listen to tomorrow's broadcast, you'll hardly believe it's actually eight o'clock!

"In other news, General Clinton Pierce, the first U.S. general to be wounded in action, has become an inspiration to our armed forces. Remember him and all our boys in your prayers tonight. . . ."

As the news broke into local headlines, Roy turned down the volume. "When they start changing the hours of the day, you know the war is getting serious."

"I think I'll like having an extra hour of light when I get home from the bank," Valerie protested, determined to overlook the minor inconvenience of getting up an hour earlier and in the dark.

"If it doesn't work out, at least it's just for the war." Rosemary snipped her thread and tied another knot before passing the doll so Valerie could stuff it. This new system of having Roy take over her portion—and more, in all fairness—of the sewing and leaving her to stuff the dolls meant unpricked fingers and less tired eyes.

Roy Benson had proved a blessing in more ways than she'd ever imagined. Rebekkah had taken a shine to him; Paul obviously enjoyed having another man around the house; Rosemary got more help with the dolls; and Valerie got the satisfaction of seeing everyone be happy—not to mention the warm tingles she got every time he smiled at her with those deep hazel eyes. He wasn't going anywhere for at least another month, too. All in all, life was good.

◆　◆　◆

"Come on, Valerie!" Roy called up the stairs.

"I'm coming!" She fairly flew down the stairs and gave him a quick frown before continuing along the hallway. "You do remember I'm the one who asked you about this?" she reminded him.

"I know." He stashed his crutches in the backseat. "And I'm glad you did."

Valerie shut the door and walked around the car to slide into the driver's seat. "I didn't mean to grump at you, Roy," she apologized as they made their way to the hospital. "It doesn't seem to matter how many times I give blood, I'm always happiest when it's all over."

"That's just because they give you juice afterward," Roy teased, knowing full well that Valerie gave blood out of nothing less than a deep determination to help others in any way possible. She'd inherited a fair portion of her mother's generous spirit.

"Ssshhh. If you tell them, they won't give me my favorite!"

"What's your favorite?" he wondered aloud. "Apple or orange?"

"I'm not telling." She pulled into a parking space and drummed her fingers on the steering wheel.

Despite her attempt to keep a lighthearted tone, he knew what she was thinking. "It's just one tiny needle. You'll be fine."

Half an hour later, they both sat at a table drinking juice and munching on cookies.

"You know, this reminds me a lot of Rebekkah's tea parties." Valerie lifted a tiny paper cup. "You're so good about attending those."

"I don't know what you're talking about." Roy feigned ignorance. "Soldiers don't go to tea parties."

"Oh, all right. I won't say anything more to spoil your image. I only wanted to thank you for how special you make her feel." She touched his hand across the table. "You have a knack for that."

"You are both special to me." He wasn't about to let the moment go. "Besides, don't think I haven't noticed how much better Rebekkah has slept since you gave her that teddy bear for Christmas."

"She's so sweet." Valerie smiled fondly. "She cuddles him on one side and her dolly on the other."

"See? You've made sure she knows she's always surrounded with love."

They simply looked at each other until a man sauntered over and plunked down onto another chair.

"Hello, Mr. Twisselman," Valerie greeted the stout fellow.

"Hello, Valerie." His moustache twitched as he spoke. "How are you?"

"Just fine. I don't like needles," she admitted to the older man, "but when I'm done, I always feel wonderful."

"Yep. Have to be careful, though." Mr. Twisselman hooked his thumbs in his suspenders and leaned back. "I come often. Good thing we butchers are hardy stock." He grabbed a paper cup.

"So true—" Valerie gasped. "Mr. Twisselman!" The butcher's face grew waxen as he slumped to the floor.

"Nurse!" Roy bellowed for help as Valerie dabbed Mr. Twisselman's forehead with a damp cloth.

"It'll be all right, miss." An orderly lifted the butcher off the floor.

"Happens all the time." A tall nurse brought out a blood pressure cuff. "He'll be fine."

"Would you like me to call his wife?" Valerie offered.

"No need. We'll keep him here a bit longer and send him on his way," the nurse assured them as she swept the now-empty paper cups into a trash can and mopped up Mr. Twisselman's juice.

As they walked out of the hospital doors, Roy smiled. *Well, Lord, I suppose being of "hardy stock" just might be overrated. If a fainting butcher can help in the war effort, why can't a lame soldier lend a hand? I'll ask the doctor at Monday's appointment just how much I can expect to be able to do.*

◆　◆　◆

"What did the doctor say?" Rosemary beat Valerie to the question before Roy so much as stepped into the room.

"Tomorrow I begin strength training." Roy's grin faded somewhat as he continued. "Of course, I'm still not supposed to try putting any weight on it."

"Bouncing is fun!" Rebekkah hopped in on one foot, a habit she'd taken to whenever the subject of Roy's leg came up. The three-year-old had to grab on to other things to manage it, but her special way of encouraging her "Uncle Roy" showed how much Roy had become a part of the family.

"Well, that's probably for the best." Rosemary's practical comment didn't seem to cheer him up any. "The streets are still icy, and we wouldn't want any accident to set you back."

"Look on the bright side," Valerie broke in. "It's a *step* in the right direction!"

Everybody groaned at her pun, but Roy smiled once again, making it all worthwhile.

◆　◆　◆

Roy looked out the window and, for the first time in months, saw a patch of blue sky. Mid-March brought the first hope of spring and the promise of change.

A lot had changed since he'd come here. The United States had declared war against the Axis powers, hundreds of soldiers had gone off to fight, and Roy had come to terms with the reality he would never be one of them. The dolls gave him a focus and purpose as his leg recovered, and he knew that although he couldn't engage in active combat, he could serve in other ways. No longer burdened by a large cast, Roy did so well in physical therapy that he'd graduated to using a cane this afternoon. He grasped it and rose from his chair, gritting his teeth and leaning heavily on the cane as he slowly made his way toward the kitchen. As his leg took the weight with only minor discomfort, he relaxed a bit and moved more easily.

Through all that, he'd become part of a real family. Roy would miss them when he left—Paul's guidance, Rosemary's mothering, Rebekkah's high-pitched giggle, and Valerie's. . .well, he'd miss everything about Valerie. Her honey curls, the mischievous sparkle in her green eyes when she teased him, the purity of her voice raised in song, how she cuddled Rebekkah, even the way she played Chinese checkers.

Before he went back, he would make a point of spending more time with her—alone, so he wouldn't have to see Paul and Rosemary exchanging smug glances. In a few days, he would be able to walk much farther. Maybe they could go for a stroll.

Lord, I complained so bitterly about my leg, but You've blessed me in so many ways through the injury. Physical strength is not the only way to be of worth. Thank You for showing me that truth.

Rebekkah tugged on his sleeve. "Snack time."

Roy grinned and took her into the kitchen, grabbing a couple of oatmeal cookies from the jar on the counter.

"Aha!" Valerie's exclamation made him turn.

"Mmmf—what?" he muttered around a mouthful of cookie. Rebekkah shoved her cookie behind her back and pressed up against the white kitchen cupboards, looking about as innocent as a girl with crumbs around her mouth ever could.

"I knew it!" Valerie's eyes flashed with suppressed laughter as she advanced into the room. "Caught you with your hand in the cookie jar."

Roy heaved a deep sigh and 'fessed up. "Guilty as charged, ma'am."

"I'll let you off with just a warning this time, soldier," Valerie intoned as she crooked a finger. "Hand over the contraband, and we'll call it even."

Roy winked at Rebekkah as his partner in crime crammed the second half of her cookie into her mouth. "I can't do that, ma'am. It's gone for good." He tried to keep a straight face as Valerie abandoned her role of authority figure to grab the green-trimmed ceramic canister and shove her arm in clear up to her elbow.

After groping along the bottom for a few seconds, Valerie gave up. "You ate the last one when you knew oatmeal cookies are my favorite?" She stared up at him in disbelief, sending a small pang of guilt through his chest. He hadn't meant to be so inconsiderate.

"Sorry, sissy." Rebekkah held up one tiny hand littered with crumbs. "All gone." Her lower lip began to quiver.

"Oh, sweetie!" Valerie scooped the toddler into her arms. "It's all right. We'll just have to break into the emergency supply!"

Roy watched in astonishment as Valerie nudged a cabinet open with her elbow and withdrew a round blue tin and set it on the counter. She popped off the lid and drew out three cookies before resealing it and nestling the tin behind some preserves.

"And you tried to make us feel guilty." Roy gazed fixedly at the cookies in her hand. "You've been holding out on us!"

She let loose a peal of silvery laughter before passing a cookie to him and handing another to Rebekkah. "When Paul moved in, we had to start making extra and putting a few aside," she explained.

"Good thinking!" Roy bit into the warm, buttery cookie and promised, "I won't tell!"

◆　◆　◆

"Here you go, Bekkah." Valerie handed her little sister a tiny shovel.

"I make holes." Rebekkah gleefully stuck her new toy in the dirt and made a shallow opening. "See?"

"Good job!" Valerie clapped. "Now do it again and make it deeper, like mine."

" 'Kay." Rebekkah rolled up her little sleeves, emulating Rosemary's habit for outdoor work, then dug in. The largest seeds, peas, sat in a bucket beside her. When Rosemary agreed the hole was deep enough, the little girl dropped in a seed and covered the hole with dirt.

"Done." Rebekkah clapped her hands and dirt powdered her little snub nose.

"One more thing. Now we have to make sure it's good and packed in there." Valerie walked over and pressed the dirt down.

"I can do it!" When Valerie stepped back, Rebekkah began stomping on the dirt.

"That's enough." Rosemary laughed. "If you keep it up, we'll never finish! Why don't you get going on the next one?"

More quickly than they would have thought possible, they filled the garden with hardy veggies like radishes, spinach, and peas. Later, when the weather warmed up even more, they'd make room for sweet corn, cucumbers, and beans.

Rebekkah hopped all around the garden for good measure as Rosemary helped Valerie rinse off their tools.

"Come on, Bekkah," Valerie called when they headed for the house.

"Comin', sissy!" She made a beeline for the house, practically zooming through the door before Valerie caught her.

"Oh, no you don't! Wipe your feet really good before you go in." Clumps of dirt dotted the mat before they all finished and trooped through the door.

"Why don't you go play with Teddy while Val and I heat up some lunch?" Rosemary watched her scamper up the stairs before fixing Valerie with a penetrating stare.

"What? I thought the garden went well." Valerie's stomach grumbled as it always did when her mother gave her that look.

"It did. I just thought it was time for a talk. Woman to woman." Rosemary sat down at the kitchen and patted the chair beside her. "While Paul and Roy are still at the doctor's."

Valerie's heart pounded in alarm. "I thought the doctor seemed impressed with Roy's progress. He's even starting to walk now! What's wrong?"

"Oh, it's nothing like that. Actually, I wanted to talk with you because he's healing so well." Rosemary reached over and clasped her hand. "He won't stay forever, you know."

"I know." Valerie didn't meet her mother's eyes.

"But he wants to."

"How do you know that? All his focus is on getting well so he can go back to the navy and risk his life." Valerie angrily swiped a tear off her cheek.

"Oh, honey, that's not true. Look at the way he's settled into this family—how wonderful he is with Rebekkah." She paused for a beat. "He'd make a good father."

"Don't say that." Valerie pulled her hand away.

"It's true."

"I didn't say you were wrong. He has other plans—he's never said one word to me about. . ." Her voice trailed off.

"About what? How deeply he cares for you? How much he appreciates this family? Honey, he's said plenty."

"Not to me. When did he tell you any of that?"

"Whenever he reads to Rebekkah or sews another doll, he shows his softness for children." Rosemary tipped her face up and smiled tenderly. "And every time he looks at you, it speaks volumes. You can't say you've never noticed it, Valerie."

"I know, Mom. I care for him, too."

"There was never any question in my mind about that. Show him."

Chapter 6

"I'll drive." Roy snagged the keys from the peg in the hallway.

"I don't think so." Valerie made a grab for them, but he moved too quickly.

"I like that zippy red Pierce-Arrow." He folded his arms across his chest, making his shoulders seem even broader than usual.

"You've only been walking for a week, and we're going to be walking all day." Valerie tapped her foot impatiently. She looked so adorable with that concerned expression that he conceded.

"Okay, but I'm driving home." He tossed the keys to her, and she snatched them in midair.

"So long as you feel up to it after a long day, that's fine with me." Her disgruntled look vanished as her eyes softened. "I just want you to be careful."

"I will be. Besides, I have a feeling today's going to be filled with fun. Bring on the fresh air!" He opened the door for her, and they walked out to the car.

"I must say it'll be nice not to have to carry a step stool around with me. You're so tall, you can tack the tops of the posters."

Roy looked at the stack of war bond advertisements piled on the backseat. "Sure are a lot of them."

"Mmm-hmm." Valerie nodded. "It's a good thing, too. The last ones I put up didn't fare too well through the February storms. We'll take them all down and put the new ones up."

"Anything for the war effort."

"After all you've done, I believe it!" She pulled into a parking space. "This is a good block to start."

"Which ones do you want to hang first?" Roy flipped through the glossy ads. "The Statue of Liberty, Uncle Sam, battleships, or. . ." He stopped as he came across a poster of uniformed soldiers parachuting onto a battlefield with the words "BACK THE ATTACK—BUY WAR BONDS" emblazoned across the bottom.

"A bit of everything. It's best to have a variety on each block so the people don't see the same thing on every corner. We don't want to be boring!"

"As if you ever could be," Roy scoffed, grabbing an assortment so they could get down to work.

"All of these need to come down." Valerie gestured to sadly faded Christmas pictures reminding that war bonds were "the present with a future."

Together, they tore down the old and tacked up the new, keeping a companionable conversation going all the while as they looked at other posters.

"I like this one." Roy gestured to a red ad for stamps with caricatures of Nazis. It asked the public to help "lick the Axis."

"Pretty clever, aren't they? Catchy, even." Valerie shoved the ratty old posters into a convenient garbage bin and strolled a bit farther with Roy at her side.

"Some of these are slogans we'll never forget." Roy stopped in front of a rendering of a battle cruiser with the reminder that "loose lips sink ships."

"I know. When you hear on the news how many ships have been attacked by U-boats and gone down, it reminds you how important it is to find the funds to replace them." Valerie tacked up another poster on a nearby fence.

"It's good to be out and doing something." Roy swiped the hammer and reached up to anchor the top. The crown of her head scarcely reached his shoulder.

"Especially when the weather's so nice." The crisp breeze put a healthy glow in her cheeks as the sunlight danced in her golden curls.

"It's beautiful." Roy drank in the sight of her as she turned to face him.

"We'd best get back to the car and move on to the next block. We're running out of posters."

◆ ◆ ◆

A few hours later, as she held up another one and Roy tacked the top, Valerie heard Roy's stomach rumble. "Hungry?"

"I could go for a bite to eat. I'm running on empty." He grinned. "Know anyplace around here with a good lunch special?"

"Hmm." Valerie thought for a minute. "Ella's makes the best chicken salad sandwich you've ever tasted. How does that sound?"

"Perfect. Let's go."

As they munched their sandwiches in companionable silence, Valerie caught sight of a newspaper. "Did you read the article about how the U.S. is moving native-born Americans of Japanese ancestry into detention centers?" She shook her head sadly. "In the midst of war so many people already lose their homes. It doesn't make sense to corral part of the population based on race."

Roy furrowed his brow. "How can we expect to have the Lord sanction our cause when we allow fear and prejudice to make us betray our own citizens?"

"I don't know." Valerie couldn't say anything to comfort him. The truth of the matter was that the discrimination against any person based on their heritage couldn't end well.

Every time she saw that determined glint in Roy's eyes, she knew she was that much closer to losing him. *Lord, he can do so much from right here. Please don't take him from me.*

After lunch they slid into the car. Valerie smiled at him. "Thank you for your help."

"I'm just glad I could do something to help." Roy grinned. "And the company's not bad, either."

"Why, I didn't peg you for such a sweet talker, Mr. Benson," Valerie drawled and batted her long lashes.

Roy laughed at her antics as she'd intended him to, then gazed at her intensely. "You know what I meant, Val."

Her breath caught when he stroked her cheek with the tip of his finger.

"You're an amazing woman."

"Roy, I—" An angry honk from an impatient driver shattered the tender moment, and Roy pulled out of the parking lot.

◆　◆　◆

"I'm glad FDR asked the commissioner to continue baseball. All sorts of interesting things are happening with the game." Paul tapped the sports section the next morning.

"Sure was good of the Yankees to let five thousand uniformed soldiers in free to each of their home games," Roy agreed.

"Did you know that the Chicago White Sox just let two Negro players work out with them?"

"About time. It's not as though white men are the only ones who can play the game. Just look at the Negro American League! I hope they make the team."

"Time will tell. Remember the name Jackie Robinson—apparently he's pretty good." Paul folded the paper. "Not that we don't have other things to discuss, you and I."

"Like what?" Roy eased into a chair and kicked up his feet on the ottoman.

"Like Valerie. What happened between the two of you yesterday?"

Roy straightened and looked the older man in the eye. "Why would you think anything happened?"

"Because of the way you two were acting—skittish as newborn colts. Besides. . ." Paul frowned. "Valerie hardly spoke ten words last night."

Roy laughed. "So that's a dead giveaway, is it? We had a nice day together. She's a special woman."

Paul chuckled. "You know it!" He sobered a bit. "Remember what we talked about your first day here."

"I will." Roy took the pledge seriously. He had no intentions of toying around with Valerie's affections. She meant too much to him.

◆　◆　◆

Two nights later, Valerie shoved the last bit of stuffing into another doll and handed it back to her mother. "We're out of filling."

"Already? But we just bought more!" Rosemary looked at the empty container in dismay.

"I think we have Roy to blame for that." Paul jerked a thumb at Roy, who busily affixed the finishing touches on a specialty Cinderella doll for Captain von Rundstedt's niece.

"Hey!" Roy took exception to being blamed.

"That's just because he's increased our productivity so much." Valerie patted his shoulder. "It's really a good thing, when you think about it."

"Not *that* good." Rosemary pulled out the list of stores where they'd purchased supplies. "I'm out of ideas on where to go. People are going to get suspicious if we keep buying cotton batting. With the war on, no one's sparing a dime for anything not absolutely necessary. We're starting to stick out like a red polka dot on a blue-striped shirt." She shook her head.

"I suppose we could travel farther," Valerie offered.

"We've already been anyplace we can reach in a day and be back before dark. It's not safe." Rosemary put a stop to that idea at once.

"I'll go with her," Roy jumped in.

"Absolutely not." Rosemary glared at them. "If you two disappear for a night, you'll both be ruined. The gossips will have a heyday, and how would you explain where you'd been?"

"We'll just have to figure something else out," Paul soothed. "What can we buy that we can use instead?" Silence fell as everyone pondered the question.

"You know," Roy mused, "mattresses are filled with stuffing to make them soft."

"That's a good idea!" Valerie perked up.

"It's too expensive," Rosemary sighed. "We can't buy a whole mattress just for the stuffing."

"Who said anything about buying?"

Blank looks met Roy's question. "We're not going to make off with mattresses, Roy." Paul glowered.

"No, of course not. We're not hoodlums. I meant going down to the junkyard and taking the stuffing out of old mattresses. Some of it will be in pretty bad shape, but the part in the very middle will work just fine."

"You can't beat free." Paul slapped his knee.

"Tomorrow's Saturday, so you and Valerie can go check it out. Just try and be as discreet as possible," Rosemary ordered.

"Sounds like we've got a plan." Roy winked at Valerie, and she couldn't help but think tomorrow would be a good day.

Chapter 7

Roy gaped as Valerie walked down the stairs early the next morning. "You're wearing slacks!" The getup made her slim legs look longer than usual. How could wearing a man's clothes make her seem even more feminine than when she wore a skirt?

"I couldn't very well go crawling around a scrap heap in a dress, now, could I?" She pulled on a pair of gloves.

"I suppose not," he grumbled. "What if someone sees you?"

"Now that women are working, slacks are far more standard. Besides, it's early and we're going to a junkyard, so I doubt I'll be running into many people anyway." With a gamine grin, she headed for the door, and Roy noticed she'd tied her curls into a shiny, bouncy ponytail. One thing was for sure—Valerie would never be predictable.

Half an hour later, they pulled into a deserted lot outside of town and opened the creaky gate to the junkyard. Piles of popped tires towered over smaller heaps of everything imaginable.

"This will be an adventure!" Valerie gawked around. "Let's get started."

"Let's walk the perimeter. Maybe there will be a pile of them somewhere." He set about surveying the site in an orderly fashion. Valerie quirked a brow and headed toward the middle of the yard, then turned left.

"Over here!" In two minutes, she'd tracked down a stack of old mattresses.

"How did you know where they were?" Roy pulled out his pocketknife and slashed the first mattress.

"I don't know. I think the Lord just led me where we needed to go." Valerie pressed down on the edge of the mattress, and dirty rainwater oozed out. "Ugh. Maybe we should try the next one. This one bore the brunt of our storms."

Together, they hefted the monstrosity over to unearth a slightly smaller mattress already boasting a hole in the middle.

"That's more like it!" Valerie opened a laundry bag and held it out as he grabbed handfuls of the well-preserved stuffing and shoved it into the bag.

They'd already filled every bag they'd brought by the time they hit the last two mattresses. "Here, let's heft a few of the other ones on top so they'll still be all right when we need to come back." Roy and Valerie tossed the already gutted mattresses back on top, then carried their bounty back to the car.

"That worked well. You're very resourceful, Roy." Valerie smiled at him as they stood by the trunk.

"Oh, it was nothing." He shrugged it off.

"Roy." She placed a hand on his arm so he'd look at her. "I mean it. You need to hear what a great help you've been. Every doll you've made is another child saved. You know that. It's the reason you've been working on them practically nonstop and gone through all our stuffing. You could've just sat around complaining about your physical therapy, how you were taken away from your job, how much you wanted to leave, but instead you did something much better. Thanks to you, we've been able to help so many more of God's children." She took a deep breath. "Earlier you told me *I* was amazing, but you're nothing short of incredible."

With a low groan, he kissed her. She rested perfectly in his arms, her lips soft as she twined her arms around his neck. When the kiss ended, he held her close for a moment longer. "I love you, Valerie Fulton."

"I love you, too, Roy." She blushed sweetly. "Let's go home."

◆ ◆ ◆

"The Gallup poll has officially named this World War II." Roy gave Valerie an update as she hung up her scarf after work on Tuesday.

"That took longer than I'd expected. Anything else I should know?"

"Just that Paul's still at the docks overseeing another shipment of dolls, and your mother and Rebekkah took some fish to Grandma Ainsley for her cat."

"It's so sweet that you call her Grandma Ainsley now, too." Valerie gave him a peck on the cheek. "Any mail today?"

"It came late, actually. There's a letter from your cousins in Denmark." He handed it to her.

"Thanks." She slid her finger beneath the flap and cracked open the envelope before reading the message aloud:

Dear Rosemary, Valerie, Paul, and Roy,

We are glad to hear that you are all doing well—we keep you in our prayers and hope by the time you get this, Roy is completely off his crutches. Please write and tell us how your latest addition to the family is doing! The merchandise is quite successful, and Captain von Rundstedt requests a Cinderella package for his niece.

All our love,
Annelise and Axel

P.S. Our friend Mr. Wright wrote and said he is in poor health. He's to see the doctor on April 30. Please keep him in your prayers.

"Who's Mr. Wright?" Roy studied the Danish stamp.

"We don't know a Mr. Wright, so it must mean something important." Valerie frowned. "Paul will know."

"What will I know?" Paul boomed from behind them.

Valerie jumped. Her stepfather's silent tread had managed to startle her on more than one occasion. "Axel and Annelise want us to pray for a Mr. Wright. He's seeing a doctor tomorrow." Valerie handed the letter to him.

"I'll go see him day after tomorrow."

"I'm coming with you," Valerie and Roy insisted in unison.

"Roy will come, but you need to go to work." Paul took Valerie's elbow and guided her away from the glass-paned door.

"If there's no other way. . .but I'll be jittery as a June bug until I know what's going on."

Roy understood exactly what she meant. If the operation was in serious jeopardy, not only would they be unable to send any more dolls, but her cousins' very lives would be in danger.

◆　◆　◆

"Good morning, Mr. Wright."

Roy noted that the mailbox designated the home as the Larson residence but kept that observation to himself as Paul introduced them.

"We're told you are in poor health."

"Come in, come in." Mr. "Wright" ushered them inside and locked the door.

"Annelise and Axel asked me to tell you that a secretarial associate with their import office has passed away, and they must find a replacement immediately. They specifically request someone who types well and knows German."

"Thank you very much, Mr. Wright." Paul shook the man's hand.

"I hope it helps."

"Your many contributions to our country will not be forgotten." Roy saluted the officer before they left and got back in the car. He waited until they were well on the road before speaking. "They can't provide the necessary documentation. That's what the message meant, right?"

"Yes," Paul affirmed grimly. "Finding a replacement will be tricky. It could undermine the secrecy of the entire operation, and with the Nazi presence so firmly established now in Denmark, they can't search on their own. Remember how last night we heard that Jews in the Netherlands are being forced to wear the star of David? Axel and Annelise's position is becoming more precarious." Paul stopped at a light and rubbed his temples. "We'll lose a lot of time while I find a permanent replacement."

"You already know someone who can fill in during the meantime, Paul. I read, write, and speak fluent German and am more than familiar with official documents. I assume they have all the supplies I'll need?"

"Yes," Paul agreed slowly. "And you get around just fine now. . . ."

"But not enough to fight. I'll need to get back to the OP-20-G in about a month, but for now this is something I can do. Send me."

◆ ◆ ◆

"Well, what happened?" Valerie demanded as she bounded into the living room without so much as a friendly hello.

Rosemary called Rebekkah into the kitchen, and the little girl scampered off.

Lord, Roy prayed fervently, *please give me the words to help her understand why I have to leave, and grant me the grace to return to her.*

"Calm down, Val. Have a seat." Paul pointed to the couch.

"I've had a horrible feeling all day." She sank onto the sofa beside Roy. "Just tell me."

"The forger died, and they have no one to create the necessary documents." Paul brought her up to speed. He smiled. "Consider yourself debriefed."

"They can't find another one over there—things are getting worse every day." Valerie jumped to her feet. "If they try, they'll be discovered and executed."

"We know. That's why I'm going to track down a permanent replacement." Paul shot Roy a sideways look. "We're concerned about the time lost while we find one."

Valerie chewed her lip. "How long do you think it'll take?"

"A few weeks, at least. Discretion is key."

"Every moment is precious." Valerie paced behind the couch. "If only there was something we could do. . . ."

"There is. I've located a party willing to fill in until the permanent worker arrives."

"That's wonderful!"

"I'm glad you think so." Roy stepped in front of her and put both hands on her shoulders. Out of the corner of his eye, he saw Paul surreptitiously leave the room to give them privacy. "I leave as soon as they draw up my passport."

He watched the smile melt from her face.

"You?" Her whisper was barely audible.

"Yes, me." He held on as she tried to pull away, tears sparkling in her eyes.

He pulled her closer to wrap her into a hug. She sagged against him with a shuddering sigh, then pounded his chest with her fist.

"No. You're. Not. Going." She punctuated each word with another thump.

He captured her hands and kissed them. "It's the only way, darling."

"Don't you try to 'darling' me, Roy Benson." She glowered up at him. "You're not going to get me to say it's a good idea to send you halfway around the world to perform illegal rescue operations right in front of countless Nazis." Her face crumpled as the tears trickled down her cheeks. "We don't even know how the last guy died."

"Remember how the letter said everyone else was fine? They haven't been found out, Valerie."

He nestled her close as she thought for a moment, then looked up pleadingly. "Don't go, Roy. I don't want to lose you."

"If I don't go, I've lost myself." The words sounded gruff to his own ears as he brushed his cheek against her soft hair.

"Why?"

"Do you remember what you said about me helping instead of sitting around complaining about my leg? I sewed all those dolls because it gave me a purpose. I even came to think that a lifelong limp was a small price to pay if my work saved even one child like Rebekkah."

"You've got a lot of nerve," she grumbled, "being so wonderful when you're telling me you're gallivanting off to risk your neck."

Encouraged, he continued. "I'll never be able to go off and fight with the other men, Valerie, but I'll always do what I can to serve God and country. It's who I am."

She gave a shuddering sigh and nodded. "I know."

He grabbed his handkerchief out of his pocket and wiped her face tenderly before pulling her into a deep kiss. "I'll come back to you."

"You'd better."

Chapter 8

Valerie stared at the blank page in her diary. *May 5, 1942*, she scribbled at the top.

> *I'm writing by lamplight with the windows shaded as nightly dim-outs along the East Coast continue. Last night my shade tore, so Mom and I hung up an old blanket to serve in the meantime. Today official sugar rationing was announced, and gas rationing is expected to begin any day now.*
>
> *I can't get my mind off of yesterday's news that German troops have taken more than four hundred prominent Dutch citizens as hostages. Each day things become more dangerous in Scandinavia.*
>
> *Has Roy really only been gone four days? I miss him so. He still won't be back for at least another three weeks. I can't call him, can't write him, can't stop thinking about him. I have no way of knowing he is well.*

She shut her diary, turned off the lamp, and knelt by her bed to pray. *Lord, will You bring him back to me? Wherever he is, please keep him safe. Help me to concentrate on the good You've sent him to do, Lord, rather than be consumed by my worries. Hard as it was to work through the grief of losing Frank, I know losing Roy would be unbearable. Please, Lord, watch over him. Amen.*

◆   ◆   ◆

Roy slung his duffel bag into the dinghy, then braced himself as the tiny craft was lowered into the water. The small splash sounded as loud as a tidal wave in the stillness of the dark night. They sculled toward the shoreline.

After five days at sea in the cramped cargo hold, he looked forward to being on dry land. He'd never managed to find his sea legs while compensating for his left knee. That, more than any other single thing, sunk home the fact he'd never serve on a naval vessel again. The dinghy hit a small, choppy wave, drenching his legs with icy salt water. The dull ache in his knee became a constant throb as he scanned the shoreline for SS officers.

They slid into a shallow bay beyond the docks, partially obscured by large rocks. With a dull scrape, the small wooden vessel met the beach. Roy shrugged his duffel bag onto his shoulder and picked his way across the sand.

By the time he reached the meeting point, his leg burned. Gritting his teeth against the pain and cold, he feigned nonchalance as he surveyed the dark streets.

A low voice from the shadows spoke in German. "Careful, stranger. Denmark no longer welcomes visitors. You must be Albrecht."

Roy shook his head and replied easily in the same language. "Jonas. Jonas Schwartz. Perhaps you know my uncle, Piet Schwartz."

His contact stepped into the light and matched the picture Paul had shown him back in the States.

"Axel Christiansen." He shook Roy's hand. "Let me show you where you can get a good night's sleep."

After a block or so, Axel casually slung Roy's duffel bag over his shoulder. As they maneuvered through dark, narrow streets, Axel changed directions frequently enough to assure Roy they weren't being followed. They continued to weave through the streets for a solid forty minutes before approaching a two-story home.

Silently thanking the good Lord that his leg hadn't buckled, Roy limped behind Axel into a blessedly warm kitchen.

"Jonas, this is my sister, Annelise, and Grams, our grandmother." As Axel introduced them, Roy noted the fact that both siblings called him Jonas from the outset.

The clever tactic reduced the likelihood of either of them being overheard or slipping up within earshot of any enemies. It also underscored the grave truth that these people depended on secrecy for survival.

He gratefully took a seat and accepted Axel's help pulling off his soaked boots while Annelise set a bowl of stew in front of him.

"This is wonderful," he praised as he swallowed the first bite, the warmth of the stew quite welcome.

"We can take your things upstairs, where you can lodge with our other guests," Annelise spoke in hushed tones, "or, if you'd prefer, downstairs."

Roy swiftly assessed the options. Paul had briefed him about certain necessary details. The attic held two small hidden rooms where Jewish children and American servicemen waited to be smuggled out. The basement held another secret room where they could develop the requisite photographs.

With the work he intended to do, Roy would need to be in the basement, and going up and down stairs every day wouldn't work well with his leg. Furthermore, one of his footsteps sounded far more loudly than the other and would be difficult to mask if he stayed upstairs.

"Downstairs will serve well," he decided aloud.

As Axel grabbed his bag, Roy stopped him. "But first, a few things from your cousins." He tugged the drawstring to the duffel and pulled out the precious items.

Annelise smiled as he brought out powdered milk and a few chocolate bars, while Axel grinned to see the coffee and peanut butter. Many simple, everyday items had become scarce in Denmark.

"I've also brought typewriter ribbons, ink, and a few rolls of film." As they'd be placed in the basement, Roy left those in the bag.

"Good. I'll show you to your room." Axel stood up when Roy finished his soup. As he crossed the kitchen toward the basement door, a row of photographs in the hall brought Roy to a dead stop.

In a picture with her mother, Valerie smiled angelically, sending a pang through his heart. He'd asked for a portrait of Valerie to bring along, but Paul shot that idea down. Apparently Paul had shown Captain von Rundstedt a photograph of Rosemary and Valerie, and the SS officer commented on their Aryan features. If Roy underwent a search, such an item would immediately tie him to Paul and Axel, placing the entire operation in jeopardy.

"May I borrow this during my stay?" He pointed to the photograph.

"So that's the way things stand, eh?" Grams shook her head and bustled upstairs, returning with a photograph of only Valerie. "The captain could notice that one missing, so this should do." She pressed it into his hands and nudged him back toward the basement door.

Roy's socks squished on the steep steps and cold cement floor until they came to the back wall. Axel pulled aside an empty trunk and a few sacks of potatoes before sliding back what seemed to be a solid wall.

A narrow room lay beyond, hardly four feet wide. Axel folded down a wooden plank topped with a thin cushion before folding it back against the wall. Similarly, another fold-down piece of wood on the perpendicular wall served as a desk.

A lumpy pillow took up residence atop a pile of blankets in the corner. An old typewriter sat next to a chair buried beneath a stack of old magazines. Roy immediately made plans to place the magazines beneath the machine while he typed. They'd absorb some of the noise.

Against the opposite wall lay two tubs of fluid and a small clothesline and clothespins for developing film. A single bare light bulb hung in the middle of the room with a pull chain.

"Perfect." Roy turned to Axel. "I think it would be best if I remain down here for the duration of my stay. It will be easier."

"Agreed. Annelise will bring you food and whatever else you will need, though you've brought your own supplies. I'll bring home more paper tomorrow, and I'll bring you the photograph film."

"One more thing." Roy caught Axel's elbow before he shut the sliding wall and pressed a bundle into his hand. "Just in case."

Axel unwound the fabric to uncover a small pistol and box of bullets. He gave a somber nod, rewrapped the weapon, and tucked it deep inside his coat before leaving Roy. Roy propped up Valerie's photo on the desk and peeled off his sopping socks before sinking onto the bed. *Lord, please help us to be successful.*

◆ ◆ ◆

The weeks passed with agonizing slowness. Roy often slid open the secret door just to feel less shut in. Sure, the cellar didn't offer a fantastic view, but at least it eased the feeling of cramped confinement.

Each day bled into the next as he rolled off the wooden pallet and took up his station in front of the typewriter and forged official-looking documents again and again.

The only bright spots of his days were Annelise's fine cooking and Valerie's photograph. Her smile beamed upon him as a ray of hope, urging him to press on. The thought of holding her in his arms once more strengthened his resolve.

As he slid another sheet of paper into the typewriter, Roy heard Axel's booming warning from upstairs: "Grams, Annelise! Captain von Rundstedt is here!"

Roy sprang into action, pulling the wall shut and jerking the chain to plunge his small chamber into darkness. *Lord, shield us with Your presence and power.*

He stood stock-still, straining to hear the muffled voices coming from above him in the kitchen.

"Captain, to what do we owe this unexpected visit?" Annelise's voice remained steady, giving away nothing.

"It's been too long since you've visited your brother's work, Annelise. I haven't seen you in weeks."

Roy frowned into the darkness as thoughts whirled through his head. If the captain's interest in Annelise brought him to the house, there was precious little they could do about it. Annelise would have to visit the office more often in order to protect the children and airmen concealed in the attic, but at what cost? Encouraging the affections of an SS officer was risky, but rejecting him outright rated equally as dangerous.

"Besides," the captain continued, "I was going to give this Cinderella doll to my niece this week, but when I took her from my bag, I noticed she is coming undone."

That sealed it. Roy had sewn that doll specially just to keep the captain off their trail. There was no chance anything had begun to unravel—sewing might not be his favorite occupation, but no Benson could ever be accused of shoddy workmanship!

The captain obviously had sabotaged the doll as a pretext to visit Annelise.

Chapter 9

O h, I can fix that in just a minute. Let me grab my sewing kit." Roy listened to Annelise's footsteps fade as she moved toward the living room, then become louder as she returned.

"Something smells wonderful."

"Here you are. Just like new." Good. Annelise had finished repairing the doll. Now, if they could just get their unwelcome visitor out the door. . . .

Roy grimaced as he heard the captain's heavy boots thump toward the center of the kitchen, away from the door.

"It's been so long since I've seen anything this fresh. Home-cooked meals are hard to come by. I'll bet these are every bit as good as my mother's." Roy bit back a groan. The man was laying it on thicker than a jar of Rosemary's preserves.

"Looks as though you made enough to feed half a contingent."

"Have you seen how much Axel eats?" Grams's laugh hardly seemed forced at all.

"Yes, well, a hearty appetite keeps a man strong."

Roy's stomach rumbled at the captain's words. After all, he'd requested tonight's dinner, a favorite dish from his childhood in the boarding school. Obviously the captain wouldn't be leaving anytime soon.

"Well, I can't guarantee it's as good as your mother's, but you're welcome to stay for dinner, if you'd like." Annelise's begrudging tone was lost on her would-be beau.

"Wonderful!" A chair scraped across the floor.

Roy sank onto his makeshift bed and waited for the meal to end. In the dark, windowless cell, he couldn't judge the passing of time nor look at his pocket watch. It seemed like hours before the captain finally took his leave and longer still before Axel judged it safe to come down to the cellar.

"Close call," Roy greeted him.

"You're telling me." Axel slumped onto the chair and held his head in his hands. "Annelise stopped coming down to the business because Captain von Rundstedt kept lurking around, and I don't want him near my sister. But since she left, he's become my shadow. Tonight he all but demanded to see her."

"We can't risk any more home visits, Axel."

"I know." He raked his fingers through his hair. "She'll have to start coming to the office again. I can only hope dinner tonight dissuades him from wanting more home-cooked meals."

"Annelise and Grams are wonderful cooks. What do you mean?"

Grams came down the stairs with two peanut butter sandwiches.

"He means that I made the food saltier than the Dead Sea." She handed the sandwiches to Roy. "And he still ate every bite." She let out a sigh. "I do hate to waste good food, but we can't have him popping up all the time for meals."

"He didn't ask for seconds, though." Axel tried to point out a bright spot.

"That's good," Roy encouraged through a mouth full of peanut butter. "By the way, good warning."

"I had to do something." Axel gave a curt nod. "Didn't hear a peep from down here all night."

"Yeah, but I didn't get any work done, either." Roy gestured to the photographs hanging on the drying line. "I have so much to do. I'd like to set up a supply of documents that need only a photograph before I leave."

"We'll be sad to see you go." Axel started back up the stairs. "You're far more productive than the last fellow."

"Thanks." Roy smiled and glanced at the photograph on his desk. "But since my replacement is on his way, I need to be off soon."

Grams gave him a measuring look and followed Axel. "Home is where the heart is," she called over her shoulder.

And I left mine in Virginia.

◆　◆　◆

Valerie heard a tap on the door. "Come in."

Her mother poked her head through the doorway. "You're up late."

"So are you."

"I was just checking on Rebekkah, like I used to peek in on you when you were smaller." Rosemary stepped across the room to stroke Valerie's hair. "Sometimes I still do."

"I know." Valerie gave her mother a brief hug.

"You've been tired all month."

"I just can't seem to sleep when I don't know if Roy is safe." Valerie felt the too-familiar sting of tears prick her eyelids.

"Oh, honey." Her mother sat down next to her on the bed and nestled her close. "He's in all of our prayers."

"I pray and pray," Valerie confessed, "but still don't have any peace about it."

"Even if you pray diligently, so long as you don't give your cares to the Lord, you won't be at peace about it."

"I just can't." Valerie grabbed her handkerchief. "I thought I'd finished grieving over Frank—that I'd come to terms with the loss."

"I thought this was about Roy!" Rosemary tipped Valerie's chin with her hand.

"It is! Don't you see? Frank is gone, and nothing will bring him back—I accept that. It's not because I miss Frank! When I fell in love with Roy, I thought he'd always be safe in spite of the war. He couldn't fight because of his leg."

"So you thought his injury made him safe for you to love." Her mother knew exactly what she meant. "You didn't have to worry about losing him."

"And now he's in Europe risking his life!"

"Valerie, do you love Roy because he can't fight or because of the man he is?"

"I love him because he's strong in Christ and kind to others, and he made me feel as though everything would be all right. And now he's not here."

Rosemary just held Valerie tight and let her cry. When the sobs subsided into tiny hiccups, she spoke again. "Honey, if you wait to love someone until you're certain your heart is safe, you'll never love. Love is the greatest gift God granted us and the heaviest responsibility." She placed her hands on Valerie's shoulders and looked her in the eyes. "If you live in fear of loss, you never really live at all."

"But I am afraid. I'm afraid for Roy. I'm afraid of being without him."

"You need to give that fear to the Lord. If you don't, you're saying you don't trust Him with what is most important to you."

"How can I?" Valerie whispered brokenly. "How did you when Paul was away?"

"Who better to trust than the One who made you? The Father who sent His Son to die for you? Didn't He assure us of His plans to prosper each of us?"

She pulled out of her mother's arms and blew her nose. "I don't know what those plans are, but I've got some praying to do. I was wrong, Mom."

"We all are, honey. That's why we need Jesus." She kissed her daughter's forehead. "Good night, Valerie."

"Good night."

◆　◆　◆

Valerie stood on tiptoe at platform 3C as she heard the train whistle. "It's coming!"

The nine o'clock train chugged into the station. Rosemary stood next to Paul, who carried Rebekkah atop his shoulders. A stream of passengers swarmed out of the cars, blanketing the platform. Valerie peered around as best she could, but Rebekkah spotted Roy before any of them.

"There! Roy!" The toddler flailed her arms so wildly that Paul tightened his grip so she wouldn't fall off.

As Roy made his way through the throng, Valerie couldn't stand still. She'd waited five long weeks to see him again—even one more minute was too long. She took off to meet him halfway. When she reached him, he wrapped her in a warm hug. She rested her cheek on his shoulder. "I'm so glad you're home!"

"Me, too."

She kissed his cheek, then stepped back. "Let me just look at you for a minute!"

"I get the better end of that bargain." His eyes drank in the sight of her, making her feel beautiful and blessed beyond imagination.

Lord, thank You for bringing him back to me safe and sound. I'm sorry I didn't put my faith in You sooner!

"My turn!" Rebekkah stretched toward Roy, wiggling her fingers.

He gave an easy laugh and swept her high into the air, grinning at her merry giggle. "Good to see you, too, Bekkah!"

"All right, all right, enough with the mushy stuff." Paul swiped Rebekkah and passed her to Rosemary before clapping Roy on the back. "Good to see you, Roy."

"Good to see you, too." He turned to Valerie. "Paul and I have some business to attend to, so we won't get home until this evening."

"Oh." She couldn't hide her disappointment. He'd been gone for five weeks, and "business" was more important than spending time with her?

"But I want you to be ready. I'm taking you out to dinner so I can have you all to myself." His smile made her heart pound. "Then we're off to the seven o'clock showing of that new Disney movie."

"Perfect!" She gave him one last hug before Paul led him away.

◆　◆　◆

"Roy, this is William Donovan."

Roy shook the stranger's hand before pulling up an office chair. "Nice to meet you, Mr. Donovan."

"You, too, Mr. Benson." Mr. Donovan leaned back and tented his fingers. "You must be wondering why we brought you in here."

Roy nodded but said nothing as Paul's friend pulled out a rather thick file and plopped it on the desk before leafing through it.

"Fluent in four languages, served the navy for eight years now. Ascended the ranks quickly to become an officer of cryptography in the OP-20-G. Very impressive, Mr. Benson." Mr. Donovan shut the folder and peered at him.

"Why so dedicated to America when you were raised in Europe? This is no time for divided loyalties."

"My father has served the United States Navy my entire life." Roy refused to let the probing question raise his temper. "Benson loyalty is steadfast, and I'm proud to follow in his footsteps. It's my heritage, my duty, and my honor to protect my country."

Mr. Donovan leaned back and gave Paul a curt nod. "Excellent. Mr. Kincaid speaks quite highly of you and your father. Let's get down to the reason for this meeting.

"As you know, we live in dangerous times when intelligence and preparation for homeland security are vital. Up until now, there has been no cohesive intelligence unit functioning at the behest of the government since the MI8 was disbanded in 1929.

"The separate cryptography divisions of the army and navy are no longer sufficient, as the Signal Intelligence Service and the OP-20-G have not established a free flow of communication. President Roosevelt has authorized me to establish an American intelligence service, which I've dubbed the Office of Strategic Services. Our mission is to collect and analyze strategic information for the Joint Chiefs of Staff and to conduct certain special operations not handled by other agencies. For instance, Latin-American intelligence will be handled exclusively by the FBI." Mr. Donovan paused for a moment, but Roy remained silent.

Lord, can this be another way You've answered my prayer to do Your work in this war?

"If you're interested, we could use a man of your background and talents."

"It sounds very worthwhile, but I have obligations to the OP-20-G, Mr. Donovan. Mr. Kincaid already had to make extensive arrangements regarding my leave of absence."

Donovan broke into an approving smile. "That Benson loyalty, eh? I already attended to the matter. Admiral Rochefort tells me that Station Hypo is now consistently breaking the Japanese naval code and has graciously consented to my request."

"In that case, sir, I'm your man." Roy rose to shake his hand again.

"Good." Donovan chuckled. "By the way, my friends call me Wild Bill." And with that, the three men went off to enjoy a fine lunch before Wild Bill left to attend to other concerns.

"So." Roy cleared his throat as Paul pulled out of the parking lot. "Where do they sell rings around here?"

◆　◆　◆

Valerie dabbed a bit of perfume on her neck as she heard Paul's car pull into the drive. She grabbed her jacket, gave her hair one final pat, and made her way to the top of the stairs.

"He'll be out in a minute." Rosemary met her at the bottom, wiping her hands on a dish towel. "You look lovely, honey. Have a good evening."

A few minutes later, Roy came out of his room, dressed in full uniform. He seemed so tall and handsome that he made Valerie's breath catch as he gazed at her appreciatively.

"You look stunning." He gallantly offered her his arm as he took her outside. On their way to Giovanni's, she learned of his time in Europe.

"I stayed in the basement the whole time. It was cold, cramped, quiet. . ." He reached over and gently clasped her hand. "And lonely. I missed you."

"I missed you, too. I prayed for your safety every day." Her grip tightened.

"Thank you." He grinned as he led her into the restaurant.

As they enjoyed warm, fragrant bread and lasagna, Valerie could tell something else was on his mind. When dinner was over, she broached the subject. "You're probably tired after your trip. We can skip *Bambi* and go home if you'd like. I'll sleep better knowing I'll see you tomorrow."

"Oh, no," he refused quickly, then gazed at her intensely. "But there is something I need to tell you."

"What is it?"

"I know how you felt about me going," he began, "but I'm called to my work. Can you support me in it?"

Valerie didn't need to think it over. "Yes, Roy, I can. I know it's a part of who you are, and I accept that. I trust you, but more than that, I trust the Lord with our love. I won't try to stop you from doing His work again."

He knelt down before her and pulled a small box out of his coat pocket. "Then, since you've captured my heart, will you do me the honor of becoming my wife?"

"Yes, Roy." She trembled as he slipped the small diamond onto her finger and swept her into his arms to seal the promise with a kiss.

"You've made me a happy man, my love."

"No happier than you've made me." She stroked her fingers through his wavy hair and smiled. "With God in our hearts and you by my side, our home will always be filled with joy."

KELLY EILEEN HAKE

Kelly Eileen Hake received her first writing contract at the tender age of seventeen and arranged to wait three months until she was able to legally sign it. Since that first contract a decade ago, she's fulfilled twenty contracts ranging from short stories to novels. In her spare time, she's attained her BA in English literature and composition, earned her credential to teach English in secondary schools, and went on to complete her MA in writing popular fiction.

Writing for Barbour combines two of Kelly's great loves—history and reading. A CBA bestselling author and member of American Christian Fiction Writers, she's been privileged to earn numerous Heartsong Presents Reader's Choice Awards and is known for her witty, heartwarming historical romances. She and her gourmet-chef husband live in Southern California with their golden lab mix, Midas!

A Thread of Trust

by Sally Laity

Chapter 1

Copenhagen, Denmark, Spring 1943

The growing darkness outside added gloom to the deserted interior of Christiansen Enterprises, casting murky shadows against the plain office walls. The eeriness heightened Annelise Christiansen's nagging sense of fear for her brother. She began pulling outdated letters from the customer files—anything to keep busy.

She checked the wall clock again. Where was Axel?

Something creaked.

Closing the file drawer, Annelise glanced through the interior window to the warehouse floor. The employees had left for the day, and only patches of light cast by dangling bare bulbs kept the blackness at bay. Stacked rows of crates and boxes of goods heading to or received from Germany and Sweden created shadowed canyons in the cavernous space.

Someone could easily hide out there. A chill prickled the fine hairs on her arms, and Annelise tugged her lightweight cardigan closer as she dismissed the notion. Being alone in this big place made her uneasy.

When she followed her brother from America to Copenhagen to take over their dying grandfather's import-export business, she never dreamed they'd be caught up in a whirl of intrigue. Imagine smuggling forged documents and money to facilitate the escape of downed British and American pilots—and more dangerous, harboring hunted fugitives! With the Nazis rounding up Jews in Germany and Poland and shipping them off to death camps, more unfortunates were flooding into Denmark needing to be hidden and given transport to neutral Sweden.

So far, Danish Jews had been spared, but for how much longer, no one knew. Everyone suspected that the Germans occupying the country were merely pretending to be friendly trading partners as they moved armed troops in to "protect the Danes," while gradually taking control of the government.

Underground resistance came into existence early on, and of course Axel had to be in the middle of it. Only the Lord knew what he'd left the warehouse three hours ago to do, since he assured Annelise her safety lay in not knowing.

Strange that he had no qualms about taking her to Nazi gatherings, convinced that a guileless female could gain useful information. She and Axel were scheduled to attend the foreign minister's dinner party in less than an hour, and they needed to go home and change. *If* he ever got here.

And *if* he hadn't been arrested.

Shaking off the thought, Annelise forced herself to focus on deciding which of her four gowns she'd don this evening. The very thought of another Nazi party with all the free-flowing schnapps and beer made her cringe. Smuggling for the Allies was hazardous enough without having to rub shoulders with those arrogant officers of the Third Reich.

Annelise exhaled, directing her thoughts to the words of a psalm she'd read in her morning devotions: "Fret not thyself because of evildoers, neither be thou envious against the workers of iniquity. For they shall soon be cut down like the grass, and wither as the green herb."

The passage still soothed her anxious mind. God's presence through these troubled times was almost tangible. He had power over all. He was stronger than the German forces, even when the opposite seemed true.

The bell above the shop's main door trilled, bringing a wave of relief. Only Axel had a key to that entrance. *Thank You, Father, for looking after him, for keeping him safe.* Breathing the silent prayer, Annelise rushed to the showroom to greet her brother.

Halfway through the furniture and artwork displays, she stopped short. The light streaming from the office illuminated not Axel, but a tall unkempt stranger in dirty seaman's clothing. Her gaze quickly assessed his unshaven face and muscular frame as she detected the stench of rotten fish and recoiled from the odor. "How did you get in here? That door was locked."

◆　◆　◆

Erik Nielsen hiked his brows and stared at the most enchanting woman ever to cross his path. Endless days aboard a British fishing trawler, hours waiting in a muddy coastal marsh for his contact, suddenly lost importance. Before him stood a vision silhouetted in a glow of backlight gilding the golden hair around her face like sunshine outlining a cloud. Only the smell of cod and herring proved this was no dream, and for some unfathomable reason, he sensed his life would never be the same.

"I said, where did you get that key?" She stepped toward him, her movements graceful. Puzzlement crested her delightfully feminine features as they came into focus, revealing eyes clear and blue as the heavens.

"Huh?" Entranced by the alluring sight, he couldn't pull his thoughts together. He'd never entertained the notion of dating, much less marriage, wanting no distractions from the life God had called him to. Now a yearning toward hearth and home, of caring for someone besides himself, swirled through him. Did the Lord have someone for him after all? Was she the one?

"The key. In your hand."

Erik glanced down. "Oh. Right." She must consider him a numbskull. He cleared his throat. "Your brother sent me to get you."

"Axel?" She frowned. "Where is my brother? Why didn't he come in?"

"He's outside, miss. Someone driving past stopped to talk. He should be along any second. He said you were late, that I should hurry you up."

"*I'm* late?" Her rosy lips tightened with a huff. "Well, wait here. I'll be back."

Gaining control of his faculties, Erik tipped his head politely and feasted his eyes on her willowy grace as she hurried away. Her light steps made whispery sounds, like the rustle of her skirt.

She returned shortly with her coat and handbag. "Might I ask your name? I don't believe we've met."

"Oh. Forgive me. Erik Nielsen, at your service." After wiping his fingers on his grimy trousers, he extended his hand.

Her nostrils flared slightly before she clasped it.

The bell announced another arrival, and easygoing Axel strode in, doffing the hat atop his fair head.

Behind him came. . .a Nazi.

Eric quickly surveyed the import shop for the nearest exit. Surely Axel hadn't ratted on him. He mentally calculated the distance to the door in case he had to make a dash for it.

"Captain von Rundstedt has honored us with a visit on his way to this evening's party," Axel announced nonchalantly, his voice and expression typically calm and collected. "He wondered why I was still in street clothes. I explained that the boat bringing my sister's fiancé was late coming in, and I had strict orders to bring him straight to her." A jaunty grin crested his callow face. "And so I have. You've kept poor Annelise waiting nearly a year, haven't you, old man?" His blue eyes twinkled with mischief.

Somewhat relieved, Erik played along, praying that the officer hadn't sensed his fear. He glanced back at the woman whose hand he still possessed. *Annelise. No one could have chosen a more perfect name for such a beauty.* "Right. Almost a year. But so far my Annelise has been keeping me at arm's length." He tugged her closer, cringing as she stiffened. "You've yet to give me my welcome kiss, love."

Impeccable in his gray uniform and spit-shined jackboots, dark-haired Rundstedt observed the exchange, his expressionless demeanor exuding the typical measure of Aryan superiority displayed by the military force occupying this small country. "How curious, Miss Christiansen. You never mentioned your engagement. Curious indeed." The crisp words, in German-accented Danish, were controlled and authoritative as his close-set, hooded eyes assessed Erik. Cold and gray they were. Like death. "So many times you conversed with me, danced with me."

Erik felt her ease slightly away. "Would that be polite, Captain? Discussing my fiancé while dancing with another gentleman? Expressing my fear for his life while he's at sea? I think not." She smiled warmly up at her intended.

Some tense seconds passed as the long-nosed Nazi continued his scrutiny. "Where, exactly, have you been fishing to be gone so long, seaman?"

Erik wondered if the man was jealous, suspicious—or both. "Mostly between

Faroe Island and Norway. But this is my last trip. Our boat was boarded at gunpoint on three occasions. Once by the English and twice by you Germans." Hoping his answer implied that his papers were in order, he drew Annelise closer and gazed down at her, drinking in her beauty again. "I know I promised to stay at sea until we had enough money for that house you set your heart on, sweetheart, but—"

Annelise touched her fingertips to his lips. "I wouldn't hear of it, love. Not with the war raging at sea these days. You've taken too many chances as it is. No amount of money is worth your life. We'll find somewhere else to live."

"If you're sure. Your brother has offered me a job here as long as I need it."

Her expression brightened. "Here with us? Wonderful." Rising to tiptoe, she kissed Erik's stubbled cheek. "Welcome home, darling. I've so much to tell you, I hardly know where to begin."

Though it was all for show, the tenderness of her soft lips touched Erik deep inside. He wondered if he could trust his voice to speak.

Captain von Rundstedt inserted himself into Erik's brief interlude. "Does this mean you will not attend Foreign Minister Scavenius's party?"

Axel gestured toward the door and ushered him toward it. "I doubt my sister would enjoy partying this evening on her fiancé's first night home. I'll be along myself, though, once I change into appropriate attire. I understand there'll be an assortment of lovely, unattached young women there, as always."

The captain halted at the entrance and raised his chin a notch as he turned to glance at Annelise. "None as lovely as your sister, to be sure."

Erik felt Annelise grow rigid.

"Until we meet again, Miss Christiansen." With a click of his heels, the officer raised his arm. "Heil Hitler."

◆　◆　◆

Positively seething, Annelise moved out of Erik Nielsen's grasp and glared in wordless fury at her too-handsome brother. What kind of mess had he gotten them into *this* time? Really. Having to take part in the pretense that this. . .this *smelly sailor* was her betrothed!

She glanced up at the man, gratified he had the grace to look as uncomfortable at this turn of events as she. Refusing to favor either of the males in the shop with another word, she huffed out to their car. At least their enterprise was valuable enough to the Nazis that they were still permitted a personal vehicle, she conceded with a twinge of guilt, since few Danes still enjoyed that privilege.

On the homeward drive, Annelise debated whether her emotions were ruled by anger or embarrassment. She'd already endured one disastrous engagement—a humiliation she never intended to repeat. The pain caused by that debacle helped her decide to leave her familiar world behind and follow Axel to Denmark.

Axel. Hmph. Once more he'd proven that no man—not even a brother—could be trusted. Compressing her lips into a determined line, she let her gaze settle on the broad shoulders of the seaman up front. Neither the stubble on his square jaw nor those fishy clothes could detract from such heart-stealing features. He had the most compelling eyes—light brown, with tiny gold flecks. And when he'd gazed down at her with them, her knees—

"By the way, sis. . ." Axel interrupted her wandering thoughts. "Erik was sent here by our American contacts to forge documents for the Allied pilots shot down over enemy territory. Originally I'd planned to set him up in the attic so he could keep out of sight. But now that the Nazis are aware of his presence, that won't be possible."

"Surprise, surprise," she groused. "So I assume this. . .forger will be working right out in the open with us. As my fiancé."

"Well," he teased, "you always claimed you didn't like being pawed by the members of Hitler's elite. Now there's someone who'll spare you that indignity."

She grimaced, though she knew they couldn't see her face. And lucky for them, she couldn't begin to put her indignation into words.

"At least spare her until Herr Captain figures out how to get me out of the picture for good," Erik added. "From the look on his face when you introduced me, I'd say the man is on the make and wants your beautiful sister all to himself."

Beautiful? Annelise allowed herself no more than a second to dwell on the compliment. "The captain has tried to get me alone lately. He's been quite persistent." *And Erik Nielsen thinks I'm beautiful, too. . . .*

"But I'm proud of the way you've handled things," Axel commented. "You did inform me he's the most loose-lipped of all those strutting Nazi peacocks." He switched his attention to his new friend. "By the way, Erik, what qualifies a person to become a forger for the U.S. government, if you don't mind my asking?"

Nielsen shrugged a shoulder. "My former occupation wasn't nearly so notorious as this one sounds. Before the war, I had a normal, run-of-the-mill job, teaching art at a college in New England. Turns out I'm particularly adept at calligraphy."

The news roused Annelise's curiosity. "How is it you speak Danish so fluently and without any hint of an accent?"

He chuckled. "It's my first language, actually. My family emigrated from Sjaellands Point, on Ise Fjord."

"Really. Where did you live in America?" Axel asked.

"The northern coast of Maine. I'm the first in my family not to make a living off the sea. I worked my way through university fishing during the summer months, though, so I know my way around a boat."

"So the smell of herring is not foreign to you," Annelise couldn't help adding.

A chuckle rumbled from deep in his chest. "You would bring that up."

"My sister and I were raised in America, too," Axel explained, seemingly unaware of the thread of tension between his passengers. "I returned in '37. Annelise came over in '39, just before the Nazis invaded Poland. I tried to convince her to go back home where it was safe, but she'd have nothing to do with that."

"My life is no more valuable than yours, brother dear. I just try to take better care of it." After a pause, she spoke to their soon-to-be guest. "No doubt Axel has informed you we do more than help downed Allied pilots. Hundreds of Jews have escaped out of Germany. Often, though, parents manage only to get their children to safety. We have a young boy and girl hidden in our basement right now. All they lack are some authentic-looking exit visas. Perhaps you've come in answer to our prayers."

"I'll do what I can. Which reminds me. . ." He slipped into English. "Before I completed my training in Virginia, your aunt Rosemary's new husband gave me some rag dolls to bring to you. They're in my duffel bag. He told me to guard them with my life."

"I must caution you never to speak English, my friend," Axel urged. "Not even when we're alone. You're not an American, remember. You're Erik Nielsen from Sjaellands Point. I don't even want to know your real name."

"That *is* my real name," he returned, reverting to Danish. "My relatives here have already been informed about this. They're all sympathetic to our cause. I am now the son of my uncle, and I've got the documents to prove it. . .even if they are my own handiwork."

Annelise smiled, despite herself. "You're also my fiancé. But. . .may I ask what a young woman of class, like myself, would be doing engaged to a lowly fisherman?" Suddenly aware he might construe her statement as flirting, Annelise felt her cheeks redden. *Don't forget how badly you were burned,* she lectured herself.

Nielsen didn't appear to notice her discomfort. "You know what the Bible says. Love is blind and all that."

"I've never come across that particular statement in any Bible I've read," she returned. "Sounds more like a myth to me."

He chuckled softly. "Maybe it just said *hopeful.*"

Annelise filled her lungs. *This one is too much of a charmer. Almost as charming as Tony was—before he dumped me for the next pretty face. So like Father. I'd better take care. There's far more danger here than merely being caught by the Nazis.*

Chapter 2

The city streets lay dark and still, and as the chatter inside the car petered out, Erik felt weariness envelop him. He remained alert by making mental notes of the route Axel took home, the landmarks illuminated faintly by the downward-slanted headlamps. At last they pulled into a narrow street and stopped before a substantial two-story house, which, in the dim glow, appeared similar to that of its neighbors. He only hoped that somewhere inside it had a bed made up and ready for him to collapse onto. He hadn't eaten since early that morning, but exhaustion prevailed over all desire for food.

"This is it," his new friend announced, dousing the lights and turning off the engine. "We live with our grandmother. I'll open the boot so you can grab your bag, and Sis will introduce you while I dash upstairs and throw on some glad rags. I should've been at that party ages ago."

Erik opened his door and climbed out, unable to discern any unique features in the dwelling since blackout shades shrouded every window along the street. He stepped to the rear of the vehicle and retrieved his duffel bag, then followed Annelise up the front steps. "You're sure I won't be imposing?"

"Not at all," she said, turning the knob, her tone indicating she'd resigned herself to his presence. "Come on in. Grams is used to our showing up at odd hours with strangers."

"At least she won't have to hide you," Axel said, bringing up the rear.

Hooking her coat onto the hall tree, Annelise shot him a stern look. "I do wish you'd stop plunging us headlong into your schemes. We can't afford to draw such constant attention."

"Point taken, sister dear." He rolled his eyes and started down the entry hall for the staircase.

Annelise straightened her shoulders. "This way." She moved toward the squared archway leading into the front room.

From a step behind, Erik assessed the well-appointed parlor with its fine upholstered furnishings and dark, gleaming woodwork. An assortment of framed watercolor seascapes adorned the walls. The plump sofa looked especially inviting to his travel-weary bones.

Then he noticed an older woman in black, seated in a padded rocking chair, peering up from a child's sock she'd been darning. She had a pleasant enough face, and silvery hair drawn into a French roll gave a frail quality to her that reminded Erik of his favorite aunt. Her small blue eyes gazed over rimless reading glasses perched on her nose.

Annelise bent to kiss her parchmentlike cheek. "We have a guest, Grams. This is Erik Nielsen. The American military sent him to provide the exit visas we need so desperately. Erik, I'd like you to meet my grandmother, Margarethe Holberg."

The woman set her work aside and began to rise.

"Please, don't get up, Madam Holberg." He touched her surprisingly firm shoulder. "I'm afraid I reek of the sea. But I'm most honored to make your acquaintance."

"Thank you, young man." Her speculative gaze took swift measure of him.

"We don't even have to hide him," Annelise added. "He can use the guest room. There's one other thing I need to tell you, though." She colored delicately. "We're supposed to pretend Erik is my fiancé come to live with us."

The woman's shrewd eyes gravitated between her granddaughter and him, and her pursed lips flattened. "This, of course, would be Axel's doing."

Annelise nodded.

Her bosom rose and fell as she studied Erik. Then her nose crinkled. "Well, take the man upstairs and draw him a hot bath. He needn't take his luggage along. It probably smells as bad as he does. We'll wash everything up in the morning, make it all fresh."

"Thank you kindly, madam." Erik gave an appreciative tip of his head. His original impression of her had been way off the mark. For all her fragile appearance, she was deceptively strong. Even persuasive. "But I shouldn't let my bag out of my sight. It contains my forging supplies and some rather...important...rag dolls."

Nothing fazed the old gal. "Don't worry. You're perfectly safe here, and so are your belongings. But this is my house, and I won't tolerate the whole place stinking like the docks."

He acquiesced. "As you wish." His glance at Annelise caught the amusement on her face.

"And to pay for your lodging, you will make exit visas for our other guests." Mrs. Holberg's expression made it a statement of fact.

"Certainly. Once I finish those needed for a downed bomber crew, I'll do the others. I believe your granddaughter mentioned there were two children here."

"That is correct. How long do you expect it will take you to get to their papers?"

Her unwavering stare nettled him. "A week maybe. Two at the most. Then I'll get right on them."

"You'll do them first," she countered, arching her eyebrows. "Planes are being shot out of the sky every day, and adults can fend for themselves. At least temporarily. But we cannot keep youngsters hidden indefinitely. They've already been shuffled around too much, been exposed to atrocities no human, let alone a child, should witness. Their trust has been shattered. They live in constant fear of never seeing their parents alive again, and the poor dears think somehow they're to blame. You'll do their papers first, so at least a fraction of their childhood might be salvaged. Otherwise, you can find someplace else to stay." She reached for her sewing supplies and resumed her chore.

Stunned by the woman's declaration, Erik recognized dismissal when he saw it, and her threat was more than a little discomfiting. He looked to Annelise.

"Come on, Grams. We can't put Erik out on the street after the Allies sent him to us. I'm sure he'll do his very best for us *and* the cause."

"Nevertheless," she insisted, "I'll do what I must. Army people think this war business is more important than anything else—this shooting at each other and anyone else who happens to get in the way. Well, these children are getting *out* of the way. This I say, and this I mean." Setting down her work once again, she crossed her arms.

"Put like that, I can understand your feelings," Erik admitted. "I'll start on those visas first thing tomorrow morning. I'll need to have their new names. Pictures, too, if you have any. You can fill me in on their ages and so forth."

Annelise shook her head. "The underground hasn't found anyone to take them to Sweden yet, so we don't have names for them. Sorry."

Perhaps it was the unwelcome news or the close confines. Maybe even a few too many hours without sleep. Erik's head began to swim. He raked his hand through his hair and gave himself a mental shake, grasping at the first idea that came to mind. "What if one of the pilots pretends to be their father? A couple of kids would make good cover. . . ."

"What?" The old woman poked her needle into the sock and dropped the darning egg. "I never heard of anything so daft! You'll not risk those dear little children to rough soldiers who can't even speak their language. Just get to work on those visas. I'll find someone myself." Muttering under her breath, she continued her work.

"I'm sure Axel will come up with somebody," Annelise suggested. "There's no reason for you to endanger yourself, Grams."

"Hmph. After this latest brainstorm of Axel's? I'd best take care of the wee ones. I've many trusted friends at the church. We'll find someone willing to accompany them to safety."

"Did I hear my name being bandied about?" Axel peeked through the archway in his crisp white shirt, bow tie, and dark slacks. His blond hair was freshly slicked back, and a dinner jacket lay over the crook of his arm. He quirked a smile at Erik. "Everything all set for you, old man?"

"Yes. Couldn't be better." Though spoken facetiously, Erik knew he'd stated the truth.

Annelise hurried to her brother's side. "Be careful. Promise? And for once, please don't do or say anything that will dig this hole any deeper."

"Whatever you say, little sis." A peck on her cheek, and he dashed off.

Mrs. Holberg frowned and sighed. "We'd better spend a good part of this night in prayer for that boy." Then her cool gaze fastened on Erik. "I assume you are a praying man."

"Yes, madam, I am." *But even if I wasn't, I'd tell you I was. I wouldn't want to be on your bad side.*

"Good. I can't abide heathens under my roof."

Erik had to grin. For a lady he'd first considered small and defenseless, she sure had spunk. And he liked spunk. In fact, he liked *her*. He liked her a lot.

◆　　◆　　◆

Annelise observed the banter between her grandmother and their new guest—whom anyone could see was dead on his feet—and admiration for the sailor-forger rose several notches. He was holding his own in the face of a woman many considered to be domineering and formidable. Perhaps it wouldn't be so bad having him around for a while to keep Grams occupied.

Still, the man *was* a perfect stranger, and beguiling smiles were something Annelise would never be fooled by again. Even if the military bigwigs considered him trustworthy, he had yet to prove himself to her and her relatives. She'd best stay on her guard. "I'll take you upstairs now," she offered, maintaining a business-like tone.

He nodded and bid her grandmother good evening, then followed Annelise to the staircase, where portraits bearing a strong resemblance to the family members he'd already met lined the walls.

Once they reached the top landing, she gestured to her right. "That will be your room as long as you're here. Directly across the hall is the bathroom. You'll find everything you need in the cupboard. I'll bring some of my brother's clothes for you to use till yours have been laundered. Leave your soiled things outside the door, and I'll take them down to the cellar to wash."

"Thank you. . .Annelise. I. . .hope you don't mind my familiarity."

She grimaced. "Why should I? It would appear we're an item, thanks to my big-mouth brother."

"Ah, yes." He flashed a completely disarming grin.

It made Annelise conscious of her less-than-friendly manner. Realizing she'd been nearly as gruff as her grandmother to the poor man, she softened her tone. "Look, I know we've made things difficult for you, and I do apologize. We're all working toward the same objective, and it would benefit the lot of us to be friends."

He nodded. "I could live with that."

"Good. Well, I know you're tired. Hungry, too, I'd imagine. I'll bring a tray to your room so you can have a bite to eat when you've finished. Is there anything else you might need tonight?"

"You've about covered everything for now. Tomorrow, though, we should get together and work on our. . .relationship. Since we're *engaged*, we need to know a little about each other, decide when and where we met and all."

She looked down. "Let's wait for Axel to get home. No telling what story he fabricated for the Nazis this evening."

"Good idea. Oh, one other thing. I had planned to visit my relatives in Sjaellands Point as soon as I can get away, to familiarize myself with the area. That part of my story needs to be kept straight, too."

"Sounds wise."

His lips spread into a knowing smile. "Of course, as my fiancée, you should probably come along and meet the folks. . . ."

A maddening sense that things were spinning out of control jolted Annelise. For a fleeting moment, all she could think of was throttling her brother.

◆ ◆ ◆

A ray of sunshine drifting through the edge of the drawn window shade warmed Annelise's face. She opened an eye and checked her bedside clock, then bolted upright. Normally she awoke before daylight. Yesterday's stress must have taken its toll. Wasting no time, she made quick work of her morning ablutions and dressed in a white blouse and navy skirt, then hastened for the stairs. Her devotions would have to wait.

Male voices drifted up from below. "The guys had to separate," Axel said. "Only five made it to a safe house."

"That's not good news," Erik answered. "Maybe a few others will—" He clammed up when Annelise entered the dining room.

"Good morning," she said brightly, masking the irritation she felt over always being kept in the dark about everything.

"Well, well," Axel teased. "If it isn't Miss Punctuality. Your clock stop or something?"

She glowered at him. "You could have rapped on my door when you got up." Even as she spoke, her gaze took in their freshly shaved guest. Axel's checked shirt and wool slacks suited Erik, though a touch small and tight-fitting. And his easy smile did strange things to her insides.

"I figured you could use the sleep, sis. Besides, this way I get to repeat what I told Erik about my conversation with the distinguished captain last night."

"Which was?" She drew out a spindle-back chair from the table and took a seat.

Her grandmother came in from the kitchen just then, bearing plates of sausage and eggs and dark rye toast for the men. She directed her attention to Annelise while setting the food before them. "I see you finally decided to make your appearance this day."

Annelise bristled as Axel and his new friend swapped amused grins.

"I'll start some more toast and eggs while you go down and fetch the children for breakfast," Grams said, returning to the kitchen.

Something about the smiles the two men had sported stuck in Annelise's mind as she headed for the cellar door beneath the staircase. Her father's smiles— just as roguish, but deceitful as well—had caused the family untold heartache. Tossing off the unwelcome reminder, she opened the door and flicked on the light to illuminate the wooden steps.

The cellar's space had dwindled when Axel enclosed secret rooms on either end, disguising the change with floor-to-ceiling storage shelves. Windowless walls made the close confines even drearier as Annelise picked her way through the cluttered maze of washtubs, food stores, and castoffs from the main floor. She carefully opened the secret door concealed with shelves of canned goods.

Two narrow cots occupied one end of the long, shallow room. A small table with chairs sat at the other end, and in between, a bookcase held schoolbooks and picture books. An assortment of worn toys lay about the rag runner covering the floor.

As always, when hearing the door opening, the children ceased their activity and huddled together in mute silence, their chocolate-brown eyes round with fear. Six-year-old Rachel peered up at Annelise, a froth of soft dark curls surrounding her heart-shaped face. She'd taken a protective position in front of her brother, Moshe, already a charmer at three. Both wore faded clothes, with their shiny curls neatly brushed.

Annelise's heart contracted at the sight of their too-thin frames. "It is all right," she crooned in the high German dialect. "I've come to get you for breakfast. Grandmother has scrambled some nice eggs for you."

The boy's brown eyes glinted, and he looked about to say something, but his sister put a finger to her lips. She relaxed her hold on him and stood, then bent to pick up his missing shoe and help him put it on. "There," she whispered. "We are ready now."

No smile accompanied the statement, but then, only on the rarest of occasions had Annelise seen either of the little ones smile. They seemed to know instinctively never to make noise, never to speak unless spoken to, never to touch things that did not belong to them. She longed to gather them into her arms and love them to pieces. . .but Grams, in her wisdom, felt it would only cause the children more grief to become attached to yet more people who'd be shipping them elsewhere. So she restrained her motherly instincts and settled for being pleasant and warm, trying to instill trust in their hearts, showing them that kind people still existed in the world.

"The cold days are almost over," she remarked as they exited the secret room. "I've been making over a new dress for you, Rachel. A pretty one with flowers, for when you're free to play in the park again."

The child's sable eyes misted, and the hint of a tiny smile appeared. But Moshe's rosy lips plumped with a pout.

"And I haven't forgotten you, sweetie." She ruffled his dark curls. "You'll have a new shirt and vest to wear."

Suddenly the door at the top of the stairs opened.

Annelise automatically reached for the children.

"It's that Nazi!" Erik said, closing the door after himself. "He and a truckload of armed soldiers just pulled up out front. Get the kids outta sight!"

Chapter 3

S haken by Erik's announcement, Annelise maintained her composure but pressed a finger to her lips. She scooped up Moshe and made her way quietly down the steps to the secret room, its shelf-laden door left open for such emergencies. Rachel trailed silently behind, clutching Annelise's skirt. "Don't make a sound, my darlings," she whispered, ushering them back inside their haven. "Though we walk through the valley of the shadow of death, we fear no evil, for God is with us."

Rachel, ever the protector, put her arms around her brother, and the pair huddled together on one of the cots. The sight of their huge, dread-filled eyes cinched Annelise's heart as she carefully closed the door on the little ones. What a pathetic existence they lived, silent, invisible. Would they ever get to be carefree children? She breathed a prayer that God would be with them. Surely He would send His angels to surround and protect such sweet darlings.

Some jars rattled from the movement of the shelves. Grabbing a bottle of her grandmother's plum syrup as an excuse for being in the cellar, she joined Erik, who waited on the top landing, his ear to the cracked door.

The sound of knocking carried from outside. "At least they aren't pounding with their fists or rifle butts as they're so fond of doing," she muttered.

"Not yet, anyway. That's their second summons. Your brother's taking his time answering."

"*God morgen*, Captain von Rundstedt," came Axel's greeting at last. "You're up and about early after last evening's festivities. What a pleasant surprise."

"*Ja*. We are on our way to Kirkgarde Engine Works to aid your authorities in breaking up a strike. Three stoppages this month alone. Traitorous agitators think they can thwart us by stirring up the workers, turning them against the cause. We will put a stop to it."

Annelise breathed more easily. The soldiers hadn't come to conduct a raid on the house; they were waiting for their captain. But before she completely let down her guard, her gaze fell on Erik's duffel bag still slumped where he'd left it last night—the bag containing forging tools, money, and stuffed dolls from America! Effecting serenity she didn't feel, she took his hand and stepped with him out into the hall to draw Rundstedt's attention.

Resplendent in his immaculate uniform and polished jackboots, the Nazi officer had his military hat tucked under his elbow. "Ah." A subtle hiking of his brows lengthened his thin face. "I see the lovebirds are also early risers."

Erik draped an arm around Annelise's shoulders, its warmth steadying her. "Why, Captain," she said airily, "we were about to sit down to breakfast. Won't you join us?"

"*Nej.* I am on duty. I stopped by to invite you all to tea on Saturday. Just a small, intimate gathering. Nothing grand."

Always stiffly proper, he never revealed emotion in his hard features, and little about the man inspired confidence. Annelise sensed his true motives were far from friendly. Certainly he suspected something amiss here. Nevertheless, refusal was no option. She smiled up at Erik. "That would be lovely, wouldn't it, sweetheart?"

"Wait a minute, sis," Axel interrupted. "We've already made plans for the weekend. Erik placed a call early this morning to the pay telephone in Sjaellands Point. A neighbor was dispatched to inform Erik's family he's back and that you'll be driving out there on Saturday to visit."

"Yes," Erik confirmed, "and Willem Larsen, who took the call, is worse than a town crier when he hears a juicy bit of news. You'll be meeting more than my family, my love. You may end up greeting the entire neighborhood."

Annelise seriously doubted that possibility would be much more enjoyable than having high tea with a German officer who was infatuated with her. "Oh, dear. I must make a good impression on your parents, your relatives, *and* the whole town?" But lest she sound too anxious, she turned to Rundstedt. "Then you must come to our home the following Saturday for tea, Captain. Surely things will have settled down by then."

"I beg to differ." Her grandmother entered the hall from the kitchen, the black attire she'd insisted on wearing since her husband's death adding to her austere demeanor.

Knowing that the outright contempt Grams had for the overbearing Nazis gave the woman a tendency toward bluntness, Annelise felt another twinge of panic.

"Not with an upcoming wedding to plan," Grams elaborated.

Eric hugged Annelise closer. "And the sooner the better." He tipped his head politely at the officer. "We hope you'll grace us with your presence on our happy occasion."

"Ah, yes. A wedding." His steely eyes fastened on Annelise. "Have you chosen the date? I should like the honor of throwing your seaman a bachelor party, if your brother has not already commandeered that duty."

"That's very generous of you," Axel replied. "But I fear the nuptials will have to wait awhile. My sister still has crucial shipments to process this month to a number of cities in Germany. It is imperative they be arranged before she leaves for her honeymoon."

"Honeymoon." Erik nuzzled against Annelise and kissed her cheek. "I like the sound of that."

Embarrassed and caught off guard by circumstances over which she had no control, Annelise eased out of his embrace. She needed time to think. Time for life to get back to the way it was before this stranger descended upon the household. In the meantime, however, she had to keep up the senseless charade. "Regardless of our wedding plans, we will make time to entertain our friends a week from Saturday."

Rundstedt took her hand and bowed over it, staring intently at her. "In appreciation, I will cancel my plans for Saturday and drive you all to Sjaellands Point in my touring car. It is far more comfortable than yours, Axel, and there'll be no necessity of using your petrol rations." He returned his full attention to Annelise. "What time shall I come by for you?"

The Nazi had yet to relinquish her hand. As Erik moved up behind her, Annelise responded with an even tone. "We'll expect you at eight o'clock. And *tak*. Thank you so much. This is most kind."

His thin lips spread into a mirthless smile. "So far from the Fatherland one has so few loyal supporters. It is the least I can do for true friends." He finally let go of her. With a click of his heels, he straightened, then raised an arm. "Heil Hitler."

A heavy silence reigned after Axel closed the door. He led them into the dining room, where they waited several tense moments for the captain's car and the open lorry lined with helmeted troops to rumble away down the cobblestone street.

Erik let out a whoosh of breath and slumped into the nearest chair. "Well. We really will have to contact my relatives now. Let them know they're going to have unexpected visitors to entertain—me, my fiancée, and a nosy Nazi."

"Do you mean to tell me," Annelise demanded, folding her arms across her chest, "you haven't even placed that call yet?" She cut a glare to her troublemaking brother. "You made the whole thing up?"

He flashed a sheepish grin. "Don't give me all the credit. Nielsen, here, added a few creative touches."

She couldn't decide which man infuriated her more.

"Breakfast is getting cold," Grams announced, breaking the strained moment. "Sit down. Eat. Axel, go get the children while I bring out their plates again. And take that putrid bag with you." She turned to Annelise. "As for you, young lady, you and that fiancé of yours need to get busy on wedding plans."

Annelise didn't dare glance at Erik. She was upset enough as it was. "But—"

Grams allowed no opportunity to protest. "That will keep you occupied so you won't have time to think about entertaining any church-burning disciples of Satan in my home. I declare. Your grandfather would roll over in his grave." With a huff, she returned to the kitchen.

◆　◆　◆

"Is it ready yet?" Axel mouthed through the window separating the warehouse from the office.

Annelise shook her head and held her hand aloft, fingers splayed. "Five more minutes."

He frowned, then turned back to the loaded truck waiting near the vehicle entrance.

Amazed she'd actually found space for the carload of cabbage on a barge to Amsterdam, in the Netherlands, Annelise hurriedly finished typing the shipping manifesto. More than likely those large crates held more than produce, since Axel displayed undue concern. He'd already come twice to hurry her along.

Erik, instead of working out in the warehouse, had spent the last few hours behind the filing room's closed door, creating documents for some downed fliers who faced the possibility of being intercepted by the Gestapo in Holland. The Nazis didn't bother with any pretense of friendship with the Dutch. They'd overrun the tiny lowland country in four days in 1940 and now occupied it with an iron fist. The active Dutch underground did all it could to arrange transport for the airmen to England, but the risks were incredibly high. Annelise prayed silently for the brave souls in Holland and Denmark, as well as the Allies.

Besides the perils involved with this venture, Annelise had to contend with having an attractive man living at home. He not only had taken all his meals with the family over the past three days, but he also constantly pumped her for personal information. That was the hardest of all: being expected to lay her heart out on the table as if it were an open textbook to be read aloud, every painful detail discussed.

She understood the reasoning behind the questions. Tomorrow they'd travel to his hometown in the company of a distrustful German officer. Something about Erik's tone and manner implied he was truly interested in her. But considering her past experiences of being betrayed first by her father and then by her former fiancé—two men she'd loved—she was hesitant to give these new illusions about Erik much credence. It didn't help having him assigned duties in the warehouse, either. All he had to do from any area of the open space was look through the office window to observe her every movement. She'd caught him doing just that on a number of occasions.

The door to the filing room opened, making Annelise jump like a nervous cat.

"Finally." Erik smiled disarmingly, devastatingly handsome now that his own clothes had been laundered and pressed and he no longer had to wear Axel's things. His grin turned smug when he patted the bulge of papers in his inside jacket pocket. "Shipping papers all set?"

"All but the bottom line." Giving the carriage return lever a last shove, she pounded the keys hard enough to print the total number, weight, and price of the cabbage crates on all four carbon copies. Then she rolled the forms up another line and leaned closer to proofread them.

Erik moved to stand behind her. "I know this whole marriage thing has you on edge," he said gently, his fingertips resting lightly on the chair back. "Especially with our having to drive to Sjaellands Point with the captain tomorrow. But since you're just now being introduced to my family, there's not much you'll be expected to know. As long as we keep our own story straight, about meeting at church—a place where a Nazi would never be caught dead—and how I was attracted by your beauty and shyness, how I kept making a point of sitting by you until you couldn't ignore me any longer, we should fare just fine."

Annelise didn't trust herself to look up at him. Not when his voice held that quiet sincerity that made the words sound true, even to her.

"And how I finally convinced you to take Sunday afternoon walks with me," he went on.

"Yes," she said, repeating the story they'd rehearsed so often, "and how on that last walk before you sailed, you asked me to marry you."

"And how you kept me on tenterhooks for the longest minute of my life before giving me that beautiful yes."

Her gaze drifted up to meet his eyes, and she lost herself in the sincerity of their light brown depths.

Axel pounded on the window.

The fragile dream popped like a soap bubble. Annelise swung back to her typewriter and ripped out the invoice forms. Fingers trembling, she tore off the last copy for her files and handed the rest to Erik. "The two of you be careful."

"Count on it," he said, hurrying out the door.

That was close, Annelise conceded. *I was almost starting to believe that pretty story he concocted.* She tightened her lips and sniffed, draping the typewriter cover over the machine. *But he was so near. And his words sounded so—so* real. *But that's just it. They're entirely made up, a script he wrote in his mind. He's merely a good actor, no more sincere than Tony. I must not succumb to such fantasies again!*

◆　◆　◆

The worn passenger seat squeaked as Erik jumped into the truck. He thought it odd that Axel, the boss of the factory, would undertake a menial chore like delivering produce. He'd seemed unusually keyed up all morning. "Is there something I should know in case there's trouble?" Erik asked as they pulled away from the warehouse.

Axel shook his head. "Not really. I just needed to stay busy, keep my mind off things." He paused. "I received some bad news. Nazis captured a flight crew—one that passed through Copenhagen last month. Some of our Norwegian contacts were trying to sneak the guys across to England and were intercepted by a wolf pack of U-boats. The Nazis removed the airmen, then sank the fishing boat with its crew still aboard."

"Oh, man. That's insane." Disturbed at the horrible news, Erik nudged the brim of his cap back and scratched his head. He switched his attention to the ancient city buildings lining both sides of the old cobblestone street.

"The submarine captain has since turned our boys over to the Gestapo in Belgium."

"I hear the Gestapo is quite accomplished at, shall we say, *persuasive* interrogation. Will this put you and your sister in danger? I can't imagine someone as delicate as Annelise at the mercy of those brutes."

Axel glanced over with a half smile as he guided the truck toward the wharfs. "Don't worry about Sis. Only one person—her contact in case something should happen to me—knows of her involvement. The Resistance has extremely strict rules. Information is given out only on an absolute 'need to know' basis. I have no idea myself how many people are connected to the underground. I do believe our ranks are swelling every day."

"So you're sure Annelise is safe? She acts so. . .guarded around me. So jittery. Maybe you put too much on her, having her pretend to be my fiancée."

He didn't answer right away. "Actually, I think it'll do her some good. Since she arrived in Denmark, she's been on a crusade to make her life count for something more substantial than being 'some man's doormat.' She used to be a naive little innocent. Now she's lost all trust in men. I guess I've only made things worse, dragging her into the middle of Nazi society."

Erik rubbed his chin in thought. "I can't imagine anyone deliberately hurting someone so lovely as Annelise, causing her to be so apprehensive."

"You can't?" Axel grinned. "Sounds like you have something in common with the captain—an infatuation with my little sister."

Erik averted his gaze, noting that the dock area was crowded with vessels, many of which were German. Pleasure boats no longer had permission to sail, but fishing trawlers, ferries, tugs, and other working boats stirred on the water. Here and there on the walls of buildings he spotted scrawled *V*s, victory signs that mysteriously reappeared again and again no matter how often the Germans painted over them. He glanced back at Axel. "Even if I did find myself attracted to her, being thrust at her out of the blue as I was hasn't endeared me to the poor girl."

"Nevertheless, I'm beginning to think throwing the two of you together was the smartest thing I've done in a long time. Annie needs her safe little mind-set shaken. It was a shock when she finally woke up and realized our dad had a number of women on the side. Then to have her fiancé do the same thing to her. . ." He shrugged. "But hey, no one gets a free ride through this life. Just ask those little urchins in our cellar or the flyboys being interrogated by the Gestapo as we speak." He inhaled a sharp breath. "I can't let myself dwell on them. All we can do is pray our guys going out today will have more luck taking the inland waterways."

As his friend reverted to silence, Erik mulled over the new revelations about Annelise. One concept his father had hammered into Erik's head since boyhood was that he really get to know a young lady before considering developing a serious relationship. He could still hear his dad's voice, see him counting off the items on his fingers as he spoke: *Is she a believer? Is she as beautiful on the inside as she is on the outside? Seek God's approval before venturing forth and choosing a wife. Bear in mind, this will be the mother of your children.*

But one thing he could not escape. Everything within him yearned to stay close to Annelise, to shield her from ever being hurt again. *Father God, if You don't want me to choose this woman, please take these feelings from me. . .even if she's like a warm, fragrant breeze after a cold, hard winter.*

"Better quit daydreaming," Axel chided, halting the truck. "Let's get these crates unloaded for the crane. The ship'll be out of here with the tide."

As Erik reached for the door handle, he spotted Nazis in pairs patrolling the docks, some with vicious dogs on leashes while they checked and poked into the various loads of cargo. *And here we are, trying to smuggle some men out with a ship-load of cabbage!* Time to get his mind on what was important. And forget this romance nonsense.

Chapter 4

Though a little early for spring to eradicate winter's drabness, gentle new greens tinted the rolling countryside as Rundstedt's shiny black touring car purred past tidy farms and red tile–roofed villages between Copenhagen and Sjaellands Point. Annelise tried to relax and enjoy the scenery, despite feeling trapped between her alleged fiancé and the German officer whose attentions she'd practically encouraged over the past several months.

"What did you say kept you away so long?" the captain asked in his heavily accented Danish. He leaned around her to focus his shrewd gray eyes on Erik. "An entire year fishing? The North Sea is rife with hazards in the winter months, is it not?"

Erik gave a casual nod. "That's what delayed us. Whenever the sea became too rough, we'd make for the nearest friendly port and sell our fish there, but for much less than we'd have gotten at home. Then we'd go out to replace our catch, only to be forced back to the nearest little fishing hamlet. The crew was determined to stay out 'til we could return with a big profit. Myself, I'd have given up sooner. I was desperate to get back to my Annelise."

"Meanwhile, I was at home," she breathed on an airy sigh, "imagining you'd thought better of your proposal or found someone else."

"Never." He smiled at her and squeezed her hand, a gentle reminder that he'd been a perfect gentleman from the first, always respectful and considerate. She returned his smile, noticing the way his dark hair caught the light among the thick strands, complementing his healthy complexion.

Annelise saw the captain's fist tighten, and knew he hadn't missed Erik's possessive gesture. Her gaze drifted ahead to the truckful of armed soldiers escorting Rundstedt's vehicle. Another followed behind them, their presence adding to the discomfiting reality that she, her brother, and their American friend were completely at the mercy of the Nazis.

She wondered how Erik viewed their current predicament. The assignment that brought him to Denmark had been risky enough without this. But to his credit, he seemed entirely at ease, answering the captain's almost nonstop questions while they covered the nearly seventy miles to Erik's hometown. Surely she'd have picked up on any nervousness he felt, sensed it in his grip. He'd held her hand in that protective way since they'd left Copenhagen. Farce upon farce. How much more would they have to endure?

Seated up front with the driver, Axel, the conjurer of this entire mess, turned around. "Looks like we're coming up on Sjaellands's Point. We've made pretty good time." Nothing about his demeanor indicated nervousness, Annelise noted. Her brother seemed made for this intrigue business.

She glanced down the gentle slope to the picturesque fishing port tucked around a sheltering cove in Ise Ford Bay. Beyond it the Kattegat Strait led out to the North Sea. With Nazi restrictions added to the danger of being at sea during wartime, idle fishing trawlers and ferries crowded the docks. No doubt countless idle seamen would be lazing about on this pleasant sunny morning.

Annelise's chest tightened as she pondered her present situation. She was coming into this town in an enemy convoy, supposedly betrothed to Erik Nielsen, a local lad whom no one here had ever laid eyes on. She needed her head examined!

The vehicles slowed to a crawl behind some milk cows plodding down the road. The herder, a gangly young man in a worn cap, turned and saw the trio of official vehicles. He gave a sharp whistle in the direction of his dog, then started purposefully for Rundstedt's car.

Annelise held her breath. Had this ruse been discovered? Had he purposely blocked the road to inform on them?

◆　　◆　　◆

"So this is the little bride-to-be." The lanky redhead's freckled nose nearly touched the car window as he spoke through the glass, giving the interior a once-over.

Erik's heart hammered against his rib cage. Betrayal? He manufactured a smile.

The stranger grinned roguishly as he looked Annelise over. "No wonder you've kept this doll to yourself. She's too good for the likes of you, old man."

Erik released a pent-up breath and winked at Annelise as he rolled down the window.

"Seems my friend has lost his tongue," the fellow said. "But I'm quite capable of introducing myself." He reached inside to shake Annelise's hand. "Jakob Kirkgarde. You must be the mysterious Miss Christiansen we've heard so much about."

"Call me Annelise. It's a pleasure to meet one of my fiancé's friends. Erik hasn't been nearly so forthcoming about you."

A cocky one-sided grin accompanied Kirkgarde's raised brow. "Now I know why."

"Driver, move on," Captain von Rundstedt abruptly ordered.

Kirkgarde stepped back. "Guess my dog's cleared the cows off the road. I'll drop by later to meet the rest of your party." He tipped his cap, and his gaze grazed the others in the car, revealing nothing.

As the vehicle drove past the herder and his cows, Erik saw Rundstedt extract his hand from a holstered pistol. He squelched a smirk. Apparently the Nazi had some fears of his own due to the growing tensions between the Danes and the occupying forces. But then, the Germans had good cause to sweat. There was scarcely a Dane in the entire country who didn't abhor their haughty presence. Just last night an explosion lit up the sky when yet another shipyard was sabotaged. This little caravan easily could have been ambushed.

Nearing the port of Sjaellands's Point, Erik prayed that everyone in town was in on his charade. The last thing he needed was for someone to try something stupid. . .or divulge his true place of origin.

The lead German truck turned onto the side street Erik had indicated, and Rundstedt's driver followed suit. A smiling couple standing on the corner waved as they passed.

"More friends?" The captain sounded already bored with the day's agenda.

"That's right. It's a small town."

Axel turned and grinned. "Methinks we're all gonna be excess baggage for you and Sis today. Perhaps after we've eaten, the captain would like to accompany me to the docks while I look for some vacant warehouses to rent."

Knowing his friend was attempting to ease the tension, Erik resisted the urge to thump him on the back.

Rundstedt seemed oblivious to the undercurrent. "We find it prudent to make our presence known wherever we go, check through a few crates, make sure all is as it should be."

The Nazi caravan drew up to a well-kept, two-story house where a group of people waited outside, smiling and waving as their returning "son" arrived.

Eager to greet them, Erik hopped out. He'd never actually seen these relatives face-to-face but had heard stories about them his whole life.

An older man bearing a strong resemblance to his real father stepped forward. Even with the receding hairline and somewhat hunched shoulders, Erik recognized his dad's younger brother from family photographs. There was no mistaking those kind hazel eyes or that Nielsen smile as the man engulfed him in a bear hug. "Welcome home, son. We've missed you."

"Don't forget about me," a feminine voice cajoled from behind. Turning, Erik saw his aunt, another familiar face from the family album. A bit shorter than he'd expected, she wore a dark skirt and white blouse, and her graying blond hair was pinned neatly in place. Already he was adjusting to thinking of the couple as his parents.

"Mom." He wrapped his arms around her plump little form and kissed her soft cheek. "I missed you, too. *And* your cooking. I sure hope you've made some of your famous *frikadeller* and *rabarbergrød*. I've been craving them for ages." His mouth watered at the thought of the Danish meatballs and rhubarb pudding, specialties of his family.

"Well, they are your favorites." She didn't bat an eye. "Your father and I are just glad you've come home in one piece. Such foolishness, venturing out to sea to fish during wartime. *Tsk, tsk.*"

Some individuals on the sidelines surged toward him then, all talking at once. Three of them were his cousin and alleged sister, Bergitte; her husband, Svend, and their baby. The others he recognized as another aunt and her husband, the local baker.

"Bergitte, Svend." He hugged the petite blond beauty and shook hands with her burly, Viking-like husband. "Don't tell me this strapping towhead is little Thor, big enough to walk already!" Then he turned to the other couple. "Aunt Lisbet. Uncle Karl. Wonderful to see you both again." Trying to respond to everyone's comments amid all the hugs and greetings, Erik suddenly remembered Annelise. He turned to see her already emerging from the car, utterly feminine in a flowy silk dress of rich violet and a gray cashmere coat with matching hat. Awed as always by her exquisite beauty, he offered his hand. "And this, everyone, is Annelise Christiansen, the beautiful woman I wrote you about, who has agreed to become my wife."

"Oh, come here, my dear, come here," Erik's "mother" crooned as the group surrounded Annelise and started introducing themselves.

"Looks like Annie has found herself among friends," Axel remarked, coming around the vehicle from the opposite side with their Nazi escort.

At the appearance of the hated uniform, the collective exuberance dimmed a fraction.

Erik cleared his throat. "Mom, Dad, everyone, I'd like you to meet Annelise's brother, Axel, and Captain Franz von Rundstedt, who graciously offered us the use of his personal car today. Axel, Captain von Rundstedt, may I present my parents, Magnus and Gjerta Nielsen. Next to Annelise are my sister, Bergitte, and her husband, Svend Dinesen, along with my Aunt Lisbet and Uncle Karl Kristoffersen."

Erik's "father" placed an arm around his wife's waist and drew her toward the newcomers. "My Gjerta and I are honored to meet you," he said cordially, extending his hand. "Welcome to our fair town."

"Yes. Welcome to our home," his wife added with a polite smile. "We're so pleased to have the pleasure of your company for the noon meal."

Watching the exchange and noting the tiny lines of strain near their eyes and mouths, Erik sensed the huge effort it cost the older pair to feign friendliness toward the German intruder. He made a mental note to express his profound gratitude later.

The group headed for the house, Annelise and Erik's pretend sister chatting about baby Thor's latest accomplishments. Erik hesitated, waiting for Axel and Rundstedt. The Nazi had gone to speak to the driver of the lead truck. Erik could not make out the conversation, but when the heavy vehicles started up and made a U-turn, he figured the troops were being dispatched to the docks to conduct searches on the various cargoes, warehouses, and ships. Meeting Axel's cagey expression, Erik prayed they'd all survive this day.

◆　◆　◆

"I'm afraid the parlor isn't large enough to accommodate all of us," Mrs. Nielsen said as they crowded into the home's appealing and homey confines. "Let's gather around the dining table instead. It's time to eat, and everything is ready."

Annelise felt Erik move up beside her and take her arm, leading her through the comfortably furnished front room and into the next as if he were familiar with the layout. She glanced around the charming dining room, where a lace tablecloth accented a long oval table already set with blue underglazed Royal Copenhagen china and his aunt's best silverware. Trays of fancy Danish pastries awaited on the buffet along the wall.

"Do I smell roast beef?" Erik's dark brows arched high on his forehead.

"That's right," his father affirmed. "Our neighbor butchered one of his cows a few days ago, and I talked him out of a sizable roast. He owed me a number of favors."

Erik chuckled. "That would be Lars, the persistent borrower of tools, no doubt."

"And before the meat dries out," his mother added, "we must serve the *klar suppe*."

"Ah, yes." Erik's cheery tone indicated how much he anticipated the clear soup with carrot bits and thimble-sized dumplings and meatballs. Annelise, too, enjoyed many of the traditional Danish dishes she'd first tasted at her grandmother's home.

"I'll help you, Mother," Bergitte said, "once I put Thor down for his nap."

Annelise watched her hurry toward the stairs as speedily as Erik's mother had left the room. Obviously the family was anxious to rid themselves of the great *honor* of wasting precious food on a Nazi officer. "I'd be glad to help, if I may," she offered.

At his place at the head of the table, Mr. Nielsen put his hand on her shoulder. "That's not necessary, my dear. Perhaps next time Erik brings you home, we'll impose on your good nature. Today you are our very special guest, and I'd like a chance to get to know my new daughter better." He paused. "My son tells me your brother has a shipping business, and you handle all his correspondence. Will you and Erik stay in Copenhagen after the wedding, or will we enjoy the pleasure of having you here near us? This is a lovely little town, coastal climate, salty breezes. . ."

It was a question neither of them had anticipated. Annelise could feel Rundstedt's perceptive stare from across the table. She chanced a glance at Erik, devastatingly handsome today in a gray tweed sport jacket and charcoal trousers, his gold-striped tie accenting the gold flecks in his brown eyes.

"With the war on," he answered, "we feel we'd be of most use in the city. Axel is too busy to get by without us."

"Oh, yes," Karl the baker chimed in, the overhead light shining off his balding pate. "Import-export. Any chance you might import some sugar our way?" He glanced at his plump wife sitting beside him. "We've exhausted our month's ration already with all the baking for your visit. Even our flour is running low. We may have to lock the bakery doors."

Axel brushed crumbs from his silk tie and gave a thoughtful nod. "Flour I can get you easily. Sugar? I'll do what I can. After all, we're family. . .or will be soon enough." His too-easy grin and twinkling blue eyes nettled Annelise. What new scheme was taking form in that handsome blond head?

Mrs. Nielsen and Bergitte returned with trays of steaming soup bowls and took their places.

Ignoring the presence of the austere German officer, Mr. Nielsen offered a brief prayer of thanks; then his wife met Annelise's gaze. "Erik never told us the date you've chosen for the wedding. Will you marry here or in Copenhagen?"

"We'd be happy to arrange for the local church," Erik's sister added. "It's lovely, in a quaint sort of way. I've always preferred the traditional-style building, don't you?"

It took extra effort for Annelise to swallow the small meatball in her mouth. Surely these people knew she and Erik weren't planning to go through with an actual wedding. Or had her *fiancé* conveniently forgotten to mention that little technicality? She smiled sweetly. "My grandmother's already making the arrangements. It keeps her happy to feel. . .useful."

"But you're all invited," Erik assured them. "The Christiansens have a large house. There's plenty of room for the family to come and stay for the festivities." He set his spoon down and sat back.

His mother, noticing that everyone had finished the first course, sent a pointed look at Bergitte, and the two cleared away the bowls in preparation for serving the main dish. The platter of beef they brought to the table moments later was richly decorated with gravy, bits of bacon, parsley, and pickled beet and garnished with green pepper and lemon slices. Potatoes browned in butter and sugar occupied one end of the large platter, and tossed red and green cabbage added a dash of color, enhancing the dish as a whole.

"It's truly beautiful," Annelise murmured, as appreciative as everyone else seemed over this respite from endless meals centering around fish.

Mr. Nielsen carved the roast and passed plates to everyone, then retook his seat. "I don't believe I caught the wedding date you mentioned." He directed his comment to Erik.

Annelise noted Captain von Rundstedt's heightened interest as he paused in eating.

"Our other son, Mikkel, is stationed over on Jutland," Erik's father went on. "He'll need to apply for a leave of duty to attend the ceremony."

"You sound like our grandmother," Axel cut in. "I've been trying to arrange time off for Sis and Erik, but with so many wartime orders hanging over our heads, it's almost impossible. Maybe by the end of May I'll be able to spare them for a short time. That's the best I can do."

Erik's aunt Lisbet beamed as she rested her forearms on the table. "That would be perfect! The flowers will be in full bloom. And we'll bake you the most beautiful cake"—she switched her attention to Axel—"*if* your brother manages to get us some sugar, that is."

"Then it's settled," Mrs. Nielsen declared. "The last Saturday in May it is. Of course you'll wear my grandmother's wedding gown. All the women in our family have worn it. The lace is most exquisite. I'll send it back with you so you can have it altered to fit."

Of course! The reason for all the talk about the wedding dawned on Annelise. There must be something that needed to be smuggled along with the gown. How comical, she decided, sneaking contraband beneath the nose of an officer of the Third Reich. "I'd be honored to be part of that family tradition."

A span of silence followed while everyone ate with enthusiasm.

At length, Axel turned to Mr. Nielsen. "The wedding brings up a much more pleasant subject—the honeymoon."

Svend Dinesen poked his wife in the ribs with his beefy arm and winked. "That's the whole purpose, right, honey-girl?"

Annelise watched Bergitte's cheeks flush and felt her own blush climbing to her temples.

Erik grinned and took her hand with a not-so-subtle squeeze, adding to her distress.

"Sis has been working pretty hard." Axel's mischievous smile matched her soon-to-be brother-in-law's. "I'd like to gift the newlyweds with a honeymoon they'll never forget. Annelise has always wanted to sail up the coast of Sweden, and late spring would be ideal for that kind of thing." He looked to Svend. "I understand your father has a yacht for charter, right?"

Flaxen-haired Dinesen flicked a stilted glance at the Nazi before answering. "It's in dry dock, same as all the other leisure boats. There's not much call for pleasure cruises with the war on." His full lips tightened at the edges.

"How about it, Captain?" Axel challenged. "Any chance of you persuading some of our naval friends to allow safe passage for a honeymoon ship? At least until she's well north of Bornholmsgat Strait?"

Annelise's insides sank. Her brother's big mouth was digging them into another hole. Honeymoon cruise. Right. No doubt he planned to help refugees escape to freedom on that yacht. Taking a sip of water from her crystal goblet, she directed a wistful look at the Nazi officer. "Oh, would something like that truly be possible? Could you actually arrange it?"

He swallowed, then blotted his mouth on the linen napkin. "I do have a few friends in the naval office." Never one to miss an opportunity to be the big man, he shifted in his chair and hiked his chin. "Perhaps I could manage something— particularly if we invite them to the wedding. If they know there will be more young ladies as lovely as the ones in this room, they might be agreeable."

Axel's good-natured laugh broke forth. "No problem, Captain. Surely you've noticed the women of Denmark are every bit as lovely as our spring tulips."

Rundstedt's cool glance slid from Annelise to Erik, and his polite smile vanished.

For what purpose had the Nazi insisted on coming along today? Annelise wondered. This family gathering couldn't be pleasant for him. It was hardly a secret that he'd love to rid himself of Erik in a way that might elevate him in her opinion. But as long as the man wore that hated uniform, nothing he could do or say would make him appealing—to her or any other patriotic Danish woman.

"Coffee and pastry, anyone?" The lady of the house nodded to Bergitte, and the two rose to clear away plates and the remaining food. In moments, the younger woman returned and set the assortment of fancy treats on the table, while the hostess poured fresh coffee. Then the two retook their seats.

Erik's uncle Karl stood to his feet and lifted his goblet in a toast. "May the good Lord bless our nephew and his lovely betrothed. May they raise a houseful of healthy children in a world of peace and harmony."

Erik draped his arm affectionately around Annelise and hugged her.

Mr. Nielsen also got up. "And may God bless this feast He provided for us on this most joyous of occasions."

Annelise heard the captain heave a weary sigh at what he undoubtedly considered an ignorant old man's ravings. But she knew that he was the real fool for thinking the Nazis could snub their noses at the Creator of the universe and get away with it forever. Retribution would one day be upon them.

Meanwhile, Axel was pulling her ever deeper into his whirl of intrigue—and Erik with her. Somehow, though, the American's presence beside her instilled her with confidence. She truly enjoyed the feel of his arm about her. And as she grew to know him, she realized she was discovering more to appreciate and like about him. Despite everything, she felt safe and loved in the midst of his warm, generous family.

Even with a Nazi staring straight at her.

Chapter 5

Emerging from the other secret room in the Christiansens' basement, Erik stretched a kink out of his back and neck. To avoid chance discovery by the Nazis, his desk and forging supplies had been brought over from the warehouse, and now he shared the hideaway with newcomer Charles Bridgeport, a lone escapee of a downed American plane. Erik's eyes burned from hours of the meticulous work, and his fingers ached when he slid the shelf-lined door partially closed behind him.

A commotion echoed from the other end of the shadowy cellar as Axel's voice impersonated a high-powered engine. "Varoom! Varoom!"

Erik worked his way to the kids' doorway and stopped at the entrance. He smiled at the sight of two grown men on the floor trying to keep pace with an energetic boy racing cars around a makeshift racetrack of boards and books.

They all glanced up, then returned their concentration to the race.

He shook his head and chuckled. "I'm going to the kitchen for a snack. Anybody else hungry?"

"We could use some of those cookies Annie baked this morning," Axel said, stopping his miniature car, "and milk. Racing's a thirsty business, buddy." After checking to see if the others agreed, they resumed the competition. "Varoom! Varoom! Varooom!"

Erik smirked and started for the basement stairs. When he'd left America for this assignment, he envisioned himself hiding out in some cold, dismal cave, suffering the life of a mole. Instead, he lived openly in this snug house with warm, caring people. People he'd quickly grown fond of. . .one in particular.

Thoughts of Annelise played through his mind in a collage of pictures, from his first glimpse of her exquisite beauty to her stunning appearance while visiting his relatives at Sjaellands Point. And her many moods—being flustered when she'd slept in on his first morning here; being annoyed when put in risky situations, yet willing to see them through; being patient and determined. And she cared for people: her aging grandmother, her foolhardy brother, children who'd been ripped away from their families, even total strangers imposing on their hospitality. *Like me.*

What a pity the wedding they talked so much about was a sham. The more time Erik spent with Annelise and the better he got to know her, the more he realized she met every single qualification his father had rattled off. And he cared about her. Really cared. Problem was, she needed a man she could trust to be with her no matter what. With a war raging around them, Erik couldn't promise to be that man.

Yes, he was going upstairs to get a snack, all right. In truth, he was yearning for some time alone with his fiancée. Reaching the main-floor hallway, he heard feminine murmurings from the dining room, where the ladies were making a new dress for little Rachel. Annelise's enchanting voice drew him down the gloomy hall toward the golden lamp glow spilling from the room.

In the archway, he feasted his eyes on his betrothed as she concentrated on pinning puffy sleeves to a small floral and lace bodice. Grams Holberg sat at the treadle machine nearby, sewing what resembled a wide sash for a dress pretty enough to be worn by a flower girl in a wedding.

His and Annelise's wedding.

No one among the family's church friends knew anyone who could take the children to Sweden, so Erik and Axel concocted the daring plan to have Rachel and Moshe march down the aisle as flower girl and ring bearer, right under the noses of the Nazis. The little pair would then accompany the wedding party to the reception on the yacht and conveniently disappear below deck before time to sail. The newlyweds would personally transport them to safety. Annelise had scoffed at the insane idea at first, but now even she was caught up in the wedding plans. Maybe in time her new enthusiasm might extend to him, too.

Erik's gaze meandered to the curly-haired darling perched on her knees in a chair by Annelise, fussing with a doll's dress made to match Rachel's special one. The rag doll was from the batch he had brought from America stuffed with money for refugees, and Rachel had latched on to one whose yarn hair was as dark as her own. Absorbed in dressing the dolly, the slight child looked so small. So vulnerable. He prayed that God would see them all through this dangerous escapade.

His attention gravitated to Annelise again, and his heart swelled with tenderness. Maybe after they'd accomplished their mission and were sailing the Gulf of Bothnia, they'd be free from the wartime tension for a while. He imagined them just being together, getting to know each other. One day she might come to trust him. To love him. . .as he was growing to love her. There was no use denying his feelings.

But who was he kidding? They'd be watched day and night by the Germans.

"See how pretty Abigail looks?" Rachel's eyes shone as she held out her stuffed doll for Annelise to see, dressed up in her fancy attire. "May I please hold my Abby under the canopy while you and Mr. Erik get married?"

Annelise smiled, admiring the treasured doll. "We won't be having a canopy, sweetie. Our wedding will be different from the ones you've seen. You'll just walk down a long aisle to the front of the church and wait quietly. Mr. Erik will already be standing there, waiting for me." A wistful smile—or *wishful*, Erik dared to hope—softened her expressive features. When she raised her lashes, her beautiful azure eyes locked on his.

For a second, he thought he detected undeniable joy. . .until her cheeks pinkened and her expression settled into one of mere politeness.

"I. . .uh. . .came up to get something to eat for me and the race-car drivers downstairs," he stammered.

Mrs. Holberg gave a wry grimace. "That's just where Axel belongs. In the cellar playing with cars instead of out in the world concocting endless messes for the rest of us to clean up."

"Did Uncle Axel spill some milk?" Rachel asked in that cute but perilous Hamburg accent. Her brown eyes rounded with dread.

"No, my dear. Nothing like that." The older woman slanted a glance at her granddaughter. "Annelise, why don't you go to the kitchen and help Erik fix a nice tray for the boys? Maybe one for us, too." She surprised Erik with a sly wink as Annelise placed her work carefully on the table.

Erik's respect for the old gal went up another notch. For all her disapproval over some of her adventurous grandson's schemes, it seemed she was in Erik's corner when it came to him and Annelise. Yep, he liked that dear lady.

◆ ◆ ◆

Acutely aware of Erik's presence in the kitchen with her, Annelise filled the water kettle and set it on the hottest part of the stove, then moved to the icebox for cheese and other snack items. "Would you mind fetching a tray and a few napkins?" she asked to keep him busy. "And there are crackers in that cupboard behind you. Cookies, too, for the children."

Erik took out a tin of cookies she'd baked earlier and brought them to her. He didn't even ask where things were! He'd gotten to know his way around the kitchen and the rest of the house amazingly quickly and seemed at home now. How had Grams put it yesterday, those old eyes of hers sparkling? *Such a good fit, he is.* Already the opinionated lady treated him like part of the family, just one more grandson. A person would think that her granddaughter and Erik really were engaged—and that the mock wedding mere days away now was legal!

Smiling at the ludicrous thought, she conceded that the American was more than pleasing. He was charming, witty, and intelligent, and he displayed a rare gentleness whenever he was around the children. Still, it seemed that Grams and Axel were caught up in a fairy tale.

How many couples really lived happily ever after? Sure, her own grandparents had enjoyed a long and wonderful life together, but that was back when marriage was considered a sacred trust, when a man presented himself to his true love's family, vowing to honor and protect her till death parted them. She couldn't imagine Erik approaching her father with such a pledge. Frederick Christiansen lacked a single honorable bone in his body.

She shook off the bitter thought. *I'll never forgive him. Never.*

"Is this everything, Annelise?" Erik interrupted her musings. . .and her idleness at the worktable.

"Hmm?" Her gaze collided with his, only inches away. "Oh." She tried to regain her poise as she surveyed the tray. She couldn't remember slicing the cheese or laying out the pickled herring, let alone arranging the apple slices, cookies, and crackers so artfully. What was wrong with her? "Yes, that's fine, except we need cups."

Erik studied her for another excruciating second before turning toward the china cabinet.

Her heart racing, Annelise asked a needless question. "The little ones will want cookies and milk. Do you think the airman will prefer those or the cheese and fruit?"

"Oh. You don't care what Axel or I want, is that it?" He looked askance at her.

"I already know that."

A mocking expression met her as he brought over the cups. "You do, do you?"

She answered too quickly. "Whenever there's something sweet, you're Johnny on the spot."

His teasing grin broadened.

"And as for Axel, he's a true Dane at heart and adores herring. But considering the wedding fiasco he's gotten us into, he doesn't deserve better than bread and water."

Erik's smile faded.

Had she hurt his feelings? She swallowed. "But you—you've been a wonderful sport about all of this. You really have."

His gaze didn't waver as he seemed to consider her words—or was it the meaning behind them? Abruptly his demeanor brightened. "Hey, for your brother to come up with a plan for me to smuggle several people out of the country by sailing up the coast in the company of Denmark's fairest flower. . ." He shrugged and gave a lopsided grin. "I'm not about to complain."

Denmark's fairest flower? He was so very entrancing. . .which only increased her jitters. For a heartbeat, a small part of her wondered what it would be like to really be married to Erik Nielsen. And part of her wished she could find out. Filling plates methodically, she changed the subject. "But Rachel and Moshe. I'm so afraid for them."

Erik exhaled a spiritless breath, as he did whenever she dodged personal subjects. "No matter when the children go, it'll be dangerous. Wouldn't you rather it was the two of us taking them out, instead of handing them over to someone who doesn't love them as we do? How much would a stranger risk to keep them safe?"

"You're right." Annelise paused and turned to face him. He'd grown as attached to the youngsters as the rest of the household had. "Whenever I look into their big brown eyes, I want to wrap my arms around them and promise them the world, make them believe everything will be all right."

With an understanding nod, he moved closer. She almost expected him to take her in his arms. . .and kind of hoped he would. Instead, he reached out to brush a tendril of her hair away from her eyes with the backs of his fingers, his touch sending a tingle down to her toes. "You've made things much easier for them while they've been here. Especially little Rachel, who understands more of what's going on. That pretty dress for her, and one for her doll. . .you'll make a wonderful mother someday." He took her hand, caressing her palm with his thumb as he gazed from it to her eyes.

Her heart skipped a beat. Unless her imagination was getting the better of her, Erik was looking at her the way a man looked at a woman he cared about in a truly special way. Her pulse throbbed in her ears.

"My dad always told me," he went on, standing much too close, "a man should search for a woman who'll be a loving mother to his children. Not just a pretty face but someone with a beautiful heart. Someone he could love for a lifetime."

Annelise could scarcely breathe.

"I—"

A deafening explosion rocked the house.

Instinctively, Annelise swayed against Erik, and he crushed her to himself.

Rachel screamed and flew in from the next room, trembling with terror.

Erik bent and lifted her up between them. "You're safe," he crooned, hugging them both close. "I'll never let anything happen to you."

Somehow Annelise sensed he was comforting her along with the child.

And somehow she believed him. She closed her eyes, reveling in their closeness.

Footsteps pounded up from below as Grams rushed in from the dining room. "From the front window, it would appear the crystal factory has blown up."

"They must have used enough explosives to level the entire block," Erik grated.

"Probably did," Axel affirmed, bursting in from the hall. "The SS stored arms there." He opened the back door and stepped out onto the porch. "Would you look at that!"

"What?" Annelise, with Erik's arm still around her and Rachel, joined him.

The night sky was ablaze. Copenhagen, beautiful, ancient Copenhagen, was being destroyed bit by bit—by its own people. And it couldn't be helped. Every Dane knew if the underground neglected to go after the Nazis, British bombers would do it for them. RAF planes roared over the country almost every day on their way to bomb strategic German sites. At least this way, the Danish people could pick and choose their targets.

"We must pray, all of us, for God's protection on all the innocent victims," Grams murmured and began to pray aloud.

Annelise pondered the fragility of life, how quickly it could be snuffed out. Within the warmth and strength of Erik's arm while they stood watching flames lick the sky, Annelise wished fervently he truly could keep her and the little ones safe. . .that he could be that fairy-tale man, the one she could trust until death.

◆　◆　◆

Annelise blew her bangs out of her eyes and peered closer at the itemized columns she'd entered in the ledger, making sure the figures matched the shipping manifests from the latest delivery truck. Axel would want the accounts up-to-date when he returned from wherever his latest "business" had taken him. She hated it when he was delayed.

The shrill of the street doorbell carried above the warehouse racket. Hoping it was her brother—or Erik, who also had been gone overlong—she glanced out the office window. How she resented Axel for risking other people's lives.

At the thought of Erik, her mind drifted to the previous night in the kitchen, to the things the dashing American had said to her. And the things he hadn't. Unless she was mistaken, he'd come pretty close to. . .to asking her to marry him for real?

Her breath caught. She had to stop this foolish daydreaming. Even if her imagination hadn't been far wrong, his actions could be attributed to high war-time emotions. Likely he was caught up in the rush of danger and excitement, the same as Axel.

Sigrid Thomsen, the birdlike woman who ran the front shop, rapped on the office door and came in, all fluttery and nervous. "Captain von Rundstedt is here to see you." She glanced toward the main entrance.

Before Annelise could respond, the Nazi brushed past the woman and strode right in. "*God morgen*, Miss Christiansen," he said in his stiff, condescending way, while Mrs. Thomsen took swift leave.

What business brings him here? Annelise wondered. Perhaps Axel or Erik had been discovered, and he'd come to inform her. . .to interrogate her. She drew on her practiced calm, returning the greeting. "Good morning, Captain. How nice of you to come by."

He gave a curt nod. "I did not see your brother's sedan outside." He peered out the inner window, scanning the warehouse.

Annelise followed his gaze, relieved that the shipping clerks had paused in their work to watch him. He'd be obliged to maintain proper decorum. "Axel's down at the harbor master's office arranging sailing permits."

He continued his scrutiny. "Let us hope it is for those mechanisms that were to have been shipped last week." He returned his attention to her.

She knew he referred to the remote homing devices for some new type of bomb that the BBC reported was being tested in Germany. Axel had been stalling the shipment while the underground made "minor adjustments" to them. "I do believe they went out, but I haven't received the paperwork yet," she answered nonchalantly. "Perhaps he'll bring it with him when he returns."

The captain gave a speculative nod. "I do not see the prospective groom around, either. Perhaps he, too, is bringing the papers." His tone dripped with sarcasm, but then, he always acted and sounded suspicious of everything and everyone.

"No," Annelise answered evenly. "He's gone to the train station to pick up a carload of fresh produce ferried over from Jutland."

"So I have you all to myself."

His insinuating leer in no way put her at ease. This threat was more personal. She attempted a small smile. "So it would seem."

Rundstedt pulled up a chair and plunked it uncomfortably close to hers, mostly below the view of the curious warehouse workers. "Now that your fisherman has been around on a daily basis, I thought you might be growing bored with him. It would not be uncommon for a young woman such as yourself to be having second thoughts about now."

When she did not respond, he spoke again. "Surely you are aware that it has been difficult for me seeing one as refined and socially elevated as you wed to such a. . .common fellow." He leaned closer. "Consider for a moment the life you would enjoy with a man of my breeding and taste. The clothes, the jewels, the finest villa. As you know, I am highly regarded in the party. And I intend to see that remains so. Once the Fatherland is victorious and controls global commerce, you could have anything in the world. Anything your heart desires. . .as my wife. Travel. . ."

Stunned by his unwelcome declaration, Annelise knew she had to be extremely careful not to offend him. She hoped her forced smile appeared sincere. "Why, Captain, I hardly know what to say. That would be a tempting offer for any woman. I haven't the slightest doubt you'd be a thoughtful and loving husband. But what my heart has desired, for a very long time, is Mr. Nielsen. Despite his humble family, my love for him has not diminished at all. Nor, I truly believe, has his for me. He is the deepest desire of my heart. All else pales by comparison to the love we share."

Rundstedt's face hardened like his rigid posture. "I see." A corner of his mouth lifted sardonically. "But surely you understand my reason for doubting this *great love*, at least on his part. I have seen no marriage announcement in the newspapers nor an application for a marriage license posted."

Annelise feigned surprise. She snatched the opportunity to stand and step back from him, her hands to her face. "You're right! We forgot all about the license. Thank you for bringing it to my attention. We must go to City Hall this very day, the minute Erik returns. We've been so busy trying to keep all the warehouse orders current while making wedding plans, writing out invitations, we've—" She forced herself to take the captain's hand. "We've even put off having you for tea as we intended. But once we return from our honeymoon, you'll be our very first guest. We'll have you to our new home, you and all of the other kind people who'll help make our wedding such a memorable event. Especially those at your naval headquarters."

The door opened just then, and Axel entered, the huge smile he always flashed on the Nazis fixed in place. "Well, well. We have a most esteemed visitor, I see."

Annelise extracted her fingers from the officer's grip.

"You'll be pleased to know, Captain, that shipment you've been concerned about is headed for Lubeck as we speak," Axel announced proudly. He patted the briefcase he carried. "I have the shipping manifests right here. I'll send your copy over with the others this afternoon."

"Good." His typical brusque nod accompanied the word. "I will inform the authorities when I return to my office." His demeanor softened a fraction as he turned to Annelise and recaptured her hand, applying pressure. "I enjoyed our little talk. Do reconsider what I said."

"Thank you again for that timely reminder," she managed, tugging free with some difficulty.

He stepped back and nodded to Axel, then clicked his heels in a smart salute. "Heil Hitler."

Axel moved to the door and cocked an ear as the Nazi's footfalls receded. Then he swung to the warehouse window, deadly serious.

Following her brother's gaze, Annelise spied two of the workers nodding purposefully at the captain and gesturing toward her and Axel. The Nazi did the same. Obviously he had issued some kind of order to them. But what was it? To watch her when he was gone? Did they have concealed weapons they'd use against her or her brother? The very thought turned her blood cold.

"What did the Kraut mean?" Axel asked. "What did he want you to reconsider?"

"Marrying Erik. He thinks I'm much better Nazi-wife material," she replied dryly.

"That's nothing new."

"Maybe not. But here's something that is. He noticed we haven't bought a marriage license yet."

"Never misses a beat, does he? But that's easily remedied. Where's Erik?"

"What do you mean, *where's Erik?* You're the one who keeps sending him out on the streets."

Axel grimaced and turned away. "I take it he's not back yet."

"Oh, no you don't. You're not getting off that easily, big brother. From what Erik told me, he didn't expect to be gone more than an hour or so."

"Things don't always go as planned," Axel hedged.

"What things?" How she detested this constant secrecy! How *could* he think so lightly of endangering a friend? Her fear for Erik intensified. "What have you got him doing this—"

He clamped a hand onto her shoulder. "Look, sis, Erik is a soldier. It's his job to do whatever he can to help win this war."

"No!" she raged back. Then, remembering they could be seen by the warehouse workers, possibly even heard, she switched to an intense whisper. "His job is to forge papers. If he's caught running errands for the underground, he won't just be shipped off to a POW camp. He'll be shot."

Axel's chuckle lacked humor. "Won't we all." His head jerked up, and he stepped nearer to the window. "Thank the Lord. That's him now." Wheeling around, he headed for the office door.

Vastly relieved, Annelise chased after him through the shop and out the warehouse door as he went to meet the truck.

Her fiancé, as maddeningly relaxed and handsome as ever, hopped down from the cab. Spotting her, he grinned.

Axel was not half as calm. "What kept you? Did you make the delivery?"

His gaze lingering on Annelise, Erik nodded. "Yep. They're all safe."

Releasing an exasperated breath, Axel gripped his friend's shoulder, drawing his attention. "Then what took you so long?"

Erik shrugged, unconcerned. "I had to take care of something." He turned back to Annelise and withdrew a tiny velvet box from his trouser pocket. "This is for you."

Realizing it was from a jewelry store, Annelise accepted the little box and opened it with trembling fingers. Inside she found a simple yet exquisite wedding band. "Ohh. . ."

"I wish I had the money to buy something more elegant," he added softly. "One that would do justice to your beautiful hands."

His tone and expression were so tender and sincere, she had the strongest urge to melt into his arms as she had last night. She tore her gaze from his and back to the ring. "It's just perfect in its simplicity. Exactly what I would've chosen."

"Really? You're not just saying that?" He released a huge whoosh of air as if her approval was of utmost importance, then plucked the golden band from its container. "When I told the jeweler you had delicate fingers, this is the size he gave me. I hope it fits." Taking her hand, he slipped the ring on her third finger.

The wedding band fit fine. . .but another band, an invisible one she could only feel, squeezed the air from her lungs. There they stood, the two of them, as if no one else in the world existed. Her hand rested in his much larger one, both of them fully aware of the ring's significance, this symbol of something so very elusive. . . never-ending love.

A tiny thought swirled through her head as delicate and iridescent as summer's first rainbow.

A girl could do worse than marry a man like Erik Nielsen.

Chapter 6

This day, their wedding day, had come so fast. Standing with his "father" at the front of the sanctuary while the ushers seated arriving guests, Erik felt his nervousness increase with each peal of the church bells. Normally the beautiful Danish chapel he attended with the Christiansens on Sundays instilled him with peace. Constructed of cut stone with a steep slate roofline, the structure's tall arched windows of jewel-like stained glass bathed the interior in a warm glow, even on dreary days. In today's sunlight they sparkled like diamonds, casting miniature rainbows everywhere. A bounty of ferns and flowers added lush fragrance that mingled with the perfumes of women dressed in their finest. So many people had come to see him and Annelise get married.

He tugged at the too-snug tie of the black suit Axel insisted on having made for him. Erik knew he looked dashing in his first tailored outfit, but that hardly soothed his nerves. Anyone would think this ceremony was the real thing!

The side door swished quietly open, and Axel came to join him, equally elegant in his own tailored attire. He was accompanied by Bergitte's husband, Svend, whose size made him appear oafish next to suave Axel. Bergitte's brother Mikkel was unable to obtain leave from military duties to be best man because of heightened tensions between the Danish army and the Germans.

Svend caught Erik's eye and patted his breast pocket with an affirmative nod, indicating the presence of the wedding license. Unknown to him, it would remain unsigned to prevent validation.

A bittersweet sadness came over Erik, but he dared not let it show. He diverted his attention to the mostly unknown faces occupying the pews, their conversations hushed against the subdued music from the pipe organ.

He easily picked out his relatives. About a hundred other trusted folk from Sjaellands Point also had come, expressly so the American, Charles Bridgeport, and several British flyers could blend in while "hiding" in plain sight. Erik spotted Charles coming to take his seat, flanked by two locals chatting brightly in Danish, little of which Charles understood. Erik tried to see if he could detect anyone who appeared British, but no one stood out.

What did stand out were the sharply dressed Nazis positioned in the back row on either side. Despite their futile attempt to maintain their superior attitude, they had to know most people detested their very presence.

Dear Lord, Erik prayed, *those particular "guests" possess terrible power. Please take control of this day and all its events. May everything go smoothly as planned, and may the Nazis leave the wedding celebration every bit as unaware as when they got here.*

Erik's "father" slipped an empathetic arm around him. "Bridegrooms are supposed to be nervous," the older man whispered, "but you look like you're about to face a firing squad." He gave Erik's shoulder a bearlike squeeze. "Put those other concerns out of your head. My friends and I will see you and your beautiful bride through all the pitfalls of this day. Just do what your grandpa told me on my wedding day." He chuckled under his breath. " 'Forget about the pomp and ceremony. Keep your mind on the prize. The honeymoon.' "

Erik knew no such prize awaited him. Yet hating that he'd deceived his relatives on that point, he mustered a grin. No one except Annelise's family and the minister knew this was a mock wedding. With so many lives at stake, Axel insisted that the fewer people who were in on the ruse, the better.

One niggle of guilt did assault Erik. His bride-to-be would be coming down the aisle in a gown worn by every bride in his family for generations, making light of a sacred tradition. In truth, she had no choice. It had been forced upon on her . . .as had this entire wedding. . .and him. He grimaced.

Three fashionably dressed young women arrived and took the pew directly in front of the Nazis. One of them turned and smiled coyly at the officers—to provide feminine diversion, Erik surmised.

He couldn't help noticing an abundance of very attractive girls sprinkled throughout the sanctuary. More of Axel's doing, he figured.

His uncle/father jabbed him in the ribs, obviously drawing a similar conclusion. "That new brother-in-law of yours must be a very persuasive fellow, to persuade so many available young ladies to attend."

Erik slid a glance at Axel and grinned. "You have no idea."

The organist abruptly increased the volume, heralding the start of the ceremony. Erik's heart leapt into his throat. The minister, garbed in his traditional formal robe, came to join him and his groomsmen, while Erik's "father" took his seat beside his wife in the front pew.

The talking ceased, and everyone focused forward.

Bergitte stepped to the doorway at the back, then started down the aisle, her steps measured to the meter of the music. His cousin's gown of rose taffeta edged with velvet and lace complemented her fair coloring and golden hair, a lovely contrast to the slim brunette who followed in a matching dress, a friend of Annelise's from church. From their dreamy expressions, neither had an inkling this wedding was anything but real.

It could have been real, Erik conceded, if Annelise would have provided the smallest bit of encouragement. He'd almost come right out and proposed to her that night in the kitchen, only she hadn't taken the hint, just gazed up at him with those incredibly sad eyes.

As Bergitte took her place at the front, Moshe started down the aisle, an adorable little tyke decked out in a new Sunday suit, his curls slicked back and shiny as he proudly carried a small satin pillow bearing a ring tied with a satin bow.

Erik watched for any indication of suspicion on the part of the Nazis to the Jewish boy's distinctive eyes and coloring, but they had yet to quit gawking at the pretty girls in front of them.

Then fragile little Rachel entered in her floral dress with its velvet sash, her sable hair a mass of ringlets and ribbons. She scattered pink and white rose petals from a white basket looped over one arm. The child took her job very seriously!

Erik almost choked when he spied the rag doll in the basket.

Halfway down the aisle, she caught sight of him and gave a shy wave, her sweet smile cinching his heart.

He winked and waved back, vowing silently to protect those two children with his life. Them and Annelise. He would die before he'd let one of them suffer at the hands of those ruthless Nazis.

The music segued into the formal bridal chorus.

Pulse racing, Erik turned his attention to the rear.

On the arm of her grandmother's brother, Annelise, the vision of his heart, paused on the threshold of the sanctuary for a breathless moment before stepping forward. Her golden beauty shimmered through the misty veil, her glory lighting up the room as she came toward him, a bouquet of pink and white roses and trailing ribbons in her other hand. The Victorian heirloom gown of handmade lace accented her fragile, priceless elegance.

Erik could barely breathe. How had he gotten caught up in a charade of this magnitude? To think he'd entertained the notion that someone like him was worthy of the perfection now coming to him on satin-slippered feet! Feeling a deeper sense of loss than he'd ever known, he let out a ragged breath.

◆ ◆ ◆

The first sight greeting Annelise as the congregation rose in honor of her walk down the bridal runner were the Nazi uniforms flanking either side. The second was the captain's ever-suspicious stare. She took a firmer hold of her great-uncle's arm, and he gave her hand an affectionate pat and a smile. Not in on the plan, he doubtless considered her a typically nervous bride.

Avoiding so much as a glance at Rundstedt, she focused straight ahead, and her gaze collided with Erik's. He stood tall and resplendent against the flowers and ferns, adoring her with his eyes. She almost forgot her own name. How unutterably sad that this whole ceremony was nothing but a charade. She'd have given anything for it to be real, to have that incredible American love her as much as he appeared to, enough to be faithful always. She almost sighed audibly.

When she reached the front, her great-uncle raised the edge of her veil to kiss her cheek, then let it fall back into place as he put her hand in Erik's and stepped away to await his line about giving her to be married.

The bridegroom took both of Annelise's hands in his and smiled at her, then turned slightly toward the minister, his gaze never leaving hers. The tenderness in his expression, the soft warmth of his touch brought a sheen of tears. She blinked to clear her vision. Intent in her struggle for composure, she scarcely heard the minister droning on in the background.

Erik repeated his vows with his eyes as much as his lips, his apparent sincerity almost tangible.

Then it was her turn. Annelise succumbed to the moment, imagining the wedding was real. But with emotion clogging her throat, she could barely murmur her own responses.

Before she knew it, the groom was putting his ring on her finger—the simple band he had chosen for her with great consideration. He gently rubbed his thumb over it, sending such a sensation of love through her that her knees felt weak.

A few final words by the minister, and Erik lifted her veil and drew her to him in a kiss so astoundingly gentle yet passionate that it was like being kissed for the very first time. Now her knees actually did wobble. Only Erik's strong arms prevented her from sinking to the floor.

He hugged her, chuckling quietly in her ear.

◆　◆　◆

The receiving line seemed excruciatingly long as Erik and his beautiful bride greeted the individuals inching past, most of whom they had never met. Still, the congratulations and good wishes seemed sincere—even those from the German officers. In their case, the joviality probably resulted from being invited to a gathering where so many unattached lovelies graced the hall.

Only one person gave him pause for concern. Rundstedt hung back on the sidelines, observing everything in silence. Did he suspect something? Or was he just being his usual overbearing self?

When the Nazi finally stepped to the end of the line, Erik felt Annelise grip his arm. Though she appeared outwardly calm, he knew she was thankful that church members had whisked the children out of harm's way, at least for now.

"I read your wedding notice in the newspaper a few days ago," the captain remarked, reaching them. He shook Erik's hand in grudging courtesy. "So I must concede the ceremony makes it official. I won't say the best man won. Perhaps merely the lucky one."

"Speaking of official," Svend piped in from down the reception line, extracting a folded document from his breast pocket. "We need to catch the good reverend and get this marriage license signed."

Erik heard Annelise's slight gasp. "You're right." He draped his arm around her shoulder, pretending to look around for the minister.

"I see him." Svend gestured to draw the man's attention. "Excuse me, sir. We require a moment of your time." He waved the paper in the air.

Observing the Nazi as he approached, the pastor maintained a pleasant expression. He smiled at the newlyweds. "Of course. Come into my office."

"And since you're standing right here," Svend tipped his head at Rundstedt, "would you mind being the second witness?"

◆   ◆   ◆

Annelise didn't dare venture a look at Erik as the foursome traipsed after the minister into his office. She fixed her attention on the man's black robe instead. He knew what was at stake here. He'd even been reluctant to be a party to a fake wedding. But now *this*.

He took his place behind the desk and held out his hand.

Svend, completely unaware of the ramifications of the affair, grinned broadly and handed over the official document.

The reverend took his good-natured time smoothing it out just so before turning it around for Erik and Annelise, as if even yet hoping for a last-minute reprieve for them. When none came, he picked up his fountain pen and offered it, his demeanor bland in the pregnant silence.

Erik took the pen and with surprising confidence bent and signed his name. He then turned to Annelise, that bravado losing a little of its power as he locked gazes with her and held out the instrument to her.

She knew she couldn't show any hesitation, either. She took the pen.

As she did, Erik closed his hand over hers. He brought her fingers to his lips and kissed them, his gaze never wavering.

The romantic gesture stopped her heartbeat for a second. But had he done it for her benefit, or the captain's?

When he released her hand, her fingers trembled. She steadied herself with her other hand and wrote her name below Erik's.

"Good going!" Svend boomed, snatching the pen from her. "That's the last time you'll ever sign your maiden name. From now on, you're a Nielsen." He scribbled his own signature, then handed the instrument to Rundstedt, who added his name and dropped the pen on the desk.

The tiny sound echoed inside Annelise's head like the closing of a great door. It was done.

It was official.

She was now Erik Nielsen's wife.

For real.

"Time's wastin' away." Svend Denison slapped one arm around her and the other around Erik and steered them toward the door. "Time to go to the yacht club for the party."

Chapter 7

No one spoke in the big black touring car transporting Captain von Rundstedt, the newlyweds, and Svend to the marina. Nearing their destination, Erik noticed wedding guests already milling about. How ironic that he, the son of a lowly fisherman, would have his wedding reception at a yacht club and honeymoon aboard a luxurious pleasure craft. But then, nothing about this wedding day had been normal, not the least of which was that he had actually married Annelise. That, of course, would have to be dealt with later. . .after the honeymoon.

Honeymoon. What an absurd thought.

Beside him, Annelise stirred, and he filled his lungs with the tantalizing scent of her perfume.

The car pulled into the parking area and stopped in close proximity to an immense yacht aglow with faint lights. Having expected a small, sleek, but cramped sailing boat, Erik could only stare at the beautiful ship. No wonder Svend's family chartered out this incredible vessel. The upkeep alone must be exorbitant.

Then Erik spied the German sentries, and grim reality returned full force. Since the Nazis no longer allowed the Danes to police their own docks, soldiers were positioned every dozen yards along the boardwalk. German naval officers were numbered among the guests, so the guards would likely remain in the background, but they appeared edgy while the throng of revelers gravitated between the yacht and the open French doors of the clubhouse.

The driver turned off the engine, then got out to assist Annelise. Erik followed close behind. As he straightened, he spied a German patrol boat anchored beyond the marina slips. It was enormously gratifying to realize that with an official escort, no other Nazi ships would bother them in the heavily patrolled southern waters of the Baltic. Obviously Rundstedt had more influence than his rank would normally grant. According to a recent BBC report, the Germans shouldn't be wasting military equipment on nonessential pursuits when they were having such a rough time trying to conquer Russia.

Axel, smiling expansively as he emerged from the club, intercepted the arriving foursome. "I've got everything running smoothly," he told Erik and Annelise. "You two go in and enjoy yourselves while you can. You'll be sailing with the tide, and that's barely an hour off. What took you so long, anyway?"

"The photographer insisted we pose for a formal portrait before we left the church," Annelise answered. "What a perfectionist. He must have taken a dozen different shots before he was satisfied."

"And they wouldn't be legally married if it wasn't for me," Svend chimed in. "We almost forgot to get their signatures on the marriage license. But it's all official now. Captain von Rundstedt and I acted as witnesses."

Axel cut a glance to his sister, then grinned in his easy way at Svend and the officer. "Lucky you two were there."

A wave of guilt over having signed the document swamped Erik momentarily. Sloughing it off, he put his arm around Annelise and steered her toward the music wafting from inside the building. "I do believe my beautiful bride owes me a dance."

◆　◆　◆

"Thank you ever so much for the lovely wedding cake," Annelise gushed, giving Erik's aunt and uncle a parting hug. "I've never seen such a pretty one in my life."

"Think nothing of it, dear. Karl and I rarely have an opportunity to do something special for our Erik. It gave us such pleasure." She beamed with pride, her heightening color glowing against her best navy dress.

"And it has been our pleasure," Erik said, "having you here today. Thank you for coming."

What if they knew this dream wedding was just part of the war effort? Annelise wondered, fighting tears.

Axel strolled toward them, arm in arm with a fashionable young brunette Annelise had never seen before. "It'd be great if you two would board the yacht. Svend and his crew are waiting."

Annelise knew the meaning behind his casual statement. The clandestine switch of crew members had been successful and the children were tucked safely away below deck. As usual, her brother managed everything without her help. With that horde of people in constant motion, the guards couldn't possibly keep everyone straight. Still, so many lives were at stake. "We should say our good-byes. It would be rude just to walk out."

"Don't worry, little sis. I'll take care of it." Axel gestured to Erik with his chin.

Erik slipped an arm around her waist. "Let's be off, sweetheart. I can't wait to check out that boat." Without waiting for her to respond, he ushered her out a side door leading to the boat slips.

The German soldier at the gate didn't bother checking their identification. "Congratulations!" he said in a thick Bavarian accent as they breezed past him.

"Thank you," Annelise called over her shoulder and clutched the long skirt of her gown in her hands. Her heels clicked on the hasty ascent up the wooden gangplank. Some wedding guests she didn't recognize were coming down just then, and she exchanged pleasantries with them. "See you in a week or so."

Svend waited at the top, a huge smile on his face. "Welcome aboard. First Mate Henrik, here, will show you to your stateroom while I ease the *Baltic Princess* out of the slip."

Annelise recognized the crewman in sailor attire as Charles Bridgeport.

"Wait!" came a shout from the dock.

Annelise's heart thudded to a stop. She and Erik whirled around.

Captain von Rundstedt and two uniformed soldiers started up the gangplank.

Only Erik's arm around her kept her knees from buckling as he took a protective stance between her and the three Germans. *It's over. All our machinations, all for naught. Someone must have informed on us.* She pressed her face against Erik's back, hoping to draw strength from him.

"I forgot to give you my wedding gift," Rundstedt announced. "Extra petrol for your trip." His men held out two gasoline cans.

"Why, thank you so much," Annelise croaked, surprised she had a voice at all as she moved to Erik's side again, a smile pasted on her lips.

"You couldn't have brought anything more timely," Erik added. "We appreciate it."

The Nazi bowed politely, his gaze never leaving Annelise's face, as if the two of them shared some secret. "Think of me when you use them."

Svend moved forward, his bearing confident in his ship's captain's outfit and cap. "We all thank you, Captain, but I'm afraid it's past time for us to be off. Henrik, Jakob, take the petrol these good soldiers have brought us down to the engine room. And, Captain, would you be so kind as to release our mooring rope when you go back down the gangplank?"

Annelise and Erik moved to the railing and waved to their guests as the large craft chugged slowly out of the slip and into the calm waters of the harbor to join the patrol boat. She didn't realize how tense she was until she noticed she had positively mangled Erik's jacket sleeve. She blushed and smoothed out the material.

He merely chuckled as he caught her hand and brought it to his lips for a kiss.

She swallowed. "Let's go below before we reach that German boat. I've used up all my pleasant smiles."

Erik's expression flattened, and he released her hand.

Had he taken her remark personally? "I really doubt I can bear the sight of one more arrogant German," she elaborated.

His face remained unreadable as he turned to Charles Bridgeport and spoke in English. "Annelise is tired. Would you show us to our stateroom now?"

Bridgeport gave a man-to-man wink. "You bet." He led the way into an elegant spacious lounge and down a steep flight of stairs to a hall that bisected the lower level. "This way." He headed toward the bow, hemming Annelise in between himself and Erik.

Bridgeport stopped at a door. "We've put the children in here with you, as requested. I know it's crowded with so many of us on board, but it'd be no trouble at all to make a pallet for the little ones on the floor of the crew's cabin."

It was a ploy to accommodate the newlyweds, Annelise knew. "I'd feel better if they were with me. I guess it's just that maternal instinct we women have."

Erik frowned at Charles. "So many of us. Are there more people than we expected?"

He nodded. "Three. And Axel also brought some ID cards for you to doctor. . . when you have time." His knowing grin evaporated when his gaze switched to Annelise. He opened the door to the stateroom so they could pass. "Herr und Frau Nielsen," he announced in fractured German and closed himself outside.

Annelise barely had time to admire the rich furnishings. The children charged out of the bathroom in street clothes, having switched outfits with other children who'd attended the wedding. Even Rachel's rag doll sported her original calico, none the worse for wear. The money inside would reimburse the new family that provided care for the children.

"You are here! You are here!" Moshe jumped up and down, his huge brown eyes as bright as his sister's. "And the big boat—it is moving!" He dashed to the nearest porthole.

Annelise bolted madly after him and whisked him away from it. "No. You mustn't look out the window. Not until the German boat is gone. Someone might see you."

"But I want to see," he whined, trying to squirm free.

"You said we'd be safe on this boat," Rachel complained.

Erik took Moshe from Annelise, then reached for Rachel's hand and walked them to the bed, where he sat on the satin coverlet, a child on each knee. "I know it's been hard on you hiding out all the time. But we need you to be patient a little while longer. By tomorrow morning the German patrol boat should be gone, and then you can play on deck as much as you want. How's that?"

But instead of the smiles Annelise expected to see on their impish faces, Rachel's expression contorted into rage as she clutched her dolly tightly to herself. "That is what everyone says. Tomorrow you will be safe. Tomorrow you won't have to hide. Always tomorrow." She shoved at Erik's chest. "Those mean old Nazis always try to catch us and hurt us. I hate them. If I had a gun, I would shoot every single one." Her lower lip pushed out as she buried her nose in her doll's yarn hair.

"Me, too." Scowling, Moshe pointed his fingers like a make-believe gun and squinted. "Pow! Pow! Pow! They are all dead."

Knowing just how the youngsters felt, Annelise began removing pins from her veil.

"Oh, now, none of that," Erik soothed, gathering the pair into his arms again. "It would be easy to hate the Nazis, I know. They've done a lot of cruel things to a lot of innocent people. But God tells us in the Bible that if we love Him, we must forgive our enemies. If we don't, He won't forgive us for the bad things *we* do."

Rachel peered up at him, only slightly placated. "But they are bad all the time. They never stop."

He nodded. "And one day, if they don't quit doing those hateful things, God will punish them worse than they hurt other people. We need to ask God to help us not to hate them and help us to forgive them. And we can pray they'll stop hurting people before it's too late, because God doesn't want anyone to harm His children." Erik kissed her cheek. "Especially His pretty little flower girls."

"And ring bearers," Moshe added importantly.

"And His big handsome ring bearers." Laughing, Erik gave him a hug and kiss, too.

Giggles erupted as Erik started tickling them.

Removing her veil and jewelry, Annelise wished she could join in on the happy moment. But Erik's words about forgiveness were deeply convicting. She had never forgiven her father. Not once had she been as concerned about his soul as she'd been about her own hurt feelings. Then, even worse, she had transferred her distrust of her father onto Erik. Yet from the very first, he'd thought of her well-being before his own, always shielding her from harm as he'd done earlier today when it appeared they'd been caught. She didn't deserve to be in the same room with a man of his caliber.

Tears stung her eyes. "If you'll excuse me," she murmured, picking up her suitcase, "I'd better change out of this lovely gown before I muss it."

In the bathroom, Annelise undressed, then took a warm shower to muffle her wrenching sobs. She had been so stupid. So heartless. Going to church every Sunday, vowing to God to forgo the love of men for the more holy calling of serving others. Having morning and evening devotions in the privacy of her room. Now she could see how pointless that was without God's love in her heart.

What had her mother cautioned her about before she left America? *Never hold on to bitterness, my child. In the end, it hurts no one more than yourself.* She was right. Annelise understood that now. Her mother had been crushed, but she'd never given up on the Lord. She'd trusted God to see her through, to give her the strength to forgive the husband who had betrayed her in the worst possible way. *Give God your pain,* she had said. *He loves us so much, He wants to take it upon Himself. Trust Him to do this for you.*

Annelise closed her eyes, letting the warm water pour over her, cleansing her body. *Dear Lord, for too long I have held on to the bitterness I feel against my father, and it has paralyzed me. Forgive me for sinning against You and causing You pain. Please give me strength to forgive him for his. . .weaknesses. Fill me with Your love instead.* As she prayed, Annelise felt her unforgiveness spilling from her, flowing down the drain with the water from the shower. For the first time in ages she felt free. . .almost weightless as she turned off the faucets and stepped from the enclosure.

Drying off with a fluffy towel, she gradually became aware of the silence in the next room. Erik and the children must have gone to get a bite to eat. It was dark outside the porthole. They had to be hungry.

She reached for the change of clothes she'd brought in with her and dressed quickly so she could join them. As she brushed her hair, the mirror revealed eyes puffy and red. Not wanting to be the cause of questions or concern, she splashed cold water on them. It helped but didn't completely banish the telltale signs caused by crying. Eventually she gave up and stepped out of the bathroom.

To her surprise, Erik and the children lay in a jumble of legs and arms on the bed, fast asleep. A tenderness enveloped Annelise as she drank in the loving, peaceful picture they made. Not wanting to disturb them, she slipped silently from the stateroom and returned above deck.

No one was in the lounge, so she walked out the door opposite the side where the German patrol boat cruised. Anything to prevent the odious reminder of the war from ruining her view or her mood.

The sun was sinking into the western horizon, its bright rays turning the sea into a blaze of glory. As the glowing orb disappeared, she closed her eyes and turned her face into the brisk salty wind, letting the breeze cool the fire in her own face. She breathed deeply. . .the pure freshness was just what she needed.

"You've been crying."

Annelise swung toward Erik's voice. Her fingers rose in reflex to her still puffy face. "Just being a silly girl, I suppose."

"No," he gently disagreed. "It's probably a little more than that, if I'm any judge. Like finding yourself suddenly married—and to such an ordinary guy as me, to boot."

She could tell he was deadly serious. She answered in the same vein. "Oh, Erik, don't you know you are anything but ordinary? You're the kind of man any woman would give her eyeteeth to find. You're everything wonderful that exists in this world."

From the doubtful look on his face, he wasn't buying it. "If I'm all that terrific, why is it you don't want me?"

Annelise had to look away. "I have nothing against you personally. It's—"

"Your father?"

She swung back. "How did you know about him?" As soon as the words left her lips, she rolled her eyes. "Axel, no doubt."

He only smiled. "He does keep himself busy."

Annelise gave a caustic laugh. "Himself and everyone else."

"Getting back to us. . ." Erik collected her hands and searched her face. "Dare I believe you've decided I can be trusted after all?"

She gazed into his eyes, nearly drowning in all they left unsaid. Hoping she wasn't seeing something that wasn't there, she took a breath and risked everything. "I trust you with my life, Erik Nielsen. From now until forever. . .if you're so inclined."

Now it was his turn to search her eyes. "*Inclined?* I've loved you from the first moment I saw you. I know it sounds crazy. You have no idea how many talks I've had with God about it."

"And what did He say?" She couldn't help smiling.

"Oh, seems it was His plan all the time." Erik's own growing smile rivaled the sunset.

He wanted her. He'd even talked to the Lord about her. How unutterably sweet. "I. . .love you, too, Erik. . .but I don't deserve you."

His eyes darkened with pleasure. "That's okay. I'll take you anyway." He drew her into his arms. "From what I hear, I'm perfect enough for both of us."

He thought that, did he? The man's head was getting much too big.

But before she could tell him so, he bent closer. "Welcome aboard my humble abode, Mrs. Nielsen." Then, lowering his head, he covered her mouth with his . . .and showed her just how perfect he truly was.

SALLY LAITY

Sally Laity has written both contemporary and historical novels, many of which have appeared on ECPA bestseller lists. She is a 1996 Romance Writers of America RITA finalist, a member of American Christian Fiction Writers, and has placed in the Inspirational Readers' Choice contest. Along with numerous romances and novellas for Barbour Publishing, she also coauthored with Dianna Crawford a three-book historical series for Barbour and a six-book series on the Revolutionary War for Tyndale House. She considers it a joy that the Lord can touch hearts through her stories. Her favorite pastimes include oil painting, quilting for her church's Prayer Quilt Ministry, and scrapbooking. She makes her home in beautiful central California with her husband of over fifty years, and loves that their four married children have made her a grandma and great-grandma.

A Stitch of Faith

by Dianna Crawford

Chapter 1

I t had been a hard day at the bicycle factory. And eerily unnerving. Sorena Bruhn expelled a weary breath as she unlocked the door to her cramped, one-room apartment. As she stepped inside, the air seemed even damper and colder than it had been on the walk home. Winter was descending faster than usual this year. She carefully removed her hat, trying not to dislodge any of the pins holding up her workday knot of hair.

Turning the light knob on, she pulled her brown tweed coat closer to her throat and quickly moved to the radiator under one of her two stingy windows. She swung the lever that would allow heat to come up from the basement, hoping to feel more comfortable once some warmth filled the plainly furnished room. Afterward she'd be able to shake the uneasiness she'd felt at work all day. . .the whispering among the women that would come to an abrupt stop whenever she stepped anywhere near the assembly line. Even though Sorena told herself they couldn't be talking about her, obviously her coworkers hadn't wanted her to hear what they were saying. Trust was a rare commodity these days.

She'd come to the city only a short time ago, and talking about herself was something she no longer did lightly. She'd divulged only that she'd come from the Isle of Fyn seeking work to help her family. She'd told no one that in the same year she'd become a bride, she'd then become a widow and fatherless. Even seventeen months after the murder of her husband and her father, she couldn't talk about the terrible loss without blurting out her hatred for the Nazis—hatred for the cruel way they'd left her loved ones to drown. Now the despised Germans overran Copenhagen, and even more despicable informers reported every suspicious word or action to the Gestapo. She couldn't risk exposing her own animosity to her fellow workers for fear of getting arrested. And without the money she sent home, her mother and sisters would go hungry.

Still, the women on the assembly line had an important secret they weren't sharing with her. But what?

Unable to shake the feeling that something was dreadfully wrong, she leaned to the side of the radiator and peeked past the blackout curtain to the dark street two floors below. All was quiet. Nothing moved. No trucks, no taxis, no pedestrians. Too quiet for six thirty in the evening. Curfew wouldn't be enforced for more than an hour.

A shiver coursed through her body. She ran her hand over the metal coils of the radiator but felt only the beginnings of warmth—still too cold to remove her overcoat. Perhaps something hot in her stomach would help take away this strange foreboding.

A mere step from the window, her sink counter, stove, and icebox ran along one wall of her narrow room. She reached into a curtained cupboard below to retrieve a pan for yet another lonely meal.

She'd thought leaving the Isle of Fyn would help her forget, but the nightmares had simply followed her. . .Papa and her beloved Curt crying out to her, begging her to save them from the sea they'd been tossed into when they'd refused to hand over their cargo ship. Every day, every time she saw a Nazi strutting up the street in his black uniform and shiny boots, her only desire was to do to him what his comrades had done to her and her family—these killers who pretended friendship as they stripped Denmark of its food and coal while waiting for the moment when Hitler would unleash his full force on their supposed allies.

Pain.

Her hands.

She opened her clenched fists and saw nail indents. Rubbing fingers across her palms, she drew comfort from the fact that not all Danes were being submissive. Every night or so, she was awakened by an explosion somewhere in the city. The underground was resisting the tyranny as best it could until the forces gathering in England came to liberate her small nation. If they ever did. The Germans had been occupying Denmark since 1940.

Perhaps the whispering at the factory today was about the Allied Forces coming. At the mere thought they might invade soon, a thrill spiraled through Sorena. She pushed aside the black cloth again, but this time to search the skies for warplanes.

A sudden pounding on the door shot through her like bullets. No one ever came to her flat.

She whirled around, her heart throbbing as she stared at the flimsy, paneled barrier.

Nazis? The Gestapo? What did they want with her?

"Open up! Please!" a woman's voice cried.

Sorena nearly sank to the floor with relief. Straightening her shoulders, she started for the entrance.

"Hurry!" came the insistent plea from the other side.

Swinging open the door, Sorena found her neighbor Mrs. Levin standing in the hall. The woman's dark eyes looked as wild as her unkempt hair. Her eight-year-old son was beside her, straining against the two-handed grasp his mother had on his arm.

The woman shoved the boy at Sorena. "Take Shimon. Keep him in there with you. Promise me. Keep him quiet, and no matter what you hear, don't let him out."

"No!" The boy wrenched free.

Mrs. Levin caught hold of his jacket collar and spun him back to Sorena. "Please. I want him safe."

Sorena pulled the rigid boy to her, trapping him within the circle of her arms, then returned her attention to his mother. But before she could question her, the frantic woman pushed Sorena and the boy back into the room and slammed the door in their faces.

"*Lock it,*" came her muffled hiss from the other side.

Shoving the bolt home, Sorena retreated from the entrance, practically dragging the dark-haired boy to the small kitchen table and chairs abutting the space between the two windows. She took hold of his bony shoulders and shoved him into one of the chairs, then pulled the other chair over and sat so she could directly face his rebellious umber eyes. "What's wrong? Tell me."

"The Nazis. They're coming for us tonight."

"I don't understand. Your father's been bedridden since I moved in. What could they possibly want with him?"

"We're Jews. They're coming to take us away tonight. Every Jew in the city. Mama said they won't check your room because you're not a Jew."

"They can't do that. They agreed not to. . ." She didn't finish what would have been an idiotic statement. All summer the Germans had been tightening their grip on the Danes, passing edict after edict, enforcing a curfew. No pretense remained when they disbanded the Danes' small army, confiscating their weapons. And now the Nazis were going to do here what they'd done in every other country they'd occupied: ruthlessly strip all the Jews of their worldly goods and ship them off to some distant slave labor camp.

But Shimon's father was dying of cancer. Surely even the heartless Nazis would see no profit in taking this small family. Yet when it came to the Gestapo, Sorena knew firsthand the evil they were capable of perpetrating.

She took the boy's hands. "Who told you the Gestapo was coming?"

The contortion of fear and hatred made his thin face look years older. "Mr. Goldstein from downstairs warned us a little while ago, but Papa's fever is up again, and he can't be moved. Papa tried to get Mama to take me and go with them, but she wouldn't leave him. She tried to send me." His eyes narrowed. "But I ran down the street and hid until I saw the Goldsteins sneaking away down the alley with their suitcases."

"No wonder your mother is so upset. You should have gone with them."

"I'm not leaving Mama. She needs me to help take care of Papa. I'm the one who goes out to buy food and fetch the doctor when Papa gets bad and. . ."

The drone of an engine and truck tires rumbling across the cobblestones carried through the window. Then the terrifying sound of screeching brakes.

Gripping Shimon's arm, Sorena moved with him to the window and inched the blackout curtain aside enough to peek.

Nazi soldiers poured off the back of a covered military truck, their rifle barrels reflecting the red of the vehicle's taillights. They charged toward the apartment building's entrance.

Sorena pulled Shimon tight against her.

The clatter and scrape of numerous boots filled the entry hall. The soldiers were inside! Pounding, banging on a door two flights below. Angry shouts echoed up the stairwell.

"They're at the Goldsteins' apartment!" Shimon's voice pitched high with fear.

Sorena covered his mouth with her hand.

His body jerked as they heard wood splintering, the crash of glass, furniture smashed against walls.

More shouts. Boot steps stampeding up the stairs. They were coming.

"Get under the bed," Sorena demanded, trying not to let her fear paralyze her. She pulled Shimon toward the single bed along the side wall.

He balked, struggling to free himself. "No. I have to go. *Mama*."

"No. You're to stay with me." She pinned him against her.

"Ma—" His shout was stopped by Sorena's hand.

She wrestled him down on her bed just as she heard the soldiers crash through the Levins's door.

Shouted demands, some in Danish, some in different German dialects, spilled over each other in a wild jumble.

"When they see how sick your father is," Sorena whispered fast into Shimon's ear, "I'm sure they'll leave them there." *Lord, let it be true,* she added silently. Mr. Levin was much too ill to walk, much less be anyone's slave.

The shrill shouting of Mrs. Levin ripped through the adjoining wall. "He's sick! He's sick! Don't touch him!"

Sorena pulled Shimon to her chest and covered both the boy's ears, wishing she could shield her own against the strident jumble of male shouts, the barrage of smashing furniture, and the shattering of glass.

Then, as quickly as the soldiers stormed in, they left, accompanied by more shouts and loud clomping. Gradually the noise faded away.

Although the boy struggled to free himself, Sorena continued to hold him until she heard the grinding of gears from the street below, then the receding rumble of the truck.

Once she loosed her grip, however, Shimon sprinted for the entrance, wrenching the bolt aside and flinging wide the door. "Mama! Papa!" Before Sorena could reach him, he ran to his apartment.

She followed close on his heels, then almost bumped into him as he stopped, frozen just inside the room.

The apartment resembled a newsreel she'd once seen of the destruction left by an American tornado. Everything was overturned and smashed. Broken glass crunched beneath their feet.

"Mama!" Shimon again shot into action. Frantically he raced around the room, flinging blankets and clothes aside, lifting mattresses in search of his parents. Then with one quick look at the front window, he dashed out of the apartment. "Mama!"

Sorena charged after him.

People living in the rooms across the hall had ventured out as far as their threshold, their expressions mirroring Sorena's own distress.

"Stop him!" she cried out. "Stop that boy!"

But before the neighbors could react, Shimon sped down the first flight.

Sorena went after him, taking two steps at a time. She had to catch him before he reached the bottom.

She didn't. He slammed out the ground-floor entry several yards ahead of her.

Reaching the sidewalk, she knew he'd be following the truck. She stretched out her legs, gaining speed as she'd done in school competitions. But this was a far more important race. The child's very life depended on her winning.

◆　◆　◆

Axel Christiansen rode the brake and clutch pedals of his sedan, slowing to a crawl as he searched for Britta Garbor's home. In the darkness, the crowded town houses all looked alike. It was vital he and his accomplice get to the party at General von Hanneken's mansion early. Axel turned the steering wheel until his tires hugged the curb, hoping the auto's hooded headlamps would illuminate Britta's green door. Tonight of all nights it was imperative to mingle with the Nazi High Command from the moment the first guests arrived, gleaning every possible scrap of information. Better yet, they needed to keep the Third Reich so amused that the high-ranking officers would neglect to check on the progress of their odious orders.

From behind, Axel heard the sound of running footsteps. He swiveled around and saw a young boy running hard, as if for his very life. The boy had curly black hair, so typical of a Jewish child. The roundup of the Jews must have already begun.

Fully aware of the danger, Axel reached across and opened the passenger door, shoving it wide. "Boy! Get in!"

Too late. The youngster had already shot past.

More rapid footsteps. A woman, her overcoat flapping out behind her, ran with equal fervor several yards behind the boy.

"Quick! Get in!" Axel shouted. He couldn't let the Gestapo seize them. "We'll catch him up ahead."

Her breathing labored, she glanced his way. An instant later, she was beside him. "Go! Fast!" Fiercely she motioned him forward.

Axel tromped on the gas pedal, and within seconds they were gaining on the boy . . .Axel, dressed in his tailored tuxedo, and this frantic redhead with much of her hair tumbled from its pins.

The boy rounded a corner.

They followed, and a second later the sedan nosed ahead of the fleeing child.

"Get him now." Axel smashed down on the brake and clutch.

The woman leaped out and blocked the boy's path.

He dodged past her.

She was just as quick. Catching him around the waist, she swung him into the auto.

Axel grabbed the youngster's arm and pulled him to the middle as the woman slid onto the seat.

"No!" the boy rasped as he gasped for air. "Mama. . .the truck. See?"

Axel's gaze followed where the boy pointed. A short half block ahead the red taillights of a German military truck punctured the darkness. In his preoccupation, Axel hadn't noticed the truck.

Two soldiers stood at the back, their rifles aimed toward the interior of the large army transport. Other soldiers disappeared inside a building.

"Climb over the seat," Axel blurted. "Get down low."

The woman didn't have to be told twice. Surprisingly agile in the limited space, she tossed the boy over, then followed, pulling him down to the floorboard with her.

Axel knew that if he turned the sedan around, it would look suspicious, and the driver of the truck would likely give chase. He'd get the numbers off Axel's license plate even if he couldn't catch the much faster auto. Axel also knew that his stopping a half block short of the truck didn't look much better, but he could easily conjure some plausible excuse. He'd spent the past three years smooth-talking his way around the Germans.

"Cover your heads with your coats," he said over his shoulder to the two on the floorboard. He then pressed down on the gas pedal while easing off the clutch, moving the sedan slowly toward the truck, hoping against hope they would not order him to halt. "If they stop us, don't breathe," he whispered, keeping the movement of his mouth to a minimum.

The woman rose up just behind him. "What did you say?"

Suddenly Axel's back door flew open.

"The kid! Don't let go of—"

The boy dove out onto the street. "Mama!"

The soldiers wheeled around.

Chapter 2

The soldiers' flashlights zeroed in on Axel's face, blinding him.

"Go!" the woman shouted as the car's back door slammed shut. "I've got the boy!"

Axel floor-boarded the sedan, swerving past the beams of light.

"Halt!" a soldier shouted. "Halt, or I will shoot!"

"Get down!" Axel raced through the intersection, then quickly shifted into second gear, striving to reach the next corner and turn before the Nazis fired.

A bullet exploded through the rear window, spraying the interior with glass.

His passengers screamed.

"Are you hurt?"

Another shot pierced the trunk.

The corner.

Axel slammed on the brake and skidded around it.

More screams came from the backseat as the vehicle tilted onto only two wheels. . .tipping. . .tipping. . .

A breathless moment later, the auto righted itself with a thud, and Axel shifted into high gear, resuming top speed. He glanced in the rearview mirror and beyond the shattered window to see if the military truck still pursued. He'd have to resort to shifting down whenever he needed to reduce speed. His taillights would be a dead giveaway.

Seeing no sign of headlamps, he relaxed slightly. "You never answered. Are either of you injured?"

"Shimon, are you hurt?" the woman asked.

No immediate answer came. Had the boy been killed?

Grabbing hold of Axel's seat back, the boy popped up and screamed into his ear. "No. Let me out! My mama's in that truck!"

The woman wrenched him away. "Your mama told me to keep you safe, and that's what I'm going to do. If she'd wanted you to go with her, she would've taken you."

Through the mirror, Axel made out the shadowy figures of the two as the woman forced the tense child onto her lap and held him tight, speaking in soothing tones.

"I know you're afraid right now, Shimon. But the best thing you can do for your mother and father is to be safe, so they don't have to worry about you. It's very, very important to your parents. Please don't take that away from them."

A pair of headlights suddenly haloed their silhouettes. *The truck?*

"Hold on!" Axel veered to the left and rounded the next corner. He pushed in the headlamp button, sending the street into instant darkness, then turned right.

The next few minutes passed with no sign of another vehicle.

"Watch for a phone booth," he called back to the pair. "It's imperative I call my family. They have to be warned."

"Why? I doubt the soldiers could identify a man inside a car on such a dark night."

"They recognized me, all right. I own one of the few Cadillac sedans in Denmark."

"I see."

Axel detected the same disdain in her voice he'd heard from others who assumed he was a collaborator getting rich off the war.

"Stop!" she blurted. "We just passed a telephone booth."

Axel slammed down on the pedal. "Which side of the street?"

"Left."

He turned around, then threw the gear into neutral and set the emergency brake. "Stay put," he ordered and hurried to the booth. Keeping watch on the unpredictable pair, he fumbled for coins, dropping one before he managed to insert another into the slot.

"Operator."

"Konig 5083, please."

He drummed his fingers on the icy instrument, waiting what seemed ages for someone to answer. He glanced down the street for any vehicle lights.

"Hello," his sister, Annelise, answered in her lilting voice.

"Hi, sis. I need to talk to Erik. Now."

"What's the matter? Something's wrong, isn't it?" As always, she had read the urgency in his voice.

"Just get him, will you? Please."

After a short pause, Annelise's husband spoke. "What's up, Doc?" he asked, carelessly slipping into English, their native tongue.

Axel answered in Danish, always Danish. The Nazis must never know he'd spent most of his life in the United States. "I think I've been exposed. The Gestapo are bound to come search the house. There's no time to waste."

Erik took in a swift breath. Axel knew that as an undercover agent for the U.S. Army, his brother-in-law understood full well the danger.

"There's a stash of money," Axel continued, "hidden in my leather jacket in the armoire. Take it and head down to the fisherman's dock where the Jews are being taken across to Sweden tonight."

"You'll meet us at the pier?"

"No. I can't chance leading the soldiers to you. I'll lie low somewhere for the next day or so and meet up with you at Grams's cousin's in Lund. Now go. Don't give Grams or Annelise time to think about it. Just tell them they have to put on their coats and walk out the back door. God be with you."

"And with you. Be careful. Don't get yourself killed."

Somewhere in the distance Axel heard shouts and a gunshot. The Germans were having a busy night.

Fortunately, this street was still dark and quiet as a shroud. But there was no time to lose. He hurried back to the sedan.

◆　◆　◆

The interior light came on when Sorena's good Samaritan opened the driver's door and leaned in, glancing at her and Shimon. Getting the first clear view of her rescuer, she saw he was exceptionally handsome—far more so than a man had a right to be—tall, tanned, blond, and impeccably attired in a rich man's clothes. A white scarf was tossed carelessly around his neck and back over a shoulder, making him look like some silly film star. Sorena hoped he had more brains than one of those vain peacocks.

"The Gestapo is rounding up every Jew in the city tonight," he said, stating the obvious. "Is there anyone you'd like to call and warn? Your family?"

That, at least, was thoughtful. "No, I'm new in the city. Besides, I'm not a Jew. I was just helping a neighbor."

"Oh. Well then, if they don't know who you are, I'll keep the boy with me and return you to whatever building you live in. They won't expect me to show up so soon in that area."

"I wish it were that easy," she countered, "but no one ever misses this flaming red hair of mine. I'm as recognizable as you and your fancy clothes. Besides, I live right next door to Shimon's apartment. Since they've just ransacked it, they'll know exactly where to go back to look for him. . .and me, for helping."

"I want them to catch me," Shimon spewed, trying to squirm free of her hold. "I want them to take me to my mama. She needs me."

"Even if you were able to catch up to them," the gorgeous man said, turning his attention to the boy, "the soldiers wouldn't let you stay with your mother, kid. They'd send you to a different work camp. Wouldn't it be better to be on the outside so you can help us find a way to rescue your parents?"

Shimon's chocolate eyes widened with hope. "You're gonna rescue them?"

The man's features softened. "We'll do everything we can."

But then, Sorena conceded wryly, he could afford to dispense hope lavishly—he'd had no problem seeing to his own people's safety. "I just wish my family on Fyn was rich enough to have a telephone, like yours, so I could warn them."

At the slight crinkling of his brow, she knew her barb had hit its mark. Not that she didn't have good reason to strike out at him and his kind. Many was the night she and her family had gone to bed hungry, while he, no doubt, had been sporting around, going to elegant parties, gorging on extravagant spreads of food.

Still, she would need to be more careful. . .at least until he drove them to safety. "From your conversation with your family—"

"You eavesdropped?"

"You weren't exactly whispering," she defended, bristling. "Besides, the window *is* shot out. Which reminds me, is it okay if we join you in the front? It's cold, and we're sitting on a pile of glass." Without waiting for his response, she grabbed Shimon's hand and tugged him outside with her, where she shook loose chunks of safety glass from their clothing before moving to the passenger seat.

The driver, too, got in and slammed his door. Once again they were cast into darkness. Just as well. He'd been wearing quite the scowl.

"As I was saying," she resumed as he shifted into first, "you mentioned your involvement with the Resistance. If you'll drop us within a few blocks of where they're hiding the Jews, I'm sure we can make it the rest of the way on foot without being seen."

"I wouldn't dream of divulging where they are. I've seen how well you two manage on your own. No, I think we'll wind our way out of the city on the back streets until we reach the road to Ballerup, if I can find it. Just before we get to the town, we can cut across the farmland to the north."

"Why? Do you know someone who can help us up there?"

"No."

"You don't? That doesn't sound like much of a plan, if you ask me."

"Plan? A *plan*? Oh, yes, that must be what I left at home in my other coat. So I guess we'll just have to wing it." The man was getting testy. "Keep your eyes peeled for street signs while I try to figure out which way is west."

Either the man really didn't know the direction, or he took great care to elude the Nazis, because he zigzagged through the narrow darkened streets of the old city until Sorena had no idea where they were. Thrice they spotted headlights on a road, and he immediately turned and went in another direction. Because he was forced to drive slowly in the pitch blackness of the overcast night, minutes seemed like hours while he strained to keep the sedan in the center of the winding streets.

At long last, he turned a corner and released a breath. "The paving on this road is different. I'm almost positive it's the one to Ballerup."

"If you'll stop, I can go to the nearest house and ask someone." Pulling her coat tighter around her, she reached for the door handle.

"It's the right road," he declared and gave the car more gas.

Shooting him a disparaging look, she pressed her lips together to hold back her retort. There was no way he could be positive, but obviously he was too full of himself ever to take advice from a mere woman.

◆ ◆ ◆

For someone he'd just saved from the Gestapo, the redhead certainly was ungrateful. But Axel knew he couldn't let her rude behavior bother him. Getting young Shimon to safety had to be his primary concern.

It appeared that the Lord was with them. The full moon peeked through the clouds, providing much-needed light. To one side of the road, he spied the rubble of the munitions factory the Resistance supporters had blown up the previous month, which meant this truly was the correct road.

His first instinct was to inform the woman. To gloat. But no, it would be more gratifying to leave her and her doubts dangling for a while. Resting back against his seat, he increased the speed, putting as much distance as possible between him and Copenhagen while the moon illuminated the way.

They'd gone less than five miles when bright points of light, headlamps, reflected in his eyes from the rearview mirror. Others crested a hill about a mile behind him. A convoy of at least three vehicles. Coming fast! With curfew in force by now, the vehicles wouldn't be civilian.

The woman turned and glanced behind her. "Do something! Quick!"

Axel noticed a country lane that crossed the road and headed into the farm fields edging either side. Much too open, but he had no choice.

"Turn right," she ordered. "Looks like the road dips down out of sight."

He took the corner, then upon reaching the slope, let the car coast into the depression. He couldn't afford to use the brakes and have his taillights announce their presence to the approaching vehicles.

As the Cadillac eased to a stop, Axel rolled down his window to better listen for motors in the stillness of the country night.

The redhead did the same, stretching up.

Suddenly she dropped back down. "Go! They're coming this way!"

"Go! Go!" the boy hollered, bouncing forward.

Judging the distance from the main road, Axel figured he couldn't gain enough speed before the vehicles overtook them. He shifted into low and made a sharp turn, driving into what appeared to be the remains of a cabbage patch.

The ground felt mushy and slick. The back tires began to slide.

He pressed harder on the gas.

The car lurched ahead, then fishtailed to one side and slugged to a stop. With the engine whirring to a high whine, the tires started spinning in place.

"Now what have you done?" the woman accused. "We're caught for sure."

Chapter 3

Axel lifted his foot from the gas pedal. He was only digging the tires more deeply into the mire. The three of them would be trapped, left at the mercy of the pursuers.

An instant later, one of the vehicles he'd spied in the distance—a smaller military truck—barreled past on the road. He exhaled a ragged breath.

Grabbing the woman's hand, Axel placed it over the interior light fixture. "Keep this covered while I open the door. I'll go see if they continue on or turn around. I really don't think they saw us."

He climbed out, closing the door behind him. His shoes squished into the mushy ground as he slogged out onto the road, and bits of mud flew from his feet when he ran up the small rise. At the top, he could make out the truck's lights where it turned off the road a mere few hundred yards ahead.

Pulse racing, Axel was just about to return to the car when the lorry's searchlight came on.

He dropped to the ground and lay motionless while he observed their actions.

The bright beam zeroed in on what turned out to be a farmhouse as the truck slowly pulled into the property. The glaring light swung back and forth, exposing a barn, then moved on to smaller outbuildings before the vehicle finally turned around and headed toward the road.

Axel released a tense breath. Maybe the soldiers were satisfied his Cadillac wasn't at the farm, but he knew better than to let down his guard yet. "Send them north, Lord. Don't let them come back this way."

When the truck complied, he grinned with relief. "Thank You, Jesus."

Picking his way carefully back to the car, he knew the next chore facing him would be to get the sedan out of the mud and onto the road again. . .hopefully without too much criticism from the outspoken woman he'd rescued.

He scoured the deeply shadowed field for something he could place under the rear tires for traction but saw nothing. His nose detected only the rotting remnants of decaying cabbage plants. As he neared his charges, he braced himself for the shrew's remarks.

Then he stopped short. *The dolls!* With the cash hidden inside them, they'd been providing assistance for Jewish children for years. Now they'd furnish a different kind of help.

"The truck drove on," he told his companion, opening the driver's door and reaching in for the keys. "I'll get us unstuck; then we can hide out at the farm up the road. We should be okay there—they've already searched it."

The dim glow of the interior light revealed the redhead's wide-set green eyes. She didn't exactly look convinced. She wasted no time opening her mouth.

He shut the door before she had a chance to utter a censure.

Trudging around to the rear, he opened the trunk. In the pitch blackness, he felt around beside the four crates of dolls, trying to find his crowbar.

The passenger door opened.

He groaned. She couldn't be getting out.

She was. He heard the sucking sound made when her foot sank into the oozy gunk, and he smirked. Even someone as stubborn as she would realize she'd have to get back into the car.

Only she didn't. Just as his fingers closed around the tool, she reached him. "Do you have a shovel in there?"

"No." *Does she think I find myself in this kind of predicament every day?*

"Then how do you expect to get us out? This stuff is. . .*awful.*" She raised a foot and banged it against the bumper. Gobs of muck spattered the mushy ground.

Axel was in no mood to enlighten the ingrate—not when he could demonstrate instead. "Can you drive?"

"Yes. But mostly boats."

"Get behind the wheel. Be ready to back up when I tell you." He braced himself for a snide remark, but amazingly, after a slight hesitation, she complied.

"I can help, too," the boy hollered.

"No," Axel countered. "No sense in all of us ruining our shoes." He couldn't squelch a wry grin as the woman slushed around to the driver's side.

After prying the heavy wooden tops off the doll crates, he jammed one lid beneath each rear tire and another right behind it. "Start the motor," he called through the gaping back window. "Put it into reverse, and back up very slowly until I tell you to stop."

The ignition caught, and the engine roared to life. That sound—along with a terrible grinding of gears when the woman shifted into reverse—echoed through the still, dark night.

Axel knew he'd made a big mistake, letting her behind the wheel. Boats didn't have clutches. "Cut the engine!"

His order came too late. The Cadillac jerked and lurched backward, spewing crate lids in all directions. One missed clouting him by a hair. The tires gained the mud again, splattering Axel with rotting cabbage and sludge.

"Stop! Turn it off!"

Shimon echoed the command, as if to make sure she heard it over the engine.

Axel didn't even want to think about the damage to his tuxedo. Seething, he gathered the crate lids and placed them back under the wheels with deliberation.

After ordering the culprit to move over, he got into the driver's side. Slowly he eased the car back a couple of feet, then got out and moved the wooden tops under the wheels again, repeating the process over and over until they finally regained the road. All the while, he debated whether or not the woman had deliberately set out to sabotage him. Grudgingly, however, he conceded that it must have been an accident. After all, from the moment she'd proved her inability to assist him, she hadn't offered a single piece of advice. In fact, she'd remained blissfully silent.

Axel guided the car cautiously in the direction of the farm buildings. The clouds were playing peekaboo with the moon, sending the dimly lit road into inky blackness every few seconds. Considering the muddy trail they were leaving in their wake, he regarded the darkness a blessing. "Keep an eye peeled for the lane to the farm," he instructed his companion. "It's no more than half a kilometer ahead."

"Are we gonna stay there?" the boy asked. "I'm tired."

Axel glanced over at Shimon, who was now between them again, snuggled within the woman's arm. Tuckered out, he didn't even resemble the fiercely determined kid of a few hours past. "I'll bet you are."

"There!" the redhead announced. "There's the lane. Turn. Turn!"

Figuring it would be prudent not to further alarm the farm's residents, Axel killed the engine and coasted past the house to the farmyard, bringing the Cadillac to a stop in front of the barn. With any luck, the three of them could sleep the rest of the night undisturbed in the sedan.

A light came on, its glow reaching them from the back porch.

The door swung open, and an older man emerged in rumpled pajamas, one hand shielding his eyes from the glare above, the other grabbing a shovel propped against the wall. "Who's out there?" Coming in floppy slippers toward the car, he raised the shovel and held it poised for attack.

"Go. Go," the redhead pleaded.

"Not yet. Let's give him an opportunity to help us first." Axel rolled down his window. "Hello, my good man."

The thin, sinewy farmer leaned down to look in, the shovel still elevated in readiness. "You the ones those Nazis were looking for?"

Axel decided to risk the truth. He'd found that most Danes hated the occupation as much as he did. "Yes, actually. We figured since they've already searched your place, this would be a good spot to spend the night. If you don't mind our imposing on you, that is."

He peered at Axel, then at his passengers. "Why're they after you?"

"They're rounding up all the Jews tonight. We're trying to save this little boy."

The man finally lowered his weapon and rubbed at a couple days' growth of whiskers. "You'll find no Nazi lovers here. We'd better get you and your car outta sight. I'll open the doors to the milk barn, and you can drive on in. I'll close up behind you." He motioned toward the structure, where a small truck with slatted sides sat parked alongside the entrance, beside a low platform holding milk canisters.

"We appreciate it, sir. Thank you." Axel gave a grateful nod.

The woman leaned past Shimon to speak. "Yes. Thank you. Thank you." Her voice sang with emotion.

The gray-haired farmer tipped his head. "We have more than enough room in the house to put you up for the night."

Axel quickly squelched the offer, not wanting to implicate the kind soul. "We couldn't do that. We'll be fine out here. Really."

"Whatever you say. Don't you folks worry about a thing. I'll fetch you some blankets, and you can bed down in the hayloft."

The sigh that issued from the depths of his passenger's being expressed beyond words all she'd suffered this night.

As Axel drove them into the wide center aisle of a barn stabling milk cows, he felt a twinge of remorse for his part in her angst. But when the farmer turned on a naked light attached to a center post, Axel got a good look at what once had been his custom-tailored tuxedo. He glared at the woman. And to think he'd felt sorry for *her*.

"Looks like you've been out making mud pies." The farmer chuckled as Axel stepped out of his sludge-coated Cadillac.

Axel shot a glance at his mouthy passenger. "Yeah, something like that."

◆　◆　◆

"Mama!"

The scream yanked Sorena out of a sound sleep. She bolted upright and searched wildly about in the thin light of morning. Her gaze landed on Shimon, bracketed between her and their rescuer on the hay, his dark eyes wide, his arms and legs flailing against the layers of blankets.

The man pulled the frantic boy into his arms. "It's all right, son. You're safe. Everything's fine." His voice was low and soothing as he held the child close and spoke against his shaggy curls.

A cow mooed and shuffled below, and Sorena relaxed. The three of them had spent the night up in a hayloft pungent with the particular odor of a dairy. Yet despite the harried events of the previous evening, she'd slept amazingly well. She'd actually felt safe...even though a man she barely knew slept a mere few feet away.

"No," Shimon moaned. "Mama's not fine. Neither is Papa. He's sick, and they took them away. I need to find them. I have to be there to help, or Papa will die."

Sorena's heart ached at the sadness of his words. Even if by some miracle Shimon managed to see his family again, she suspected his world would never be the same.

"If you *had* gone with your parents," Axel assured him, "the Nazis wouldn't have let the three of you stay together. Your father will probably be sent to a hospital, your mother to a women's work camp, and you'd go to a different camp with men and boys. You'll be more help to them if you stick with me." He lifted Shimon's chin and looked him in the eye. "I promise you, just as soon as the American and British forces land, we'll join them and go get your parents back, along with all the other people the Nazis stole."

Shimon choked back a sob. "Promise?"

The man, who in the growing light looked more like a clodbuster than a playboy, gave the child a sincere nod. "You bet."

Sorena watched him comfort Shimon. Perhaps she'd misjudged him. The tuxedo and fancy car could be a ruse to fool the Germans, and he truly might be just an ordinary person. Maybe even a seaman like her husband and father had been. One thing was for sure, though—even with his blond hair going every which way, he was still one good-looking bloke. She blushed at the ridiculous sentiment that had come from out of nowhere.

His gaze drifted her way, his expression unreadable.

Suddenly conscious of her own sorry state, Sorena rose from the hay to make a quick exit. Smoothing down her dress and tweed coat, she glanced around for the shoes she'd removed last night. She spotted what must be her everyday walking shoes, though they were so caked with mud they were unrecognizable.

Would they even be salvageable?

As she slipped her feet into them, the previous evening's fiasco flashed in her memory, renewing her irritation. If her *hero* had driven ahead as she'd suggested, her shoes wouldn't be ruined. But no, he had to do things his way, even if it meant getting them all stuck in that marshy mess.

Then another certainty dawned on her. He'd paid a high price for his choice. The man himself had ended up covered with mud from head to toe. A grin slipped into place as she glanced back to view the evidence in the rays of sunshine slanting through the barn windows.

Alas, his back was now turned away, and he had the blankets pulled up over his shoulders.

But that was all right. His Royal Highness would have to come out into the light of day sometime this morning, and when he did, she'd be right there to revel in the sight.

Chapter 4

Axel stirred in his sleep, and a sharp piece of straw poked through the blanket he lay upon, awakening him. He yawned and glanced around the loft, careful not to disturb the still slumbering Shimon. The high angle of the sun's rays streaming through cracks in the barn, indicated they must have dozed off again after the redhead took her leave earlier this morning. But extra rest was little more than they deserved, considering the harried experiences of the previous night.

And what about his own family? Had Grams, Annelise, and Erik managed to elude the authorities and flee to Sweden? Until he received news of them, Axel could do nothing but leave his worries to the Lord. He breathed a silent prayer for them all.

Reaching over to the boy's sleeping form, he gently roused the youngster awake, then rose to his feet.

Shimon grimaced and stretched his thin, seven- or eight-year-old body, then squinted up at Axel as he rubbed the sleep from his eyes. "Time to get up?"

Axel nodded, brushing dried flakes of mud from his rumpled clothes. "I think we slept a good half the day away already. And I'll bet that lady friend of yours will make sure we know it." The thought of the wild-eyed redhead brought a grin. That one sure was a handful. Always ready for a fight. Nothing like the women he normally chose to spend time with. "By the way, what's her name?"

"Sorena. That's all I know." Shimon kicked out of the blankets. "She's only been our neighbor for a couple of months. She lives in an apartment down the hall from us. And she works all the time."

Sorena. Such a gentle-sounding name for a shrew. Finding his dress shoes, Axel banged them against the floor of the loft, dislodging most of the caked dirt, then slipped them on. "Let's climb down from here and find out what Sorena's up to." Hopefully this day held more promise than yesterday had offered.

Stepping from the last rung of the ladder to the ground, Axel noted that all the stalls that had housed cows the night before were now vacant. Had he actually slept through the milking and feeding, the clanging of bells as the cattle were turned out to pasture? Incredible. Even if the dairyman had seemed wholly trustworthy, Axel couldn't recall having let down his guard so completely since the outbreak of the war. Not good for one's health in today's Denmark.

"Oh, wow! Look at this!" Shimon pointed to a spot on the filthy black Cadillac parked just inside the barn doors. The boy ran a finger across one of the bullet holes marring its once pristine exterior.

The gouges and the shattered rear window attested to last night's narrow escape. "Oh well, we're alive. That's the important thing," Axel replied, calculating the time and expense the repairs would involve—not that he could ever be seen driving the car again. "Let's go up to the house. Maybe we can borrow some soap and a towel."

Shimon eyed him with disdain. "Not me. I don't need to get cleaned up. I was inside the car the whole time. I didn't get dirty like you."

"Maybe not," Axel said, cautiously surveying the uncluttered barnyard and beyond to the road before they stepped into bright sunlight. "But you know how women are. I'm sure the lady of the house will insist on both of us washing up."

The youngster cast him a scathing look.

Something moved off to the side.

Axel spun to face it, then relaxed. A dairyman near his own age came sauntering from the edge of the barn, a pitchfork in hand. Obviously not a Nazi.

"Morning," the wiry, muscular fellow said, a broad grin displaying a mouthful of healthy teeth. He leaned the tool up against the lower stone half of the structure, then hooked a thumb around the strap of his overalls as he studied Axel and the boy with undeniable interest. "Or maybe I should make that *afternoon*. It's lunchtime."

Axel offered the wavy-haired stranger a good-natured shrug.

Shimon surprised Axel by taking his hand as they started toward the square clapboard dwelling a short distance away. Gone was the bravado he'd displayed earlier.

Axel made a mental vow to keep the child safe. "Lunch, eh?" he remarked as they neared the dairyman. "That'll sure hit the spot." His stomach growled at the mere thought of the substantial meal the farmer's wife would likely serve. He'd missed supper last night and guessed that the boy had, too. "I'd introduce myself, but it's probably safer for your kind family if I don't. You understand."

"Don't see how knowing first names could hurt." The young fellow wiped his hand on his pant leg, then offered it. "Name's Knud. I live here with my folks."

Axel liked his open friendliness immediately. "Glad to meet you, Knud. I'm Axel, and my buddy here is Shimon. You have no idea how grateful we were last night to happen on such a welcoming farm right when we needed it most."

Knud nodded, his lopsided smile a bright slash in his sun-reddened complexion. "Oh, I have a pretty fair idea of it. Come on. Let's go see what Ma's cookin' up." He led the way to the house.

After scraping off the remaining dried dirt on a worn scrub brush that had been nailed to the floor near the back door for that purpose, Axel followed Knud and Shimon through the service porch. Loaded shelves held a variety of canned goods, stored items, washtubs, and galvanized pails. But all thought of the practical and functional faded as the aromas of good country cooking met Axel's nostrils.

"You've a bunch of hungry men to feed, Ma," Knud commented as they entered the old roomy kitchen, where an assortment of hanging pots and utensils above a worktable reflected the light from calico-curtained windows. He removed a twill cap from his back pocket and looped it on a wall hook beside the door.

A sturdy woman in a simple gray cotton housedress and floral bib apron glanced up from setting the oblong table in the center of the room. Only the most cursory of smiles appeared on her round, weathered face as she silently resumed her work. Understandably she was less than thrilled over the danger her husband had invited into their home.

"Good morning, madam," Axel said, his mannerly greeting and friendly tone implying his appreciation of her sacrifice. But all the while, he knew he had to be a ridiculous sight in his irreparably ruined tuxedo. He hoped there were no bits of dirt falling from it onto her shiny varnished floor.

The enticing smell of sizzling potatoes reached him, and he turned.

Sorena stood at the cast-iron stove flipping potato pancakes. The sight of her didn't make things any easier. Having risen hours before he and Shimon, she wore a fresh dress and crisp apron, her long hair brushed into an attractive pageboy. Even her freckles looked somehow at home in this setting with this family. But he knew her superior smirk was for him alone.

Axel cleared his throat and directed his attention to their hostess. "My name is Axel, madam," he said with his best smile, "and my young friend is Shimon. I cannot tell you how much we appreciate your kind hospitality."

The older woman reached up a hand to tuck a stray hair from her bun back into place. She raised her chin a notch and gave a resigned nod as her humorless gaze raked across them. "I suppose a welcome is in order, considering your plight. Let's just hope your trouble doesn't become ours as well." Her attention switched to her son. "Knud, take these two upstairs to wash. Food's about ready."

◆　◆　◆

So his name is Axel. Sorena began removing golden-brown pancakes from the skillet onto a warming plate. *He was certainly pleasant and forthcoming with these farm folk. But then, it is to his advantage, after all.*

His display of gentlemanly manners began to wear thin, however, after a good fifteen minutes had passed without him or the other two reappearing from upstairs. With nothing left to do but wait, Sorena sat at the table with the older couple. Polite conversation had petered out some time ago, so now she avoided their eyes and gazed about the homey room while the elaborate cuckoo clock on the wall announced a new hour and the delicious-smelling spread of food grew cold. Hands in her lap below the plain linen tablecloth, she tapped her fingertips together in agitation. Part of her felt guilty for ruining their nice meal, even though she knew exactly whose fault it was. Undoubtedly the playboy was upstairs trying to restore himself to his former glory.

"The wife says you work at a bicycle factory in the city," Knud's rawboned father said from the table's head, his words more a query than a statement. Plucking gold-rimmed spectacles off his nose, he swiped the lenses with a kerchief from his overalls pocket.

"Yes." Thankful for the diversion, Sorena elaborated a bit more. "I worked there until yesterday. I don't think I'll be able to go back, though. Not after helping Shimon to escape. It won't be safe to return to my flat, either."

"What will you do?" his wife asked, empathy evident in her tone. "Where will you go?" But before Sorena could answer, the woman's focus shifted to the hall doorway and the sound of approaching footsteps.

Axel strode into the kitchen first, his evenly tanned features and incredibly blond hair making even the cambric work shirt and coarse trousers he wore look stylish.

Sorena deliberately averted her gaze back to the farmer's wife. "Thank you, ma'am, for your concern, but I really can't think about anything else until I know Shimon is safely situated." She glanced at Knud, also in a fresh shirt, his light brown hair neatly combed into a high wave above his forehead, most likely to impress her as he'd tried to do every time he'd come in this morning.

She centered on the boy, and her mood lightened. She couldn't help smiling at the effort that had gone into slicking down those unruly curls. "Come sit by me." She patted the wooden chair next to her—the only empty one on her side of the table. Far more comforting to have Shimon there than either rude Axel or the oversolicitous Knud.

The youngster, seeming to appreciate the invitation, ran to join her and scooted into his seat. He grabbed his fork and grinned up at her, exposing a missing eyetooth. "Sure smells good."

"I agree," the gray-headed man of the house said, wagging his own fork at the boy. "How about we all sit down so I can ask the good Lord to bless the food."

Sorena bowed her head but barely heard the rumble of the lanky dairyman's prayer as the two young men took their places directly across from her. Even with a wave from her side-parted hair falling across her brow and shielding her a little, she felt their gazes burning her cheek.

Shame on them. They should be respectfully listening to the man.

Shame on me. I'm the one who should be listening instead of judging others.

Amens sounded from around the table, proving Axel had been paying more attention to the prayer than she had.

Heat sprang to Sorena's face when she raised her head and found both men still staring at her. She snatched the nearest serving bowl and spooned some sauerkraut onto Shimon's plate, then passed it on and accepted the platter of potato pancakes from her host.

"Shimon," their hostess began, her stern features softening. "I brought the sausage up from the cellar just this morning. It was made from ground goose, not pork, so I do believe everything on the table is kosher."

"Thank you," he said, diving in. "I'm very hungry."

"And you, Mr. Axel," the older woman said, a jovial smile lighting her face, "I must say, your appearance has improved considerably from when you first walked in."

Axel matched her smile with an easy one of his own. "I do apologize if I tracked any dried mud onto your spotless floor."

Sorena tuned out the woman's next gushing remarks. Apparently Axel's practiced charm had completely won the old gal over. Instead, Sorena kept filling her own plate and Shimon's. But once the food had made the rounds, she was obliged to politely chew and swallow her meal across from the two entirely too attractive younger men. . .who seemed to be sharing some private joke. She made a point of concentrating only on her eating.

"Knud and I were talking upstairs," Axel said out of the blue, directing his comment to her.

Knowing she'd started at the sound of his voice, Sorena gathered her composure and settled back in her chair. "And?"

"He's agreed to take the crates of rag dolls I have in the trunk of my car into Copenhagen this afternoon along with his milk deliveries."

"Dolls?" Axel certainly didn't look like a doll vendor. She arched her brows. "Don't you think we have more important matters to attend than selling your merchandise?"

He studied her a moment, then glanced around the table, his expression sober. "What I'm about to say cannot leave this room. That *merchandise*, as you call it, happens to be dolls that were smuggled into this country from America. They're stuffed with money and occasional donated valuables to help finance the escape of Jewish refugees. Considering the events of last night, even you can see they're needed now more than ever. And since I can no longer deliver them personally. . ."

Sorena flinched. He'd put her in her place. Royally. Perhaps she deserved it, always thinking the worst of him when in reality she knew next to nothing about the man. What had he done since she'd crossed his path except try to help her and Shimon, endangering himself in the process? Being rich and heartstoppingly gorgeous didn't automatically make him callous and superficial. She cringed just thinking of her judgmental attitude.

The farmer's wife leaned forward. "What about the risk to our son? He goes through checkpoints on his way in and out of the city, you know. The last thing we need is to draw undue attention from the Gestapo."

"We thought about that," Axel answered earnestly. "We'll remove the funds from several dolls on top of the lot. Give the empty ones to the guards if they're interested. Knud will tell them you've been working on them in your spare time to sell during the Christmas holidays."

Her rail-thin husband kneaded his whiskered chin. "Sounds believable to me."

"Yes," his son said from beside Axel, taking on a self-important air. "And when I hand the dolls over to Axel's contact, I'll have the fellow arrange transport for our three guests across the sound to Sweden." His gaze reached past the table and held Sorena's, and he hiked a brow as if she were on the menu. "Unless you'd like to stay behind. I'm sure we could keep you busy and out of harm's way right here on the farm." An unmistakable gleam sparked in his blue eyes.

"That's true," Axel said thoughtfully. "There's no reason for the young lady to make that journey. I'd be happy to escort Shimon the rest of the way. Right, buddy?"

The comment stung Sorena. He wasn't missing his chance to rid himself of her.

"Of course," Axel went on, giving the boy a playful wink, "you'll need to carry a doll or two along."

Shimon stiffened. "Who, me? I'm not carrying a sissy doll."

"And I'm not deserting Shimon," Sorena announced, glowering at Axel. She then turned to the farmer's son. "I thank you and your family for that most generous offer, but I promised Shimon's mother I'd keep him safe, and I cannot and will not renege on something so vital."

The farmer's wife placed a hand over hers and gave it a squeeze. "You're a decent, hardworking girl. No one can fault you for standing by your promise."

Kind words for sure. But Sorena had a strong suspicion that the woman would be more than grateful to see the last of the three fugitives. Life would be much safer for this farm family without any strange faces around.

And Axel? He'd be far happier if she stayed.

Chapter 5

Soon after the noon meal, Knud left for Copenhagen, his old gray farm truck loaded with canisters of rich milk. Axel immediately made himself useful by volunteering to do chores around the dairy. As the afternoon dwindled, his latest task consisted of raking out cow stalls and laying fresh straw. . .anything to stay busy and keep away from Sorena. For some reason, he felt a strong attraction to her—freckles, sassy mouth, and all. Aware of a strong personal tendency toward competitiveness, he was pretty sure Knud's interest in her was what had piqued his own.

"That has to be it," he muttered as he leaned the pitchfork against the wall and strode out of the barn, brushing straw from his borrowed work clothes. He glanced down the road toward the city and stretched a kink out of his back. It was nearing dusk, and the farmer's son had yet to return. So many things could have gone wrong. Or, he surmised, Knud may have been delayed merely by waiting for Underground Resistance contact Johann Zahle to organize an escape plan for Axel and his charges.

Cowbells clanged across a deep stretch of pasture, and Axel saw the seasoned dairy farmer and Shimon bringing in the herd for milking. He grimaced. More work to be done. Peering toward the road again, he hoped to discover the man's strapping son and his two toughened hands coming to help.

But the chore of milking a score of cows was almost finished before Axel detected the rumble of the truck and the clatter of empty galvanized cans bouncing in its bed. As he'd been instructed earlier, he stripped the last of the creamy liquid from a brown Jersey he'd been milking and hurried out to hear how the young man had fared.

Uneven light from the house and barn blended with the truck's headlamps as Knud hopped down from the running board, a pleased expression on his ruddy face.

Axel exhaled a breath of pent-up worry and went to intercept him.

"I have good—" Knud stopped talking mid-sentence when the back door squeaked shut, revealing Sorena.

She appeared almost mysterious, even beautiful, the way the light and shadow played across her feminine features as she approached them warily. "Yes? Finish what you were saying." Her tone had lost last night's demanding quality and now sounded merely eager.

Knud grinned. "The dolls are delivered." He moved closer to her like a moth drawn to flame, then stopped and looked back at Axel. "You were right about the sentries. When I told them my mother makes dolls to sell for the Christmas season, they weren't the least suspicious. Of the eight we emptied of money before I left, only one remains. The guards bought the others to send home to Germany for their own children."

"And Johann?" Axel asked. "Did you find him okay? Talk to him?"

"That I did, and I gave him the dolls and the leftover money." The dairyman glanced again at Sorena and visibly sighed. "I'll tell you all the details. But first I have to hose out the cans for tomorrow's milk."

"I'll help," Axel blurted. After the hour he'd just spent in the barn with those smelly bovines, perhaps the spray would wash off some of the stench.

As he and Knud unloaded the large-handled cans and set them on the slatted platform, Shimon banged out the back door, munching on a spicy muffin. He ran after Sorena coming across the barnyard. "We're not leaving before supper, are we?"

Axel chuckled. The growing boy had not lost his appetite. Mercifully, Shimon didn't comprehend the kinds of senseless horrors his parents faced.

Knud looked much too athletic, muscling off a can in each hand as if he were lifting weights—plainly for Sorena's benefit. "No. You'll be needing a good hot meal in you first."

Sorena looked up from a length of hose she was uncoiling next to the barn. "Why is that?"

Her voice, Axel noticed, had a pleasing huskiness to it, sounding nothing like the shrew she'd first seemed to be. Maybe that shrill tone hadn't been a normal part of her nature. He shouldn't have judged her so harshly during last night's extreme threat.

"You'll be crossing the sound tonight in a rubber raft." Knud set down his cans and regarded her.

Axel frowned. He couldn't have heard right. *A rubber raft?* "That's the best Johann could do?"

"Yes." Knud continued to study Sorena as he spoke. "Your friend said you're lucky to get even that. Everything that floats has been put into service to take the Jews across." He finally averted his gaze from the redheaded beauty. "You'll be happy to hear, though, that the Germans weren't as successful as they might have hoped. They managed to round up only a few folks. Thousands of Jews have already made it to safety."

"Not my mama and papa," Shimon lamented, his young voice full of hurt.

Bringing the hose to the men, Sorena detoured and came up behind the boy. She wrapped a motherly arm around his shoulders. "I know. And we won't forget them. Will we, Axel?"

"Absolutely not." Placing a can on the platform, he mustered a smile for the youngster. "Shimon, would you run in and find out when supper will be ready? I'm so hungry I could eat one of those cows I just milked."

Axel waited until Shimon sprinted away before resuming the earlier subject with Knud. "What about transportation to the coast? It would be too risky to take my car."

"True. Tell you what. If you'll permit me to siphon the petrol out of it, I'll drive you there. We're only allotted enough for milk deliveries." Knud turned to Sorena and straightened to a rather impressive stance. "I'll take you also, if you still feel you must go. I'm sure that with Axel's experience in the Resistance, he's more than capable of seeing Shimon to safety. If they did happen to get caught, what help could you be if you were imprisoned, too?"

"He's right, Sorena," Axel agreed. No longer all that interested in ridding himself of the spirited redhead, Axel's concern was solely for her safety. Her staying behind would be best. . .even if Knud's offer had an underlying motive.

◆　◆　◆

Sorena, dressed in dungarees and a heavy coat, sat scrunched between Knud and Axel on the truck seat, her knee knocking against the gearshift every time the tires hit a bump. As the vehicle sped through the night, the roar of the engine precluded all hope of conversation. For that she was grateful, considering neither man wanted her along on the forty-kilometer ride north to Helsinger.

Shimon had fallen asleep in Axel's lap, with one leg draped across hers, shortly after they began the trip. She hoped he wouldn't awaken until they reached their destination—the home of the Resistance worker who would take them to the raft.

Trying to keep her mind off the dangerous journey at sea awaiting them, Sorena toyed with the yarn hair of the rag doll she held and gazed out the window, counting the thinly scattered lights of the farmhouses they passed. Knud had been careful to slow down as they drove through the town of Hillerod, and it seemed the Lord had been looking after them, because they hadn't had to detour around any roadblocks.

"I see some lights up ahead," she said, pointing. "Is that Helsinger?"

"What?" Knud leaned closer.

"Helsinger," she repeated more loudly in his ear.

"Yes. Axel!" he shouted, rousing Shimon in the bargain. "Give your little friend to Sorena. You get down on the floorboard."

Sorena's heart started pounding as she stared hard, trying to figure out what exactly Knud saw.

Axel, too, hesitated a moment, then did as he was told.

Knud reached into the crack behind the seat and pulled out a smelly dark tarp. "Sorena, cover Axel up. Then drape your legs across him and rest against the window as if you're relaxing. Shimon, pull that cap down over your curls, grab hold of the doll Sorena is holding, and lean against her. Pretend to be asleep."

After checking her own beret for stray hairs, Sorena tugged the boy close as she cut a glance over at Knud. "You didn't have us do this at Hillerod."

"Hillerod isn't sitting next to the narrowest spot between us and Sweden, either. The Nazis keep a tight lock on this place."

"The road. It'll be blocked?"

"Most likely."

"And you plan to go right up to it."

He shrugged. "Don't worry. Leave it to me."

Don't worry! "Isn't there some way we can drive around it?"

"No. Besides, that's what they expect from folks who have something to hide."

It sounded plausible, especially since Knud seemed composed and sure of himself. But Sorena felt as if they were driving right into the barrel of a loaded cannon.

Axel, on the floorboard, squeezed her ankle. "Relax. Play it cool."

Easier said than done. Within seconds, a bright spotlight zeroed in on them as a military truck edged out, blocking the road.

"I'll do the talking," Knud said, shifting into a lower gear.

"But we don't have any papers!"

Shielding his eyes from the glare, he ignored her and slowed to a gradual stop just short of the Nazis. He rolled down his window, the motor idling.

A German soldier with a flashlight in one hand and a rifle in the other came up to the driver's side of the farm truck. Another walked around to the rear.

The closest one hopped up onto the running board and searched the cab's interior with his light.

Half frozen with fright, Sorena silently pleaded with God to help her appear calm and to blind the man to the bulky tarp concealing Axel.

The guard aimed his torch at Knud's face. "What are you doing out on the road after curfew?" he demanded in his heavy German accent.

"Some of my friend Einar Klipping's cows have come down with a fever. He asked if I could help him out. I'm delivering some milk to make up for his shortfall."

The casual tone of his voice eased Sorena's panic, but only slightly. She felt the truck dip as the other soldier climbed up into the bed. She had to stay calm, but with Axel beneath her feet and a Jewish boy clutching her waist, her every instinct spurred her to run for her life.

"Give me your papers." Slinging his rifle strap over his shoulder, the guard stuck out a gloved hand.

"Sweetheart," Knud said, offering Sorena a nonchalant smile, "get my authorization out of the glove compartment, would you?"

Noticing the tremor in her hand as she reached to comply, she quickly used the other to still it, then opened the glove box and retrieved the forms. "Here you are, dear."

While the soldier scanned the documents with his light, the other German hopped off the back and joined his comrade. "Is only milk in back. Nothing more."

His cohort gave a nod. "Good. And these papers seem to be in order." He handed them back. "Now give me the woman's."

Sorena swallowed a gasp, her every sense on edge. Slowly sneaking a hand to the side, she wrapped her fingers around the door handle.

"Sweetheart, did you bring your identification?"

Her mouth dropped open. He was the one who was supposed to have all the answers. "No," she shot back, outrage choking off her voice. "You said you'd get it."

Knud turned back to the guard and winced. "She's right. I did say that. I reckon we'll have to turn around and go back for it."

The guard looked from Knud to Sorena, then frowned and rolled his eyes. "I will let you through this time. But do not let me catch either of you without them again. Do you understand?"

"That I do. Thank you, sir." Shifting into gear once again, Knud pulled slowly away.

Sorena heard some muffled huffing at her feet. Axel. Was he crying?

"You can get up now," Knud announced. "It's safe."

Axel eased up from the cramped position. And he wasn't crying but laughing. He scooted onto the seat, still chuckling. "Good job, Knud. Be sure to wait for the changing of the guard before you come back through here."

His mirth obviously was infectious, because Knud joined him, then Shimon.

Sorena supposed that was as good a way as any to release the tension, though she'd prefer to cry. Or better yet, faint.

Finally the laughter tapered off, and Axel did something most unexpected. He pulled her and Shimon close, as if he truly cared. "Knud, I'd like to introduce you to my secret weapon. Miss Smart Mouth. No man can stand against it."

◆　◆　◆

Once the truck reached the outer edge of Helsinger, caught in the fingers of a wispy fog, Knud took a cobbled side road leading toward the sound. He stopped at a small cottage, whose address he said he'd been instructed to keep to himself.

"You're to knock three times," he told Axel. "Then two. When the door opens, ask for Peter."

As soon as Axel piled out of the crowded cab with Sorena and Shimon, he checked up and down the street just to be sure no one was about. Then, after Knud drove away into the night, he followed the instructions. Fortunately, the person who answered the summons claimed to be Peter. The small trim man ushered Axel and his charges inside.

Axel had to duck to go through the low entrance. The smell of burning coal oil assaulted his nose, but the simple, dimly lit parlor was quite warm, considering the coastal dampness outside.

A woman of medium build in a faded pink chenille robe sat in a rocker near the gray stove. She looked up from her knitting and scoured the heavily dressed threesome as Shimon quickly hid the hated rag doll behind his back.

"Emma," the man said, addressing his wife, "I'll be gone a little while. You needn't wait up for me."

"Another of your midnight trysts?" the woman asked, her brows arched high in skepticism.

Her husband headed toward the back of the house without replying. His only words were for Axel and company as he gestured for them to follow. "Out this way."

Wherever they were headed in the foggy darkness, the man didn't waste time. He set a swift pace.

Axel hefted Shimon up onto his shoulders and hurried after Peter, trusting that Sorena would be able to keep up on her own. Would she call out if she couldn't? She hadn't uttered a word since he'd termed her *Miss Smart Mouth*. Knowing her, he'd probably hear plenty about it before this night was over. Still, he felt a niggling guilt for being so insensitive.

After a fast walk of about ten minutes, they started down a sandy slope toward the gentle sound of lapping water. Where the ground leveled out, the sand was damp, and tall reeds crowded the path on either side.

Peter slowed to a stop. "We'll be leaving the trail here," he said under his breath.

Axel stepped off into mush and reeds. He couldn't imagine who could possibly hear them so far out in the marsh, but he appreciated the fellow's caution nonetheless.

Behind him, Sorena gasped.

He knew she didn't enjoy experiencing a second night of sloshing in mud.

As if understanding her plight, a muffled giggle came from Shimon as he nuzzled within the warmth of the woolen scarf Knud's mother had insisted he wear.

Moments later, the man stopped. "We're here. I've put some blankets in the raft. It'll be bitter cold out there on the water."

Axel strained his eyes but couldn't see anything for the sea grass. He lowered Shimon to the soggy ground. "I'll help our friend haul the boat down to the water. You stay back with Sorena and hang on to that doll. Could be we'll need the money."

When he joined their guide, the man had one end of the raft above the reeds, a rounded black silhouette against a horizon almost as dark.

Running his hand along the smooth rubber skin, Axel felt along for the opposite end. He found it much too soon. Grabbing the handle, he lifted it up and gauged the distance between him and Peter. "This isn't more than six feet long."

The man shrugged. "Best I could come up with on such short notice. The Germans are watching every craft they know about. Besides," he added as he led the way toward the water, "this is less likely to be spotted. You can launch in water half a meter deep. The patrol boats won't expect to find anyone crossing from here." He paused. "Watch that you don't drift toward the docks, though. The tide's going in that direction. Fix your position on one of the stars and keep going straight."

Trudging along behind him, Axel looked up into a sky of mostly clouds with a lone star peeking out here or there. He had limited experience at this sort of thing and didn't relish having to row across the sound in such a dinky raft with only the illusive stars to guide them.

"I know the stars," Sorena said quietly.

Her voice surprised Axel. He'd been unaware of her presence right behind them.

She touched his arm. "I'll see we maintain a true course."

"Once you get out in the sea lane," Peter said, "there's more than patrol boats to watch out for."

More good news.

The man continued. "From what we hear, the Nazi wolf packs have been taking a real beating the last few months. Scores of their subs have been sunk or crippled. Something about the Allies having improved sonar. To keep us from observing the extent of their losses, they no longer come sailing in during broad daylight. Now they sneak in by night with no running lights. Watch for them, too. Even if they don't see you, their wake could swamp the raft."

"Right." Axel caught his breath as he stepped ankle-deep into bone-chilling water, then recovered. "On my shortwave radio, I heard they'd taken major losses back in May. I'm glad to have it verified. We're winning this war, you know."

"Yes. We have to." The man stopped and set down his end of the raft. "This is far enough. But before you set off, sir, I need a private word with you."

"Sure." Maybe the fellow had some word of Annelise and Grams. "Sorena, you and Shimon climb into the raft while I speak to our friend."

Once they slogged the several yards to a drier surface, Axel was first to speak. "When you were contacted to help us, were you by any chance given word of my family? Did they reach Sweden safely?"

Peter shook his head. "No mention of anyone in particular, but my contact reported a miraculously successful night, and they hope to get the remaining people across in the next couple of evenings. I did hear some rather disturbing news, though. Remember all those Danish soldiers the Germans shipped off to work camps in August? A few of our boys escaped and made it back to Copenhagen. They said the Nazis were working the boys eighteen, twenty hours a day on starvation rations. Some have already died, and it won't be much longer before the rest go, too. They're faring no better than the Jews."

Axel clenched his teeth. He couldn't help but think of the Danish mothers and fathers, and what it must feel like to lose those sons who were the promise of the future. Then there were Shimon and all the other Jewish children he and his family had sheltered over the past three years. Every day that passed, the Germans turned more of them into orphans. "Yes, the Allies have to invade soon. With all the losses the Germans are taking on the Russian front, they're getting frantic. And more vicious wherever they still have control."

"Keep that in mind while you're out on the water. No matter what, don't let them take you alive. You *or* your wife and son."

Peter started back toward the raft before Axel could correct his misconception. But then, what did it matter? They'd probably never meet this fellow patriot again.

When the two of them reached the water, Axel saw that his two charges had settled into the small craft with Sorena holding it in place by grounding an oar. They looked impossibly vulnerable. Too vulnerable. This whole plan was insane. "Get out. Between the patrol boats, the subs, and the possibility of springing a leak in icy water, I can't risk taking you two out there. We'll hide out in Helsinger until a motorboat is available."

Sorena swung to face him in the darkness. "Every minute we remain in Denmark we're in danger. But even if we take our time, we can be across in four hours. It's only seven kilometers across at this spot."

"How would you know that?" The woman always had to argue.

"Because I've traveled these narrows transporting cargo hundreds of times. I'm the oldest of five daughters. There were no boys in the family, so I started going to sea with my father by the time I was eight."

Shimon piped up. "You did? Really? When you were my age?"

"That's right." She focused her attention on the boy. "Taking my turn at the wheel and everything. Of course," she added, her voice becoming testy, "I wasn't required to dig out of the mud."

She never missed a shot.

Sorena turned back to Axel. "Have a little faith. I know these waters. I can get us safely across. Besides, I need to get someplace where I can earn some money as soon as possible. Now that my father and my husband are..." She swallowed. "The funds I send my family are all they have to live on. The authorities sank our freighter."

Husband? Dead? And her father? The Germans had taken so much from her, and he'd been angry and upset about losing a few possessions. "Don't worry about your family. I'll see they're provided for. But this is much too dangerous. God entrusted you to me, and I won't risk your lives like this."

"If it was just you, you'd take the risk."

"That's different, and you know it."

"Do I?" She jerked the oar out of the mud and hooked it into its slot. "Shimon and I have already decided. We're going. With or without you."

Chapter 6

Sorena couldn't make out Axel's features in the darkness, and she preferred it that way. She'd openly defied him and knew he would be furious. She could hardly blame the man. For some reason, he brought out the worst in her.

He stood there, unmoving in the shallow, chilly water, facing her and Shimon for several minutes. Finally he spoke. "Shimon, this is very dangerous. If we're sighted out on the water, there's no place for us to run and hide."

"The night will hide us," her little trooper replied confidently. "And so will God." With a resolute nod, he adjusted the woolen scarf Knud's mother had given him more snugly about his neck.

Sorena loved his mettle. Seated behind him on one of the strips of canvas stretched between the raft's sides, she reached forward and squeezed his shoulder.

"Very well," Axel muttered, stepping into the raft between the two. "But this is on your head, lady."

He was angry.

"I shouldn't have said that."

An apology?

"Move up to the seat with Shimon. I'll paddle. You keep your eyes on the stars."

Although Sorena figured she knew more about rowing than he did, she decided it was best not to argue. She handed Axel the oar she'd been using to steady the raft, then grabbed hold of one side and edged past him to join the boy.

"I'll help you, Sorena," Shimon said. "You just point out the star we're going to follow."

His words brought to mind the nativity story and the wise men being led by a star. She patted the child's knees. "I'll do that. The fog seems to be breaking up."

"Well, Peter," Axel said to the man who'd led them there, "I guess we're off. *Mange tak.* A thousand thanks. We appreciate your help."

He gave a somber nod. "God be with you." He gave the little raft a shove, sending it out of the reeds toward the inky expanse of the channel.

Axel slotted the oars into the rings, then maneuvered the clumsy inflated boat around until his back was to the sound.

Sorena appreciated his knowing enough to do that. Perhaps he wasn't a total novice. She swung her legs over to face forward—and to face him.

Shimon did the same.

"God in heaven," Axel said quietly, "our lives are in Your hands. Keep a tight hold."

"And thank You, Father," Sorena added, placing an arm around Shimon as Axel leaned into the oars, "for sending a godly man to watch over Shimon and me."

As soon as the words were out, she realized she'd placed herself in a vulnerable position where Axel was concerned, admitting that she needed him. Truth was, she did. Who knew what might have happened to her and the neighbor boy if it hadn't been for Axel? What other individual would have come to their aid with no thought regarding his own safety? She busied herself by unfolding one of the blankets their latest benefactor had supplied and wrapping it around Shimon. "If we see a boat, duck your face into the folds and get down low."

She shook out another. Then, despite her hesitancy to be too close to Axel, she stood cautiously on the unsteady floor and wrapped the second blanket around his shoulders while he continued to row. She could actually feel the warmth of his breath on her hands as she drew the wool beneath his chin. Trying to keep her gaze occupied with her task, she caught a flash of his white teeth when he grinned.

It had a strange effect on her insides. Heat rushed to her cheeks. She sat back down and gathered a blanket for herself. Knowing how red her freckled face could become, she was grateful for the darkness.

"I see some stars over there," Shimon said, jutting his chin in their direction.

Sorena looked up. The light fog seemed to be drifting toward the west. She spotted a bright star near the northern horizon along with a cluster of smaller ones. Lyra. "Shimon, look just above the hills across the sound. Do you see the star peeking over? That's the one we're heading for. Keep us going straight for it, okay?"

"I will." His words sounded confident, even though his teeth had begun to chatter.

Sorena picked up the last blanket and bundled his legs.

When the splash of rowing slowed to an even pace, she became aware of Axel again.

He leaned forward and spoke quietly. "You're good with children. Do you have any of your own?"

"No. But I helped raise my younger sisters. What about you?" she ventured. "Do you have a wife and children home waiting for you, worrying over your return?"

He put his back into rowing again. "Nope. I've been too busy fighting the war." He hesitated for a heartbeat. "I. . .was sorry to hear about your losses. I hope they didn't suffer."

His kind comment brought a flood of memories. Sorena closed her eyes against the pain and struggled to find her voice. "The North Sea is even colder than this. I don't imagine they suffered very long."

"I see." He started rowing with more fervor.

She was glad he did. That was hard to talk about, hard to think about. And she didn't want to go into detail, especially in front of the boy. "When you get tired, I'll row awhile."

◆　◆　◆

Axel, with Shimon snuggled against him, silently thanked the Lord for keeping them safe. They'd been on the water close to three hours, and not a single vessel had passed. He watched with admiration as Sorena rowed with the efficiency of an old salt. Just a little longer. Sweden's shore couldn't be much farther.

A rumble carried from off in the distance.

The noise came from the east, but a mist hugged the water. Axel could see only a muted glow. He removed his arm from around the boy and stood.

About half a kilometer away, more defined light slowly scanned the water.

"What is it?" Sorena asked urgently.

"A patrol boat. Coming in our direction."

"Straight for us?"

"No. As long as it doesn't change course, it won't run us over. But to be sure, stop and row the opposite way for a few seconds." Axel tried to sound calm for their sakes. Taking his seat once more, he regretted having agreed to bring them out here. Sorena had already been through so much, and so had Shimon. The possibility of failure weighed heavily on Axel's shoulders.

The searchlight popped out of the mist.

"Cover yourselves and get down in the bottom," Axel ordered.

Sorena lifted the oars out of the water and laid them aside as Axel pulled Shimon down with him and covered them both with a blanket. "I'm sure a black raft this small will be hard to make out, even with a searchlight."

He felt Sorena crowd in beside Shimon.

The boy started shivering again, and Axel rubbed his back. "It's okay. They won't see us."

The patrol boat roared closer.

Listening to the approaching motor, Axel worried that his earlier assumption had been off the mark. It sounded like it was heading directly for them! He raised the edge of his blanket enough to peek over the side.

"Are they near?" Sorena asked anxiously, her voice no more than a whisper.

"If it stays on course, it should pass about ten meters away."

He heard her swift intake of breath. "We'll be caught in its wake for sure."

Seconds later, the vibrating roar became deafening.

Axel reached across Shimon and put a protective arm around Sorena, pulling her closer. If anything happened to them—to her—he would never forgive himself.

Light pierced the blanket covering Axel. The searchlight! His pulse throbbed. The glare lasted less than a second as it moved across them.

He held his breath, waiting for the beam to zero in on them again. . .for the *rat-tat-tat* of a machine gun. But he heard no shouts, no change in the engine's rhythm. Still, his heart pounded so hard he thought it would burst. "I think we're—"

A powerful wave cut off his statement. Paralyzingly cold water sloshed over the bow. The little boat emerged and rode down, only to be hit by a second surge not quite as strong, sending in more water.

Sorena rose and threw off her drenched covering. "Quick. Soak up as much as you can with your blankets. Axel, you're stronger than I am—wring them out while I row. We've got to keep Shimon warm, get him to shore before hypothermia sets in."

The woman did have a way of taking over. But Axel couldn't deny she made good sense. Far better to have a woman with pluck than some helpless female prone to tears and fainting spells. His admiration for her went up a notch, and he wondered what other hidden qualities she possessed. He plucked up a dripping blanket and wrung it out. Then he reached for Shimon's. The shivering boy's teeth were chattering audibly as he clutched the soggy doll to his chest as if trying to shield it. Axel took the doll and squeezed the water out of it, then returned it to Shimon and began rubbing the boy's arms and back through the blanket to increase circulation. The worst of the crisis was over.

◆　◆　◆

Axel had just relieved Sorena at the oars when he noticed a faint light in the east. The sun would be up within the hour.

"Look." Facing him in the dimness, Sorena gestured straight ahead. "I see the shore. We're almost there." She grabbed hold of the shivering boy and hugged him close. "Just a few minutes more, and we'll get to a nice dry place, find some good hot food."

Axel felt like laughing with relief. Digging the oars in deeper, he put all his remaining muscle into getting them there as fast as possible. They were going to make it to Sweden's neutral ground.

By the time they were within a hundred meters of shore, the predawn light brought glorious color back to the wisps of damp hair that had escaped Sorena's beret. Axel was stunned by her beauty. With the way she cradled Shimon, he would have sworn she could've posed for a painting of the Madonna. But as lovely as she was on the outside, her appearance couldn't hold a candle to the glow of beauty that came from within her. He couldn't help staring.

At that moment, she lifted her gaze up at him and kept it there. Her expression did not change, but a subtle warmth came from her eyes to his. Approval. . . and maybe admiration. Maybe even more.

When she finally looked away, he felt bereft, as if something precious had been taken from him.

Suddenly she turned to him, her eyes wide. "The patrol boat! It's back!"

He swung around. It was heading right for them at full speed. A man in the conning tower had his attention trained on them. Where was the fog when they needed it?

Axel rowed as hard as he could.

Sorena stumbled past him.

He felt the raft dip as she leaned over the front, frantically scooping water away with her hands. Any second now they'd be in range of the mounted machine gun.

◆ ◆ ◆

Sorena glanced over her shoulder as she madly swept her hands through the water. She cringed at the sight of the uniformed soldier at the bow, the machine gun aimed at them. They weren't going to make it. The three of them would die right here, within fifty meters of the beach. Even the innocent child Shimon.

"Dive!"

Before she had a chance to react to Axel's command, he shoved her over the side. She and Shimon plunged into the icy, breath-stealing waves beneath Axel. He shoved them down farther.

Bullets pierced the water, but she couldn't go any deeper. She'd struck bottom. It was no more than a meter deep.

On top of her, Axel buckled. Sorena knew instinctively that he'd been hit. His grip on her grew slack.

Seconds later, the firing ceased abruptly.

Beside her, Shimon flailed about in a frenzy. Had he taken a breath, swallowed water?

Sorena grabbed his arm and gathered him to herself. Planting her feet on the sandy bottom, she broke the surface enough for them both to gasp for air while she searched for the enemy.

The speed of the chase had taken the Nazi boat past them. But now, out in deeper water, it was reversing its engines to slow while circling. In less than a minute the machine gun would be in position to fire again. As long as the three of them remained in the water, the Germans would consider them fair game.

She looked around for Axel and found him facedown in the icy shallows, drifting away from them!

"Shimon! Grab my neck. I need to help Axel." Reaching for him, she used all the strength she possessed to flip his big frame over. Then she clutched his collar and slogged on numb legs toward shore. Shimon's stranglehold nearly pulled her under.

A faint cough let her know Axel was still alive. She nearly cried out with relief.

"Kick your feet out behind you, honey. Help me!"

The roar of the patrol boat's engines grew louder in her ears, but she couldn't spare the time or energy to look back. She made for some tall reeds hugging the shore.

The boat's engines shifted into forward, plowing straight for them.

Sorena feared the reeds would not provide a good enough hiding place. The gunner would surely strafe the shoreline.

Driftwood lay scattered across the beach. And nearly covered by accumulated sand sat a log! "Thank You, Father," she breathed aloud. "Shimon, you can let go now. It's not deep here. Take one of Axel's arms and help me drag him up onto the beach."

The boy's entire body was shaking, but he didn't hesitate. With God's help and precious few seconds, they managed to position Axel's lifeless weight behind the log.

"Stay down," she commanded, ducking out of sight of the patrol boat.

As Sorena moved to check Axel for wounds, the machine gun shattered the air, splintering driftwood in a steady stream of blasts.

Bullets ricocheted in every direction.

A line of shots raced across the log.

Sorena shielded Axel's body with her own as flying sand peppered her hands and the back of her neck.

Then, as suddenly as it had begun, the firing stilled.

The enemy's engines continued to throb at idle as the boat hovered beyond the shallows.

Would the Nazis challenge Sweden's neutrality by coming ashore?

For eternal moments, she strained her ears to listen for their movements above the sound of her labored breathing. At last the patrol boat revved its engines and chugged away.

Weak with relief, and beginning to shake uncontrollably, Sorena raised up to make sure the vessel was gone.

"Look at all the blood."

Shimon's statement jolted Sorena. She moved off Axel and peered down at him. On one side of his head, his blond hair and the sand beneath it were crimson. He was bleeding profusely.

She pressed her hand over the source. "Shimon, your scarf. Give me your scarf."

When he thrust it at her, she wrapped it around Axel's head as quickly as her numb, trembling fingers would allow. "Run up the bank, honey. Go to the first house you see and get help. Fast. Go!"

Wide-eyed, his teeth chattering, the boy took off, scrambling up the crumbling bluff with amazing speed.

Sorena looked down at her fallen hero, this man who had shielded the two of them with his own body. That's when she saw another red stain seeping into the sand—from his leg.

He's been shot twice!

Her fingers stiff from the cold, she unbuckled the belt at her waist for a tourniquet. "Please, Lord, don't let him die!"

Chapter 7

P anic and anguish gripped Sorena as she knelt beside Axel, pulling the belt from her borrowed dungarees. His lifeblood was seeping from him. . . because of her stubbornness. With freezing hands she threaded the leather strip beneath his leg, then tugged it tight across the wound and buckled it.

Was he still breathing? Her hands shook as she saw the nearly imperceptible rise and fall of his chest. She touched his arm. His skin felt so cold. She glanced around for something to use to cover him. Nothing. Heaven help her, she had to keep him warm. She lay beside him, spreading her soggy coat over them both. Thoroughly wet and cold herself, she doubted she'd be much more than a windbreak, but she didn't know what else to do.

"Please, God, help Shimon to find help quickly," she pleaded through chattering teeth. "I've already lost two loved ones to the Nazis. I don't think I could bear to lose Axel, too." She felt him take a deeper breath beneath her, and hoped that was God's way of saying He'd heard and cared.

"Down there!" The young voice sounded like Shimon's.

Already? He'd left only an instant ago. Struggling to her feet, Sorena scanned the top of the low bluff.

One fellow, then another popped into sight. They charged down the bank with the energy of men not yet thirty. Close on their heels, Shimon followed, swaddled from neck to ankle in one of their coats.

Sorena had never felt such relief. She blinked back pooling tears.

"How bad was he hit?" the first yelled in a Swedish lilt.

"He's unconscious," she called, "but still alive. You got here so fast!"

"We heard the gunfire," the coatless man offered as he neared, "and were coming to investigate."

His companion dropped down to examine Axel. "Good. You've stemmed the bleeding." He glanced up at the other fellow, sturdy and muscular as himself. "Olaf, help me lift him. We must get these folks inside before they freeze."

Moving to assist, Olaf eyed Sorena, then nodded in the direction of the shore. "You came across in that rubber boat?"

She peered toward the water.

The bullet-flattened raft was being dragged along on the swell of a gentle wave. *And the rag doll!* Surely God's work. Caught in a fold of the collapsed rubber, it bobbed listlessly in time with the raft's movements.

"Yes," she answered past numb lips as she went to fetch the money-stuffed toy. "It was our only choice. Everything else was being used to ferry the Jews across."

"Don't we know it." The one called Olaf grunted as he and the other man hoisted Axel's dead weight. "For two nights now they've been landing all up and down the coast from Hoganas to Falsterbo. So many folks needing shelter and food."

"But we'll manage to find places for them and for you, too," his friend added as Sorena hurried to catch up to them, the doll in her hand. "We always do."

◆　◆　◆

The men carried Axel to one of a cluster of small homes set back from a boat-yard and marina cluttered with nets and buoys.

When Sorena opened the door to make way for the group, a blast of heated air hit her face like a thousand needles. She couldn't remember the last time she'd been this cold.

But no colder than Axel, she surmised as his limp body was carried past her.

Or Shimon. She caught the skinny boy's hand and hurried him inside, monumentally grateful that one of their rescuers, the man called Olaf, had loaned the child his coat.

"Sven," he directed, "we'll put him in the front bedroom."

Watching after the pair attired in the sturdy rubberized boots and knit caps of fishermen, Sorena concluded the home must belong to Olaf since he knew its layout.

A petite blond woman with a pleasant face stood in an archway leading from the tidy front parlor to the low-ceilinged kitchen. Drying her hands on her apron, she motioned to Sorena. "I am Greta Lagerlof. Come. Bring the boy in here. It's warmer by the cookstove."

"Thank you, Greta. I'm Sorena, and this is Shimon."

Shimon balked, planting his feet. "What about Axel?" he asked, oblivious to his own chattering teeth. "I need to stay with him. He's hurt bad."

With her thumb, Sorena smoothed the worry lines pinching his brow and attempted a confident smile. "We wouldn't want to be in the way just now, sweetheart. And you're very cold. As soon as you're warm again, we'll see if it's okay for you to go sit with him. In the meantime, we'll both pray very hard that God will make him better. Is that a deal?"

"I guess," he said grudgingly. "He has to stay alive, you know. Me and him have important things to do."

"I know. So you have to be well and strong, too, not sick in bed."

He nodded and went with her to the kitchen, where their hostess was pouring a kettle of hot water into a large pan.

"Greta," Sorena began, "I'd really appreciate it if you would help Shimon out of his wet clothes and into something dry."

"Of course. And you, too." A kind smile deepened the fine lines on the woman's attractive face as she nodded toward the stove. "I've also made some cocoa."

"That sounds wonderful. But I need to check on Axel first." She gave Shimon a nudge toward Greta. "I'll only be a little while, I promise."

As she started through the homey confines of the house for the door to the bedroom, Sven came out, his sharp blue eyes halting her in her tracks. "I am going for the doctor. I'll have him here in a few minutes." Adjusting the knit cap he'd pushed back on his head, he left.

Sorena's heart contracted in alarm. Hurrying to Axel, she joined Olaf, who was bent over the bed. The man had unconscious Axel lying on his side while he worked off the soggy wool coat.

Still holding the equally limp rag doll, Sorena dropped it on a nightstand. "I'll help you," she told the brawny Swede, and together they eased the jacket off, then Axel's shoes and socks.

His feet, she noted, were even colder than her hands. She began rubbing them brusquely to create some warmth.

"That'll help, madam," Olaf said, "but I think we can do better. Go ask my wife to fill a hot water bottle for his feet. And have her put some flannel sheets in the oven to warm."

When she returned a short time later with the rubber bottle, she noticed Axel's clothing on the floor. The blankets had been pulled up to his neck. She moved to the foot of the bed and lifted the covers just enough to place the hot water container at his feet. "How does Axel's leg look?" she asked Olaf. "Is it very bad? When you took off the belt, was it still bleeding a lot?"

"Ah, so Axel's his name. Good to know. As for the bleeding, with him being so cold, that probably helped keep it to a minimum. And your name is?"

"Sorena Bruhn. The boy in the kitchen is Shimon." She noticed a bloody white cloth beneath the scarf at Axel's head, and all effort at making polite conversation fled.

Olaf saved her the trouble. "Yes, the head wound is still seeping a bit. That's natural. Those are always the worst for bleeding. But his breathing is steady, and your man looks to be in good shape."

Sorena was more than ready to latch on to any scrap of hope. "Do you really think so? Oh, yes, Greta said it'll be a few minutes more for the flannel sheets."

"Fine. Now how about going and getting out of your own wet clothes while I wait for Dr. Heidenstam to get here?"

"I'd rather not leave Axel in case he wakes."

"And I'd just as soon not have two invalids on my hands. Go on, now, before you come down with pneumonia." He gestured toward the door with a nod of his head.

The man spoke logically. After all, she'd said nearly the same thing to Shimon moments ago. But. . .

Her gaze was drawn to Axel again. He looked so pale, so. . .

The sturdy fisherman took her by the arm. "Go. Now."

Momentarily, Sorena found herself seated next to Shimon in front of the open oven door, both of them wrapped in blankets, with their feet soaking in pans of heated water. Mrs. Lagerlof had been a godsend, and Sorena had never felt more coddled in her life—especially when the lady handed them cups of hot cocoa. She was beginning to believe that becoming warm again was possible. She sipped the sweetened drink and let it trickle down to the cold reaches of her insides. "You have no idea how wonderful this is," she said, hoping to express her thankfulness.

Greta smiled. "This is hardly the first time someone's come in freezing. My Olaf's gotten drenched a time or two himself."

"I know what you mean." Sorena chuckled at her own memories. "I come from a seafaring family, too. Our home port is on the Isle of Fyn." The smile faded. "Or was before the war."

The blond woman placed a hand on her shoulder. "And it will be again. Soon. Our government wouldn't have had the nerve to stop the Nazis from using our railroads to cart their troops across to Norway if they thought Germany was still capable of doing something about it."

"That's encouraging. But the Nazis still rule the Baltic Sea. I can attest to that."

"Not for long. I truly believe God is on our side."

"Yes. He has to be." Sorena glanced at Shimon, a child of God's covenant with Abraham. His eyelids had drooped along with his curly top. Poor little tyke. He'd been through so much in the last few days and hadn't slept much, yet he'd been amazing throughout the whole ordeal. She reached over and deftly lifted the cocoa from his hands.

Greta came forward and took the cup from her. After placing it on the table, she stooped and removed the sleeping child's feet from the pan, then dried them. "I'll take him into Hildy's room. It's time for her to get up for school anyway."

School? It was hard for Sorena to digest such an everyday happening. "You have a daughter?"

"Yes. Hildy's seven," she whispered, reaching down for Shimon. "This is her first year, and she's very excited about going."

As the hostess carried Shimon through a door adjoining the kitchen, Sorena wondered how long it would be before he, too, would be returning to a classroom. At least that could now be a reality for him.

But had it cost Axel his life?

Urgency overtook her again. She lifted her feet out of the water. Bending to dry them with the provided towel, she heard a quick knock at the door and turned toward the entrance.

The man called Sven burst in, his cheeks flushed.

Right behind him came a distinguished older man in faded black, carrying a worn leather satchel.

"This way," Sven directed.

Before Sorena could get up and secure the blanket around herself properly, the two men had disappeared into the front bedroom.

Hiking the edge of the blanket off the floor, she flew after them. She had to be there when the doctor examined Axel. Had to know if he would live.

He has to.

For Shimon's sake. . .and for hers. There was so much she needed to say to Axel, so much to take the blame for. She was the very reason he lay at death's door. She and her stubborn determination.

Chapter 8

Good evening, Sorena." Still wearing fishy work clothes, Olaf Lagerlof strode into Axel's antiseptic hospital room. "Thought I'd stop by on my way home and see how you're doing. Maybe talk you into coming along for supper."

Sorena appreciated the many kindnesses the Lagerlofs had extended to her and Shimon over the past week while she'd waited, hoped, and prayed for Axel to awaken. She rose from the bedside chair. "Thank you. But he's had some eye movement recently. I don't want to leave him yet."

"He's come to?" Olaf glanced at Axel, who lay as still as the day they'd brought him to Helsingborg's only hospital.

"No, his eyes were closed. But the nurse said the movement was a good sign."

"I see." Though he appeared unconvinced, Olaf's demeanor brightened. "I do have some good news for you. I received a radio message from the *Herring Hound* a few hours ago. Your mother got the money you sent. Captain Perrson said they were faring well."

"Oh, thank you. That is such a relief."

"I'll tell you who else would be relieved. Shimon—if you'd come to the house with me. You didn't leave here at all yesterday. Greta enrolled the boy in school with Hildy this morning, hoping to get his mind on something besides you and. . ." He nodded toward Axel.

Sorena gave a defeated sigh. "I suppose that's best. Dr. Heidenstam isn't handing out any promises. But Axel must wake up. He has to. There's so much I need to say to him."

"Maybe. But what *you* need is to get out of this room. Breathe some fresh air. Have a good, home-cooked meal. Even if he should come around while you're gone, he'll still be here when you get back. Think of your own health. If he wakes up—"

"You mean *when*. . ."

"*When* he wakes up, you don't want to be sick in bed yourself." The big man grasped her shoulders. "Take a look at those dark circles under your eyes. If it was me lying there and you were my wife, I'd want you to get your rest."

Her face warmed at the intimate reference, and she smiled. "I will, Olaf. I promise. Tell Shimon I'll be there before bedtime to say good night."

"We'll hold you to that," he said with a mock frown. "Greta will keep a plate of food in the oven for you."

◆ ◆ ◆

Greta. Olaf. Axel couldn't wrap his mind around those names. If only he could get his eyes to open.

"An hour more. Two at the most," came the familiar voice. "Tell Shimon I'll be home soon."

"Will do. See you then."

Footsteps faded away. The man Olaf had left. But the woman was still here. He could hear her moving closer, hear her breathing.

She'd mentioned another name. Shimon. . .a Jewish name.

Shimon! Clarity returned. Axel's lashes sprang open, and he lurched up. "Shimon!" Pain exploded in his head. He fell back to his pillow and closed his eyes.

"Axel?"

Slowly raising his eyelids, he focused on the flame-haired woman leaning over him.

"You're awake! Thank God." Tears flooded her wide-set green eyes. She took his hand. "You're awake."

He recognized her. Sorena. She didn't appear to be injured, but what about Shimon? "Is the boy all right?" The words came out hoarse.

Tears rolled unchecked down her pale cheeks as she nodded. "Yes. Shimon is fine. Terribly worried about you, but otherwise. . ." She took a shuddering breath. "Just fine."

Axel raised his free hand to check the source of his head pain. "How long have I been out?"

"Eight days. You were shot. One bullet grazed your skull; another went through your leg." She swiped at her flooded eyes. "I'm so relieved. We didn't know if you'd ever. . . I'll get the nurse." She squeezed his hand and gifted him with a heart-stealing smile. "I'll only be a moment."

Pausing at the door, she looked back. Fresh tears streamed past the radiance of her smile. "You're with us again." Filling her lungs, she disappeared into the corridor.

Axel gazed after the redhead. She sure was emotional about his regaining consciousness. Had she somehow come to care for him while he was asleep and unable to talk back? He marveled as he explored the thick bandage along the left side of his head. Sorena.

He preferred to think she'd started to care before he'd been shot. He'd sensed her softening during that long night in the raft. Even before that, he'd begun to see her with—he hated to admit it—a tenderness. But then after sharing a life-threatening experience, being thrown together night and day, all pretense had been stripped away. They'd come to know each other in a short span of time.

Now that he thought back, there wasn't anything about her he hadn't grown to love. Not even her mouth. She'd seen right through his most devastating smile, just like Grams always had. . .and he dearly loved that old gal for it. Grams knew him for the spoiled, reckless guy he was and loved him anyway. From the look on Sorena's face, she did, too. Possibly.

As his head cleared more fully, other disturbing memories surfaced. Grams. Erik and Annelise. He had to get to a telephone. Find out if they'd made it safely across the sound.

A large-boned woman in crisp white marched in ahead of Sorena. "Splendid, Mr. Bruhn. You've decided to rejoin the world of the living." She came brusquely to his bedside and shoved a thermometer into his mouth, then caught his wrist to take his pulse.

Mr. Bruhn? Puzzled at the address, Axel refrained from speaking around the glass tube. Sorena must have had a good reason for giving the attendant that name.

"Good. Good." The nurse released his wrist. After checking his bandage and fussing with his blanket, she removed the thermometer and read it. "Better. It's coming down. I'll fetch your doctor. He'll want to examine you now." With an efficient smile, she left, leaving him alone with Sorena.

For the first time, he noticed the dark circles beneath her eyes. She couldn't have slept much in days. She had to care!

She pulled a chair close and sat. "You're probably wondering why Nurse Almquist called you by my last name, Bruhn. I don't know yours. Everything happened so fast," she said with a slight smile, "we never really introduced ourselves."

"Ah." Axel's mouth began to curl. "I'm Axel Christiansen, at your service, milady."

"Another thing," she added, pinkening, her lashes lowering. "I've let them think I'm your wife. Otherwise, they wouldn't have allowed me to stay here through the night."

Axel blinked in surprise. "You've been here day and night for over a week?"

She shrugged. "I did go to check on Shimon every day to bolster his spirits. He's been so worried about you. The doctor wouldn't let him visit while you were unconscious. But now that you're awake, there shouldn't be a problem."

"Yeah, I'd like to see the little guy myself. He really grows on you, doesn't he?"

Sorena met his gaze again. "He does. The people we're staying with, the Lagerlofs, have offered to keep him till the end of the war. They're nice people with a daughter a year younger than he is. But I'm not ready to let him go." Her exquisite features softened. "And he keeps reminding me you two have plans."

"I did promise we'd go after his parents once the Allies march into Germany. I know it's far-fetched, but I'd like to keep my word if there's any way possible."

"Then you agree," she breathed on a sigh. "We won't leave Shimon with the Lagerlofs."

She was discussing the boy's fate as if he were their child. *Fascinating!* Axel decided to test the waters even further. "Then for the time being, we'll just keep him with us at my great-aunt's manor house in Lund. It's big enough to billet a regiment."

"We'll live with you? At a manor house?" Her sea-green eyes reflected a mixture of emotions.

He knew if he wasn't careful, he'd scare her off. "Don't worry. It's old and drafty with separate wings. We might not see each other for days on end. And since the economy was so bad before the war, it's desperately short of servants. You won't be living in any more luxury than before."

"I didn't say—"

"You didn't have to. Those beautiful, expressive eyes said it for you."

Her cheeks grew rosy, and she turned away.

This woman would never be able to lie to him.

"What's keeping the doctor?" She checked the wall clock. "He said he wouldn't leave for home until six."

As if by command, a dignified, gray-haired gentleman appeared at the door, a stethoscope draped about his neck.

Axel watched Sorena quietly withdraw and turn her back to them while the physician poked and probed him for what seemed a quarter hour.

"No signs of paralysis or loss of eyesight or hearing," the man commented as he worked. After he recorded his findings on the chart at the foot of Axel's bed, he turned to Sorena. "Mrs. Bruhn?"

She turned back to face them. "Yes?"

"I'll release your husband to your care in a day or two, once the swelling on the brain is gone and he no longer has a headache. Of course, he'll be on crutches for a few weeks, but his leg is healing nicely. There seems to be no permanent damage."

"Oh, thank you. That's great news." The sincerity of her words warmed her expressive eyes. . .and his heart.

"I would imagine. Just one more thing, madam. I suggest you have a serious talk with your man about taking such risks. You could've both been killed—and the boy as well." Finishing in a stern tone, he started for the door.

"But it wasn't. . ." Sorena gave up as he hurried away. She turned to Axel. "I don't know what to say. Dr. Heidenstam shouldn't blame you. It was me. Me. You almost died because I forced you to go."

"No." Axel caught her hand. "I wanted to make the crossing. It was taking you and Shimon I objected to. I couldn't bear the thought of anything happening to you. Or him."

"And nothing did." Her lower lip quivered. "You took the bullets for all of us." Her eyes glistened with renewed moisture.

"Hey." He squeezed her hand. "Didn't you just hear the doctor? I'll be good as new in a couple of weeks."

The statement didn't seem to help. "Why must you act so noble?" she practically wailed. "Offering me a place to stay—and after all the mean things I said to you. . ." Her words lost power as she drew a ragged breath.

She looked absolutely stricken. Axel couldn't abide having her feel so down. Not his spunky Sorena. He raised up on his elbow, ignoring the pounding in his head, and quirked a grin. "You know, I'm really starting to like this, you all contrite and apologizing. I'll have to get shot more often."

That did the trick. Her jaw dropped, and she started sputtering, but no sound came out.

Axel's grin broadened. He'd rendered his mouthy redhead speechless. . .at least for the moment.

With bewilderment written across her freckles, she tugged free of his grip and back-stepped toward the door. "I promised Shimon I'd go get him the instant you woke up. I'll have him here in a little while."

"I'll be waiting," he called after her.

When Axel lay back on the pillow, he noticed a buzzer and pushed it. He needed to learn of his family's fate.

Shortly, he was being wheeled along the gray linoleum floor to the front desk, where a phone awaited his use. Once the local operator transferred his call to Lund, he heard ringing on the other end and imagined the sound echoing off the ancient stone walls of the manor.

On the eighth ring, his chest tightened with concern. Someone should have answered by now.

"*Hejsan?*" came his sister's voice in Swedish.

Thank You, God. He released his breath and responded in their customary Danish. "Annelise. You're there. For a minute I thought. . ."

"Axel? *Axel!*" Her shout pierced his eardrum. "Grams! Erik! Come quick. Axel's alive! Where are you?" she asked only slightly calmer. "Why haven't you called before? We've been sick with worry."

"It's okay, sis. I've been taking a little nap, but the doctor says I'll be just fine."

"Doctor! Where are you?"

"At the hospital in Helsingborg."

"Hospital? In Helsingborg?"

"The phone, give it to me," Grams demanded in her gruff voice. "Axel?"

"I'm fine, Grams," he avowed. "I'm supposed to be released in a day or two."

"You are sure? I need to see for myself. We'll take Hannah's Rolls and be there in. . . How far away is that?"

"About sixty kilometers. But I'd rather you wait, Grams. I'll be out in a couple of days, and you can come get me then. No sense wasting precious petrol. Oh, by the way, I've invited a couple of people to come stay with us."

"Axel, Axel," she said in exasperation. "You always manage to find someone, don't you? Who is it this time? Jews passing through or airmen or sailors you found out in the sound?"

"Actually, I'm hoping these two won't be just passing through. I want them to stay."

"Oh? Why is that?"

He could just picture the arch in those silver brows. "You'll understand when you meet her. I mean *them*."

"Her? Did I hear right?" Annelise obviously had been listening along with Grams. "Don't tell me your bachelor days are finally coming to an end, brother of mine!"

Axel had to think about that one. But not for long. "If I have my way about it."

"I can't believe it!" she exclaimed. "The Axel has fallen!"

◆　◆　◆

The second Sorena pointed out Axel's hospital room, Shimon forgot her instructions regarding being quiet. He bolted for it, his leather soles slapping loudly on the linoleum, the water-stained rag doll he'd insisted on bringing dangling haphazardly from his hand.

Reaching the doorway, she saw the surprising sight of Axel sitting in a wheelchair, his head still bandaged and his leg propped. He'd already engulfed Shimon in a bear hug and was grinning so broadly his azure eyes crinkled.

So did her heart. She could see he truly loved the boy.

"I knew you'd wake up," Shimon declared, not quite releasing his hero's neck as he remained beside the wheelchair. "Me and Sorena been praying and praying." He eased away slightly, focusing a direct look at Axel. "Besides, me and you still have a job to do, saving Mama and Papa. And God knows that. That's why He didn't let you die."

Out of the mouths of babes and sucklings hast thou ordained strength because of thine enemies. Awe filled Sorena as she pondered the familiar scripture verse. For Shimon to have such faith in the face of so much evil bolstered her own.

Axel must have been affected, too. He shot a glance to her, then took Shimon's slim cheeks in his hands and kissed the top of his curly head. "You bet. Just as soon as the Allies come."

Reluctant to intrude on their man-to-man moment, Sorena didn't venture forward. Watching the two of them together was so touching, she could've cried. But she'd already done too much of that this evening.

"And look!" Shimon shoved the moldy, smelly doll in Axel's face. "I still have this. We didn't lose it, no matter what."

"I'm real proud of you." Axel took the weathered toy and looked up at Sorena. "Both of you."

"But Sorena already took some of the money out and sent it to her mother." She cringed. She'd wanted to divulge that news a bit later.

"Good," Axel said. "That's what it's for, to help refugees. And that's us."

"Yes, sir," Shimon agreed. "For sure. But not for long." He flicked a glance at her. "Sorena says when you get out of here, we're gonna go live in a great big house with your family. With plenty of food—like at Knud's house. You and me and Sorena."

Axel looked over the child's head and met her gaze. "That's right. Until the Nazis are run out of our country and we can go back home. You, me, and Sorena—if she's willing to put up with us, of course."

"Sure she is," he announced. "She's been taking care of you and praying for you, just like Mama does Papa. And she won't leave you now just when you're better, 'cause my mama would never leave my papa." He turned to her. "Right?"

The child was making too many assumptions. *What must Axel think?* She felt the blood drain from her face.

"I think we're rushing the lady, Shimon," Axel said gently. He flashed her one of his most charming grins. "She's already promised to come with us to Lund. That's enough for now. Once she's all settled in and feeling at home, we'll show her what a fine couple of chaps we really are."

Axel sported his bandages like badges of honor, and his hopeful grin was almost comical. So was Shimon's gap-toothed giggle. Sorena couldn't help smiling herself. "It doesn't look to me like you're waiting."

Still grinning, Axel reached back for the metal water pitcher on his bedside table and handed it to Shimon. "Be my buddy and go have the nurse fill this for me?"

Obviously proud to do his hero's bidding, Shimon scampered off.

"Come closer, Sorena," Axel coaxed, his tone husky. "We don't have much time, and there are some things I really need to tell you."

When she stepped to the side of his chair, he took her hand, and before she realized what he was doing, he put it to his cheek.

The gesture made her heart skip like a schoolgirl's.

"I know we got off to a rough start. And I know it's sudden, but this experience has changed me forever. It's as if I've spent my whole life standing outside myself looking in. I never took anything seriously. . .until now. The way I feel about you I'm taking very seriously. You're the first woman I've ever met who's seen me at my worst. And by jingle, you're still here."

Hesitating only a second, Sorena knelt down beside him. "I think we've both seen each other at our worst. But don't forget, I've seen you at your best, too."

He leaned nearer. "And did you like what you saw?"

She could barely speak. "I. . .yes."

His gaze gentled. "Did you know I love every one of your freckles?" he asked softly, his breath feathering her face, he was so close. "Especially this one." His lips brushed her cheek.

Sorena's pulse missed a beat.

"And this one." He kissed her nose. Releasing her hand, he cupped the back of her head, and his mouth claimed hers.

Unbelievably, her playboy was kissing her. And it was fine. Perfect. Even exhilarating. With awakening love, she slipped her arms around his neck and returned his kiss. After endless months of grinding sorrow, joy was filling her again. To the brim, and overflowing. . .

From somewhere in the distant swirl, she heard a child's thin voice. "Wait here, nurse, 'til they're done kissing. Kisses make everything better, you know."

Sorena couldn't argue with that.

DIANNA CRAWFORD

Dianna Crawford, a bestselling author with two RITA nominations, has published twenty novels and several novellas. Widowed a few years ago, she has four grown daughters and several very active grandchildren. She lives in foothills above California's San Joaquin Valley and is the librarian at her church. In her leisure time she loves to paint and travel with friends.

Letters from Home

by Lynette Sowell

Dedication

To Connie, Margie, and Eileen—thanks for grafting me into "the posse" as we
developed our stories together.
It was a joy to research with you as we drifted
from one time period to another.

To those from the "Greatest Generation," example
of tenacity and courage to all who've come after you.
Truly these were your finest hours.

A big thank-you to the Pioneer Museum in Fredericksburg for answering
questions during our research trip
to your sweet town.

*My people will live in peaceful dwelling places,
in secure homes, in undisturbed places of rest.*
ISAIAH 32:18 NIV

Chapter 1

C'mon, Trudy! C'mon!" Eric Meier tugged on his sister's arm. "We're going to miss the parade! We can find a good spot to watch if we hurry."

"Hold your horses. I'm right here with you." Trudy didn't mean to drag her feet, because part of her wanted to see the parade and hear the band and some of the Hollywood performers passing through Fredericksburg. Listening on the radio wasn't the same thing, or reading about it in a magazine. Little Fredericksburg wasn't a regular stop for many Texas visitors. Not until their own Chester Nimitz had risen to the top ranks of the navy to show the world that even from landlocked Fredericksburg, someone could go on to do great things.

But today Trudy felt closer to forty-one than twenty-one. Her legs felt like lead weights, her muscles tired from working at the beehives until sundown yesterday. She fought away the fatigue, clutched the Brownie camera that hung from a strap around her neck, and tried to be positive. Maybe today she'd get some good shots. Of course, she'd need to order more photo paper, something at a premium during these lean years.

She paused at her parents' bedroom door. "Mama?" She heard nothing, so she pushed the door open a few inches. Her mother's low snore filtered through the space. It was best she let her sleep, all worn out from her volunteer work at the hospital. She'd arrived home early that morning.

The front door banged. "Tru–dy! Come *on!*"

Trudy shook her head and closed the door. Eric could tear all over the countryside on his bicycle, yet for some reason he couldn't make it to town without her presence at his side? "I'm coming, Eric."

The May morning sun promised a toasty afternoon. If she had her way, she'd bicycle down to the creek with a book, a pen, and her camera. She'd sit under her favorite live oak tree and watch the wind blow the puffy clouds across the sky. The favorite tree would remind her of Kurt and the promise they'd made to each other under its branches.

Trudy blinked at the momentary pain and let it pass. She closed the front door to the house behind her, as if that could close off the memory. Today, she'd definitely win the bike "race" to town that Eric always tried to egg her to join.

"They have a midget submarine, you know." Eric's voice jolted her. He bent over to check the chain on his bicycle. "All the way from Japan. I wonder if we can touch it."

"I'm sure you'll make it your mission to find out if you can." *Thank You,*

Lord, that Eric can keep his childlike wonder, even during the war, even with Father away. It seemed like everyone gave something up once their country had entered the war. A lifetime of days had ticked away since December 7, 1941, a little less than eighteen months ago.

Soon they were off, down the winding road that led into town. Trudy could close her eyes and feel each curve in the road, anticipate each landmark, no matter how minor. The sameness should comfort her, but instead it itched her like a wool scarf that her grandmother had made.

Trudy thought of the ring that still lay inside the jewelry box on her dressing table. Kurt had released her from her promise to marry him after he returned from the war, before his last letter...

He deserved someone who'd be by his side at the peach farm owned by his family, someone who was satisfied with Fredericksburg, with the small-town routine. Once, she'd shared with him her wild dream of seeing the world. Kurt had blinked and asked, "Why?"

Less than a month later, his orders came and he shipped out, leaving her behind. Jealousy fought against fear inside her.

The town hadn't changed much since her childhood. She caught sight of the first few homes on the outside of town, a snug row of Sunday homes, the middle one owned by her family. Her *oma* had lived there until her passing over the late winter. Trudy slowed down. If things were different, she'd ask her mother if she could stay in the house by herself and have a measure of independence. Of course, her help was needed most at home.

Next door was the Zimmermann family's home. How she'd loved Sundays growing up in Fredericksburg, all the comings and goings and visiting. And the food. *Oma, I miss you, and every time I see the house, it reminds me of what we've all lost.*

Eric left her literally in his dust. He rang the bell on his bicycle and the jubilant sound joined with the sounds of celebration ahead of them on Main Street. The war bond tour had descended on Fredericksburg. It wouldn't surprise her if nearly the whole town assembled along Main Street.

Instead of following Eric, Trudy moved off the road and circled back. She might as well leave her bicycle parked at the Sunday house. She could negotiate any crowd on foot, where a bicycle might get in the way.

"You're just in time for the parade." Her longtime friend Kathe exited the Zimmermann family's Sunday house. Kathe Zimmermann, soon-to-be Kathe Mueller, grinned.

"Eric made sure." Trudy tried to pop her kickstand down, but the contraption stuck so she leaned the bicycle against the house, just past the porch. "So how are you? I've been such a poor bridesmaid, and I should be helping you prepare for the wedding."

"You've done plenty," Kathe said as she linked her arm through Trudy's. "Peter and I are keeping things simple, especially now. But my cake is going to be made with white sugar, not brown, and have gobs of buttercream frosting."

The thought of a rich, creamy wedding cake with plenty of frosting made Trudy's sweet tooth ache a little. "I'm so happy for both of you."

"Thanks." Her friend's expression fell. "I know this must be hard for you, with Kurt..."

Trudy shrugged. "It's all right. Like I said, I'm happy for both of you. The fact that Peter survived, came home to you, and now you get to have your happy ending, I'm just glad someone else is finding some joy in the middle of all this."

She didn't have to mention the Wagner twins who'd perished and now lay buried in a Fredericksburg cemetery. The war had cost Fredericksburg so much already, even with their favorite son, Chester Nimitz, commander in chief over the Pacific theater.

Kathe hugged her. "Thank you. I'm praying you'll have your happy ending, too."

"I hope so, someday." A lump swelled in Trudy's throat. *Gertrude Meier, I see now why you wish to travel the world and see life beyond Fredericksburg. That has never been my desire, and I release you to find your way. Lord willing, once this war is over and you have traveled, maybe we will find our way back to each other again.* Trudy shoved the letter's words away, burned into her memory. "Let's go. I wonder if Mitzie Harmon looks the same in person as she does in the movies."

Kathe laughed and the sound propelled Trudy back to more innocent times, to childhood. She echoed the laugh as they ambled the rest of the way to Main Street.

◆　◆　◆

Bradley Payne stepped off the bus, the dust of Main Street Fredericksburg swirling around him. He slung his duffel bag over his shoulder. The bag contained all his worldly goods—well, everything that he'd been toting since leaving Washington, DC, just over three weeks ago.

He adjusted the brim of his hat as he scanned the street lined with people, its buildings resembling something out of a Wild West show combined with European charm he'd seen in Germany. Fredericksburg. Home of his father's family, the family he never knew. *Father, why did you leave the family who accepted you and took you in?*

Bradley continued to the Nimitz Hotel, a curious-looking, three-story structure on the corner of Main Street and North Washington. A flag flew from the roof, the building resembling a ship. Charles, the old man who'd built the hotel, was once a sea captain. Ironic that he'd build a hotel like this far from the ocean.

Ironic that Bradley's travels should take him here as he and his fellow journalists followed the war bond tour that stopped in the hometown of Admiral Nimitz. Chester Nimitz, grandson of the man who built the Nimitz Hotel, was born right here in a small Texas town hundreds of miles from any body of water large enough to float a battleship, yet he'd risen through the ranks after graduating from the United States Naval Academy to achieve the highest-ranking position in the Pacific theater. Hopefully, Bradley would find someone well acquainted with the Nimitz family, as Chester hadn't been back to Fredericksburg in quite some time.

Growing up in the family's hotel, Nimitz had likely seen a myriad of people pass through its doors. If anyone new came to town, the Nimitz family would know.

Nimitz had grown up without a father, who passed away before Chester was born. At least Nimitz's father hadn't deserted him and he'd had the love and support of his extended family during his childhood. Admittedly, Bradley had had the love of his mother, who told him to love his father and pray for him.

A long-ignored bitterness oozed from Bradley's soul in sharp contrast to the merry tune played by the band on the town square. This was no way to meet the town he'd be exploring during the tour. This was no way to find his story. *Help, Lord,* Bradley prayed silently as he ambled in the direction of the music. The town square lay just past Adams Street, opposite the library and the courthouse.

His editor, Frank McAffrey, had clamored during the entire trip about finding the story everywhere he went. *"Letters from the Homefront is one of our readers' favorite columns. So don't disappoint them,"* Frank had said before Bradley left.

No one ever disappointed Frank McAffrey and kept their job long, or at all. Plus, there were too many other journalists wanting to write for *This American Life*. Bradley had worked hard to get this position, and even harder to convince Frank that following the war bond tour would bring an even more personal touch to his column.

Find the story, find the story, he reminded himself as he studied faces in the crowd. Wherever the tour had gone, they'd encountered a similar atmosphere, yet with a character unique to the people of the local area.

The voices of the crowd rang out in laughter at Mac Mackenzie, the traveling comic's antics on the makeshift stage festooned in red, white, and blue. Bradley allowed himself to remain at the edges of the crowd, close enough to observe but not so close that he'd miss something if not having the eyes of an outsider.

Then he saw a pair of young women who grabbed his attention. A proverbial willowy blond with eyes the color of the waters of the Mediterranean. Now, she was a looker. She chatted with her friend, pushing wayward strands of hair over one ear. But her cool, tall figure didn't keep his attention.

Instead, he focused on her friend, a brunette with dark honey tones in her hair, eyes the color of amber. She bit her full lower lip with her teeth, holding up her camera, her eyes narrowed while she studied the scene through her lens. Her tall skinny friend giggled at the comedian and bumped her shorter friend's elbow.

The brunette murmured something and shook her head, then laughed, lowering the camera. Her gaze traveled across the square and locked with his. She'd caught him staring, and he refused to look away.

A half grin quirked in his direction, and she lifted the camera and pointed it at him.

Chapter 2

"You took his picture?" Kathe glanced at Trudy. "I can't believe it."

"He was staring at us, like he knew what we were thinking." Trudy wound the film in her camera until she felt the familiar click. What on earth had compelled her to snap a picture of the man? Okay, he was handsome enough. He could stand beside any of the silver-screen heartthrobs and hold his own. He definitely wasn't from Fredericksburg.

"Now he's coming this way."

"So's your Tante Elsie." Trudy nodded toward Kathe's aunt. "She can set him straight."

"Ha. She can set anybody straight." Kate smiled.

"Girls, hasn't it been a wonderful show?" asked Tante Elsie.

"You couldn't go all the way to Austin to see a finer one at the Paramount," said Trudy.

"Good afternoon." A rich baritone voice tugged Trudy's attention away from the older woman.

Trudy turned to face the man she'd brazenly snapped a photograph of less than two minutes before. The townspeople were used to her bicycling around town during her free moments, photographing this and that, waiting for the correct light conditions. But to photograph a complete stranger?

She felt Kathe's elbow in her ribs. "G–good afternoon, Mr.—"

"Ah, so you're going to ask my name, now that you've taken my photograph?" His smile made a bolt of heat shoot through her insides.

"It's only proper that I can identify my subject." She felt a grin tug at the corners of her mouth.

"Bradley Payne." He removed his hat and nodded.

"Trudy Meier." She extended her hand. "And this is my friend Kathe Zimmermann, and her aunt, Miss Elsie Zimmerman."

Mr. Payne hesitated a fraction of a second before putting his hat back on. "Zimmermann, you say. . ." Then he cleared his throat and continued. "It's a pleasure to meet you all while I'm visiting your fine town. I'm here following the tour."

"I assumed as much, since I didn't recognize you." Trudy clutched her camera in front of her.

"You must take some time and get to know our town." Tante Elsie was studying him thoughtfully. "You know that Admiral Nimitz, commander of the entire Pacific theater, comes from Fredericksburg."

Trudy glanced at the older woman. Was that a tear in her eye? She met Kathe's gaze. Kathe shrugged.

"That I do, Miss Zimmermann." He looked at Trudy again with those dark eyes of his. "I actually work for *This American Life* magazine."

"You do?" Trudy's heart beat even faster. "I try to buy it when I can." The name Bradley Payne should have seemed familiar to her, as much as she read the magazine cover to cover.

"That's swell. It's always fun to meet a reader." He eyed her dangling camera. "I take it then you're a camera buff?"

"Yes, yes I am." She clutched her Brownie again. "One day I'd like to get a better camera, but for now, this one does fine." Now she felt like a nincompoop for taking his photograph. He was probably a seasoned traveler, working for such a renowned national magazine.

"Do you do your own developing?"

"I do. My closet doubles as a darkroom, and it works fine as long as my little brother doesn't come charging in." Her cheeks flamed.

"Excuse me," Kathe interjected. "I see Peter's mother over across the way, and I need to ask her a question about the wedding rehearsal."

Sure. Leave her here, floundering as she tried to untangle her snarl. This would teach her to be impulsive. Truly, she would never try anything so foolhardy again.

"We'll see you soon," Tante Elsie said, looking from Mr. Payne to Trudy, then back to Mr. Payne again. "Where are you staying while you're in town, Mr. Payne?"

"At the Nimitz Hotel, of course. Only for tonight, I think. The troupe is moving on in the morning."

"Well, should you need to stay in Fredericksburg longer, you might inquire to see if one of the local Sunday houses is available." Tante Elsie placed her hand on Kathe's arm. "Let's see about talking to Mrs. Mueller."

Trudy watched them leave. Now, how to extricate herself from the conversation. "I hope you enjoy your visit."

"What's a Sunday house?"

"It's a weekend home, here in town," Trudy explained. "Those of us who live on farms outside town, our families built them years ago so we didn't have to travel back and forth on the weekend to do business and go to church. They're generally quite tiny. It's easier to drive back and forth to town now that we have cars. But we've kept our houses. Sometimes now they're rented out, or our grandparents move into them to be closer to town. That's where Miss Zimmermann lives now."

"Ah, I see." Mr. Payne glanced around the town square as the crowd filtered away. "Did you know they're having another performance tonight at the high school?"

"I do. But I only came to see the one today." Trudy bit her lip as reality bit into her. "I'll be needed back at home tonight."

He nodded. "Do. . .do you know if there is a Sunday house close by that I might rent for a time? The tour will be moving on, but I think I might stay for a while." He slung his jacket over one shoulder.

Trudy thought fast. She'd wanted to escape the conversation, the feelings swirling inside her at merely talking to this handsome stranger, but times were tough and she knew her family's coffers could use the money. "My family has one. It's empty right now. How. . .how long were you planning to stay?"

"I–I'm not sure. A week or two?" His expression was unreadable.

"We charge twenty dollars for a week, one dollar a day extra if you want us to provide a food basket." She hadn't consulted Mother, but the house had been empty since Oma's passing. Other families rented out their empty homes, why not the Meiers? The food basket was an impulse as well. First, snapping photographs, then renting out the Sunday house. What was with her?

"That's fair enough." He nodded at her, the shadow of his hat brim slanting across his face. "I'll want a food basket, too. I'll be spending my time writing, not hunting down meals."

"All right then, Mr. Payne. It's a deal." She extended her hand and they shook again, their grip lingering. Her breath caught in her throat. Now she needed to explain to her mother what she'd done.

"Deal." Mr. Payne released her hand. "How will I know which house?"

"I—I can meet you with a key at the Nimitz Hotel when you check out tomorrow, and show you the way."

"I'll see you at noon." He smiled again. "And, call me Bradley."

"I'll see you, Bradley." Trudy fled in the direction of the library.

◆　◆　◆

The sun had set on Fredericksburg, not long after 9:00 p.m. That was a switch for Bradley, who was used to the sun setting earlier in the Northeast. He ambled along Main Street, the quiet soaking into him.

Tante Elsie Zimmermann. Tante Elsie. His aunt. Only on his deathbed had his father talked about the kindness shown to him as a child by his cousin and his wife, Hank and Amelia. Hank was his father's cousin, but with the age difference, he'd addressed them as aunt and uncle. He'd left home as soon as he was grown and hadn't looked back. Father never allowed anyone to fill the empty space yawning inside him after his parents' death. As a child, he'd moved on, but as he'd grown older, he'd started questioning the family's love for him. Micah Delaney Zimmermann's scars from nearly being sent to an orphanage by his own grandfather—Hank's father—had never healed. Consequently, Bradley had a close bond with his mother, who had been an only child and had no family close by. The pen name, Payne, came from his mother's side of the family.

He supposed he should introduce himself fully to Tante Elsie and the rest of the family. Would the Zimmermanns acknowledge him as family?

He entered the lobby of the Nimitz and found Heinrich, the concierge, at the desk. "Mr. Payne, I have that line to Washington, DC, you needed."

"Thank you very much." Bradley accepted the telephone receiver from Heinrich. "Frank, are you there?"

"You're calling me from Texas? This had better be good." Frank's voice held an edge to it. "It's after 10:00 p.m. here."

"I want to stay in Fredericksburg for a while instead of heading west with the rest of the group."

"You'd better have a good reason."

"I want to show a different slant, letters from home, but from the hometown of Admiral Nimitz. I want to get to know its people. You know most of them are German. I think they'll have a unique perspective of the war."

"You don't say. Well, I'll give you a week to begin with. Get me some good stories."

"Thank you, sir. I won't let you down."

"Of course you won't. I'll send Briggs to meet the group in New Mexico and we'll see how it goes."

"I'll wire a story to you in a week."

"Have it wired by Friday."

Three days. Bradley sucked in a breath. "You'll have it."

He hung up the phone and glanced at Heinrich. "Thank you, sir."

"You're very welcome, Mr. Payne."

Bradley nodded then strolled out of the lobby and out again into the Texas night. His mind drifted back to Trudy Meier and her funny little camera. She'd been so earnest, and he saw a glimmer of the same curiosity that he had as a writer. She stood on the fringes, like he did, and watched. He understood that.

She liked him, too. Pretty girls were a nice distraction, but that was it. A distraction. Maybe someday, he'd settle down when he met the right girl. Not that he had a family to bring her home to, with Father and now his beloved mother gone.

He'd watched from the edges for most of his life, having worked his way out of high school and then through college, making his mother proud. Most of the other boys had had money. He had a scholarship and hard work. Even there at university, he'd felt on the outside.

But now here he was in Fredericksburg. His father had told him years ago that he was related to Hank and Amelia Zimmermann in Texas, that they'd adopted him after his parents had died. Here he had a pile of family, and all he had to do was make himself known. He realized that Trudy's tall, skinny friend was even a cousin of his.

The thoughts swirled in his head. What did he want, here in Fredericksburg? He wasn't sure. But knowing he had a scrap of family here, well, he had to see where this trail led him. Spending some time with Trudy Meier wouldn't be unpleasant, either. Maybe she had someone off fighting in the war. It wouldn't surprise him if she did. He'd follow that trail, too, if only out of his journalist's sense of curiosity, nothing more.

Chapter 3

Trudy parked her bicycle at the front of the Nimitz Hotel and popped the kickstand in place. She was on time to meet Bradley, but she'd had to hurry. Her mother hadn't been terribly pleased about renting their Sunday house to a stranger. Trudy agreed to accept the responsibility if anything went awry. Which, of course, it wouldn't. She'd spent the morning at the house, sweeping and scrubbing and airing the place out. The mustiness was gone, at least. It would be a tragedy if the scent of Oma's lavender disappeared forever. Now the Sunday house was ready for its first tenant. Mother couldn't argue with the extra income Mr. Payne would bring them.

Bradley. One of the last things he'd said was his first name, Bradley. She tried not to fuss over the wisps of hair that pulled out of her headband. Headband. Like a schoolgirl. She stuffed away the thought. She needn't worry about what Mr. Payne thought of her. It was a business transaction with a visitor to town. She knew nothing about the man. But dreams of travel and everything he'd seen followed her home.

Trudy yawned. She'd sat up too late, poring over her old issues of *This American Life*, with its photos of adventures throughout the country. A few articles from Bradley Payne. His head shot looked glamorous, half a grin spread on his face and his jacket slung on his shoulder, as if he'd just returned from a fabulous trip. Now here he was in tiny Fredericksburg.

"Here I am, Miss Trudy Meier. It *is* miss, or. . . ?"

"Yes, it's miss." So he wondered if she was married. . .but that meant nothing. "But just Trudy is fine."

"You don't seem like a 'just' anyone."

She found no response that would make sense and tried not to stammer as she said, "I—I have the key here, although you shouldn't need to worry about keeping the house locked. We watch out for each other here." Heat rushed through her face.

"That's nice to hear." He shifted a duffel bag on one shoulder. "Lead away."

Trudy nudged her bike's kickstand up into place and pulled it away from one of the pillars. "It's not far, just down a side street and almost at the southern edge of town."

"Have you lived here all your life?"

"Yes, all my life. My parents have a farm, and we keep bees and grow peaches like a lot of people around here do. My father is away, in France the last we heard. I have a younger brother who's twelve and I try to keep him out of trouble as best I can." Her mouth was running along at a steady pace, like the train that chugged into Fredericksburg regularly from Austin.

"So how did you get interested in photography?" Like a gentleman, he slowed his pace to match hers.

"My father. . .he brought home *National Geographic* magazine, and the pictures were so beautiful. Then I got to go on a trip to see Ansel Adams's photography in a gallery in Dallas. I knew I wanted to take pictures of anything and everything." Her cheeks flamed. Her photos weren't of any exotic or dramatic subjects, though.

"Of course, you had to try. Did you take photographs when you were in high school?"

"Yes, I did. We even had a small club. I was the president. Everyone else took it for kicks, but. . ." She didn't tell many people she wanted to be a photographer, more than portraits of families and children.

"I'd like to see some of your photographs sometime. I've shot some photos for the magazine before."

"Really? I'd love some pointers. But I know you're here to work."

"I won't be working all the time." His grin made the temperature shoot up at least ten more degrees. *Oh dear. Slow down. He's here now, but he'll be gone soon enough.* She had grown up knowing Kurt Schuler and had loved him once, probably still loved him a little, but the feelings clamoring for attention inside her, well, she'd never experienced these with Kurt.

"All right, then. I'll bring my portfolio." She suddenly felt shy again as she led him down the street. Two more blocks and they'd be at the house. Time to ask him some questions of her own. "So, why Fredericksburg for your magazine?"

"Why anywhere? For one thing, there's Nimitz. What kind of atmosphere did he grow up in that made him the leader he is now? That answer is here in Fredericksburg. Plus, like many small American towns, your town has given a lot."

She nodded. "That it has. . ." The twins. Kurt. Plus dozens of other fathers, sons, husbands, away without any word of when they would return.

"And then there's the obvious. Most of the town is German. Has that affected the way you're treated, here in Texas?"

"Ah, now that's always a good question." She paused, pondering how best to answer him. She never thought being of German descent would be a problem, but as the war escalated, it didn't seem to matter to some people that her own people were fighting for the right side. "Well, there are some who won't do business with us. But we've been pretty self-sufficient here."

Bradley nodded. "I've seen lots of small gardens in town."

"Yes, the idea of having a victory garden is nothing new to us. We've always grown what we needed." Funny. He'd changed the conversation back to Fredericksburg, away from himself. They approached the first in the small row of houses. Tante Elsie sat on the porch in her rocking chair, fanning herself, a jar of cool tea beside her foot.

"Hello, you two," Tante Elsie called out.

"Hello, Tante Elsie." Trudy smiled at the woman. She treasured the friendship with the Zimmermanns even more now that her own oma had passed on. Even Tante Elsie was almost like an oma to Kathe, with her own grandmother passed away.

"Miss Zimmermann." Bradley tipped his hat to Tante Elsie, an elegant gesture. "We're going to be neighbors for a while." There was something refined about him, yet somewhat unpolished. Trudy glimpsed a dark shade of stubble on his chin. She envisioned him hunched over a typewriter, clacking away at the keys into the night, rubbing his chin as he thought of the right word.

"Ah, so I see." There was a sparkle in the woman's eye. "I'm sure the Meiers will take good care of you."

Trudy dreaded the familiar sensation of blush. She tried to act normally, as if walking with Bradley Payne were something she did every day. She pulled the sack from her bicycle basket. "All right, there's not much to show you here." She balanced the sack on one hip and unlocked the door to the house. "We only kept this locked since it's been empty, but now that you're here, you can leave it unlocked."

She stepped into the familiar space, now clean and swept. The one room contained a narrow bed in one corner, covered. Her dusty sneakers thudded on the wooden floor. Oma's braided rag rug made a circle in the center of the room.

Bradley entered behind her and moved to shut the front door.

"No, please leave it open." Trudy stepped toward him. "It's better that way. People won't, um, talk. . .about us being alone in here, behind a closed door."

A half grin appeared on his lips. "Okay, you've got it. Door open. Nobody talks."

"So," she said, placing the sack on the square wooden table, "in that small cupboard in the corner, you'll find some bowls and cups. The woodstove works, but you likely won't need it. I've brought a few things for you. My mother's biscuits and a jar of peach preserves, as well as a jar of honey. Plus a sandwich. I hope that will do. I can bring more biscuits by tomorrow, plus some of mother's chicken potpie."

"Sounds tasty. This will be fine for now. I have to write, and I don't eat much when I'm on deadline." He paused, the breeze from outside swirling into the small space and lifting the front of his hair. "There's something else I'd like you to bring, though. I'd hoped you would today."

"What's that?"

"Bring some of your photographs. I'd like to see them."

She almost smacked her forehead. "Oh, I did. They're in the sack, in a folder." She pulled it out. Mr. Greiner at the newspaper office didn't care much for her photographs. Maybe Bradley wouldn't either.

He accepted the folder from her and opened it. "The light's not very good in here. I'm heading outside. C'mon."

She followed him and settled onto the swing beside him. The friendly, almost intimate seating arrangement made her heart flutter. That, and the fact her heart was shown through the photos.

"This is beautiful." Bradley held up the print she'd made of a field of bluebonnets and Indian paintbrush, sweeping up to an old barn that filled the sky. She'd lain on her stomach, shooting uphill to get that shot. "When did you take it?"

"That was this spring, in April. I wish you could see the colors."

"You have an eye for composition, and contrast. The lightness of the flowers, with the barn looming at the top of the background." Bradley moved to the next print.

Her throat caught. Oma's hands, kneading out bread dough, the sun slanting into the window. Then a photograph of the schoolchildren of Fredericksburg, linked arm in arm in front of their scrap collection piles, proudly celebrating what they'd done to support the war effort.

"What's this?" Bradley asked. "A scrap king and queen?"

"Sounds silly, but they had a contest at the high school for who could bring in the most scrap metal." Trudy shrugged. "It was newsworthy. Mr. Greiner even bought that photograph for the newspaper."

"Nice job. You're a pro." Admiration filled his voice. Or was that her wishful thinking?

She looked up at him and met his gaze. No, not wishful thinking. "I'm not a real professional."

"You were paid for your work. And that"—he poked her arm—"makes you a pro."

"I sort of always dreamed of being a real photographer, traveling and taking pictures," she admitted. "My former teacher told me I should open a studio and take portraits. But—"

"But you don't want that."

"No, I don't."

He smiled. "I understand. I'd rather be traveling and writing than staying in one place."

"What about your family?"

"My. . .my father left when I was young. He was in and out of my life. A year ago, my mother passed away. I was an only child." A shadow passed across his eyes.

"I'm sorry. What about grandparents, or cousins?" She placed her hand on his arm. "Surely you're not completely alone."

"No, not completely." The shadow grew darker in his eyes. "Well, Miss Trudy, I hope you'll bring me more photographs. Or maybe, we could go for a walk sometime. I'd like to see more of Fredericksburg and it would be nice to see it through a local's eyes."

She nodded slowly. Whatever secrets he held, he was welcome to hold them. "I'm developing a roll from yesterday. I can bring those prints. The good ones, anyway. Sometimes I get some duds."

"I'd like that, Trudy Meier." The shadow in his eyes disappeared with his smile.

"Tomorrow then, Bradley Payne." She returned the grin.

◆　◆　◆

The sun slipped toward the horizon and Bradley watched the shadow of the porch railing stretch longer and longer. He sat at the simple wooden table, writing out his thoughts on the last evening's show.

The small borough of Fredericksburg...

He crossed out *borough* and wrote *town* above it.

The small town of Fredericksburg welcomed the war bond tour with a greeting as big as the Lone Star State.

Not bad. He thought of the Japanese Ha-19 midget submarine they'd wheeled down Main Street, a reminder of the proverbial last straw that had catapulted the United States into the thick of the Second World War.

With the ocean many hours away, the Japanese Ha-19 midget submarine spurred the people into action, to give to a cause that lies thousands of miles away, where many of their men are serving in harm's way.

Not *spurred*. These people didn't need to be spurred. The town, over seventy miles west of the capital city of Austin, might be far from any typical civilization, but it wasn't immune or isolated from the effects of war. He circled the word. He'd find the right one before he wired his story to Frank.

His thoughts drifted to Trudy. She'd started to pry, gently, and he didn't blame her. He'd quizzed her about her family and the town. Of course she was curious about him. Something about her was comforting, familiar. Maybe it was the photographs, the common wanderlust they shared. He could see it in her eyes.

"Hello there, young Mr. Payne," a voice called out.

Bradley snapped his attention toward the porch. He wasn't a betting man, but a hunch told him it was Miss Zimmermann come calling. He set down his pen and left his papers on the table.

Sure enough, the woman stood beside the single step that led onto the porch. "Miss Zimmermann."

She regarded him with sharp eyes. "I see you've settled in."

"That I have. I'm very grateful to the Meiers for renting me the house while I'm here."

"You look like someone I know, only that was many, many years ago. He left the day he turned eighteen, broke all our hearts." She leaned on her cane as she helped herself onto the porch. "You're the spittin' image of my little brother, Micah Delaney. Our sister, Joy, is going to become a grandmother any day now."

He swallowed around a lump. "Wow, you don't say. It's funny how that happens."

"Becoming a grandparent, or you resembling my brother?"

He wanted to squirm under her look. He'd encountered tough interview subjects, but seldom had found himself under someone else's spotlight.

"Miss Zimmermann," he heard himself say, "I believe you're my aunt. Micah Delaney was my father."

"Of course he was," Tante Elsie whispered. "Was, you say?"

"He. . .he passed away two years ago. But he told me about all of you before he died."

His aunt sank onto the porch swing. "I'm glad he did." She patted the seat beside her. "Sit, sit. We have a lot to talk about."

Bradley complied, not sure what else to add to the conversation.

"Well, you have a large family here, and I know they will all be glad to hear about you. Micah, your father, was the youngest of the three of us. But what you don't know is that our adoptive mother and father had three more children after they took us in. Kathe is Lily's daughter. We lost Lily to sickness and Kathe's father is away fighting, so I've been keeping an eye on her. Kathe and your new friend Trudy are thick as thieves, best friends since they were in pigtails."

"I noticed that the other day."

"We're having a wedding soon, in June, at my parents' house. Your grandfather, Hank, is still alive, too."

Bradley's throat caught. Grandfather. "I'm looking forward to meeting him." So much to take in. He knew his father had family, but to have ignored them for so many years. Bradley realized how much he'd missed out on. *Father, if you'd only told me years ago. . . .*

Tante Elsie patted his arm. "So. Tell me about you. You're a writer. How did you decide to do that?"

"I always wrote from the time I was a kid. Then after high school, I studied journalism at the university in Ohio, where I grew up. Then I got a stringer job in Washington, DC, reporting. A friend helped me get an assignment for *This American Life* magazine and the rest is history."

"What? That's it? Is there a ladylove, someone special waiting for you back in the capital of our country?" She gave him a sideways glance.

"No, no one."

"Why not?"

"Time. It takes time to know someone, time I don't have. Writing sort of takes over everything, and some women don't understand that." Bradley shrugged. He'd been up past midnight, writing out his first piece in longhand, then walking, bleary-eyed, in the morning to the mercantile to wire his story.

"It sounds like it's *time* for you to slow down." Tante Elsie smiled at him. "You're not here by accident. Of course the war bond tour brought you here. But it's your choice to stay and take some time with your family. I think it's a good one. And who knows what can happen in a few weeks?"

He waited for a comment, linking him with Trudy Meier, but none came. "You're right, who knows?"

Chapter 4

The light hanging from a hook inside Trudy's closet glowed red. The aroma of photo processing chemicals filled Trudy's nostrils, and she tried not to sneeze.

"C'mon..." She placed the photo paper into the chemical bath and waited for the exposure to take place. A series of photos hung to dry from a narrow width of clothesline stretched from one side of the closet to the other. She'd clipped each of them to a hanger and in turn hooked the hanger from the line.

The photo of the small Japanese submarine looked pretty swell. Eric would love it. She'd definitely make another copy of the photograph for him, if her chemicals held out. The newest photo image in the chemical bath emerged from the blank paper. A sunlit crowd on the town square, with everyone facing toward the bandstand. Everyone except Bradley Payne.

His smile came to life, lit by the summer sun, the shadow from his hat brim shading one of his eyes. Charming, friendly, curious. Holding secrets. Did she dare ferret them out?

Mr. Payne's assignment here was a temporary one, so what did it matter? A sadness lurked deep in his eyes. Was it her job to help him? Maybe that was someone else's task.

Her mother warned her of strangers, that people weren't always what they seemed. Wolves in sheep's clothing prowled, looking for unsuspecting lambs to devour, or so she'd been told. Trudy would admit that she wasn't worldly wise. But she wasn't quick to trust strangers, either.

Yet there was something in Bradley's eyes, despite how he tried to push people away.

Dear Lord, we've all been through so much. We can use some hope, some joy. It's hard to believe sometimes that You're in control when the news talks about the insanity of war. Trudy slammed the brakes on her thoughts, especially the ones surrounding her doubts. It seemed, though, no matter how much anyone prayed and believed, the longed-for answers didn't come.

Bradley's image shimmered beneath the surface of developer. There. The photo was done. She snatched it out with her tongs then slid it into the water tray. After a rinse, she hung the photo to dry like its companions.

She clung to the faith she'd had since childhood, but as a grown woman, the answers of childhood didn't satisfy her as much. *Some answers I can live with, that's all I ask. And how can I help someone like Bradley Payne, when I don't have answers for myself?*

"Trudy!" Eric bellowed outside the closet door, the shrillness in his voice making her jump.

She bit her lip. "What is it? I'm only in the closet, not hard of hearing."

The door handle jiggled.

"Don't open the door, you'll ruin everything."

"Mama's home early. She's real tired. She wants to know if you picked the vegetables yet."

"No. Tell her I'll be right there." She sighed. Although, she had to admit that she found gardening relaxing. The first few vegetables were maturing now with an early onset of spring back in March.

"Don't be mad, Trudy."

"I'm not mad, Eric." She turned out the light and the closet filled with darkness. She reached with her toes to pull the towel away from the crack between the door and the wooden floor of her bedroom. She pushed the door open.

The room was empty. Evidently, Eric had scampered off to his next adventure. Oh, to be twelve again, when the biggest care was if your friend could come outside to play. She scolded herself. Eric didn't have it easy. A boy needed his father, and their father was an ocean away.

Trudy left her trays of developing solution in the closet and padded barefooted downstairs to find her mother in the kitchen.

"You're home early," she said.

Mother nodded. "They didn't need me today at the hospital. So I thought you and I could pick vegetables."

Of course this meant Mother wanted to talk. It seemed they all had battles with worries and cares since the war came to their doorstep. Within a few minutes, they both carried a basket to the back garden.

The first baby potatoes were ready, along with lettuce and tiny cucumbers. By summertime, they might have enough to put up jars of pickles. The soil felt cool to Trudy's feet as she squatted to pick some tomatoes.

"It's a good garden this year," Mother said. "Your father would be proud of us."

"I—I hope we get another letter soon," Trudy said aloud. "After what happened to Kurt, missing in action. . ." Missing. Not dead or wounded. But somewhere that no one knew about. And if someone did, they were likely the enemy.

"Are you sure you made the right decision, calling off the engagement?" Mother inspected the tops of the carrots, then passed them by.

"Yes. Not like it matters now."

"He might come back. Would you reconsider?"

"I don't think I would."

Her mother sighed. "Everything has changed. I never imagined this for our family. Here you are, twenty-one, halfway out our door. I just dread the thought of someone coming and taking you away. . . ."

Trudy listened to the sound of the breeze whistling through the branches of the peach trees at the end of the garden. "I don't think anyone will take me away. But if I ever do leave, Fredericksburg will always be my home."

"I—I have a confession to make." Her mother retrieved a narrow envelope from her apron pocket. "Here. . .this is for you."

Trudy sat in the middle of the row of plants, not caring that her dungarees would get dirty. The return address was for *Texas Wildflowers* magazine. Back in April, she'd sent them a photograph of a field of bluebonnets, the Texas state flower.

Dear Miss Meier,

We find your photograph of the bluebonnet field of great interest to our magazine and intend to use it in our late summer issue. Please find a cheque for three dollars. We will also send you five complimentary copies of the summer 1943 issue of our magazine. If you have more photographs of our lovely wildflower landscape, we would like to see those as well.

Regards,
Terrence Irvine
Editor-in-chief
Texas Wildflowers

"When did this come in?" Three dollars. Someone paid her money for her photograph. Real cash money, once she brought the check to the bank.

"Last week." Mother dipped her head. "I'm afraid you're going to leave, go off hither and yon, taking photographs like you see in those magazines you love so much."

"Mother, I have no plans to leave just yet. This editor invited me to submit more photographs. He likes them. That doesn't mean I'm going to move to Austin or anything. They don't have wildflowers in the city, anyway." Trudy scrambled across the row of plants and hunkered down next to her mother, then embraced her.

"I'm sorry I hid it from you, and I'm sorry you're seeing me like this." Mother looked at the squash as she spoke. "I try to be strong for you, and your brother."

Trudy gave her a hug. "You don't have to be strong for me."

"I know you're all grown up. Just look at you, renting out our Sunday house. I'm not sure what your father will think about it. I'm not sure what I think about it." Mother wiped her brow with the back of her gloved hand. "To be sure, the extra money is nice, but—"

"But what?"

"Be careful, *schatze*. He's a reporter. I don't trust him."

"I'm careful, *Mutti*."

◆ ◆ ◆

Bradley set his napkin on the table. "Thank you, or should I say, *danke*? I really don't know any German." The smiling faces that lined the dining room held no judgment of his lack of German. This little pocket of society was far from a large city, and its older residents held to their native language. But the younger people his age spoke little German, if any.

"That's all right," said his opa, Hank. He brushed off Bradley's apology with his wrinkled hand, callused from decades of woodworking.

The old man had cried when Tante Elsie introduced him as Micah's only son.

"My Amelia and I loved him as best we could. We built a family together, all of us." Opa shook his head, with the faintest of a tremor accenting his movement. "But my father was harsh. I'm sorry I didn't realize how deeply that affected Micah."

"Now Papa," Elsie interjected. "Don't apologize. Micah knew you loved him as a son. That should have more than made up for what your father tried to do."

Bradley didn't want to share with them about the last conversation he'd had with his father, so he held his tongue. If loose lips sank ships, the hurt that his late father's words could inflict would hurt many assembled at the Zimmermanns' home for supper.

He found himself the guest of honor, and although he was nowhere near a prodigal to this family, they'd killed the fatted calf and embraced Bradley as one of them. That, and there was cause for double celebration with the upcoming nuptials of his second cousin, Kathe, in several weeks.

"Will you still be with us?" Elsie asked.

"I–I'm not sure," Bradley managed to answer. "My job brought me here and is letting me stay on for several weeks. I'm writing a series of articles about Fredericksburg on the home front, actually."

"Please stay," said his cousin Kathe. "You are welcome at my wedding. We need a celebration around here, and having you here will add to it."

"I'll talk to my boss." He took a sip from his coffee cup. Never had he expected his writing journey to take him here.

"Have you ever been to Europe? Did you see any fighting?" asked one of his younger cousins—Walter, Bradley thought his name was.

"Yes, I was in Germany, briefly, as well as France and England. Then the war bond tour brought me here," said Bradley. "When my number came up, they sent me home because of my ear infections. I'm hard of hearing in one ear. They thought that was a liability, I guess."

"I'll be glad when the war ends," said Tante Elsie. "I know we all will."

A whistle echoed outside, followed by a call from a bullhorn in the street. "Lights out, lights out!"

Then, just like in many neighborhoods in many cities across the country, the younger Zimmermanns scampered around, turning light switches off and pulling down shades.

Bradley wasn't sure the little hamlet turning off all their lights and hunkering down would help the war effort, but maybe it made them all feel as if they were doing something instead of watching news reports.

"So, you're renting from the Meiers," Grandfather Hank stated.

"I am. I met Trudy right after the parade yesterday."

"I think she's quite taken with you," said Kathe.

"Kathe," Tante Elsie chided.

"Well, I haven't seen her like this, especially after Kurt." Kathe shook her head.

"What if he comes home? Then she has a choice to make." Tante Elsie rose from the table. "More coffee, anyone?"

"So she has someone, then." Bradley lifted his coffee cup. "I don't mind more coffee."

"No, not exactly." Kathe sighed. "Kurt is MIA, somewhere in France. He's been missing for three months now. His unit thinks he's been captured."

"That's horrible." It definitely gave a personal edge to the news. "His poor family. . ."

"So, I bet you'll want to know more about Fredericksburg's favorite son," said Hank. "I knew the old captain well, Chester's grandfather, Charles."

"You did?" Bradley pulled his notepad from his pocket.

"Put that thing away. Tonight's just for listening, not for working." Hank waved his pointer finger at Bradley.

"Yes, sir." Bradley tucked the notepad away, trying not to smile at the older man's gesture. So this was how it felt, being part of a family.

Chapter 5

Good afternoon," Trudy called into the Sunday house where Bradley sat at the table, pen in hand. She shifted the folder under one arm and tried not to drop the basket she carried in the other hand.

He looked up and a smile spread across his face. "Good afternoon."

"Here's some chicken potpie my mother made." Trudy set the basket on the table.

"A wonderful smell"—Bradley leaned toward the basket, where the pie lay inside, wrapped in a cloth napkin. "I haven't had homemade potpie in...a very long time. I miss my mother's cooking."

"Did your mother cook a lot?"

"She did. She was the best. Even though it was just her and I for a long time." Bradley corked the inkwell and set down his pen. "My father left when I was nine. He still came around, though."

"I–I'm sorry." The conversation had taken a more personal turn, but this was what she'd hoped for. Something about him made her want to learn more.

The shadow passed from his face when he looked up at her again. "Enough about that. Did you bring more pictures?"

"That I did. They're the last roll I shot, including the parade and war bond show." She pulled the photographs from an old school binder. "Here. . ."

Bradley thumbed through the set, nodding as he did so. "Good shots. You might want to up the exposure on the one with the midget submarine. A few of the details are lost."

"Okay." She knew she had much more to learn about photography.

"Do you have plans today?"

"I always have something to do, especially with Father gone. We manage as best we can."

"Will you take me around town and introduce me to people? I want to get a good picture of life here during World War II." The intensity of his tone compelled her to look him straight in the eye.

"I can, today." Spending the afternoon with Bradley? Her heart raced.

"Do you have your camera? Maybe I can see if my editor could use some of your images."

"I always have my camera with me." She was on her last roll of film and didn't

376

know where she'd find some cash for more. Unless that editor of Bradley's would pay for photos.

"Perfect." He stood, picking up a slim notepad. "Where shall we go first?"

"You said that people look differently at us because we're German. We have nothing to do with the actions of that insane man and the people who blindly follow him. People need to see what we've given." Her throat caught. "You need to meet the Wagners. They had twin sons, both killed in the service and both buried in a Fredericksburg cemetery. Mr. Wagner runs the soda shop in town, and Mrs. Wagner is a seamstress."

"We'll go there, then." He followed her out into the sunlight.

◆　◆　◆

As they left the Wagners' home, Bradley fought the emotions rising inside. Trudy dabbed at her eyes with a handkerchief that she slipped into her pocket. "I don't know what to say," was all he could manage.

"I know." Trudy nodded. She gripped her camera strap, her fingers trembling. "I take my brother to get a soda, and it's hard to watch Mr. Wagner. I can see the memories in his eyes, remembering how his own boys were the same age as Eric once."

He touched her elbow, and she released her hand's grip on the strap and allowed him to take her hand. "May I?"

She studied their hands, fingers interlocked, and nodded. "Can I take you somewhere?"

"All right. Lead the way."

"I want to show you a place of beauty here. It's where I shot some of the pictures you've already seen." Her hands were soft, her fingertips having the tiniest bit of callus from working with chemicals.

He needed to tell her about his ties to the town, that one day he'd be back. Instead, he let her talk, pointing out the landmarks from the creek, to where she completed high school, to the historic school building where her mother and grandmother went to school.

"Here we are," she said, leading him under the shade of a trio of oak trees. "These are live oaks, probably at least one hundred years old."

The trees had massive trunks, so thick that Bradley could wrap his arms around only half of a trunk. Their thick, gnarled branches spread wide before reaching up to the sky. "These are something else. They're not as tall as the redwoods in California, but just as majestic in their own way."

"I'm glad you understand, not being from around here and all."

"Actually, I've been wanting to tell you something." He took her hand again. "It turns out, I do have ties to Fredericksburg. My father, Micah Delaney, is related to your friends, the Zimmermanns."

"Really? You're part of their family then?"

He loved watching a smile bloom on her face. "Yes. He was Tante Elsie's younger brother." Bradley explained about his father leaving Fredericksburg and never returning, then about his parents' untimely deaths.

"I'm so sorry, Bradley." She covered his hand with her other hand. "Your father was so alone, and he had people here who loved him all along."

"His loss, and I wish he'd realized that before it was too late." Bradley shrugged. "I wasn't sure what the Zimmermanns would think, but they've been very accepting. Aunt Elsie recognized me right away, it turns out."

Trudy had a musical laugh. "I'm certain she did." Her eyes held a curious light, with the breeze catching the ends of her hair.

"I haven't felt so at home since. . .ever." His throat tightened and he pulled Trudy close, and kissed her. The rosewater scent she wore surrounded him, and the remainders of the soda they'd drunk at the Wagners' shop were sweet on her lips. She molded perfectly against him. It was as if they'd known each other far longer than two days.

Then she pulled back, giving a little gasp. "Bradley, we hardly know each other."

"Maybe we know each other better than you want to admit. As far as the day-to-day things go, those are things we can easily learn about each other."

"But—"

"Is it Kurt? Well, I'm not Kurt. I'm sorry about what happened to him, and I hope they find him." He allowed himself to touch her chin and raise her gaze to meet his. "You can't let yourself be in limbo. The war will end, we'll start moving on with our lives, and where will you be? I'm thankful and blessed to have a job that somehow makes a difference in people's lives. You have a wonderful talent as well. Are you going to let yourself stay here?"

"Who told you about Kurt?" Trudy stepped back and crossed her arms over her chest. "I should have been the one to tell you. Not someone else."

"So you do have feelings for me."

"Of course I do. I've felt it from the moment we met, and it frightened me. There's so much uncertainty in life right now, I don't see adding to it." Her brow furrowed, and she lowered her arms to fiddle with her camera strap.

"Even without war, life is still uncertain. That's where trusting God comes in." Unspeakable relief washed over him. She cared for him. She'd felt it, too, that instant connection that neither of them were expecting or looking for.

Trudy nodded. "Of course it does. Without my faith in God, I wouldn't have hope."

"Well, then. Have faith that whatever's happening between us will have a happy ending."

One corner of her mouth twitched. "I'll try." But her eyes held an uncertain expression.

Chapter 6

Trudy couldn't avoid Bradley over the next two weeks. She wanted to know him better, as he'd said. Everyday things were easy to learn about someone else. Likes, dislikes, little annoying or endearing habits.

What she'd intended to be a weekly ritual turned into an everyday happening. She would bring Bradley food, intending to drop it off and leave. She'd tote along either biscuits or rolls from her mother, or leftover meat or something for Bradley to make himself a sandwich. Instead of her heading straight back to the farm, she and Bradley would end up walking the streets of Fredericksburg, occasionally running into yet another friend or a distant cousin of his.

The day before Kathe's wedding, Bradley was grinning when Trudy arrived at the Sunday house. A brown paper–wrapped parcel sat on the table, addressed to him in care of the Nimitz Hotel. "Look what I have here. I was hoping it would arrive."

Trudy studied the parcel, securely tied with string. "A package. Good. You mentioned the other day about waiting for something to arrive."

He tapped the brown paper. "Go ahead, open it. It's for you."

"For me?" She worked at untying the string, which didn't work, so Bradley worked at it with his pocketknife. The paper unfolded to reveal a book, cover side down. She turned the book over.

Photography Fundamentals and Beyond: A Professional's Primer.

"Bradley—" He understood her. It wasn't a romantic gift, by any definition of the word. Any fellow could buy a girl flowers or chocolates, but this, this was personal. "I studied what I could, but I always had to return the photography book to the library."

"Well, now this copy is yours forever." He took her hand and squeezed it.

"Thank you, thank you so much."

"I think you could be a professional photographer, and not just portraits. You could work anywhere."

"It means a lot to have someone believe in me like this, especially you." The air grew thick, just like it did weeks before under the live oak trees.

"I do." He raised her hand to his lips and kissed it.

◆　◆　◆

The memory of his gift followed her through a sleepless night until the following afternoon, when she stood inside her cousin Kathe's bedroom, where the temperature soared with early June heat. Kathe stood in front of a small circular fan, moving as it oscillated.

"I'm melting, Trudy. Oh, why, why didn't Peter and I wait until autumn to marry?" Kathe frowned, but Trudy laughed in spite of her own somber thoughts. "And here you are, my maid of honor, laughing at me."

"It's too late to turn back now," Trudy said. "Besides, Peter is well enough to get married."

Kathe nodded. "He's going to walk me during the recessional—oh dear, I can't cry. Not yet." She fanned her face and glanced at Trudy. "Okay, you. 'Fess up. What's going on with you and my handsome, young journalist cousin from Washington? You've been seen around town nearly every day."

"I don't know. I wish I knew. But"—Trudy shivered at the memory—"he kissed me once."

"No. Scandalous, and him so new in town." Kathe's eyes were wide, but she followed the fish-eyed expression with a smile.

"Don't act shocked." Trudy studied her friend's face. "Wait. Did you tell him about Kurt? Because the other day, he brought up Kurt and knew what happened."

"Um. . .well, we sort of all did, the first night he had supper with us." Kathe started moving back and forth in front of the fan again.

"I wanted to be the one to tell him. . . ." Trudy sank onto the bed. She should have told him herself, but she hadn't wanted to press the issue as if she were trying to prove to him that she was "available." She picked up the pink gown, simple, with an A-line skirt. The idea of getting into her maid-of-honor gown wasn't pleasant. Although the gown was beautiful and lovingly sewn by Tante Elsie, she'd melt just like Kathe would.

"I'm sorry. Bradley wanted to know, and it all just sort of came out."

A soft knock sounded at the door. "Are you almost ready? The guests have almost all assembled in the backyard," said Tante Elsie.

"Almost," Kathe called out. Then she continued in a lower tone. "You're not mad at me?"

"Of course not. We—he and I—well, we agreed to continue getting to know each other."

"Why don't you look happy about it?"

Trudy stood and ran her fingers over the fabric of her dress. "For one thing, he's going to leave. That's a given fact. He can't write about Fredericksburg forever and his boss wants him to move on eventually. And another thing, how do I know that this isn't moving so fast? He makes me feel. . ."

"Like you're flying on air, like you've been running for a day and can't catch your breath?" Kathe asked.

"Something like that. . .yet I look at my parents, and I don't think I've ever seen them like that." Trudy frowned. "I don't want to chase some dream that will only leave me heartbroken in the end."

"I'm sure your parents felt that way about each other, as did mine," Kathe said. "We've just never seen them young and in love. Everyone starts somewhere."

"You're right." Trudy nodded.

Kathe took her dress from the hanger and held it up to herself, studying her reflection in the mirror. "I prayed long and hard about Peter. He'd come home injured, and I knew that now was the time for us to marry. But I wanted to be sure that it wasn't just me going all 'hearts and flowers' over the whole thing. One morning I woke up and I just. . .knew. . .beyond a doubt, that Peter was the man for me and I was ready to do everything I could to have a good marriage. And, here we are."

"Here you are." Trudy smiled at Kathe. "Let me help you get dressed. We need to get you downstairs so you can have that long-delayed wedding."

Silently, she added, *Lord, show me the way. . .*

◆　◆　◆

Bradley watched as Trudy glided down the grassy lawn of the Zimmermanns' main house. Her hair swept up into a pile of curls on her head. Her light pink dress skimmed her knees with a wide skirt, and her bouquet of fresh flowers from the garden made a pretty contrast.

Her eyes met his, and a faint blush swept down her neck and toward her shoulders. What a two weeks it had been since taking up temporary residence in Fredericksburg. His first set of columns had won praises from Frank. That had earned him more time here.

But time here would be coming to an end, regardless of how much Bradley tried to prolong it.

"There's a war going on, Payne," Frank had told him. *"I appreciate the fact you've brought a human interest angle to the stories about Fredericksburg and your family, but our readers always want something fresh and new. If it starts to get stale, I'm pulling you out of there for your own good."*

"I understand, Frank," Bradley had said.

That conversation came roaring back into his memory as he watched Trudy pass by where he stood. He'd found a treasure here in this Texas town, a treasure of family and the promise of more with Trudy.

The minister asked them to rise as Kathe Zimmermann walked toward the outdoor altar. She leaned on Hank's arm. She made a beautiful bride, her dress simple yet just as elegant as any Bradley had seen in his travels. His grandfather gave him a slight nod as they passed.

Grandfather. Opa. *Thank You, Lord. Please don't let me make the mistake my father did by pushing people away and running from people who love me.* He didn't know how to act with a family. He was used to keeping his own hours, his own

381

time and schedule, without anyone except his editor to give him a timetable for anything. Now people were asking for him, wanting to be involved in his life. He'd never found himself in a family gathering like this.

Kathe had asked if he wanted to read a scripture during the short ceremony. At first he declined, until his grandfather talked him into reconsidering. He could scarcely drag his gaze away from Trudy, who stood at her friend's side. If there was any indication that she had dreary thoughts about this not being her own wedding day, Bradley didn't see it. He did see the woman who'd stolen his heart. First, her talent and sense of adventure inspired him, but then he saw her love for her family and her town.

"And now, a few words from Paul's first letter to the Corinthians," said the minister. He nodded at Bradley, who rose from his chair and walked to the small arbor. He took the open book that the minister held, already turned to the correct passage.

He cleared his throat. "Though I speak with the tongues of men and of angels. . ." The familiar poetic words of truth came from his lips. "Charity suffereth long, and is kind. . .beareth all things, believeth all things, endureth all things. . ."

He allowed himself a glance at Trudy, whose gaze held his for a millisecond before she lowered her focus to her bouquet. A blush swept over her features.

"When I was a child, I spake as a child, I understood as a child, I thought as a child: but when I became a man, I put away childish things. For now we see through a glass, darkly; but then face to face: now I know in part; but then shall I know even as also I am known. And now abideth faith, hope, charity, these three; but the greatest of these is charity."

Lord, help me, I'm in love with Trudy Meier.

The rest of the ceremony ticked by without his conscious thoughts directed at the newly married couple. This wasn't in his plans. What could he do now that his heart was held by a honey-haired photographer from a tiny Texas town? Certainly she talked about adventure and wanting to see the world. There were drawbacks. He knew them. Tough travel conditions, uncertain accommodations. There was occasionally some danger. He wasn't guaranteed a permanent position at the magazine. What if he ever found himself out of work, with a wife to take care of?

He knew Trudy's mother had expressed a few objections to the idea of her only daughter being paired with a freelance journalist. He didn't blame her. The practical part of him understood all too well. If it were his daughter, he'd want her tucked safely into the shelter of a town like Fredericksburg. But then, Trudy wasn't a child, but a grown woman capable of making adult decisions.

Someone nudged him. Opa Hank. "You going to hang back and not try to get a piece of wedding cake?"

"Huh?"

"You were anywhere but here, young man."

"Sorry. It was a nice ceremony. I'm honored that I was included."

"I know that the young Meier girl had your attention."

"Was it obvious?"

"Of course it was." His grandfather walked beside him in the direction of a long table filled with delectable dishes. Someone had baked a ham, another friend or family member had brought homemade sausage. Plenty of potatoes and garden vegetables. And—the cake.

"Hello." Trudy's voice came from somewhere off to the side, close to his right shoulder.

He turned to face her. "Hello, yourself. You look beautiful."

"Thank you." She colored at his words. "It was a lovely wedding, wasn't it? I'm glad you said yes to Kathe about reading the scripture. I know it meant a lot to her." Trudy waved off a fly, who'd developed an interest in her bouquet.

"It meant a lot to me, too. It'll be one of my favorite memories of Fredericksburg and meeting my family." He took a step closer to her.

"You sound as if you're leaving. . ." Trudy bit her lower lip.

"Eventually, I am." He tried not to put a damper on the day. "Okay, probably sooner than eventually. I knew I would be. . ." He didn't add, *and you did, too.* The pain in her eyes almost made him wince.

"I'd heard the rumors, but didn't want to believe them," a female voice said. Bradley didn't know the woman who'd come to stand beside them. She looked to be a few years younger than Aunt Elsie, and she glanced from Trudy, to him, then back to Trudy again.

"What rumors do you mean, Mrs. Schuler?" Trudy asked.

"You've taken to running around town with this man who claims to be a Zimmermann, while my son—my only boy—is somewhere missing in Europe." The woman's eyes crackled with anger, but Bradley saw the fear inside them, too. One of his friends had gone missing after an air raid in London a year ago. No one had heard from him since. Sad, how life kept going even when someone's sudden absence left a gaping hole.

"I miss Kurt, too, and I wish he were here." Trudy stood her ground. The words she said sounded odd. How much did she really miss him? Bradley couldn't guess. Today wasn't the right place or time, but eventually they'd have to square off and face each other, all cards on the table, and both of them would see what the other held.

Chapter 7

"You ready for bigger and better things, Payne?" Frank's voice roared over the telephone line, the Wednesday following the wedding. "Genius, I tell you. Genius, profiling Nimitz and the town that helped him become the man he is now."

"I'm glad you're happy, Frank." Bradley had hunkered down, finishing the last of the series of articles featuring Admiral Chester Nimitz. A feeling like being stuck on the downward turn of a Ferris wheel entered his stomach. The day was coming when he'd be on his way, especially if he wanted to keep his job. Which, he did.

"I've got something coming up, something big that *This American Life* has never tried before. It's one of America's next frontiers, and if all goes well, I'll have you there in less than ten days."

"Ten days?" His own tone surprised him. Usually he was raring to go to the next assignment.

Trudy had barely stopped by the last several days, especially since the Zimmermanns had sent him home well stocked with leftovers from the wedding. He missed her. But considering the latest developments, maybe it was best this way. If she wasn't absolutely sure she could see herself having a traveling life—or even having a husband traveling much of the time like him.

Husband. . .him, a husband? He'd only been here for the story. . .and his family—

"Payne?"

"Yes, Frank?"

"Did you get what I just said? Because I have a feeling you didn't hear me."

"So, you can have me there in less than ten days?"

"Wind up the series. Get some photographs that we can use for a photo page, then hightail it up here to my office. We'll give readers enough to expect that your next setting will be something they've only seen in the news reels. You can cool your heels before you ship out again."

"I understand."

"Don't sound so glum. This is the chance of a lifetime."

"You're right." Bradley ended the call and set the phone back on its cradle.

"Are you okay, Mr. Payne?" asked the shopkeeper.

"Yes, yes I am. I'm going to be leaving sooner than I thought."

"Well, we've enjoyed having you in our fair town."

"Thank you, thank you. I've—I've enjoyed it as well." He slid some cash across the counter to help pay for the long-distance phone call. "I'll be back at some point, to see my grandfather and the rest of the family."

But back for Trudy—he wasn't a hundred percent certain of that. In a perfect world, he would come swooping back and they'd have themselves a grand reunion.

◆　◆　◆

Trudy fumbled with the knife as she sliced the potatoes. Beef stew was the fanciest she could manage for a nice supper. She'd used garden tomatoes for the base and added fresh chopped vegetables from the garden. She'd bartered honey for a small end piece of beef from the butcher. Some people didn't want to buy the cast-off pieces, but others knew how to coax the toughness from the end pieces after cooking the meat for hours.

Bradley would enjoy this stew, or at least she hoped so. After the wedding, Trudy had done some long, hard thinking and praying. She loved Bradley, and it had hurt her the way Mrs. Schuler had talked to them. Yet she didn't want him to misunderstand about Kurt. She realized that loving Kurt had been a first love. She didn't think a first love had to be her only love.

Mrs. Schuler, to give the woman credit, had apologized after the Sunday service. *"I'm sorry for what I said to you at Kathe's wedding, Trudy. You and your family have been a great support to mine. Kurt told me in a letter as well that you both decided not to marry. It's just hard to see other people going on with their lives, when Kurt. . . when Kurt and his father and I have no chance to go on with ours."* Sobbing, she'd embraced Trudy and whispered in her ear, *"I know Kurt will always love you."*

Trudy hadn't known how to answer the woman and even now, had no answer. She'd mumbled that she would be praying for them. All of Fredericksburg did a lot of watching and praying, it seemed.

She gathered the diced potato from the cutting board and dropped it into the bubbling stew. Soon enough, the meal would be done. A fresh loaf of bread, wrapped in a dish towel, waited on the counter. Cookies would round out the meal.

Within thirty minutes, she'd tucked a ceramic-covered pot of stew and the bread into the bicycle basket, plus her small battery-operated radio. It would be a clear night tonight, or at least she hoped so. Maybe they'd get a signal and listen to a show from Austin.

It was the least she could do for Bradley, especially after his gift of the beautiful photography book. The gift had touched her to the core. She'd spent her free time studying it, learning where she intuitively made good composition choices, and other places in her developing that she could improve upon. She bumped along the road on her bicycle, her blouse sticking to her back. It had been a silly idea to try to look fancy for him tonight, as if they were going out. As a reward, she'd be hot and sweaty by the time she arrived at the Sunday house.

Trudy pedaled along. The sight of the Sunday house's open door made her heart sing. Good. Bradley was home. Before long, the shadows would be stretching and the sun going down. As if he knew she was approaching on her bicycle, Bradley emerged from the house and squinted. A grin spread onto his face when he saw it was her.

"Hello there," he called out as she glided to a stop on the hard-packed dirt, dust swirling around her tires.

"Hi." She popped the kickstand down, got the bicycle balanced, and pulled all the food from the bicycle basket. "I hope you're hungry."

"Just a little." He rubbed his stomach as he stepped off the porch. Bradley picked up the pot, while she gathered up the bread and the radio.

"It's beef stew, made with real beef," she said as she followed him into the house. The single, open room felt cozy. They left the front door open and the breeze drifted in.

"Real beef? I'm impressed." Bradley pushed aside a stack of papers and set the pot on the center of the table.

"I know we're in Texas, but our beef has been going elsewhere the past couple of years. And most of us don't ranch around here. We farm. However, I managed to secure some fresh meat." She smiled and patted the top of the pot. "And if you don't mind, I'm inviting myself to stay for supper."

"Of course you can stay." He pulled out a chair for her. "Please, sit down."

"Why thank you." Her heart sang. She knew he'd be leaving. He hadn't mentioned it lately, but his rent was paid up for one more week.

Bradley headed to the corner cupboard. "I must admit, I've missed you the past few days."

"I knew you had plenty of food after the wedding, when I saw Aunt Elsie packing a basket for you." Trudy removed the lid from the stew and inhaled. Hopefully, it was as good as her mother's.

"Here. I have bowls and spoons." He set one in front of her and kept one for himself. "Welcome to Payne's Café, madame."

"Why, thank you, Mr. Payne." She laughed. If only they could pretend there wasn't a war going on. She served them each a bowl of stew, then divvied up the bread.

"Oh Trudy. . ." Bradley reached for her hand. "I'm going to miss you."

"You're leaving soon, aren't you?"

He nodded. "I talked to my boss today. I'm wrapping up the series and heading back to Washington early next week."

She'd been preparing herself for this, but even so, the edges of her heart crumbled. She tried to smile. "We—we can keep in touch."

"Of course we can." Then he cleared his throat. "You know, I'll be back to see my family, when I can."

"But you don't know when that will be." She blinked to clear her burning eyes. No, she wouldn't let him see her tears. Not tonight. Tonight was supposed to be a night to remember.

"You're right, I don't. But you can be sure I'll be back to see my family, when I can."

"If you didn't have family here. . ."

"I'd still come back, somehow."

Trudy nodded. "I'm glad. But—"

"I can't ask you to wait for me, though. That's not fair to you."

"What if I want to wait for you?"

Bradley sighed. "Even after the war, I'll still travel a lot."

"I know." Trudy fumbled with the spoon beside her bowl.

He squeezed her hand. "I'll ask the blessing over our meal."

Trudy nodded and bowed her head.

"Lord, we thank You for this day. I thank You for this food. Bless the hands that prepared it, and strengthen us for Your service. Amen."

"Amen." Trudy pulled her hand away from his. "Here, maybe we can find some music to play for supper, and we can pretend we're somewhere exotic." She almost sounded like a child, acting out make-believe.

"That's a great idea."

The strains of "Taking a Chance on Love" filled the air, with only a hint of static. They ate their stew, talked, and laughed. Trudy imagined that tonight was all they had, and refused to let her mind ponder the fact that Bradley was leaving in four days.

All too soon, the stew was finished and the pot empty. The music kept playing. Thankfully, no news reports broke in to shatter the moment.

"It's probably cooler outside," Bradley said. He stood and gathered the bowls together before she had a chance to reach for them. "I'll clean this up later."

Bradley took her by the hand and led her outside. "Oh, my sweet Trudy. . . this is much harder than I thought it would be."

She wanted to tell him, *Take me with you, please*, but she kept silent. She wasn't going to beg, or plead. Instead, she said, "I know. I feel the same way. . .what are we going to do?"

He pulled her close into the circle of his arms and she responded in turn, listening to his heartbeat through his shirt.

"Would you come with me?"

Trudy opened her mouth, but the roar of a car's engine bit through the twilight and made them both jerk apart. Trudy glanced toward the road. Her mother, behind the wheel of the family's car.

She honked the horn and the car ground to a halt. "Trudy! There you are." Her mother's tone made her stand bolt upright. Was it Father?

"What's wrong?"

Her mother leapt from the car. "Not wrong—Kurt's mother got a telegram. Kurt's been found, alive, and will be sent to a hospital in Washington in a few days."

387

Chapter 8

Trudy and her mother hurried, hurried, hurried down the corridor of the army hospital, the scent of antiseptic making Trudy's stomach turn. Kurt. . .asking for them. For her. Alive. What he must have been through. Of course she had to come. It was the least they could do. Exhaustion pricked her eyelids. They'd taken a train and had sat upright for three days in the car. She wished they'd had the money to get a sleeping car. But at least they were here, now, in the nation's capital.

Kurt's parents had fallen ill suddenly, too ill to travel, so they begged Trudy and her mother to go in their place. "If he can't see us, we know he'll want to see you."

Making the trip with Bradley helped. Neither she nor her mother had traveled this far before, and he made the process smooth. He attended to what they needed, whether it was securing a pillow or a blanket, and helped them connect to the right trains. They laughed when they could. Laughter was an antidote to the pain of war, to the constant reminders from the radio and newspapers. Even Mother relaxed, although she kept worrying that someone was going to steal her purse. That and if Eric was behaving for the Zimmermanns, who volunteered to let him stay with them.

From the taxi, Trudy glimpsed the Capitol building and Washington Monument as they made their way outside the city to the hospital. If her trip hadn't been so urgent, she'd have loved to stop and take photos.

"I'll see you to the hospital," Bradley had promised. He even accompanied them inside the hospital, inquiring at the desk about where to find Kurt. He followed them along the hallway like a silent shadow.

Trudy held his hand, regardless of her mother's opinion at the moment. She smiled at Bradley. "Thank you for everything." He replied by kissing her hand.

Now each step drew Trudy closer to Kurt. For a few moments, she remembered their childhood promises, their romance that seemed so perfect—to everyone else, but not her. What was romance or true love? She knew that bottle rockets and swooning didn't last. But weren't you supposed to feel something for the one you loved? Of course, she felt some affection for him.

But Kurt had never made her feel like Bradley did, like she was on the brink of some discovery or big adventure.

"They said he's in ward two," Mother whispered. Trudy nodded. A nurse passed them, efficient and neat in her crisp, white uniform and cap. Somewhere, a man sobbed about needing more medicine.

Oh Lord, please don't let that be Kurt. But then, she wished it wasn't anyone. This was the side of war she wanted to hide from, the reason she tried not to read the newspaper much, the reason she turned the radio off if it played anything but music. She glanced at her mother. The times her mother had volunteered at the hospital back in Texas. . .what had she witnessed? Trudy had never bothered to ask.

"Here we are," Mother said.

Trudy felt her feet seal themselves to the tile floor. "I—I don't know if I can go in."

"You can do this." Bradley slipped his arm around Trudy's shoulders. "I know you can."

"I—I want to go in by myself first," she said. The Schulers had been vague about his injuries, other than that he was malnourished and had had a fractured leg, and some facial lacerations.

"We'll be right here." Mother gave her a hug before she entered the ward.

Sunlight streamed through the large window at the end of the two rows of beds. Trudy tried not to stare, but some images still seared themselves into her eyes. Bandages, tubes, bruises. Which one was Kurt? It had been well over a year since he'd left Fredericksburg.

"Trudy." One of the figures spoke. But which one? She glanced from face to unfamiliar face. It had been so long, but how could she not recognize him?

One of the men cracked a grin at her. "I wish you were here to see me, doll." His left eye was covered with a bandage, but his right eye, a shade of robin's egg blue, winked at her.

"I–I'm sorry," was all she could stammer to the wounded soldier. She did pause at the foot of his bed and until she found her voice. "I hope you get well soon." Just because she was here to see Kurt didn't mean she had to ignore everyone else.

"Over here." A feeble, bony hand waved from the second bed from the end, then lowered to the starched white blankets.

Trudy willed herself to walk tile by tile to Kurt's bed and stop at the foot, by the arched metal frame of the footboard. She tried not to clamp her hand over her mouth or gasp when she saw him.

Kurt Schuler wasn't the young man she'd once known. Sunken cheeks, skin stretched taut over bones. His hand reminded her of a skeleton, covered with a layer of skin. Scars marred his once clear face. She remembered how she'd liked his strong jaw, his boyish shock of blond hair, now cropped close. Some had fallen out in patches, likely due to malnutrition. One leg was gone, with a stump left that didn't come close to matching the other side. All this she took in within a few seconds that ticked by one painful second after the other.

"Kurt, I—we've been so worried. . .all of us have been." A sob caught her throat. "I'm sorry. I wasn't going to cry. But I'm so happy you were found. . ."

He reached for her hand and she refused to let herself recoil at the boniness of its touch. "I counted every day I was captured. I think. After a while, I lost track. They fed me once a week, twice if they remembered."

"Well, you're here now, and all you have to think about is getting better." She swallowed hard. "My—my mother is here. We came because your family can't right now. . .soon, though. I needed to see you because of your last letter. I hope you got mine. . ."

"I did." She tried not to stare at his bruised face, the stitches. Her fingers felt numb in the grasp of his hand.

"Trudy, I can't promise you much more than a simple life in Fredericksburg. But even with my leg gone, I plan to walk again. I'm going to farm like my father did. He promised me at least fifty acres of my own, with peach trees, and enough space to build a house and have room for a garden." Kurt sucked in a breath then started to cough.

"Kurt. . ."

"I know I released you from our engagement, because I knew we were both so young, but now, I can't help but ask again. . ." He coughed, then spoke in a clear voice that rang out through the ward. "Gertrude Meier, will you marry me?"

"I—I—" Trudy sighed. "Oh Kurt. . ."

◆　◆　◆

Bradley had heard enough, standing in the hallway opposite Trudy's mother.

"I'm—I'm heading to my office now, Mrs. Meier. Do you think you'll be able to order a taxi to bring you to your hotel? Here." He slipped her some coins for the fare.

She nodded. "I can do that. . . Mr. Payne, I know you care for my daughter, and I know she cares for you. But right now, with Kurt coming home again, it will be very complicated for her."

He nodded. "I don't know when I'll be back." In fact, he knew he was doing the right thing by leaving for his office immediately. Part of him wanted to march into the ward and talk to the former prisoner of war, now found and returned home. But it wasn't the place or the time. Kurt Schuler wasn't the issue, either. Even without Kurt, they both had difficult decisions to make.

"I understand. It's probably best to give her some time." Mrs. Meier glanced into the ward. "I'll tell her for you."

Bradley tipped his hat to Mrs. Meier. "Thank you, ma'am."

With that, he walked away without a backward glance. Maybe this was a sign that Trudy and Kurt were meant to be together, and his own summertime affection for her had been merely a distraction. Either way, he knew she needed distance now, not two suitors pressing her, one of them barely alive.

Numbly, he took a cab back to the office and headed straight to see Frank.

"Payne, you did amazing work in Texas. I wasn't sure about letting you stay like that, but you captured the hearts of those people and shared them with us."

Frank pumped his hand and clapped him on the back. "Phenomenal work. Pulitzer worthy, and I'm not pushing it to say that, either."

You captured the hearts of those people. No, it was his heart that had been captured. Bradley rubbed his stubbled chin. He'd barely been back, only dumped off his rucksack at his desk before speeding off to the hospital with the Meier ladies.

"Thank you, sir." He blew out a pent-up breath. "So, this next frontier. Where am I headed?"

"I hope you like coconuts and pineapple, because you're going to Hawaii." Frank clapped Bradley on the back as if he'd just won a prize. "The housing isn't fancy, but you'll have room to spread out. I want you to cover the Pacific angle of the war. Keep up on the news there. Lucky dog, writing from paradise."

But paradise didn't appeal to him without Trudy by his side.

Chapter 9

Mother, I can't believe you let Bradley leave like that," Trudy said as they entered their hotel room. Small, but tidy. "I wanted to introduce him to Kurt."

"He said he needed to go to the office, and I agreed with him." Her mother set her handbag on the dresser.

"What did you tell him?"

"I told him you needed time."

"Oh Mother. I need to call him as soon as possible." Trudy found the telephone number for *This American Life* and dialed from the hotel room telephone. The efficient-sounding operator put her straight through to the editor-in-chief's office.

"Frank McAffrey's office," a woman said.

"I'm—I'm looking for one of your staff writers, Mr. Bradley Payne," said Trudy. "He's been in Texas, in my town actually, but is now back in Washington."

"Yes, he's been to the office, but he's not here at the moment."

Her hope deflated a little. "Is there a way I can leave a message for him, next time he comes by? I'm Trudy Meier, a photographer from Texas."

"You don't say." The lady rustled some papers. "Well, I'm not sure when he'll come by again. We've sent him to Hawaii. He's going to lead our Pacific division for the rest of the war."

"I—I see. Thank you anyhow."

"If he calls, I'll tell him you asked about him."

"Thank you." Trudy ended the call. Hope deflated? No, this was hope dashed to pieces. She'd wanted to tell him about Kurt, that there wasn't going to be an engagement, or a wedding. Kurt had been disappointed, but she'd sat with him for hours, talking about the goings-on in Fredericksburg. She left him with a light in his eyes and a promise to always be his friend.

She turned from the phone to see her mother standing there. "Did you reach him?"

Trudy shook her head.

"Maybe it's for the best. You don't want a man who's the leaving kind. He ought to fight for you, to stay around long enough."

"But his job—"

"His job alone means no stability." Her mother hugged her in a warm embrace, but that didn't help ease the sore spot in her heart.

Bradley Payne was gone, and he wasn't coming back.

◆　　◆　　◆

"I'm going to write every week, Tante Elsie," Bradley said to his aunt.

"I'll hold you to that promise." His voice was warm and soft. "I feel like I have my little brother back again."

"I'm glad I found the family I never knew I had for the longest time." Bradley's throat caught. He wanted to ask about Trudy, but dared not. He'd thought that he'd found someone, someone who understood what it was like to have wings, yet someone who taught him the importance of having strong roots.

"You know, your Trudy isn't getting married."

"What?"

"No. Kurt will be home in Fredericksburg soon, but Trudy told him no, that she wouldn't marry him. I think some in town were hoping they would make a match of it after all."

"Trudy. . .not married."

Tante Elsie stood and hugged him. "Well, I know you came here just to tell me good-bye, but you do know the way to her house. Go, go after her, Bradley."

"Yes, ma'am." With that, Bradley left his family's Sunday house and stepped into the sunlight.

◆　　◆　　◆

The small space of the Sunday house felt like a gaping hole that echoed with emptiness. Of course Bradley Payne had left. He'd gone on to his next story, his next big thing. Hawaii, imagine that. Briefly, Trudy had dreamed of traveling at his side as Mrs. Bradley Payne, photographing the world, yet always having Fredericksburg to return home to. He did have her address. Maybe he'd write, or send a postcard. Or something.

Trudy sank onto the bed, covered with her grandmother's quilt. "Oh Lord, I love him. So much. This came as a complete surprise to me, and even better, he's part of the Zimmermann family. . ."

She dashed away a tear. No time for tears. Now was a time to be strong, like her father had always encouraged her and Eric to be. Reality meant that sometimes things turned out, sometimes they didn't.

Enough of feeling sorry for herself. She stood, the floorboards creaking under her feet. She crossed a few steps and stopped at the table. Bradley had left pens and a bottle of ink behind. Trudy picked them up. He'd left that, plus she had a few photographs of them together. Sentimental girl. . .she allowed herself a sigh. She might as well head home.

A shadow blocked the sunlight. "Trudy—"

"Bradley." She dropped the pens and the bottle of ink, which rolled off the table. "You're—you're here? But you're supposed to be going to Hawaii."

"I am. I took a moment to stop here on the way. Out of my way, but I wanted to see Tante Elsie and Opa before I left."

"I'm sure she's happy you did." She wanted to tell him that there wasn't going to be a wedding, that she'd looked for him, and she wanted to ask him why he left that day at the hospital. But she didn't.

"My aunt told me something interesting, though." He stepped inside the Sunday house and closed the gap between them.

"What's that?"

"You're not getting married."

"No, I'm not." She shook her head. "Not to Kurt. He's a good man and has a long road to healing, but. . .but we called off the wedding before he went missing. He needs someone who'll be content to stay here, to be a farmer's wife. And, I'm not. . ."

A smile bloomed on his face, and Trudy wished she could capture the expression with her camera.

"I know it's been a fast summer for both of us, but when I met you, I felt like for the first time ever, I'd come home." Bradley took her hand. "You're beautiful, sweet, kind, and you have an adventurous spirit that pulls me along. I—I love you, and I want to spend the rest of my life with you, wherever God takes us."

"I love you, too."

He pulled her into his arms and kissed her until she was breathless. Surely, this was a dream. He released her, but still kept her in the circle of his arms. "I think we should talk to your mother."

"She'll be dubious. She thinks you're one who leaves."

"I left because of Kurt. I knew that you both had a lot to talk about, and he's been through a lot. But now that there's no Kurt. . ."

"You came back."

"I did. . .then when Tante Elsie told me you weren't getting married, I knew I had to find you." He frowned.

"What's wrong?"

"I need to be in Hawaii as soon as possible. Will you wait for me?"

Trudy shook her head. "No, I won't wait for you."

"What?"

"Because I'm coming with you, as Mrs. Bradley Payne." She kissed him back. Truly, he brought out her reckless side. No proper woman proposed to a man.

"Is that a proposal, Miss Meier?" His eyes twinkled at her.

"Indeed it is, Mr. Payne."

"Actually, I'm thinking of going by Zimmermann."

Epilogue

Nine months later

Trudy would never tire of seeing the ocean, much as she missed the hill country of Texas, and the German accents of her people. The bluebonnets of spring were vivid in her memory. But she wished she could capture the blue of the ocean to show her parents. A letter arrived from Mother every week. She'd heard from Father, who was doing well, but long past ready to return home.

Please forgive me for making things so difficult for you and Bradley. A mother only wants to protect her child. One day, I am sure you will understand, her last letter had read.

Trudy snapped another photo of a palm tree at the edge of a sandy beach, then wound the film. For a wedding present, Bradley had given her a brand-new camera.

"Are you out of film?" Bradley asked.

She nodded. "I can't wait to see how these come out." They'd turned their pantry into a darkroom, much to her delight.

"Frank is pleased as punch with your photographs, as am I." There was talk of eventually bringing *This American Life* into a color print format, one day. There was also talk of Trudy Meier Zimmermann winning a photography award as well, but Trudy wasn't thinking of that overmuch these days.

"I'm thankful that I get to do what I love, and that you and I are together in such a beautiful place like this. Our apartment isn't much to speak of. . ." She didn't mean to sound as if she were complaining, because they were often out and about on their assignments together.

"I wish it were more. . ."

"But I love it because we're together." She smiled at her husband.

Bradley kissed the tip of her nose, then touched her stomach. "Have you felt the baby move?"

"Not yet." She smiled. "It's too early. I think. My mother would know." Sometimes homesickness struck Trudy in waves, but the wonder of discovering the world around her kept that at bay most of the time. Now, she felt sickness for a different reason. Bradley had been over the moon when she told him about the baby.

"Now it's my turn with surprises." Bradley held up an envelope.

"What's that?" She reached for it, and he whipped it away from her grasp, then handed it to her with a smile, the ocean breeze ruffling his dark hair.

Trudy opened the envelope. "Plane tickets? Where are we going?" Their first stop would be Los Angeles. She didn't page through the tickets after that.

"Washington, with a detour by Texas first. I know you've been missing your family." He wrapped his arms around her and she leaned into him as they looked out at the crashing waves.

"That I have. I enjoy reading their letters, but I would love to visit before I can't travel anymore." A mother. She was going to be a mother.

He nodded. "That's what I thought. And I know just the place we can stay when we get there."

Trudy smiled up at her husband. "Our Sunday house will do just fine."

LYNETTE SOWELL

Lynette Sowell is an award-winning author with New England roots, but she makes her home in Central Texas with her husband and a herd of five cats. When she's not writing, she edits medical reports and chases down stories for the local newspaper.

A Light in the Night

by Janelle Burnham Schneider

Dedication

With love and gratitude to three very special nurses, who I am honored to call friends—
Catherine, Diane, and Cathy.
And to Mark, for all you do to help
bring my stories into being.

*"Therefore, since we are surrounded by such a great cloud
of witnesses, let us throw off everything that hinders
and the sin that so easily entangles,
and let us run with perseverance the race marked out for us.
Let us fix our eyes on Jesus,
the author and perfecter of our faith."*
HEBREWS 12:1–2 NIV

Author's Note

The Atlantic Ferry Command is a little-known part of World War II. This was the means by which men and matériel were transported from North America to England to aid on the European front. Goose Bay was only one of several locations involved in this endeavor. First the Canadians carved an airfield and supporting military base out of the wilderness of Labrador, then the Americans made their own space. Though the focus at the bases was the flights made by the Royal Air Force of England, the Royal Canadian Air Force, and the U.S. Army and Air Force, thousands of support personnel also contributed.

In *A Light in the Night*, I've chosen to highlight the efforts of the nurses who were posted at Goose Bay. Though this base was far from the front, medical services were still needed for routine ailments, as well as for the injuries sustained during the many crash landings and other accidents that occurred.

We owe just as much to those who served on this little-known base as to those who fought overseas. Without the Atlantic Ferry Command and other supporting organizations, those overseas would have had no resources for their struggle against the Axis powers.

On a personal note, this story is particularly special to me for two reasons. First, the romance between Ian and Elisabeth mirrors some of the experiences in the courtship between my husband and me. My husband, Mark, was an engineer with the Canadian Forces and, as such, spent much time away from home. From the earliest days of our romance, the moon has remained our joint symbol of our love for one another.

Second, just as I was beginning to write this story, a small hero passed from this life into the Father's arms. Grifin Alexander Rochat was born to a dear friend of mine and experienced a heart transplant at just three weeks of age. Though he fought valiantly to remain with us, his body couldn't continue the struggle. He had a true warrior's spirit. His parents and his older brother have continued to display incredible courage as they adjust to their loss.

Experiences like war and like Grifin's death sometimes cause us to ask how a God of love can permit such heartache. I have no answers. All I know is that God is faithful in all His ways, and He carries us through the storms of grief.

The cloud of witnesses to which the writer of Hebrews refers has a whole new meaning for me. I find great comfort in knowing Grifin is watching with all those who have gone before and waiting for us to join him. May we, too, be found faithful.

Janelle

Chapter 1

Accompanied by chattering coworkers, Elisabeth Baker tugged her parka hood securely over her auburn hair as she stepped outside the doors of the nurses' quarters. Here in Goose Bay, Labrador, winter's chill could freeze exposed skin in a matter of minutes. The fur around the edge of her hood shielded her face from the wind as they walked to the officers' mess.

The walk did nothing to decrease her dislike for what lay ahead. She didn't enjoy these weekly "social evenings." She preferred to watch, to observe unnoticed from the sidelines. That wasn't possible here. A collection of young men always hovered around the nurses, wanting to chat or even wanting to dance. Her adopted father would tell her it was a good "stretching" experience.

She felt the affectionate smile tug at her lips while the cold stung her cheeks. Just the thought of Papa Johan, as she called him, brought a sense of security and courage. He and Mama Glorie had always understood her shyness yet encouraged her to step beyond it. Mama would remind her of her duty. Somehow, when Mama used the word, it didn't sound like drudgery. It sounded like honor, part of the honor of being a nurse, following in Mama Glorie's footsteps and those of their nursing ancestors.

The sounds of the festivities could be heard long before Elisabeth reached the swaths of light pouring from the windows. Piano music seemed to float above the roar of conversation mingled with laughter. As she and her friends passed through the doorway, welcome warmth embraced them. The sheer volume of conversation made her think briefly of retreat. Instead, her gaze searched out other nurses while she unzipped her parka and hung it by its hood on one of the many wooden pegs that bristled from the wall.

The room was large and open. The rectangular tables that usually filled it had been stacked and pushed together along the long wall across from the main doors, to open up the floor area for dancing. One of the soldiers sat at the beat-up-looking upright piano in the corner to Elisabeth's right, providing better-quality music than often graced these gatherings. Urns of hot water for tea and fragrant coffee sat on a couple of tables against the wall to her left, along with bowls of fruit juice punch and plates of cookies. Just above the tables, a large opening allowed a view of the large kitchen area, staffed tonight by two soldiers who kept the refreshments supplied.

In the far corner, beside the refreshment tables, Elisabeth spotted the group of nurses. She threaded her way toward them, through clusters of conversing men. While her small stature made it impossible to see over the shoulders of the crowd, it also enabled her to slip through unobtrusively. By the time she reached the corner where she had seen the other women, they'd already been claimed for dances.

Dancing hadn't been part of her life before she was stationed here. Though many of her Christian friends viewed dancing as immoral, Elisabeth's reasons for not dancing were more personal. She simply didn't want a stranger holding her that close. Even though dancing was one of the few recreational options here at this remote post, she still couldn't bring herself to participate. Nevertheless, she enjoyed watching others have fun. These Friday evening socials enabled them all to put aside for a few hours the grim reality of their daily lives.

The approach of a tall, blond-haired soldier in a Canadian uniform made her palms suddenly feel clammy. She hated being invited to dance. While some accepted her gentle refusal, others became insistent. When she tried explaining that she didn't know how to dance, they offered to teach her. The situation always made her feel put on the spot. Even though her job as a nurse required that she know how to assert herself when necessary, her confidence always deserted her in social settings.

"May I bring you a cup of tea?" His bass voice penetrated through the noise around them.

Having braced herself to refuse a dancing request, she was caught off balance by his less-threatening inquiry. "S–sure," she stuttered in reply. "Uh, that would be nice."

His deep-set gray eyes softened with his smile. He gave no verbal reply, making Elisabeth feel as if he didn't fault her for her social awkwardness and perhaps even understood it. She almost laughed aloud at the thought. His blue uniform and the gold wings below his left shoulder told her he was a pilot. Pilots were known for their confidence. What would she say to him when he came back? She hoped the other nurses would return soon to carry the conversational burden.

"Do you take sugar?"

Again, his deep-voiced question made her stumble mentally. "Um, well, sometimes."

He extended the cup toward her. "In that case, this shouldn't be too offensive. I dumped a spoonful of sugar in just to be safe." His twinkling eyes invited her to share his amusement.

She felt her tension ease enough to make her smile genuine. She raised the volume of her voice to be heard. "A nurse can't be too picky about her refreshments. We learn to take whatever is available."

"Contrary to common belief, pilots are the same. One has to take whatever food and drink might be offered at a refueling stop or go hungry." He leaned back against the wall, his knees slightly bent as if he were used to relaxing without benefit of chairs. He inclined his head toward her, giving the impression he wanted to be sure to hear whatever she wanted to say next.

But nothing clever came to mind. She enjoyed the warmth of the tea as it slipped down her throat, but it wasn't worth commenting on. She could hardly tell him she felt surprised to be enjoying his company. The piano player moved easily from a familiar wartime tune to a melody Elisabeth hadn't heard before. She tilted her head, letting herself absorb the music and sensing that this tune would replay in her mind for days to come. She noticed the pilot smiling at her just before he spoke.

"Is the song a favorite of yours?"

She shook her head. "I've never heard it before. It sounds like the words would be wonderful."

"They are. Would you like to go see if they're written on the sheet music he's using?"

Nerves assaulted her again. This corner felt comfortable, unnoticed. If she followed him across the room to the piano, she would be seen. But his eyes communicated quiet encouragement as he silently extended his hand, as if inviting her to trust him. The music drew her as nothing else could have. She took a step toward him. He pushed away from the wall, grasped her elbow gently, and began to maneuver them through the crowd.

At the dancing area, her steps hesitated. The open area lay between them and piano. Crossing it meant making herself conspicuous, but gentle pressure on her elbow steadied her. Her tall companion guided her along the edge of the crowd, seeming to take care not to draw her into the dancing area. Once they reached the piano, she stood just behind and to one side of the man seated there. Her companion took up a position between her and the rest of the room. The musician slowed the tempo, clearly drawing the song to a close.

The soldier quickly reached into his pocket for a quarter and made a circling gesture with his hand, asking the musician to play the song again. The man grinned and segued from ending notes back into the introduction. Elisabeth couldn't help but smile. She felt almost as if she were back home, singing beside the piano with Mama Glorie while Papa Johan accompanied them, adding his bass to their higher voices.

Now as she read the words on the sheet music, the pilot's strong, deep voice began singing along in perfect pitch.

Early in childhood, she'd learned to harmonize with her parents. Since the pilot was carrying the melody of this song, she quietly found a simple, high soprano harmony to add to the refrain.

"No matter where I go you'll be with me in my soul.
Though we have to part for now in our hearts we're never far.
When I see the sun, I'll feel your smile.
When I look at the moon, I'll think of you."

Their voices blended so perfectly that her gaze sought his in pure surprise. They maintained eye contact throughout the refrain, then Elisabeth had to turn back to the sheet music for the words to the next verse, which they sang in unison. The din in the room slowly faded to a listening silence. Elisabeth didn't realize they'd become the focus of attention until the second verse. She hated the tremble in her voice. Her singing partner shifted slightly closer to her and put a reassuring hand at the small of her back. Somehow it steadied her. The pianist must have felt the mood in the room as well, because he didn't end the song but took them through the refrain two more times. As the final notes of music hovered in the air, applause swept through the room. Elisabeth felt a blush heat her face. When the clapping subsided, she offered a smile and inclined her head graciously. No matter how much she disliked being on display, she could do no less than acknowledge the appreciation.

To her immense relief, she felt the pilot's hand at her elbow, guiding her toward the exit. She reached for her coat, and he took it from her fingers to hold while she slipped her arms into the sleeves. As she zipped it and slipped the hood into place, he shrugged into his own coat.

The cold struck her face like so many invisible needles as they stepped into the starlit night. He guided her around the edge of the building, where they were sheltered from the blast of the wind.

The cold felt tolerable here, even welcome after the heat of being on display. She couldn't believe she'd followed this man into the seclusion of the dark outdoors, but his presence felt more sheltering than the noise and crowd indoors.

After a few moments of silence, he commented, "Now that we can hear each other clearly, introductions might be in order. I'm Ian MacDonald."

She had to tilt her head back to look up into his face. "I'm Elisabeth Baker."

"Too bad we already have jobs." Even in the darkness of the northern evening, she could see the humor in his eyes. "I think we could go on the road as a singing team."

"Not me." She shook her hooded head. "I like to sing, but only in private."

"I guessed as much." He reassured her with a smile that seemed to come from his heart. "You were very courageous in there."

"Courageous?" Conviction made her voice more forceful than usual. "That was just manners. It would have been rude to turn my back on the appreciation they were showing. No, courage is what I see every day at work when young men struggle to recover from injuries they shouldn't have in the first place."

"I haven't thought much about the hospital, to be honest. Is it busy?"

"It seems like we always have at least half the beds filled with routine afflictions—flu, pneumonia, frostbite, and various injuries."

"I guess this far from the front, you wouldn't see many battle wounds."

"For which I'm grateful," she responded fervently. "It's bad enough seeing the casualties from crash landings. You'd know as well as anyone about the number of planes that miss the runway, or slide off the end, or otherwise end up in a heap. One of these days, someone is going to get killed." She could hear the emotion in her own voice and fell silent. She was here to serve, not give commentary.

"Any part of war is risky, even being part of the supply line," Ian remonstrated softly. "We all know that's part of the package."

"It still doesn't make it right."

"Do you also see that it's necessary?"

The gentleness in his voice made her want to confide her distress. Their purpose here haunted her day and night. She'd come because it was part of her responsibility with the Red Cross. In no way, however, did it make her a believer in the "cause." But this wasn't the time for her to voice those thoughts. Instead, she deliberately shifted the subject. "I'd rather hear about your family."

He looked off into the distance with tenderness in his expression. "My mom, Sarah, is a widow from the Great War. My dad was killed toward the end. She supported us by working in a bakery. I have younger twin sisters, Megan and Millicent. Megan's fiancé is an infantryman overseas. How about your family?"

"I'm an only child, adopted. My adoptive dad, Papa Johan, is a veteran of the Great War and has worked ever since as a politician. My adoptive mother, Mama Glorie, was an army nurse in the Great War and still works as a nurse."

"Is that why you became an army nurse?"

"Actually, I'm not real army. I trained under the Red Cross. But when America joined the war, all qualified Red Cross nurses were automatically enlisted in the U. S. Army Nurse Corps. It's not my choice, but it is my duty."

"Which brings me back to my original question. Don't you see that our being here is necessary?"

Apparently this man could be stubborn as well as charming. "I know our governments think it's necessary. My belief is that war is never necessary. If people want peace badly enough, they can always find a way."

The pilot turned to face her directly. "May I tell you how I see it?"

She nodded again.

"We didn't seek out this war—not Canada, not the United States, not Britain. Britain was forced to defend itself, and Canada's loyalty to Britain made her a part of it as well. The U.S. suffered an unprovoked attack by Japan, and she had no choice but to become part of the conflict. We're in it because we have to be, not because we want to be."

The intensity of her feelings forced her to speak. "I'm not questioning our involvement but rather the war itself. It's so senseless. How many people are losing their lives, or their health, because of the Axis' determination to control the world? What's the point of it all?" Her voice broke. Silently, she berated herself for even opening the conversation. Why bare her heart like this when she knew he'd never understand?

He remained silent for a long time. Finally he inquired in a soft, yet respectful voice, "Elisabeth, are you a believer?"

"Yes, I am. Why do you ask?"

"I wanted to be sure we have the same frame of reference." He turned to face her and took both her mittened hands in his own. "Since we believe in Jesus as Savior, we also have to believe in God as the Controller of all things. We don't know why He allows the things He allows, but we can be at peace knowing He is in control."

She shook her head in disagreement. "That's not good enough for me. I believe He is in control, but I want to know why He doesn't stop it."

Again he didn't respond immediately. Finally, he shrugged. "I can't even pretend to have an answer for that, Elisabeth. For me, it's enough to be doing what I can to help stop the war. I wish I could give you answers, but since I can't, I'll offer to pray until peace comes to you. In the meantime, I'd better get you back to where it's warm. Shall we return to the mess or would you rather go back to your barracks?"

"The barracks, please." She appreciated his perception of her mood. She needed quiet now, not a noisy roomful of people. To her surprise, he kept her hand tucked in the crook of his elbow and let the walk pass in silence. When they reached the nurses' quarters, she smiled up at him. "Thank you for listening and for the company."

"My pleasure." A smile lit his face once more, as if he'd just thought of a wonderful secret. He saluted her then walked away into the night.

Chapter 2

Elisabeth woke at reveille the next morning, feeling as if she'd barely slept. Her conversation with the tall pilot had replayed itself in her dreams. It wasn't typical of her to voice her thoughts, and especially not to someone she barely knew. What was it about the Canadian that had drawn such openness from her?

She thought back over the evening as she loosened the braid that had confined her long, heavy hair while she slept. The words to the song she'd learned began to replace her self-conscious thoughts, and she found herself humming the poignant tune. As always, picking up the silver-backed brush from her dresser top made her think of home. The brush had been a Christmas gift from Papa Johan and Mama Glorie, and it matched the silver picture frame that always stood beside it. The frame held a sketch of a curly haired tot and a woman smiling at one another. The love between the two glowed from the picture. Elisabeth slid her fingers over the images, giving thanks yet again for Papa Johan's artistic skill. He'd drawn the portrait of Elisabeth and her mother, Grace, in the hospital where he'd been recovering from war injuries. Just weeks later, both of Elisabeth's birth parents succumbed to the flu epidemic. She paused to say a quick prayer for the health, safety, and happiness of her adoptive parents. Then, as she began to brush her hair, her gaze drifted to the small metal brooch pinned to her dresser scarf.

Shaped like the lamp carried by every nurse's heroine, Florence Nightingale, it had been created by Elisabeth's great-grandfather. Elisabeth's adoptive mother, Glorie, had inherited the pin, and had presented it to Elisabeth just before her departure for Happy Valley-Goose Bay. More than anything, Elisabeth wanted to live up to the traditions of dedication and service it represented. How could she be worthy of it with so many questions in her soul? She wished she could replace the questions with certainty as easily as she replaced her nightclothes with her nursing uniform.

With the ease of frequent repetition, she gathered her hair into a low ponytail at her nape, then twisted the hair into a tidy bun on the back of her head. A few pins secured it. She set her white nursing cap in place and secured it as well.

She checked her appearance in the mirror one final time. To her relief, none of her doubts showed in her blue eyes. Instead, a competent-looking nurse stared back at her. Her soul might not be as steady as Mama Glorie's, but her appearance was every bit as professional. The thought brought a smile to her lips as she bundled into her army-issue Arctic parka and boots.

From her first day on duty she had enjoyed the short walk from the nurses' barracks to the hospital. The distance was just long enough for her to enjoy a bit of fresh air and yet short enough that walking on even the coldest days wasn't unbearable. At ten minutes to seven, she saluted her nursing supervisor. "Good morning, Captain."

"Good morning, Lieutenant." Of average height, Captain Thompson had straight, graying hair that seemed always to be perfectly ordered beneath her nursing cap. Laugh lines around her brown eyes indicated a sense of humor Elisabeth had seen only rarely. Most of the time, the captain projected an image of military precision that made Elisabeth feel like a stumbling recruit. "It was a quiet night, so I sent the night nurses home a few minutes early."

"Yes, ma'am." Elisabeth saluted again as a third nurse, Sandra Carter, arrived. She and Elisabeth shared the same rank, so the salute wasn't strictly necessary. However, Elisabeth didn't want to neglect any detail in Captain Thompson's presence.

Lieutenant Carter had received her training through the Army Nurse Corps, so she had as much military training as medical. She and Elisabeth had become friends soon after Elisabeth's arrival, and she had helped Elisabeth adapt to the military environment. With blond curly hair, which often escaped its confining twist, and twinkling green eyes, she had an air of relaxed confidence that always put Elisabeth at ease. For the next four days, the two women would work the same shifts. Elisabeth enjoyed working with the tall nurse. When their duties allowed, they often traded confidences, which made Elisabeth feel as though Sandra were the sister she'd often craved.

But today gave them no time for confidences. They served breakfast to the six patients under their care, and by lunchtime, a series of accidents had filled the ward to capacity. Two soldiers had encountered "soft ice" on the lake and were brought in with hypothermia. A plane returning from a reconnaissance mission over the Atlantic missed the end of the runway, resulting in broken bones for all four crew members. The navigator had escaped the plane first but returned to drag the pilot from the burning wreckage. The pilot had a few minor burns on his face, but the navigator's hands were much more severely burned. A pneumonia case and two men suffering dehydration from the flu filled the remaining beds.

"The nurses on Ward A are just as busy," Captain Thompson informed them. "It looks like influenza has hit the Signal Detachment hard."

Elisabeth felt grateful for the busyness. The tall pilot and their conversation the previous evening kept returning to her thoughts. Something about him piqued her interest beyond anything she'd ever experienced. But the demands of the day forced her to focus on other things, enabling her to ignore the strange attraction. By the end of the eight-hour shift, she wanted nothing more than to prop her aching feet on a stool and just sit still. The next shift of nurses arrived, she and

Sandra gave them an overview of the patients, and then the two women walked together back to the barracks.

"Any plans for tonight?" Sandra asked with an odd gleam in her eyes.

Elisabeth laughed in spite of her exhaustion. "Yes. I have a hot date with my footstool and a shower. Cynthia is away, so I have the room to myself."

"Where is she off to this time?"

"She left yesterday for Iceland to airlift some patients to Halifax."

"Hmm. Maybe you should have become a flight nurse." Sandra grinned at Elisabeth, her eyes dancing with mischief. "You might have met your pilot sooner."

"My pilot?" Elisabeth tried to stem the blush that warmed her cheeks.

Sandra winked at her. "I hear you two made quite an impression in the mess last night. I'm sorry I missed it. I figure he has to be someone special if he got you to come out of your corner."

From anyone else, the comment could have been hurtful. But Elisabeth knew Sandra understood her shyness. In fact, the other nurse often deflected attention away from Elisabeth when she sensed Elisabeth's discomfort in social situations. Elisabeth shrugged and grinned back. "He bribed me with that song. I'd never heard it before, and the music was wonderful. He suggested we go look at the words, and the next thing I knew I was singing along with him. I didn't realize everyone was listening until it was too late to stop."

Sandra put an arm across Elisabeth's shoulders in a quick hug. "Good for you! From what I heard, you two sounded great together."

Elisabeth shrugged. "He's with the Canadian Air Force, so it's not like he'll be at our mess on a regular basis."

"Maybe so, maybe not," Sandra replied cryptically, reaching for the door of the barracks building. "Do you feel like playing some Ping-Pong later?"

"Sure. You know I'm always ready for a game."

On either side of the entry area a long hallway led to nurses' quarters. Sandra's room lay down the hallway on the left, while Elisabeth's was on the right. Elisabeth looked forward to what promised to be a quiet afternoon and evening. She opened the door and almost stepped on a folded white piece of paper that lay just beyond the threshold. She unfolded the paper to reveal small, neat printing.

Dear Lt. Baker:

Please do me the honor of accompanying me to dinner in the Canadian offi-cers' mess tonight at 1900 hours. With your consent, I will provide transporta-tion at 1830 hours.

Sincerely,
Ian MacDonald

A thrill shot through her, quickly replaced by trepidation. Why did he want to seek her out? She noticed the absence of rank in his signature, seeming to put their fledgling acquaintance on a personal level. Yet, the respect in his form of address showed he didn't want to presume anything, either. It conveyed a comfortable balance between formality and friendship. But of all the nurses he could have invited, why her?

She pondered the invitation while she traded her uniform for her flannel housecoat, then slipped down the hallway to the communal shower room at the end of the barracks. With a plastic cap covering her hair, she enjoyed a quick but warm shower that eased the day's tightness out of her muscles. Back in her room, she stretched out on her bed for a rest. What would she do about the pilot's invitation? Her impulse was to turn it down. She had no way of making contact with him before his arrival at 6:30, but she could easily leave a note for him taped to the front door.

Yet just as her thoughts had been pulled toward memories of their meeting last night, so now a strange sort of instinct pulled at her to accept the invitation. She argued with herself that she'd already made plans with Sandra. The strange "something" argued back that Sandra wouldn't mind the change in plans—would, in fact, encourage it.

With a grunt of frustration, she stood up. She might as well talk it over with Sandra right away. She wouldn't be able to relax until she'd made her decision. Regulations permitted the wearing of civilian clothing within the barracks, so she pulled on a white turtleneck sweater, navy wool pants, navy socks, and white tennis shoes. Around her hairline, wisps of hair had curled from the steam of her shower, but her hair remained tidy enough for a visit to the other nurse's room. She grabbed the paper off her bed and hurried down the hallway.

She found her friend lounging in her housecoat, a book in hand. "What story are you into now?" she teased.

"Nothing I can't put aside for you." Sandra closed the book and set it on her dresser. "It must be important to bring you out of your room before supper. Sit down, honey." She patted the edge of her bed.

"I found this under my door after our shift ended." She held out the note, and Sandra took it. Elisabeth remained silent while Sandra read. At Sandra's wide smile, Elisabeth held up a cautioning hand. "Don't jump to conclusions. He's invited me for dinner, that's all. Not a one of us nurses goes a week without at least one dinner invitation. It's part of being only a handful of women among thousands of men."

Sandra raised her eyebrows. "Which explains why a Canadian pilot seeks out an American nurse and offers to take her to his mess?"

Elisabeth shrugged, willing down the blush that warmed her face again. "How do I know what he's thinking?"

"That's not as important as what *you're* thinking. The fact you're even considering this invitation tells me there's some kind of spark between you two."

"He just wants to be friends, that's all." She accepted the paper as Sandra returned it to her.

"How many dates have you had?" Sandra's gaze turned perceptive.

"You mean invitations or dates I've accepted?"

Sandra's smile was indulgent. "Ones you've accepted."

"Just here at Goose Bay or in general?"

"You're stalling, my friend." Sandra stood and beckoned Elisabeth to take the chair, then began rubbing the other woman's shoulders. "How many dates have you actually accepted in your lifetime?"

"None." She felt ashamed to admit she'd never participated in an activity that seemed a normal and frequent part of many people's lives.

"How many invitations have you received?" Sandra's fingers worked at a particularly tight spot beside Elisabeth's neck.

"I don't keep track."

"And that's my point," her friend offered. "You never lack for attention from men, but you always turn it away. For the first time since I met you, you're actually thinking about going on a date. Not only are you considering spending time with someone you barely know, but you're even willing to go somewhere unfamiliar. It seems to me your heart might be speaking louder than your brain."

Heart? What did her heart have to do with it? Heart implied affection, and affection could lead to falling in love. There was no way Elisabeth wanted to let her emotions get entangled. But if she voiced that resolution, Sandra would grill her about her reasons, and she wasn't ready for that. "How can my heart have anything to do with this? I met him just last night."

"He's obviously smitten with you. Sometimes the best things in our lives happen in mere moments. So, are you going?"

"I don't know." Elisabeth took in a deep breath then let it out slowly. "You and I already had plans for the evening."

Sandra laughed as she moved around to sit on the edge of her bed. "As if those plans were anything special. Girl, you have a chance to spend time with a man who must appeal to you in some way. Just go with it. Besides, I've decided I'm too tired for Ping-Pong tonight. After you leave to get ready for your date, I might just lay down for a nap and let myself sleep right through supper." She tried to pull her face into an exhausted expression, but her eyes twinkled.

Elisabeth couldn't help but laugh. "As if you've ever slept through any meal!" She sobered. "This must be another of those experiences that my Papa Johan calls a 'stretching experience.' I can't say I enjoy them."

"Silly woman!" Sandra leaned forward to give Elisabeth a quick hug. "It's just dinner and some pleasant conversation, not ward inspection. Go and let yourself have a good time." She stretched out on her bed. "I'm going to sleep."

Elisabeth left her friend's room, wishing her decision were as simple as Sandra made it sound. Yes, a part of her felt drawn to the tall, charismatic pilot. But she didn't want to be. She wanted no attachment to any soldier. If she fell in love then lost her love to this horrible war, she doubted she'd ever recover. Better to stay firmly unattached until the world returned to normal.

She changed back into her housecoat and lay down on her bed. Pulling a wool, army-issue blanket over herself, she snuggled down into her pillow, willing her body to relax for a nap. If she woke in time to get ready, she might just take this adventure. If she didn't, then Ian MacDonald would arrive to pick her up and would probably assume she'd had to work. But that was the cowardly way out. It would also show lack of respect for a fellow officer and, even worse, an officer from another army. Her integrity rebelled against the thought.

Two choices remained—compose a note of regret for him or get dressed to accompany him. Both options gave her the jitters. Slowly she remembered Papa Johan's advice. How often she'd seen him wrestling with difficult choices in his diplomatic career. "I just need to listen to my heart," he'd say. "The still small voice of God will tell me what to do." Then he'd lie down on the sofa in their living room and close his eyes. She and Mama Glorie knew not to disturb him when he lay in that pose. Rarely did more than half an hour pass before his eyes would open. He'd look at Mama Glorie and say, "I see the clear path."

As Elisabeth was growing up and she faced her own difficult decisions, neither he nor Mama Glorie dispensed advice. Papa Johan would always ask, "What is your heart telling you?" Her heart had led her first to train as a nurse and then to join the Red Cross. Even though service in the Red Cross had then required that she become part of the Army Nursing Corps, she still knew her choices had been right.

But now she faced a different kind of decision. This wasn't so much about her future as about vulnerability. She closed her eyes and willed her thoughts to still. She could remain emotionally safe and turn down the pilot's invitation. She imagined herself writing the note then spending the evening quietly with some of her coworkers. The prospect held appeal, except she knew she'd wonder how the evening could have turned out. What if she never experienced a second opportunity to get to know Ian MacDonald? That thought filled her with unease.

What if she "took her courage in hand" as Mama Glorie would say and accepted the invitation? It would mean unfamiliar people in an unfamiliar setting. Not her favorite way to spend an evening, but it would also mean a chance to find new friendship. As much as she felt terrified, she also felt a tingling anticipation.

Kind of like the day she started nurses' training. And like the day she boarded the plane to come to Goose Bay.

She saw a clear path. . .with Ian MacDonald as her dinner companion this evening. She couldn't predict where the path would lead, nor did she think she wanted to try. It would take all her courage to follow her heart just for tonight.

Chapter 3

I an escorted her to a small round table. Elisabeth couldn't decide whether she felt relieved or disappointed when she noticed another Canadian officer obviously waiting for them. He wore a clerical collar, indicating his status as a chaplain. She felt even more intrigued by her companion—an outgoing, confident pilot who shared a close friendship with a chaplain.

Apparently, the same standards of informality existed in the Canadian officers' mess as in the American, as the men did not exchange salutes. The chaplain stood as they approached, and the pilot made introductions. "Miss Baker, I'd like to introduce my friend, Don Landry. Don, this is Miss Elisabeth Baker, with the U.S. Army Nursing Corps."

"Pleased to meet you, Miss Baker," the dark-haired chaplain replied, extending his hand to shake hers. "I hope you don't mind that we don't use rank here in the mess. It's a neutral environment, so we don't have to keep track of protocol." Standing, the top of his head barely reached the pilot's shoulder. Dark eyes and a swarthy cast to his skin indicated native heritage. His gaze held a sturdy peace that intrigued Elisabeth.

She felt immediately at ease with his soft-spoken manner. "It's the same in our mess, Chaplain. It's nice to have a place to get to know one another as people, rather than just as officers."

"Then in that case, I'd like you to feel free to call me Don. Chaplain sounds just as formal as Captain."

"Don it is, then." She wondered if she should invite him to use her first name as well, but the moment was interrupted by the arrival of their server with steaming plates of food. The server departed, and Elisabeth felt no surprise when both men bowed their heads. She joined them. Don offered a quick and quiet blessing over their food, concluding with, "And we ask for a speedy ending to this conflict in which we feel compelled to take part and for Your peace and comfort to sustain those who have already lost loved ones because of it." She added a heartfelt amen to his.

The three of them enjoyed easy conversation over the thick slabs of meat loaf which turned out to be more flavorful than she expected. The canned green beans were just as mushy as those served in the American mess, confirming her opinion that canned vegetables simply couldn't be made appealing. A well-roasted potato rounded out the meal.

Elisabeth had never felt so comfortable around new acquaintances. Before the plates had been half emptied, she discovered she could easily address each of the men by first name, and she invited them to use hers. Don's use of her name felt comforting, while every time Ian said it, a strange tingle ran down her spine. By the time dessert arrived—squares of chocolate cake accompanied by scoops of ice cream—she found herself able to voice the question that refused to leave her alone.

"Don, how do you reconcile the concept of God's love with this awful war?" She hoped she hadn't offended Ian. A quick glance at his face showed his empathy for her quandary.

The chaplain, or padre, as she'd heard others in the mess address him, didn't answer immediately. He studied her face for a moment, then dropped his gaze downward as if looking deep inside himself for the right words. "To be honest, Elisabeth, I don't think there is an answer to that question. If I could explain everything about God, He wouldn't be any bigger than my concept of Him. As participants in this war, we simply have to hang on to faith."

The initial question had fallen from her lips as a theoretical discussion. Now she wished she'd kept her mouth shut. The food she'd just eaten turned to an indigestible lump in her middle. As much as she wanted now to change the subject, she somehow couldn't hold back the disgraceful admission. "Sometimes I wonder if I have any faith left."

"Do you still love Him?" Don's tone held nothing but kindness.

Again, she glanced at Ian to see what his reaction might be to this conversation that had suddenly turned very personal. The encouragement in his eyes made her feel as though anything she said next would be accepted and understood.

She had no doubt what her answer would be. "Yes, I do. I don't know how I'd get along without knowing Him."

"Do you believe that He loves you?"

"Oh, yes." Mama Glorie and Papa Johan not only had taught her of God's love but had lived it before her so convincingly that she was as certain of His love as of theirs. "But that's where I stumble. If He loves all of mankind as I know He loves me, then how can He permit the killing and suffering?"

Again Don fell silent for a time. When he looked back at her, there was deep compassion in his eyes. "I could talk to you about how God lets each of us make our own choices and suffer the consequences, but I don't think it would answer your questions. I suspect you already understand the concept of free will. Sometimes we can only cling to what we do know of Him and leave what we don't know in His hands."

"Leaving it is the hard part," Ian put in. "It's not easy for me to let go of something I can't understand or resolve."

"Of course it's not," Don offered with a teasing smile. "We all like to feel we understand and are in control of our circumstances, but I think you pilots have it worse than the rest of us."

Ian accepted the good-natured jab with a chuckle. "No comment."

The conversation drifted into easier topics. Elisabeth enjoyed watching the interplay between her two companions. Their rapport spoke of more than acquaintance by circumstance. "How did you two meet?" she finally asked.

They looked at each other and started laughing simultaneously. "We happened to be on a military flight together," Don explained. "We were seated across the aisle from each other, and Ian was as nervous a passenger as any I've ever seen. I finally asked him if his pilot's wings were fake."

She could hardly envision the scenario they described. "You're honestly not pulling my leg?"

"Padres don't lie," Don informed her solemnly.

"Though they might exaggerate," Ian added. "I wasn't as bad as he describes."

Don merely raised his eyebrows in unspoken question.

Ian lifted his chin and asserted, "I wasn't nervous. I simply wasn't used to not being in the cockpit."

Don turned to Elisabeth. "What were we saying about being in control?"

"Don't you have to be somewhere in ten minutes?" Ian asked, but with a smile that assured Elisabeth he could poke fun at himself.

Don grinned back. "Honesty hurts, doesn't it, pal? But sadly, you're right. I promised to meet someone at 2030 hours. It was good to meet you, Elisabeth, and I hope you'll be our guest here again soon."

Somehow Elisabeth didn't feel awkward being alone with Ian. In fact, it felt very right. "I enjoyed meeting your friend."

"Don is one of the best," Ian replied, his words underlined by the deep feeling in his eyes. "He helps keep me from getting that overconfidence pilots are famous for."

Elisabeth smiled, thinking of some of the pilots she'd encountered. One in particular had pestered her with invitations for weeks, unable to believe she honestly didn't want to socialize with him. The memory brought to mind an audacious question. "What would you have done if I hadn't been waiting outside for you?"

His eyes twinkled. "I wondered myself. I thought I might stand outside and serenade you until you'd be forced to come out just to make me shut up."

"Good plan," she acknowledged with a mockingly solemn nod. "One small problem—my room is on the opposite side of the barracks from the front door. I likely would not have heard you."

"Hmmm." He appeared to be thinking deeply. "I suppose I could have stormed the barracks, then."

"Even bigger problem." Elisabeth felt a full-fledged laugh building in her throat. "Captain Thompson would have skinned you alive."

"She's not in awe of pilots?"

"Captain Thompson isn't in awe of anybody but God, as nearly as I can tell." The laughter in Ian's eyes enticed a story from her. "She's the nursing superintendent at the base hospital. She was a nurse in the Great War and is as tough as an old sailor. Just a couple of weeks ago, we had a two-star general come for a base inspection. He's also a veteran from the last war, and everybody is scared of him. He's been known to strip his officers' rank for saluting improperly. He had airsickness on the way here. From what I heard, he just about passed out leaving the plane. He absolutely refused to come to the hospital for examination, so Captain Thompson went to see him. I didn't get to witness the encounter, but the captain returned with the general meekly in tow. He was badly dehydrated, and she had him in bed sipping fluids in less time than it took us to realize what she'd done. Apparently, she convinced him that Allied defeat was imminent if he didn't allow himself to be treated."

He grinned. "She runs a tight ship, then?"

Elisabeth basked in his appreciation as she nodded. "She's good to work for because we always know what's expected—nothing less than our best. She's quite strict about the rules in the barracks, but only because she feels they make us better nurses."

"Like what?"

"One example that really rankles some of the other girls is that she frowns on civilian clothes, even in the barracks. The official rules say we can wear them in the privacy of our rooms and between each others' rooms, but she prefers we be in uniform all the time."

"Does she have uniform pajamas?"

Ian's mischievous eyes made Elisabeth feel like laughing again. "No one has seen her out of uniform, so we have no way of knowing. We suspect she does, though."

He responded with a story about someone similar he had met, and their conversation flowed effortlessly from there. Elisabeth had never enjoyed such comfortable interaction with anyone outside her family.

As she lay in bed later that evening, she could still feel the warm companionship she'd sensed at supper, the feeling of absolute safety. Her last thought before sleep was, *I could even let him teach me to dance.*

Chapter 4

As Elisabeth expected, Sandra stood waiting beside the front doors the next morning. "Since we're going to the same place, I figured we might as well walk together," she announced in what seemed to be a casual manner.

Elisabeth knew better. "Besides, if we're busy at work today, this will be your only chance to find out about my dinner last night."

Sandra winked at her. "Absolutely right. So, tell all. Quick, before we get there."

"He took me to dinner where we were joined by his friend, who is a chaplain. The three of us talked. He brought me back here. The end."

"Oooh. This is good. He's introducing you to his friends already. Way to go, Elisabeth."

For the first time since meeting her, Elisabeth found Sandra's enthusiasm bothersome. She didn't want to think about last night in the context of a date. It had been a pleasant evening with friends. Nothing more.

The rest of the day and the two that followed were too busy for contemplative thoughts. No sooner did one patient become healthy enough to be discharged than two more took his place. She felt like she started each shift on the run and didn't stop until she reached her room nine hours later. Sandra seemed to sense she shouldn't push discussions about Ian, enabling Elisabeth to stay silent on the subject. Yet in the privacy of her room before sleep overtook her each night, her thoughts were anything but silent. She had enjoyed the evening with Ian and Don more than she thought possible. She thought a lot about Don's comments about faith, but it was Ian's smile that drifted through her dreams.

Monday was her last day on morning shift, which gave her twenty-four hours before she had to report for duty at 1500 hours on Tuesday. She luxuriated in the extra sleep. After waking, she stayed in her room in her bathrobe and crocheted slippers. Cynthia had returned from her overseas mission the night before, but she always took care to give Elisabeth solitude on her mornings off. Elisabeth revelled in the privacy. She pulled a chair close to her bed so she could prop her feet on the edge. Using a book as a lap desk, she wrote to her parents about meeting both Ian and Don. She carefully screened out any references to her feelings about the war in general, limiting herself to closing with a quote from Don's prayer.

I pray, as I'm sure you do, for a speedy end to this conflict in which we feel compelled to take part, and for God's peace and comfort to sustain those who have already lost loved ones because of it.

> With all my love,
> Elisabeth

With an hour yet before lunch, she decided to take a walk. She rebraided her hair and wrapped the braid around her head, securing the end with pins. She pulled on the navy wool sweater issued for Arctic wear, as well as pile-lined trousers, Arctic boots, and her parka. Snugging a wool knit toque over her head, she then pulled the fur-trimmed hood of her parka into place.

The day was stunningly beautiful. Bright sunshine didn't occur often here at Goose Bay, but today the clouds had parted. Sunlight glinted off ice particles in the snow, creating a brightness that demanded sunglasses. She set off away from the hospital; she saw that view often enough. Today her feet led her toward the airfield before she realized the direction they had chosen. Even after she became aware, she couldn't muster the resolve to turn around. She wouldn't be looking for Ian, she reasoned, especially since she stood no realistic chance of meeting up with him. She was simply taking a walk.

She reached the edge of the airfield, which vibrated with activity. On the distant runways, she saw planes landing and taking off. Numerous vehicles maneuvered around the various buildings and parked aircraft, and even more people hustled here and there. While at first glance the scene seemed to be one of confusion, it took only moments for her to feel the sense of purpose throbbing in the air. As she watched, an awareness began to grow in her. For the eight months that she'd been here, her focus had been limited to the sick and the injured. Her profession demanded that focus.

But here on the edge of the heart of Goose Bay, she could acknowledge her world as just a small part of the overall work accomplished at this location. The bombers and fighters using the runways so continuously were desperately needed in skies far distant from where she stood. It required an immense amount of manpower to accomplish that objective. Her role was to help the personnel involved when their bodies succumbed to illness or injury. Turning back toward the base with a lighter heart, she sensed a faint understanding of a brand-new perspective. Rather than seeing her patients as victims of wretched circumstance, perhaps she'd now be able to view them as important elements in an effort much bigger than any one person or country. Her work wasn't so much rescue from misfortune as it was enabling her patients to take their part in the bigger purpose.

Those thoughts carried her through four more busy days. Though she worked with Sandra on Wednesday and Thursday, they had little time for mundane conversation. They usually ate dinner together in the dining room and enjoyed games with the other nurses in the evening, but there was no opportunity for the exchange of confidences. Elisabeth felt relieved. She'd seen or heard nothing from Ian all week. She told herself she didn't mind, that there was nothing between them other than casual acquaintanceship. Still, when Friday came, she felt a twinge of regret that she wouldn't be off duty until 2300 hours. Not that she would seriously consider going to the evening social, even if work were not a factor. She refused to start pining for someone she'd met only twice.

Still, she couldn't deny that she missed him. She kept reminding herself that it wasn't likely she'd ever see him again, stationed at different bases as they were. Saturday brought another shift change, this time to night shift. Though she felt exhausted by the time she got off work Sunday morning at 0800 hours, she set her alarm to wake her in time for the service at the chapel at 1100 hours. It wouldn't be easy to stay awake, but she needed the spiritual sustenance.

She slipped into a back pew a few minutes late. The congregation had already begun singing the opening hymn, "Great Is Thy Faithfulness." It was a favorite of Papa Johan's and brought tears to her eyes. She felt in her soul that this was part of what Don had talked about at dinner the week before—God's faithfulness in spite of inexplicable circumstances. The chaplain's message came from the text in Joshua 1:6, "Be strong and of a good courage." After the service, she remained in her seat for awhile, mulling over what she'd heard.

"Good afternoon, Lieutenant."

The familiar voice both startled and delighted her. "Captain MacDonald! I didn't expect to see you here."

"I'm sure you didn't." The smile that had danced through many of her dreams lit his face. "I just thought I'd pop over here this morning to see if I might catch up with you."

Elisabeth's weariness fell away. "I got off night shift at 0800, so I might not be the best companion."

A throat-clearing to her left attracted her attention. Somehow Sandra had slipped up beside her without Elisabeth knowing it. "Captain MacDonald, this is my friend, Lt. Sandra Carter. Sandra, this is Capt. Ian MacDonald, pilot with the Royal Canadian Air Force."

The two shook hands, and Sandra offered, "Would you join us for lunch, Captain?"

Elisabeth looked at her in shock and dismay. While they were permitted to invite guests for meals in the nurses' dining room, she didn't feel ready to bring Ian as "her" guest. She knew some of the nurses would jump to conclusions, and she would become the focus of attention.

As if understanding Elisabeth's thoughts, Sandra added, "You can be my guest, and no one will know you're really here to see Elisabeth."

The comment made Elisabeth's face flame, even while she was grateful for the intervention.

"I won't be keeping you up when you should be sleeping, will I?" Ian inquired of Elisabeth, genuine concern in his eyes.

She managed a smile. "I have to eat anyway, and you're welcome to join us."

◆　◆　◆

As she had expected, Ian's presence did attract attention. Worse yet, Captain Thompson joined the gathering. Everyone sat around one large table, with Captain Thompson at one end. After being introduced to Captain MacDonald by Sandra, she invited Ian to sit opposite her at the other end. Sandra quietly suggested Elisabeth sit to his left, and she took the seat across the table to his right.

Lively conversation swirled around the table as the other nurses directed a multitude of questions and comments at Ian. He fielded them all with both respect and laughter. Elisabeth watched in awe. Had she been in his position, she knew she would have been a stammering mess. Every once in awhile, he glanced her way with the slightest of winks, just enough to let her know he remained aware of her.

The meal concluded when Captain Thompson left the room. The nurses on afternoon shift departed shortly afterward. Elisabeth knew Sandra also needed to leave for her shift but appreciated her continued presence as a buffer until everyone else had left. At long last, the other nurses drifted over to the recreation room, leaving Ian, Sandra, and Elisabeth alone in the dining room.

"Thank you for the lovely lunch, ladies. I felt like a rooster in a henhouse, but it was fun." Ian turned to Elisabeth. "Thank you for keeping yourself awake. I'll leave so you can get to bed, but I'll be in touch."

Elisabeth walked him to the front door. When it closed behind him, she turned back to find Sandra still watching.

For once, Sandra's face looked solemn. "I hope someday someone looks at me the way Captain MacDonald looks at you." She held up a hand to stop Elisabeth's protest. "I know you think you don't want this. But consider carefully. What's budding between you two is too precious to throw away just because you might lose it."

Chapter 5

Pure physical exhaustion caused Elisabeth to drop into slumber, but she slept lightly. Cynthia tiptoed into their room and back out again, and other nurses murmured in the hallway. But all of those disturbances were minor compared to her inner restlessness over Sandra's parting words. Was there really something special between herself and Ian? If so, did she want it or, worse yet, did she even have a choice?

She dragged herself to the ward for duty at 2300 hours. Three nurses typically covered both wards for the night shift. As the junior nurse, Elisabeth moved back and forth between the wards as necessary. In spite of a heavy patient load, the night was quiet enough to allow her thoughts to continue tumbling over each other like pebbles tossed down a slope.

Her rest didn't improve on Monday afternoon. By the time she got off shift at 0800 hours Tuesday morning, she felt as though she were walking in a stupor. She fell into bed without a meal and slipped into sleep. When she woke, it took her a few minutes to orient herself. A glance out her window showed deep darkness. Cloud cover obscured the stars. The shadowy shape of her roommate huddled beside the window. "Cynthia?"

The other woman turned her head, her long brown hair black in the semidarkness. "Sorry to wake you."

"You didn't." Elisabeth sat up and draped a blanket around her shoulders against the chill in the room. "What time is it?"

"It's four in the morning." Her voice sounded as though she might be smiling. "Sandra stopped by around eight last night to see if you were okay. You didn't even stir."

"I was beat. So what are you doing awake at this hour?"

"Just thinking about things." Her voice now sounded distant and sad.

"I know the feeling." Elisabeth sank down on the bed and studied her hands. All the uncertainties of the past few days flooded her mind once again.

Cynthia moved to sit on her own bed, opposite Elisabeth. "If you want to talk about it, I'd love to think about someone else's problems."

Elisabeth looked toward the other nurse, even though the night obscured her expression. "A couple of weeks ago, I met a Canadian pilot." Somehow, being unable to see her roommate clearly made her words form more easily, even made her feel eager to talk.

423

"Ah, a man," Cynthia commented in a quiet tone. "Many a nurse's sleep has been disrupted by the opposite sex."

Elisabeth smiled. "We haven't spent a lot of time together, but he's different than any other man I've ever met. I want to be able to trust him."

"What's stopping you?" Gentleness filled the other woman's voice.

"I don't want to fall in love with someone who might not live past next week." For the first time, she voiced the crux of her fear, laid it out bold and bald.

"Do you have any idea how he feels about you?"

Elisabeth shrugged. "We've seen each other only three times, so we haven't come close to discussing our feelings, or lack of them. Sandra is sure there's something between us, though."

Cynthia sighed deeply. "Elisabeth, I don't claim to have a lot of wisdom, but I do know this war has put us all in a place where everything about life seems more urgent than it did before we became involved. We look death in the face every day—you and I in helping the wounded, your pilot in his sorties over the Atlantic. In times like this, we don't have the luxury of slow and easy courtships. More than once I've seen two people meet, and it's like their hearts recognize each other instantly. I don't know if that is what is happening between you and your pilot, but I would advise you not to throw away the possibility just because you're afraid of loss. Loss is going to touch all of us personally before the war is over. We can't hide from it, so we might as well embrace the joy that comes our way, no matter how unexpected."

Elisabeth had never heard her roommate sound so philosophical—or so urgent. Usually, she remained calm and quiet, with not a lot to say. She didn't battle shyness as Elisabeth did, but she didn't speak unless she felt it necessary. Her usual reticence made these words all the more weighty. "Cynthia, what's happening with you? Something serious is bothering you."

Cynthia sighed again. "Later today, I fly out on a cargo plane bound for England. I'm needed to accompany a planeload of wounded back to Gander. My mind has been buzzing all night with the what-ifs."

Elisabeth knew exactly what she meant. Cynthia's trips as a flight nurse had been mainly to and from the Arctic bases, as well as a couple of rescue missions over the Atlantic—but still close to the North American coastline. This trip would take her right over some of the worst of German U-boat activity. She pushed back her covers and moved to sit on the edge of the other bed. She found her roommate's hands in the semidark and clasped them tightly. "I don't know what to say, Cynthia, other than you'd better come back."

"I'm not so much afraid of death for myself." Cynthia talked as though thinking out loud. "I know Jesus is my Savior and heaven is where I'll go. But what about those wounded men I'll be responsible for? They've already been through so much. What if we get shot down and I can't do anything but watch them drown in the ocean?"

Elisabeth didn't want even to imagine the horror of the experience. She didn't consciously think the words before they came out of her mouth. "I have no doubt you'll know exactly what to do if the worst happens. You'll do the best you can, and God will take care of the rest."

Tears seemed to hover in Cynthia's reply. "Thanks, Elisabeth. That was just what I needed to hear. The same holds for you. He'll show you what to do, as long as you're not afraid to listen."

Elisabeth enfolded her friend in a tight embrace, then returned to her own bed. Was she ready to listen for what God might say about this attraction between her and Ian? She lay down to think about it and drifted into a dreamless sleep.

When she woke at midmorning, she felt peace in spite of her uncertainties. With the rest of that day off as well as the following day, she had plenty of time for long walks, more rest, and opportunities to enjoy friendly Ping-Pong competitions in the nearby recreation hall. She'd heard nothing from Ian since his Sunday dinner with the nurses. When her thoughts drifted in his direction, she reminded herself that there could be nothing between them. Obviously, time and circumstances weren't going to allow even a basic friendship. Before she could acknowledge the sliver of disappointment, she redirected her thoughts by saying a prayer for Cynthia's safety. She did her best to ignore the ball of fear in her middle every time she thought of the extreme danger the flight nurse would have to experience.

Her first day back on shift was Thanksgiving Day. The hospital kitchen had managed to create a full-course dinner, which Elisabeth and Sandra served to the patients at noon. Though the two of them had been on different shifts for the past two weeks, Elisabeth felt gratitude for their togetherness on this one day. Sandra's cheeriness helped alleviate some of the loneliness Elisabeth felt for her own family. One of the youngest soldiers seemed to become more despondent during the meal. She made an opportunity to stop by his bed for a quiet chat.

"Are you okay, Private Keller?"

He looked up from his half-eaten meal with naked homesickness in his eyes. "It's the dinner, Ma'am. Puts me in mind of Thanksgiving dinners at home, with both sets of grandparents there and a ton of aunts, uncles, and cousins. Since I can't be fighting, I can't help but wish I were home. Tomorrow they'll put up the Christmas tree."

Elisabeth forced a smile. "I don't have a huge family like yours, but I miss being with them today as well. Being away from them is part of doing our duty, but that doesn't make it easy."

"No, ma'am," he whispered, looking back down at his tray.

But her words must have helped, because when it came time to clear the trays away, Private Keller had eaten every scrap and had found a crossword puzzle to work. The rest of the afternoon was hectic as the captain opened both wards for unlimited visitors. "It's bad enough that our boys have to be away from home on Thanksgiving; I want them to be able to be with their comrades, at least," she explained to her staff. It meant that the first shift of nurses had to work an hour later, but seeing the brightened spirits of all the patients, none of them seemed to mind.

Elisabeth returned to the barracks that night with her spirits heavier than ever. As she'd told Private Keller, she missed her family terribly. But she hadn't told him about Papa Johan's Thanksgiving dinner prayer. Usually his blessings over meals or his prayers for other occasions varied according to circumstance. He wasn't given to ritual or flowery language, but every year on Thanksgiving Day, he used the same words. Elisabeth came to understand them as the only words he could find to express his gratitude for what he valued most—his family and world peace. She pondered the words now:

"On this day of Thanksgiving, our Father, we thank Thee for our blessings too numerous to count. Dearest to our hearts is the gift of family You have bestowed on the three of us, brought together by heartache and war. We also thank Thee from the depths of our hearts for the gift of peace that You have bestowed on our world. We ask Thy guidance in the year to come as each of us continues in our work to ensure continued peace. In the name of the Prince of Peace, amen."

Elisabeth's homesickness only made her more aware that this prayer from Papa Johan's heart had not been answered. What had he prayed this year? Something in her soul told her he'd still asked for peace in the world but had also added a plea for her safety and happiness.

She knelt by the side of her bed and repeated the first part of the prayer. Then she added, "Though I cannot understand why You would allow war to sunder our world again, I thank Thee for the opportunity to serve those who would do their duty in the fight. Please bless Mama Glorie and Papa Johan and keep them safe. In the name of the Prince of Peace, amen."

Tears fell onto her hands for just a few moments. Just as she was getting to her feet again, Cynthia came through the door. The two women collided in a joyful hug. "Welcome home, Cynthia! How was the trip?"

"Not bad," the flight nurse replied, her brown eyes shining. "The Germans tried to nail us, but we got our boys home. I'm supposed to leave on another mission on Sunday."

Apprehension almost forced words of protest from Elisabeth's lips, but her training held them back. As members of the Army Nursing Corps, they were trained to render service anywhere. She could not dishonor herself or the Corps by speaking of her fears. But the sick dread didn't vanish for being left unspoken. On the contrary, it finally brought resolution to her questions about Ian. She could not, must not, risk more than the most casual friendship with him. To allow herself to become attached to his companionship would only put her at risk for a broken heart. This war had already demanded more than her heart felt able to give. She simply could not give more.

With her decision made, Elisabeth plodded through her days. Cynthia once again returned safely from her overseas mission. That Friday night, Elisabeth accompanied Sandra and a few other nurses to the officers' mess for the Social Evening.

Though she tried to tell herself she wasn't looking for Ian, she couldn't deny the disappointment she felt over not seeing him. She sidestepped the many offers to dance, though she did try to maintain pleasant conversations with those who approached her. Thankfully, no one seemed to remember the duet she'd sung with Ian, or if they did, they didn't mention it. For her part, she just tried to ignore the piano on the other side of the room. She couldn't look at it without remembering how well their voices had blended in song. Sandra had to leave at 2200 hours to get ready for her night shift, so Elisabeth accompanied her back to the barracks. She promised herself she wouldn't visit the mess again. The memories were simply too vivid and the uncertainties too unsettling.

The next morning she awoke after a restless night, resolved to let Ian MacDonald occupy no more space in her thoughts. Nursing was what she'd come here to do, not pine over someone she barely knew. As an ever-present reminder of her determination, she fastened the clasp of Mama Glorie's lamp pin over the chain of her dog tag so she could wear it under her uniform.

She glanced over at her roommate, who had donned her flight suit. "Where to now?"

Cynthia grinned. "Just to Gander and back on a training flight. We should be back tomorrow night."

Elisabeth hugged her roommate, relieved beyond words that she would be out of range of enemy fire. "If you get home early, I promise to let you win at Ping-Pong."

"It's a deal." Cynthia hurried out, and Elisabeth pulled on her outdoor clothing for the walk to the hospital. She reported for duty, determined to focus on her nursing duties to the exclusion of anything else. When a few moments of unoccupied time occurred between patients' needs, she helped the corpsmen with their cleaning and scrubbing.

Toward the end of her shift, she looked up from making a newly emptied bed to see Captain Thompson talking with the other nurse on duty in Elisabeth's ward. Both nurses looked over at Elisabeth then continued their whispered conversation. After a few moments, the captain approached. "Lieutenant, I need to speak with you outside the ward, please."

Elisabeth checked the nursing supervisor's face for a sign of censure but saw none. "Yes, ma'am." She followed the other woman out into the hallway.

"Lieutenant, I have difficult news for you. We just got word that Lieutenant Jenkins's plane crashed at Gander. All the crew, including Lieutenant Jenkins, were killed."

A horrified numbness settled over Elisabeth. The only words that would come out of her mouth were, "Are you sure?"

Captain Thompson's voice remained brisk and matter-of-fact. "Yes, Lieutenant, we're sure. I trust I can count on you to finish your shift."

Elisabeth shook her head as if to clear away the fog of disbelief.

"Lieutenant?"

The sternness in her supervisor's voice penetrated the cloud. "Yes, ma'am. I'll be fine." Elisabeth returned to the bed she had been making and finished the job mechanically. She had no idea how she finished that last hour or even how she managed to return to the barracks.

But in her room the grief broke over her. Never again would she turn to the soft-spoken woman for advice or even just for company, when homesickness became too intense. She felt something precious had been ripped away from her. She lay facedown on her bed and let the sobs shake her. Into her pillow she cried out, "God, how could You let this happen?"

But no answer came. After awhile the tears abated, leaving only an ache just under her rib cage. She stayed in her room as the twilight deepened into nightfall. Supper would be served soon, but she had no appetite. It just made no sense. Cynthia had survived two round-trip flights across the enemy-patrolled Atlantic. How could she have died on a training flight?

Elisabeth sat by her window staring into the night, as Cynthia had just a few days ago. A hush seemed to have fallen over the entire barracks. Only faint sounds of other nurses' activity reached her ears. Then came a knock at her door. She opened her mouth to respond, but the tears spilled over and choked out her reply. The knock came a second time, and this time the door opened slightly. Sandra's worried face peered through the semidarkness. "Are you okay, Elisabeth?"

Elisabeth couldn't move, other than to nod.

"You don't look like it. May I come in?"

Again Elisabeth could only nod. She heard her friend's approach, then felt comforting arms slide around her. She tried to hold back the tears, but they refused to be denied. With her head resting on Sandra's shoulder, she sobbed afresh.

Sandra murmured quieting words, barely more than nonsense. Then Elisabeth felt a dampness on her own shoulder. With it came the awareness that she wasn't alone in her grief. There were so few of them among so many men that they were like their own extended family. This loss would scar them all.

Chapter 6

Elisabeth forced herself through the days that followed. A memorial service took place three days after the crash, but she refused to attend. Her loss only felt bearable when she focused stubbornly on her nursing responsibilities. Regulations forbade any communications home about the loss, for which she felt grateful. This way she didn't have to decide whether or not to tell her parents.

One evening, as she sat alone in her room, a diffident tap at the door startled her. When Elisabeth opened the door, a fellow nurse stood on the other side with a piece of paper in her hand. "One of the Canadian pilots asked me to give this to you."

Before her brain could absorb the information, a jolt of delight went through her. With shaking hands, she opened the note. "If you would join me outside, I have a surprise for you." It was signed simply, "Ian."

She dismissed the other nurse with a smile and a "thank you," then shut her door and began pulling on outerwear as fast as her hands could move. All the while, she reminded herself that she needed to tell Ian she couldn't date him anymore. Regardless of what she felt she had to say, her heart refused to let go of its happiness.

Well-bundled against the cold, she hurried outside. There he stood, off to one side, looking more handsome even than in her dreams. He held a basket on one arm, and with the other, he beckoned her. "I figured it's a good day for a picnic, since it's too cold for bugs."

Elisabeth laughed, the first time she'd felt any kind of joy since the awful news ten days previously. She tucked her hand into the crook of his elbow and smiled up at him. "It's good to see you."

He began walking at an easy, wandering pace. "I'm not supposed to tell you I've logged more hours in the air than I think I can count. I no sooner get one plane delivered than they whip me back here for another one. So, how have you been?"

She studied the snow in front of her feet. How much should she tell him? Since this would be the last time she would see him, she might as well be honest. "My roommate was killed in a crash landing at Gander a couple of weeks ago."

"The flight nurse?" His voice quivered with disbelief.

"Cynthia." She could barely say the name.

"Oh, no. I saw the rubble on a couple of landings before they got it cleared away. They told me a nurse had been killed, but I had no idea it was your room-mate. I'm so sorry, Elisabeth. How are you doing with it?"

She shrugged. "I'm coping, I guess. Don't have much choice."

He let the silence hover for several strides. Then with a gentle nudge, he turned her toward a snowbank as high as her waist. "Let's sit for a few minutes. The snow-bank will break the wind." He pulled a blanket from the basket on his arm and laid it out on the snow, then gestured for her to take a seat. She expected to be chilled quickly. Instead, with the diminished wind, she felt cozy in her Arctic gear. He lifted an insulated container from the basket, then filled two mugs with steaming liquid.

"Hot chocolate?" she asked incredulously. "How did you come by this?"

"Connections," he responded with a saucy grin.

Not until they had finished the drinks and resumed their walk did she find the courage to voice her thoughts. "Ian, I don't know how to say this, so I'm just going to be blunt. I don't think I should see you anymore." She couldn't bear to look up into his face. If she had hurt him, she wouldn't be able to forgive herself. Still, she had to protect herself. The past two weeks had reinforced her resolution.

When he spoke, his voice remained as conversationally friendly as ever. "Would you mind telling me why, other than the fact that I'm never around?"

"I don't want to get attached." The words sounded cold, but she had to make her point.

"Are you talking about friendship or about romance?"

"Both."

"Elisabeth." He paused and turned her to face him. The intensity of his gaze, even in the gathering dusk, compelled her to maintain eye contact. "I don't have to tell you we're living in terrible times. I know better than anyone how easily I could take off on a flight and never return. Not once do I take off from a runway without thinking of my mother and two sisters and the loss they'll feel if something happens to me. I feel horrible about making them live with that. But I couldn't live with myself if I didn't do what I do."

He set the basket on the ground and took both of her gloved hands in his. "I'm not one to date just for the sake of dating. I know there's something special between us, but I don't want to try to define it. I cannot let myself become part of a romantic attachment until I know for sure that I'll be alive to fulfill any promises I make. Does that make sense to you?"

She nodded, no longer sure of her own feelings. Just to hear him say the words "something special between us" filled her with both joy and foreboding. She couldn't care about him any more than she already did. She simply wouldn't let herself.

"Are we still friends?" Once again, his gaze held hers.

Once again she nodded, incapable of further response.

"I do want to keep you as a friend for as long as God allows." He tucked her hand around his arm again and picked up the basket, resuming their walk. "I know you're going through a horrible time right now, and I hope it helps to know that I think of you often."

For some strange reason, it did help. The ache that she'd begun to think would be a permanent part of her began to ease.

"Look up there." He pointed into the sky ahead of them. The cloud cover was sporadic tonight, providing a clear view of a large, full moon. "That's your reminder, little friend. Whether I'm in Gander, Iceland, England, or someplace as yet unknown, I'll see the same moon and I'll be thinking of you." Then in the wonderful baritone she'd heard once before, he began to sing,

> *"No matter where I go*
> *You'll be with me in my soul.*
> *Though we have to part for now*
> *In our hearts we're never far.*
> *When I see the sun, I'll feel your smile.*
> *When I look at the moon, I'll think of you."*

She tried to hum along, but emotion clogged her throat. He finished with a grin, and they returned to the barracks in silence. At the doors, he wrapped her in a quick hug. "Remember the moon," he whispered, then he stood back as she went inside. Not until she reached her room did she realize he hadn't agreed that they shouldn't see each other again. Rather, he'd offered a promise of friendship that her heart seemed determined to cherish in spite of her good intentions.

And so, each day as she trudged through the snow and darkness to and from work, she couldn't help but look upward. She was surprised at how often she could see the moon, however faintly, in spite of the seemingly permanent cloud cover. Whenever she saw the steady glow, a matching glow lit her soul.

Just ten days before Christmas, a package arrived from home. She invited Sandra to join her as she opened the treasure. Tissue swathed the top layer. She gently pulled the packing aside to reveal a small wreath woven from dried stalks of grain and decorated with bits of green felt and tiny red yarn pom-poms. Beneath that lay a box of fudge, from which they each took an immediate sample, and a tin of her favorite shortbread cookies. A cedar box lay at the bottom of the package, with an envelope attached.

Dearest Elisabeth,

The note began in her mother's tidy handwriting.

> *While Papa Johan and I were praying for you the other day, I felt the time had come to send you this. The letters and the journal were written by*

431

my grandmother Lucy, your great-grandmother, while she served as a nurse during the Civil War. Her thoughts encouraged your papa and me during some dark days when our circumstances were similar to yours, and I hope they'll do the same for you.

With all our love,
Mama Glorie

Elisabeth gently lifted the cedar lid. Carefully folded within lay sheets of paper already yellowing with age. She felt startled by the unfamiliarity of the rounded writing. In the years before Great-Grandma's death, she'd often sent little notes to Elisabeth. That writing had been shaky and sprawling. But as soon as she started reading the words, she knew her great-grandmother's spirit hadn't changed a bit with age. Her courage and determination showed through each sentence.

She laid the box aside with regret. With only an hour until time to report for her shift, she couldn't let herself get involved in the story she was sure to find. But distant memories of her great-grandmother accompanied her throughout her hours on duty. It had been years since she'd thought of Lucy as anyone other than the heroic first owner of the pin Elisabeth still wore on the chain beneath her uniform.

Over the course of the next three days, she found opportunity to read the letters a bit at a time. Sunday would be her next day off, and she promised herself she would spend the entire afternoon with the little cedar box. But as she left the chapel after the morning service, she saw a familiar, though unexpected, figure in the crowd ahead of her. The top of his head was visible above those around him, and anticipation rippled through her. She pushed it away with the reminder that she'd told him they shouldn't see each other again. For that reason, she shouldn't expect his presence on the American base to mean he'd come to see her.

But as she stepped outside the chapel, there he was, a short distance away, obviously waiting for her. She didn't try to stop the grin that felt like it might split her face. No matter what she wanted to tell herself about her intentions, she simply couldn't deny her joy in seeing him. Because they were both in uniform, she couldn't greet him with anything less than a very proper salute.

Formalities out of the way, they stood facing each other in the cold winter air. "I really wanted to see you this afternoon," he explained. "I hope you don't mind."

She smiled again and shook her head. "I'm glad to see you."

"Are you?"

She knew why he asked and couldn't blame him for being uncertain. "I don't want to be, but I am." She expected him to be offended by her honesty.

Instead, he looked at her with understanding in his eyes. "We seem to have been given a gift neither of us wants. May we have lunch together?"

"Yes. I'm off today, so my time is my own. Would you like to join us again in the nurses' dining room?"

"Is there someplace where we might have a semi-private conversation?"

"The officers' mess might have a quiet corner."

He nodded, and they both turned toward the building that stood just a few doors away from the chapel. Neither said anything more until they were settled at the end of a large table with full plates in front of them. Ian sat at the end, while Elisabeth sat on the side immediately to his left. Though there were other officers at the table, two empty chairs created a gap for privacy.

After asking a quick blessing over their meal, Ian didn't reach for his fork right away. Instead, he looked solemnly at Elisabeth. "I came over today because I need to talk with you about something. There's no easy way to say it, but since I told you I want to be your friend, I feel I have to tell you this." He studied her face as if trying to discern how she would react then took a deep breath. "I can't give you any details, but it may be awhile before you see me again. I've been assigned to go on patrols."

Elisabeth didn't need any further explanation. She had heard patients talking in the ward about "Jerry Patrols." German U-boats had penetrated partway up the St. Lawrence Seaway and were suspected between Labrador and Newfoundland. While ferrying planes took Ian right over enemy-patrolled waters, this assignment would be even more dangerous. "Jerry Patrols" meant the planes went looking for a fight. The U-boat captains were known for being relentless when attacked. The exchange of gunfire usually ended only when either the submarine or the attacking airplane was destroyed. At that moment, she wished she could take back the evening when they met. If she had known then what she knew now, she would have walked away rather than accept the cup of tea that started their acquaintance.

Instead, she had to sit still and endure the wave of terror that broke over her. Involuntarily, she recalled the early morning conversation with Cynthia before her first flight to England. She'd felt this same clammy fear that morning, and it had proven prophetic. But she couldn't voice that thought to Ian. He didn't need her fear. Yet no heartening comment came to mind. Instead, she put a forkful of food into her mouth. It could have been straw for all she knew.

Ian looked closely at her. "I wish I could promise you I'll come back safe and whole. I'd feel less guilty if I could. All I can tell you is that we want the same thing—an end to this war. You work toward that goal by patching people up. I work toward it by flying a plane wherever they tell me to fly it. We each have to go where duty takes us."

"I know." She finally found safe words. "As long as enemy soldiers risk their lives, we have to do the same."

Chapter 7

Elisabeth reported for work Monday morning feeling as if the last bit of hope had drained from her. It no longer mattered whether or not she should care for Ian. It didn't even matter whether she felt mere affection or longed for something more. Whatever words she chose to define her feelings, they had been shredded by his announcement yesterday. Her hours on duty became her refuge. At least on the wards, others' need for her care kept her mind off her own troubles. She felt relieved that she knew none of Ian's comrades. It would have been unbearable to catch a glimpse of someone who knew him, but not see *him*.

With Christmas only six days away, activity buzzed around her. The nurses started with the barracks, decorating as best they could with a variety of handmade items. The tissue from boxes received from home became bells and lacy paper chains. Someone's mother sent popcorn, which the women threaded into long chains in the recreation room. To add even more excitement, the nurses had divided themselves into two "teams." The team that made the longest popcorn chain by Christmas Eve would be treated to foot massages and back rubs by the other team.

Then, as time allowed, the nurses on night shift created little bits of cheer for the wards. They used green and red crayons to color mini wreaths to hang at the end of each bed. A set of paper bells hung in each doorway. Captain Thompson made no comment about the decorations, either positive or negative, so the day shifts left them in place.

Still, Elisabeth couldn't get excited about the holiday. "Joy to the World" and "Peace on Earth" were simply too far removed from the emotions with which she coped every day. Christmas Eve morning, she decided to go for a walk. She turned away from the barracks toward a trail that wound around the perimeter of the base. Approaching the main road, she heard someone call her name. "Lieutenant Baker!"

It sounded like "Left-ten-ant," which was the Canadian pronunciation. She knew only two Canadians. The exceptional height of one of them made him easily identifiable, which meant that this man could only be the padre, as the Canadians called him. "Captain Landry!" In the instant of recognition, she knew his companionship would be exactly what she needed.

Once they were within conversational distance of each other, Don explained, "I saw Ian for a few moments last night and he asked me to be sure to let you know he's okay. He had just a few hours for some sleep before he had to leave on another patrol."

Her relief lasted only long enough for her to hear that he was probably on another patrol as they spoke. "Thank you for coming."

"Ian told me of your loss. How have you been?" His tone told her he cared, but without pity.

For a few moments she considered dissembling, as she'd done with everyone else. After a week of hearing her reply "Just fine" to every inquiry after her well-being, her fellow nurses stopped asking. Even Sandra didn't try to dig further. More than once, Elisabeth had sensed Captain Thompson's gaze on her. But no matter who asked, she simply couldn't admit that she lived in moment-by-moment terror of bad news, or that Cynthia's death still ate at her spirit. She hadn't even tried to befriend the nurse who now shared her room. "I'm struggling." She watched Don's face, alert for any sign that she shouldn't have confided in him.

But his brown eyes remained steady and watchful. "Struggling isn't a sin. In fact, it's healthy."

She shook her head. "I don't think so. My mother was an army nurse in the last war, and somehow she didn't let stuff like this bother her."

"Do you know that for sure, or is it just the image you have of her? We often remember our parents as being more heroic than they actually felt at the time. As children, we don't know the agony of heart they experienced."

"I don't think she could have made it through the war if she felt the way I do."

"Can you tell me what your worst feeling is?"

She pondered the question. It felt good to stop hiding from herself. "If God could stop the war, then why is it necessary for good people to die in it? He didn't protect Cynthia, so I can't even ask Him to protect Ian. And yet if something happened to Ian, I wouldn't be able to forgive myself for not praying for him."

"Dear girl, Ian's safety rests in God's faithfulness, not in yours. If He wills to preserve Ian's life, nothing can destroy it—not your lack of prayers and certainly not German ammunition."

"But where was God's faithfulness when Cynthia's plane crash-landed? It wasn't even enemy fire that killed her. It was an accident!" She ended on a sob. The tears poured in hot streams down her cheeks, and she buried her face in her hands. A gentle arm came around her shoulders and pulled her close. She wept against him, not caring about the cold or what anyone who saw them might think. It felt good to let out the grief and confusion. When the sobs no longer shook her shoulders, she remained with her head against him. It was foolish, she knew, but it felt, just for a few minutes, like he had absorbed the burden she'd been carrying alone for so many days.

He fumbled beneath his jacket, then handed her a crisp white handkerchief. "Shall we find some place warmer to continue this discussion?"

Embarrassment set in. She started to shake her head, to tell him she felt fine now, but he grasped her elbow lightly and turned them back toward the buildings.

"It's my job to listen and to help people work through their troubles as best I can," he said in a tone no different than if he were commenting on the latest snowfall. "Tears are part of the process." As they passed the chapel, he paused. "Shall we go in here?"

To Elisabeth, the suggestion seemed perfect. The little building offered her both a sense of safety and of privacy. No one would think twice about them being alone together there. Once inside, she sat in silence, absorbing the peace but also wondering what she should say next.

Don seemed to sense her dilemma. He didn't wait for her to reopen the conversation. "I could offer you any number of trite reassurances, such as that Cynthia could just as easily have died from a fatal illness in peacetime. But I don't think that would answer what's disturbing you most. May I ask a really personal question?"

She nodded, certain she would tell him anything if it would help unravel the knot of misery that had been tightening inside her ever since she had found herself part of the Army Nurse Corps.

"Who else have you lost in your life?"

She looked straight into his eyes in astonishment. Of all the questions she might have expected, that was not one of them. Equally surprising to her, her eyes filled with tears. She could barely push the words past the lump of agony in her throat. "My parents."

His ungloved hand touched hers. "When?"

"At the end of the Great War. A flu epidemic."

"How old were you?"

"Three. My mother's twin sister and her fiancé took me in and raised me as their own."

He honored her grief with silence, then slowly and gently began talking again. "That was a monumental loss for one so young. Though you probably can't remember the details, I would guess that at the time, you felt as if your entire world had been ripped away. You would have been too young to comprehend any explanations, so you were left with terrible confusion as to why the parents you loved disappeared."

The tears started slowly, seemingly a continuation of her mourning for her roommate. Childhood memories came with the tears. How often she'd sat in her room as a teenager, wishing she could meet her parents. Papa Johan and Mama Glorie had been wonderful about keeping her parents' memory alive for her, but she wanted to feel the hugs of those who had given birth to her, to look in their eyes just once and see their love for her. She'd never voiced the feelings aloud, much less shed tears over them. Her adoptive parents had given her so much. Mourning would have seemed so ungrateful.

But now, a profound sense of loss rose within her, feeling as though it came from the deepest part of her soul. She felt as though it would swallow her completely, leaving nothing but the empty shell of her body. She wrapped her arms around her waist as if to hold herself together, and was barely aware of the way she rocked back and forth. This time she didn't merely sob. She keened with agony that could be released no other way. She wept until she felt limp from the emotion. Don's patient presence felt like an anchor that kept her from being swept completely away. Only when her rocking stilled did he move close enough on the bench to again put his arms around her.

"It is a huge loss, Elisabeth. You've carried this grief for so long. Now you can let it go."

When she was finally able to look at him again, his eyes were red-rimmed with unshed tears of empathy. "The book of Hebrews says that those who have died form a great cloud of witnesses that cheers us on as we continue our lives here on earth. I know your parents are watching you, Elisabeth, and I know they're proud of who you've become."

"But I still have so many questions. I can't simply accept war, sickness, and death as His will and leave it at that." She felt surprised at the lack of bitterness in her tone. Where there had been anger and frustration, now there was only a clean hurt, one that felt like it would heal, rather than fester for years to come.

"I wish I had answers for you. All I know is that God is big enough for our questions. He knows how we feel and doesn't blame us for feeling that way."

"But isn't it lack of faith that brings us to ask Him why?"

Don gripped both her hands in his. "Knowing Him doesn't mean we have all the answers. It only means we have a safe place for our questions. As long as we take those questions to Him, rather than clutching them to ourselves and running away, I believe they serve His purpose."

"That's not an easy concept to get used to. I wish you were around here every day, so you could keep reminding me." The first genuine smile she'd felt in weeks lifted her lips.

"God has promised something even better than that. Jesus told His disciples that the Holy Spirit's mission is to remind us of those things we've been taught. The Spirit is with you at all times, so there's never a moment when His encouragement is too far away for you to hear." He released her hands, then looked at his watch. "It's almost lunchtime. Would you like to join me at the mess?"

Elisabeth shook her head. "Thanks for the offer, but I couldn't handle a crowd right now. I'll get something at the hospital kitchen before I go on shift."

"Are you working tomorrow?"

"Yes. This is my first of four afternoon shifts. I don't mind, though. I came here to be a nurse, and I'd rather be with the patients on Christmas Day than anywhere else." Except maybe with Ian. But she couldn't voice that thought, not even to this wonderful man.

"Then you're just the person they need to have around on a day when they're bound to be missing home and families. I'll be praying for you."

She wanted to ask him to focus his prayers on Ian's safety, but the words wouldn't come. Instead, she stood, zipped her parka, and pulled on her mitts. "Thank you so much for taking time for me today. I know something has changed inside me, and it feels good."

He winked. "That's what I'm here for. I'll keep Ian in my prayers, too."

They left the chapel together then parted. Don went left, toward the base entrance, and Elisabeth went right, toward the nurses' barracks. Back in her room, she picked up the cedar box containing Grandma Lucy's journals and letters. The small bound book was ragged from handling and fragile with age. Gently, reverently, she opened it. From the first entry, she felt gripped by the emotions expressed by her ancestor. They were the same thoughts that she, Elisabeth Baker, in 1943, had been thinking, the same questions she'd been afraid to ask God, the same confusion. She read the girlish handwriting until so late that she had to run all the way to the hospital to be on time for work.

She felt strangely energized as she went about her duties until the end of her shift at 11 PM. Her patients were no longer symbols of families torn apart by war. As in her early days of nursing, they were once again individuals in need of the education and skills she'd gained, the solace she could give. When she returned to her room late that night, her heart remained sore from loss, but healing had begun. She lay her head on her pillow, snuggled under her covers, and fell into a dreamless, deeply restful sleep.

Chapter 8

Anew peace accompanied Elisabeth during the following days. While on duty, her mind felt clearer than it ever had. For the first time since Mama Glorie had presented her with the heirloom lamp pin, she felt no unworthiness in wearing it. The pin no longer symbolized an ideal; rather, it made her feel connected with those who had gone before. After every shift, she hurried back to her room to read more in Lucy's journal. Once she finished the journal, it felt like the most natural thing in the world to pick up her pen and begin writing letters of her own. But instead of letters to God, these were letters to Ian. She wanted desperately for him to know the changes taking place in her and what had sparked those changes.

Two days after the turn of the year, Sandra caught up with Elisabeth as they were both heading out the door for duty. "Where have you been hiding, friend?"

Elisabeth grinned. "No place special. I thought you were the one hiding. You haven't pounded on my door in weeks."

Sandra's smile faded. "I didn't want to bug you too much. You seemed to need time alone after. . .I mean. . ." Uncharacteristically, her words trailed off.

"You mean after Cynthia's death. Yes, it has been an awful time, but I'm doing better now."

Sandra studied her, then nodded. "I can see that. What made the difference?"

"It's a long story, but the short version is that my mother sent me her grandmother's journal. Great-Grandma Lucy was a nurse during the Civil War."

"Oh, wow! How does it feel to hold a journal almost one hundred years old?"

"Scary." Elisabeth laughed. "I'm afraid it's going to fall apart in my hands at any moment. When I get back to the States, I want to find someone who can help me preserve it. It's something that has to be handed down to the generations of family to come."

"Thinking that far ahead, are you? Is there something you're not telling me?"

The two laughed together as they reached the door of the hospital, and then their duties ended the conversation. Elisabeth recorded her thoughts later that evening in her letter to Ian.

Sandra's comment made me realize that for the first time in my life, I'm looking forward to the future, rather than dreading it. I feel like I've finally

439

been able to leave the past in the Father's hands and rest in His care for the present.

She still didn't feel comfortable telling him all she held in her heart. Specifically, she held back how her thoughts continually turned to him—wondering where he was, praying for his safety, asking God for an awareness that He was with Ian as he did the duty for which he'd been trained.

Being that it was midwinter, daylight appeared for only a few hours each day. Thus, most of her treks to and from the hospital took place in darkness. She enjoyed it, though, because whenever the cloud cover allowed, she'd catch glimpses of the moon. Even while chatting with Sandra, or any other nurse who happened to accompany her, she still looked for the moon and felt a link with Ian whenever she saw it.

One afternoon, toward the end of her shift, Elisabeth found a note at the desk where the nurses did their record-keeping.

Lieutenant Baker, report to my office at the end of your shift.
                                                                Captain Thompson

A shiver of apprehension went through her. More bad news? She touched the lamp pin through her uniform, reminding herself of the divine strength that had helped Lucy Danielson through difficult circumstances.

But when she approached the nursing supervisor's desk with a crisp salute, the captain looked friendly. "At ease, Lieutenant. Have a seat."

Elisabeth sat in the indicated chair, taking care to keep her posture straight. She folded her hands in her lap to hide their shaking.

"Are you aware it's time for your fitness report?"

"No, ma'am." Elisabeth had completely forgotten about the annual evaluation.

"You've had much on your mind."

"Yes, ma'am."

"In fact, I was beginning to fear we might have to send you back to the States."

Elisabeth's heart rate accelerated. Two months ago, she might have jumped at the chance. Now she felt as if she had finally found her purpose here. "May I ask why?"

"Lieutenant, I know you took your roommate's death very hard. I felt concerned it might lead to a breakdown. Though we're not under enemy fire, service here is every bit as demanding as at the front. We would have sent you back for your own health, Lieutenant, not because you had failed in some way."

Not sure how to respond, Elisabeth waited for her to continue.

Captain Thompson looked through a file, which Elisabeth assumed to be her personnel record. Finally the captain looked up. "You're a good nurse, Lieutenant. You care deeply, and that communicates itself to our patients. It's exactly what they need to help them recover so far from home. But caring also puts you at risk for emotional exhaustion. We've been pleased to see that since Christmas, you seem to be recovering. Would you care to tell me what has made the difference?"

Elisabeth's mind raced. She felt compelled to say something, but it was contrary to her nature to confide in someone who still intimidated her. "I had a long talk with Captain Landry, a chaplain on the Canadian side. He helped me find peace."

The captain nodded. "I'm glad to hear it. And the Canadian pilot? What do you hear from him?"

A wave of dizzy shock passed over Elisabeth. How had the captain learned about Ian? Would she forbid Elisabeth any further contact? Granted, the stipulation against married nurses no longer existed, and thus there was no discouragement against romance. But Captain Thompson was known for being "old school." Elisabeth sent up a quick prayer for help, then gave the only answer possible. "I haven't seen him since before Christmas, ma'am."

"Not by choice, I take it?"

"No, ma'am."

Captain Thompson's gaze softened. "Lieutenant Baker, though some days it seems quite the contrary, this war won't go on forever. You have a lot of your life ahead of you still. Don't be afraid to let your heart plan for that day." She cleared her throat, and her voice resumed its gruff tone. "I have been very pleased with your contributions to our unit and to our hospital and will be recommending you for promotion."

Elisabeth stood and snapped to attention. "Thank you, ma'am."

"Dismissed."

Elisabeth returned to her quarters feeling dizzied by the conversation. Not only had she been complimented in her professional life, but if she hadn't misinterpreted the captain's comments, she'd also been encouraged in her personal life. A door of hope opened ever so slightly within her. Did she dare? Even if Ian survived his missions, did he care enough about her for her to dream about a future with him?

More unanswerable questions. Her letter writing slowed to nothing. The only thing she wanted to discuss with him was something she couldn't write. It had to come in person, and it had to come from him first. She followed Lucy's example and turned her pen toward prayers. As she wrote, the peace that was becoming ever more familiar settled her heart.

Just two nights later, she left the ward at 2315 after an afternoon shift. The moon shone bright and full in a clear sky. She wandered off in the direction she and Ian had taken for their snowbank picnic, drinking in the sight of that luminous connection between them. Was he flying tonight? Was he able to see the moon?

Lost in thoughts and prayers, she didn't notice anyone approach until a pair of hands settled on her shoulders. Even before her startled gasp left her lips, she recognized the touch. "Ian!" She whirled about in his arms for a joyous hug.

He returned the embrace with equal enthusiasm and a laugh. "I didn't expect to be greeted this enthusiastically! How have you been, little friend?"

"What are you doing here at this hour?" The question fell from her mouth without any forethought. She clamped her hand over her lips. "I'm sorry. That sounded rude and didn't answer your question."

"It's okay." He hugged her again. "I know it's late. I arrived at the airfield less than an hour ago. Since I was so close, I decided to hang around and see if you might be getting off shift. Good intuition or what?"

She couldn't have stopped smiling if she'd wanted to. "Good intuition, Captain. In answer to your question, I'm doing well."

"I can see it in your face. I'm glad." Moonlight illuminated his face so clearly, she could see the expression in his gray eyes. Tenderness showed in his gaze. Her heartbeat quickened and her ability to make conversation vanished. Mesmerized by what she saw, she barely noticed his face coming closer until his lips touched hers. The kiss was brief, but their hearts touched. He drew back slightly, his arms still holding her close.

"Elisabeth?" His whisper was ragged, as if he were afraid to say more.

"Yes, Ian?"

"I haven't been able to stop thinking about you. I know you don't want us to fall in love. I didn't want it either. But I think it's happening anyway. Do you mind?"

"Mind?" She laughed softly. "I've been hoping you wouldn't mind if I fell in love with you."

"It won't be easy, little one. I can't stop flying until the air force tells me to park my plane. I can't even promise I'll come back safely. But I also can't leave one more time without letting you know how much I care."

"I know." This time she was the one to pull them together in another embrace. "I can wait, and pray, and hope."

He pulled back again to study her face. He gazed into her eyes as if trying to see her soul. Elisabeth willed her heart to show itself in her gaze. "I'm not afraid anymore, Ian."

"I can see that. Neither am I. I've actually written you some letters to tell you what's been on my mind. I don't have long on the ground between flights, but I can meet you for lunch tomorrow if you have time."

"I have letters to give to you, too."

"Then let's each go grab some sleep. I'll come to the mess here and meet you at the doors. Okay?" He tucked her arm into the crook of his elbow as if to hold her close to him as they walked to her barracks. At the door, he touched his lips to hers again in another meeting of their hearts. "Good night, my little friend. I'll see you in a few hours."